PRAISE FOR SHANE

'Maloney is top shelf.' *Australia*

'One of the genre's most gifted

'For the first time in the vicinity of Australian crime-writing, the true national voice of comic futility, a literary voice which is rich, ridiculous and tawdry, which can set itself up with a soaring rhetoric and slide on the banana skin of its own piss-elegance…Maloney is terrific… he could be the Australian Chandler.' *Age*

'Maloney is a literary writer who some will feel is wasting his time in the detective business. He takes characters that are stereotypes (the public servant, the minister, the arty type) and depicts them with subtlety and originality and compassionate humour. He also writes a ripping yarn.' *Eureka Street*

'I look forward to the next Murray Whelan book with the same anticipation of pleasure that I feel for the new Carl Hiaasen or Elmore Leonard.' *Sydney Morning Herald*

'The funniest meanstreets-style writing on offer these days.' *Sunday Age*

'To the list that contains Charles Willeford's Florida Keys, Jim Thompson's West Texas, Pete Dexter's Philadelphia, James Crumley's Montana and Carl Hiaasen's Miami, you can add Shane Maloney's Melbourne.' *Herald Sun*

THE BIG ASK

'The best Maloney yet.' Graeme Blundell, *Australian*

'Shane Maloney's books brighten up my day…Spiky wit and good humoured cynicism.' *Sunday Telegraph* UK

'Whelan's distinctive voice drives the story along with considerable zest and wittiness…Another triumph for Maloney, who is one of our best

and most consistently original crime writers. Highly recommended.'
Canberra Times

'A rollicking good read of sex, political intrigue and murder.'
Brisbane *Sunday Mail*

'Gloriously politically incorrect…Shane Maloney writes like an angel, always in control of his plot and pace. Not that many readers will notice this: they'll be too busy laughing…Maloney just gets better, and Murray Whelan remains one of the most reliable and rewarding sleuths in the business.' Ian Rankin, *Age*

'Maloney, the great exponent of the Australian crime genre, has done it again. *The Big Ask* is full of laugh-out-loud humour as well as jaw-dropping accuracy in describing Australian political life.' *Marie Claire*

'Maloney…paints a wonderfully grainy, gritty picture of Melbourne, while clearly loving every inch of its flat surface.' *Sydney Morning Herald*

'All great cities have their literary interpreters…now Melbourne has found a fresh spokesman – Shane Maloney.' *West Australian*

'Crime fiction is often a stylish genre: preferring the first person, it can become a virtuoso performance linguistically speaking. Maloney is no exception.' *Overland*

SOMETHING FISHY

'Hilarious and unmissable…highly recommended.' *West Australian*

'Sometimes the pleasure of Maloney lies in the small things: a description of a teenager having "something chippish in the shoulder region"; or a Chandleresque simile: "He made a noise like a chihuahua being dropped down a lift-shaft"…Whelan is ageing well, and his creator remains at the top of his game. Not just a fine crime writer, but a fine writer full-stop.' Malcolm Knox, *Sydney Morning Herald*

'Admirers of Shane Maloney's hero, Murray Whelan, will be relieved to learn that his elevation to State Parliament has not in the least affected his ability to put himself in the most absurdly funny, and dangerous, of situations…We can only hope that, with the continued success of Labor in Victoria, it won't be too long before Murray makes Premier.' Barry Maitland, *Age*

'A new Murray Whelan adventure from Shane Maloney is always warmly welcomed and his latest certainly lives up to expectations.' *Canberra Times*

'Hilarious and pacey, this will keep you on the edge. You'll probably read it in one sitting.' *Weekly Times*

'Maloney's ironically faceted style is elided, almost laconically; the extraneous is struck out, leaving cinematic vividness in his choice of the most significant detail, and a sense of motion and change. He also does the colloquial better than anyone in local crime fiction.' *Australian*

'A great read…There are plenty of laughs and heart thumping action in *Something Fishy*. You'll enjoy it.' *Victorian Police Association Journal*

SUCKED IN

SHORTLISTED, AGE BOOK OF THE YEAR AWARD 2007
SHORTLISTED, NED KELLY AWARD FOR BEST CRIME FICTION 2008

'Shane Maloney is one of the funniest writers in the land, and Whelan one of the great comic creations of Australian literature.' *Courier Mail*

'Brilliant…He has Elmore Leonard's gift of making things go wrong in a seemingly natural sort of way…His style, realised in spare, necessary prose, is so acutely colloquial in rhythm, you can almost hear Maloney reading aloud for rhythm and cadence. Like Leonard, he strikes out the extraneous, leaving the impression of a kind of cinematic clarity in his choice of the most significant detail…Maloney is on his own now as a highly original crime writer.' *Australian*

'From the opening pages, the story gallops along, powered by Whelan's laconic observations and Maloney's rare ability to make the complexities of Labor Party machinations interesting and entertaining.' *Canberra Times*

'Shane Maloney is the master of a genre of his own making—apparatchik lit. Stories from the murky, lurky world of Australian politics (especially inside the Labor Party and union movement) have no better teller in contemporary Australian fiction.' *Age*

'Maloney's sixth Murray Whelan mystery is a joy…In a word: compelling.' *Gold Coast Bulletin*

'Clever stuff as usual, and full of hilarious Labor in-house bitching.' *Geelong Advertiser*

'This series is an absolute cracker and Murray Whelan our most noble dag. No city has been better served by its leading man.' *Hobart Mercury*

'How does Maloney do it? This must have been written at least a year ago and it's so spot-on topical it sends shivers up your spine at the same time as you're rolling on the floor with laughter…It's the engaging characters, the rapid-fire colloquial style and the sassy satirical one-liners that make Maloney addictive.' *Adelaide Advertiser*

'Wonderfully wry…A colourful cast, an intriguingly twisted plot, a convincing background and Maloney's skill with language (particularly dialogue) make this novel more entertaining than a homicide investigation really has any right to be.' *West Australian*

'Sucked me in right to the end. Maloney's writing is full of class and depicts the shenanigans with verve and wit. If only real politicians were as interesting.' *Bulletin*

'Brilliantly written rollicking story, enhanced further by the witty dialogue. The Murray Whelan thrillers are priceless.' *Herald Sun*

THE NEXT MURRAY WHELAN TRILOGY

THE BIG ASK + SOMETHING FISHY + SUCKED IN

SHANE MALONEY

t

TEXT PUBLISHING
MELBOURNE AUSTRALIA

The paper used in this book is manufactured only from wood grown in sustainable regrowth forests.

The Text Publishing Company
Swann House
22 William Street
Melbourne Victoria 3000
textpublishing.com.au

Copyright © Shane Maloney 2000, 2002, 2007

All rights reserved. Without limiting the rights under copyright above, no part of this publication shall be reproduced, stored in or introduced into a retrieval system, or transmitted in any form or by any means (electronic, mechanical, photocopying, recording or otherwise), without the prior permission of both the copyright owner and the publisher of this book.

First published by Text Publishing: *The Big Ask* 2000,
Something Fishy 2002, *Sucked In* 2007
The Next Murray Whelan Trilogy first published 2009

Printed and bound by Griffin Press
Designed by Chong

National Library of Australia
Cataloguing-in-Publication-data:

Maloney, Shane

The next Murray Whelan trilogy : the big ask, something fishy, sucked in /
Shane Maloney.

ISBN: 9781921351914 (pbk.)

Maloney, Shane. Big ask.
Maloney, Shane. Something fishy.
Maloney, Shane. Sucked in.

A823.3

All the characters in this book are fictional. Any resemblance to real people, living or dead, is unintentional.

THE BIG ASK

This book is dedicated to Christine, Wally and May.

I have no choice—they know where I live.

The author of this book, its setting and its characters are entirely fictitious. There is no such place as Melbourne. The Australian Labor Party exists only in the imagination of its members.

The smart money was home in bed.

It was 4.30 a.m., a Monday morning at the arse-end of winter, and I should have been there too, clocking up a few hours sleep before the eight o'clock flight to Sydney. My son Red was somewhere in Sin City, missing and possibly in danger.

Instead, I was sitting in a greasy spoon cafe at the Melbourne Wholesale Fruit and Vegetable Market, nursing a bruised forehead, drinking over-brewed coffee and talking to a truck driver named Donny Maitland about his campaign to unseat the leadership of the United Haulage Workers.

Dawn was still two hours away and a frigid wind was sweeping off Port Phillip Bay, one of those bone-chilling breezes that descend on Melbourne in late winter and make us wonder why we bother to live here. Vendors were standing in front of their stalls, stamping their feet and rubbing their hands together. Beyond them, past rampaging forklifts and crates of vegetables, the tower blocks of the central city were etched against the sky above the railway switching yards, dark on dark.

Donny had just arrived, five hours from Nar Nar Goon with a load of spuds. He breezed through the door in a gust of arctic air, a craggy, cleft-chinned, stout-featured bloke in a woollen pea-jacket. One of those men, you knew if he was ever hit, wouldn't fall down. Not that I could imagine anyone trying it on. Donny wasn't that type. His body was a fact, not an assertion. Something he lugged around to do the work.

He spotted me straight up, plonked his frame onto the stool beside me and laid a hefty hand on my shoulder. A flush of good cheer rose across his cheekbones like old sunburn, almost managing to conceal the fatigue in his amiable brown eyes. He must have been shagged, a night behind the wheel, but he wore it well. Donny was a stayer, all right. More than once over the years, he'd drunk me under the table while the women came and went, talking of Michelangelo. Or Solzhenitsyn. Or Sinatra.

'Sorry to keep you waiting, Murray,' he declared. 'I stopped to help some bloke who'd lost his load on the South Gippsland Highway. Hope the bastard votes for me.'

'It'll take more than random acts of kindness to win control of the Haulers,' I said.

Donny jerked his thumb over his shoulder. 'Don't worry, comrade. The rest of the crew are on the case, spreading the word among the cabbages. And the kings, too, if they find any. For the time has come, as the walrus said.'

I glanced through the glass wall of the eatery and caught sight of one of Donny's running mates, a scarecrow of a bloke called Roscoe, as he disappeared into the hurly-burly of the market, distributing handbills. Donny extracted a sheaf of flyers from his pea-jacket and thrust one into my hand. 'Vote UHW Reform Ticket,' it was headed. 'Fight for a Union that Fights for Its Members.'

As I read, Donny squinted at my forehead. 'Where'd you get the bump? You look like you've gone three rounds with a revolving door.'

I touched my hairline and winced. 'Must be this all-male environment.'

'You've been brawling, haven't you?' Donny tilted his chin up and stared at me with astonishment. 'In the twenty years we've known each other, I've never once heard of you swinging a punch.'

'The other bloke swung first and swung harder,' I said morosely. 'Name of Darren Stuhl.'

'Bob Stuhl's son?' Donny puffed his cheeks and exhaled. 'Runs the Stuhl Holdings depot down here for his old man. Did he realise he was taking a poke at a senior adviser to the Minister for Transport?'

'This was personal, not professional,' I said. 'We had a run-in a couple of nights ago. I never expected to see him again. Then, five minutes after I arrive here at the market, he turns up and decides to go for a repeat performance.'

Donny grinned and shook his head. 'You're a wild man, Murray Whelan. What's Angelo Agnelli going to say when he finds out his trusty lieutenant has been trading punches with the heir to the biggest private trucking company in the country?'

'What the boss doesn't know won't hurt him.' My gaze extended over Donny's shoulder, out to where a dark-haired man in a grey leather jacket was leaning against a crate of oranges. He had a face like a cop in a French movie and his thousand-yard stare was turned in our direction. 'And right now we've got a more pressing problem than some bad-tempered rich kid,' I said. 'You know a Haulers' organiser by the name of Frank Farrell?'

Donny looked at me over the rim of his cardboard cup. 'I do indeed,' he said. 'He's an all-purpose goon. Ex-shearer, ex-army. Works both sides of the street. A head-kicker for the union who does freelance favours for Bob Stuhl.'

'Well, he's spotted us,' I said. 'And right now he's putting two and two together and concluding that you and I didn't just happen to bump into each other. Come office hours, he'll be on his mobile phone reporting to Hauler headquarters that a member of the minister's staff was cooking something up with a rank-and-file activist in the market cafe. And I don't mean toasted sandwiches.'

Government interference in the internal affairs of a union was the dish Angelo Agnelli had in mind. A little stirring of the industrial pot. But the success of the recipe would depend on whether Donny could stand the heat of the kitchen.

He turned to look, but I clamped my hand on his forearm. 'Farrell told me he was here to deal with some sort of irritation,' I warned.

'That'd be us.' Donny looked pleased. 'Word must've got back that the natives are restless.'

'And Farrell's not alone. He's got a bunch of roughnecks with him, lurking around the Stuhl Holdings depot.'

'Told you they consider us a threat,' said Donny. 'I'd better warn the others to expect trouble. We can't ask anybody to vote for us if we can't hold our ground, so we should put on a bit of a show.' He checked his watch. 'It's 4.40 now. We'll rustle up a campaign rally in the parking lot in thirty minutes, show the flag before the place closes for the day.'

'I can't stay that long,' I said. 'Something's come up. You remember Red, lives in Sydney with his mother, Wendy?'

'Never understood what you saw in that woman,' nodded Donny.

'One of the eternal mysteries,' I agreed. 'The thing is, Red's done a bunk. Disappeared. I'm on a flight at eight. Thirteen years old. I've got to tell you, mate, I'm worried sick.'

'Ah, jeeze,' said Donny. 'Thirteen, eh? Last time I saw the little tacker he couldn't have been more than five or six. Anything I can do?'

'You can tell me where I can ring a cab,' I said. 'I need to get home, change my clothes, pack a bag.'

'Forget the cab,' he said. 'Stick around. The rally won't take long and then I'll run you home. Drive you to the airport, too, if you want. It'll be faster that way, I guarantee. You can't leave before you've had the chance to see us in action.' Donny glanced across the cafe and grinned. 'Hello, here's Heather.'

Heather was Donny's sister-in-law and the partner in his trucking business. Once upon a very short time, I was a frog that she'd kissed. She was, I feared, still on a quest for my inner prince. And she was steaming towards us, weaving through the tables, denim skirt swirling at mid-calf, a chunky little Dolly Parton. Heads turned, tracking her progress.

'Uh-oh,' I said.

Heather joined us at the counter and signalled for a coffee. 'Well, well,' she said, a devious smile dimpling her cheeks. 'Look who's here.'

'What an unexpected surprise,' I said.

'I'm here to talk to clients,' she explained. 'Try to hustle up some jobs. Times are tough and this union crap isn't going to make life any easier.' She nodded at the leaflet in my hand. 'You should know better than to encourage him.'

Donny climbed off his stool and surrendered it to Heather with a sarcastic bow. 'Leave the boy alone,' he said. 'Can't you see he's been in the wars. Here five minutes and some dickhead tries to rearrange his face.'

'You're kidding?' Heather registered the swelling on my forehead and her tone softened. 'You're not kidding, are you? You look like shit.'

'She's a real charmer, isn't she?' said Donny. 'See you in the parking area in half an hour, Murray. Tough customer like you might be handy, push comes to shove.'

I nodded. Another thirty minutes weren't going to make much difference, one way or another. Donny took his campaign leaflets and his impregnable confidence and vanished into the vegetal world of the market.

'So,' demanded Heather. 'What happened to you?'

It was too humiliating to recount. I stared down into my coffee, brown sludge, lukewarm and oversweetened. 'Long story,' I muttered.

'It always is.' She shook her head, no stranger to the infinite foolishness of the male species. 'And I thought you were a nice boy.'

'You should know better than that,' I said, absently probing the tender spot.

She dug in her bag and found a pack of aspirin. I washed down a couple of tablets and rubbed my eyes. 'Sorry,' I yawned. 'I haven't been to bed yet.'

'C'mon, then.' She took my elbow and stood me up. 'If you're going to stay, we might as well do something about your war wound.'

She had the burger flipper put some ice in a plastic bag, then she led me back through the market, greeting and being greeted. Across the shed, I saw Donny's mate Roscoe in animated conversation with a forklift driver, pressing a handbill on him. A man in a football beanie and leather apron came out of a vendor's stall and rousted him away. Above the stall was a sign with the proprietor's name. It was one I recognised from newspaper stories about pre-dawn slayings in suburban driveways. Incidents attributed to a well-known Italian self-help association.

'It's a world of its own,' said Heather. 'They'll have Donny for breakfast.'

'I'm sure he can look after himself.'

'Yeah?' she said.

A fine drizzle alighted on our shoulders as we stepped out into the parking area. Trucks and vans of every size, age and make crowded the asphalt. Motorised trolleys darted between them, ferrying all the roots and leaves it takes to feed three million hungry mouths. An ethereal light leaked down upon the scene from the distant pinnacles of towering stanchions, casting murky shadows between the parked rigs.

The Maitland truck was slotted between a big refrigerator

rig and an old Bedford with the word 'Foodbank' stencilled on the tailgate. 'Strange name,' I said.

'A charity,' explained Heather. 'They collect perishable foodstuffs, then distribute them to worthy causes.'

I'd be the one perishing if I didn't get out of the cold.

Heather opened the cabin door. 'Up you get,' she instructed, indicating the narrow sleeping ledge behind the bench seat. 'Make yourself comfortable.'

Compliant to orders, I shucked off my shoes and clambered up. Heather, kneeling on the passenger seat, covered me with a blanket and pressed a cube of ice gently to my brow. 'Poor baby,' she cooed. 'Does that feel better?'

Much better. I closed my eyes and sighed.

'You know what you need, Murray?' murmured Heather. 'A bit of tender loving care, that's what.'

She spoke a simple truth. 'Hmmm,' I agreed.

A kind of blank exhaustion settled over me, a state of suspended animation. Time must have passed, but I had no sense of its progress. Then the truck swayed slightly and the door swung shut. I heard the click of the lock and opened my eyes. Heather's face filled my field of vision, her eyes brimming with compassion.

Nope. It was something else. She leaned closer and touched her lips to mine.

It was so long since I'd felt a woman's kiss that I couldn't summon the power to resist. The kiss lengthened, widened, deepened. Heather's mouth was infinitely inviting, wordlessly eloquent, irresistibly persuasive. I felt myself succumbing.

'Yummy,' she breathed.

Her hand slid under the blanket and tugged at my sweater. Shivers ran down my spine and a low moan escaped from somewhere deep within my chest. Goosebumps rose as her cool fingers found my skin.

'No,' I protested, perhaps less than insistent.

'Sssh.' Heather's tongue traced a wet path across my cheek and explored my ear. 'Don't say anything.'

Then she was up on the ledge beside me, backing me deeper into the narrow space. She pinned me against the curtained rear window, her thigh flung across mine. Her hands were busy between us, probing, unbuttoning, delving.

Pop, pop, pop went the stud-buttons of her quilted vest. Pop, pop went her shirt front. She pushed my jumper up around my neck and the lace of her bra scraped across my exposed chest. Another furtive groan escaped my lips.

'You like that,' she whispered. 'Don't you?'

The evidence was in hand, the *corpus* was in *delicti*. More kisses devoured my face, fed by every feeble move I made to elude them. My willpower was melting in the heat of our mingled breaths. To prevent Heather tumbling, half-undressed, backwards into the driver's seat, I put an arm around her. Jesus, I thought, I'm in big trouble here.

'Just like old times,' she said, hiking up her skirt.

We writhed together on the narrow ledge. It was like trying to have it off in a horizontal phone booth. And there was nothing long-distance about the call that Heather was placing.

'Heather.' I used my most forceful tone. 'This is not a good idea.'

Heather was not of the same opinion. She unfastened her bra and smothered my objections. I tried to turn away, honest I did. It was useless. My resistance was wilting. It was the only thing that was.

'Relax,' she purred, her hair falling around my ears, her abundance stoppering my mouth. 'I'm not going to do a *Fatal Attraction* on you.'

I didn't want to give her the wrong impression about my true feelings. But those breasts, Christ Almighty. A man would have to be made of stone. Part of me felt like it already was.

A veil of condensation had formed on the truck's windows, hiding us from the world outside. I pressed my palm against the glass and smeared the cool moisture across my face. Heather's face was elsewhere and not at all cold.

'Please,' I moaned. Through the hole in the condensation, I glimpsed the corporate slogan on the rear bumper of a Stuhl Holdings truck. 'Bob Stuhl Is Big.' Mine was too.

Further across the parking area, Donny was climbing onto a stack of pallets, his pea-jacket buttoned to the neck. He raised a bullhorn and the muffled sound of his voice swept across the bitumen, echoing off the sides of the sheds. I could just make out Roscoe, standing beside the pallets as if on sentry duty. A small, tentative cluster of onlookers began to form.

'The rally,' I said. 'Donny'll notice if I'm not there. Heather, please stop.'

She did, raising her eyes and fixing me with a wicked smile. Then, suddenly, she tried to pull my sweater off. 'Skin,' she demanded. 'I want more skin.'

Her recklessness was exhilarating. Her knees were planted on either side of my chest, blanketing my nether regions in the tented folds of her skirt. She reached down and began to tinker with my front-end alignment.

'Um,' I said, not meaning a word of it. According to

Saint Augustine, a standing prick has no conscience. Neither, for that matter, does a reclining one.

Donny's voice rose and fell and his arm pumped the air. More figures materialised in the pre-dawn gloom, converging on the pallets. Among them I recognised Frank Farrell, the Haulers' enforcer, his fist raised. Heather, meanwhile, was engaged in a complex docking manoeuvre. 'Murray,' she said sternly. 'It takes two, you know.'

An overcoated figure broke from the fringe of the crowd and vaulted up beside Donny. 'Something's happening,' I reported.

It certainly was. Heather bore down, mission accomplished. A rare pleasure suffused my loins. I closed my eyes and surrendered. At that moment, Donny's oration ceased.

With Heather's clutch fully engaged, I strained to see through the smeared glass. The man who'd jumped up beside Donny was reaching into his coat. He pulled something out and pressed it to Donny's temple. The crowd began to scatter. A confused tangle of bodies contested the rostrum. A sharp crack rang in my ears.

And again. And again.

In her amorous enthusiasm, Heather was pounding the top of my head against the wall of the cabin. Interesting cure for a headache. Unless she stopped, I'd have a cerebral haemorrhage. I squirmed out from underneath her and tumbled down onto the seat.

'What's wrong?' she pleaded. 'I thought you liked me.'

I fumbled on the floor for my shoes, levering my camshaft back into my pants. 'I do,' I said. 'I'm just not ready for a relationship.'

'A relationship?' She started tucking her upholstery back into place.

My shoes were under the seat, along with a hefty shifting spanner. 'It's a bit sudden, that's all,' I said. Laces dangling, spanner in hand, I hit the bitumen.

'A relationship?' Heather repeated plaintively. 'I'd settle for a bit of slap and tickle.'

The air was thick with exhaust fumes, the smell of burnt rubber and decaying vegetable matter. Everywhere, trucks were in motion, great wheeled walls of steel and chrome, pumping a grimy haze into the air, their towering bullbars advancing before them.

I picked my way through the obstacle course of vehicles, some moving, some stationary. By the time I reached the stack of pallets, the crowd had vanished. It was like it had never been there, as if I'd imagined everything. The only evidence that anything had happened was a broken megaphone. It lay in a shallow puddle, its handle shattered, batteries strewn across the ground.

I climbed the pallets and scanned the scene. The drizzle was thickening into a solid rain. The parking area was rapidly emptying. Here and there, hunched pedestrians flitted through the semi-darkness. I headed for the floodlit shelter of the main shed and loped into the market. Stalls were closing up. Loads of produce were being shunted into coolrooms. Nothing for me there. Breathless, wondering what was going on, I sprinted back towards the truck.

Head down against the rain, dashing past the Foodbank truck, I slammed head-on into Frank Farrell.

He dropped his mobile phone and it skittered across the wet asphalt. As he bobbed down to snatch it up, the hard man ran his hard eyes over the spanner in my hand. 'Been tightening somebody's nuts?'

I ignored him, kept going and found Donny with one foot on his driver-side step, beginning to climb aboard. He was wild-eyed, hyper-energised, rain streaming down his face. 'Did you see the crowd? Twenty-five, thirty, that's good for here,' he babbled. 'When Farrell and his hoons realised we were prepared to stick up for ourselves, they put their tails between their legs and took off.'

'Was that Darren Stuhl?' I interrupted. 'Was that a gun he was waving around?'

'Fucking idiot. Trying to prove what a big man he was. I knew he didn't have the guts to use it. Not in front of witnesses, anyway. Don't say anything to Heather, eh? She gives me a hard enough time already.'

He dragged the door open and swung himself up into the driver's seat. I headed for the passenger side, skirting the front of the truck. Checking for oncoming vehicles, I glanced back in the direction of the market. Frank Farrell had reached the canopy and slowed to a casual amble, heading inside with his hands rammed into the slit pockets of his jacket.

I climbed aboard, tossing the spanner back where it belonged. Heather scooted to the centre of the seat, bone-dry between two dripping men. She gave me a withering look, then folded her arms across her ample chest and stared straight ahead. 'You two had your fun?' she sniffed.

Donny tapped the top of the steering wheel impatiently as he pumped the accelerator, revving the engine. 'We can do it,' he muttered, half talking to himself. 'I had my doubts before, but I'm certain now. We can win this thing.'

Noise filled the cabin. The roar of air from the demisters, blasting the fog from the windscreen. The slap and sluice of the wipers, the percussive pounding of rain on the metal roof. I checked the time and felt a surge of panic.

Heather saw me look at my watch, registered my anxiety. 'Murray's a man in a hurry,' she told Donny. 'Isn't that right?'

Absolutely. Thanks to Heather's ministrations, time had got away from me. It was past 5.30. We were cutting it fine. If I missed the plane, it would definitively prove my failure as a father.

Donny slammed the stick into first and the gears screamed like a Jimi Hendrix solo. We inched forward, a wall of heavy-calibre traffic blocking our way, bottlenecked at the exit gate. A gap opened, Donny swung the wheel and we lurched forward. Heather put her hand on my knee.

'Shift it,' I muttered. I was talking to the truck in front. Any slower and it would've been going backwards. An air horn sounded behind us, one long continuous blast, on and on.

Then came a pounding on Donny's door, the bang-banging of a balled fist. His arm pumped and his head went out the window. Somebody shouted up at him, staccato sentences, inaudible against all the background noise. Donny cursed, slammed the truck into neutral, hauled on the handbrake and climbed down.

'With Donny there's always something,' muttered Heather.

I swung open my door and craned back. A curtain-wall truck was pulled up behind us at an angle. The name on the side ended in a vowel. A dwarf-like Sicilian in a leather apron was remonstrating with Donny. Even by the usual standards, he was agitated, jabbering and gesturing into the space we'd just left.

A dark shape lay there on the ground. Whatever it was,

we'd made a mess of it. Rolled over it with the rear trailer wheels, burst it open and smeared its contents across the asphalt.

'We've run over something,' I told Heather. 'Sack of tomatoes, by the look of it. Donny's getting an earful from some Italian bloke.'

'Damn,' she said. 'It'll be pay up, or spend all day arguing the toss.'

Not what I wanted to hear. And now more of them were arriving. The United Nations General Assembly, plenary session. Donny was down on one knee, assessing the damage. Slap, slap, slap went the windscreen wipers, escalating my impatience, now at the jiggling, buttock-clenching stage.

'I'm going to leg it, try to get a taxi,' I told Heather. 'I've got a plane to catch. Donny will explain.'

She eyed me sceptically. 'Is it just me, or are you like this with all women?'

I hoisted my jacket over my head, took a parting glance at the damaged-goods conference and trotted towards the gate, shoes slipping on the rain-greasy asphalt. I felt bad about running out on Donny, but not bad enough to stay behind and risk missing my flight.

If I'd looked back, even for a moment, I might have seen what was looming. I might have seen the great tidal wave of shit that was about to break over me. Just one backward glance and Donny might still be alive. And I wouldn't be languishing in the place where I am now.

It was all Angelo Agnelli's fault, of course.

If it wasn't for Angelo, I would never have been at the market in the first place. I wouldn't have been trying to play funny buggers with the most powerful and dangerous union in the state. I most certainly wouldn't have found myself trying to second-guess a man like Frank Farrell.

The Honourable Angelo Agnelli, member of the Legislative Council, was the Minister for Transport in the sovereign state of Victoria. And it all began in his office on the previous Friday evening. His Parliament House office, to be precise, in the majestic old legislature atop the gentle rise at the eastern edge of Melbourne's central business district.

As government leader in the Upper House, Ange was entitled to one of the building's more imposing bureaux. Its antique desk, french-polished bookcases, overstuffed chairs, velvet curtains, flock wallpaper and moulded cornices dated from the time when our city was a shining colonial jewel in Queen Victoria's crown. His office, in short, looked a cross between Lord Palmerston's study and a Wild West bordello.

It was August 1991 and even Blind Freddy could see that his enjoyment of these facilities was nearing its conclusion. After a decade in office, Labor had lost the plot. It was common wisdom that our defeat at the next state election was inevitable. But the election was still a year away. In the meantime, the sorry business of government went on.

There were three of us, men in suits. Agnelli was standing behind his desk, his waistcoat unbuttoned. Pushing fifty, he was no longer the boy wonder and his once-beaming dial had turned into a doughy ball in which his wary eyes were set like raisins in a slab of stale fruitcake.

Out on the floor of the chamber, Angelo did his best to project an image of senatorial gravitas, grey of temple, thick of waist, measured of speech and glad of hand. In the privacy of his office, during the parliamentary dinner recess, he dispensed with any such pretence. He held a tightly rolled newspaper in his fist and was smacking it against his thigh as he spoke.

'As if I don't have enough on my plate, *thwap*, what with Treasury screwing me to the floor over the budget estimates,' he said. 'Now I've got a *thwap* bushfire to fight. What am I paying you for, Nev, *thwap*? If it isn't to keep this sort of crap, *thwap*, out of the papers?'

Neville Lowry was Agnelli's press secretary. He was a tall, sad-faced ex-journalist with a permanent stoop, a reedy voice and about as much hair as it would take to stuff a pincushion. He was perched like a heron on the arm of the office chesterfield, his shoulders slumped forward in the melancholic posture appropriate to his vocation. 'It's the *Herald*, Ange,' he pleaded. 'You know what they're like.'

Lowry did not need to elaborate. Melbourne's afternoon

broadsheet had never been sympathetic to the Australian Labor Party, in or out of office. And its current editor, a Murdoch hack with the physique of Jabba the Hut and the morals of a conger eel, had made it his mission in life to torment us at every opportunity.

'But the *Herald* wouldn't have it, *thwap*, if somebody hadn't, *thwap*, leaked it.' Agnelli turned his ire on me. 'And that's your *thwap* department, Murray.'

Neville Lowry was a comparatively recent addition to Angelo's staff and he still tended to pay the boss some degree of deference. Not a mistake I was likely to make. I leaned forward in my chair and displayed the palms of my hands. 'What am I now?' I said. 'The resident plumber?'

For almost seven years I'd worked for Angelo. Stoking the boilers of policy analysis. Tending the vineyards of administrative superintendence. Fixing his fuck-ups and burying his boo-boos. Almost seven years. It was beginning to feel like eternity. First I was Angelo's electorate officer, inherited with the fittings and fixtures when a factional deal handed him a safe seat in the northern suburbs. Back then I managed his constituent affairs, fending off cranky voters and stroking the local party apparatus. And when, in our second term, he was appointed Minister for Ethnic Affairs, he took me along for the ride. This was designed to fend off any suspicion of wog favouritism. As he pointed out at the time, with his characteristic mastery of the bleeding obvious, Murray Whelan is not an Italian name.

Other portfolios followed, rungs in Angelo's ascent up the ladder of political preferment. We'd climbed them together. Local Government. The Arts. Water Supply. Agriculture and Fisheries. And now the big one, the jackpot. In a Cabinet reshuffle the previous month, Angelo had been catapulted into the job of head honcho of the state's rail, tram and road networks.

In better times such a promotion would've been cause for celebration. Unfortunately, Transport had become a poisoned chalice, claiming the careers of two of Angelo's predecessors in less than a year. The problem was money. The government had run out of it. The boom days of the eighties were over and the chickens of fiscal profligacy had come home to roost. With the state deficit running at Brazilian levels, the minister's task was reduced to screwing as much revenue out of the system as possible while presiding over a one hundred million dollar budget cut.

A man of conviction and inner resource might have been able to cope. But those terms had never been applicable to Angelo. In the previous three weeks he'd veered from steely resolve to catatonic retreat to blustering bravado. Now he was tearing strips off his advisers. 'A leak,' he repeated, *thwap*. 'Somebody's got it in for me.'

'That's a pretty wide field, Ange,' I said.

'You know what the *Herald*'s like,' moaned Nev Lowry again. 'And the Buzz doesn't even pretend to be factual.'

The Buzz was the *Herald*'s gossip column, a vehicle for all manner of kite-flying and bait-laying. It was a gadfly in that day's Buzz which had flown up Angelo's trouser leg, a snippet headed TRUCK CASH GRAB.

'The Buzz has it that incoming transportation supremo Angelo Agnelli has been cooking up plans to slap a hefty new tax on trucks. Makes you wonder how the government's union cronies will react to attempts to slug their members. Not to mention the big wheels of the Transport Industry

Association. Somebody should warn the minister that you tangle with the truckies at your peril.'

This was a complete beat-up.

Okay, it was true that a Treasury proposal had recently crossed Angelo's desk, arguing for a tonnage levy on heavy trucks to help defray the damage these multi-wheeled behemoths inflicted on the public highway. It was also true that the last time the government tried to make the private transport industry pay its way, irate truck-owners had blockaded the state's milk supplies, forcing a humiliating backdown. Angelo's response to the Treasury proposal had been to bin it. Our administration might have been terminal but it wasn't suicidal.

'Nev here has issued a press release denying any planned increase in motor registration charges,' I said, throwing a bridge over Angelo's troubled waters. 'And, if you want, I'll interrogate the girls in the Treasury typing pool.'

Angelo nodded, tossed the newspaper aside and sat down, as though content that his clumsy minions were now showing some evidence of competence. But we both knew that the real cause of his agitation wasn't the piece in the paper. Nor the possibility of a leak. The entire government administration, after all, leaked like a prostate patient with a prolapsed bladder. No, the gossip column item had merely triggered an inevitable event, one that Angelo had been dreading.

'Howard Sharpe's got a damned nerve, turning up on my doorstep like this,' he said. 'If the state secretary of the United Haulage Workers has something to talk about, he can make an appointment like anyone else.'

Nev Lowry unfolded his legs and began edging towards

the door. Not that he wasn't interested in relations between the government and the unions. As a young journalist Nev had often dreamed of covering first-hand the horrors of war and pestilence. He just didn't want to be around when the Haulers arrived. Who could blame him? Angelo flapped his wrist, dismissing his press secretary.

'Just tell Sharpe it's a typical piece of *Herald* mischief,' I said. 'A minor variation on their usual union-bashing theme. Or a bureaucratic cock-up. Disavow all knowledge. Better still, I'll go out and tell him you're not available. Like you said, he should've made an appointment.'

'Might as well front him now, get it over with,' said Angelo. 'If it isn't this, it'll be something else. Soon as I got this job, I knew that Sharpe'd be looking for a pretext to ambush me, to let me know what a tough customer he is. This job's difficult enough already. It'll be impossible if Sharpe thinks he can just waltz in here and throw his weight around any time the mood takes him.'

Howard Sharpe's weight was considerable. The United Haulage Workers was bigger than some of the government departments that Angelo had headed. Its twenty-five thousand truck and tanker drivers, aircraft refuellers, baggage handlers and forklift operators moved everything from beer to bricks. Or not, if Howard said so. As well as buildings and cash assets totalling at least twenty million dollars, the Haulers controlled a pension fund in the region of five hundred million. And, not least, a sizeable block of votes on the Labor Party's central administrative panel.

But the Haulers were more than an association of honest toilers, more than just a power base for the right wing of the party, more than just Howard Sharpe's personal fiefdom.

They were a law unto themselves. Judge, jury and, it was whispered, executioner.

'Perhaps this is an opportunity to mend some fences, get a bit of dialogue happening,' I suggested, not altogether facetiously.

'Too late for that,' said Angelo. 'Sharpe's got a long memory and he's a man who knows how to nurse a grudge.'

Agnelli was referring to an encounter during his pre-parliamentary incarnation as an industrial relations lawyer. Acting on behalf of the Construction Labourers' Union, Ange had successfully sued the Haulers after several of their members, cement-truck drivers, crossed a CLU picket line at the urging of Haulers' officials. In the ensuing scuffle, a CLU member was drowned in wet concrete. No criminal charges were ever laid but Ange won the CLU handsome civil-action damages, which it used to foil attempts by the Haulers to poach its members.

'Howard Sharpe came here for a test of strength,' said Angelo, standing up and buttoning his voluminous midriff into his waistcoat. 'And that's exactly what he's going to get.' He inflated his shoulders, tugged downwards to firm the fit of his suit, adjusted the knot of his tie and stiffened his upper lip. 'Time to grasp the nettle.'

'The United Haulage Workers isn't a nettle,' I muttered, falling into step. 'It's the spinning blade of an electric blender.'

The entrance hall of Victoria's Parliament House is paved with mosaic tiles in the pattern of the state bird, a forest-dwelling litter-fossicker. The ceiling of this grand vestibule is so high that you can get a crick in your neck just trying to find it. It is a space designed to impress. The three representatives of the United Haulage Workers did not look impressed. They rose as one from a padded bench and advanced to meet us.

'Gentlemen,' declared Agnelli. 'What a surprise. Just happened to be in the neighbourhood, I suppose. Thought you'd drop in and say hello. Very considerate of you.'

Howard Sharpe was a florid-faced, obese man in his early sixties. His belly preceded him in a bullish, self-satisfied way and his bibulous nose seemed to be glowing even more ominously than usual. He returned Agnelli's greeting with a cursory nod. 'You know Mike McGrath, don't you?' he grunted.

McGrath was his deputy secretary, a thin-lipped individual with round, horn-rimmed glasses and the tapering face of a high-minded ferret. Despite his title, Mike would've had trouble distinguishing a tip-truck from a tenor trombone. His true function was that of Howard's bag man, number cruncher, head-kicker and general gofer. He was being groomed, it was widely believed, for a safe spot on the Senate ticket. To Mike McGrath's way of thinking, anybody entering politics with motives other than ulterior was a *prima facie* idiot.

'And this is Frank Farrell.' Sharpe indicated the third man. 'Our membership welfare officer.'

Sharpe and McGrath were wearing suits, strictly off-the-rack. Farrell wore a grey leather blouson-type jacket over a black turtleneck sweater and neatly pressed jeans. He was somewhere between forty and fifty with thick, brushed-back hair and pumice-stone skin. He shook Angelo's hand, then mine. He had a breezy, masculine manner and a grip that left no doubt about his physical capabilities. Despite his job title, there was no hint of the caring professions about Frank Farrell. Nor was there any hint of the extent to which our destinies would intertwine. If there had been, I probably would have turned tail and fled.

Muscle, I thought. When it came to finesse, nobody beat the Haulers.

'Better come into the parlour,' said Agnelli, leading us down the corridor and back into his office. 'Sit, sit,' he urged, assuming the power position behind his desk.

Sharpe and McGrath glanced around as if trying to decide what to smash first. Or, in McGrath's case, steal. Eventually, they figured out the purpose of the chairs. Farrell remained standing, leaning against the door frame, well behind the action. I took up a position beside Agnelli's desk, put my hands in my pockets and did my best to impersonate an innocent bystander.

The boss leaned back in his chair and spread his arms. 'Fire away,' he said. I hoped that our visitors would not take his words literally.

Sharpe was out of breath from his waddle down the corridor and the exertion of sitting down. 'So, Agnelli,' he wheezed. 'Tell us about this plan of yours.'

'Plan? What plan?' Agnelli raised his shoulders theatrically, a gesture bred into his Latin genes. 'Do we have any plans, Murray?'

'Plenty of plans,' I said. 'No shortage of plans around here.'

'You want to talk plans, Howard,' said Agnelli, 'you should drop in on the Minister for Planning. He's got plans coming out his arsehole. Isn't that right, Murray?'

'Arsehole,' I agreed.

Sharpe leaned forward, his shirt buttons straining, and rested an elbow on his broad knee. He wanted it clearly understood that he was not to be mocked. 'Cut the crap,' he barked. 'You know very well what plan I mean. This truck tax increase. We're not going to wear it, you know.'

'Ah, yes.' Angelo pressed his fingertips together and contemplated the ceiling for a moment. 'The item in this afternoon's paper. Had somebody read it to you, did you? And then you thought you'd drop around, demand to know where I got the temerity to think I might have the right to read my own departmental correspondence without first asking your permission.'

'So it's true,' said McGrath.

'Maybe,' said Angelo. 'Maybe not. Either way I certainly don't intend to be made to account for myself on the basis of an item of gossip in a rag like the *Herald*. Nor do I appreciate being bushwhacked like this, Howard.'

To Sharpe this was no more than preliminary small-talk. He'd come to flex his muscles and nothing Agnelli said was going to stop him. 'Because a tonnage levy is the most stupid fucking idea in the entire fucking history of stupid fucking ideas,' he fulminated. 'And if you think we're going to sit still for it, you need your head examined. The big outfits might be able to afford it. My blokes, the owner-operators, out there busting their guts every day just to survive, you might as well put them out of business, be done with it.'

Agnelli nodded sagely, as if ruminating upon some ancient, imponderable mystery. 'Your loyalty to your members is commendable, Howard. More of whom, by the way, work behind the counter in the airport cafeteria than own semitrailers. And while I'm always perfectly willing to consult with their duly elected leaders, that doesn't mean I'm prepared to have an ugly fuck of a bull-elephant wander into my office any time he likes and shit on the carpet.'

Perhaps he was being a little provocative but I had to admire Angelo's moxie. This was Sharpe's ambush, after all, and he could hardly expect Ange to cop it sweet. He was in Agnelli's backyard now and if a dog can't bark in its own kennel, where can it? Not that a bit of barking ever deterred the Haulers. One time, story was, Sharpe wanted to make a point to an adversary. Bloke came home from work and found the Fido nailed to his front door.

If Agnelli's attitude was designed to aggravate, it was doing the trick. Sharpe flexed his jaw and I thought his nose was going to explode.

During all of this, I was studying Frank Farrell as he leaned against the deep frame of the closed door, his manner both relaxed and attentive, his hands clasped in front of him. He was a confident one, that was for sure. His face was expressionless but from time to time his black Irish eyes lit with a kind of sardonic glint, as though bemused that grown men could behave in such a manner. He was no mere meathead, that much was evident.

McGrath now spoke, the voice of moderation. 'You know that you're going to have to deal with us, Angelo,' he cooed. 'So why make a stick to beat yourself with? Time like this, the Labor Party on the nose with the punters, we should all be pulling together. And you wouldn't want to jeopardise your preselection, would you?'

Melbourne Upper was one of the safest seats in the state. Safe for Labor, safe for Angelo. In all the time he'd held it, Ange had easily retained the endorsement of both the local branches and the party central office. Challengers had come and gone, of course, for ours is a democratic party and any clown is welcome to a tilt. But as the incumbent member, and a minister, Angelo had a secure grip on his seat. Despite the premier's attempts to convince the factional bosses to nominate more women as parliamentary candidates, the outcome of the preselection ballot in a little over a month's time was a mere formality.

'You must think I came down in the last shower, Mikey-boy,' said Ange, leaning forward and putting his elbows on the desk. 'But since you've raised the subject, aren't the Haulers due for an election in a few months? Your members must be getting pretty jack of officials who treat their union as no more than a launching pad for private political ambitions. It wouldn't surprise me if you boys find yourselves facing a bit of competition for once. There's a contender lurking in the wings, I hear.'

'Bullshit,' growled Howard Sharpe, his eyes narrowing. 'What would you know about it?'

Angelo tapped the side of his nose. 'All in good time, my friend. All in good time.'

Mike McGrath, meanwhile, was peering through his spectacles at the bookcases, first at the calfskin-bound volumes of Hansard, most of which had not been opened since before the Boer, and then at Angelo's personal collection of political philosophy, which had not been opened at all.

McGrath started reading the titles aloud. '*A Critique of Political Economy*,' he sneered. '*Retreat from Class: The New Socialism*.' He stood up, removed a volume, flipped through it and returned it to the shelf. 'This is pretty dry stuff, Angelo. Where's your copy of the *Kama Sutra*?'

'That your idea of a witticism, is it?' said Agnelli. 'A subtle hint that I should change my position.'

Howard Sharpe gave a wheezy chuckle. 'A word to the wise, that's all,' he said, his belligerent tone now transformed into one of infinite concern. 'We all have our weak spots. Especially those of us in the public eye.' He formed a circle with his thumb and forefinger and made an illustrative gesture. If there'd been an Eskimo or a Hottentot in the room, even a member of the Liberal Party, Sharpe's meaning would have been obvious.

Angelo wasn't taking the bait. He shook his head with an air of disappointment. 'Stop pulling yourself, Howard,' he said. 'You'll go blind.'

An insistent ringing erupted in the background. The bells announcing the end of the dinner break and summoning members back to their places on the parliamentary benches. Angelo put his palms on the desk, applied his full weight and stood up. 'It's been lovely chatting,' he said. 'But some of us have work to do. Don't hesitate to drop in again. No need for the bodyguard next time, Howard. Murray here isn't half as dangerous as he looks. Now fuck off.'

That was my cue to open the door. As Farrell stepped aside, he gave me a collegial nod. Nothing personal, it seemed to say. All in a day's work for the likes of us, the common foot soldiery.

Sharpe continued to sit in poisonous silence, a lump of surly malevolence. He grunted at last, made a Darth Vader noise in the back of his throat, got up and lumbered out the door, his associates in his wake. 'Round one,' said McGrath as he filed past. 'Nil all.'

The moment I closed the door, Agnelli flopped back into

his chair and heaved a small hurricane of relief. 'Is that the best they can do?' he said.

I doubted it. This was no more than a courtesy visit, a presentation of the Haulers' calling card. A reminder, just in case he needed it, that if Angelo ever contemplated making a decision that might impinge on the Haulers' interests he should expect the worst for his political career and personal reputation.

'So who's this mystery contender?' I said, leaning back against the closed door as if to bar any attempt at re-entry by Sharpe and his associates.

'You,' said Agnelli.

'Me?' I tilted my head to one side and tapped my ear, like maybe my invisible hearing aid was on the fritz. 'What do you mean, me?'

'I mean that Howard Sharpe and his cronies have been re-elected unopposed for as long as anyone can remember. It just occurred to me that rather than sitting around waiting for them to come to us, we should be taking the battle to them.'

Angelo had come up with some crackpot schemes in his time, but this one took the tortellini. If I was hearing him right, he was instructing me to run against Howard Sharpe in the upcoming United Haulage Workers election. What button had been pushed in my employer's febrile temperament to generate such a deranged plan, I wondered?

Surely not the suggestion that he was involved in some kind of sexual impropriety. As well as being a tired and feeble scare tactic, the implication that Angelo was putting it about a bit would only have served to boost his middle-aged ego. He'd been married to the same woman for twenty years and there was nothing in his history to suggest Casanova tendencies. You only had to look at Ange to realise the idea was preposterous.

Could it have been the threat to his preselection? The Haulers had clout in the central party processes by dint of their delegate entitlements at the state conference and the funds they contributed to the organisation's coffers. But Angelo's allies in the left-wing unions more than matched the Haulers' baleful influence. And the Sharpe gang cut little mustard among the rank-and-file party members in the electorate, the other component in the preselection equation.

'There is just one small obstacle to your plan, O Wise One,' I said. 'How can I run in the United Haulage Workers election? I'm not a member of the union.'

Agnelli heaved an impatient sigh and began gathering papers off his desk, budget briefs to review while he was sitting in the chamber, making up the quorum. 'Don't be so literal-minded,' he said. 'Of course you can't do it yourself. But a man of your broad acquaintance shouldn't have too much difficulty finding somebody to give it a shot. We throw a few dollars into the pot, stir gently, and then maybe Howard Sharpe's got something better to do with his time than think up ways to bust my balls.'

'There's a very good reason why nobody challenges Howard Sharpe and Co,' I reminded him. 'It's a health hazard. Last time anybody so much as nominated, the poor bastard spend the next six months in traction.' Or so the story went.

Agnelli tucked his papers under his arm, strode across the office and put his hand on the doorknob. 'I have every confidence in your abilities, Murray,' he said. 'And turn off the lights when you leave. We're on an economy drive, don't forget.'

I stood for a long time at the window, staring down into Spring Street. Rush hour was over, the working week at an end. The city was slipping into evening clothes. Across the road, a crowd was milling in front of the Princess Theatre. Its shingled roof was the shade of ashes and the highlights in its stained-glass windows glowed the colour of clotted blood. A golden angel stood poised upon its roof, trumpet in hand, as if sounding the summons to Judgment Day. The words *Les Misérables* were blazoned across its marquee. I knew what they meant.

Out on the parliamentary terrace, the broad sweep of steps leading down to the street, stood a horse-drawn carriage, an open-topped landau. A top-hatted coachman sat stiffly at the reins, brass buttons gleaming, tall whip in hand. A bride and groom cavorted in the passenger seat, striking romantic poses while a photographer snapped away, framing his shots against the facade of Parliament House. It was a common enough Melbourne sight, a wedding album cliche.

In the stroboscopic stutter of the photographer's flash, the horse raised its tail and deposited a stream of steaming turds. The driver immediately reached under his seat and produced a whisk and a shovel.

That was me, I reflected. And I didn't even have shiny buttons or a broom. I headed for the door.

A trickle of honourable members was emerging from the

dining room, braced with lamb cutlets and cabernet shiraz for a long and drowsy night of law-making. Howard Sharpe and Mike McGrath had waylaid one of them at the entrance to the main lobby, the Queen's Hall. A Labor back-bencher from a marginal seat, he looked like a startled rabbit caught in the headlights of a runaway road train.

As I padded through the foyer, a woman bustled past, the press secretary of the deputy leader of the opposition. She looked the part, a snooty brunette in her late twenties with serious legs and a fiercely businesslike bearing. And a penchant for older men if the salacious scuttlebutt was to be believed. Obviously, I didn't qualify. She gave me a brusque nod and continued on her way. Considering that all the Liberals needed to do to win government was wait until it fell into their laps, I found her self-important manner mildly amusing. Her pins, on the other hand, warranted serious consideration and I sneaked a second appreciative look before heaving open one of Parliament House's massive bronze-inlaid entrance portals and slipping out into the night.

The sky was inky black, the air colder than a conservative's heart. The honk of a saxophone was faintly audible above the rhythmic clatter of a passing tram. At the foot of the terrace, overcoated couples strolled arm-in-arm beneath the fairy-lit trees of Bourke Street. Bound for dinner, I supposed. At Pelligrini's or Il Mondo, perhaps. Mietta's or the Florentino, if they could afford it. Maybe somewhere in Chinatown, a scant block away. Or one of the Greek joints on Lonsdale Street. To any of the cafes, brasseries, bistros, curry houses, pancake parlours and sushi salons that made Melbourne the epicurean epicentre of the nation. If it was edible, we'd eat it. If it wasn't, we'd suck it and see.

I paused for a moment, considering my options. A flame flickered a few paces away. Frank Farrell was standing in the colonnade, having a cigarette while he waited for his employers to emerge. We exchanged nods.

'Off home to the missus, then?' he said.

These were the first words Farrell had spoken since we were introduced. His tone was amiable, his voice a melodious baritone with residual traces of the bush. 'No missus,' I said. 'No pets, either. Sorry to disappoint.'

He chuckled and extended his pack of Marlboro. My daily limit was four and I'd already smoked three. I usually saved the last for after dinner but I found myself accepting his offer, bending to light it from a flame he conjured from a gold lighter in the cup of his blunt fingers.

'Bit rich, don't you think?' I said. 'Sharpe and McGrath toting you along to put the frights on a government minister. No personal offence intended.'

'None taken,' said Farrell. 'I was there to make up the numbers, that's all. Any meeting he ever goes to, Howard likes to know he's got the majority.'

'He's quite a character, your Howard,' I admitted.

'How about Agnelli? What are you doing working for a dipstick like that? No personal offence intended.'

'It's a living,' I shrugged.

'Not for much longer, it won't be. Plan to stick around until the election, sink with the ship?'

'You're not offering me a job, are you?'

'Something can always be found for a friend,' he said.

'Ah, there's the rub.'

Farrell nodded at the Windsor Hotel, catty-corner across the intersection. 'Got time for a beer?'

I consulted my watch. 'Thanks, but I've got a previous.' And drinking with toughs was not high on my must-do list.

Farrell tossed his cigarette butt aside. 'If you change your mind, give me a call.'

'About having a beer?'

'About going down with the sinking ship.' Abruptly he extended his hand.

I shook it. No union of any size, whatever its ideological disposition, can operate without a bit of brawn. Farrell at least had the virtue of not pretending he was anything else. Doubtless we would have dealings, and neither of us wanted to poison the wells yet. Like we both said, nothing personal.

I continued down the steps. The previous appointment was a fib. I had no plans. If I turned right and walked briskly, I'd be home in Fitzroy in less than fifteen minutes. But home exerted no irresistible attraction. I headed down Bourke Street, shoulders hunched against the cold, hands thrust deep into my pockets, my breath advancing before me in a white mist that vanished even as it appeared, ephemeral as an election promise, enduring as a good intention.

Three minutes later I was shouldering open the door of the Rumah Malaysia, breathing deep the aroma of ginger and chilli. The small restaurant was crowded, rackety with the clatter of cutlery and good cheer. The waiter held a single finger aloft, just in case I didn't speak Malay. 'One,' I agreed, and was led to a tragic, tiny table beside the kitchen door.

That was the way it had been for longer than I cared to contemplate. There had been the odd woman in my life since my divorce from Wendy. Odd as in infrequent, not peculiar. But none of them lasted. Not Helen the librarian or Claire the art restorer or Phillipa the doctor.

Phillipa was the most recent. I consulted her about my cigarette habit. She prescribed nicotine patches. Therapy proceeded to dirty weekends at charming little country hotels. But general practice was a tad dull for Dr Phillipa Verstak. And so, apparently, was I. Six months earlier, at the end of summer, she'd gone back to her old job, fitting artificial limbs to land-mine victims at an Austcare hospital in Phnom Penh. How could I compete with legless Cambodian kiddies?

I would've felt a whole lot better about it if she'd managed to cure my cigarette habit. The very thought was enough to make me fire one up. I smoked it while I drank a bottle of Crown lager and waited for my meal to arrive. Four, five, what was the difference? I could die of lung cancer and nobody would shed a tear. Except my son, Red. He'd care. But Wendy probably wouldn't even bother telling him.

The laksa came rich and spicy, helped down with another bottle of beer. By the time I paid the bill, my blood was warm and my head was light. I sauntered back to Bourke Street, half thinking of catching a tram home, half drawn by the tinkle of feminine laughter coming from a line of people extending along the footpath to the front door of the Metro.

Time was, the Metro was a movie house, one of the town's grandest picture palaces. In the seventies, Callithumpian evangelists used it to stage spiritually uplifting productions of *Puff the Magic Dragon and His Technicolor Dreamcoat*. Recently, fashionable architects had transformed it into what the entertainment pages described as a cutting-edge dance club.

I wasn't entirely sure what that meant. Back when I was a barman at the Reservoir Hotel, we used to get some bloke with a panel van to bring in a mobile sound system and one of those modular disco dance floors with the flashing lights underneath. But that was hardly a dance club, was it?

Only one way to find out, I thought. The night was not yet middle-aged. Nor was I, if you counted forty as the starting point. And those bottles of beer had taken off at least a couple of years apiece. I checked out the queue.

I put the median age at twenty-eight, give or take five years. Take, mainly. I was ten years older, but not offensively so. The boys tended to designer jeans and white T-shirts, the girls to scoop-neck dresses and balcony bras. Despite the nip in the air, there was plenty of skin on display. And some of the women were definite lookers. But I was hardly an impartial judge. After six months of celibacy, I was starting to get an erotic frisson from the dummies in shop windows. Nobody screamed when I joined the queue.

The screaming would come later. And I'd be the one doing it.

A matching pair of blondes in micro-minis and stiletto heels stood sentinel at the Metro's entrance. They cast an appraising eye over my navy-blue Hugo Boss suit, concluded that I was pathologically unhip but otherwise both harmless and solvent, and raised the red rope. Doof, doof, doof, came the beat from the interior. Wang, wang, wang.

Twenty-five years earlier, I'd sat in the Metro and watched Gregory Peck and David Niven destroy the guns of Navarone. There was still plenty of smoke and noise and flashing light, but no sign of David Niven. Not his scene at all.

The seats had been ripped out, replaced by a dance floor. The movie screen was now a wall of video monitors, an animated matrix of MTV images, winking and blinking. DJs in white overalls tended a console of turntables, the bridge of the Starship Enterprise, warp-factor nine imminent. A central bar dispensed back-lit liquors and bottles of Mexican beer with wedges of lime shoved in their necks. Beams of coloured light zapped from gimballed prisms set in huge robotic arms that swung out above the dance floor, flexing and pumping to the relentless beat. Doof, doof, doof.

It was still early, not quite eleven, and the place was only half-full. Hardly a thousand people were milling about, crowding the bars or bopping on the dance floor. There were so many blond tips that I wondered if they were spiking the drinks with peroxide. I shed my tie, left my jacket at the coat-check counter, rolled my sleeves to the forearm and elbowed my way to the booze. The happy-hour special was bourbon. To my surprise, it wasn't watered.

Glass in hand, I surveyed the dancers. Criss-crossed by searchlights and enveloped in clouds of artificial fog, they moved with jerky, pixilated movements to a persistent, all-encompassing, unvarying bass thump. Doof, doof, doof.

A suspended gangway led to the balcony where I'd once sat between my parents and watched *The Parent Trap*. It was now a lounge, booth seats with waitress service and a view of the video wall. There was no sign of Hayley Mills. Instead, clusters of frighteningly glamorous women sat around elaborate cocktails, checking the prospects. Even if I'd had the courage to approach one of them, I couldn't imagine bellowing pick-up lines over the top of Tina Turner. If the music got any louder, I'd start bleeding from the ears.

What I had in mind was a statuesque redhead with a come-hither look, the ability to read lips and a lapel badge that said 'Take Me, Murray, I'm Yours'. It looked like she hadn't arrived yet.

Some sort of VIP area occupied the topmost level, admission by membership key-tag only. Doubtless this was where the real fun was being had, the stuff involving rolled-up hundred dollar bills and celebrity cleavage. Techno-beat clanging in my cranium, I retreated to a glassed-in area with a bar along one wall and a half-dozen pool tables covered in blue baize. It was less crowded and marginally quieter.

I took a stool at the bar, ordered another Wild Turkey and pondered my instructions from Agnelli. Any attempt to find a proxy challenger to the Hauler incumbents was bound to be noticed, further aggravating existing antagonisms. And if I persuaded some sucker to stick his head in the lion's mouth and he got hurt, I wouldn't feel very comfortable, ethics-wise.

In this sort of situation, the best way of handling Agnelli was the go-slow. His attention would soon turn elsewhere. First thing Monday morning, I would begin to drag my feet. Meanwhile, I'd clock off, loosen up and try to make the most of the weekend. The hooch was a good start. A bit of female companionship would be even better.

At the nearest pool table, three guys were putting their moves on a trio of girls. All six were in their mid-twenties, well oiled and kicking on. One of the girls was bent over a cue, poised on the toes of one foot. She was slender, fine-boned and wide-eyed, her dark hair cut short. An Audrey Hepburn lookalike, I decided.

The notion amused me. I began to think of screen equivalents for the other players. Nobody too recent, that was the rule. It had to be someone I might conceivably have seen in this very theatre.

The tallest of the girls had long, straight hair and a wide

mouth full of perfectly even teeth. Seen from a distance of several miles by a man with glaucoma, she might have passed for Ali McGraw. The fleshy one with the sultry lips was definitely Maria Schneider. *Last Tango in Paris.* Butter on that popcorn, please.

The short dark guy was playing to type, doing a Jean-Paul Belmondo. Cigarette at the corner of his mouth, up-from-under smoulder as he bent over his cue. Maria Schneider was buying it. Give them a couple of hours and they'd be propped on post-coital pillows, swapping subtitles. The tall thin bloke was a limp-limbed Montgomery Clift. He was doing a line for Ali McGraw.

Male number three was a stocky, cocky, corn-fed Steve McQueen. Whenever Audrey Hepburn potted a ball, he grabbed her hand and hoisted it aloft, referee-style. If she bent to take a shot, he draped himself across her, the better to deliver a coaching tip. Any excuse to touch her. She didn't like it and kept skipping free. Bullitt persisted, convinced of his irresistibility.

The others were too busy pairing off to notice. Lover boy caught me watching and tried to stare me out. I let my eyes drift elsewhere. The last thing I needed was amateur aggravation. One more drink, I decided, then bye-byes for Murray boy.

The crowd was thickening by the minute. I found myself doing the arithmetic. Fifteen hundred people, say. Five bars, all working flat out. Three drinks per person per hour, absolute minimum. Spirits at six bucks a pop, champagne at five a glass, imported beers at top dollar.

For three generations, Whelans had owned and operated licensed premises. Nothing in this league, of course.

Country and suburban pubs, no smoke machines or six-foot door-blondes. Fifteen years since my father sold up, retired to Stradbroke Island, the last of the publican line. Hard to guess the margins, joint like this. Any way you figured it, somebody was doing nicely.

Unlike Steve McQueen. The more Audrey eluded him, the more he drank. And the more he drank, the more pissed-off he got. You could read his growing frustration in the curl of his lips and the way he held his bottle by the neck when he drank. His mates were well on the way to scoring. He was starting to look like a loser. What was wrong with this bitch?

An ugly drunk is an arid source of amusement, even if he's playing pool with a goddess. When he caught me looking again, I held his hostile stare. Same to you, I thought. Not my problem if you flunked out of charm school.

Madonna vogued across the video wall, dividing and multiplying like some collagenic amoeba. Seamlessly the music segued into a track by the artist then still known as Prince. Doof, doof. Wang, wang. Time to hit the frog.

As I skirted the dance floor, I felt my tail-feathers begin to twitch. Weakened by alcohol, my body was succumbing to the all-pervasive beat. Some of these women are here to find a man, my libido wheedled. Perhaps one of them will show a little pity. 'You should be so lucky,' warbled Kylie Minogue.

What the hell. I shuffled into the fray. The dance floor was sardine-tight with bodies, a roiling cauldron of half-glimpsed faces and lurching torsos. As I sashayed deeper into the throng, Audrey bopped into frame, dancing by herself, flushed and radiant, a picture of pulchritude.

Sweet dreams were of this, and who was I to disagree?

I hove-off at a respectable distance, took in the view and gave myself over to a little gentle grooving.

Then Stevie-boy appeared, hot on Audrey's delectable tail. He sidled up close and proceeded to get as grabby as ever. But the bits he was trying to grab were strictly off limits, at least in a public place and without prior permission.

Audrey's expression made her annoyance apparent. Girls just wanna have fun, not be mauled by monomaniacal morons. She removed his hand and mouthed something succinct and unmistakeable.

Clearly, Audrey was a girl who knew how to take care of herself. Gallantry, on the other hand, did not permit me to stand there, swaying on the spot, waggling my buttocks. When McQueen lunged again, I shoulder-shimmied into the breach and wang-dang-doodled him aside. He tried a flanking manoeuvre but I headed him off with a series of rapid-fire John Travolta arm-thrusts. Then I blocked all further attempts at advance with a space-invading frug-jerk combo enhanced with Elvis-inspired pelvic thrusts and I-Dream-of-Jeannie neck wobbles.

Hep, I hoped, to my chivalrous intent, Audrey took the opportunity to vanish backwards into the crowd. Her foiled suitor scowled and gave me the finger. I flexed my groin in his general direction. Steam appeared to come out of his ears, but it was just artificial fog. Then he, too, melded into the crowd and disappeared.

My innovative terpsichorean technique had attracted a certain amount of attention. Beautiful people of every sex, gender and lifestyle orientation began backing away at a rapid pace. My career as a babe magnet was in tatters.

Hip-hop melded into rap. I collected my jacket and

headed for the exit, pausing only to visit the men's room. The original urinals were still intact and fully operational. I gave one of them the traditional greeting, then turned to the hand basins.

Despite the heavy bar traffic, there was only one other customer. It was Steve McQueen. He must have followed me in. I could see at once that he wasn't there to relieve the pressure on his bladder. 'Reckon you're clever, don't you?' he slurred.

For a drunk, he was very fast. He swung wide and his fist connected with the side of my head before I saw it coming. I stumbled backwards, skidded on something slippery and landed flat on my backside on the floor.

Vicious Steve said something in Anglo-Saxon and cocked his foot for a kick. I rolled sideways and started scrambling to my feet. He grabbed the back of my collar and propelled me into a toilet stall. My fingers grabbed for the frame but found no purchase. A white ellipse rose to meet me. Pressure bore down on the back of my head, shoving my face into the toilet bowl. A flushing sound thundered in my ears. Niagara Falls descended.

I fought it hard, gripping the rim of the bowl and arching my back, legs flailing and kicking, my mouth and eyes screwed shut against the torrent of water. The grip on my neck was relentless.

I'm drowning, I thought. What a way to go. Ducked to death in a dunny. I thrashed and heaved and jerked, gasping for air, spluttering and retching. My head banged against the bowl like the clapper in a bell. My mouth collided with the hard enamel and I tasted salty blood.

'Jesus,' declared a distant voice. 'Not again.'

Feet scuffled in the cubicle. Abruptly, the downward

pressure ceased. The cavalry had arrived. My head flew backwards and I sucked at the air, triggering a coughing jag. Stars exploded in my eyes. Wrenching myself upright, I spun around. The men's room was empty. I rushed towards the door. Angry. Dizzy. Intent on revenge. Justice. Something. Anything. A towel would've been good.

The doors swung inwards and my path was blocked by a pair of pretty boys in knit tops and bell bottoms. They stopped dead in their tracks and exchanged scandalised looks. Beyond them, the Metro was a seething mass of bodies, an inferno of swirling lights and deafening noise. My assailant was nowhere in sight. My hair was dripping, my shirt soaked. 'Are you all right?' inquired one of the tweenies.

Not according to the mirror above the wash basins. My lips were a pulpy red mass. My fingers went into my mouth and confirmed what my tongue had just discovered. My two front teeth were gone, sheared off just below the gum line. The canines jutted down on either side of the yawning gap, giving me the countenance of a drenched vampire. Dracula meets the Creature from the Black Lagoon.

A ponytailed punter brushed past me, entered the stall and commenced to decant. I jerked him aside, narrowly avoiding a hosing. Down beyond the lip of red-smeared white porcelain, way down in the yellowy murk, lay something that might have been a pair of shirt buttons.

As I stared down in disbelief, it suddenly occurred to me that maybe they could be re-attached, restored by the miracle of modern dentistry. Averting my eyes, I thrust my hand into the liquid.

'You pervert,' gasped the evicted pisser.

Just as my fingers touched their target, he slammed down the lever and a torrent of water flushed my fangs from my grasp.

'Security!' yelled a voice.

Security was a brace of gorillas in black polyester James Brown tour jackets.

'Walk into a door, didja?' insinuated the one trained to speak.

The other one thrust a wad of cocktail napkins into my hand, something to stop me bleeding all over the floor. My white linen-blend shirt was a write-off. Only worn twice. Sixty bucks at Henry Buck's winter sale.

'I've been athaulted,' I complained, spraying pink saliva. 'He'th about twenty-thicth, medium height, brown thuede jacket.'

Grudgingly, they escorted me around the premises in search of my assailant. He appeared to have absconded. Nor was there any sign of the rest of the cast, Montgomery and Ali, Jean-Paul and Maria. Audrey, too, had made the great escape.

'Call the copth,' I demanded.

This got me nowhere but the front door. One of the blondes indicated a payphone across the street, slammed the velvet rope behind me and turned her pretty face to stone. The phone had been trashed, the handpiece torn off. I toyed with finding another, but not for long. The result was all too easy to predict. An extended wait on a freezing-cold street corner. The eventual arrival of a couple of teenage coppers. Unsubstantiatable allegations against an absent and unknown perpetrator. The pointless taking of details. Polite inquiries as to whether sir had been drinking at all this evening. The inevitable suggestion regarding a taxi and a good night's sleep.

Might as well cut out the middle-man, I figured. Save myself the forty cents. Flag down a cab and get myself home, take a proper look at the damage in the privacy of my own bathroom. At every breath, frigid air whistled thorough the gap in my pearly whites. After a couple of failed attempts to hail a taxi, I turned my face north.

Damp and shivering, I trudged past the now-dark Princess Theatre. *Les Misérables*, I reflected, had nothing on me. Compared with the nightclubs of Melbourne, the sewers of Paris were the fields of Elysium. This was going to cost me a small fortune. Already I could feel the pressure on my hip-pocket nerve.

This sort of thing doesn't happen in Melbourne, I told myself. Ours is not a violent city. We have our share of bank robberies, to be sure. The odd terrorist outrage, for ours is an international city, even if it happens to be located at the far end of nowhere. From time to time, a psychopath goes berserk, opens up on the passing public with an automatic weapon. The police training manual was written by Dirty Harry. But things like this, a vicious attack in a public place, don't happen to people like us. Men in suits. Respectable citizens.

Almost respectable, anyway. No member of the Australian Labor Party is entirely respectable. Not to himself, at least.

The late-night streets had a ghostly air, misty at the edges as though viewed through a vaseline-smeared lens. Traffic was minimal and the office buildings had the abandoned, monochromatic feel of some 1950s science-fiction movie. *The Day the Secretariat Stood Still* or *Attack of the Killer Memorandum*. Here and there, cleaners could be seen silhouetted in windows, vacuums strapped to their backs like the life-support systems of a visiting race of anally retentive aliens.

Other windows showed To Let signs, a reminder that we were in the midst of a recession. The recession we had to have, according to the federal treasurer. We deserved it. It would cut the national flab, make men of us. Lean and mean and competitive men. Men like that arsehole known to me only as Steve McQueen.

God, I hated him. A gutless wonder, groper of women and cold-cocker of innocent ministerial advisers. My tongue kept worrying the stumps of my departed dentition, probing the sharp edges of the fractured enamel, reminding me of my victimhood. Perhaps I should vandalise a public telephone, I thought. That'd show him.

But I passed no phone. Even if I did, I wouldn't have had the energy to attack it. Exhaustion was replacing outrage. I soldiered onwards, past St Vincent's Hospital and the Academy of Mary Immaculate, its walls topped with broken glass. Perhaps the nuns knew something, after all. Perhaps there was more to be feared in this world than the chastening hand of Sister Mary Ursula.

'Why did God make me?' she'd demand.

'To know Him, to love Him and to be with Him forever in heaven,' I'd recite.

Fat lot of good the catechism had done me. God's protecting hand obviously didn't extend to the men's toilets of cutting-edge dance clubs.

Abandoned by the Almighty, a mouth like steak tartare, I entered the narrow residential streets of Fitzroy. The tight-packed terrace houses of my neighbours were dark, shut up against the night. Their occupants were already abed, dreaming of childhood in some Calabrian village. Or bonged into oblivion. Or out the back in the new renovations, sipping a Sambuca at the conclusion of another successful inner-city dinner party.

No light burned in the window of my humble single-storey abode, no fire in the hearth. The framed Spooner caricatures on my hallway wall and the kilim runner on the floor had a reassuring familiarity but they emitted no welcoming warmth. Shit, I didn't even have a cat.

Nor did I bother to look inside as I passed the open doorway of my bedroom. Nobody, I knew for a certain fact, was waiting for me in the bed. The same nobody who'd failed to straighten the covers and clear last weekend's newspapers from the floor. I continued down the hall past Red's room. No point in looking there, either. I knew what I would see. His skateboard, his Spiderman posters, his boxes of dog-eared comics. All untouched in the five months since he last slept there.

Sometimes, occasionally, I'd come home at night, flick on the light, and stand there in the doorway, trying to visualise the outline of his body beneath the covers. Trying to frame the shape of his face in my mind. Imagining that my son was living here with me, not an hour's flying time away, sleeping beneath another man's roof, carried thence by his witch of a mother, Wendy.

Wendy wore the big banana's trousers in the public affairs department at Telecom, a busy career woman with a busy career husband and a house with a view of Sydney Harbour. According to the terms of our no-fault divorce, I was entitled to regular access visits from Red. For practical reasons, this usually meant he came down for the school holidays. But a sporting obligation had nixed the May stay and the upcoming September break had become a victim of Wendy's new maternal status.

Pushing forty, my ex-wife was a mother again. Twins. A matched pair of infant girls were barfing Gerber all over her Chanel suits. And giving her yet another excuse to monopolise Red.

'I think Redmond should come to Noosa with me and Richard instead,' she informed me, when I rang to confer on the September visit arrangements. Richard was the new husband, a hot-shot blueblood lawyer. 'Melbourne's too cold, you'll be busy with work and we've rented a house on the beach. It'll give Red a chance to bond with his new sisters.'

'Can't they bond at home?' I protested. 'Surely he doesn't need a beach to bond.' What were they, babies or fucking mermaids?

Wendy sucked in her breath and, through a thousand kilometres of fibre-optic cable, I heard the skin around her mouth tighten. 'That's the trouble with you, Murray,' she said. 'You're so selfish.'

'Selfish?' Twenty seconds into the conversation and I was already on the ropes. 'I'm lucky if I get to see Red four times a year.'

'And have you ever considered how emotionally disruptive he finds those visits?'

You can't argue with a line like that, and I knew better than to try. I had her put the kid on the phone and we traded a few masculine monosyllables about getting together later in the year. 'See you, son,' I said. But I didn't know when. Christmas, I supposed, unless the bonding didn't take or Wendy found another novel excuse.

It seemed such a long, long time since Red and I were bachelor boys together, hunkered down in congenial suburban squalor while Wendy gadded about the countryside, pursuing her brilliant career. He was seven, then, and we were a collective of two, socialism in one kitchen. He was a teenager now and our time together was gathering dust in an empty bedroom.

I continued down the hall. My living room was as I'd left it. Untidy and smelling slightly of those liberties a man who lives alone permits himself. The good elves, I was not surprised to discover, had yet again failed to visit the kitchen in my absence. But three fingers of whiskey remained in my medicinal bottle of Jameson's. The first mouthful stung, the second burned, the third numbed.

Examining my reflection in the tarnished chrome of my toaster, I could just make out the stumps of my frontal tusks peeking from outraged gums. A fortune, I mumbled. An absolute fucking fortune.

On the other hand, I told myself, things are worse in Cambodia. And self-pity is a mug's game. Count your blessings. I counted them out in the back courtyard, pissing on the lemon tree.

For a start, I had a job. This was more than many of my countrymen could say for themselves. Nearly a million at the last count. But Frank Farrell was right. A little over twelve months remained until the election it was universally understood we would lose. After which, my prospects were anyone's guess. First Monday after the vote, I'd be down the dole office.

Previous experience? the form would ask.

No form in the world had enough space to answer that one, not if I told what I could. Which I wouldn't. Secrets were safe with me. Good old Murray Whelan. Party member from the age of sixteen. Assistant secretary of Young Labor, Northern Metropolitan Region. Research officer for the Municipal Employees Union, retired injured. Associate director of the Labor Resource Centre, now defunct. Electorate officer for the Member for Melbourne Upper, Charlene Wills, since deceased. Ministerial adviser to the Honourable Angelo Agnelli, loose cannon.

My lemon tree and I, upon reflection, had a lot in common. Much pissed upon, but still bearing fruit. 'Buck up,' I told myself. 'Or bugger off.' The Whelan family motto.

The telephone began to ring. Past midnight and somebody was calling. I was not alone, after all. I foreshortened my micturition and rushed through the back door just as my answering machine kicked in with the message that I was not available.

'Yeth,' I gasped, snatching up the handpiece. 'Hello, hello.'

The caller had hung up. I noticed then that the counter on my machine had registered a half-dozen other calls in my absence. I pushed the playback button and listened to the messages.

The first was an invitation from a cold-canvassing telemarketer, an exciting offer on time-share resort accommodation in New Zealand. As if things weren't bad enough, I thought. The second was a jackal of the gutter press, trawling for the inside running on the tonnage levy. Then came a series of hang-ups, three in a row. Maybe I should change my message, I thought. Make it more alluring.

I wondered who my most recent caller had been. But I didn't wonder long. I was battered, bruised, miserable and alone. My head was thumping and I sprayed when I spoke. Bed was looking like a very attractive proposition. Dumping my damp, blood-spattered shirt into the laundry tub, I gingerly brushed what was left of my teeth and crawled between my cold and loveless sheets. Nobody had remembered to turn on the electric blanket. Again.

As I lay there in the dark, shivering slightly, knees drawn up to my chest, the pillow cool against my cheek, I fixed my despicable assailant's features in my memory. That well-fed smirk, that air of entitlement, that flop of rufous hair. I'd remember him always, I vowed. And if I ever saw him again, I'd punch his fucking head in.

'Come on,' I sighed, losing the battle against sleep. 'Have a go, you mug.'

While I slept, a front of low pressure advanced across the continent, sucking moisture-laden air out of the icy wastes of the Southern Ocean and depositing it on the lower edge of the land mass. By the time I awoke, a steady drizzle was drenching the city, rendering the roads slippery and the outlook gloomy.

Mine in particular. I steamed my lips open under a hot shower, rinsed my mouth with orange juice and worked my way through the telephone book until I found a dentist who was open for business on Saturday mornings. Dr Freycinet had a cancellation, his receptionist informed me, in half an hour. His emergency ministrations, she did not need to add, were going to cost me plenty.

With that thought in mind, I pulled on a sweater, donned a waterproof jacket, sprinted to the end of the street and climbed aboard a city-bound tram. Sitting among other glum-faced, wet-shouldered passengers, I scanned the morning tissues. To my considerable relief, it appeared that the tonnage levy beat-up had withered on the vine. Then, as I flipped through the business section of the *Age*, I noticed a half-page spread headlined STUHL SLAMS GOVT COSTS.

Bob Stuhl was the founder and CEO of Stuhl Holdings and nobody had more clout or more trucks than Bob. Over seven hundred of them at latest count, readily identifiable by their distinctive orange livery and the punning brag that each bore on its rear bumper bar: 'Bob Stuhl Is Big.'

Big Bob was a legend. A rough-nut among the silvertails. The man they couldn't root, shoot or electrocute. Not just trucks but shopping centres, hotels and a major stake in an airline. You name it, Bob had a piece of it. Net worth, according to the *Business Weekly* annual rich-list, in excess of eight hundred million dollars. But doing it tough, he wanted us to believe. The story quoted him as warning that transport industry margins were tight and the rumoured state government tonnage levy would send freight costs soaring and bring the economy to its knees.

Wondering if an economy could really be said to have knees, I studied the photograph which accompanied the piece. The *Age* had chosen Stuhl's corporate portrait, head-and-shoulders, full-face. It showed a besuited bulldog with heavy jowls and a thick neck, his luxuriant head of silver hair teased into a grizzled quiff with matching sideburns.

Although he looked like some kind of superannuated old rocker, Bob Stuhl managed to project a potent aura, an amalgam of physical bluster, raw willpower and grasping ambition. Nothing, it was clear to see, had ever been handed to Bob on a silver platter. What he had, he'd wrung from the world with his bare hands. Wrung it until its arteries burst. His eyes, staring out from their sacks of flesh, had an unflinching hardness that made the Ayatollah Khomeini look like Bambi.

In the manner of all great tycoons, Stuhl's ruthlessness was matched by his philanthropy. His largesse included an entire intensive-care wing, donated to the Mercy Hospital after his eldest son was brain-damaged in a swimming pool accident.

The story was a put-up job if ever I'd seen one. First the Haulers, now Bob Stuhl. Head throbbing, I could sense Angelo's irritation turning into a full-blown persecution complex.

I got off the tram at the top end of Collins Street, a block from Parliament House and the Metro. Flecked with drizzle, I hurried along the footpath, counting off the street numbers. At the entrance of almost every building were the brass plates of specialist quackery. Fellows of the Australasian College of Radiology. Dermatologists, haematologists, ophthalmologists and gastro-enterologists. Every one of them with a string of hungry polo ponies or a daughter at a Swiss finishing school. Even their poor cousins had shingles on display. Podiatrists, osteopaths, physiotherapists, contact lens practitioners and dentists.

Dr Freycinet's surgery was in one of the street's few remaining art deco buildings. He had a mottled pink scalp and well-scrubbed fingers like hairy little weisworst sausages. Prodding me with chromium implements, he stared down at the poignantly truncated stumps of my tusks. 'Bet that hurt,' he tut-tutted, with all the cheerful certainty of a man well on his way to his second million.

I scarcely had time to agree before he snapped on a pair of rubber gloves, jammed a dental dam in my mouth, plunged a syringe into my upper gum and proceeded to drive a pair of self-threading stainless-steel posts into the front of my face.

'Relax,' he urged. 'A couple of temporary crowns and we'll have you out of here in a jiffy.'

Ninety minutes later, I was teetering in front of his receptionist's desk, numb from the navel up, wearing a pair of interim plastic incisors. 'Have a nice day,' she chirped, handing me a bill. Four hundred dollars, plus an estimate for the installation of permanent porcelain crowns. Grand total, two thousand three hundred dollars.

The sum reverberated like a gong in my befuddled brain. Twenty-three hundred dollars could've bought me a business-class return trip to Los Angeles, including eight nights accommodation, car rental and a family pass to Disneyland. Two mobile phones with carry cases and battery recharger units. A second-hand car, if I wanted one. Five months of child support payments.

Not that I'd made any recently. Not since Wendy decided to be bloody-minded about Red's access visits. Anyway, Wendy and Richard were probably pulling a cool quarter million a year between them. My maintenance cheques, intended to keep the boy in tennis shoes and subscriptions to *Marsupial Monthly*, were probably going on pool-care products or subsidising Richard's marina fees.

To compound the issue of cost, I felt like I'd just escaped from a cement mixer. All that drilling and grinding, compacting and scraping had taken its psychic toll. Waves of peevish misery sloshed around inside me, searching for an object upon which to break. Had my cowardly assailant been there, I would gladly have throttled him on the spot. Taken my revenge in full view of the passing traffic, confident that no jury in the country would have convicted me. But the prick wasn't there, was he? I didn't even know his name.

Back home, I devoured a handful of industrial-strength aspirin, crawled back into bed, pulled the cover over my head and once again sought catatonia's embrace.

Occasionally, the jangling of the telephone hauled me up from the depths. But I let the machine answer in the other room, slipping back into a dazy doze as soon as the ringing stopped. Probably Angelo, I thought, aerated about the story in the *Age*. Let him share his hair-trigger insecurities and hare-brained schemes with somebody else. His departmental bureaucrats, for instance. There were plenty of those. His other advisers. His factional cronies. His press secretary. His wife.

Even Angelo had somebody to share his bed, I grumbled to myself. Could he really be getting a bit on the side as well? It was just too ludicrous to contemplate. Not to say unfair. I was single and the closest I ever got to romance was the occasional fling with Mrs Palmer and her five daughters. And I wasn't even in a fit state for that sort of consolation.

A bang woke me, an insistent rapping on the back door. A six-year-old child stood on the step, her face beaming up at me, a tiny moon in the murky twilight. 'Mum thed to come and have dinner at our plathe,' she lisped, the gap in her milk-teeth mirroring my recent condition. 'If you want.'

Her name was Chloe and she lived on the other side of the cobbled lane that ran behind my house. Her parents,

Faye and Leo Curnow, were my closest friends. Family almost. The sort of people who take an active interest in a man's misfortunes. Faye was a journalist at the *Finance Weekly* and Leo lectured in something mathematical at Melbourne University. Their other child, Tarquin, was the same age as Red and the two boys had been pals since kindergarten.

Now passably fit for human intercourse, I accepted the invitation. While Chloe rushed home to lay me a place at the table, I dressed and checked the phone messages. Four calls, all hang-ups. Crossing the lane, I stepped into the fug of domesticity, the heady aroma of drying laundry and vegetable soup, the reassuring cacophony of the television: 'Hey, Hey, It's Saturday'.

Reading glasses perched on the tip of her nose, Faye was simultaneously whisking the contents of a saucepan and consulting a cookbook. Leo was wrestling the cork from a bottle of red wine. The kids were arrayed on beanbags, glued to the box. Tarquin glanced up, then did a double take and squinted at my lips. 'Have you got cold sores or something?' he demanded. 'You look really gross.'

'Somebody smacked me in the mouth,' I said. 'If you're not careful, it could happen to you.'

Faye hitched up her glasses and took a closer look. 'You're kidding?'

'I wish I was.'

As I reprised the Metro massacre, Faye rolled her eyes and shook her head reproachfully. Trouble, she firmly believed, didn't just happen.

Leo, however, was impressed. 'Brawling in a nightclub,' he grinned through his beard. 'There's life in the old dog yet.'

When I got to the bit about the dentist bill, Faye leaned close and scrutinised my temporary prosthetics. 'They're very white,' she said. 'But apart from the fact that they glow in the dark, they almost look better than the originals.'

I tried them out on her gourmet experiment, a *tagine d'agneau a la Morocco*. It melted in the mouth, for which I was grateful. Apart from the thrashing it had copped in the Metro toilet, my cavity had taken a fair buffeting from Dr Freycinet's tubby fingers and shiny appliances.

'How come this stew's got apricots in it, Mum?' said Tarquin.

After dinner, the children watched television while the adults sat around the kitchen table, chewing the cabernet sauvignon. Faye, cat on her lap, took up a recurrent theme. 'You know what you need, Murray?' she said. 'A woman.'

The next morning I got a call from one.

Her name was Lyndal Luscombe and she was my successor as Angelo's electorate officer. She had a husky voice, a throaty laugh and she gave great telephone.

I was lingering over breakfast in the pale sunshine that was filtering through my kitchen window when she rang. I'd slept late and woken to a succession of minor miracles. My head was clear. My mouth felt almost normal. There was nothing in the papers about the tonnage levy. The sun was shining and I was considering how I might fritter away the rest of the day, make the most of the unseasonably fine weather.

'Hello Murray,' she said. 'It's Lyndal.'

'Murray's not here,' I said. 'He died of a broken heart. The woman he loves left him for another.'

'Really?' she said. 'The way I understand it, he dithered around, never declared his intentions, left his play too late. She had no idea about his true feelings.'

'He didn't think it was right to make a pass at a professional colleague,' I said. 'He's a very proper person.'

'As well as being dead?'

'Only from the waist down,' I said. 'And the sound of your voice has fixed that. To what do I owe the pleasure, Lyndal?'

'The usual,' she said. 'Our lord and master.'

Lyndal had been running Agnelli's constituency office in Melbourne Upper for the previous three years, the reward for some highly effective voter-profiling work for the state secretariat. She was a psychology graduate, a one-time crisis counsellor whose experience with the depressed and suicidal amply qualified her to run a local Labor Party office. And, usually, to deal with our boss.

'He's cutting the ribbon at the opening of our new community cultural centre today,' she said. 'When I rang this morning to brief him, he interrogated me about threats to his preselection. Went right off the deep end, reckoned somebody was plotting against him, wanted me to draw up a list of potential traitors. I think he's flipping out, Murray, and I'd really like your advice. Any chance you can come out to this wing-ding today?'

It seemed I'd found a place to do my frittering. And I couldn't think of anybody I'd rather fritter with. 'Can you hold on a moment?' I said.

I put the phone down and went to the bathroom mirror. My lips were still a little crusty and my frontal fangs glowed several shades brighter than their next-door neighbours, but I was not unsuitable for general exhibition. I picked up the phone again. 'Will Nick be there?' I said.

Nick Simons was Lyndal's designated other, the man who'd snaffled her, struck first while I had hesitated.

'That's for you to find out,' she said.

Half an hour later, I was dolled up in my best Country Road casuals, boarding the Number 11 tram to Preston.

Out I rode, out beyond the cafes and terraces of Fitzroy. Out across the Merri Creek, dredged now of its industrial effluent, home again to the migrating eel, green with young eucalypts and threaded with bike paths. Out past the Greek Orthodox monastery, its bell tolling noonday prayers across the heathen roofs of weatherboard bungalows and brick-veneer dream homes. Out past discount clothing stores and fried chicken franchises and the temples of gimcrack Protestantism with their couch-grass lawns and peeling facades. Out past second-hand office furniture showrooms and the wire-meshed windows of licensed grocers. Out into the heartland of the party of the proletariat, to the electorate of Melbourne Upper.

Lulled by the swaying of the tram, I thought about Lyndal. About how I should've made my move when I had the chance. How we met during the '88 election campaign and more than once exchanged the kind of signals that give rise to a man's hopes. How I'd held back, justifying my timidity with spurious reservations about getting involved with a workmate. How I'd let her be snatched away by Nick Simons, a organiser with the Amusement, Entertainment and Theatrical Employees Federation. A ticket seller to the ticket sellers. How Nick was a nice enough bloke, but that didn't mean I wasn't entitled to try to rectify my mistake. Lyndal didn't have children and, by definition, a childless woman is always fair game. She has not yet mated for life.

When the tram reached the terminus depot, I got out and walked. At the Doug Nichols reserve, a little-league football game was in progress, half-pint ruckmen contesting the slippery pigskin across a trampled patch of mud, parents howling encouragement from the sidelines. The kids were younger than Red, eight or nine, but I could imagine my son, socks around his ankles, dashing for the goal posts, a look of fixed determination on his face, trying to hide his disappointment when the kick went wide. I turned away and hurried on.

A hundred metres up the road I reached the Northern Region Performing Arts Centre, a post-modern assemblage of corrugated steel and tinted cement that rose from a car park between a railway line and an arterial road. 'Official Opening Today', proclaimed a banner suspended above the entrance, 'Join the Fun'.

The fun was already well advanced. Lambs were being spit-roasted and sausages sizzled in a row of open-faced rent-a-tent pavilions. Boys in bum-fluff moustaches, embroidered waistcoats and Nike runners tuned fretted instruments beside the stage door. Girls with coin-fringed headscarves rehearsed dance steps between parked minibuses. Community groups had set up stands in the foyer. The Nursing Mothers' Association and the Movement against Uranium Mining. The Local History Society and the Committee for a Free East Timor. Beside the face-painting stall, an environmental Leninist tried to sell me a copy of *Green Left Weekly*.

Slipping into the auditorium, I found a vantage point against the side wall. Formalities were in full progress, the mayor presiding, a former butcher with a face like a slice of corned beef. On the stage behind him sat a row of dignitaries, including the federal and state members of parliament.

Agnelli's wife, Stephanie, was seated beside him, the very figure of wifely rectitude in a russet-toned, knee-length suit and sensible shoes.

The crowd was doing its best to keep the chatter down to a roar. 'We are here to salivate the pre-forming arts,' the mayor proclaimed, testing the new acoustics to the limit.

I scanned the audience. Nick Simons was nowhere in sight. I found Lyndal in the second row. She was wearing a cable-knit sweater and stretch slacks, leaning forward in her seat, compact and muscular, her chin pointed forward like the figurehead of a sailing ship. Her face was a mask of dutiful attention but the edges of her lips were curling slightly in wry amusement at His Worship's malapropisms.

A country girl, six years younger than me, Lyndal had been drawn to the Labor side of politics by a temperamental disposition towards social justice and an intellectual disdain for the self-serving nostrums of the Liberals. She modestly concealed these attributes behind a flip manner and a technocratic fascination with the intricacies of bureaucratic procedure. She had full, luscious lips and tight curly hair.

How I longed to federate with her, to capture her preferences, to scrutinise her affiliations. To man her booth, to poll her quorum, to table her amendments, to join her in congress, to have her sit on my administrative committee.

She swivelled in her seat to survey the room. Her green, cat-like eyes caught mine and she tipped me a conspiratorial wink. I replied with a little salute and we turned our faces back to the microphone. To Angelo, our boss and our cross.

He wore a sports coat and striped tie, neither too formal nor too casual. Just one of the folks, if a slightly more important one. His speech was mercifully brief. He praised the creativity of the local community, referred modestly to his own role in getting the centre funded, thanked all the right people. He read from cue cards, doubtless prepared by Lyndal.

Ange's address concluded the formalities. Lyndal swooped, escorting the distinguished couple to the door, whispering names in his ear as Angelo pressed the flesh. People stood, stretched, hailed friends. A choir filed onto the stage. I nodded to some familiar faces and drifted outside.

Lyndal was standing on the auditorium steps, observing Agnelli as he mingled with the punters, handing out the howdy-doodies. I propped beside her, shoulder-to-shoulder. Our heights were almost equal and it was all I could do not to step behind her, wrap my arms around her waist and scratch my itch on the small of her back.

Angelo had stopped to chat at one of the food stalls. Somebody handed him a sausage in a bread roll. Mustard squirted onto his tie when he bit into it, and he jumped backwards like the victim of an unwelcome practical joke.

'He's never been very comfortable with his constituents,' said Lyndal. 'But I've never seen him this edgy. Any idea what's spooking him?'

'He's had a recent visit from the Haulers,' I said. 'They threatened to jeopardise his preselection.'

'The Haulers are a very spooky outfit,' she said, 'but they don't have any influence out here. Angelo should know that.'

Choral keening erupted inside the auditorium in an unfamiliar language. English, probably.

'I'm sure he does,' I said. 'But I'm beginning to suspect that our employer has finally been promoted beyond the level of his incompetence. He could barely handle the burden of his minor portfolios. Transport's a major nightmare and he may not be able to cope.'

Lyndal considered this information for a while. It seemed to reassure her. 'So it's just general anxiety, then? He doesn't have some specific suspicion?'

'All I know is that he needs a lot of hand-holding at the moment,' I said. 'Although I'd prefer if it was my hand being held. By you. Where's Nick, by the way?'

'On the road as usual,' she said. 'Warracknabeal, Ararat, Horsham. Doing a membership sweep of the country racetracks.'

If this woman was mine, I'd be superglued to her, not chasing turnstile attendants in the boondocks. 'Great,' I said. 'Then there's nothing to stop you flirting outrageously with me.'

'Nothing but that man down there,' she said, nodding towards Angelo.

A cluster of constituents had captured their representative and were getting into his ear. A problem with domiciliary nursing-care benefits, possibly, or a wrangle with the office of Consumer Affairs, the Liquor Licensing Commission or the land valuation board of review. A matter, in any case, either beneath Angelo's dignity or beyond his capacity. He put his hand up and started waving in our direction like a drowning man signalling a lifeguard.

We started down the steps. 'You've got it cushy out here in the electorate,' I said. 'The worst Angelo can do is alienate a few pensioners. Back at the ministry, he's at war with the entire trucking industry.'

'What do you mean, cushy?' she huffed. 'Some of these

pensioners can be savage. The worst that can happen to you is an overdose of country and western.' As she dived into the scrum surrounding Angelo, the lambent twang of a steel guitar wafted from the far end of the car park.

The music was neither country nor western. It was rockabilly, and its source was a band on an outdoor stage beyond the blow-up jumping castle, the flat-bed of a truck trailer. Figuring I'd continue to pitch my woo at Lyndal when she finished bailing out Angelo, I bought myself a can of beer and joined the meagre gaggle of toe-tapping onlookers in the watery winter sunshine.

They called themselves 'Over the Limit'. Two guitars, a slap bass, a vocalist and drums. Middle-aged amateurs, paunches over their belt buckles, they laid with cheerful abandon into a repertoire of Hank Williams and Carl Perkins standards. Jambalaya Joe and his Blue Suede Shoes.

The drummer's name was Donny Maitland. I never knew he played the drums, but it didn't surprise me. Nothing Donny did could ever surprise me.

I was sixteen when I met Donny Maitland. One hot summer afternoon, he sprung me reading a novel in the cellar of my father's hotel, the Carters Arms, shirking my chores in the cool of the stainless steel beer barrels. He threw back the pavement doors and stared down at me, nimbus-headed in the furnace of the afternoon, bare-legged in his work shorts, the sleeves of his brewery-issue shirt rolled to the shoulders.

'What have we here?' he declared, eyeing my Penguin paperback. 'An intellectual?' He must have been in his late twenties then. A man to my boy. A man unlike any other I'd met, and you meet a lot when your father owns a hotel.

I slipped *The Plague* into my back pocket and helped him unload his consignment, taking the strain as he rolled the eighteen-gallon kegs down the ramp. Not that he needed much help. Donny was solid muscle, strong as an ox.

Afterwards, he went into the public bar to get the delivery docket signed and have a beer. They always had a drink, the brewery drivers. I tagged along, drawn as if by gravitational force. Raising a silent toast to our comradeship of labour, he lowered the entire contents of his glass down his throat in one smooth swallow. 'You ought to be careful,' he warned, wiping his mouth with the back of his hand. 'That existentialism shit, it'll rot your brain. Start reading Camus, you'll end up on Kafka.'

I wasn't sure who Kafka was. But I'd heard the name, so I asked about him.

Donny and I talked books for the next half-hour, during which he consumed several more glasses of beer. His views were trenchant, visceral, political. Drawn from the certainty of his class, sharpened by his intellect and confirmed by his experience. And he talked to me like an equal. No grown man had ever done that before.

From then on, through school and university and beyond, Donny was a comet that blazed intermittently on the periphery of my vision. A promiscuous reader and tireless talker, he was equally conversant with the thoughts of Mao Tse-tung and the licks of Lightning Hopkins. A hard drinker at bohemian parties, he somehow managed to combine unmoderated radicalism with steady employment. Women loved him. Loved his energy, his humour, his unruly mop of sandy hair and his big, expressive hands.

Hands that were now wrapped around drumsticks, pounding out a steady four-four beat on an el-cheapo beginner-level drum kit. The passage of time had thinned his hair a little and softened the flesh on his frame. He was whiskey-raw at the cheekbones, too. You can get that in your fifties.

Over the Limit weren't bad for a scratch band, though their title was not entirely inaccurate. My attention moved from the impromptu stage to the prime mover. It was a flash rig, a snub-nosed Kenworth with chrome bullbars and vertical exhausts. White with navy blue trim. Hefty horsepower in high-gloss livery. A name was painted on the door, wrought in the ornate copperplate beloved of the trucking trade. *Maitland Transport.*

Last I'd seen of Donny, a couple of years back, he was still at the brewery, twenty years on the job. By the look of it, he'd cashed in his chips and struck out on his own. I struck out, too. Tossed my empty can and scouted the crowd for Lyndal.

It was slow going. At every turn I ran into familiar faces. Old mates from the neighbourhood whose children were in need of my admiration. Minor ethnic luminaries. Chronic conspirers from the local party branches. By the time I arrived back at the auditorium, Angelo's official car was gone from the kerb. And his electorate officer, sadly, was nowhere to be found.

I drifted back to the twang just as Over the Limit were finishing their set with a thumping rendition of Lonnie Mack's 'Down in the Dumps' that set the friends-and-family crowd whooping and hollering. Donny spotted me as he cleared his kit from the stage and vaulted down off the trailer, surprisingly light on his feet. He greeted me with a slap on the shoulder and a wide smile. 'Well?' he demanded. 'Whatta you reckon?'

'Tragic old farts,' I said. 'Should be called Over the Hill.'

'Call us what you like, it's thirsty work,' he said. 'And since you're looking so prosperous, Murray, how about you buy me a beer.'

We went into the bar tent, popped the tops off a couple of tinnies and stepped back into the open air. A Latin combo was setting up on the stage, lots of percussion.

'You can't be exactly poverty-stricken yourself,' I said, waving my drink at the big Kenworth. 'Looks like you've become a capitalist.'

'Nah.' Donny chugged on his can and shook his bearish head. 'I'm just the wage slave of a petty proprietor.'

The owner's name on the door, he explained, was that of Heather, his sister-in-law. 'Ex, rather. My little brother Rodney did the dirty on her, shot through with a new cookie. Sold the business, panel beating, twelve on the payroll. Took the money and ran. Heather's got her lawyers on the case, but everything takes forever. Only thing left was the truck. Rodney had it in the wife's name for tax reasons, leasing it out. Lease expired and she tried to sell it, couldn't get a decent price. After I copped the flick from the brewery, she made me an offer. I drive and she handles the business side. No regular contracts, unfortunately. Just bits and pieces. Fruit and vegetables, mainly.'

I clearly needed some updating on Donny's recent history. Turfed by the brewery? Before I could ask what this was about, he grabbed me by the elbow and glanced around, acting scared. 'You're not still working for that Angelo Agnelli, are you?' he said. 'If Heather finds out, she'll be into you about this tonnage levy scheme. She'll make mincemeat of you, mate.'

I heaved a weary sigh. 'The tonnage levy's bullshit,' I said. 'Nothing but media mischief. The trucking industry'll be free to pothole the public highway for the life of this administration, I guarantee it.'

'Well your boss'd better get the message out pronto,' advised Donny, releasing his grip. 'The tom-toms are beating in every roadhouse in the state and the CBs are crackling with rumours.'

'Being spread by the Haulers, no doubt,' I said. 'They're keen to keep the government on its back foot. With friends like Howard Sharpe, who needs enemies?'

'Amen to that,' nodded Donny. 'The bastard stitched me up good and proper.'

'Yeah?' I said. 'What's the story?'

'The usual one. But I'm planning to rewrite the ending. Let's get something to eat and I'll tell you all about it. Come and meet Jacinta.'

'Who's Jacinta?'

'*Mi corazon,*' he said, as the Sandinistas of Samba kicked in.

He led me into the sit-down eating area, a cluster of green plastic garden tables, and introduced me to two men and a woman sitting at a spread of chicken pilaf and pork rolls. 'Roscoe, Len and this is Jacinta.'

The men gave me curt but friendly nods. They had the same all-weather, hard-living complexions as Donny although they were a little younger and firmer in the body. Roscoe was lank and rangy. Len was the nuggety pug-eared type.

Jacinta was fortyish, tawny skinned with cow eyes, masses of raven hair and a generous gap-toothed smile. 'Sit down,' she urged. 'Help yourself. There's plenty to go around.' She had an accent, a glottal sort of American-Asian cross. A Filipina, if I guessed right. Donny beamed at her proudly. Last time I looked, he was flying solo. She seemed nice and I was glad for him.

We sat down and tucked into the food. The band was loud

and I butted my seat against Donny's, raising my voice to be heard above the music. 'You were saying about Howard Sharpe,' I prompted. He put his plate down, as if the subject had ruined his appetite, parked his elbows on the table and gave me the oil.

Twelve months back the brewery fell into the hands of corporate raiders. The new owners immediately set about carving it up, stripping the assets, flogging off everything that wasn't nailed down. Including the fleet of trucks. The delivery contract went to Bob Stuhl, a known associate, who proposed to lay off the drivers on the brewery payroll. The union stepped in and brokered a deal. In exchange for improvements in productivity, the men would keep their permanency and conditions.

'Before long, the squeeze was on,' said Donny. 'Longer hours, double shifts. Anybody quit, they didn't get replaced. Country runs, blokes were falling asleep at the wheel. Three fatals in three months.'

Donny was the shop steward. The men sent him to talk to Howard Sharpe. The union had done all it could, he was told. The men could like it or lump it. Instead, at Donny's instigation, they pulled a wildcat strike.

'Just before Christmas, it was. The period of maximum demand.'

Under pressure from his corporate cowboy cronies, Stuhl folded, agreed to new schedules and overtime allowances. Three weeks later, Donny was offered a beer after making a delivery. 'Used to be part of the culture. Some blokes'd drink ten, twelve pots a day. Reckoned the trucks knew their own way home. But that era's long gone. Drinking on the job's a sacking offence these days.'

The publican insisted. Just the one, he said. No harm in that. Made an issue of it. Wouldn't sign the docket until Donny had a drink with him. 'Soon as the glass touched my lips, one of Stuhl's managers tapped me on the shoulder, fired me on the spot. It was a set-up, but Sharpe washed his hands of me. Said I'd dug my own grave, undermined the union leadership's credibility with employers. Twenty-five years a member and the self-satisfied sack of shit sold me down the river.'

I nodded sympathetically. 'He came to visit Agnelli a couple of days ago. Paraded his credentials as the champion of the working truckie. Problem is, he's had uncontested control of the union for so long that he thinks he can get away with anything. And that'll never change until somebody steps on his tail.'

'Well, that might just be on the cards,' said Donny. 'I'm not the only one who's had a gutful.'

'That right?' I said. 'I don't suppose you'd know anybody who might be interested in taking a crack at our fat friend?'

Donny gave me a sly, sideways look. 'Our new transport minister wouldn't be looking for a chance to ruffle Howard Sharpe's feathers, would he?'

'Put it this way,' I said. 'Anybody prepared to tackle the current Haulers' leadership might well find himself the beneficiary of an anonymous donor.'

Roscoe and Len were angled back in their chairs, legs extended, beer cans on their laps, soaking up rays and watching the band. Donny reached across the table with his fork and prodded Roscoe in the arm. 'Murray here's got a line on some prospective campaign finance,' he said. 'Show him your T-shirt.'

Roscoe looked me up and down with new interest, then unbuttoned his denim jacket and displayed the slogan emblazoned across his chest. *Vote Reform Group*, it read, *Stop the Sharpe Sellout.*

'Reform Group?' I said. 'Who's that?'

'Us,' said Donny. 'Me, Roscoe and Len. We're putting a rank-and-file ticket together to run for the state executive.'

'You'll need more than a T-shirt to knock Howard Sharpe off his perch,' I said. 'And you'd better have good medical insurance. Those boys play rough, by all accounts.'

'We're not exactly cream-puffs ourselves,' said Donny. 'Right, comrades?'

Roscoe and Len made clenched-fist gestures and grimaced militantly. 'If you don't fight, you lose,' declared Roscoe.

And sometimes you just lose. But these blokes didn't look like babes in the woods and, since they already had a campaign up and running, perhaps it'd be possible to meet my brief from Angelo after all. And do my old mate Donny a favour at the same time.

'You got any other backing?' I asked. 'Running a state-wide campaign costs money.'

'Early days,' said Donny. 'The vote's still four months away and we've only just lodged our nominations. But I reckon I'll be able to round up some resources from Sharpe's enemies in other unions. He's got plenty.'

'And you wouldn't mind getting into bed with Agnelli?'

Roscoe leaned forward and breathed beery fumes into my face. 'Listen, mate,' he told me. 'We'll lie down and spread 'em for anybody who helps us stick it up Howard Sharpe.'

'Roscoe's another of the brewery casualties,' said Donny, waving his associate back into his seat.

I eyed Donny's running mates sceptically. 'Angelo'd want some bang for his buck. He's not a soft touch.'

'Naturally you'll want to run the tape over us, see if we're dead-set,' said Donny. 'Come down to the wholesale fruit and vegetable market tomorrow morning. We'll be in campaign mode. If you like what you see, you can square us with your boss.' He rubbed his thumb and forefinger together. 'Let's say about three-thirty, four o'clock.'

'In the morning?' I said. 'Forget it. Agnelli doesn't pay me enough to get up that early. I only assess campaigns conducted in daylight.'

The bongo beaters finished their bracket and some sort of ethno-pop ensemble moved onto the stage. Clarinet, accordion, bazouki and tabla. A woman in a down-filled vest arrived and tapped Donny on the shoulder. She was short and busty, her plentiful cheese-blonde hair pinned up with a pair of tortoiseshell combs. Moon-faced, well-preserved, mid-thirties.

'How long before this finishes?' she demanded impatiently, indicating the stage. 'Don't forget you've got to be in Nar Nar Goon in time to load those potatoes.'

'How could I forget with you around to remind me?' said Donny resignedly. 'Murray, meet my slave-driver, Heather.'

She checked me out, head cocked to one side, scrunching her eyes against the low-slung sun. 'Murray?' she said. 'Not Murray Whelan?'

I looked at her more closely. It was not painful but it made me none the wiser as to how she knew my name.

'Coburg Town Hall, 1970,' she said, smirking a little. 'The debutante ball. I was Heather Dunstable then.'

The deb ball was the highlight of the municipal social

calendar. A chance for the favoured maidens of the suburb to don elbow-length white gloves, chisel-toed satin shoes and A-line evening gowns and play at being princesses, escorted beneath a flower-decked trellis archway by young men in hired dinner suits, dragooned for the occasion from the ranks of local likelihood.

A university student, I was well beyond such things. Or so I thought until I got the call. The mayor's daughter, it seemed, had a best friend, a lovely young lass whose intended partner had broken his collarbone when an engine block dropped on him during a clutch-plate replacement. As a prominent member of Young Labor, I was considered an ideal stand-in escort. And since the council provided the venue for our annual conference for nix, the mayor was sure I'd be only too happy to oblige. All I had to do was pick the girl up, lend her my elbow during the presentation ceremony and waltz her around the parquetry a couple of times. His Worship would even swing for the tux rental and the corsage.

And thus it came about that I rang Heather Dunstable's doorbell, boxed orchid in hand, wearing a ruffled apricot shirt and clip-on velvet bowtie. I found myself facing a vivacious little butterball, her hair in coiled ringlets, the front of her dress dropping away to a view that all but sucked my eyeballs out of their sockets. 'Pick your jaw off the floor,' she said. 'We don't want to be late.'

By the time I'd met her parents, posed for photos in front of the mantelpiece, bundled her into my Zephyr and driven to the town hall, I'd learned that Heather preferred the Kinks to the Rolling Stones and could hardly wait to start secretarial college.

She could hardly wait for other things, too, but I didn't find that out until later, after we'd ascended the red-carpeted steps of the town hall stage and she'd curtsied before the mayor and the lady mayoress. After she'd got giggly on Brandivino and lemonade and suggested we stop off on the way home and take in the view of Coburg Lake in the moonlight.

'That's not moonlight,' I told her as we parked under the trees. 'It's the glow from the searchlights at Pentridge prison.'

'I'm not stupid, you know,' she said, slipping off her shoulder straps. 'Let's get in the back seat.'

Compared with the pimply adolescents who'd squired her peers, I was probably a bit of a catch. Or so I fancied. 'Don't worry,' she breathed. 'I'm not in love with you or anything.' Then she said something that no other girl had ever said to me, certainly none of those stand-offish snobs at uni. A phrase which every red-blooded male of my generation longed to hear. 'It's okay,' she assured me. 'I'm on the pill.'

All this flashed through my mind in a nanosecond, sending a rush of heat to my face. 'Heather Dunstable,' I blurted. 'Of course I remember. You haven't changed at all.'

'And you're still a smooth talker.' She smirked, enjoying my discomfort. 'I was only sixteen, you know.'

'Yeah,' I said. 'But advanced for your age.' More than I was, still a virgin at nineteen.

She pulled up a chair, moved closer, got chatty. 'You were doing law, weren't you?'

'Politics,' I said.

Donny was observing Heather's moves with ill-concealed amusement. 'Murray works for the transport minister,' he said. 'He's been telling me how he managed to get this tonnage levy quashed. And I've been telling him about our campaign.'

'Your crackpot crusade, you mean,' she said. 'If you spent as much time behind the wheel as you do plotting to take over the union, we could almost afford to go broke.'

Jacinta paused in the middle of packing up the remains of the food. 'Choo have to stand up for what choo believe,' she flared.

This was clearly a well-gnawed bone of family contention.

'Murray's coming to the market in the morning,' Donny told Heather, as though the matter was settled. 'He's thinking of getting behind the campaign.'

The reedy wail of snake-charming music came from the stage. Heather put her bosom against my shoulder and leaned into my ear. 'So tell me,' she purred. 'Is there a Mrs Murray?'

According to the calendar, spring was only a few weeks away. But spring in Melbourne is an elusive phenomenon, a largely theoretical construct. It finds expression less in the behaviour of the elements than in the expectations of the population. It arrives because, having endured winter, we deserve it.

But we didn't deserve it yet. Not by a long chalk. Battalions of black clouds were rapidly advancing from the south-west horizon. By the time the Felafel Quartet went into their big finish, blasts of wind were sending litter flying and up-ending the plastic tables. In the sudden rush of activity to pack up before the rain arrived, I slipped away.

By the time I got home it was pushing 7.30, and rain was drumming on the iron roof. Running into Donny had been a stroke of luck. What with one thing and another, I was due for a win. And what could be better than a win-win deal with an old friend? As I thawed myself in front of the wall furnace and scanned the television guide, the phone rang. I let the machine answer and cocked an ear.

'For God's sake, Murray,' a woman's voice pleaded. 'If you're there, pick up the phone. Please, please, please.'

It sounded a lot like my ex-wife, although pleading had never been part of Wendy's repertoire. The snarl was Wendy's customary mode of address where I was concerned.

Curious, I answered. 'Hello, Wendy? Is that you?'

'At last,' she said. 'At last.' A more familiar, hectoring tone came down the line. 'Why didn't you answer my calls? I've been trying to reach you all day.'

'What is it, Wendy?' I sighed, resigned to a lecture on my evasion of financial duty, cursing my better nature for suckering me into taking her call.

'It's Red,' she blurted, her voice quivering at the name. 'Our little boy. He's gone.'

'Gone?' I said. 'Gone where?'

She didn't know. And that was only part of it. She didn't know when, either. 'It must have been some time on Friday night. The school didn't realise he was missing at first.'

'What do you mean, the school? Was he at a camp or something?' I imagined some character-building three-day adventure in hutments on the edge of a national park. Obstacle courses and nature walks, possum-spotting by torchlight and dishwashing duty in the communal kitchen. Then a wrong turn taken on a hike. Search parties thrashing through impenetrable bush, police helicopters, rescue crews abseiling down cliff-faces, an injured child shivering all night in some wombat hole.

'Oh, yes,' said Wendy, like she'd just remembered. 'I've been meaning to tell you. We enrolled him as a boarder at Richard's old school. It's very hard to get into.'

But not, apparently, out of.

'You put Red in a private boarding school?' I could hardly believe what I was hearing.

'He wasn't being challenged in a government school.' For once, Wendy was on the defensive.

'Or thrashed or sodomised.'

'That's terribly unfair,' she snapped, back in familiar form. 'Brookside isn't like that at all. We were just doing what we thought was best. I've got my hands pretty full, you know, with the new babies and work. And Richard's job is very demanding. We both have to travel a lot. We felt that Red would benefit from the experience. Anyway, he comes home most weekends.'

'But not this one? A fact that somehow managed to escape your attention, what with your busy lifestyle and all.'

That really got the acrimony going. When it abated a little, I managed to learn the little that Wendy knew. It seemed that Red had vanished some time after lights-out on Friday night. His absence was noted on Saturday morning yet, due to some crossing of the procedural wires, it was assumed that he'd simply gone home for the weekend. Wendy spent Saturday and most of Sunday oblivious to this misunderstanding. 'He left a message at my office on Friday, said he'd be staying at school for the weekend,' she sniffed.

'Bonding with the chaps?' I said.

Lashing out at Wendy gave cold comfort. There would be time for recriminations later. In the meantime, our thirteen-year-old boy had been missing for forty-eight hours and nobody had the slightest idea where he was. The police had been notified, inquiries made, bulletins posted, potential accomplices interrogated. It looked like he'd done a bunk.

Emptied his bank account, packed a bag, gone over the wall.

'We're looking everywhere, all the usual places runaways go.'

Wendy didn't need to specify what that meant. My bushland visions were replaced by urban images: street-kids, gutter crawlers, used syringes. It was a nightmare so precise, an apprehension so specific, that it even had a name. Kings Cross, sleaze capital of a nation.

This wouldn't have happened if I'd been more concerned about Red, I told myself, and less preoccupied with exchanging long-distance artillery salvos with Wendy. 'How could you let this happen?' I demanded. 'I'll be on the next plane up there.'

'What earthly good will that do?'

I had no idea. But I knew for sure that I couldn't just sit on my backside in Melbourne and await further bulletins. If necessary, I'd turn Sydney upside down. First I had to get there. I rang off and called the airlines, couldn't get a seat for at least twelve hours. The next available flight was eight the next morning. I booked the ticket and stood beside the phone, flexing and unflexing, my guts churning. What now?

An accident would have been easier to cope with. An illness. At least Red would be there, visible, tangible. With a jolt of dismay, I remembered the mysterious hang-ups on my answering machine, those pregnant silences. It was him, no doubt about it. He'd reached out, time and time again, and found me wanting.

I checked the machine in case he'd called again. There was only the rebuking hiss of erased tape. Clutching at straws, I rang Telecom, hoping my phone records might identify the source of incoming calls and provide some clues about Red's movements. Call back during office hours, I was told. I rang Wendy instead, urged her to use her insider clout, pull whatever strings she could wrap her senior executive hands around. 'I'll be up there by eleven tomorrow morning,' I told her.

'I really don't see the point.'

'I'm coming anyway,' I insisted, teeth clenched. 'In the meantime, ring me the moment you hear anything. Anything at all.'

I felt powerless. There was so much I couldn't even guess at. I'd never met Red's Sydney friends, didn't even know their names. Not to mention this shit with the boarding school. My derelictions reared before me, full of reproach. I went into Red's room, paced among his boxes of comics, chastised myself, fingered his clothing as though I might conjure him up out of sheer willpower. His clothes seemed so small. He was still just a baby. Now he was somewhere out there in the jungle, fresh meat for the wolves.

There was nothing I could do until the morning. A headache ticked at my temples. Alert for the jangle of the phone, I went across the back lane, tapped on the Curnows' kitchen door and beckoned Faye into the yard. Tarquin stared goggle-eyed through the glass as his mother wrapped her arms around me and rocked me side-to-side. 'Wow,' he said, when he heard the news. 'Unreal.'

Faye and Leo sat with me into the night, watching me smoke far too many cigarettes. Faye rang Wendy, made clucking noises, learned there were no new developments. Around midnight I convinced the Curnows that there was nothing else they could do, chased them off home.

A mantra echoed in my head. *A child is always better off with its mother.* For years, my whole relationship with Red had been predicated on that single assumption, the reason I had not contested custody. Now it sounded like a hollow rationalisation for abdicating my responsibilities. A child needs its mother, certainly. But a boy needs his father, too. Whether either of them fully realise it.

Occupying myself with mindless and repetitive tasks, I cleaned and tidied, willing the phone to ring, the news to be good. Eventually, I put myself to bed. I'd be no use to anybody if I arrived in Sydney ragged as a rat's arse.

At 3.15 I was still wide awake, lying on my back, staring at the pattern on the ceiling where the streetlight seeped through a chink in the curtains. I was out of cigarettes, out of ideas, out of things to tell myself.

I pulled on a waterproof and walked the empty streets. Past the silent tower blocks of the Housing Commission high-rise, down Gertrude Street, on and on, washed by squally little showers that ended almost as soon as they started. At the all-night 7-11 on Victoria Parade, I bought cigarettes, put one between my lips and walked another three blocks before I realised I didn't have a light. Went back for matches, wet hair plastered to my forehead. 'You all right, mate?' said the Lebanese kid behind the counter.

A taxi came up the hill, the only car on the road. I put my arm out. Where do you go at four in the morning, killing time? 'Wholesale fruit and vegetable market,' I told the driver.

I hunched in the back seat, staring out the window, fending off the cabbie's attempts at conversation. I was all talked out, exhausted from futile speculation, from picking at the balled knot in the pit of my stomach. Silence was better. To contain was to control. To forestall, somehow, the worst possibilities. That Red had been lured away, enticed, entrapped.

In fifteen minutes we were on Footscray Road, an industrial artery running between the docks and the railway yards, a hard-edged world bathed in a space-port glow. The road margins were a pulverised wasteland of busted-up concrete, broken glass and shredded tyres. Trucks appeared out of the night, throwing slush onto the taxi windscreen. We joined their flow, converging on a boom gate in a chain-mesh fence. I paid the cabby, sucked damp air into my lungs and tramped up the access road.

The market was somewhere up ahead, beyond a parking apron crowded with manoeuvring trucks, big refrigerator rigs, bug-splattered eighteen-wheelers, minivans, the runabouts of suburban fruit shops. A motorised cart stacked with boxes darted from between two semitrailers, missing me by inches. 'You wanna die?' yelled the driver.

I headed for safer ground, scanning the scene for Donny's truck, half grateful for the distraction, half wondering what the hell I was doing there. Open-fronted buildings bordered the parking apron, the depots of major freight companies. A small cluster of men loitered in front of the Stuhl Holdings shed, hands in the pockets of their work jackets. One of them detached himself from the group and advanced to meet me, a mobile phone in his hand. It was Frank Farrell, the Haulers' welfare officer. Up to some skulduggery, no doubt.

'Morning, Murray,' he declared cheerfully. 'Or is it still last night?'

'Bit of both,' I said, nodding towards the group of men. 'Attending to your members' welfare, are you?'

A figure emerged from the building. He was wearing a stylish woollen overcoat and the splash of a too-bright tie showed against the white of his shirt. His features were indistinct in the murky half-light but there was something familiar about them.

'Who's that?' I asked.

Farrell followed my gaze. 'Him? That's Bob Stuhl's son, Darren.'

As I narrowed my eyes, straining for a clearer view, head-lights swept the man's face. No doubt about it. It was Steve McQueen, the truculent party-boy who'd rammed my head down the toilet at the Metro.

'Did you say Darrell or Darren?'

'Darren,' said Farrell. 'Bob Stuhl's got him familiarising himself with company operations down here.'

'Hey, Darren,' I called.

He sauntered over, answering to his name. As he closed the twenty paces between us, my pulse soared. Play it cool, Murray, I told myself.

Darren Stuhl's skin was pasty and razor-scraped. By the look of it, he was hungover and not long out of bed. He glanced at me without a glimmer of recognition. 'Yes, what is it?' he demanded, his tone peremptory, managerial. He slid back his plush cashmere cuff and looked at his watch. He was an important man with important things to do.

'Forgotten me already?' I said.

He peered at my face for a couple of seconds, then shrugged.

'The Metro,' I reminded him. 'Friday night.' For all my efforts at cool, the words had a squeezed, slightly hysterical tone.

A memory began to take shape somewhere in Darren's recesses. His eyes flicked to Farrell, then back to me. He gave a dismissive shrug. 'So what?'

'Two grand's worth of dentistry, that's what,' I blurted. 'You knocked out my front teeth, you arrogant prick. And now I know who you are, I know where to send the bill.'

He gave a contemptuous snort. He had better things to do with his time, it said, than stand in a car park listening to the pathetic bleating of some wild-eyed loser. 'Your teeth look okay to me, pal,' he said. 'It's your head needs fixing.'

As he turned away, I felt a flush of humiliation. 'Before you go,' I said, putting my hand on his sleeve, 'I think you owe me an apology.'

He stared down at my hand like it was freshly extruded from a dog's rear end. It occurred to me that his overcoat was worth more than all the teeth in my mouth. When he tried to jerk his arm away, I grabbed a handful of the fabric. 'Say you're sorry, Darren.'

'Get rid of this idiot, Frank,' he ordered.

Farrell stood blank-faced, immobile as a statue.

Darren put the palm of his free hand on my chest and shoved. Not a smart move. I saw red. I saw purple. I saw a seething mass of ugly vengeful images that erupted up out of my guts and blew the top right off my fragile self-control. Lashing out, I smacked him across the chops. He reeled back, even more astonished than I was. Then he took a swing.

This time, I was ready. I dodged, grabbed his lapels and sent him sprawling onto the ground. I stared down at him, reckless with rage. If this jerk thought he could assault me with impunity, just because Daddy was worth a couple of hundred million dollars, he had seriously underestimated the mettle of Murray Theodore Whelan.

'C'mon,' I urged, beckoning him to his feet. 'Have a go, you mug.'

The half-dozen men from the depot rushed forward and formed a circle of spectators. The Marquess of Queensberry was not among them.

Darren got to his feet, dragging the back of his hand across his mouth. He peeled off his overcoat and tossed it to one of the onlookers, then squared off and shaped up. A brawler with an audience, relishing it. Not without reason. Hungover or not, he was fifteen years faster and ten kilos fitter. Rolling his shoulders beneath his fashionably baggy olive-green suit, he tilted his chin upwards, urging me on. I was seriously outclassed, over my head in very deep shit.

He led with his bathroom-proven right hook, aiming for my face. I dropped my shoulder and ran at him, feeling the blow land on my ear as I slammed into his chest. If he thought I was going to box him, he'd mistaken me for a man who knew what he was doing. Get in close, I thought desperately. Compensate for my lack of skill by kneeing him in the knackers.

We scrabbled and scuffled across the wet tarmac. I tried to topple him over, wanting nothing so much as to be somewhere else. Anywhere else. His breath was in my face, his eyes wild and savage. The guy was cut-snake mad, completely off his fucking tree. A forearm jolt to the throat sent me reeling backwards. Then I was on the ground.

A pair of shoes filled my field of vision. Black leather brogues, wing-tipped, buffed to a shine, spattered with mud and patterned with little punched holes. A swift kick to the stomach drove the wind out of me and flooded my eyes with spinning red atoms. My left arm shot up to shield my face. The taste of bile filled my mouth, mingling with shame and anger and confusion.

Darren took a backward step, taking his time now, enjoying the moment. He unbuttoned his jacket and cocked his leg for the *coup de grâce*. In the pit of his arm, he was wearing a leather holster, the butt of a gun clearly visible. The kick came towards me. I shut my eyes.

Nothing happened. I took a peek and saw that Frank Farrell was dragging Darren backwards, pinning his arms to his side, wrestling him under control. 'Enough,' he was saying. 'Easy, easy.'

As fast as I could, I clambered to my feet. Darren was still trying to get at me, struggling against Farrell's restraint. We glowered at each other, chests heaving. But the fisticuffs were finished and we both knew it.

'Go,' Farrell ordered me. 'Just go.'

Go? It was all I could do not to turn tail and run. But the tattered remnants of my pride could face no further humiliation. 'Come near me again, you useless piece of shit,' I panted, my legs as firm as instant noodles. 'You won't know what fucking-well hit you.'

Darren shrugged off Farrell's grip. 'Any time,' he sneered. 'Any time.'

'Break it up, you two,' growled Farrell. 'This isn't the time or the place.'

Brushing the mud from my sleeves with as much dignity as I could muster, I turned on my heels and strode away. I had no idea where I was going.

Ahead of me, the wholesale produce market was a cavernous, floodlit hive of activity. I let it swallow me. It was either that or fall twitching to the ground, a gibbering wreck.

Mountains of oranges reared up before me. Ramparts of onions. Avenues of avocadoes and corridors of celery. Mesh sacks bulged with butternut pumpkins and waxed cartons glistened with iced broccoli. Red peppers and purple eggplants. Uncountable heads of cauliflower and crate-loads of cabbages. And everywhere the frenetic lurch of forklifts, the squeal of brakes, the flash of banknotes peeled from tight-rolled wads by men in leather aprons.

I went deeper and deeper into the vast, high-roofed building. Above the stalls hung the names of the vendors. A lot were Italian and Greek but there were Asian names, too, Vietnamese and Chinese, above bundles of bok choy and white radishes the size of torpedoes.

Adrenalin was pounding in my ears, my abdomen ached and a lump was rising at my hairline. Fuck, what a psycho. And Frank Farrell, what was that all about? For a lowly union head-kicker, he seemed pretty familiar with the son of one of the biggest plutocrats in the country.

This is insane, I thought. Trying to kill time, I'd nearly got myself killed instead. And now I was wandering aimlessly through a gigantic shed full of tubers and foliage, dodging trolleys and forklifts, wondering what the fuck had possessed me to come here. My hands, I realised, were trembling. Where was Red at this moment, I wondered? How was he passing the night? Was he alone? Safe? What had impelled him to strike out into the big, bad city?

Donny and his mates were nowhere to be seen. The place was so big, so busy, they could easily not notice that I was here. I felt a sense of relief at that fact. I just wanted to call a cab and go home. If I wasn't at the airport by seven o'clock, they'd sell my ticket to somebody else. I calculated the travel times. Half an hour back to Fitzroy, same again to shower, shave and pack. Forty-five minutes to the airport. A total of two hours, say. It had just gone four, giving me nearly an hour up my sleeve.

I arrived at the market cafe, a steaming, glass-walled hubbub of muffled conversations and toasted sandwiches. I went in, looking for a payphone, didn't find one. Sleep was now off the agenda. Caffeine and nicotine were the order of the day. I bought a cup of cardboard coffee, sat down at a battle-scarred formica table and sucked hungrily on a cigarette. My son, I said to myself, your father is a fool.

The coffee was crap, but it was warm and wet. Halfway through it, Frank Farrell came through the door. He sat down and laid his cell-phone on the table between us. Big man, I thought, flashing his big, expensive status symbol. 'You okay?' he said.

I crushed my stub in the overflowing tinfoil ashtray. 'Never better.'

'Pompous prick, aren't you?'

I had to agree with him. 'Okay, so I didn't exactly cover myself in glory. But a man can forget his manners when he runs into the total stranger who attacked him in a nightclub and rammed his head down a toilet.'

'Darren did that?'

'Hilarious, eh?' I peeled back my top lip and tapped my teeth with the crooked knuckle of my forefinger. 'Twenty-three hundred bucks.'

He gave a low whistle. Whether this was in disgust at Darren's behaviour or amazement at the high cost of dentistry was not immediately apparent. 'Send me the bill,' he said. 'I'll make sure Bob pays it. And something in the way of compensation, too, if you'd care to put a figure on it.'

'Sounds like you've done this sort of thing before,' I said. 'I've heard the Haulers are snug with Stuhl Holdings but I didn't realise you also babysit the owner's children.'

Farrell gave a resigned shrug. 'I prefer to call it managing the management.' He lit a Marlboro. I could see him up there on the horse, squinting into the distance, riding herd on the herd. 'There's background here,' he said.

'And I suppose you want to share it with me?' I drew back my cuff and looked at my watch. 4.15.

Farrell rested his elbows on the table and leaned into his cigarette, considering where to begin. Then he started. 'Bob Stuhl has two sons, right. Half-brothers. Adrian's the child of his first marriage. High achiever. MBA, champion rower, the works. The apple of his father's eye, the very nectarine. Being groomed as future chief executive, seat on the board at twenty-seven.'

'Until he had an accident,' I said. 'Read about it. Dived into the shallow end of a swimming pool.'

'That's the public version,' said Farrell. 'Real story's a bit more interesting. Involves your friend Darren.'

'Surprise, surprise,' I said.

'Darren's ten years younger than Adrian. Never what you might call foreman material. Piss-poor academic record, no good at sport. Generally failed to meet his father's expectations.'

'Boo-hoo,' I said. 'Low self-esteem, so he turns into a delinquent.'

Farrell narrowed his eyes. 'You want to hear this or not?'

I yawned. 'Wake me up when it gets interesting.'

Farrell waited until the silence got uncomfortable, then started back in. 'The accident was about six years ago. Darren's in his last year of school. He's supposed to be doing his homework, but he's bored. Bob had him at one of those places where they don't mind if you're dumb as dogshit, long as the cheques keep coming. Anyway, Darren decides to climb out his bedroom window onto the roof. This is the Stuhl family compound in Toorak, a thirty-room French chateau.'

'I see Bob more as the Graceland type.'

'You got it,' said Farrell. 'This is more the wife's speed. The number two, Darren's mother. Social climber. Anyway, it's a hot summer night and Adrian's down below, taking a dip in the French provincial swimming pool. Darren's up on the roof, arsing around. Accidentally dislodges a sheet of slate. Eighth of an inch thick, edge like a blunt machete. It shoots down the incline, frisbees off the guttering and lobotomises big brother. Cost Bob a hospital wing to bury the truth. Also cost him fifty million when the market expressed its sympathy by shaving 10 per cent off the Stuhl Holdings share price on account of succession uncertainties.'

Good story. As stories went. 'Lifestyles of the rich and famous,' I said. 'Your point being? I should consider myself lucky that Darren only cost me my front teeth?'

Farrell tapped the edge of the ashtray with his cigarette. It didn't have any ash on it.

'My point being that Bob lost his heir apparent,' he said impatiently. 'Suddenly dipstick Darren was the great white hope, promoted into his brother's shoes. First Bob shipped him off to America so he could get himself some sort of ticket in business administration. Now he's back with a vengeance, learning the family racket from the ground up. Running around making a nuisance of himself at every Stuhl depot and office from here to the Black Stump. Not only isn't he up to it, he's a chip off the old block. Thinks the way to get things done is to be the meanest dog in the yard.'

The adrenalin had ebbed away and I was suddenly very, very tired. 'Okay, I understand your problem,' I said. 'Bob employs, what, nearly a thousand of your members. And Darren represents what you might call an occupational hazard. So you keep a close eye on him. You drag him away when he's about to give some poor prick a kicking. You manage the management. I can sympathise. But I'm not going to roll over, help poor benighted Bob with his dynastic succession problems. Now that I know who Darren is, I'm going to lay a complaint of aggravated assault, have him charged, brought before a magistrate.'

Farrell's mobile phone chirped. He pushed a button and

hoisted the black plastic brick to his ear. 'Yeah?' He listened briefly, frowned, then turned it off and laid it back on the table, its stubby antenna quivering. I considered asking him if I could use it to call a cab. But I was already obliged to him for saving me from a kicking and wasn't inclined to go begging petty favours.

'You'd be well within your rights,' he told me, straight back onto the topic of Darren Stuhl. 'But why take him to court, deal with all that shit, when a private settlement can be reached, put some dollars in your pocket?'

'Because it's not just a private matter,' I said. 'The guy's a public menace.'

'Up to you,' he shrugged. 'I know what I'd be doing. His lawyers'll make mincemeat of you.'

He was probably right. I was in no fit state to think about it. Four-thirty. Time to be making tracks. I nodded at Farrell's phone, wondering again why he was here. 'Darren bites again?'

'Not this time. Minor irritation. Nothing we can't handle.'

'Especially with Darren on the team,' I said. 'And all tooled up, too.'

'That thing?' said Farrell dismissively. 'Rich kid's toy. Darren's got himself a gun club licence, not supposed to take it anywhere but the firing range. I've warned him before about toting it around like some sort of fashion accessory. Might go off and blow his tiny dick away.' He shook his head with weary exasperation. 'The things a man has to deal with'.

We both stood to leave. 'You didn't say why you're here,' said Farrell.

'I came for the colour and movement. Got more than I bargained for.'

'If you change your mind, send me your bill. Bob can be a very reasonable man. And go home to bed. You look fucked.'

Good advice. I should've taken it.

I went to the counter to ask the whereabouts of the nearest public phone. The chief sandwich toaster was flat out filling orders. While I was trying to get his attention, Donny Maitland arrived. He breezed through the door with his handbills in his pocket and greeted me as though there'd never been an iota of doubt in his mind that I'd be there waiting.

So I ordered more coffee and told him about my run-in with Darren Stuhl. Then I warned him about Frank Farrell's lurking presence and accepted his offer of a free ride after the campaign rally. Half an hour later, I was pinned against the back window of the Kenworth with Heather's lipstick on my dipstick.

Through the mist-smeared glass, I witnessed Donny's campaign rally descend into a wild affray when Darren Stuhl decided to start waving around his artillery. Then came the frenzied burst of activity as I quit the truck and went hunting for Donny.

And then I was jogging through the rain, not looking back, thinking only that I'd barely have time to swing past the house and throw some duds into an overnight bag before zooming to the airport. I trotted through the exit gate, past the clog of departing vehicles, and made for the Mobil roadhouse on the other side of Footscray Road. A mustard-coloured smudge was beginning to stain the sky beyond the office towers of the city centre. Maybe Red had turned up. It occurred to me that I'd forgotten to turn on the answering machine when I went out to buy cigarettes. Shit, shit, shit.

Footscray Road was a death trap, eight lanes of speeding trucks. I sprinted across, nearly getting skittled in the process. Drying my face on a paper towel at the pumps, I went into the roadhouse, found the payphone and called the cab company. Fifteen minutes, I was told. My watch said 5.42. By the time I'd finished waiting in line for a doughnut and bought a copy of the *Sun*, it was saying 5.55.

On the dot of six o'clock, a police car came screaming down the road, lights flashing, and turned into the market. Shortly after, an ambulance did the same.

Had the squished tomato incident gone ballistic, I wondered? I hoped Donny was okay but I figured he could look after himself. Was he not the victorious general who had just swept his foe from the field of battle?

I sipped what Mobil called coffee and thumbed through the paper, looking up every time a car pulled into the forecourt, frantic for the roof-light of an arriving taxi. MOSCOW COUP SHOCK, read the *Sun*'s front-page headline. Hard-liners had seized power in Moscow. Mikhail Gorbachev was missing, location uncertain.

Fuck Gorbachev. It was my son's whereabouts that concerned me. Was it raining in Sydney? Was Red sleeping rough? Five past six came and went. Another cop car turned into the service road leading to the market. What the hell was going on over there? Had some mafioso greengrocer decided to get antsy about a few dollars worth of hothouse tomatoes? Had hot-blooded Heather decided to take the situation in hand? She'd handled me so well that I was still sticky with her transmission fluid. I wished I could get Lyndal's motor racing like that.

The news from Moscow was late-breaking, too recent for the *Sun*'s cartoonist. He'd found a more parochial topic. Angelo was depicted as an uncomprehending wombat, caught in the headlights of an oncoming semitrailer. Bob Stuhl was behind the wheel and the grille bore the words 'Tonnage Levy'.

Fucking Stuhl family, I thought. They're out to get me. I'd have to ring Angelo as soon as I got to Sydney, explain my absence, try to smooth his feathers. At least I'd found him a stalking horse to back against the Haulers.

At 6.07:14, a taxi pulled up and tooted its horn. For once, the driver was the silent type, a pockmarked Somali with skin like a chocolate-coated biscuit. I slumped low in the back seat, my fingers beating a fretful tattoo on the vinyl. Shrouds of cloud were swirling around the city office towers, lights beginning to appear in house windows, traffic building. To what kind of dawn was my baby boy waking, eight hundred kilometres away? Where and how and with whom had he passed this night? This one, and the one before it?

We reached the house and I told the driver to wait while I bolted inside. There was no time for personal hygiene or even a change of clothes. Wendy would have to take me as she found me. I rushed into the bedroom, pulled out an overnight bag and was feverishly ransacking my laundry basket, sniffing for packable jocks, when I heard a voice from the living room.

'You wascally wabbit,' it said.

A gangly prepubescent boy was standing in my living room, shovelling cereal into his mouth and watching Elmer Fudd chase Bugs Bunny around a tree with a blunderbuss. 'Hi, Dad.' He spoke through a mouthful of Weeties, taking his eyes off the screen just long enough to acknowledge my presence. 'Where have you been?'

A wave of relief buckled my knees. 'Don't you fuckingwell "Hi, Dad" me,' I said. 'And never mind where I've been. Where the hell have *you* been? Your mother and I have been worried sick.'

'I took da wrong toin at Alba-koiky,' said Bugs.

'And switch that fucking TV off,' I said, moderating my tone. 'You're lucky I don't put you over my knee.' I would've had my hands full if I tried. Red had shot up a good three inches in the months since I'd last seen him and his knees and elbows bulged in his baggy clothes like a handful of coat-hangers in a sock. If he was a girl, it suddenly struck me, he'd be sprouting tits and getting his period. In Angola, he'd be in the army.

'Sorry, Dad,' he said sheepishly. 'I didn't know what else to do. You won't make me go back, will you?'

'That depends,' I said.

'On what?'

I widened my arms. 'On whether you're too big to give your father a hug, for a start.'

His expression said he thought he was, but his better judgment prevailed and he submitted to a long paternal embrace. I added a light cuff around the ears for good measure. 'Now tell me what's going on. No, wait.' I dashed out the front. The meter said fifteen dollars. I gave the cabby twenty and told him to keep the change. He was lucky I didn't hug him as well. 'Okay, start talking,' I told Red. 'And this had better be good.'

Red sat on the couch with his knees tucked under his chin and poured out his plaint in a continuous, meandering stream. It boiled down to this. His situation sucked. Big time. The reasons were numerous and well-rehearsed. For a start, there was his new school. Everything about it was stupid. The teachers were stupid, the rules were stupid, the uniform was stupid. 'We have to wear a straw hat,' he said. 'It's called a boater. How stupid is that?'

Pretty stupid, I had to admit.

He'd been enrolled in the middle of the year, filling a vacancy created when the son of a Singapore businessman was required to leave because his father had lost his fortune gambling and could no longer afford the fees. He didn't have any friends and he didn't like all the rules and regulations.

Red, that is. Not the lad with the bankrupt dad. When he complained to Wendy and Richard, they insisted he'd soon settle down and learn to like it, that many new boys underwent a similar adjustment period.

'Richard said he cried for months when his parents first sent him there and it hadn't done him any harm. And Mum, all she thinks about is Nicola and Alexandra.'

Wendy's choice of names for her twin daughters never failed to bring a smile to my lips.

'They cry all the time. And I mean all the time. Totally. They've been through four nannies already.'

'So you decided to run away?' I said, doing my best to sound stern.

'I told Mum I wanted to come down here,' he said. 'Live with you, go to Fitzroy High with Tarquin. But she said that was out of the question. That you weren't responsible enough.'

That was Wendy, all right. 'If you were so unhappy, you should've called me,' I said. 'We could've talked.'

'I rang and rang, but you were never here.'

The reproach struck home. 'You can't just disappear because things aren't going your way.' But that was exactly what he had done. He'd fled to Melbourne to front me in person. Crack of dawn Saturday morning, he walked out of Brookside, used a teller machine to empty his bank account, then went to the Greyhound terminal. He'd done his research. The bus was cheaper than the train. Thirty-nine dollars, student price.

'In case you had to be sixteen or something, I asked this older kid to buy the ticket for me. Except he ripped me off. Took my money and never came back. I only had twenty dollars left and it wasn't enough.'

He spent the rest of Saturday trying to hustle small change. 'I said I'd lost my bus fare, which was true, so I wasn't lying or anything.'

But panhandling is hungry work for a growing boy and food purchases ate into his takings. When night arrived, he was still twelve dollars short. He rang me again but got no answer. I thought back and worked out that I must have been at the Curnow's place. He snuck into some bughouse screening a midnight-to-dawn Star Trek marathon and dozed off during *The Search for Spock*. 'I'd seen it before,' he said. 'So I knew where he was.'

The next morning, figuring he was in too deep to change his plans, he shook down a couple of Klingons for the balance of the fare. This time, he braved the counter himself, bought a ticket on the next bus to Melbourne, the overnighter.

'That reminds me.' I interrupted his saga for long enough to ring the airline and cancel my booking. 'I was flying to Sydney to look for you,' I told him.

'You were?' He swelled with momentary gratification, then realised that remorse was the more appropriate response. 'Sorry, Dad.'

The story continued. Ticket in hand, he lashed out on an Egg McMuffin, killed Sunday in a succession of video arcades, then spent fourteen hours beside a fat lady who snored all the way from Gundagai to Tallarook. Arriving on my doorstep at six o'clock, he retrieved the spare key from its hiding place, let himself in and proceeded to eat every flake of cereal he could lay his hands on. At which point, I arrived.

'Have you got a girlfriend?' he said.

'Several. That's why I look exhausted.'

Jesus, the kid could've got a job writing low-budget travel tips for Lonely Planet. I didn't know whether to laugh or cry. But I did know two things for sure. Never again would my son be forced to wear a straw boater. And never again would he spend an entire night in a darkened room full of Trekkies. Not unless I was there, too. 'So what do you think we should do now?' I asked, a leading question.

'Ring Mum?' he ventured. 'Tell her not to worry any more.'

Correct. I placed the call, told Wendy that I wouldn't be coming to Sydney, after all. She was right, I could do nothing useful up there. 'Red's here with me. And he'll be staying here until we get a few things sorted out.'

'What things?'

'Stupid things.' For once I was holding the trump card in the access game. 'Things that suck.'

Red took over then, faced the maternal music like a man. 'I *do* love you, Mum,' he insisted. 'It's just that…'

Respectful of his privacy, I withdrew into the bathroom and splashed water on my face. All things considered, I didn't feel too bad. In fact, I felt great. Not only was Red safe and well, he'd flown to me for sanctuary, forgiven me my negligence, offered me the opportunity of fatherhood once again.

On top of which, I now knew the identity of the shithead who clobbered me in the kisser at the Metro, marring my haunting good looks. Okay, so I'd embarrassed myself with a pathetic attempt to even the score. But an offer of compensation now lay on the table. I'd taken the high moral ground with Frank Farrell, blathering on about having Darren

Stuhl locked up. In the cold light of my bathroom mirror, though, I was more inclined to take the money. Darren's delinquency, I decided, was going to cost Bob Stuhl plenty.

I'd even had my wing-wang wiggled for the first time in living memory, although not in a manner with which I was completely comfortable.

Red, his contrite conversation with mama completed, appeared at the bathroom door. 'We're out of cereal,' he announced.

I scrambled us some toast and we ate in silence, content with full mouths and each other's company. In the middle of his fourth slice Red nodded at my plate. 'You going to finish that?'

'Keep this up,' I told him, 'and I may not be able to afford you.'

Thanks to the snores of his travelling companion, the runaway had got little sleep on the Greyhound red-eye. He readily accepted my proposal of a few hours kip. Within minutes, he was unconscious. For a long while I stood in the doorway of his room, gazing at the lump beneath the covers.

That's when it came to me, fully formed and with dazzling clarity, as if it had been waiting in the wings for the right instant to step forth and declare itself. For too long I'd been content to drift, to let other people set my agenda. The time had come to take the bullshit by the horns. Red's arrival was a sign that it wasn't too late for a second chance in the lottery of life.

Time was, even a minor political flack could see himself as part of a larger project, something from which he could draw pride sufficient unto the day. But that day was long gone. My life's work was reduced to helping a clapped-out mediocrity retain his fragile grip on an office whose powers he was incapable of exercising. Not a lot of *amour-propre* to be derived from that. The moment had come to tell Angelo that I was popping outside for a little walk in the snow.

My requirements, after all, were modest. Employment that provided a modicum of self-respect, kept the bank at bay and the refrigerator stocked. Time to devote to the long-neglected tasks of fatherhood, to cultivate my own garden. If I couldn't find an employer to replace Angelo, I could always work for myself, set up shop as a consultant. Use my contacts in the public sector to build a client base. Flog my experience as a bureaucratic fixer. The more I thought about it, the more I liked the idea. I could get a card printed. *Murray Whelan & Associates.* It always looked more impressive if you had associates. Maybe I might even get some.

It was past eight now. I rang Faye. 'Naughty little sod,' she said. 'Tell him to come visit Tarquin after school.'

Doubtless I'd be seeing a lot more of Tarquin from now on. I set the alarm for 1 p.m. and had just hit the hay when the phone rang. It was Agnelli's private secretary, Trish. 'Are you coming into the office this morning?'

'Not if I can help it.'

'He's very keen to talk to you.'

'About what?'

'About eleven-thirty.'

I got out of bed and began drafting my resignation.

Transport House was a spit-coloured office tower at the western edge of the downtown grid. Its fifteen floors were dedicated to the administration of the public transport system, the undertaking of feasibility studies into the implementation of multi-modal ticketing systems and the issuing of fifty thousand weekly pay cheques. This work was conducted by men in comfortable trousers and women in bum-freezing skirts, who spent their coffee breaks standing on the pavement outside the main entrance, smoking the sort of cigarettes that come in packs of fifty.

The Minister for Transport's office was located on the top floor. When not fulfilling his obligations in the legislature, or conferring with his factional colleagues, its current tenant could usually be found there, in his ministerial suite, surrounded by ambitious schemers, cynical cronies and time-serving paper-shufflers. And me.

By the time I stepped into the elevator, showered and suited, a note for Red on the refrigerator door, I'd done my homework.

According to my calculations, taking into account the full gamut of accrued leave and sick days, unpaid overtime, severance pay and sundry other entitlements, the total sum due to me on resignation would amount to exactly four-fifths of five-eighths of fuck-all. Or approximately three months' wages, whichever was the lesser. Not much, after all my time with the firm. And now, with my mortgage rate topping 13 per cent, plus the additional outlay on Frosty Flakes and other juvenile sundries that would be required, my decision to quit was not ideally timed. So I'd torn up my letter of resignation. I had another strategy. I'd get myself sacked.

Dismissal would trigger various premature termination clauses in my contract, netting me six months' salary in lieu of notice. Double what I would get if I merely quit. Plus, if a new job proved elusive, the fact that I'd been laid off would entitle me to claim forthwith my birthright as an Australian citizen, a fortnightly dole cheque.

As I entered the ministerial suite, Trish glanced up from her keyboard. 'Walk into a door or something?' She fluttered a yellow message slip in the air between us. 'Your wife wants you to call her.'

'My ex-wife, as well you know.' I crushed the slip into a ball and tossed it into the nearest WPB. Wendy was nothing if not predictable. She thought she'd have more luck convincing me to send Red back to Sydney if she got to me at the office, away from the boy's influence. 'If she calls again, tell her I don't work here any more.'

'You wish,' said Trish. 'Go straight in. He's waiting for you.'

Angelo's Transport House office was bigger than the one at Parliament House but it was strictly utilitarian. Its only feature of note was the view, a panoramic vista that occupied one wall like a gigantic photorealist painting. In the middle distance, the cooling tower of the Newport power station was a gigantic cigarette, wisps of white wafting from its red-painted rim. Cars the size of ants crawled across the twisted parabola of the Westgate Bridge. A seething stratosphere pressed down upon this scene, the writhing clouds as black as Bible-binding.

Angelo was standing in front of the window, hands clasped behind his back, Napoleon crossing the Alps. Neville Lowry sat primly on the edge of a chair, knees crossed. His hairless pate was glowing like an oiled halo.

Angelo waved me inside with an impatient gesture. 'You see the cartoon?' he said, rocking on his toes. 'Made me look like an idiot. Cabinet meets this afternoon and I want to demonstrate that I'm taking action to nip these leaks in the bud. I've decided to make an example.'

Neville moved his attention to a point beyond the clouds. To the hole in the ozone layer, perhaps, or an orbiting satellite. Angelo, too, turned to the window, avoiding eye contact with me. I waited, very alert, my mouth suddenly dry. Did I dare hope, I wondered, that the head to drop into the basket would be mine?

Angelo turned to face me. 'Nev here has agreed to accept full responsibility,' he said. 'I've just terminated him.'

Neville smirked and gave me an amiable shrug. For a man whose cue-ball head was rolling across the carpet, he was inexplicably buoyant.

'In six weeks,' continued Agnelli, 'when the dust has

settled, he'll be taking up a new position within the department. Deputy director, Corporate Communications. Not a political appointment, you understand. A purely administrative one.'

I understood all right. Nev Lowry wasn't responsible for the leak. He'd simply used the opportunity to engineer a move from the political to the civil service payroll, thus ensuring job security beyond the election. 'Such self-sacrifice,' I said. 'It borders on the heroic.'

'Ours not to reason why,' said Neville, standing up. 'Ours but to take a long overdue holiday. Anything you want me to bring back from Bali?'

'Tropical ulcers,' I suggested.

'Just try to look a bit more contrite, Nev,' said Agnelli. 'At least until you're out of the building. And shut the door on your way out.'

I sank into the sofa, wondering if I shouldn't be considering a similar game plan. Angelo resumed his imperial stance before the window. 'Any advance on the Haulers front?' he demanded.

'I might have found a taker,' I said. 'A bloke named Donny Maitland is putting together a rank-and-file ticket. Reckons he can tap into the disaffection with the incumbent regime.'

'You think he can knock off Sharpe and McGrath?'

'That's about as likely as the water-fuelled jumbo jet,' I said. 'Still, he's hard to frighten and he might have some impact, given the resources.'

'Then see that he gets some. Bury the cost in the policy-development budget, call it industry research or something. How does ten grand sound?'

Like enough to get Donny's little show on the road, pay for some printing and postage. 'I'll get onto it,' I said, standing up.

Angelo waved me back down. He began pacing, sure sign that he was screwing himself to some sticking point. What absurdity now, I wondered? Upon what madcap mission was I about to be dispatched? 'I saw you speaking with Lyndal yesterday at that community arts crap,' he said. This was both a question and an accusation.

'She's an asset to the team,' I said.

'Get your hand off it, Murray,' said Angelo. 'There's backstabbing afoot out there, I'm sure of it. I could feel it in the atmosphere.'

'You're being paranoid,' I said.

'I'll be as paranoid as I like,' he said. 'Anyway, it's not paranoia. It's instinct. When you've been in politics as long as I have, you sense these things. Somebody is plotting to knock me off.'

Jesus, I thought. Hark to the man. He's dragged me out of bed to pour oil into the storm-tossed teacup of his ego.

'Face it, Angelo,' I said. 'Nobody in their right mind wants to talk to you. You're a bully and an unprincipled careerist. You take your constituents for granted and treat your employees like shit. Frankly, it's a miracle you're not still chasing ambulances for a living, you slimy arsehole.'

Angelo slapped his hands together, rubbed them energetically and beamed at me. I tried again. 'You think I'm joking, don't you,' I said harshly. 'Well that just proves what a dopey cunt you really are.'

Insubordination. Personal abuse. Sexist language. He'll have to fire me now, I thought.

Ange looked even more pleased. 'You're absolutely right,' he enthused. 'That's the great thing about you, Murray. You're the only one who's prepared to be up-front with me. None of these toadies'—he flapped his wrist vaguely—'none of them would ever talk to me like that. That's why I know I can trust you implicitly. You're the only one who tells it like it is. Which is why I wanted to talk to you today. I want you to do something for me. It's a big ask, I know. But you're the only one I can turn to. The only one I know I can truly rely on.' He paused dramatically.

'I want you to nominate for preselection for Melbourne Upper.'

That damned invisible hearing aid was on the blink again. 'You're quitting parliament?' I said.

'Don't be ridiculous,' Ange scoffed. 'I just don't want to leave anything to chance with my renomination. If you run against me, it'll help split any potential opposition. Then you swing your support behind me in the final ballot and bump me over the line. Simple.'

Sure it was simple. It was the oldest trick in the political book.

'Like I said, it's a big ask. But I'm worried, Murray. I wouldn't suggest it otherwise.'

I sat there, speechless, staring at him.

'Don't interrupt,' he said. 'I know what you're going to say. You're going to say that I might be worried, but that you'll be the one at the rough end of the pineapple. End of the day, I'll be back in parliament, you'll be the man who knifed his boss, got the sack. After all, I can hardly keep you on my staff after you declare your intention to run against me. Stands to reason. So there's not much incentive in it for you.'

'Not much,' I agreed.

'That's why I'm prepared to make it worth your while.'

A crack opened in the clouds and a beam of sunshine fell upon the container gantries of Appleton dock. Don't move, I told myself. You'll break the spell.

'You're shocked, I can see,' said Angelo. 'Please, don't be offended. I know I can't buy your integrity, but I'd be grateful if you give me this opportunity to express my appreciation for your years of loyal service. You know I can't guarantee your job security beyond the election, but at least I can cushion the blow, money-wise.'

'Money?' I said, as though the filthy subject never crossed my mind.

'Your current employment contract provides for, what, three months' pay in case of dismissal?'

'Six,' I said, a mere point of information.

Angelo was undeterred. 'We'll make it nine. Nominations for preselection close in two weeks. Plenty of time for us to amend the relevant clauses. Then wham, bam, ink's barely dry and you decide to run against me—which is your prerogative as a party member. And I give you your marching orders—which is my right as your employer. You pocket the payout and away we go.'

'Nine months' severance pay?' I closed my eyes and squeezed thumb and forefinger across them. Any second I was going to wake up, find myself at home in bed, realise this was all a dream.

'Okay then, twelve,' said Ange quickly. 'A year's pay, lump sum. How's that for a golden parachute?'

Why did I need a parachute? I'd sprouted wings. I tried to look riven.

'I know what you're thinking.' Agnelli was a veritable clairvoyant this morning. 'You're thinking that you'll have a job until the election anyway. But keep in mind there's a lot of pressure on me to cut costs. Other ministers are shedding staff.'

Act now, in other words, to avoid disappointment. 'Suppose I agree,' I said tentatively. 'Hypothetically speaking. For this to work we'll have to put up a pretty good show. I'd need to have a really proper go at you.'

'Absolutely,' said Angelo, moving in for the kill. 'Boots and all.'

'In that case, I'll have campaign expenses. Phone bills, entertainment, postage.'

'Chicken-feed,' said Ange. 'I'll pay out of my own pocket. A grand, shall we say?'

The fucking cheapskate had just donated ten times that to Donny out of government funds. 'Two,' I said, feeling generous, 'and it's a deal.'

I extended my hand and he nodded in its vicinity.

'Amend your contract and have it on my desk for signature by the close of business,' he said. 'And mum's the word, okay?'

Trish buzzed to say Angelo's next appointment had arrived, a senior official from the Railways Union. I got out while the going was good and went into my office, a cubicle adjacent to the ministerial document-shredder.

Once I'd located my job contract, it took me all of five

minutes to pencil the new details into the margins, ready for retyping. Then I pulled out the phone book, found the listing for Maitland Transport, highlighted the address, copied the details to a cheque requisition form, added the relevant budget codes and marked it for immediate payment. Not a bad day's work, all up.

I was about to take the paperwork out to Trish when she buzzed me. 'There's a gentleman here to see you,' she said. 'A Noel Webb.'

I knew Webb. He was no gentleman.

Surf was up. The waves of shit were about to start breaking.

Noel Webb was a copper.

We'd had dealings a couple of years back when Angelo was Minister for the Arts, a little matter concerning forged paintings. It was not a happy encounter. I took a couple of deep breaths, asked Trish to send him in, slipped the contract back into my top drawer and stood at my desk, waiting.

Webb filled the door frame. He had the build of an icebox and a personality to go with it. His hair was cut to an assertive two-millimetre burr and his ears stuck out the side of his head like the handles on a cast-iron casserole. He had the sort of face you could strike a match on. It wouldn't light but you'd get a lot of satisfaction doing it.

'Hello, Noel.' I didn't offer him a seat. 'How's life in bunko?'

'Wouldn't know,' he said. 'I'm on other duties now.'

'Let me guess. Public relations?'

Webb leaned idly against the door frame and surveyed my broom closet as though it confirmed his estimation of my net human worth. 'I understand you were at the wholesale fruit and vegetable market earlier today.'

It wasn't a question. 'So?'

'Why were you there?'

'To buy some asparagus.' Until Webb eased back on the attitude, gave me some explanation, I saw no reason to answer his questions. 'I'm planning on making a quiche.'

'It's not the asparagus season.'

He was right. The asparagus season didn't officially begin until they put up a sign at the Melbourne Club requesting that members refrain from urinating in the umbrella stand. 'I was misinformed,' I said.

Webb sucked in his cheeks. 'Still a smartarse, I see, Whelan.'

'So this a social call, then?'

Noel Webb liked to be the one asking the questions. 'When did you leave the market?'

'Before the asparagus arrived,' I said. 'But after the last of the stone fruit.' Provoking Noel Webb was like shooting fish fingers in a supermarket freezer. I relented. 'Five thirty-seven,' I said. 'Or eight.'

He thought I was still winding him up. 'Looked at your watch, did you?'

'Matter of fact, I did.' I made a show of looking at it again. 'It keeps very good time. Which is a valuable commodity. So how about you stop wasting mine with the quiz-show routine and tell me what this is all about.'

'Happen to see Darren Stuhl at the market?'

If he was here asking, he already knew the answer. Shit, I

thought, Darren's reported me. Got in first, claimed that I was the one who attacked him. Which is what it must've looked like to those blokes who witnessed the fight. Men who, conveniently, were Stuhl employees, unlikely to contradict the boss's son, even if they knew the true story. Which they didn't. Shit. There went my *quid pro quo*. 'I saw a lot of people,' I said. 'It's a very busy place.'

Webb ran his tongue around his teeth and pursed his lips. His repertoire of facial expressions was limited but communicative. He wanted me to understand that he could barely restrain his irritation. In that regard, nothing had changed since we were in the same class at Preston East Technical High School.

'And if you blokes were doing your job properly,' I said, 'you wouldn't be harassing innocent people. You'd have Darren Stuhl behind bars. He's a vicious prick and it's only a matter of time before he does someone a serious injury.'

'Not much chance of that,' said Webb complacently. 'He's on a slab in the morgue.'

That gave me pause. 'What happened to him?'

'Run over by a truck. Squashed flat as a tack. Raspberry jam from arsehole to breakfast.'

Call me uncharitable, but I felt a momentary flash of elation. 'Nasty,' I said. 'Then again, accidents do happen. And they couldn't happen to a bigger jerk than Darren Stuhl.'

'Whether it was an accident or not remains to be seen,' said Webb. 'And your comments about the deceased are not exactly well-chosen, considering.'

'Considering what?'

'Considering that you were in the truck that ran him over.'

My insides rose, then fell, as if I was in a plummeting

elevator. The burst sack, the smear of red on the asphalt. Then another thought jostled forward. Holy moley, I thought, this is about my parting words to young Dazzer. If he came near me again, I'd told him, he wouldn't know what hit him. Now something had.

I sank into my seat. 'Do forgive me, detective sergeant,' I said. Fortunately I had not yet called Webb by his boyhood nickname, Spider, a usage he deeply disliked. 'In my understandable excitement at seeing you again, I forgot my manners.' I gestured at the visitor's chair. 'Please.'

Webb sat down. 'That's detective *senior* sergeant.' He pulled out a small spiral-bound notebook and laid it on his knee. For the moment, he left it closed. 'Let's begin again, shall we?' he said. 'Why were you at the market this morning?'

'I had insomnia. Couldn't sleep. I was wandering the streets, looking for distraction.' I put my hand on my heart. 'And that's the living truth.'

He looked at me sceptically but let it ride. 'And you saw Darren Stuhl there?'

'Like I said, we spoke to each other.'

'You knew him from your work here at the Transport ministry?'

'We met informally,' I said. 'He punched me in the face and shoved my head down a toilet.'

'An understandable reaction. Must happen to you fairly regularly.'

My turn to let it ride. 'Happened at the Metro nightclub last Friday. At the time I had no idea who he was. Thought he was just an aggressive drunk. Check with the bouncers if you like. By sheer coincidence, I saw him again at the market this morning, fronted him, suggested he might care to pay my dental bill.' I flipped back my top lip and bared my fangs. 'Two grand he cost me.'

Webb's eyes flicked from my teeth to the graze on my forehead. 'And what was his reaction?'

'We agreed to disagree,' I said.

'What time was this?' Webb took a pen from his inside pocket and opened his pad.

'About four o'clock.'

'What then?'

'Nothing really. We went our separate ways. I ran into Donny Maitland. He was there making a delivery. We had a coffee. He offered me a lift home.'

'And what's your relationship with Maitland?'

I shrugged noncommittally. 'I've known him since I was a kid. Took his sister-in-law to the Coburg ball in 1970. She was there, too, as you're no doubt aware. Heather. As we were leaving, we got caught in traffic, all those trucks and whatnot. I was running late, had a plane to catch, so I took off, legged it, caught a cab home.'

Webb consulted his notes. 'This was at 5.37 exactly?'

I nodded. 'Just before I took off, we ran over something. I thought it was a sack of fruit or something. But Donny's already told you this, hasn't he?'

'Catch your plane?'

'Obviously not. Circumstances changed and I cancelled the trip. A family matter. The reason for my insomnia, if you must know.'

He seemed to accept my assurances on that point, or at least he did not pursue the matter. 'Know anyone who had a grievance against the deceased? Who might want him dead?'

The deceased. The word had such a blunt finality to it.

My acquaintance with Darren Stuhl had been nasty, brutish and short and I'd wished him nothing but ill—but I derived no great satisfaction from his death. Not once my initial surge of *Schadenfreude* dissipated. Apart from anything else, it meant that I could kiss my two grand goodbye. Under the circumstances, presenting a dental bill to his father would have smacked of squalid opportunism. Even in death, Darren Stuhl managed to make a pest of himself.

'Based on my brief contact with him,' I said, 'Darren was not what might be called congenial. He could've had hundreds of enemies. Thousands, even.'

Webb was hoping for something a little more specific. 'What about your old mate Donny Maitland? Bit of a stirrer, I understand.'

I flashed on Donny, turbo-charged and babbling, grinding his gears. 'Donny's got some industrial issues with Stuhl senior's corporation,' I said. 'And he's got the T-shirt to prove it. But taking things out on the son, that's not his style. Anyway, what makes you think it wasn't an accident? It was pissing down rain, there were vehicles everywhere. Slippery road. Hazardous conditions. And some of those trucks are real monsters, bullbars sticking out a mile. He might've slipped, fallen under. Could happen to anyone.' If Farrell's story about the roofing tile was true, Darren had a history of clumsiness.

Webb wasn't there to speculate on possible scenarios. 'So the last time you saw Stuhl alive was at approximately 4 a.m.?'

It was, apart from a quick glance through a misted window across a crowded parking lot in the pre-dawn gloom while having my motor tuned. At which time he was holding a pistol to Donny Maitland's head. If I'd seen him then, so had others, men with a better view. And if they wanted to share their recollections with the police that was their business. For my part, I preferred to wait until I had a clearer idea of what was going on. I had no wish to feed an old friend into the maw of the law.

'Yep,' I said.

Webb jotted something down, flipped his notebook closed and stood up. His glance alighted on the phone book, open on the desk between us, where Donny's entry was highlighted. 'I sincerely hope you're not trying to play funny buggers with me, Whelan,' he said. 'Because if you are, rest assured that you'll live to regret it.'

'I have no reason to want to play anything with you,' I said, also standing up. 'And I've answered your questions to the best of my ability. If you have any other queries, you know where to find me.'

Webb put his notebook in his pocket and turned for the door. When he reached it, he looked back. 'You should be careful how much you bite off, Whelan,' he said. 'Make sure you can chew it all.'

As soon as he was gone, I slumped back into my seat. My mind was racing or at least hobbling as fast as it could. It was more than twenty-four hours since I'd slept. Hectic and draining hours, many of them. Fatigue was beginning to tell. I could scarcely string two beans together.

The note I left for Red on the refrigerator, the one place I was sure he'd find it, said that I'd be back about midday. It was that now. Before I went home, however, I needed to make a call.

I looked down at the phone book and started to dial.

A machine answered the Maitland Transport number. I started to leave a message for Donny to call me when Heather picked up.

'How's Sydney?' she said. 'Any news about your son? Donny told me he's gone missing.'

'Red turned up here in Melbourne,' I told her. 'Made a unilateral decision to come and live with me.'

'Well, at least you've got something to be pleased about,' she said. 'That thing we ran over, it was Bob Stuhl's son.'

'So I heard,' I said. 'How's Donny?'

'Shook up, as you can imagine. It was a pretty grisly sight. The police didn't finish with him until ten o'clock. First the uniforms, then the plainclothes lot. They took him up to Citywest station to sign a formal statement. He kept your name out of it, by the way. Thought you had enough on your plate, what with your kid missing. Save you any hassle. I didn't say anything either.'

The only other person at the market who knew my identity was Frank Farrell. He must have supplied that information to the cops. 'I appreciate the thought,' I said. 'Any idea how it happened?'

'Beats me,' she said. 'He was a fair way under when the wheels went over him, that's all I know. Soon as you left, there were people coming from everywhere. You could've sold tickets. Until the cops arrived, that is. Then the cone of silence descended. The only one left to do any talking was Donny.'

'Any suggestion of culpability?'

'Why should there be?' said Heather, slightly alarmed. 'It was an accident wasn't it?'

'Let's hope so,' I said. 'Get Donny to call me when he can, okay. I'll be home in bed.'

'Alone?'

'Asleep. Five minutes with you and I'm all shagged out.'

I got off the line before she could come back at me, gathered up my paperwork and took the contract to Trish for typing. 'That Webb guy was a cop, wasn't he?' she said.

'Road trauma squad,' I said. 'I'll be out for the rest of the day.'

I took the payment requisition down to accounts, kissed some bean-counter backside, extracted a promise that Donny's cheque would be cut by the next morning, then caught a cab home. Red was on the couch, watching 'The Young and the Restless' in pyjamas that were three sizes too small. 'Sorry, mate,' I said. 'I had to go to the office for a while. Work.'

He was familiar with the concept, if not the practice. 'No worries. A man's gotta do what a man's gotta do.'

Clearly what these particular men had to do next was go shopping. Apart from the clothes he was wearing, Red had arrived with a Walkman, some tapes, a pair of Nike cross-trainers and a towel he'd filched from boarding school. Thanks to his hyperactive growth hormones, nothing in his room fitted him. 'Just ring Mum and tell her to send all my stuff down,' he suggested.

That pleasure would have to wait. We lunched at a local pizzeria, then schlepped down the street to the Brotherhood of St Laurence thrift shop near the Housing Commission flats. The choice was not choice. Eventually we hunted up a couple of pre-loved tracksuits. Perfect condition. Twelve dollars the pair.

'I look like a bogan,' Red complained.

'If you want to make a fashion statement, you're welcome to catch the next bus back to Sydney,' I told him. 'I understand that boaters are all the rage up there.'

He didn't push his luck. 'Can we go to Tark's place now, before anyone sees me dressed like this?'

Tarquin and Chloe had just arrived home from school. Tarquin was grudgingly babysitting his little sister until Faye finished work. The two boys greeted each other as long-lost soul mates, exchanging high-fives in the time-honoured Australian manner. 'Hey, man, lookin' like a bogan,' declared Tarquin.

'It's the look, man,' said Red. 'It's the happening look.'

They immediately retreated to Tarquin's room to conduct secret boys' business, while Chloe remained, watching television: a 'Wonder World' segment about guinea-pig care. I pulled up a beanbag beside her and rested my eyes for a moment.

'Use plenty of straw,' said a voice. 'So the little feller is all snuggly-wuggly.'

Snuggly-wuggly, I thought. A snoozy-woozy on the couchy-wouchy, that's what I need. Not a kicky-wicky in the heady-weady or a rumpy-pumpy in a trucky-wucky or a squishy-wishy on the roady-woady. Just an incy-wincy nappy-wappy.

The sound sting for the six o'clock news hauled me back into consciousness. The guinea pigs had been replaced by tanks in the streets of Moscow. Gorbachev was still incommunicado. There was no news from the Crimea. Faye came in from the kitchen to catch the headlines, wiping her hands on a kitchen towel. 'You'll stay for dinner?' she asked.

My attention was back on the television screen. A reporter was standing in front of the wholesale vegetable market, an umbrella in one hand and a microphone in the other. It was broad daylight, a light rain was falling and the parking apron was deserted except for a couple of police cars, Donny's truck and fluttering yellow ribbons of crime-scene tape.

'The victim, son of prominent business identity, Mr Bob Stuhl, was discovered just before six this morning,' the reporter was saying. 'The notoriously close-lipped market community is reported to be mystified by his death. At this stage, police have refused to rule out foul play.'

Faye noticed my interest. Her journalistic beat lay in the territory of interest-rate fluctuations and the impact of exchange rates on the balance of trade but she was not unacquainted with the nation's premier trucking dynasty. 'Apart from the coup in Russia, the Stuhl family was the hot topic at the *Weekly* today,' she said as the news went into a commercial and I followed her into the kitchen. 'Apparently this Darren was quite a handful. Not that Bob's any angel. The rumours have been around for years that he isn't as legitimate as he'd have us believe. You don't parlay a couple of clapped-out old trucks into a business empire worth millions without cutting a few legal corners.'

I decided to wait for a more opportune time to reveal that my interest in the story was based on more than idle curiosity. This was an occasion to celebrate Red's deliverance from perils real and imagined, not for revelations about bare-knuckle brawling and visits from a dick called Spider. Leo burst though the front door, bellowing his hellos and extracting the cork from a bottle of Hunter Valley red.

While pasta percolated and sauce seethed, I sat at the kitchen table, recounted Red's saga and declared my resolve to fight his mother for custody, if necessary.

'Wendy's not just going to roll over and take it,' said Leo.

'She never did,' I said. 'But that's another story.'

'This will mean a lot of changes, Murray,' warned Faye.

'I've already started to make them,' I said. 'Can't talk about it yet, but I've had an offer.'

'Headhunted?' asked Leo.

'Cannibalised would be a better word. In any case, I'll be able to spend more time with Red.'

'And so you should,' said Faye, ever the moralist. She dumped a writhing mass of spaghetti into a colander, tilted her head back and bellowed at the ceiling. 'Dinner!'

An avalanche of children fell down the stairs and onto the food. 'Can Red stay here tonight?' slurped Tarquin.

'Wait your turn,' I told him. 'There'll be plenty of time for that sort of thing from now on.'

'Look what I can do,' giggled Chloe, siphoning a strand of spaghetti through the gap in her smile.

'You must be the grossest little girl I have ever met,' I said. She beamed at the compliment, bolognaised from chin to cheekbones.

This was the life. Happy families. Here in Fitzroy at least. Not so joyous in French provincial Toorak, I mused. Poor old Bob Stuhl. Rich as Croesus and tough as nails. But what did it profit him? One son was parsnip puree, the other tomato concasse.

As the kids cleared the dishes, Faye reached into the freezer. 'Strawberry crush or tutti-frutti?'

The phone jerked me from an uneasy sleep soon after eight the next morning. It was a woman. Unfortunately, it wasn't Lyndal Luscombe.

'You can't do this to me, Murray,' she started in.

I swung my bare feet onto the floor, wondering if it was too early for a cigarette. 'This isn't about you, Wendy,' I sighed.

The ability to relinquish control had never been my ex-wife's strongest suit. And when it came to custody of her flesh and blood, she had no compunction in unleashing her inner pit bull. 'You clearly haven't given any thought to Red's future,' she accused. 'Knowing you, you'll send him to a government school. He'll miss out on his chance to sit the International Baccalaureate and end up at some third-rate university. There goes his MBA. God, you are so selfish.'

Red's decision to vote with his feet had put Wendy in an untenable position. Short of kidnapping him, she couldn't force the boy to return to Sydney. And it wasn't as if I didn't have previous experience in the prime parenting role, I reminded her, back when it was me who kept the home fires burning, made the playlunch, ran the bath, applied the band-aids, read the bedtime stories. We finally reached a compromise. Red would remain in my care, subject to review at the end of the year. In the meantime, I was to make sure that he rang his mother regularly.

'He'll turn out like you,' she warned. 'And we don't want that, do we?'

I rang off and stood in the doorway of his room, watching him sleep and contemplating our new life together. My little boy was beyond storybooks now. Beyond bathtime and peanut-butter sandwiches, folded not cut. He'd become a streetwise bus-fare hustler. An illicit crosser of state borders. A fugitive from boarding school. His will was his own. He could be guided but not constrained, enlisted but not compelled. And, whatever Wendy might say to the contrary, I could be a good father to him. I could love him and feed him and watch over him while he slept. And enrol him in a government school.

I proceeded into the kitchen, phoned Fitzroy High and made an appointment with the principal. Then I togged up, put a note on the refrigerator and nipped into Transport House to make sure Angelo had countersigned my revised job contract.

'It's still on his desk,' said Trish. 'He's been too busy selling his budget cuts to the public transport unions to sign it.'

My trip was not entirely wasted, however. The paper-shufflers in accounts had set a new benchmark for efficiency. The check for the Maitland consultancy job was waiting in my in-tray. Since I hadn't yet heard from Donny, I gave him a call.

'Are you awake?' I said, phone in the crook of my shoulder, staring out my twelfth-floor window at a sky that was now the colour of dirty bandages.

'I ought to be,' he said. 'I've just had a visit. A copper, and not nearly as civil as yesterday's lot. Bloke named Webb. Head like a garden tap, personality like a duodenal ulcer. Accused me of obstructing the course of justice. To wit, concealing the fact that you were present when I ran over Darren Stuhl.'

'Sorry if I dropped you in the shit,' I said. 'Webb came to see me yesterday, knew I'd been at the market. I assumed you'd told the cops, didn't realise otherwise until Heather told me.'

Donny wasn't fussed, said he'd explained to Webb that he thought I'd gone to Sydney to look for my lost kid, that he didn't think my momentary presence in the truck was relevant to the accident report. 'Good thing Jacinta's at work. She'd freak if she knew I'd had a house call from a member of the homicide squad.'

'Homicide?' I said. 'Webb didn't tell me he was from homicide.'

'Very interested in you, he was,' said Donny. 'Wanted to know if I'd ever seen you with Darren Stuhl. Implied you're involved in some way and I was covering for you.'

'He suggested the same to me about you.'

'Standard procedure,' said Donny. 'In my experience, the best thing with coppers is to say as little as possible.'

'A man in my position can hardly refuse to talk to the police,' I said.

'And what position is that, Murray?'

Good question. 'We need to talk,' I said. And the telephone, by implication, was not the place to do it.

'Come on over. I'm not going anywhere. They've impounded the truck, pending forensic tests. They've probably got it down the watch-house, belting a confession out of it with a telephone book.'

I told him I'd be there in a couple of hours, after I'd attended to some pressing domestic issues. The first of these was a visit to the supermarket for fresh supplies of cereal. The second was to return home, rouse Red and inform him of our imminent appointment at his new school. 'If you're serious about wanting to live here, then the sooner we get into a settled routine the better. Deal?'

'Deal.'

A box of Nutri-grain later, we set out for the tram stop at the end of the street. 'We could save quite a bit on fares if I had a bike,' Red remarked casually. 'Tarquin rides to school and he hasn't been killed yet.'

'We'll see,' I said, thinking we'd be needing a car, too. A little second-hand runabout, easy to park, fuel-efficient. In a couple of weeks, the departmental taxi account would be a thing of the past. In the meantime, we trammed the kilometre to the Edinburgh Gardens, then walked between skeletal elm trees to the red-brick high school with its cluster of portable classrooms, its asphalt basketball court and peeling community mural.

The principal, Ms Henderson, was an ample woman with a Sapphic haircut, her daunting demeanour somewhat moderated by the laugh lines at the corners of her caftan. It may have been my first day at high school, but Red was an old hand, well versed in the jargon. By the time the lunch bell rang, we'd completed the paperwork and taken the tour. 'Is it okay if I stay for the rest of the afternoon, Ms Henderson?' Red pleaded, ear cocked to the burble of voices in the yard.

'If it's all right with your father.'

The student prince extended an upturned palm. 'I can catch the tram home with Tarquin, Dad.'

'Thought you said he rides his bike?' I coughed up five dollars. 'Make it last.'

'Keen, isn't he?' remarked Ms Henderson dryly as Red disappeared into the throng.

So was I. To see Donny, to find out what was going on. I trotted back to Brunswick Street and hailed a cab.

Reservoir was two suburbs beyond the Northern Region Performing Arts Centre, an undulating expanse of cream-brick working-class suburbia. The sort of place, it was said, where old greyhounds go to die. Donny's place was typical, a low-fenced double-fronted bungalow with a patch of lawn at the front and driveway leading down the side to a backyard garage. An off-white Commodore with a dinged rear tail-light stood in the drive.

A chink creased the venetians as I stepped from the cab and the front door was open by the time I reached it. Donny looked like he'd been through the wringer. He was shoeless and unshaven, his flannelette shirt hanging loose over saggy track pants, the bottoms tucked into a pair of thick socks. 'Heather told me about the kid,' he said. 'Must be a weight off your mind.'

'If it wasn't for this shit, I'd be the happiest man in the world,' I said.

Donny led me down a short hallway lined with overstuffed

plank-and-brick bookcases and we emerged into a combined kitchen–living room warmed by a wood-fired heater. The furniture was mix-n-match. Filipino folk art hung haphazardly on the walls. Donny's drum kit stood in the corner and a geriatric labrador snoozed in front of the fire. Sliding glass doors overlooked a redwood deck with hanging plants and a Webber barbecue. We were in absolutely no danger of being interrupted by a photographer from *Vogue Interiors*.

'What a mess,' I said, meaning the general situation.

'You should've seen Darren Stuhl. That's what I call a mess. Nearly lost my lunch, and I hadn't even had breakfast yet. You want a beer?'

'Bit early for me,' I said. 'Cup of tea'd go down well. If homicide's involved, they must've made their minds up pretty quick that it wasn't an accident.'

Donny lit the gas under the kettle and unhooked a couple of mugs. 'You'd have to wonder how he got so far under the wheels.'

'So what do you think happened?' I said. 'Any ideas?'

'I leave the theorising to you intellectuals.'

I sat at the table and stared at my hands. 'You tell the cops he pulled a gun on you?'

Donny cocked a worldly-wise eye. 'Yeah, sure. And volunteer myself a motive for killing him? Not bloody likely. Besides which, I'm trying to present myself as a credible union leader. If I go bleating to the constabulary every time some twerp tries it on, I might as well toss in the election right now.'

'So the campaign's still on?'

'My oath,' he said. 'I'm not going to let this distract me.'

'Don't take this the wrong way,' I said. 'But what about

Roscoe or Len? Maybe one of them decided to engage in a little hand-to-hand class warfare.'

'Believe me, if either of them were responsible, they'd be lining up to tell me all about it. Whatever happened back there, it wasn't down to us. You can take my word for it.'

'Well it wasn't me,' I said. 'I swear.'

'You don't have to tell me that, Murray,' he said. 'But you might have a bit of trouble convincing the cops. Like I said, Webb was very interested. Knew about your punch-up with Darren.'

'I told him that part myself,' I said.

'So how come the cops knew you were at the market?'

'I assume Frank Farrell told them. Apart from you and Heather, Farrell was the only other person there who knew my name. And he'd have no reason not to tell the cops. In a situation like that, a man dead, even a deadshit like Darren Stuhl, I wouldn't expect anyone to withhold information.'

Donny plonked a steaming mug in front of me. Garfield the Cat. 'There's withholding,' he said. 'And there's volunteering. And a man like Farrell doesn't talk to the cops out of a sense of civic duty. He's making mischief, Murray.'

'I've got nothing to hide, so he's not going to get very far.'

'That's not going to stop him trying. Situation like this, a man would be well advised to keep his wits about him.'

Through the window I saw a recent model Magna pull into the driveway behind Donny's Commodore.

'Here's trouble,' said Donny. 'It's Heather. She's been to the bank, telling them we'll have a bit of a cash-flow problem while the truck's impounded. She still doesn't know about the gun, by the way.'

Heather stomped through the back door in her bossy boots

and shoulder pads, groomed to within an inch of her life. 'Oh,' she said. 'It's you.' Her tone was frosty, preoccupied.

'What did they say?' said Donny.

'What do you think they said?' She didn't bother to conceal her exasperation, both with Donny and the bank. She pulled a printout from her handbag and slapped it flat on the table. 'You've been dipping into the truck expenses account to pay for your stupid bloody campaign handbills, haven't you?'

Donny made a dismissive gesture. 'Relax. I'll pay it back.'

'With what? Jacinta's wages?'

Donny flushed. 'What Jacinta chooses to do with her money is her business.'

'Professional psychiatric help,' snorted Heather. 'That's what you need.'

I tried to make myself as inconspicuous as possible. Total invisibility would've been good. Then Heather turned in disgust from Donny and directed her lasers at me. 'If you were as much Donny's friend as you pretend, you wouldn't be encouraging this nonsense.'

'Fair go, Heather,' said Donny. 'This isn't Murray's fault.'

She folded her arms and glowered down at us, a woman at the end of her tether. Always a dangerous place for a woman to be.

'Cup of tea?' I said inanely. She tightened her lips and gave a hard little shake of her earrings. I took the cheque from my pocket and placed it on top of the bank statement. 'How about ten thousand dollars then?' I said. 'Would that make you feel better?'

Donny snatched up the cheque. 'Jesus, you move fast.'

Heather thought I was making some kind of joke. 'What's that for?'

'To secure the services of Maitland Transport to undertake an ongoing, open-ended, industry-based research project on behalf of the policy development section of the Ministry of Transport.'

'What research project? We don't do research.'

'We do now,' beamed Donny.

I gave him his riding orders. 'Clear any debts you've already incurred,' I said. 'Then use the balance to pay yourself a salary equal to your income from driving the truck. Enlist support from sympathetic unions. Recruit enough candidates to field a ticket. Beef up your publicity. Start getting up Howard Sharpe's nose.'

Heather twigged. 'Is this legal?' she said, taking the cheque from Donny and examining it carefully.

'It's from the government,' I said. 'How could it be otherwise?'

Her mood began improving. The cheque disappeared into her handbag and she decided that a cup of tea would be nice, after all.

'Agnelli is to be quarantined from any responsibility for this exercise,' I told Donny.

'My lips are sealed.'

'You know I don't agree with Donny about this union election thing,' said Heather. 'But I'm grateful for the help.' She put a warm hand over mine and squeezed. 'Very grateful.'

'Goodness,' I said. 'Is that the time? I really must be off. Got to pick my boy up from school.'

'Here we go again,' she said. 'The Incredible Vanishing Man.'

Heather was not the only person whose attentions I was keen to avoid.

In case Angelo's mental compass suddenly swung about on the backstab pay-out offer, I thought it wise to keep out of the way until his signature was firmly appended to the contract. As soon as I got home, I rang Trish to report that I'd come down with a dose of the Texas flu and wouldn't be fit for the office for the rest of the week.

When Red arrived home from school, I had him call his mother to discuss which of his possessions she should ship south. Then we went into the city and spread some plastic around the retail end of the teenage apparel industry. Despite the intermittent nature of our contact over the previous five years, the old father–son adhesive had stood the test of time. In little more than thirty-six hours, we'd segued into an easy domesticity.

'So when do I meet these girlfriends?' asked Red as he set out on Wednesday morning for the second day of his third-rate education. 'This harem of yours.'

'Never,' I said. 'In honour of your arrival, I've taken a vow of celibacy.'

'It's not natural, Dad,' he advised. 'A grown man has certain needs.'

'Right now my greatest need is for you to pick your clothes off the bathroom floor,' I said. 'And for Christsake, turn off the fucking television before you leave the house.'

The tonnage levy issue finally bit the dust on Thursday. An item appeared in the *Sun* reporting that the transport minister had issued a firm denial of any intention to implement the tax. This was described as 'an embarrassing backflip'. I was glad I wasn't at the office.

But that didn't mean I couldn't be found. Just before six, I went to the corner store for a loaf of multigrain and a litre of low-fat. Spider Webb cruised past in a shiny maroon Falcon as I was returning. When I reached the house, he was waiting on the doorstep, legs apart, hands on hips, his centre of gravity somewhere around the keyhole. I resisted the temptation to stick my key into it. 'You don't look very sick to me,' he leered. 'Your office said you were bedridden.'

'So you dropped around to offer your best wishes for my speedy recovery, did you?'

'You know your problem, Whelan?' he said, like he was the world's leading expert on the subject. 'You don't know your own best interests. Let's go inside and talk about it.' His tone suggested I didn't have any choice.

'The house is already full of germs,' I said. 'And you've had nothing from me so far but my full co-operation. So let's talk here, shall we? What do you want this time, Spider?'

His scalp bristles bristled. 'To give you a bit of friendly advice, that's what. We've got more officers working on this case than you've had hot dinners, smartarse. Nothing is escaping our attention. And if you think your fancy political contacts can protect you, you're a bigger fool than you look. And that'd take some doing.'

'Thanks for the tip,' I said. 'But I've got no idea what you're talking about.'

'Yeah?' he sneered. 'Well you might be interested to know that we've now got Darren Stuhl's post-mortem results.' He delivered this information like a man playing an ace.

'And what do they say?'

'They say you should take this opportunity to come clean, save yourself a lot of trouble.'

If there was any logic here, it defeated me. 'You'll have to give me a hint,' I said. 'I don't speak Neanderthal.'

Webb rocked back and forth on his heels, giving me the slow burn. 'You remember a bloke called Brian Sutch?' he said.

'Vaguely.' Sutch was a notorious standover man. He'd given us a few headaches back when I was at the Municipal Employees Union, extorting money from our members.

'Heard what happened to him?'

'Shot, wasn't he?' This was a good fifteen years back. The closest I'd come to the incident was reading about it in the papers.

'That's right,' said Webb. 'Three rounds to the head in the public bar of the Brickworks Hotel. Twenty-five eye-witnesses. All swore blind they were in the gents at the time. Ever been to the Brickworks? The bog's even smaller than that rathole office of yours.'

'And?'

'We knew who did it, but couldn't make the case without a witness. Fortunately, there was quite a bit of old evidence lying around the squad room. Turned out that some of it could be made to fit one of the witnesses. Amazing how fast his memory improved when that fact was pointed out to him.'

I reached around Webb and slid my key into the lock. 'If you have any other queries, Sergeant Webb,' I said, brushing past him. 'Don't hesitate to give me a call. I'll be more than happy to consult my schedule. And my lawyer.'

I shut the door in Webb's face and leaned my back against it. This is blatant intimidation, I thought. Spider acted like a big swinging dick at school and he clearly believed that membership of the police force was a licence to do likewise in adult life. His belief that I was covering for Donny Maitland was now out in the open. His threat to frame me unless I came clean, however, was a waste of breath. I had nothing to come clean about. If Spider Webb thought I'd perjure myself, he needed his head read. In Spider's case, that was a job for a phrenologist.

The sound of Webb's departing car leached through the woodwork. I took my bag of supplies down to the kitchen where Red was on the phone to his mother, adding further essential requirements to his initial list. 'Don't worry about sending the bike,' he was saying. 'It's too small now and, anyway, Dad's going to buy me a new one.'

In accordance with newly instituted practice, the television was running unwatched in the living room. Breaking open a meditative beer, I slumped on the couch, letting the six o'clock news bulletin wash over me. Webb's line about the post-mortem, what the hell did that mean?

A man in a police uniform with silver-studded epaulets appeared on the screen. Spider's boss, the Chief Commissioner of Police. He was fronting the microphones at a press conference, an update on the Darren Stuhl case. If Bob expected top-level service, he was certainly getting it.

According to the C.C., Darren Stuhl's autopsy indicated that the cause of death was a blow to the head with a blunt instrument, rather than traffic injuries as initially assumed. The task force undertaking the investigation was confident of an early result. Heavy rain and a high level of vehicular activity in the area at the time of the incident had, however, hampered police in their inquiries. Anyone having relevant information was urged to contact the police.

Red threw himself onto the couch beside me and heaved an exhausted sigh. 'Mum said that Richard's upset I can't crew with him in the regatta on Saturday. As if.' He reached for the remote control. 'Can't we watch something else? This is boring. And what's for dinner?'

'A blow to the head,' I said absently.

'I'd prefer a poke in the eye,' said Red. 'Or how about some of those beef-burgers in the freezer.'

I was more concerned with what was cooking in the minds of the police. I could appreciate their difficulties. A wash-out crime scene. The market tighter than a fish's arse. Bob Stuhl breathing down their necks for a result. But the only blunt instrument I could recall at the market was the one Heather had in her hand. And nobody had beaten Darren Stuhl over the head with it. Not as far as I could remember.

'Turn the grill on,' I told Red. Then I went into the bedroom and rang Donny Maitland, planning to do some grilling of my own. 'See the news?' I said.

'I'm too busy cleaning up,' he said. 'Mr Plod's been back. Tossed the place. Did a right royal job of it, too. Joint looks like a tornado's been through it.'

'What were they looking for?'

'Didn't say. Whatever it was, they didn't find it. They came, they ransacked. Three hours later they left empty-handed. Fishing expedition, that was my impression.'

'They have a search warrant?'

'No, I invited them in,' he said sarcastically. 'Mistook them for interior decorators. What's this about the news?'

I told him about the chief commissioner's announcement and Spider Webb's visit.

'Sounds to me like Webb's just shaking your tree, see if anything falls out. As for Darren getting decked, it stands to reason. If they were looking for the murder weapon here, they didn't find it. How could they? I didn't do it.'

'I think you should get a lawyer,' I said.

Donny scoffed. 'What good would a shyster do me? I've got better things to do with your boss's money. You want to help me, get off the line so I can finish cleaning up this mess before Jacinta gets home.'

Donny was right, I decided. The cops were beating the bushes. Webb and his task force colleagues were probably putting pressure on every potential informant in town, hoping that something useful would turn up. Well, it wasn't going to turn up from my direction. How could it? I didn't know anything.

Nor, evidently, did the press. Both of Friday's morning dailies carried stories about the Stuhl case. In the absence of hard facts, they fell back on speculation. The market-murder clippings file was dusted off and long-dead, bullet-riddled tomato vendors again got their photos in the paper, although the connection between whitebread Darren and the garlic-munching godfathers remained obscure. To compound the issue, it was reported that some kind of turf war was happening between Vietnamese newcomers and some of the longer established market interests.

Darren's funeral was held that afternoon at St John's in Toorak. Bob's elevated status ensured a big turnout. Several former federal Cabinet ministers attended and many a crocodile tear was shed in the memory of a promising young man so untimely squished. Among the shedders, caught briefly in the sweep of the television cameras as the casket was borne down the front steps, was the entire state executive committee of the United Haulage Workers. Watching it that night at home, I glimpsed Frank Farrell's face in the congregation.

Unlike that of his older brother, though, Darren's fate had no appreciable impact on Stuhl Holdings' share price.

Monday saw me back at the office. In my absence, Angelo had signed the contract. It was waiting in my in-tray along with a preselection nomination form and a copy of the party membership rolls for Melbourne Upper. The message was clear. The skulduggery was to commence.

I phoned a real estate agent and made arrangements to rent a one-bedroom flat in Preston. This would allow me to claim to be a resident of Melbourne Upper, always a useful sop to local sensibilities. I spent the rest of the morning poring over the membership list, mapping known factional allegiances, ethnic affiliations and personal networks. When I returned from lunch, I found a telephone message slip on my desk. It stated that Senior Sergeant Webb had called requesting that I ring him regarding an appointment.

As a general operational principle, I avoid lawyers. They leave bits of paper everywhere and cost a poultice. But since push was coming to shove, it seemed advisable to share my burden with somebody more acquainted with police procedures. I rang a man named Pat O'Shannessy, known to me only by reputation.

Commonly called One-Stop, O'Shannessy was a criminal lawyer who plied his trade in places where more fastidious eagles feared to fly. He listened to the bare bones of my situation, took Spider's direct line and rang me back fifteen minutes later.

'Citywest police station, three this afternoon. See you at my chambers at two.'

One-Stop's chambers were smack in the middle of the legal precinct, in a Queen Street high-rise commonly known as the Golan Heights. The reason for this was apparent when I read the directory in the lobby. Unless I was mistaken, few of O'Shannessy's fellow tenants had been educated by the Jesuits.

One-Stop was a man of Falstaffian proportions, proprietor of the largest collection of chins I'd ever seen. So many that I thought for a moment he was wearing a neck brace. He gazed at me through half-moon glasses from behind his redoubt of a desk, the hem of a red linen napkin wedged into his barely visible collar.

'Lunch on the run,' he explained, waving me into a chair with a baseball mitt that might have been a hand. 'Care to join me?'

Declining his roast beef sandwiches, I went straight into my spiel. Told him pretty well everything. Apart from

Heather going the lunge, of course. And the bit about seeing Darren threaten Donny with a gun. 'I don't believe that Donny Maitland killed Darren Stuhl,' I concluded. 'Apart from anything else, why would he implicate himself by shoving the body under his own truck? It doesn't make sense. And I'm not going to let the cops railroad me into implicating him.'

Except for the steady motion of his jaws and the occasional smacking of his lips, One-Stop heard me out in silence. When I finished, he licked his enormous fingers and wiped them delicately on the napery. 'It is the task of the police to separate the circumstantial sheep from the evidentiary goats,' he pronounced. 'The extent to which you are prepared to assist them in that process is up to you. My advice is this. If you cannot be entirely candid, at least be consistent. If you cannot be consistent, say nothing.'

'I've done nothing wrong,' I said. 'Nothing unlawful, at least.'

'Glad to hear it.' O'Shannessy ripped the napkin from his neck, stood abruptly and brushed the crumbs from his lapels. 'Onward, then,' he declared, 'into the valley of death.'

It was amazing how fast the man could move. He barrelled down the footpath like a galleon under full sail, alarmed pedestrians leaping aside at his approach, while I bobbed in his wake like a dinghy. By the time we'd covered the four blocks to the Citywest cop shop, I fully expected him to barge straight through the front doors without waiting for them to open. One-Stop's legal skills were still an unknown quantity but there was no doubt about his capacities as a morale booster.

'If I think you're getting into hot water,' he said, 'I'll pull the plug.'

Citywest was a low-slung, box-like building across the road from the Flagstaff Gardens. It might have passed for the regional headquarters of a computer software company if not for the pervasive smell of truncheon leather and the Uphold the Right motto above the bulletproof reception desk. Noel Webb appeared promptly, beady-eyed and hot to trot. 'One-Stop?' he sneered into my ear as he fed us into the elevator. 'You must be desperate.'

He took us to an interview room, a windowless cube with washable vinyl walls, and we were joined by a horse-faced man in his mid-fifties with tired, watery eyes and a bad case of the sniffles. His breath smelled of throat lozenges and he carried himself with the resigned air of one kept from his sickbed by the unremitting demands of a thankless job. He introduced himself to me as Chief Inspector Voigt and croaked that he appreciated my co-operation. This pleasantry fooled nobody.

'Consider yourself honoured,' said One-Stop, 'Reg here is *le grand fromage* himself. Head of homicide.' He and O'Shannessy were clearly old sparring partners.

We all sat down and One-Stop opened the batting. 'I am instructed that my client has already answered a number of your questions. He advises me that he is happy to assist in any way he can. But stick to the straight and narrow, please gents.'

Voigt fixed me in his rheumy gaze. 'Mr Whelan,' he sniffed. 'Can you tell us why you were at the Melbourne Wholesale Fruit and Vegetable Market on the morning of Monday 12 August?'

I explained about Red going missing, that I was unable to sleep and walking the streets in search of distraction.

'But why the market?'

'Impulse,' I shrugged. Professional discretion constrained me from disclosing my other reason. It was, after all, irrelevant to the matter at hand. 'I was quite upset about my son. And, like I said, I was looking for distraction.'

Voigt's inner bullfrog made a sceptical sound. 'You didn't go there with the intention of seeing anybody?'

'Darren Stuhl, you mean? Not only didn't I go there to see him, I was unaware of both his identity and the fact that he'd be there.'

'But you did know him.'

'We'd met,' I said. 'But I didn't know who he was.'

For what felt like the hundredth time, I described our encounter at the Metro. As he listened, Voigt nodded and dabbed his nose with a crumpled tissue. 'You were assaulted, yet you made no official complaint at the time.'

'I complained to the nightclub bouncers,' I said. 'There seemed little point in raising it with the police as there were no witnesses and I didn't know my assailant's identity. I only discovered that when I spotted him at the market. A man called Frank Farrell identified him for me.'

'And how do you know this Farrell?' said Voigt.

'Professionally,' I said. 'He works for the United Haulage Workers. I've had contact with him in my capacity as an adviser to the Minister for Transport.'

Noel Webb, who was doodling idly on a writing pad, smirked at this, as though I'd exposed myself as a fatuous big-noter.

'So you approached Stuhl,' continued Voigt. 'What happened then?'

'I suggested he apologise and pay my dentist bill.'

'What was his reaction?'

'He was dismissive.'

'But you persisted.'

One-Stop cleared his throat. Not, I assumed, because he'd caught Inspector Voigt's influenza.

'He pushed me away. I pushed back. There was a minor scuffle. It was all over in a few seconds.'

'But you did threaten him.'

'I warned him that I'd take legal action if he came near me again,' I said firmly.

One-Stop, observing this over the top of his half-moon glasses, gave me an encouraging nod. So far, so good.

'Then what?' said Voigt.

'I walked away. I wandered around the market, took in the sights, had a cup of coffee in the cafe. Donny Maitland turned up, offered me a lift home, so I went and waited in his truck with his sister-in-law Heather. I've told all this to Sergeant Webb.'

Webb continued to toy with his pen, as if waiting for the pussy-footing to finish.

'This is in the parking area, right?' said Voigt.

'Yes.'

'At approximately 5.15 a.m.?'

'Yes.'

'And you didn't see Darren Stuhl there?'

'Like I said, I was sitting in a truck with Heather Maitland. We were engrossed in conversation. The windows were misted up.'

'Were you aware that Maitland was conducting a union election rally in the vicinity at the time?'

'I could hear him making a speech,' I said. 'But I wasn't really paying attention.'

'And you remained in the truck until Maitland returned?' said Voigt.

This was where the ice started to get thin. 'No, I stepped out briefly. I was booked on a flight to Sydney to look for my son. I was beginning to get anxious that I'd miss it if we didn't leave soon, so I went looking for Donny.'

'Alone?'

'Heather stayed in the truck while I did a quick circuit of the area,' I said, kissing my alibi goodbye. 'Donny turned up, we pulled out, ran over something. I thought it was a bag of fruit, decided I couldn't wait around while it was sorted out. I went across to the Mobil roadhouse and called a cab. When I got home, my son was there, so I rang the airline and cancelled my booking. They've probably still got a record of it.' Even as I provided it, this corroborative suggestion seemed ludicrously irrelevant.

'And when was the last time you saw Stuhl?'

'I wasn't even aware that Darren Stuhl was dead until your colleague here informed me later that day.'

That was it. End of story. I turned to One-Stop and shrugged.

'And you definitely didn't see Stuhl in the parking area?' Voigt persisted. 'You're sure?'

'I've told you what happened,' I said.

'And you have nothing to add?'

'Like what?'

Spider Webb ended his reverie and gave an incredulous snort.

'DSS Webb believes you haven't been entirely frank with us, Mr Whelan,' snuffled Voigt. 'Isn't that right, sergeant?'

'I do indeed, sir,' said Webb.

This exchange was conducted in a slightly flippant manner that was intended to convey that the tenor of the interview was about to undergo a distinct change.

'We are now going to show you something, Mr Whelan,'

said Voigt. 'I want you to take a close look at it and tell me if you have ever seen it before.' He nodded to Webb, who laid down his pencil, got to his feet and strode from the room.

One-Stop tilted his head back, stroked his neck flaps and peered at me quizzically through his spectacles. I shrugged apprehensively, wondering what this mysterious exhibit might be. Voigt took advantage of the pause in the interrogation to draw a series of deep nasal breaths, clearing his sinuses.

Then Webb was back. He dropped something on the table in front of me. It landed with an emphatic clunk and I found myself staring down at a clear plastic bag containing a fourteen-inch, drop-forged Sidchrome shifting spanner.

Shit. How had I managed to let that slip my mind? Frank fucking Farrell, I thought. This was down to him. And it was mischief, pure and simple. Nobody else had seen me with the damned thing. Christ, I'd even forgotten about it myself. And to explain why I was carrying it, I'd need to tell them what I'd seen out the truck window. And if I did that, I'd risk dunking Donny in the doo-doo.

'Well?' said Voigt.

'It's a spanner,' I said.

'I think we're agreed on that much, Mr Whelan,' said Voigt. 'The question is, have you seen it before?'

My mind was racing, figuring the angles. Some of them were acute. Others weren't so cute. None of them were guaranteed to make me look blameless. I fell back on the truth, hoping I wasn't impaling myself. To be on the safe side, I blunted its edges a little. 'Possibly,' I said.

'Would you care to elaborate?' invited Voigt.

'A spanner similar to this dropped out of the truck when I opened the door,' I said. 'I held onto it until I got back in. If you found this under the seat of Donny Maitland's truck, then it's probably the same one. If you're implying that I hit Darren Stuhl over the head with it, I categorically deny it.'

Webb was still standing. He put his palms on the table, leaned forward and stuck his pie-crust face into mine. His aftershave smelled like formaldehyde. 'How about we cut the crap,' he said. 'It's as plain as day what really happened here. This arrogant, vicious, spoiled rich kid sticks your head down a toilet, humiliates you, costs you an arm and a leg in dental charges. You run into him again, take a perfectly reasonable tone, he tries for an encore. You tell him you're going to have him prosecuted, walk away. A bit later, he finds you alone. He threatens you. This time, you've got a spanner. You defend yourself. But you hit the prick a little bit too hard. You kill him. You panic, shove him under the nearest truck, try to make it look like an accident.'

He leaned back, arms wide, QED. Inspector Voigt was looking contemplative, as though this novel and unexpected interpretation of the events might warrant consideration.

'It would've been pretty stupid of me to attack a man with a spanner, knowing he was carrying a gun,' I said.

Voigt shot Webb a sideways glance. This wasn't part of the scenario he'd been sold. 'What do you know about the gun?' he demanded.

'Only that I noticed Stuhl was carrying one when we were scuffling.'

'So why didn't you mention it earlier?' harrumphed Webb.

'Because you didn't ask me.'

'And what else haven't you told us?' said Voigt.

There was a scraping sound as One-Stop pushed his chair back. 'My client,' he announced, 'came here of his own free will and in good faith. He came to answer your questions, which he has done. He is not here to engage in hypothetical speculation or to play guessing games. If you have evidence to substantiate your allegations, I suggest you produce it and give my client the opportunity to refute it. Otherwise, I am advising him to terminate this interview forthwith.'

Spider ignored him. 'Take this chance, Whelan. Clear the air. Don't dig yourself deeper into the shit.'

Voigt had stopped sniffling and the two cops were staring at me very hard. Their gaze was about as relaxing as Dr Freycinet's high-speed drill.

'If Sergeant Webb wants to talk to my client again, Inspector Voigt,' said One-Stop, 'have him contact me first.'

Voigt sniffed wearily and nodded. Spider backed away and sulked.

'I'd like to go now,' I said. 'If that's all right.'

'Amateur theatrics,' concluded One-Stop. 'That spanner wasn't even tagged for evidence.'

He made these reassuring remarks in the bar of the Golden Age Hotel where he took me for a stiffening belt after we left Citywest.

'I told you Webb was threatening to frame me,' I said.

'His *modus operandi* undoubtedly contains a degree of bluster,' agreed One-Stop, signalling for another round. 'But I don't think you need worry too much. They've got no witness, no admission, no evidence and therefore no case. It's a hollow threat. Sit pat. If they want to talk to you again, they have to call me first.'

Heartening advice and a snip at eight hundred dollars. But I wasn't going to do nothing while Frank Farrell took advantage of the situation. As soon as I got back to the office I rang the United Haulage Workers.

Mr Farrell was not currently in the office, I was informed by a sing-song female voice. 'Is it a pressing matter?'

'It's pressing on me,' I said.

'You could try his mobile. The number's changed. I'll give you the new one.'

I dialled the string of digits and Farrell came on the line. He sounded like he was speaking from inside an industrial vacuum cleaner.

'It's Murray Whelan,' I said. 'I'm calling to congratulate you on your good citizenship.'

'The cops been asking you questions, have they?' he said. 'I just told them what I saw, that's all. Why should I keep my trap shut for you? For all I know, you had a hand in it.'

'That's bullshit and you know it,' I said. 'Why would I kill Darren when you'd just offered to negotiate a generous compensation payment? Get real, Frank. You saw an opportunity to associate a member of Angelo Agnelli's staff with Darren Stuhl's death. Howard Sharpe and Mike McGrath must be very happy with your work. You know I had nothing to do with it.'

'All I know is that you were sticking your bib where it didn't belong,' he said. 'Don't tell me that you weren't at the market to connect with that stirrer Donny Maitland.'

I stared down at the floor between my shoes and wished I'd cooled down before I made this call. Spider Webb had stoked me up and I'd gone off half-cocked in Farrell's direction.

'Anyway,' said Farrell benignly, 'how do you know Maitland didn't do it?'

'Thanks again for nothing, Frank,' I said, hanging up.

My gaze moved from the phone to the window. It lingered long on a flotilla of battleship-grey clouds while

I considered my position. With a week remaining until pre-selection nominations closed and our deal went into effect, the last thing I wanted was for Angelo to discover that I'd been implicated in the death of Bob Stuhl's son. Fortunately, Ange was out of town until Wednesday, crawling cap in hand through the corridors of Canberra, hunting up federal finance for a raft of redundancy packages for public transport employees. After that, I could only hope that the cutting and slicing required by the Treasury bureaucrats would keep him busy.

And the best way to avoid further implications of collusion with Donny Maitland was to have no further contact with him, at least for a while. Donny was a big boy. Donny was capable of looking after himself. And I had loyalties closer to home. Red should be my most immediate priority.

Do what the man said, Murray, I told myself. Sit pat. And that's exactly what I did for the next seven days.

Sat behind the wheel of a number of bargain-priced second-hand cars, test driving prospective purchases. Sat through *Dances with Wolves* with Red. Sat in on a parent–teacher information evening with Faye and Leo. Sat in Dr Freycinet's chair while he fitted my new porcelain crowns. Sat and wondered when Spider Webb would next appear on my doorstep. Wondered, too, who had killed Darren Stuhl. And why.

Sat on the phone and trawled for indications of potential challengers to Angelo's preselection. Only one blip appeared on that particular screen. A seventy-year-old ex-communist named Jack Butler. Old Jack was a seasoned activist, a perennial combatant in the ceaseless struggle for universal justice. He'd set up a group called Save Our Trains to campaign against government plans to close the Northern Line of the metropolitan rail network, a community resource that had been losing money since the day it opened in 1884. According to rumour, Jack planned to run against Angelo in order to focus opposition to the closure of the line.

But Jack Butler was a minor-league player. And as a single-issue candidate he represented no threat to Angelo's tenure. So had Angelo's finely calibrated antennae picked up evidence of a more dangerous contender lurking in the wings? Or was I simply the beneficiary of a bad dose of the heebie-jeebies?

On the afternoon before nominations closed, Angelo summoned me to his Parliament House office. 'Perhaps you won't need to run after all,' he announced. 'Apart from that old commo from Save Our Trains, mine's the only hat in the ring.'

'Fine by me, Ange,' I said. 'But it's play or pay. I'm sick of jumping through hoops.'

'On the other hand,' he said, 'nominations don't close until noon tomorrow. And it never hurts to have an extra iron in the fire.'

That settled, we got down to brass ballots.

The process employed by the Australian Labor Party to select its candidates for public office is fully understood by only three people. Two are dead and the other is still awaiting release back into the community. As far as the rest of us can work out, half the votes come from party members in the electorate and the other half from a panel elected at the state conference.

In this instance, the vote was scheduled to take place in three weeks' time when an exhaustive ballot would be conducted over the course of a weekend. Since Angelo's factional allies held a slim but firm majority on the central panel, he needed less than half the branch votes to re-confirm his nomination. Short of Nelson Mandela deciding to stand against him, the result was a foregone conclusion. Or so it looked.

My task was to muster the strays. Disaffected individuals, the shell-back left, up-for-grabs ethnics. Convince them that voting for me was the best way to send a salutary signal to the powers that be, then deliver their preferences to Angelo in the second round of the ballot. Easy money for three weeks' work. Better still, there was no penalty for failure. What could Angelo do, fire me?

'You're an independent candidate with an open mind,' he instructed. 'I don't want anyone to know what's really going on, including Lyndal Luscombe. By the way, she's waiting for you at the Southern Cross Hotel. I asked her to meet you, discuss the lay of the land.'

'The lie, don't you mean?'

'Bit late to get moralistic, Murray,' he said. 'I'm headed down there myself to say a few words at the annual cocktail party of the Victorian Coach and Bus Operators Association. Let's go.'

A group of Labor parliamentarians were coming along the corridor as we stepped out of Angelo's office. When we were almost abreast of them, Ange turned to me, his face swelling with rage.

'After everything I've done for you,' he sputtered, waving an upraised finger in my face. 'You two-timing turncoat. Clear your desk and get out of my sight!'

As interested faces turned our way, I set my jaw angrily.

'You're an incompetent disgrace, Agnelli,' I hurled back at him. 'And the sooner the party wakes up to you the better.'

I stormed off, through the foyer and down the parliamentary declivity into the gathering twilight. Five minutes later, Angelo found me loitering in front of the Society restaurant. 'I think they bought it,' he said. 'But there's no need to get personal.'

We walked a block down the Bourke Street hill to the Southern Cross, once the city's only truly modern hotel, now just another airport Hilton, indistinguishable from dozens like it. While Angelo went upstairs to the Epsilon Room to bestow his benediction on the captains of the coach industry, I rang Red from the lobby and told him I'd be home a little later than usual. Then I went into the lounge.

The place was beginning to fill. The after-work trade, tourists in pre-dinner mode, business travellers on expenses. A blouse with puffy sleeves was inflicting show tunes on a Steinway in the corner. Felines, nothing but felines.

Lyndal was perched on a stool at the bar, glass in hand. A tad more dressed-up this time. Gunmetal grey suit, hem above the knee. A coastguard clipper. On the next seat, angled towards her, was a fleshy man with a nailbrush haircut, tie loosened, getting mellow.

'Hello, Murray,' said Lyndal. 'This is George from Hamburg. George has been buying me drinks. He thinks I'm a hooker. Isn't that right, George?'

Hamburger George made a noise like lobster climbing out of a hot wok, grabbed his room key off the bar, muttered something about time zones and beat a hasty retreat. As I took his place, I tried not to look at Lyndal's legs. Tried not to imagine lace and a hint of garter. 'You're in fine form,' I said.

'Nothing a conversation about Angelo Agnelli can't fix.'

'Say what you like about Ange,' I said. 'He has a rare gift for inspiring loyalty in his staff.'

'Loyalty in his staff, rapture in the ranks.' She hailed the barman, a silver-haired lifer in a tartan cummerbund and matching bowtie, and ordered a gin and tonic. Her third, at least, judging by the emphatic flourish in her gestures. I booked a double Jameson's to catch up.

'So how's he travelling?' I said. 'The branches still solid?'

'Solid?' Lyndal graced me with a wry twist of the lips, an arch of her sharp-edged eyebrows. 'The local membership doesn't exactly regard itself as the Angelo Agnelli fan club, you know?'

'Diversity of opinion is the lifeblood of the party. Any specific grievances?'

'All the usual ones. He doesn't spend enough time in the electorate. He's out of touch. He's getting too big for his boots. The left think he's too close to the right. The right think he's a prisoner of the left. The Turks reckon he favours the Greeks, the Greeks the Turks, the Anglos the Italians.'

'Business as usual, then,' I said. 'Point is, can at least half of them be relied on to put their hands in the air for him when required?'

'Will they do as they're told, you mean? Of course they will.' Behind her flippancy, the *lingua franca* of our trade, I could hear something else, a brittle contempt.

'All that crap about gender equity,' she said. 'Fact is, you men think that sex is just one of the perks of the job.'

We seemed to have jumped ahead a page. I wondered

what she was talking about. Our drinks arrived. I took a snort and jiggled my ice cubes. Lyndal did likewise and stared at me like she'd been reading my mail. The items that come in a plain brown wrapper.

'Christ,' I said, the loose threads coming together. Mike McGrath's crack about the Kama Sutra, Howard Sharpe's obscene finger gesture in a meeting that seemed to have happened a lifetime ago. 'He's having an affair, isn't he?'

'How do you know?' said Lyndal, astonished. 'Is there talk going around? God, how embarrassing.'

'Embarrassing?' I said. 'It's almost unbelievable. Although you never know what some people find attractive. And there's the power thing, I suppose. Henry Kissinger and all that.'

'He's not that repulsive,' she said, defensively. 'I mean, I've slept with him, after all.'

Now it was my turn to be astonished. 'You've slept with Angelo?'

She nearly choked on her drink. 'Agnelli? Ugh, what gave you that idea? God, it'd be like fucking Toad of Toad Hall.'

'So who are you talking about?' I said.

'Who are *you* talking about?'

'Angelo.'

'Angelo's having an affair?' She looked at me like my marbles had taken a hike. 'Who with?

'I thought you might be able to tell me.'

'Margaret Thatcher?' she hazarded. 'Indira Gandhi?'

'Indira Gandhi's dead.'

'That just proves you can't keep a good man down.'

'I have absolutely no idea what you're talking about,' I said.

She drained her glass, slid to her feet, tugged her hem

down and smoothed her skirt. 'This gin's going to my head,' she said. 'And it's time the tonic went somewhere else.' She slung the strap of her bag over her shoulder and wove her affirmative way towards the amenities.

McTavish the Barkeep cleared the debris, wiped the puddles and laid out a bowl of complimentary nibbles. 'Nuts, sir?'

I put a ten on the bar to reserve our seats and followed Lyndal's lead. The washrooms opened from a vestibule off the lobby containing a cigarette vending machine and a deep telephone alcove. By the time I lightened my load, I'd figured out that I'd been holding my telescope to the wrong eye.

I dallied in the vestibule, pretending to use the cigarette machine, then collared Lyndal when she emerged. 'It's Nick, isn't it?' I said. 'Your boyfriend, whatever you call it. Your designated spouse equivalent.'

'What about him?'

'He's the one having the affair?'

'How do you know?'

'You just told me.'

'Yes, I suppose I did,' she admitted. 'All these trips to the country. Turns out he's been shagging his way across rural Victoria.'

'You don't seem very upset.'

'I don't give two hoots. Nick and I decided to separate a while ago. It's just a matter of getting the timing right.'

'Right for what?' I said. 'Are you involved with somebody else, too?'

'You'll find out soon enough,' she said.

I wondered who'd beaten me to the punch this time. 'Is it anyone I know?'

'What makes you think there's anybody?'

'I'd just like to know, before I make a complete fool of myself,' I said.

'It's a bit late to worry about that, Murray,' she said, smiling.

'If you were more upset, I could comfort you,' I said. 'Or if you were angry, I could offer you the opportunity for revenge. If you'd had more to drink, I could take shameless advantage of you.'

'Talk,' she said. 'That's all I ever hear from you.'

'Well, try this for talk.' I backed her into the phone alcove, wrapped an arm around the small of her back and drew her hard against my torso. I met no resistance, French or otherwise. I put my mouth on her throat and nuzzled my way upwards until I found her lips. They were pretty much where I expected them to be, just south of her nose, tasting slightly of gin. After I'd tasted them for a moment, they moved.

'Not here,' they breathed. 'Not in a phone booth.'

'I'll get a room,' I said. 'Don't go away.'

I detached myself and bolted for the front desk, dizzy with near-success.

'Do you have a reservation, sir?' asked the clerk. Gus, according to his name tag.

A reservation? Until five minutes ago, I didn't even have a hope. 'Not as such,' I said.

In that case, Gus would see if there was anything available. Lowering his eyes, he began to peck at a keyboard, invisible below the raised edge of the desk. Tap-tappety-tap-tap, he tapped. Tap and peer, tap and peer. Tap, tap, tap. What was he typing down there, I wondered. Madame fucking Bovary?

I looked back the way I'd come. Lyndal had emerged from the vestibule and was loitering beside the fountain in the centre of the lobby. She contemplated its marble nymph. Her expression was worryingly pensive. Tap, tap, went Gus. Lyndal began towards me, then hesitated. Gus reached chapter 47, wherein Emma anxiously awaits the arrival of her lover Rodolphe. Hark, the clatter of hooves on the cobblestones. Tap, tappety, tap.

Lyndal was chewing her bottom lip now, definitely besieged by second thoughts. You've overplayed your hand, I thought, beginning towards her, words of passionate reassurance forming themselves in my mind. At that moment, a bell in the elevator bay pinged and Angelo Agnelli emerged, his duties upstairs with the bus proprietors concluded.

Oblivious to my presence behind him, he hailed Lyndal and began to speak with her, drawing her along as he moved towards the main doors. She must have said something unexpected, because he pulled up with a start of surprise. She cast me a quick glance across his shoulder. Sorry, it said. Can't be helped.

Then they were walking again, deep in conversation. Right across the lobby and out the door. Gus finished his manuscript. 'I'm afraid I can't help you, sir.'

'That's okay,' I sighed. 'I know a little place in Fitzroy. A sort of boutique operation. There's always a bed for me there.'

An empty one, unfortunately.

I went out the front and let a man dressed like an admiral whistle me up a cab. Had it drop me at the Khyber Pass, the Indian takeaway nearest the house, then walked home with a chicken mukhani, two vegetable samosas and a tub of saffron rice. Desire, according to the Buddha, is the fountainhead of all unhappiness.

I found Red toiling over a hot television. 'Hard day, Dad?' he said, clocking my comportment, bless his hundred-dollar Nikes.

'It was only hard for a while,' I said. 'But not any more.'

We ate our curry in front of 'Sale of the Century', then tackled Red's homework, ancient Egypt. 'You haven't forgotten?' he inquired as we whittled pieces of cardboard into a simulacrum of the Great Pyramid of Cheops. 'Term holidays start tomorrow.'

'How could I possibly forget?' I said, asking myself the

same question. 'I'll have a bit of free time, changes at work and whatnot. We can go to the museum together, stuff like that.'

Red looked underwhelmed. 'It's just that Geordie's invited me to go to Mount Buffalo. He's asked Tarquin, too. Can I, please?'

Geordie, if I remembered right, was one of the new peers, a freckly kid, very polite. Considering that Red's move south had cost him two weeks in sub-tropical Noosa, I could hardly stand in the way of a tobogganing expedition. 'What's it going to cost me?' I said.

'Nothing. It's free. His parents have got a lodge.'

So Red rang Geordie and set up a teleconference. Geordie's mother remembered me from the school information night, and I pretended likewise. Then we trooped across to the Curnows to filch a sleeping-bag. Faye was working late and Leo was helping Tarquin with the death mask of Tutankhamen.

'That job prospect,' I told him. 'It's running for Agnelli's seat in parliament.'

Leo was a mathematician. He knew how to put seven and nine together. 'I'll open a bottle,' he said. 'Hold this scarab while the glue dries.'

When we got back home, there was a brisk message on the machine from Angelo. 'Call me,' it said. I didn't. I was tired of being Angelo's yo-yo. As far as I was concerned, tomorrow couldn't come fast enough. When it did, I dispatched Red to school with a cut lunch and the Nile Valley in his backpack, zipped my jacket against the breeze and walked up the hill to Carlton, to the Cafe Caruso, a small espresso bar just off the main strip.

The old place had been tarted up since I was last there,

the zinc counter replaced by a slab of polished granite, mirror tiles installed in place of the dusty bottles of almond cordial. The card-playing *paesani* had been banished and the ancient aluminium coffee machine superseded by a flash new apparatus of vaguely fascistic design, all bronze eagles and curvaceous chrome. The ancient laminex tables had been transposed into Memphis-style structures with surgical appliances for chairs.

'Looking prosperous these days,' I told Claudio, the diminutive proprietor.

'Whatta can you do, Murray?' he shrugged. 'You gotta keep up.'

Apart from a couple of truants playing Space Invaders down the back, I was the only customer. I stood at the bar and ordered a short black, then slid my nomination form across the burnished granite. 'I need your signature, Claudio. It's just a formality.'

Claudio read the form solemnly, twice. 'Angelo, he know about this?'

'Angelo is comfortable.' I tapped the side of my nose, then jerked my chin towards the telephone. 'Any questions, ring him.'

That was good enough for Claudio. He shrugged, signed with a flourish. I finished my coffee, thanked him for his assistance, then went down the street to Bernini's bistro and repeated the procedure.

By the time I reached the end of Lygon Street, I had the requisite number of signatures on my nomination form, all Labor Party members in good standing, registered residents of Melbourne Upper. I also had so much caffeine coursing through my system that my heart was fluttering like a distressed damsel's eyelashes. At party head office, a big Victorian terrace in Drummond Street, I lodged the form with the receptionist, watched while she thumped it with a stamp that said 'Received'.

'Any others for Melbourne Upper?' I asked.

Her nibs was an old warhorse, a stickler for protocol. 'Seventy seats, you can hardly expect me to know the candidates in all of them.' She indicated the clock. It was eleven, one hour until close of nominations. 'You'll find out soon enough.'

I walked back to Fitzroy and did a load of laundry. According to the machine—phone, not washing—Angelo had called again. The washing machine didn't say much at all. Probably because it was too busy trying not to gag on the smell of Red's socks.

At midday, the beginning of the rest of my life, I was standing in the backyard, my mouth full of clothes pegs, staring up at the gathering strato-cumulus and wondering if I hadn't made a very big mistake. Wondering if I had blown it with Lyndal. Wondering what Noel Webb and his task force associates were doing, if they were any closer to a result. Wondering if Red had enough warm clothes for five days in the snow.

Agnelli rang half an hour later. 'I won't tell you to clear your desk,' he growled down the line. 'There's been nothing on it but dust since last week. But, as of now, you're officially fired.'

'After seven years together, Angelo, this is a profoundly emotional moment,' I said. 'Before I get all choked up, how did the field close?'

'No other takers,' he said. 'Unless you count Lyndal Luscombe.'

'She's nominated?'

'She told me last night. Sprung it on me as I was leaving the Southern Cross.'

It all made sense now, sort of. Her vacillation at the birdbath fountain, what I took for second thoughts, could just as easily have been misgivings about the timing. She'd said something about timing, getting it right. Then Angelo's sudden appearance had tipped the balance, probably her last chance for a face-to-face before nominations closed. Even her siren call to the opening of the cultural centre fitted the scenario. Her concern about Angelo's state of mind was an oblique way of asking if he'd tumbled to her intentions.

My love life, my political machinations, were all turning into scenes from a French farce.

'I should have guessed,' I said.

'You didn't say anything last night, did you?' demanded Angelo anxiously. 'You didn't give the game away?'

'My lips were sealed,' I said. Most of the time. 'I thought she was about to come across with something, then she suddenly left.'

'She claims it's a matter of principle. If the factional bosses won't select women candidates, it's up to women to stand anyway, try to force the issue. It's cost her her job, of course, and she realises she can't win. But it's her business if she wants to make a martyr of herself. My problem is that it's hardly a vote of confidence, two of my closest aides turning traitor. Confirms the wisdom of my decision to have you run.'

Forget Aristotle, Angelo's logic was in a category of its own. A thesis which he immediately confirmed. 'We can't be seen together from now on,' he said. 'There's this motel in

Carlton, the Gardenview Mews. Whenever I want to meet, I'll book a room in your name, give you a call, let you know the time. Okay?'

'Bit cloak and dagger, isn't it?'

'Don't talk to me about daggers. I've just been stabbed in the back. Twice.'

For a year's salary, lump sum, Angelo could be as absurd as he liked. 'You're the boss,' I said. Force of habit. I'd just hung up when the phone rang again. It was Lyndal.

'About last night,' she started.

'I think I've got last night figured out,' I said. 'I can't help but wonder if you were going to tell me.'

'About nominating? Of course I was,' she said. 'I just felt I owed it to Ange to tell him first. How about you? When were you planning on coming clean?'

'Upstairs in the honeymoon suite,' I said. 'If Nick's still out of town, I could come around to your place tonight. Since things are out in the open, there's nothing to stop us taking up where we left off.'

'Except the fact that we're running against each other.'

'That's just politics,' I said. 'I'm talking lust.'

'Goes to credibility.'

'Mine or yours?'

'You don't have enough credibility to worry about,' she said. 'It's pretty obvious that you've cut some kind of deal with Angelo. What's he offered by way of inducement? A permanent public service job?'

'What do you take me for?' I tried to sound offended. 'A hooker?'

She laughed at that, a nice teasing sound, rich with possibilities. 'See you on the hustings, Murray.'

177

My next call was from Mike McGrath, deputy secretary and chief weasel of the United Haulage Workers. I didn't ask how he got my home number. 'I've just heard the news, mate,' he said. 'Thought I'd call to offer my felicitations. Not that you need them. Agnelli must be making this little charade worth your while.'

'Do I detect a note of cynicism?' I said. 'Did it never occur to you that I might merely be exercising my rights as a member of our great, democratic party?'

'If that's the case,' he said, 'I take it you'll be willing to accept our support?'

'You're offering me the opportunity to crawl into your pocket, Mike? Gee, that's generous of you. Thanks, but no thanks.'

'I wonder if Ms Luscombe will take such a high moral tone?' He put a mocking spin on the Ms.

'The enemy of my enemy, is it?' I said. 'Anything to keep Agnelli on the back foot. I think you'll find that Lyndal has more sense than to let you poison her wells.'

'Maybe,' he said. 'Or maybe she won't know until it's too late.'

'What's that supposed to mean?'

'If you change your mind, give me a call.'

'You lot should change your name,' I said. 'From Haulers to Spoilers.'

The phone began to ring constantly as word spread through the grapevine. I stuck to the script, reciting the pre-arranged formula. That I had no personal grievance with Angelo. That I believed the voters of Melbourne Upper should be given a choice. I repeated it so often that I almost convinced myself.

One caller who hadn't yet heard the news was Donny Maitland. He rang to update me on the progress of his campaign. 'The Haulers' traditional union enemies have been less than forthcoming with their support, I regret to report,' he said. 'But that hasn't stopped me setting up a base down by the docks to get the word out direct to the rank and file.'

I explained that I was now out of the ministerial adviser racket and was challenging Agnelli for preselection. 'I'll give you the full story when I can,' I said. 'There's also something else you should know.' I told him about my visit from Webb and the interview at Citywest.

'The cops must be getting desperate for a result,' he said. 'Any result. I told you Farrell was up to no good. But your lawyer's right. Sit pat. That's what I'm doing. It'll all come out in the wash.'

'I wish I had your confidence,' I said. 'Good luck with the cops and good luck with your campaign. And keep your eye on that dog of yours.'

'Don't worry about me,' he said. 'I've taken your tip. Got myself some medical insurance.'

First thing the next morning, Red left on his trip to the snow, piled with the other kids into Geordie's parents' Pajero. 'We'll have him back on Thursday night,' said Geordie's mother, a reassuringly athletic type. 'It's a six-hour drive, so expect him about ten o'clock.'

The armed men arrived a little earlier.

It happened on rubbish night.

In the six days that Red was away, I began the spade work for my preselection campaign. This was not demanding. I called some prospective supporters. I arranged appointments to speak at branch meetings. Mostly, I shopped for a car.

About 9 p.m. on Thursday, I put the bin out and stood for a moment on the kerbside, contemplating the silver-grey 1986 Honda Civic I'd purchased that afternoon. One owner, four new tyres, eleven months registration, $11,250. Easy to park, cheap to run, and perfect for my campaign image as the unpretentious, thrifty, environment-conscious offspring of hard-working local parentage.

Just as I was stepping back through the front door, I heard rushing footsteps behind me. Before I could turn a blow struck the back of my head. Down, down I went, the walls sliding past. Then hands gripped my arms and I was being dragged forward. Then came a white radiance. I swam towards it as if from the bottom of a bucket of red jelly. Hello, I thought. Be with you in a minute.

It came to me that I was lying on my living-room floor, looking up at the ceiling light. My arms were twisted behind my back. I told my limbs to move, get out from underneath me, to straighten themselves. They wouldn't. Perhaps they'd gone deaf. Perhaps they couldn't hear because of the thumping inside my head. I tried to speak but my mouth wouldn't open. It was taped shut. Strange, I thought.

About as strange as the two figures looming above me, staring down. They were wearing powder-blue boiler suits and yellow rubber washing-up gloves. They had blobby faces; their noses and lips were all squashed. One of them was holding his penis in his hand. He began to urinate, directing the spray at my face. A hot, stinking stream stung my eyes.

'Wakey, wakey,' said the other one, his voice muffled by the stocking over his head.

But I was more than awake. I was thrashing against the tape that bound my ankles and wrists, trying to struggle upright, trying to shout. Something hard jabbed into my chest, pinning me to the floor. When I realised it was the barrel of a shotgun, I got the message.

'Do we have your attention?' said the one holding the gun. He bent over me, a shrink-wrapped pug-dog face.

I nodded. Certainly. Absolutely. Most assuredly. Yes indeed.

'And you know why we're here, Murray?' His voice was calm and relaxed. Very much in control and utterly unfamiliar. I ran the socio-geographical nuances of his accent and drew a blank. He raised the gun barrel a little and tapped me under the chin with it. 'Eh?'

I shook my head.

His twin finished buttoning his flies and kicked me in the side. Just hard enough to make the stars tap dance.

'No idea?' said the gun one. 'Think about it.'

I thought about it, hard. They probably weren't from the Labor Party. Not state, anyway. Nor reporters from the *Herald*. Too articulate. They knew my name, so this wasn't some random home invasion. The Haulers could have nothing against me, now that I was no longer Agnelli's sidekick. Which left only one possibility. This had something to do with Darren Stuhl.

'Ughhgh,' I said.

The urinator sat down in my Ikea armchair, sprawled back and let gun-boy do all the talking.

'I'll get straight to the point, Murray, just so there's no misunderstanding,' said the voice at the end of the shotgun. 'We can blow your head off. We can blow your knees away. We can knock you out and burn your house down around you. We can do anything we like, any time we like. You understand?'

If he was trying to frighten me, he was doing a sterling job.

'Understand?'

I nodded.

'That's the spirit. Now listen very carefully. You listening?'

I nodded.

The muzzle of the shotgun moved up until it was resting on the bridge of my nose. The barrels had been sawn short and the edges filed. I noticed this because they occupied my entire field of vision.

'You haven't been entirely truthful with the police, have you?'

I nodded. Force of habit. Jesus, I thought. It's the cops. Webb has stepped over the line.

'You're covering up for your friend Maitland, aren't you? You forgot to tell them what he did to Darren, didn't you?'

'Urgh,' I pleaded. 'Grnghf.'

'But you're going to tell them now, aren't you?' He tapped my forehead with muzzle of the shotgun. 'Because Bob Stuhl is not going to let some pissant like Maitland get away with murdering his son. Understand?'

I was beginning to. These guys weren't overzealous cops looking to cut a few procedural corners. They were representatives of the private sector.

'And Bob's not going to stand back and watch while some vindictive pen-pusher helps his son's killer walk free. Understand?'

By then, my head was nodding faster than the chorus line in a Bombay musical. Bob Stuhl, Christ Almighty. The cops might threaten me, but a threat was all it would remain. But Bob Stuhl? The Prince of Darkness had a better reputation.

Pug-face swung the shotgun aside and leaned closer. 'What are you going to do?' Abruptly he ripped the strip of tape off my mouth, taking a layer of lip with it. 'Tell me.'

'Aya,' I said, gulping air.

The shotgun came back up into my face. 'Tell me what you're going to do.'

'Aya um going to tell them Donny did it.'

'Or?'

'Or you'll kill me.'

'Good boy.'

The tape went back over my mouth. The silent pisser put his heel against my hip and rolled me over onto my front. The shotgun moved to the nape of my neck. Then the light went out. I lay there in the dark, listening to the air surge in and out of my nostrils, the pounding of my heart, feeling the metal against my skull.

'If you haven't done the right thing by this time next week, we'll be back to remind you. We won't be so polite next time.'

Then they were gone. Out the back door, across the yard and down the lane.

For a long time I just lay there, trussed up like a Red Cross food parcel, inhaling ammonia-scented wool-blend carpet fibres. I'd been threatened before. I'd been frightened before. But I'd never before been systematically terrorised.

My buttocks gradually managed to unclench themselves. Rolling onto my back, I brought my knees up to my chest and threaded myself through the loop of my arms. I hopped into the kitchen, fumbled in the dark for a steak knife and sawed the plastic tape from my hands and feet. Then I ripped the gag from my mouth, walked calmly into the bathroom and vomited into the toilet.

Red would be home soon. He couldn't find me like this, pissed-on and hyperventilating. I locked every door and window, gathered up the scraps of plastic tape and dumped them in the kitchen tidy. Then I stripped off my clothes, dropped them into the laundry sink and stood under a scalding shower, scarifying my skin, willing myself to wake up from this nightmare.

Sitting pat was no longer an option. Complaining to the

police would be pointless. Even if I could persuade them that this had really happened, they could offer me no protection against men like this. Action was being forced upon me. Action I did not wish to take. Still trembling, I wrapped myself in a bathrobe and punched the digits of Donny Maitland's phone number. Jacinta answered from somewhere on the other side of Jupiter.

'He's at the campaign office,' she said. 'He told me what you did to help him, getting the money and everything. Thank you so much.'

I muttered a pleasantry, extracted the number for the campaign office, rang off and punched again.

'Rank-and-file ticket,' yawned Donny's voice. 'Stop the Sharpe–Stuhl collusion.'

'It's Murray, I said. 'I've had some unpleasant visitors.'

'Cops?'

'Worse than that, I'm afraid. I need to talk to you urgently.'

'You want me to come over?'

'Yes, please. No. Wait, let me think.'

Red would be through the door at any tick of the clock, full of stories to tell. If Donny then turned up and we went straight into a closed-session conference, the boy would wonder what was going on. Lies would be required. On top of which, I wanted to get out of the house. The place felt like a trap. I didn't want Red there.

'Better if I come to you,' I said. 'How do I find the place?'

As Donny gave me directions, a horn tooted in the street. I opened the door and found Red heaping his luggage on the step. One arm waving thanks to the departing Pajero, I went down on my knees and embraced the startled boy. 'Dad,' he protested. 'Somebody'll see.'

I pointed to the Honda. 'Our new wheels,' I said. 'Let's go for a spin.'

He ran an appreciative eye over my purchase. 'Only if you get dressed first,' he said.

I threw on some clothes, cranked up the batmobile and drove. While Red babbled about chairlifts and nursery runs and snowball fights, I steered a course for the docks, following tram lines that glistened like drawn swords beneath the streetlights. A painful bump was swelling at the back of my skull. I felt like I was wearing a subcutaneous yarmulke.

'Is this to test the shockers?' said Red as we juddered down a pot-holed service road, barbed-wire alley.

'Since we're out and about, I thought we might visit a friend.' I turned into a compound marked by a hand-sprayed sign.

Our headlights swept a quadrangle walled by stacks of shipping containers that rose four-high like gigantic Lego blocks. In the centre of the yard stood a white box, a portable site office. Donny opened the door and stood watching our approach. In his black pea-jacket and knitted cap he looked like an extra from *On the Waterfront*.

I parked beside his dinged Commodore and we walked towards the office, gravel crunching. Red nudged me and pointed up. Above one of the container-stack walls, the superstructure of a ship loomed in silhouette against a backdrop of moonlit clouds. 'Cool,' he said.

Donny read at a glance both the alarm in my eyes and the situation with Red. 'Welcome to the liberated territories,' he said, spreading his arms. 'And this must be the boy.' He extended a beefy hand to Red. 'Haven't seen you since you were knee-high to a hubcap.'

Red shook hands tentatively, somewhat overwhelmed by the sheer masculinity of the situation, and we followed Donny inside. Maps, whiteboards and posters covered the walls. A photocopier was churning out leaflets. Behind a partition was a galley kitchen with a Cafe-bar and a refrigerator plastered with stickers. Beer $2, read a note on the door.

Donny steered Red towards a computer with winged toasters fluttering across its screen. 'There's supposed to be some games in there, but nobody can find them. How about you take a crack while I talk with your old man?'

Within a few clicks, Red was putting Pacman through his paces. Donny tilted his chin towards the door and I nodded. As we started back outside, the phone rang. Donny picked it up. 'Rank-and-file ticket.'

He listened intently for about twenty seconds, then started rubbing the back of his neck. 'Of course I'm pissed off,' he said at last. 'We're trying to present ourselves as a credible alternative, you pull a stunt like this, makes us look like feral crazies.'

He listened some more. The fluorescent light made him look old and tired and brought out the boozer in his face. 'If that's your attitude,' he said wearily, 'we're better off without you.' He listened a bit longer, then dropped the handpiece back in its cradle with a shake of his head.

'Problem?' I said. It couldn't be as bad as mine.

'Roscoe,' he explained. 'He was driving past the Haulers' head office in South Melbourne a little while ago and noticed the lights were on. It seems the organisers were all there having a meeting. So Roscoe unilaterally decided to mount a guerrilla raid. The fucking idiot aerosoled our slogans all over their fleet of cars. When I expressed my disapproval, he accused me of lacking militancy and quit the ticket.'

'Very mature,' I sympathised. 'Can you find somebody to fill his spot?'

'It won't be easy. Len's dropped out, too. His wife got the jitters. The bastards were parking in front of the house while he was at work. A couple of them'd just sit there all day. Tell you the truth, things aren't going quite as well as I'd hoped.' He glanced at Red, his face lit by the glow of the screen, then chucked his chin towards the door. 'Anyway, enough of my troubles. Come for a walk.'

We crunched slowly across the yard, hands sunk deep into our pockets. A milky moonlight filtered though the clouds. The air smelled of exhaust fumes, the sea and wet gravel. I fired up a cigarette. 'Haven't you heard?' said Donny. 'Those things can kill you.'

'There's faster ways to go,' I said. Then I told him about my visitors, pouring it out in a breathless stream. 'They threatened to come back and kill me if I don't do what they want within a week.'

Donny's face became redder as he listened. 'He *pissed* on you?' he said. 'And you reckon these guys are working for Bob Stuhl?'

'They definitely gave that impression. Dropped his name a few times. He must have a direct line to the cops. They share their suspicions, he expedites the process.'

'Bob fucking Stuhl,' muttered Donny. 'What a ruthless bastard. Got his start in business cutting the brake lines of his competitors. I wouldn't put it past him to engage in a bit of vigilante action if he thought it'd nail his son's killer. But maybe it wasn't him who sent them. Could've been the Haulers, trying to set me up. Or even the cops themselves.'

I crushed my cigarette into the wet gravel and lit another. The smoke churned my empty stomach. 'Whoever they were, they scared the shit out of me,' I said. 'So what am I going to do, Donny?'

He tilted his head. A growl was coming from the road, the gear-shifting roar of an approaching truck. It was moving fast. Donny grabbed my arm and tugged me towards the parked cars.

Suddenly, a blinding bank of headlights exploded into the compound. A towering prime-mover rocketed towards us, hit its anchors and carved a path through the gravel, fish-tailing wildly. As it slowed, the passenger door flew open. Frank Farrell leaned out, one foot on the step. A bottle flew from his hand, tumbled through the air and burst against the site office, spreading a sheet of flame across the wall. The truck revved up again and disappeared behind the portable. Above the roar of its engine I heard the sound of shattering glass.

I ran for the door and wrenched it open. The rear window was shattered and the photocopier was an oily chemical blaze. Flames licked the ceiling and acrid black smoke belched everywhere. Red was stumbling backwards, arm raised to shield his face from the heat, coughing and spluttering. Donny rushed past me and grabbed the boy by the collar. We all fell out the door, retreating crab-wise into the yard, crashing to the ground in a cursing tangle of limbs.

The truck was speeding away, heading for the gate, engine shrieking. Donny sprinted after it. As it turned up the road, he pulled a pistol from his waistband and fired after it. Pam, pam.

That was Donny Maitland. Never a dull moment.

The office was going up like a bonfire, crackling and popping as its contents were incinerated. Another few seconds and Red would've been among them.

'Holy shit,' the kid declared. His attention was so firmly fixed on the fire that he hadn't noticed Donny's fusillade.

Cinders were raining from the sky and we retreated further from the heat. Donny began trudging back from the road, eerily lit by the leaping flames. The gun was nowhere in sight. I ran my hands over Red. Satisfied that he was uninjured, I bundled him into the Honda, its sales-lot paintwork already flecked with thumbprints of soot.

'What's going on, Dad?' the boy pleaded, subdued and bewildered.

'Wait here,' I ordered. My tone brooked no contradiction. For once, it got none.

Donny and I stood watching his headquarters burn.

'Roscoe wanted to turn up the heat,' he said. 'Looks like he got his wish. A bit of tit-for-tat, Haulers style.'

'First spray cans, then Molotov cocktails,' I said. 'Now gunfire. What next? Hand grenades?'

Shadows danced across the towering container-stack walls of the compound and the stench of burning plastic poisoned the air. The yard was a desolate inferno, one of the rings of hell.

Donny said, 'You're right. I acted without thinking.' He patted his hip. 'These things can be a real temptation.'

'You should've told me you were planning an armed struggle,' I said. 'I could've asked Agnelli to fund some guided missiles.'

'This isn't usually my speed, Murray,' said Donny. 'You know that. Call it a lapse of judgment. I realise I can't shoot my way into the union. And, let's face it, I'm never going to get elected either. The wheels were already starting to fall off. Now it's gone way too far. Jesus, Murray, the kid could've been killed. I'm tossing in the towel. It's not worth it. Fuck the union.'

Headlights swept across the yard. A security-service patrol car came through the gates. It screeched to a halt beside us and a watchman stuck his horseshoe moustache out the window. 'What happened?' he said.

'A cigarette in a wastepaper basket,' Donny told him. 'Spread to a can of fuel. Nobody hurt. Can you get on your radio, call the fire brigade?'

The driver obliged then got out to watch the show. Donny and I paced around to the far side of the fire. 'Where'd you get the gun?' I asked. Across the other side of the yard I could see the pale shape of Red's face peering through the window of the Honda.

'Off a crim who didn't need it,' said Donny dismissively. 'These guys, your visitors. They gave you a week, right?'

'That's what they said.'

'And you trust me, right?'

After what had just happened, I felt entitled to a degree of scepticism. 'I'm in a hard place here, Donny,' I said. 'If it was just me, I might be able to deal with it. But I've got the kid to think about.'

The big truckie fixed me in his gaze. 'I did not kill Darren Stuhl,' he stated firmly. 'And I'll get you out of this fix, if it's the last thing I do. Just give me a couple of days, okay? I'll see you right, I swear.'

The wail of a siren wafted over the horizon. Donny glanced around, took a small automatic pistol from his pocket and thrust it towards me. The burnished metal of its stainless steel barrel glowed in the canyon between our bodies. 'Do me a favour, will you?' he said. 'Chuck this in the river.'

The siren grew louder. My hand reached out and the gun disappeared into my jacket pocket, dead weight. Donny jerked his thumb towards the gate. 'I'll be in touch. And try to be more careful where you throw your cigarette butts in future.'

I left him standing there, watching the guttering slagheap of his ambitions, and drove out the gate. Red's curiosity filled the car's interior, palpable as gas under pressure.

'Those men in the truck don't want Donny running against them in a union election,' I explained. 'Matter of fact, they don't want anybody running. They're not big fans of democracy.' Or having their cars aerosoled.

'Are they after you, too?'

'Nah,' I reassured him. 'We just happened to be in the wrong place at the wrong time.' Other men were after me.

A fire engine sped towards us, crowding the centre of the road, lights searing the night. 'Exciting, eh?' I grinned, needing to say something, making a joke of it.

'Shit, yeah,' Red agreed. 'Wait until Tark hears about this.'

'You think this could be our secret for a while?' I said.

'How come?'

'Put it this way, how would your mother react if she found out I'd taken you somewhere that got fire-bombed?'

'But Tarquin won't tell Mum,' he said.

'Not your mum,' I agreed. 'But what about his mum? Thing like this, he'd be bound to want to tell her. Could be a bit of a weak link in the chain. He tells Faye, she tells Wendy, one thing leads to another. You with me?'

He was with me, all right. Shit like this didn't happen at exclusive boarding schools. And getting rescued from a burning building outclassed a ride in his stepfather's yacht any day of the week.

We turned into Footscray Road, a stream of thundering trucks even in the midnight hour. Their aggressive bulk dwarfed the two-door Honda, a pitiful trespasser in the kingdom of the whopping leviathan. Contemptuous of both common courtesy and the rules of the road, they cut and wove around us, buffeting our tiny sedan in their slipstreams. The human hands that guided them were invisible, indifferent, somewhere high above. Braking for a red light, I read the slogan on the bumper of the colossus in front of us. *Bob Stuhl Is Big.*

And his reach is long, I thought.

Despite Donny's alternative scenarios, I remained convinced that Bob Stuhl was behind my unwelcome visitors. Cut the red tape, that would be Bob's attitude.

Red twiddled the radio dial through snatches of music and the somnolent drone of late-night chat shows. Dark water beside us, the floodlit gantries of the container terminal on the edge of my vision, we drove into the empty places where the city washed against the sea. *Dirty deeds*, came the refrain. How cheap, I wondered, did a pair of hired gunmen come? For a man as rich as Bob Stuhl, such men could be bought for the price of a decent lunch.

We crossed a bridge over the Maribyrnong River and I turned to follow its course. Further upstream, it ran between playgrounds and golf courses, taverns and boathouses. Down here, near the bay, it was an industrial canal, a black ribbon flecked with litter. I pulled into the undercroft of an electro-plating works, Customer Parking Only, and told Red that I needed to take a leak.

Cutting through a construction site, I followed the embankment until I was well out of sight of the car. Inky water lapped at the pilings as a dredge motored past. An oily slick glistened in its wake like plankton rising from the deep. When it was gone, I stepped from the shadows, took the gun from my pocket and tilted it into the dull moonlight. Donny was right. Sometimes the temptation is irresistible.

This was the first pistol I had ever held. My knowledge of guns extended no further than the stock phrases of a million movies. Rack it. Lock and load. Safety off.

There should be a catch somewhere, a button or lever to release the magazine. Yes, there it was, where the trigger guard met the butt. I ejected the magazine, slipped it into my pocket. I gripped the slide firmly between thumb and forefinger and drew it back. A shell popped out of the breech, flew over my shoulder, bounced off the concrete and rolled over the edge of the wharf.

The slide remained locked open, displaying the empty breech. I pulled the trigger, felt firm resistance. The thing was empty now, inert. I examined it more carefully, reading the inscription on the barrel. S & W Compact 40.

Okay. Compact was the model. Forty was the calibre.

S & W needed no deciphering. The magazine held six bullets. I slid it back into the grip and released the slide. If I had this figured right, there was now a round up the spout. Drop the safety catch and squeeze the trigger, it would fire. Feet apart, I aimed down at the water. Two-handed grip, the classic stance. Squeeze, don't jerk.

The gun bucked slightly and a sharp bang echoed off the blank face of the cold-storage depot across the water. The sound was swallowed up by the emptiness of the night. The spent shell tinkled at my feet. A faint smell of cordite mingled with the salt tang of the air. I peered down at the water, its surface unmarked. What did I expect? A dead fish to come floating to the surface?

I flicked the safety back on and kicked the spent casing into the water. I tucked the pistol into my waistband, zipped my jacket and walked back the way I had come.

Fuck with me now, Bob, I thought.

That night I slept soundly, the automatic beneath my pillow.

I was a man packing heat. Nothing could unnerve me. Not a damned thing. Not the cat that crossed my roof at one o'clock or the slam of a neighbour's door just after two. Not the rattle of a windowpane at three or even the twitter of birdsong at five-thirty.

At eight, when a garbage truck came down the street dragging an aircraft carrier behind it, I gave up the battle and brewed myself a cup of breakfast. According to the radio, the Soviet Union had ceased to exist as of midnight, Moscow time. The things that happen, I thought, when you're not paying attention.

While Red snoozed on, I showered and shaved and examined my face in the mirror. It looked desperate. Donny had asked for a couple of days. I couldn't wait that long. At 9.15, I rang Frank Farrell. He answered with a grunt shrouded in static.

'Hello, Frank,' I said. 'How's the Citizen of the Year this morning? Or should I say the Haulers' resident terrorist?'

The line fizzed and hissed, an overlay of white noise. For a moment, I thought I'd lost him.

'That you, Whelan?' he crackled. 'What are you bitching about this time?'

'I was ringside at your arson attack last night, Frank. Saw the whole thing. Donny Maitland won't go to the cops, but there's nothing to stop me.'

'And tell them what? That your mate was party to the malicious damage of a fleet of vehicles belonging to this union? That he's taken to firing pot shots at passing traffic?'

'That I saw you torch a building with a child inside.'

'What child?'

'My son, Frank. You nearly incinerated him.'

'Jesus,' said Farrell. 'I had no idea. Is he okay?'

'If he wasn't, you'd be behind bars right now. Not that you should discount that possibility. Assault with intent to do bodily harm. Reckless endangerment of a minor. Can't see Howard Sharpe and Mike McGrath going in to bat for you over charges like that. They'll hang you out to dry, leave you twisting in the wind.'

There was another long pause. 'I'd never knowingly hurt a child, I swear.'

'Convince me in person,' I told him. 'Midday at the main gate of Luna Park.'

'This is a joke, right?'

'Can you hear me laughing?' I said. 'Just be there.'

Red emerged from hibernation and stuck his head into the refrigerator. If he'd been traumatised by the previous night's events, the emotional scars were not immediately evident. His appetite was certainly unimpaired.

'Let's do something together today,' I suggested.

'Not the museum,' he begged, his mouth full of oven-popped grain treats. 'Anything but the museum.'

At 11.30, we were cruising St Kilda, looking for a parking spot. Spring was putting in a tentative appearance and a good-sized crowd had turned out to express its appreciation. Volvo station wagons choked the streets and the bike-rental operators on the foreshore were doing brisk business. The bay was a sheet of burnished silver, flecked with yachts and wet-suited windsurfers. Lycra-thighed roller-bladers whizzed along the pier and seagulls wheeled and dived in the breeze like squadrons of demented Messerschmitts.

I found a park beneath a palm tree on the Upper Esplanade and we walked down the slope to the open-mouthed clown face that formed the entrance to Luna Park. The old funfair was showing its age, though there remained something irresistible about its tawdry attractions. The screams of rollercoaster riders advanced to meet us, echoing the cries of the gulls.

Red had invited Tarquin along and the three of us merged with the masses. Two juveniles in baggy jeans and windcheaters, a fatherly figure in corduroy trousers and a hiking jacket, a .40 calibre semi-automatic in his pocket.

We went to the cashier's window and I bought a wad of ride tickets. 'Go pick up some girls,' I told the boys, dispensing cash and tickets. 'See you in two hours.'

At noon, right on schedule, Farrell was waiting at the entrance, leaning against a fortune-telling slot-machine. He was wearing his grey leather blouson, his hands thrust into the front pockets of his tight-fitting jeans, thumbs out, framing his crotch. 'Now I see why you chose this place,' he said. 'The joys of single fatherhood, right?'

'Save the soft soap,' I snarled.

'You're pissed off,' he said. 'I can appreciate that. How was I supposed to know there was a kid there? I'm not the only one to blame here. It cuts both ways.'

'You nearly roast my son alive and it's *my* fault?' I said. 'Your logic defeats me.'

He fell into step as I headed back into the carnival, past the pinball arcade and the hall of mirrors. 'Maitland would never have got that office together if somebody wasn't bankrolling him,' he said. 'It's pretty obvious that Agnelli's behind it and that you made the arrangements. If you start a war then take a kid into the combat zone, you can't blame other people if he gets hurt.'

We reached the Ferris wheel. The great machine advanced in fits and starts, one set of riders alighting and another taking their place, swinging seat by swinging seat. A paradigm of the democratic process. When an empty cage dropped into the loading position, I stepped forward and handed the attendant two tickets.

'Let's talk about Darren Stuhl,' I said, climbing aboard.

Farrell hesitated, then grudgingly followed me. 'What about him?'

A roustabout dropped the safety bar into place and hauled on a lever. Our swaying seat jerked forward and upward. The Big Dipper thundered past, girls screaming, then we began to revolve smoothly, rising high above the swallow-tail pendants on the turrets of Ye Olde Giggle Palace, far above the calliope cadences of the carousel, up into the open air.

The bay extended before us and the crystal towers of

the city rose in a cluster that seemed close enough to touch. A gusty wind had begun chopping at the water, raising whitecaps, and the light off the sea was harsh in our faces.

'You've caused me a lot of needless aggravation, Farrell.' The wind tore and snatched at my words.

Farrell eased a pair of sunglasses from the narrow slit of his jacket pocket and put them on. 'Like I said, I just told the cops what I saw.'

'Darren Stuhl was a shit,' I said. 'But I didn't kill him.'

Farrell didn't answer. He just stared out to sea, as if the row of tankers inching their way along the shipping channel was the most compelling sight in the universe.

'I imagine the cops weren't the only ones you talked to,' I said. 'You offered to talk to Bob Stuhl, or his people, about compensation for what Darren did to my teeth. So I imagine you must have communicated with him on the circumstances surrounding his son's death.'

Farrell folded his arms across his chest. 'What if I did?'

'Well since you're Mr High Level Contact,' I said, 'I want you to tell Bob Stuhl something else.'

'You want me to tell him that you didn't kill his son?'

The momentum of the wheel increased. We crested the top and began to descend, gathering pace. The pendants on the turrets of the mock-medieval castle snapped and cracked like whips. I plunged my hands into my jacket pocket and gripped the butt of the automatic.

'Masked men came to my house last night,' I said. 'They stuck a shotgun in my face and threatened to kill me unless I tell the cops I saw Donny Maitland kill Darren Stuhl.'

Behind the lenses of his sunglasses Farrell's face was as

unreadable as a Patrick White novel. 'And you think Bob Stuhl sent them?'

'I think a grieving father, impatient for justice, might be tempted to take things into his own hands,' I said.

Farrell pondered this, then nodded. 'Could be,' he said. 'Are you going to do what they told you?'

'No, I'm not. And since you have access to Bob Stuhl, I want you to see that he gets that message. If those men come near me or my son, I will kill them without hesitation. Then I'll come and kill him.'

'Is that right?' Farrell didn't bother to conceal his scepticism at this brave declaration.

We reached the bottom and began to ascend again. I took the automatic out of my pocket and held it casually in my lap, finger curled loosely around the trigger, thumb resting on the hammer. 'Tell him that this is not an idle threat,' I said.

Farrell's gaze dropped to the gun. He studied it. 'Where'd you get that?'

'Won it in a fucking lucky dip,' I said. 'Never mind where I got it. The point is, I've got it and you're going to tell your pal Bob that I won't hesitate to use it.'

Farrell puffed his cheeks and blew out a long, hard breath. 'Then I hope you can shoot better than you use your fists.'

'Only one way to find out.' I thumbed back the hammer and pressed the muzzle into his side. 'And if this is part of some job you're doing on Maitland, the same goes for you.'

Farrell stiffened, getting it now. 'Take it easy,' he said. 'I get the message. You're quite the hairy-arsed individual, aren't you?'

'When I want to be,' I said. We reached the top. There was nowhere else to go. Slowly uncocking the gun, I slipped it back into my pocket. 'A little understanding, Frank, that's all I'm asking for.'

'I'll see that Stuhl gets your message, if that's what you want,' said Farrell. 'No skin off my nose. But why don't you just go to the cops, tell them you're being stood over?'

'Let's just say I'm covering my bases.' I patted my pocket.

The ride was ending. Our cage dropped to the loading step and lurched to a halt. The bar came up and we stepped back onto terra firma. A little firmer, I felt, than before we boarded. We walked towards the main gate.

'Very cinematic,' said Farrell, folding his sunglasses. 'The only thing missing was Orson Welles and a zither.'

'Make no mistake,' I said. 'I'm in deadly earnest.'

He held his hands up in a mollifying gesture. 'I was wondering about that gun,' he said. 'Compact automatic, chrome slide. Looks a lot like Darren's yuppie toy.'

'So what?' I said. 'There must be thousands of guns like this.'

'But it's an interesting coincidence, isn't it? Did you know that Darren's gun was never found? Word is, the cops think whoever killed him must have taken it.'

'Well I didn't kill him,' I said. 'And I didn't take his gun.' I now understood why Voigt and Webb lit up when I mentioned it.

'But you were at Maitland's office last night. And Maitland just happened to have a gun there. This wouldn't be the same one, by any chance?'

We'd reached the pinball arcade just inside the entrance. Red and Tarquin saw us passing and dashed out to block our path. Tarquin brandished an inflatable plastic baseball bat.

'This is a hold-up,' said Red. 'Give us more money.'

Farrell sidestepped him and continued towards the exit. 'I'm sure Bob'll be very interested in everything you've told me,' he said.

The implication of Farrell's words hit me like a locomotive. As my head swivelled to watch him go, my mouth dropped wide open. It was a wonder nobody stuck a ping-pong ball in it.

Tarquin, meanwhile, was pummelling me with his inflatable cudgel and Red was thrusting forth an imploring palm. 'Donkey Kong ate all our money,' he explained. I peeled off fresh cash, recommended the Whip and allowed gravity to draw me down the slope to St Kilda pier. My mouth was now closed but my brain was spinning faster than a fairy-floss machine.

The water beneath the pier deepened from shimmering transparency to impenetrable jade. I walked its length, out past the Victorian pavilion where the concrete pilings ended and the rock groyne threw its protective arm around the yacht marina. Roller-bladers zipped past, mobile phones clutched to their ears. Old Greek men sat on Eskys, jigging for squid with long rods and barbed lures. 'Penguin Viewing Cruises', said a sign on the railing. 'Japanese Spoken'.

Clever penguins, I thought. A damned sight more intelligent than me. When I arrived at Luna Park, I was merely terrorised. Now I was catatonic. And this time, it was all my own fault.

Donny said he got the pistol from a crim who didn't need it. I now realised that he'd been finessing the point. By Donny's lights, Darren Stuhl was born into a criminal class. The fact that he was also a thug only confirmed the definition. And Darren didn't need the gun because he was dead. So did getting it mean taking it? If so, when had that happened? And how? And why?

Whatever the answers to those questions, there was one thing I did know for sure. Nothing could have been better calculated to inflame Bob Stuhl's belief that Donny Maitland killed his son than what I had just done. Not only had I blithely brandished a missing item of evidence which linked Donny directly to Darren at the time of his death, I'd found exactly the right messenger to convey that connection to Darren's vengeful father.

I began to pick my way across the rocks of the breakwater, the hollow of my head echoing with the rattle of rigging against the masts of the yachts in the marina. Gulls swooped and bickered. A cluster of English backpackers had stripped off their tops and were sunning themselves in the lee of the wind, their skin ghostly white against the blue-black of the granite boulders.

Bob Stuhl's minions had given me a week. Would Donny last that long? If Big Bob was willing to use terror tactics at the investigation stage, how far would he go as Director of

Private Prosecutions? What penalty would he feel entitled to exact?

My hands were in my jacket pockets. One was closed around the butt of the automatic. The other fingered the bullets. I knew better than to walk around with a loaded gun. Test-firing the automatic was one thing, I'd concluded as I tossed and turned through the night, but using it was another. The state I was in, lunging for it nervously every time a shadow crossed my windowpane, I was more likely to shoot Red than to fend off a posse of professional toughs.

My objective in showing the automatic to Farrell was deterrence. After that my plan was to throw it into the sea. Near the end of the breakwater, I found a sheltered spot between two large boulders. Squatting at the water's edge, I marked a suitable place in the deep green of the marina channel and slipped the pistol from my pocket.

Donny had sworn that he hadn't killed Darren Stuhl. But real doubts now hung over that assertion. Could he have been lying? A version of the events at the market that morning swam before me. Darren waving his gun in Donny's face. Donny somehow getting the better of him. Donny taking Darren's gun, then pulverising his body to escape detection. But why bother? Why not just plead self-defence? Unless, in the heat of the moment, Donny's low opinion of the law's claims to impartiality had got the better of him.

The breeze was cool at the water's edge and I hunched deeper into my hiking jacket, the gun pressed between my palms. The wind pushed a row of triangular sails over the horizon, then pushed them back again. The wake of a passing speedboat slapped the rocks by my feet. Still I squatted there, thinking.

Donny had promised to see me right. But how did he propose to deliver on that assurance? Was it possible that I was putting myself and Red at risk on the basis of a misplaced trust? Donny Maitland was a good man yet he was unpredictable. I needed to talk to him again. Soon. I put the pistol back in my pocket and walked back along the breakwater to the pavilion. There was a payphone inside.

Heather answered the Maitland Transport number. 'Donny's gone to collect the truck,' she said. 'The police have finished with it at last. And he's decided to give up this union nonsense, so we can finally get back to business.'

'Can you let him know that I need to speak with him urgently?'

'It's not about the money, is it? We'll have a problem paying it back. Donny wasted most of it on office equipment and there's been a fire at his campaign headquarters, whatever he calls it. I don't think he'd got around to insuring it yet.'

Insurance. Even when you take it out, you're never entirely sure you're covered. There's always some risk you haven't considered, some caveat you've failed to read.

I told her I'd square the money with the ministry but I still needed to see Donny. Then I got off the line before she could ask me if I was alone. The answer this time was yes. Very much alone.

I walked back up the hill to the rictus mouth of Luna Park. The boys had long exhausted their funding and were waiting with bored impatience. 'You said two o'clock,' whined Tarquin. 'It's already ten past three.'

'I was thinking,' I said. 'You should try it.'

'I'm hungry,' Red remarked.

We went down the road to the Hebrew bakeries on Acland Street and I fed them to bursting with pastries. By the time we'd finished eating, the sun was losing its lustre and the pleasures of St Kilda were exhausted. We drove back to Fitzroy and I checked the messages on the machine.

Donny hadn't called but Angelo Agnelli had. The preselection process was now a week old and it was time for our first clandestine conference at the Gardenview Mews motel. The agreed place, as Angelo's message gnomically described it. Six o'clock.

Angelo's shadow play was the least of my immediate priorities. Until Donny got in touch, though, I decided I might as well go through the motions. I chased the boys off to Tarquin's place, swathed the gun in clingwrap and buried it in a shallow hole at the base of the lemon tree in the backyard. Then, so that I'd have something to report to Ange, I called Jack Butler and mooted a strategic alliance with Save Our Trains.

Old Jack had no illusions that he would survive the first round of the exhaustive ballot. On the second round, his handful of votes would be up for grabs. I offered him an inducement to swing them my way. He agreed to think about it.

I checked the day's papers in case some new crisis had set a cat among Angelo's pigeons. Nothing jumped out at me. But beyond all the end-of-an-era stories about the demise of the Soviet Union, the *Age* ran a piece about women candidates for ALP preselection. Lyndal Luscombe was quoted as urging Labor to honour its commitment to greater gender equity. The party, she warned, was at risk of appearing hypocritical. As if that wasn't a danger with which we had long learned to live.

At 5.45, I trudged through the Exhibition Gardens to my assignation. A damp chill was rising from the lawns and the tail-lights of the Friday rush-hour traffic blazed red to the horizon.

The Gardenview Mews was on Rathdowne Street, across the road from the park, set inconspicuously into a row of terrace houses. The name was spelled out in foot-high brass letters above an entrance archway. Nothing indicated that a place of public accommodation lay within. From Angelo's point of view the place had two great advantages. Not only was it unlikely that he'd be noticed as he came and went, but Parliament House was a scant ten-minute walk away. He could meet me at the Gardenview Mews and be back in his office before anybody noticed he was gone.

I walked through the arch and found myself in a motor court overlooked by a double tier of balconies. These were trimmed with cast-iron lacework, as was the ground-floor walkway that ran around three sides of the quadrangle. Cars were parked nose-in against the walkway, recent model sedans mostly. At the open door of one of the rooms, a young couple with the look of the landed gentry were unpacking a designer-togged toddler from an upscale station wagon. A paunchy man in a business suit, his tie loosened, came down the stairs from the upper levels and began filling an ice-bucket from a machine on the walkway. We all nodded at each other amiably.

The have-a-nice-day clerk in the office at the end of the walkway confirmed that a phone reservation had been made in my name, took an impress of my credit card and handed me a brass-tagged key to a room on the ground floor. I let myself in, admired the three-and-a-half-star rating and turned on the television. Agnelli's arrival coincided with the sting for the six o'clock news.

'You haven't got much to report yet, I imagine,' he announced, shedding his jacket and sprawling on the settee. 'But no harm in touching base.'

I killed the set and gave him the rundown on my approach to the Save Our Trains candidate, making my phone conversation with Jack Butler sound like a round of shuttle diplomacy.

'What'll he settle for?' asked Angelo, rooting about in the minibar. 'Bottom line.'

'Public support for the issue while wearing my hat as a former transport adviser, personal solidarity and a five hundred dollar contribution to his campaign expenses.'

'And what's Lyndal Luscombe offering?'

I shrugged. 'Jack's not giving much away.'

Ange settled on a pack of peanuts and reclined on the bed, munching. 'She's the main game. Get close to her. Offer her a preference swap, then renege in the final round. If she wants to play with the big boys, she'd better learn how the game works. Your pay-out cheque's in the mail, by the way.'

Angelo then spent twenty minutes giving me the benefit of his opinion on the key ethnic powerbrokers in the electorate. Venal idiots, one and all, he concluded. My mind, however, was elsewhere. 'Any further aggravation from the Haulers?' I asked. 'Our decoy duck has gone under, I'm afraid.'

'Good.' Angelo dismissed the issue by lobbing the empty peanut package into the wastebasket. 'Save you having to close him down. The Haulers are back on the reservation for now. They've agreed to suspend hostilities in the interest of the party's overall electoral prospects.'

'Our man will be glad to know his failure has not been in vain then,' I said.

Angelo had moved on. He picked up the phone, dismissing me with an airy wave. 'I'll drop the key off on my way out,' he said, 'after I've made a few calls.'

'Long as they're not international,' I said. 'And leave the minibar alone.' He was already dialling, a million miles away.

As I crossed back through the Exhibition Gardens, avoiding the deep shadows, sticking to well-lit paths, it occurred to me that the Gardenview Mews would make a useful bolthole if I got the heebie-jeebies at home later that night. The room was paid for, after all.

A soot-smudged white Commodore was parked in the street outside my house. Donny climbed out as I approached and eyed me anxiously. 'You rang,' he said. The statement contained an obvious question.

I shook my head. 'They haven't been back. But I need to talk to you.'

'Good idea,' he agreed. 'I've got a proposal for you.'

I unlocked the door and waved Donny inside. He lumbered down the hall ahead of me like a bear going into a wardrobe. 'How's the boy today?' he said. 'That fire must have given him a hell of a scare.'

'A mother like Red's got,' I said. 'He can handle anything.'

Donny loitered in the living room flipping through my CDs while I screwed the top off a new bottle of Jameson's. 'Chris Isaak,' he said approvingly. 'Roy Orbison with a creepy edge.' He'd already had a drink or two; in the confined space I could smell it.

'I hear the cops are very interested in the whereabouts of Darren's gun,' I said, handing him a glass of neat whiskey. 'Word is it wasn't found on the body.'

He picked up my wavelength. 'Probably at the bottom of some river by now.'

We sat down in the easy chairs, the bottle on the coffee

table between us. 'I've been trying to imagine what happened that morning,' I said.

Donny avoided my gaze. 'Better if you don't know.'

'Yeah?' I said. 'And why is that?'

Donny took a sip, then stared down at the pale liquor, rotating it meditatively in his glass. A silence hung between us. Donny was measuring his words, finding the right way to distribute the load.

'There's only two people who know what happened,' he said at last, raising his eyes. 'Me and the man who killed Darren Stuhl.'

'And who was that?'

'Farrell.' He said it as though stating a self-evident truth.

'Farrell? Why would Farrell kill Darren Stuhl?'

Donny's great shoulders rose and fell. 'Dunno,' he said, abjectly. 'Looked to me like he might've just done his block.'

My glass was suddenly empty. I reached for the bottle and refilled it. 'And you saw this happen?'

Donny sipped again, heaved a reluctant sigh and proceeded to his confession. 'I get up on the pallets, right, start speaking my piece. About fifteen, twenty people gather around, Farrell and his pals included. Farrell starts giving me the raspberry. Nothing to write home about. As soon as I start talking about Bob Stuhl and the way he puts his drivers at risk, Darren appears. He jumps up beside me and sticks his gun in the side of my head.' He mimed the action, finger and thumb cocked. 'Then Farrell jumps up there, too, and starts dragging Darren away.'

'All part of the Haulers' service,' I said. 'Managing the management.'

'Farrell's lot start shoving chests, telling people to piss off, it's all over. Roscoe takes a swing and an all-in brawl erupts. Len's getting clobbered so I jump down to help. Then, fast as it started, it's over. Everybody takes off. I go scouting for Len and Roscoe. Out of the corner of my eye, I register a flash of movement between two parked trucks. Farrell's got something in his hand and he's slamming it down on Darren Stuhl's head.'

I stopped him there. This was a matter in which I had a particular interest, thanks to Noel Webb's Theatre of the Spanner. 'What was it?'

Donny shrugged again. 'Dunno. But it must have been solid because when I saw Darren's body later, he had a bloody big gash on his forehead. Anyway, Darren goes down like a ninepin. Just then, Roscoe calls out to me. A bunch of Farrell's mongrels have got him cornered. I dash over and help him sort things out. When I look again, there's no sign of either Farrell or Darren.'

'Did Farrell realise you'd seen him?'

He shrugged again. 'He had his back to me,' he said. 'He might have spotted me in the wing-mirror on one of the rigs. I don't know for sure.'

'So why didn't you tell all this to the cops?'

Donny shook his head ruefully, sagged back into his seat and showed me his palms. 'Perhaps because Farrell had done me a good turn hauling Darren off me like that. But mainly it was because I liked the idea that I had something on him. I thought I'd bide my time, see if I could use it during the union election campaign.'

'Use it how?'

'That's a question I've been asking myself ever since,' he said. 'Let's just say it seemed like a good idea at the time.

Even when Darren turned up under the truck and it was obvious that Farrell was trying to set me up, I still didn't say anything. To make things worse, I pinched Darren's gun off his body when nobody was looking, just in case.'

'Just in case of what?'

'In case it came in handy,' he said. 'If things got rough in the campaign.' He was a punctured tyre, still holding its shape even though the air was gone.

'You've got to go to the cops,' I said.

'I've left my run too late. They won't believe me. I was too confident early in the piece. I didn't think they'd believe I was stupid enough to kill Darren Stuhl then stick his body under my own truck. Well, they were wrong about Darren but they were right about the stupidity. I could win an Olympic medal for idiocy. And now that I'm a suspect, they've got even less reason to believe me. Like you said, why would Farrell kill Darren Stuhl? I've set myself up for a fall here, mate. And it all came to a head last night. First your visitors. Then me, blasting away at Farrell's tail-lights like a madman.'

I struggled to process the implications of Donny's words. And to cross-reference them against my own actions in showing the gun to Farrell.

Donny might have been first ashore on Fuckwit Island, but he wasn't Robinson Crusoe on the atoll. Now I'd have to tell him what I'd just done. That I'd given Frank Farrell the opportunity to finish the frame-up job he'd commenced when he dumped the deceased Darren under Donny's Dunlops. 'Darren's gun,' I began.

Donny leaned forward, squared his sagging shoulders and interrupted me. 'Thanks to my mistakes, Murray, you've got a sword hanging over your head,' he said. 'I said I'd see you right and that's exactly what I'm going to do. Remember I said I had a proposal to put to you?'

'I'd be lying if I said you had my unalloyed confidence at the moment, mate,' I warned. 'And like I was about to say…'

'Jacinta's been on my back about taking a trip to the Philippines,' he interrupted. 'Very nice at this time of the year, I understand. Especially if you've got local contacts who can show you some of the more remote places, the ones off the beaten track.'

'Some men are going to kill me and you're talking about taking a holiday?' I said incredulously.

Donny ignored me. 'It'll take me a couple of days to get a visa and book a ticket,' he said. 'But I reckon I can be there well before your deadline expires. Soon as I arrive in Manila, I'll give you a call. Then off you toddle to the cops. Say exactly what you were told to say. That I killed Darren and you've been covering up for me. Tell them whatever you think it'll take to get the bastards off your back. The cops, Bob Stuhl, whoever they are.'

I considered what he was saying. Not only would it take the pressure off me, it would place Donny out of range of Bob Stuhl's vigilantes. There was only one problem. 'You realise this means spending the rest of your life on the run?' I said.

'That remains to be seen,' said Donny. 'Once the legal wheels start to turn I can play it by ear. In the meantime, it's not like I've got anything to keep me here. The union campaign's history and I'm sure Heather can find somebody else to boss around. The main thing at the moment is to get you off the hook. And since I hung you there in the first place,

I don't want to hear any argument about this, Murray. I've made up my mind.'

The back door slid open. 'Honey, I'm home,' yodelled Red. 'What's for dinner?' He erupted into the living room, then pulled up short, sensing the sombre atmosphere.

'G'day, young feller,' said Donny. 'Enjoy our little barbecue last night? Your dad's just been helping me plan my holidays.'

Red idled in the doorway, grinning sheepishly. Donny downed the last of his drink and stood up.

'Red,' I said. 'Isn't it time you rang your mother? And before you go, Donny, I've got a travel tip for you. Come out the back way.'

When we reached the lemon tree, I scraped at the dirt with the side of my shoe until a plastic-sheathed parcel appeared.

'Darren's gun isn't at the bottom of the river,' I started. 'You might still need it.'

Donny's determination to head for the hills of Mindanao was only strengthened by the news that I'd flashed the pistol at Farrell. 'I've got even more reason to go now,' he declared.

'Thanks to me,' I said.

'This whole fiasco is my fault,' he insisted. 'Wait for my signal, okay? If you haven't heard from me by Thursday, go to the coppers anyway. Until then, do whatever you'd normally do. And, listen mate, I can't tell you how sorry I am for the trouble I've caused you.'

After extracting an oath that I would obey his instructions, he gave me a parting slap on the shoulder and disappeared along the back lane. I stood there watching him go, wondering how long it would be before I saw him again. Wondering, too, if Frank Farrell had whispered into Bob Stuhl's ear yet. Or the ears of those who had Bob's ear.

Donny's decision at least had the virtue of being a plan,

or so I told myself. A desperate plan, to be sure, however, one that would allow me to meet the twin terrorists' demands. I slept a bit easier that night. But not before double-checking the locks on all the doors and windows and leaving a light burning in the living room.

By the next morning, Saturday, spring's cautious reconnoitre had become a full-blown advance. The sky was a blanket of baby blue. For the first time in months, the sun shed warmth as well as light. The air refreshed rather than braced. Blossoms emerged from swelling buds with an almost audible pop.

It wouldn't last, of course. It never does. Soon the rain would return, blooms would rot on the branch and Antarctic fingers would again stick themselves up our trouser legs. But, according to the forecast, we could reliably expect at least another five fine days. By then Donny would be out of harm's way and I'd be down the cop shop buying a reprieve with a lying oath. Until that moment arrived, I did as Donny had urged and pretended things were normal. It was either that or take up permanent residence under the bed.

Sunday was Father's Day, a fact which had escaped my attention until Red woke me with a tray. Rock-hard boiled eggs, desiccated toast and a little gift-wrapped something from the Sox'n'Stuff spring sale. 'You shouldn't have,' I said, pleased as Punch.

'They said you could change it if you didn't like it.'

'Not like it?' I was scandalised by the very idea. 'A tie like this could stop a charging elephant.'

We spent the afternoon in the park playing frisbee, intermittently discussing Red's career plans. Acting, he thought, or maybe directing. Possibly special effects, pyrotechnics maybe.

Donny rang while we were out, left a message on the machine saying that everything was on track. He'd soon be in that warm place we discussed. As a peace-offering to Heather, he was making a final run, a one-off job up the bush, too good to pass up. On the road, I thought, was probably the best place for him. Out of town was out of sight.

A week remained of the school holidays. A bike was bought for Red. Skateboards cluttered the yard. The television stayed on continuously. We hosted an all-night sleepover for a bunch of the guys. And I went into campaign mode.

I realised, of course, that my imminent confession to conspiracy to pervert the course of justice would do little for my standing in the community. That was a hit I would take to see Donny safe. But until that moment arrived, I buried my fears in the most prosaic pursuit I could imagine. Cold canvassing for votes.

I erected a collapsible card table in my bedroom by way of an interim office, broke open the membership lists and began grubbing among the grassroots.

As I tested the litmus of Angelo's standing, I found the situation much as Lyndal had described. While he was far from universally popular, his status as the sitting member ensured that most of the troops felt obliged to support him. Either that, or they took their cue from ethnic heavyweights who delivered blocks of votes in return for the kind of largesse that could only be dispensed by a government minister. But Ange's footings were not set in quite as much concrete as he might have hoped. With the electoral tide ebbing, there was a growing mood of recrimination within the ranks. And, with patronage reaching its use-by date, some of the clients were sniffing about for fresh sources of pork.

Lyndal was siphoning some of his support, mainly from areas that I, too, was targeting. While many of the comrades agreed in principle that the party should beef up the participation of women, they saw in Lyndal a bit too much of the self-serving apparatchik. Uppity chick, in other words.

On Monday evening, while Red was playing Nintendo at Geordie's place, I toured Melbourne Upper branch meetings, pitching to tiny gaggles of true believers huddled in underheated supper rooms at Mechanics Institutes and municipal libraries. On Tuesday morning I took coffee and biscotti with Maestro Picone, *eminence grise* of the Italian senior citizen set. In the afternoon, I bought drinks for members of the local schoolteacher intelligentsia at a popular after-work watering hole. I also rang Ayisha Celik at the Migrant Resource Centre.

Back in my days at the electorate office, Ayisha ran the Turkish Welfare League. Over the years she and I had done the odd favour for each other. Not quite as many as I would've liked, but that's the way the kebab crumbles. Now, according to the word around the traps, she was Lyndal Luscombe's campaign manager.

'Mr Shifty,' she said, in her lilting wog-girl voice. 'We wondered when you'd be in touch.'

After a bit of banter, I raised the subject of a meeting with Lyndal. Ayisha proposed lunch the next day in the restaurant in the National Gallery where a competing-candidate *tete-a-tete* was unlikely to be observed by some motormouth from Melbourne Upper and fed into the rumour mills. I knew the place well from the days when

Angelo was the arts minister and I dabbled in the cultural mysteries.

'Tell Lyndal I'm looking forward to seeing her again,' I said.

'Put it back in your pants, Murray,' joked Ayisha. 'Or I'll have you arrested.'

'Too late for that,' I said. 'I'm already planning to surrender myself to the authorities.'

Red had just left for a reciprocal sleepover at Geordie's place when I switched on the six o'clock television news. I was only half-listening as I fixed myself a cup of coffee and it took me a moment to register the headline story. Something about the discovery of a body that morning in the cabin of truck on a remote backroad near Warracknabeal, 400 kilometres north-west of Melbourne.

The boiling kettle screaming in my ears, I spun around to face the set. A helicopter shot panned across a truck parked in a stand of she-oaks on the shoulder of a dirt road beside an endless paddock of yellow-flowered canola. A white Kenworth with blue trim. According to the newsreader, the dead man had been identified as Donald Maitland, a fifty-two-year-old truck driver. He had been shot in the head at point-blank range.

I cut the gas beneath the kettle. The words and images struck me like a series of rolling punches.

A reporter with a handheld mike stated that the truck had been there for two days before a local farmer made the grisly discovery. And that a suicide note found in the cabin connected Maitland to the recent high-profile slaying of Darren Stuhl, son of transport magnate, Bob Stuhl. A hand gun belonging to Darren Stuhl, missing since his death, had been retrieved from the truck.

A suicide note? Where had that come from? It could only have been extracted under duress. Threats? Torture?

Inspector Voigt appeared, standing near the truck with his tie flapping in the wind. In gratified tones, he told a cluster of reporters that he believed speculation about Darren Stuhl's death would soon be laid to rest. His inference was clear. The police believed that Donny had killed Darren, then blown his own brains out with the dead man's gun.

By the time the bulletin moved to the next item, I was punching Donny's number into the phone. The line was busy. I rang at five-minute intervals for the next hour with the same result. The seven o'clock news brought no additional information. Same story, same spin.

I tried again to reach Jacinta or Heather but either the phone was off the hook or they were under siege. Family, friends, the media, whoever. I called police headquarters and asked for Inspector Voigt, hoping that the homicide chief was back in town. My name was taken and I was put on hold. After a long wait, Noel Webb came on the line.

'What do you want, Whelan?'

'To talk to one of the grown-ups.'

'About what?'

'About this story you're feeding the media. Donny Maitland would never top himself. It's just not plausible.'

'Gun in one hand, suicide note in the other,' said Webb. 'Looks pretty plausible to us.'

'And very convenient, too. Gives you a result in the Stuhl case. I saw Donny just a few days ago and he definitely wasn't suicidal.'

'Always the expert, aren't you?'

'I know Donny.'

'And do you also happen to know what Darren Stuhl looked like when they scraped him off the ground? What a man looks like after the rear wheels of a ten-tonne truck have rolled over him? Try to picture it in your tiny mind, Whelan. Try to imagine doing that to another human being. Think what it'd be like to see that image every night when you close your eyes. Then tell me it mightn't start to eat at you.'

'I don't believe that Donny killed Darren Stuhl and I don't believe he killed himself.'

'Believe what you like. Us dumb coppers, we believe the evidence. Maitland was aggrieved at being sacked by Stuhl Holdings. Stuhl junior threatened him with a gun. He had the motive, the opportunity and the means.'

'What means?'

'Any blunt object, plenty of which were readily to hand. Anyway, it's all academic now. He left a handwritten confession. Said he couldn't live with himself any more, after what he'd done.'

'It must have been coerced out of him.'

'I know he was a mate of yours,' said Webb, 'but face facts. Ever since Darren Stuhl's death, Maitland's been acting in a highly erratic, unstable manner. He concealed information. He was an unco-operative witness. Last week, a building he was leasing burned down. A cigarette, he said. Petrol, according to the fire brigade. He claimed his union had colluded with Stuhl Holdings to get him sacked. The real cause was drinking on the job. His body, by the way, was found with elevated blood-alcohol levels. You want me to go on?'

What could I say? That I could provide different explanations for all of those events, mostly based on information

I'd concealed from the police?

'Perhaps if you'd been more forthcoming about your own relationship with Maitland, things might've turned out different,' said Webb.

'What do you mean?'

'You seem to think we've been sitting around here for the past three weeks with our thumbs up our quoits. Maitland's bank records show he received money from the transport ministry, funds that you authorised immediately after the events at the market. Nobody else in there knows anything about it, only that you wanted it done urgently.'

Again, there was nothing I could say. So I didn't say it.

'If you want to go down this road, Whelan, be my guest. I'll put you through to the chief. But I doubt very much if he's going to reopen the case on your say-so.'

'You haven't heard the last about this,' I said.

'I won't hold my breath,' said Webb.

I hung up and stood staring down at the phone, sick to the core. Donny Maitland had paid too high a price for his mistakes. And now the only eyewitness to Darren's killing was dead. Any attempt I made to set the record right would be dismissed as the hearsay testimony of a self-interested party.

Conjecture about Donny's last moments flooded my brain. By what vile means had the confession been extracted? Had he begged for his life? In his position, I would've gone down on my hands and knees and blubbered like a baby.

But outrage and indignation were not the only emotions washing over me. I also felt relief. Bob Stuhl had found his sacrificial victim so I was off the hook. The shotgun men had no reason to return.

And with the relief came guilt. Spider Webb was right. I

was not without blame. Donny had given me Darren's gun to throw away. Instead, I'd used it to betray him. And then I'd thrust it back into his hands, to become both the method of his execution and the means to conceal it.

This was all down to Frank Farrell. The prick would be hearing from me. And he wouldn't like what I had to say. First I needed a drink. Opening the kitchen cupboard, I reached for the Jameson's, untouched since Donny and I had broached it together four nights earlier.

The glass touched my lips and I wondered if one drink would be enough.

When the bottle was empty, I lurched to the pub on the corner for another, my head spinning in the rush of night air. The stars looked down at me from infinite space. We are tiny, they said, but you are insignificant.

Bob Stuhl, on the other hand, was big. And the CEO of Stuhl Holdings had heavy buffers. Nobody would ever be able to tie him directly to Donny's death. The dirty work had doubtless been done by men who performed tasks for people who arranged things for blokes who did favours for guys who occasionally played golf with friends of a friend of Bob's former chief mechanic's cousin. Probably the same men who had come calling on me.

But Bob's minions had got the wrong man. And, come the dawn, I'd make it my business to find a way to bring that fact to his attention. Then Bob's vengeance would descend on Farrell. In time it might even be possible to make the great panjandrum himself pay for what he'd had done to Donny. In the meantime, I sat in the dark and poured liquor onto the fire blazing in my brain. The fire raged and I danced around it, plotting my revenge. Standing at the lemon tree, I pissed into the hole where the gun that killed Donny had been buried. Had it still been there, I would've dug it up and made my way to a certain French provincial mansion in Toorak.

As I staggered inside it occurred to me that the phone was ringing. 'Is that you, Whelan,' said a voice. 'It's Frank Farrell here. I just wanted you to know that Bob was very appreciative of your information. He's forgiven you for not coming clean with the cops. Says to tell you it's evens now. Live and let live. He says he's sure you'll understand, being a father and all.'

I held the telephone so tight my fist began to tremble. 'And what's he gunna say when I tell him that he got the wrong man, that you're the one who killed his son?' I demanded.

A sucking came down the line, a sharp intake of air. 'Well, well, well,' said Farrell. 'I wondered if Maitland told you what he saw. Dumb of him not to tell the cops, wasn't it? But he didn't and that's the main thing. Anything he said is hearsay. And nobody's going to take your word against mine, least of all Bob Stuhl.'

'That won't stop me trying,' I slurred.

'Get real, Whelan,' said Farrell. 'Drunk or sober, nobody's going to believe you. You were Maitland's crony. And you were the one uttering threats against Darren. I was the trusty babysitter. I'd been hauling that psychotic bastard out of scraps for years.'

My hand found the neck of the whiskey bottle. I poured another slug down my throat. I was scarcely tasting it any more. 'Until one day you got fed up, eh?'

Farrell gave a dry chuckle. 'You can relate to that, can't you? Darren was riding for a fall. First he stuck his gun in Maitland's face. Then, when I tried to hose him down, he did the same to me. I made my displeasure known. Hit him harder than I intended and accidently put the prick out of his misery.'

'Then set Donny up to take the blame.'

'You've seen how Bob Stuhl works, so you'll appreciate how keen I was that he didn't find out it was me,' he said. 'Maitland just happened to be the most likely culprit.'

'You arsehole,' I fumed. 'I don't give a fuck about what you did to Darren Stuhl. But Donny was innocent and he's dead because of you.'

'Because of you, too,' Farrell reminded me. 'Don't forget that. The gun was the clincher. You shouldn't have given it back to him, should you? Get off your high horse, Whelan. It'd be a brave man indeed who decided to make an issue of this. Are you a brave man, Murray?'

Farrell's tone was genial but the note of menace was unambiguous. I held the phone to my ear, listening to his breath, wondering how to answer his question.

'It's the way things are,' said Farrell into the silence. 'And there's nothing that you can do about it.'

He hung up. I was glad he did. I was beginning to see his point of view. We live in a dog-eat-dog world. And sometimes there just aren't enough dogs to go around.

I went back to the bottle, mired in the realisation that Farrell was so right that he didn't even have to pay me the courtesy of duplicity. He could come right out and rub my nose in it. I had no credibility with the cops. My chances of getting to Bob Stuhl were zero. If I tried, I risked putting myself back in danger. It stuck in my craw to admit it, but there was sweet fuck all that I could do.

The booze eventually did its job and I crashed out, fully dressed, seething with self-contempt and impotent rage, on top of the bedclothes.

The next voice I heard was not my own. It was Red's. He was ringing from Geordie's place to inform me of his plans for the rest of the day. The gang was going to the movies: *Terminator 2*.

My alarm-radio said it was eleven o'clock. I dosed myself with caffeine and aspirin, shaved and showered, ironed a shirt and eased myself into my Hugo Boss. At 12.30, wretched but mending, I crept into the restaurant at the National Gallery.

The place was full of Taiwanese tourists bustling about in polyester leisurewear. Lyndal and Ayisha were sitting at a table with a view of the sculpture garden, picking at salads. Both were power-dressed. Not the salads, the women. The elegant silk scarf at Ayisha's throat was just bright enough to emphasise her dark Levantine beauty without undercutting her masters degree in public administration. Lyndal was in a plum-coloured pants-suit. Her businesslike demeanour reminded me how much I longed for her community welfare services, to fall into her safety net.

I steered my way through the Taipei ramblers and announced my arrival by clearing my throat and straightening my tie. Not the one Red had given me. That was at home, locked in a sound-proof container. I'd chosen my Versace, teal with orange-yellow flecks, in the hope that it might deflect attention from my ravaged eyes.

But there was no fooling Ayisha. 'Night on the tiles, Murray?' she said, bouncing her generous eyebrows in a salacious manner.

'I wish,' I sighed. 'A touch of the flu.'

'Poor dear,' said Lyndal sweetly. 'We can do this later, if you're not up to it. A couple of weeks, say?'

Cute, considering the reason for our meeting was only eight days away. 'Angelo would never forgive me,' I said, sitting down. 'He's paying me very good money to come here and lie to you.'

'How much?' said Ayisha eagerly.

She reached for their lunchtime bottle of chardonnay,

offering me a glass. I shook my head, not up to it, and turned to signal for a coffee. Failing to get the waiter's attention, I settled for the wine. It couldn't make me feel any worse.

'Let's just say I negotiated a generous redundancy package,' I said. 'And that for purposes of public consumption, my decision to run came as a complete shock to my employer. Just as your surprise decision, Lyndal, was no doubt prompted by a firm conviction that Melbourne Upper is ready to rally to the feminist standard.'

Lyndal speared a cherry tomato. 'I wasn't going to sit around forever, waiting for the faction bosses to tap me on the shoulder to tell me, it's your turn now, girlie.'

'Particularly since there'll be a party room spill after the election,' I said. 'And Angelo, one of the old guard, tarred with the brush of failure, will probably be consigned to the backbench. There's not much kudos in being an opposition backbencher's constituency assistant.'

'None at all,' agreed Lyndal. 'But after we go down in the state election, the national office will start to worry about the next federal poll and begin looking for new blood.'

I gave a low, admiring whistle. 'A federal seat? You're aiming high.'

'And why not? I couldn't do worse than some of the fools already in Canberra. But I'll only get noticed if I make a decent showing in Melbourne Upper. Which I intend to do.'

'Coming off a cold start?' I said. 'Without factional support? Against an incumbent backed by the machine?'

'The machine's short a cog,' interjected Ayisha. 'Ange couldn't find Melbourne Upper in the street directory without his electorate officer to tell him the page number. You of all people ought to know that.'

'The fact that Lyndal's job is vacant is a plus for Angelo, not a minus,' I pointed out. 'He can put it up for auction, dangle it in front of twenty different interest groups in exchange for their support. What can you offer?'

'Not enough to buy me the seat, I admit,' said Lyndal. 'But that's not my objective. All I want is a creditable performance and a decent second-placing. Show some form and I might qualify for a better starting position in a higher stakes race.'

Now we were getting down to it. 'So what do you reckon you'll get in the first round of votes?' I plucked a figure from the air, testing her confidence level. 'Thirty per cent?'

'About that,' she shrugged nonchalantly. Meaning she was thinking higher. And straw-polling was her professional speciality. So maybe closer to 40 per cent. 'And you'll get, what, 10 per cent?'

'Fifteen,' I said. My current guesstimate was closer to eight.

She looked at me sceptically. 'Okay, so there's your fifteen, plus my thirty, plus the Save Our Train's three. That's 48 per cent. Angelo gets the other fifty-two. And since a majority of the central panel is already committed to him, he's over the line in the first ballot. Even taking into account shrinkage, slippage, leakage and drift.'

God, this was great. Lyndal talked numbers like some women talked dirty.

'First ballot, second ballot, whichever way you slice it,' I said. 'Angelo's going to win.'

Of course these projections were so rubbery they could be dribbled like a basketball and shot through any hoop in sight. The entire system was constructed so that a voter could look at least two candidates in the eye and truthfully swear to have voted for him. Or, less often, her.

Ayisha pounced. 'You're saying that Angelo doesn't really need your preferences. So why not sling them to Lyndal. Long as Ange wins, your conscience'll be clear.'

'What's my conscience got to do with it?' I said. It was a strange word to hear on the lips of a member of the Labor Party. 'I've got a clear-cut deal with Angelo. What can you offer that would induce me to break it?'

'Ayisha,' said Lyndal, 'would you mind waiting for me outside?'

Ayisha smirked knowingly, drained her glass and stood up. 'I'll be in the gift shop,' she said.

We waited until she'd gone, eyeing each other with wary amusement. 'Your campaign manager's very keen,' I said.

'And capable. She'd make a good member of parliament, don't you think?' It sounded like the girls were laying some pipe.

'You too,' I said. 'If I hadn't already made a commitment to Angelo...'

'Yeah, yeah,' she laughed. 'That's what they all say.' She scrutinised my face. Despite my tie, the effects of recent events must have been evident. 'Are you okay?'

I cocked my head towards the door. 'If you think I look bad, you haven't seen the abstract expressionists.'

We went into the gallery proper and strolled among the pictures, side by side. As we warmed ourselves in front of a Rothko, she slipped her arm through mine. 'We both know you didn't come here today to propose a preference swap,' she said. 'So why are you here?'

'I think you know that,' I said.

'You want to frot me in a telephone booth?'

'You were tempted. Don't deny it.'

'A girl likes to be romanced. Not have her bones jumped when she's half-tanked and keying herself up to quit her job.'

'Is that why you agreed to meet? So you could tell me that another try wouldn't be unwelcome.'

'Possibly,' she said. 'Depends how it's done.'

'So I shouldn't shove you against that Jasper Johns and stick my tongue down your throat?'

'Not unless you fancy a swift kick in the Jackson Pollocks.'

'So it's dinner at Florentinos, candlelight, champagne?'

'That'd do for a start. Not until after the ballot, of course.'

'What if I can't wait that long?'

'Do what you usually do.'

'The popcorn girl at the Wangaratta drive-in?'

'Don't push it, buster.'

She handed me one of her business cards, the electorate officer stuff crossed out and her phone numbers handwritten on the back, home and mobile. 'I hope you're feeling better soon.'

'I hope I'm feeling you soon.'

'That depends on how you play your cards,' she said.

Turning on her heels, she proceeded briskly towards the gift shop. As I watched her go, I noticed a large painting in the contemporary Australian section. It depicted a red-eyed man with his hands sunk into the pockets of his coat. He was standing on a blasted plain beside a burning city while brimstone rained from the sky. A sturdy and independent dog was his only companion.

I knew how he felt.

All my contacts, all my skills, were useless. Donny's death cast a pall, but it was one in whose shadow I had no choice but to keep living. Like some poor fucking Bulgarian in a polluted shithole of a industrial town, I trudged each day to the coalface knowing no other way of life. In my case, the mineshaft was a card table and my pick was a telephone. And it was the press that spewed out the degraded crap that sustained the commerce of our city.

Two days after my meeting with Lyndal, the *Sun* led with one of its perennial stories about factional brawling in the Labor Party. Although the editorial line was predictable, certain facts resonated with whispers I'd been hearing on the grapevine. I spent the day on the dog and bone and found nothing but confirmation of the story. The tectonic plates were shifting, ructions were brewing, long-forged alliances were going weak at the welds. Factional deals were coming unglued faster than discount-store furniture.

Mid-afternoon I got a call from Angelo's secretary. 'He said same time, same place, usual arrangements,' she said. 'Whatever that means.'

It meant the Gardenview Mews. Angelo prowled the motel room like a caged lion as he grilled me about my progress with Lyndal on the preference swap offer.

'She's taking it under advisement,' I told him. 'But I'm optimistic. I think my chances are good.'

It was what he wanted to hear. I moved the topic to the situation at the centre. 'Heavy seas,' he said, making it sound more like a meteorological phenomenon than a committee of union bosses and party apparatchiks. 'Although I think I can ride out the storm.'

So much for the shipping news. I left him sitting on the edge of the bed, running up my phone bill. He could call Brazil for all I cared. My easy-money termination pay had finally appeared in the electronic coffers of my bank account.

I walked home and cooked dinner for Red. Grilled steak and baked vegetables. I didn't have much of an appetite but Red was happy to take up the slack. In little more than a week, I told him, my current work arrangements would be at an end. It was time to equip the corporate headquarters of Murray Whelan & Associates.

The next morning, Saturday, we went shopping. My deputy director of Technical Support recommended a 386 with one meg of ram. 'State of the art,' he assured me. 'Fully upgradable.'

While we were at it, we bought a printer, a pile of games discs and a book called *DOS for Idiots*. The computer set-up cost me almost three grand. A fax machine set me back another nine hundred dollars. Inevitably, I'd have to get myself a mobile phone, join the wankers. But I wasn't quite ready for that yet. The 99-memory Motorola was priced at twelve hundred dollars. The more memory the better, I figured. Preferably something with a spanner-gripping facility.

But a four-grand outlay in a single shopping expedition was my personal limit so I put the mobile on hold. 'I'd need a handbag to carry it around in,' I told Red. 'Let's wait until they start making them small enough to fit into a man's pocket without it looking like he's got a canoe in his pants.'

We took our infrastructure home and set it up in Red's bedroom for convenience. Convenient for him, since he promptly invited Tarquin around to test its game-play capabilities.

I wangled enough access on Sunday to write a brief circular, 'What Murray Whelan Can Bring to Melbourne Upper', then spent most of the afternoon pecking it out with two fingers and playing around with fonts. Red, meanwhile, was also enmeshed in paperwork, rushing to finish neglected assignments in time for his return to school. Fortunately, we both finished our chores in time to watch *The Blues Brothers* on television.

Monday morning, after Red went back to school, I took my flyer to Qwik Print, then spent the rest of the day stuffing and addressing 800 envelopes. By the time I'd mailed them and spent a couple of hours calling names on the Melbourne Upper register, the news was out. Predicated on Labor's loss of the next election, a new faction had emerged, an alliance between the hard-left, the medium-right and the double-adaptors. Suddenly all bets were off in the dozens of preselection contests currently in progress.

Tuesday was Donny's funeral. I drove out to the

crematorium chapel at Fawkner cemetery and took a pew at the back beside a contingent of his old workmates from the brewery. For the requiem of a murderer-suicide, the numbers were respectable, about forty of us, all up. Some of the faces were familiar from parties of the left, both the boozy and political varieties. There were enough old flames in evidence to do credit to the deceased's memory as a lover.

Jacinta sat in the front row, ashen-faced under a black mantilla. She looked like she hadn't slept a wink since the discovery of the body. She and Donny had been together for little more than a year, so her status as official widow was somewhat tenuous. Meg Taylor, to whom he'd been legally married for most of the seventies, didn't appear eager to contest the title. She was sitting further back, paired with a woman in her mid-twenties that I took to be Ellie, the little daughter she'd taken into the relationship.

Donny's brother Rodney sat across the aisle beside a couple in their seventies who could only have been the parents. The mother was withered and shrunken, her claw-like fingers hooked over a walking stick. The father was more robust. From time to time during the service, he glanced disapprovingly back over his shoulder, as if those assembled were the bad company he'd warned his son against, the ones who'd led him to a sticky end. Heather was sitting beside him and she didn't need to look around for me to know she agreed.

In accordance with the known wishes of the deceased, there was no god-bothering and the bare minimum of ceremony. A civil celebrant conducted the proceedings, possibly an employee of the funeral company. Reading from notes, he summarised Donny's life in tones of anodyne sincerity that conveyed the man's biography but none of his essence. The only allusion to the circumstances of Donny's death lay in the use of the words 'tragic' and 'untimely'.

Donny perished a paid-up member of the union, so the Haulers sent the customary wreath. It was one of a number, including mine, that sat atop the Eureka flag that draped the coffin, half buried in the individual long-stemmed red carnations that we were each handed as we arrived. A pair of drumsticks lay there, too, placed by the bass player from Over the Limit, who tiptoed with awkward reverence up the aisle in his cowboy boots. Roscoe and Len, Donny's putative running mates, turned away shamefaced when I looked their way.

The only surprise, to me at least, was provided by a large-boned, soft-spoken woman in her early thirties who got up after Rodney had done his brotherly recollection bit. Hesitantly, she introduced herself as Donny's daughter, born without his knowledge and adopted by an Adelaide couple. When she recently contacted him, after careful consideration, she said, Donny had expressed surprise and delight to find that he had a long-lost child. The two of them had spoken on the phone several times and planned to meet at Christmas during her annual leave. Although that encounter would now never take place, and she had never actually met her birth-father, she wanted to add her farewells to those of his legitimate family.

For some reason, this brief and barely audible announcement, delivered by a diffident stranger, struck me as providing the most compelling argument yet that Donny had not killed himself.

As the remains rolled slowly through the portals of immolation, the John Lennon version of 'Stand By Me' came over the PA. Somebody was doing their best to lend occasion to the occasion. It succeeded only in sounding cheesy. In the silence that followed, an off-key voice began to sing 'Solidarity Forever'. We battened onto the familiar anthem with collective gusto but began to falter when we got to the verse about nothing being weaker than the feeble strength of one. After the first chorus we took it no further.

Afterwards, as the crowd dispersed into the overcast afternoon, I approached Jacinta. We shook hands and shared our bereavement in a moment of mutual silence. If Donny had discussed our last conversation with her, she gave no sign of it. When I turned to go, she touched my arm.

'You have my vote,' she said.

'Excuse me?'

'For preselection. You have my vote.'

'You're a member of the Labor Party?'

'You sound surprised. Did you think I was a mail-order bride? I used to work for the Textile Workers Union. That's how I met Donny, trying to organise a blackban on the transport of garments made by out-workers.'

'I didn't know,' I said. Hardly a novel phenomenon when it came to the multitudinous facets of Donny's life.

'Twenty of us Filipinas are members of the Reservoir branch,' she said. 'I'll make sure the others vote for you, too.'

I thanked her, somewhat disconcerted that my bullshit activities had raised their head at such a time.

'Donny would've wanted it,' she said. 'You were a true friend.'

Others hovered, waiting their turn. I kissed Jacinta on the cheek and went out into the leaden afternoon, thinking about truth and friendship. And about their obligations.

Three days before the preselection poll an item arrived in the mail. Bearing only a franking stamp and a printed address label, it gave no external clue as to its sender. Inside was a printed flyer headed 'Why Angelo Agnelli is Unfit to Represent Melbourne Upper'.

Because, it stated, he was an oppressor of women. A sexual harasser and serial sleazebag. Instead of putting his hand to the tiller of state, he'd been sticking it up every skirt in sight. Or words to that effect. The overall tone was a melange of lesbian separatism, pop psychology and fundamentalist moralising. The spelling was appalling. No examples were cited, no names named, no evidence presented. This, the communiqué claimed, was out of respect for the privacy of the women who had been so shamefully used by the 'contempteble predater Agnelli'.

There is only one alternative, concluded the document.

SEND THE CHAUVANIST PACKING—VOTE FOR LYNDAL LUSCOMBE.

For the benefit of readers from non-English-speaking backgrounds, these charges were repeated on the obverse in all the main food groups—Greek, Italian, Turkish and Arabic.

Since I'd been sent one, it was reasonable to assume that everyone else on the Melbourne Upper party roll had also received a copy. I took Lyndal's card from my wallet and started dialling. It took some trying, but eventually I got through. She was not a happy camper. In between taking calls she'd tried to ring me, unable to raise an answer because the phone was unplugged.

'It wasn't me,' she said.

'I didn't think so,' I assured her. 'Your spelling's better that that.'

'This isn't funny, Murray. It's a dirty trick. Whoever did this has really screwed my credibility. Makes me look like a complete bitch.'

'Doesn't exactly make Angelo look great,' I said.

'An anonymous shit-sheet? Malicious, unsubstantiated allegations, barely literate. He doesn't even need to dignify it with a reply. Meanwhile, I look like I'm peddling half-baked slander. This sort of thing is a male nightmare. Not only will it cost me support in Melbourne Upper, it'll frighten the horses in Canberra. God, I wish I knew who was responsible. I'd strangle them with my bare hands.'

'Issue a statement refuting it,' I said. 'Disavow all knowledge, say that you've been set up, your name used without your permission or approval.'

'And add fuel to the fire? It'll look like I'm having a two-way bet, running with the hares and hunting with the hounds.'

'If you don't want to put out a statement, then I will,' I proposed. 'I can deplore it as both an attempt to blacken Angelo and a bid to discredit you. Try to minimise the damage all round.'

'And make yourself look terrific in the process.'

'That's unfair,' I said.

'Probably. Right now I think my only option might be to withdraw from the ballot. Demonstrate my good faith with an act of self-sacrifice, try to cut my potential losses with the boys in the national back room.'

'Might be a better idea to find out who's responsible first,' I suggested. 'See if you can expose the source.'

'Spend the last couple of days of the race running around interrogating people, come across as a complete paranoid? No thanks. Face it, Murray, there's only one person who really stands to benefit. And I never dreamed he'd stoop to something like this.'

I wasn't going to ask who she meant. I might not have liked her answer. Leaving her pondering her options, I rang Angelo. He took some tracking down, but I ran him to ground at party headquarters.

'Of course I've seen it,' he said. 'And naturally I don't like it, leaves a bad taste in the mouth and there's always a risk that a little bit of the shit might stick. But for a man like me, a public figure, this sort of thing is an occupational hazard. And, on the up side, our Ms Luscombe has really shot herself in the foot this time.'

'You don't actually think she's responsible, do you?'

'Probably one of her rabid femo-nazi supporters,' he said. 'Whoever did it, it's a potential windfall for us. If I react, I'll look defensive. But you can capitalise on the opportunity. Put out a statement. Independent non-aligned candidate deplores the use of underhanded tactics. Parliamentary aspirants should be able to keep their more extreme supporters in line. Unwarranted attack on a man of unimpeachable character. So on and so forth. Criticise the policies, not the man. Perhaps not that bit. I'll leave the exact wording to you. I've got my hands full maintaining my outright majority on the public office selection committee, so I need a thundering endorsement from the branches. We've got to wipe the floor with this woman. Get cracking and I'll see you on Friday, usual time and place.'

Mumbling something about him being the boss, I rang off and made myself a sandwich. Angelo was entitled to his money's worth, however, a declaration like that wouldn't do anything for my stocks with Lyndal. Better to drag my feet, see which way the cards fell. I thought about who might have been behind the letter. The potential beneficiaries, as Lyndal so pointedly pointed out, were limited. Just how desperate was Angelo getting?

I got my answer late the next morning as I was making out a grocery list. It came via a phone call from the deputy secretary of the United Haulage Workers, the ferret-faced Mike McGrath.

'Heard the news?' he said. 'Lyndal Luscombe has tapped the mat. Withdrew her nomination half an hour ago. Decided that shit-letter wouldn't look very good on her resume.'

'You were behind it?' I said. 'You arsehole. Why do something like that, just for the sake of a bit of gratuitous slander? Just can't help yourselves, can you?'

'Don't be like that,' he said. 'Your time has come, my friend. I'm calling with a proposition.'

'What proposition?'

'Bag Agnelli. Attack his competence as transport minister. Come out with a public statement as his former long-time adviser, say he isn't up to the job.'

'Why would I do that?'

'Because we want him out of the portfolio. There's still a year to run before the end of the government's term, don't forget.'

'That's your motive, McGrath,' I said. 'What's mine?'

'Bit slow on the uptake this morning, Murray. A safe seat in parliament, that's what. If you can pick up enough of the lovely Luscombe's stray sheep to get even 25 per cent of the branch vote, I can deliver the support of our allies on the central panel. The nomination will be yours. How's that for motivation?'

'Let me get this right,' I said. 'All I have to do is shaft Angelo, change my allegiances, conceal my secret backers and get into bed with you.'

'Don't be prissy. Haven't you heard, flexibility's the name of the game at the moment. I'm offering you the chance of a lifetime.'

He was right. I thought about it. Long and hard. For about five seconds. 'Get fucked, McGrath,' I said.

'You're a bigger fool than I thought, Whelan.'

'Yes, but I'm my own fool, not yours.'

'You'll come crawling,' he said.

'Go fuck your mother, McGrath.' I hung up, added mouthwash to my shopping list, and dialled Lyndal's mobile number. She answered in a coffee shop, judging by the background noise. Either that or a steam laundry.

'It's Murray,' I said. 'I found out who sent the letter.

McGrath at the Haulers. It's all part of their destabilise-Agnelli strategy.'

'Makes sense,' said Lyndal. 'I suspected I'd been caught in somebody's crossfire. I appreciate your efforts, Murray, I really do, but I've bailed. My best bet was to get out while the going was good. Sorry, I can't talk now, I'm breaking the news to a coven of my supporters, but give me a call next week. We'll talk about it over dinner and whatnot.'

I liked the idea of the whatnot. 'I'll ring you Monday.'

'Make it Tuesday. I don't want you to think I'm easy.'

As distinct from hard. That would be my part. If I passed the audition. I felt my credentials firming, so I hung up and reviewed my immediate priorities.

Where does a man go who has just passed up an offer of a safe seat in parliament? On the balance of probabilities, all things considered, I figured that my best bet was Safeway in Carlton. Free undercover parking with every purchase over five dollars. The amount of food Red was going through, I'd spend that much, easy. And the way the rain was pissing down, undercover parking was an inducement too good to refuse.

I was turning the Honda into Brunswick Street, wipers slapping, the condensation on the inside of the windscreen thinning in the warm-air blast of the demister, when suddenly the word 'Foodbank' materialised. It was stencilled onto the tailgate of the Bedford truck in front of me.

As we inched along, the traffic thicker than a National Party voter, I recalled that Foodbank was a charity that collected perishable foodstuffs for distribution to worthy causes. I remembered, too, where I had learned that fact.

In an instant I was transported back to the wholesale fruit and vegetable market, to the interior of Donny's Kenworth.

Okay, so my zucchini wasn't tangled in the knicker elastic between Heather Maitland's alabaster thighs. But I could clearly recall the occluded view through the smeared mist of the rear window. I could see the Foodbank truck parked beside us. Like a film projected onto my windscreen, a scene unfolded before me.

Head down, I was sprinting through the rain towards Donny's truck. As I rounded the tailgate of the Foodbank Bedford, I slammed head-on into Frank Farrell. The impact of our collision knocked his mobile to the ground.

Then Farrell was scooping up his phone, casting an appreciative eye over the spanner in my hand and continuing on his way. A few moments later, I glimpsed him again as he ambled into the market, jeans tight around his backside, hands thrust into his jacket. His grey leather jacket with its cinched waist and narrow slit pockets. Pockets suitable for a pair of sunglasses, but far too small to contain a bulky mobile phone.

So where was it? One moment it was in his hand, the next it was gone. No more than fifteen seconds had elapsed since our collision. At some point during that time, he must have ditched it. But why toss away a thousand dollars worth of communications equipment? And where?

When the Foodbank truck took a left at the lights, I stayed behind it.

The traffic was crawling. My mind was racing.

Spider Webb described the murder weapon as a blunt object, of which there were plenty 'readily to hand'. And if you happen to be holding one, what could be more readily to hand than a mobile phone?

When I'd called Farrell at the Haulers, ten days after Darren's death, I was given a number for his mobile. The *new* number. If he had a new number, surely that meant he had a new phone. So what happened to the old one? Was it possible that Farrell had tossed it into the load on a parked truck? Might Foodbank have driven away from the market that morning with more on board than just a consignment of on-the-turn vegetables?

We turned into Victoria Parade, four lanes wide. The traffic thinned and the Bedford picked up speed. I stayed with it, tracking it past the edge of the central business district. I hunched over the steering wheel, my eyes glued to the words on the tailgate in front of me. A desperate hope had begun to take root in my mind.

The only eyewitness to Darren Stuhl's killing was dead. But if Farrell's phone could be found, and if it could be shown to be the murder weapon, then the police would be forced to reconsider the case. Once that happened, Farrell's whole fabric of deceit would begin to unravel. It was even conceivable that Bob Stuhl's role in Donny's alleged suicide might come to light.

Whoa, I told myself. You're drawing a very long bow here, Murray. As an object to clutch, the idea didn't even amount to a soggy straw.

By the time we reached the workshops and warehouses of North Melbourne, reality had begun to shine its cold light on my fantasies. For all I knew, the Foodbank truck was bound for Perth or Darwin or Dar-es-Salaam. Even if I followed it to the ends of the earth, what were my chances of finding Farrell's mobile phone when I got there?

I broke off the chase, dropped back and flipped on my indicator, angling for a break in the traffic. At that moment, the Bedford turned down a side street and vanished into a warehouse between a radiator replacement joint and an airfreight dispatch centre. The sign above the entrance read 'Foodbank Central Depot'.

Doubling back, I pulled into the kerb in front of the building. Through the slap of the windscreen wipers, I watched a station wagon emerge, slow to check for oncoming traffic, then drive away. The driver was a man in a Salvation Army uniform. He was a big bloke, one of gentle Jesus's burlier devotees. He probably believed in miracles. I didn't, but I got out of the Honda anyway.

Foodbank was a drive-through operation, a medium-sized warehouse with a roller door at each end. Down the centre ran a row of metal racks containing trays of bread and baked goods. Styrofoam cases of fruit and vegetables were stacked against the walls. A coolroom opened to one side, curtained with heavy strips of clear plastic. A woman in a tracksuit was helping herself to the fruit, loading her choices into a transit van with the words 'Street Kids Mission' on the door. Three men in dustcoats were carrying crates of fruit juice from the back of the truck into the coolroom, working efficiently but with no great sense of urgency.

They had about them the fate-buffeted air of individuals who might once have been on the receiving end of the charity they now helped to dispense, who lifted and toted but harboured no illusions about the redemptive value of physical labour. I thought I recognised one of them from the market parking lot, a scrawny old lag, one of the first arrivals at the scene of Darren's pulping.

If Farrell had tossed his phone into the Foodbank truck, then it was possible that this man had found it. It was also possible that the police had already covered this territory as part of their general inquiries. Since I was there, I decided to find out.

The man paused in his work as I approached, leaned against the Bedford's mudguard and pulled out a tobacco pouch. 'Help you?' he said, a cigarette paper stuck to his bottom lip.

I opted for the direct approach. 'You were at the wholesale market the morning that bloke got killed, weren't you?'

He tilted his head to one side, fingers working at the

makings. 'You a reporter? Bit slow off the mark, aren't you, mate?'

I took the opening. 'I'm doing a bit of follow up. Progress of the investigation, that sort of thing. Tracking down some of the people who spoke with the cops.'

He parked a thin rollie in the corner of his mouth. 'Who says I talked to the police?'

I tapped the side of my nose. 'Can't disclose my sources, mate.'

'Well you'd better get more reliable ones,' he said, an aggressive edge creeping into his voice. 'I didn't say nothing to the cops. And that's because I didn't see nothing. End of story.'

The shutters were coming down fast. I shrugged helplessly. 'Looks like I've had a wasted trip, then.'

'Looks like it.'

Time for a different approach. I nodded apologetically and made as if to leave, then turned back. 'While I'm here, I might as well make a contribution.' I took out my wallet and offered him a twenty dollar bill.

He picked a shred of tobacco off his bottom lip and shot a glance over his shoulder. 'Can't give you a receipt, mate. We're not set up for cash donations.'

'Don't worry about the paperwork.' I folded the bill and slipped it into the breast pocket of his dustcoat. 'I'm on expenses.'

He lit his cigarette and inhaled hard, waiting.

'You didn't happen to find anything unusual in your load that morning, did you?' I said.

He sucked his cancer stick and meditated upon the matter. 'Found a python once, in a load of bananas. And a rusty hand grenade in a bag of spuds.' He rubbed his stubbled chin. 'Can't say I found anything that morning.'

That was it, then. I had my answer. 'Thanks anyway, mate,' I shrugged and started to go, for real this time.

'But then I didn't do the unloading that morning,' he added, almost as an afterthought. 'We had a couple of young blokes at the time, some sort of youth training program. Anything turned up worth keeping, they'd've kept it. Anything else would've got chucked in the lost and found.' He twitched his cigarette towards a large cardboard carton at the end of the vegetable bins.

I nodded thanks, went over to the box and fished among the accumulated odds and sods. These consisted of a dirty check apron with the strings missing, an ancient football jumper with the sleeves torn off and a baseball cap that appeared to have been fed through a hay-baling machine. Some heavier items had settled on the bottom. I tipped the box over and dumped its contents onto the concrete floor. Out tumbled a lidless lunchbox, a fractured thermos flask, a John Deere tractor badge and a black mobile phone.

My mouth went dry and my pulse went through the roof. I squeezed my eyes closed and counted to ten. When I opened them the phone was still there.

Before it melted into thin air, I crouched down on my haunches and prodded it with a pen. Its casing was intact, the display panel cracked and the antenna bent. When and where this happened was impossible to tell. It seemed reasonable to assume that it was kaput when it arrived at Foodbank or it would have been snaffled by the youthful trainees.

There was no doubt in my mind that this was Frank Farrell's phone. And that it had been used to deck the despicable Darren. Problem was, would anyone else believe it?

To my dismay, no convenient clumps of reddish hair adhered to the casing. No clots of blood were visible in the crevices of the keypad. But Donny had talked about a bloody big gash and Farrell had disposed of the object in haste, so there must have been at least some prospect that evidence remained of its lethal use. I was no expert, but I'd watched enough police shows on television to know that every contact leaves its traces.

If my discovery was to lead anywhere, I would have to find those traces. Only after that would there be any chance that the police would take me seriously. And since I had no forensic facilities at my disposal, my only hope was to trust to luck and try to wing it.

Taking care not to touch it, I bundled my find into plastic wrapping from a package of date-expired Danish pastries and carried it briskly out of the building. My dustcoated informant made a conspicuous show of not noticing me leave. Our conversation, I understood, had never taken place.

Once back in the car, I resumed my trip to the supermarket. As well as toothpaste, tinned tuna and enough cereal to feed a team of draught horses, I purchased a pair of tight-fitting rubber dishwashing gloves. At the office-supplies store on Elgin Street I bought a magnifying glass.

Back home, I restocked the refrigerator and the pantry, moved my reading light to the kitchen table, snapped on the rubbers and set to work.

Gingerly tweezering the phone between thumb and forefinger, I examined it closely with the magnifying glass. No fingerprints were visible. But a fine seam, I discovered, ran along the plastic moulding above the earpiece. This was the most likely point of impact if the phone had been used to strike a blow. Running the tip of a safety pin along the crack, I extracted a minute quantity of dark-brown crud.

Which told me exactly nothing.

I transferred the gunk to the rim of a saucer and turned

my attention to the keypad. There were twelve number keys, eight function keys, * and #. From the gaps around these I extracted more tiny samples of muck. What I needed was an electron spectrographic crudometer.

Or the nearest equivalent. I went into Red's room and dusted off the microscope that had been languishing on top of his wardrobe since a week after his tenth birthday. It wasn't the most sophisticated piece of scientific equipment in the world, yet it was more than just a toy. I set it up on the kitchen table and adjusted the mirror until the lens revealed a luminous white circle. Then I sorted through the glass slides and eliminated those labelled Angora Rabbit Hair, Butterfly Scale and Fowl Feather.

Science had never been my strongest suit at school but I'd studied biology until my final year. If any of the stuff I was dredging from the nooks and crannies of the phone were blood, I'd need a sample with which to compare it. I pricked the tip of my middle finger with the safety pin and smeared a drop of blood on a clean slide. I laid another on top and took a squiz. What I saw looked pink and bubbly, like the froth on a strawberry milkshake.

Laying aside the control slide, I proceeded to scrutinise the various bits of detritus I'd dredged from the phone's clefts and crevices, first mixing them to a slurry with a droplet of water. I got the Mekong Delta, mosquito diarrhoea and the hide pattern of a Friesian cow. Nothing remotely resembled my specimen of blood.

This was getting me nowhere. I turned the phone over and tried the other side. Releasing the latch button, I removed the battery. A layer of soft residue caked the seam. I smeared some of it on a slide and squinted through the lens. What I saw was caramel rather than strawberry but its bubbly cellular structure was almost identical to my self-sourced sample.

If that's not blood, I thought, I'm Louis Pasteur.

The more I squinted through the eyepiece, the more convinced I became that I had uncovered an item of evidence capable of nailing Frank Farrell for Darren Stuhl's homicide. And thus of putting paid to the canard of Donny Maitland's suicide. Possibly even triggering an investigation that might even reveal Bob Stuhl's role in Donny's death.

Unless, on the other hand, it wasn't Darren's blood. Or Farrell's phone. These were matters that could only be determined by the police. Proper scientific scrutiny might also find fragments of Farrell's fingerprints and further bits and pieces Darren's biology. His hypochondrial DNA or whatever it was called.

But Inspector Voigt would not respond well, I imagined, to the suggestion that an amateur sleuth had discovered more in three hours than his crack team of Spider Webbs had brought to light in a month of flatfooted fossicking. Persuading the coppers would be a substantial job. It would take a substantial man.

I put Red's gunkoscope away, then went into my bedroom and began looking among my papers for One-Stop O'Shannessy's number. The phone rang. It was Ayisha Celik.

'News from the battlefront,' she lilted. 'With Lyndal out of contention, you are now the thinking woman's candidate of choice. Not that there's much choice. So if you want to reconsider your deal with Angelo, I reckon I can swing a fair few of Lyndal's votes your way.'

'Angelo's a done deal,' I said. 'The money's in the bank.'

Ayisha was undeterred. In an attempt to swing me across, she launched into an exhaustive analysis of the current factional fluctuations, with particular reference to the role of the rank and file.

'It's Thursday,' I reminded her when I finally got a word in. 'Two days before the vote. Even if I reneged on him, Angelo would still have it in the bag. But thanks for the offer.'

As soon as I hung up, the phone rang again. It was Agnelli's secretary, Trish, calling to confirm our regular Friday meeting at the Gardenview Mews. I didn't see much point, considering that Angelo's only genuine competition was now out of the race. Still, it was typical of Angelo to want his full pound of flesh. Only when the poll was declared on Monday would I be truly free of him. 'Tell him I'll be there,' I said wearily. 'Same time as usual.'

I hung up and dialled One-Stop's number. It was busy so I headed down the hall to my kitchen table crim-lab, wondering if I had a zip-lock bag large enough to hold the mobile. It occurred to me that Red would be home from school any minute.

Too late. He already was. And the moment I saw him, a chill ran up my spine.

Red was crouched over the kitchen table, his baseball cap reversed, spraying Farrell's phone with window cleaner and rubbing it furiously with a tissue. I rushed forward and snatched it from his grasp.

'I've cleaned off all the crap,' he said brightly. 'But the battery needs recharging. If you want my opinion, you haven't got a hope in hell of making this thing work.'

I thrust the phone into the beam of the reading light and stared at it. Farrell's Motorola was spotless. Not an iota remained of Darren's protoplasm.

'Why are you wearing rubber gloves, Dad?' asked Mister Helpful.

'So I can strangle you,' I cried, lunging for his throat.

Red scooted away, warily eyeing the flecks of white foam that had appeared on his father's lips. 'It's not my fault,' he pleaded. 'Whatever it is.'

I counted to ten. He was right. If a lad comes home from school and finds an item of gadgetry semi-disassembled on the kitchen table, the impulse to tinker is bound to be irresistible. 'Sorry,' I grovelled. 'I'm a bit pre-menstrual.'

Red got out from behind the couch. 'It's the testosterone, Dad. You've really got to find an outlet for your male needs.'

I fed him a line about the phone being on loan from a friend, how I'd accidentally dropped it down a drain. Then I stashed it in my laundry basket, slunk down to Brunswick Street and sulked in a coffee shop, smoking cigarette after filthy cigarette. My thoughts tangled in the smoke. For a fleeting moment I'd held in my hand the Achilles heel capable of unlocking the tangled ball of wax that had led to

Donny's murder. The missing link that would unravel the house of cards and blow the lid off the hidden hand of Bob Stuhl. But the possibilities that fate had dangled before me had been cruelly snatched away by the fruit of my own loins. Chagrin gnawed at my vitals.

Jesus, was I pissed off.

Nevertheless, the serendipitous discovery of Farrell's phone had raised hopes that could no longer be suppressed. The worm had turned and it was rearing up on its hind legs. If I couldn't use the fucking thing in the way I had intended, perhaps it might yet serve a useful purpose. But what?

I remembered One-Stop O'Shannessy's advice after my little chinwag with the cops at Citywest. No witness, no evidence, no admission, no case, he'd said.

The witness was dead, the evidence was disinfected, so all that remained was the possibility of an admission. Farrell had candidly admitted to killing Darren in our phone conversation on the night that I learned of Donny's death. Perhaps he could be induced to repeat the performance.

But Frankie-boy hadn't been trading idle banter that night. His candour served a purpose. It cowed me into silence. If I wanted him to discuss the subject again, I'd need to provide some pretext. Some bait.

The phone was cactus as evidence, but Farrell didn't know that. Until the fix firmed on Donny, he must have been shitting himself that it would turn up. Well, now it had. Better late than never. I decided to call him. We'd bat the breeze about dear departed Darren. And I'd keep some record of the occasion for posterity. For the police. And for the moment when I told him I'd found his phone.

Now I was thinking fast. Farrell would wonder about my

motive in drawing his attention to my discovery. What if I offered to trade the phone for something? Something a dickless pen-pusher like me would really be hot for, that would convince him I'd come to terms with what he'd done. Something suggesting a form of petty revenge to stroke my pomposity. Something plausible.

By the time I ran out of cigarettes, all this had begun to formulate itself into the inkling of a scheme. I paid the black-garbed waiter for my coffees and walked home to mend my fences with Red. The rain had cleared, the pavements were drying and the only clouds that remained in the sky were smeared in glorious technicolor across the western horizon. Shot with the beams of the lowering sun, they glowed yellow, purple and orange like crumbs from some gargantuan marble-cake. The boy will be wanting his dinner soon, I thought.

I found him with a mouthful of clarinet, his weapon of choice in the junior school band. While I made tuna casserole and encouraging remarks, he practised the first three bars of the Pink Panther theme. Over and over again. 'Enough with the dead ants,' I screamed after half an hour. 'Or I'll go back into strangulation mode.'

'Shut up,' he retorted. 'Or you'll damage my self-esteem.'

My bedroom ceiling copped a lot of staring that night. But when sleep finally came my scheme had firmed to a plan.

After Red left for school the next morning, I called the Haulers' office to check that Farrell was in town. No show without Punch. He was at the Mobil refinery, I was told, on a picket line of striking tanker drivers. He'd probably be there all day. But if the matter was pressing he could be contacted on his mobile.

'I think I've got his number,' I said.

At ten o'clock, I strolled up the slope to the Carlton shops. It was a good day for it, fine and clear with a forecast top of eighteen degrees. Young mothers in skin-tight jeans and tattoos emerged from the Housing Commission flats to smoke cigarettes and push their offspring around in strollers. Blossoms were turning to mush on the gutters. Spring had truly sprung. There was no turning back.

My first stop was the office-supplies store in Elgin Street where I'd picked up the magnifying glass. This time, I bought a palm-sized microcassette recorder, batteries and a box of tapes. I only needed one tape, but they didn't sell them singly. I consoled myself with the thought that even if things didn't work out as I planned, the purchase was tax deductable for a man in the consultancy racket.

I stuffed the surplus tapes into my pocket, put the batteries in the recorder and walked back down to Rathdowne Street. As I went, I dictated to myself, getting the hang of the gizmo. Just after eleven, I arrived at the Gardenview Mews. The desk clerk, a thick-set young man with work-out shoulders and the cocky deference of a recent hospitality studies graduate, recognised me from my previous two check-ins.

'We have your reservation, Mr Whelan,' he said. 'But you're a little earlier than usual. I'm afraid you'll have to wait for a room to be made up.'

This meant that the place was fully occupied. Which was just the way I wanted it. I asked for the room I'd first had, if possible. The one at the end of the ground-floor walkway, right next to the ice machine. 'Sentimental reasons,' I explained.

The clerk consulted his keyboard. 'No worries, sir,' he confirmed. 'Room 23. It'll be yours in a jiffy.'

During the jiffy I went into the parking quadrangle, soaked up some rays and admired the way the wisteria drooped from the cast-iron lacework around the balconies. Guests arrived and departed. Cars came and went. A tired-looking housemaid dragged her trolley along the walkway, unlocked Room 23 and set to work. At a rough count, her arrival was visible from the doors of at least thirty other rooms. Excellent.

I was thinking about the set-up for the swap-meet. No clever-clever stuff this time, I'd decided. No Ferris wheels. No guns. Just a well planned, cautious exchange. That's what Farrell would expect and that's what I'd give him. And while we were swapping, we'd chat.

Taking the tape recorder from my pocket, I pushed the record button and laid the device on top of the ice machine. It didn't stand out a mile. It didn't stand out at all. 'One, two, three,' I said, stepping out the paces to the open door of Room 23. 'The time has come, the walrus said, to speak of many things.'

The housemaid looked up from her bed-making. 'Can I help you, sir?'

'Just thinking out loud,' I said. 'Thank you very much.'

I pocketed the tape recorder and walked up the steps to the balcony rooms. At the first landing, I replayed the tape. It wasn't going to win an Emmy, but every word came back at me crisp and clear. When I got back downstairs, the housemaid had trundled away. I collected my key, walked home through the gardens, made myself a cheese and pickle sandwich and rehearsed what I'd say to Farrell.

I imagined the picket at the gate of the Mobil refinery. Twenty or thirty shuffling tanker drivers. Hand-lettered signs flapping on the mesh fence. Shoulders hunched into windbreakers. A fire burning in a forty-four-gallon drum. A radio turned up loud. Thermos flasks and cut lunches. Boredom the main enemy. Frank Farrell prowling the perimeter, on stand-by in case of rough stuff. Or maybe sitting in a folding chair, awaiting developments, his phone in his lap.

Just after 2.30, I crossed my fingers and made the call.

'The mobile telephone you are calling is switched off,' announced a Telecom robot. 'Please try again later.'

Shit. I was ready to rock'n'roll. Farrell was being inconsiderate, fucking with my schedule. I mopped the kitchen floor, watched it dry, then tried again. Same message. I vacuumed the living room, then went into the backyard and smoked a cigarette. Somehow I was back up to twenty a day. Not in the house, of course. I tried Farrell's number again and got a busy signal. Progress. I started working the redial function.

Twenty minutes later I got the ringing tone. Then Farrell barked his name.

'It's Murray Whelan,' I said. 'How are things at the barricades?'

'All quiet on the western front,' he said. 'What is it this time, Whelan?'

'The same matter as we last discussed, Frank. Seems you mislaid your mobile phone that morning. After you decked Darren with it, I mean. Anyway, I thought you'd like to know that I've managed to lay my hands on it.'

'You're breaking up,' he said. The signal was crystal clear.

'Give me your number, I'll call you back on a land line.'

I recited my number and hung up. So far, so good. Since he was taking precautions against eavesdropping, I'd definitely found his frequency. I went into the backyard and stared up at the wild blue yonder. That was where I was headed, flying solo. Flapping my arms and hoping I didn't fall. Flap, flap. Ring, ring.

I went back inside and picked up, hoping nobody else had chosen this exact moment to call. Farrell's breathing was laboured and traffic roared in the background. Now I could see him in a payphone beside an arterial road, rigs whizzing past, phone pressed to his ear.

'What are you crapping on about, Whelan?' he said. 'I didn't mislay any mobile phone.'

'Suit yourself,' I said. 'My mistake. Sorry to disturb you.'

I hung up and started counting. I got to nine. This time, Farrell's voice had a steely edge. 'This phone you reckon you've got,' he said. 'Where'd you get it?'

'I saw you throw it away,' I said. 'Lucky for you it took me so long to put the pieces together. You took a big risk tossing it away like that. Darren's blood in its tiny crevices. A quick wipe with a hankie just doesn't do the job in the face of modern forensics, Frank. You must've been feeling pretty confident, I guess.'

A long silence came down the line. It did not sound like a denial. I swung into the pitch. 'Naturally my first impulse was to go to the police,' I said. 'Good citizenship and all that. My credibility might be shaky on the hearsay front but physical evidence cuts a lot of ice. Particularly if it happens to be the murder weapon. But dealing with the cops can be very time-consuming. And as you know, they're not always as fast off the mark as they should be. On top of which, once the wallopers get in on the act, who knows what other sleeping dog might get woken up, eh? So I've decided to offer you first option.'

Farrell didn't say anything. I gave him all the time he needed not to say it. 'Go on,' he grunted, eventually.

'I've taken on board what you told me last time we spoke,' I said. 'What's done is done. Let the dead bury the dead. I've come around to your point of view, Frank. I don't like what you did, but I don't think that should stop us doing business.'

'What sort of business?'

'A trade,' I said. 'It so happens that I'm in urgent need of a job at the moment. And you're just the man to help me get one.'

'You want me to find you a job?'

'In a manner of speaking, Frank. Like you once told me, something can always be found for a friend. This is what I'm thinking. If I was able to provide Angelo Agnelli with some sort of ammunition to use against the Haulers, he'd be very well disposed to finding me a cushy position on the government payroll. Maybe even an overseas posting. You supply that ammunition and I'll give you back your mobile. It's a win-win situation, Frank. So what do you say? You want your mobile back, or should I take it to the cops?'

'What do you mean by ammunition?' he said.

'Nothing more than a piece of paper,' I said. 'If you want in, go to the Haulers' office. I'll call you there in half an hour. If you don't answer straight away, I'll assume you're not interested. Getting you sent up for killing Darren will take time. And there'll be nothing in it for me from a personal point of view. But I don't have anything better to do at the moment. Not having a job and all.'

Farrell did a little contemplative breathing. 'Yeah, all right,' he said. 'I'll be there.'

'By the way,' I added, 'I've got the trade item in a safe place. So don't get any clever ideas about dropping around to pick it up.'

I hung up. Farrell was cagey, but he was sniffing the bait. I thought I'd hit just the right note of venality. My lunch-hour gruyere sandwich didn't agree. It was trying to work its way back up my gullet. There were ants in my pants. Not dead ones, either.

Fifteen minutes later, Red lolloped through the back door, home from school with a bunch of the guys in tow around 4 p.m. I drew him aside, told him I had a commitment for the next few hours and suggested he try to wangle an invitation to dinner at Tarquin's place.

'Hot date?' he said.

I most sincerely hoped not.

I'd budgeted to meet Farrell before my six o'clock confab with Angelo. Thanks to the delay in getting through to him, we'd now have to meet afterwards. This meant keeping him in cold storage for a couple of hours.

Joggers thundered past me in damp T-shirts as I headed back to the Gardenview Mews. I was wearing a lightweight spray jacket over a polo shirt and jeans. Farrell's mobile was under my arm in a family-size zip-lock freezer bag. I walked through the archway, nodded hello to a bloke in a well-cut suit getting into a rental car in the motor court, checked that the ice machine wasn't vibrating and let myself into Room 23.

I put the mobile and the tape recorder on the dresser, hung my spray jacket over the back of a chair and took a miniature of scotch out of the minibar. I thinned it with tap-water and sipped very slowly, getting my full six dollars worth. And keeping Frank Farrell waiting a half-hour longer than the specified time. At 5.30, I called the United Haulage Workers.

A machine started to tell me the office was closed, then Farrell cut in. 'Is that you, Whelan?'

'Personing the desk yourself?' I said.

'What do you expect, this hour on a Friday?' he said. 'They've all gone home. So what's this piece of paper you want?'

'Go to the stationery cupboard,' I said. 'Get yourself some union letterhead. Write me a statement that you witnessed Howard Sharpe and Mike McGrath concocting a false and slanderous letter accusing the Minister for Transport of sexual misconduct.'

Farrell snorted derisively. 'Fuck off,' he said. 'Agnelli starts flashing something like that around, I'll be run out of here on a rail.'

'Would you prefer to be taking suicide-note dictation from Bob Stuhl's death squad?'

Farrell made a noise like oatmeal going cold. 'Like that is it, eh? You want to have your bit of flesh as well. Make you feel better, does it?'

'I'm helping you get away with murder, Frank,' I reminded him. 'Your job at the Haulers is a small price to pay. A man of your talents can always find work. If he's not in jail, that is. Or dead.'

'Okay, you'll get your ammunition,' he said. 'When do I get the other thing?'

'Start writing,' I said. 'Keep it simple. Nothing too fancy. I'll leave the wording up to you. I'll call back shortly and tell you where to bring it.'

I rang off, cracked another miniature, lay back on the

bed, stared at my shoes and thought about Donny Maitland.

I thought about the time we'd stood in a crowded kitchen at a loud party. We were drinking flagon claret and arguing about whether Ho Chi Minh was a communist or a nationalist. To the best of my recollection, the only conclusion was a terrible hangover. I remembered, too, that I still had his copy of *The Unbearable Lightness of Being*. And how he'd brushed me aside in his haste to rescue Red from the burning site office. How it was exactly three weeks since our last conversation. And how his last words to me were an apology.

This rigmarole with Frank Farrell, I reminded myself, was just the first step. Maybe I was tilting at windmills, but one day Bob Stuhl would pay for what he'd done to Donny. At five to six, I swung my feet onto the floor and dialled the Haulers' number. 'Written it?' I said.

'I've done what you told me,' he said. 'What now?'

'Be in the lounge bar of the Southern Cross Hotel at seven o'clock,' I said. 'Bring the statement. You can read it to me there. And you won't need your phone or any other weapon. Come alone.'

I hung up, wrapped Farrell's mobile and the tape recorder in my jacket and put it on the luggage rack. Then I opened the door and stood in my shirtsleeves on the walkway and waited for Angelo to arrive. Dusk was beginning to fall and the floodlights had been turned on in the quadrangle. Doors were opening and shutting on the balconies. An elderly couple with Queensland accents bickered their way cheerfully down the stairs and into a station wagon. He hadn't, he told her, driven all this bloody way to eat bloody Eye-talian.

A couple of minutes later, Angelo strode through the archway. For a man whose nomination was now assured, he looked less than entirely gruntled.

'How's Lothario this evening?' I asked.

'That bloody sexual predator letter,' he scowled, slinking disconsolately into the room. 'The press have got hold of it. Under normal circumstances, it wouldn't merit a second glance. But now that there's blood in the water, they're trying to dig up dirt on everybody in sight, discredit the entire government. Some hack from the *Sun*'s been trying to corner me all day. I only just managed to give him the slip.'

'Stop bleating.' I followed him inside and shut the door. 'And quit pacing about. You're giving me claustrophobia. Sit down and shut up.'

He did as he was told, shedding his suit-jacket and sinking into the sofa. I took a half-bottle of champagne from the minibar and filled two plastic tumblers. 'To your imminent renomination, Comrade Shoo-in,' I toasted. 'And the end of our long association.'

Ange raised his glass. 'You don't know how much help you've been to me, Murray,' he said, adopting his most sincere expression. For an awful moment I thought he was going to get sentimental. 'And I hope you never find out.'

We bumped our plastic cups together and sipped. By this small gesture, it was mutually acknowledged that my obligations to Angelo were now fully acquitted. My hand-holding days were over.

'Remember the time you invested the party election funds in that dodgy company?' I said. 'Every last cent. On the day before it went bankrupt.'

Ange unbuttoned his waistcoat, loosened his tie and

levered his shoes off. 'You were nothing when I found you,' he said. 'I made you what you are today.'

'Unemployed?' I said.

'And I think I can truthfully claim,' continued Ange, 'that I've taken you as far as you can take me.'

In other circumstances my departure from Angelo's employment might have been marked by a small gathering in the office and a farewell card signed by my co-workers. Instead, the two of us lolled in a motel room and exchanged low-level insults over a dribble of South Australian brut and an overpriced bag of crisps. Before long, Ange's eyes were drifting towards the phone on the bedside table.

'Just a couple of quick calls,' he said. 'Won't be long. No need for you to stick around.'

Angelo's idea of a couple of quick calls meant factoring at least another half-hour into the time I'd need to keep Farrell dangling. I gave a resigned shrug and left him to it, engaged in conspiracies about which I no longer gave a twopenny toss. Before I left, I pocketed the room key. I took my bundled-up spray jacket with me, donning it on the walkway outside the door. Farrell's mobile and the tape recorder fitted easily into its large pockets.

It had just gone 6.30. A cobbled lane ran behind the motel and I followed it towards Lygon Street, my footsteps echoing up the narrow alley. If Farrell was obeying my instructions, he was somewhere between the Haulers' office in South Melbourne and the Southern Cross Hotel.

Lygon Street throbbed with life. Low-slung cars cruised, motors throbbing, music pulsing behind their tinted windows. The sidewalk tables were filling fast and the aroma of tomato paste and oregano hung heavy in the air as prospective diners window-shopped for tagliatelle con vongole and fritto misto.

I strolled the length of the street to the Astor Hotel, an old-style pub with tiled walls the colour of a lung disease, and drank a whiskey at the bar. Then I walked back the way I'd come. Dusk had given way to night and the floodlit cupola of the Exhibition Building glowed above the dark treetops of the gardens. At a phone booth on Rathdowne Street, I rang the Southern Cross, had Frank Farrell paged and waited an anxious five minutes for him to pick up the house phone.

'Slight change of plans,' I said.

'You wouldn't be fucking me around, by any chance?' he growled.

'Do exactly as I say and you'll have what you want very soon.'

The Southern Cross was only four blocks away. I gave Farrell directions to the Gardenview Mews, told him to enter through the archway to the parking quadrangle and said I'd be waiting for him there in exactly fifteen minutes.

Traffic hummed along Rathdowne Street, the theatre and cinema crowd streaming into town, late commuters heading the other way. A black BMW turned from the northbound lane and drove through the archway into the motel. I recognised the driver as the leggy press secretary to the deputy leader of the opposition. What was she up to, I wondered?

I didn't wonder for long. I confronted more compelling questions. Would I be able to get Farrell to talk? Would my little tape-machine trick succeed?

I had a ten-minute start. I used three of them to smoke a cigarette and stare across the road at the sign on the back entrance of the Exhibition Building. *The National Boat and Fishing Show*, it read. I had the bait in one pocket and the hook in the other. All that remained was to land the catch. I ground my butt underfoot and went into the motel quadrangle.

The black BMW was nose-in to the walkway, two doors away from Room 23. Its driver was nowhere in sight but there was a healthy degree of coming and going along the upper balconies. So far, so good. A public place, but not too noisy for recording purposes. We'd be out in the open, so Farrell would be unlikely to attempt to overpower me and snatch the phone. The most important thing was that he should believe that the swap was the main game. All the while, the tape would be running.

I went along the walkway to Room 23 and tested the handle, assuring myself that Ange had left the room locked when he left. I stripped off my jacket and stuffed it behind the ice machine. Goosebumps rose on my bare arms but I wanted Farrell to see that I wasn't wired. Every possible suspicion was to be allayed.

Pressing the record button, I placed the microcassette on top of the ice machine. Then, clutching the clear plastic bag that contained the mobile, I stood in front of Room 23 and waited.

Thirty seconds later Farrell prowled through the archway.

He was wearing a denim jacket, a denim shirt and crotch-hugging jeans. At fifty metres, his eyes were caverns of impenetrable darkness. But when he tilted his head back to scan the scene, the light caught the tautness of the skin over his cheekbones, the hardness of his face.

Until that moment I hadn't really thought of him as a physical threat. Not to me, at least. Perhaps I should've made provision for the possibility. It was too late for that now. I was so far out on a limb I could've got a job as a ring-tailed possum.

I waited until he saw me, then dangled the bait and beckoned. He stalked forward warily, scoping the set-up, eyes darting from side to side. When he was four steps away, I signalled for him to stop. The tape recorder was a metre beyond his right shoulder. I willed myself not to look at it.

'We'll do it here.' I nodded towards Room 23. 'When I tell you, shove the statement under the door.'

He raised his eyebrows. 'Think I'll try to snatch it back once I've got what I want?'

'Absolutely,' I said. 'You can hardly blame me for not trusting you, Frank. You're a devious bastard and you've got a terrible temper. Look what you did to poor Darren Stuhl. Analogued him off. Would that be the right expression?'

Farrell didn't rise to the topic. He took a folded sheet of paper out of his breast pocket and extended it into the space between us. In response, I took the phone from its bag and lay it on the ground at my feet. One swift kick and it would be under a car, out of reach. The zip-lock bag went into my back pocket, a crumpled ball.

'Read it to me,' I said.

Farrell read quickly and without expression, like a courtroom clerk speeding through the ticket. For recording purposes, however, his volume and diction were perfect.

'I, Frank Farrell,' he read, 'an official of the United Haulage Workers, do hereby state that I was present when Howard Sharpe and Mike McGrath, respectively state secretary and deputy secretary of the aforesaid union, did maliciously conspire to fabricate and disseminate a libellous letter alleging sexual misbehaviour on the part of the Minister for Transport, Angelo Agnelli. Signed and dated.'

'A bit bush-lawyerish,' I nodded. 'But it'll do.'

Not that I gave a stuff what it said. It was just a stage prop. A rubbery little tentacle designed to conceal the hook. What I needed now was a tongue-loosener, something to get the dialogue flowing.

'Pity you killed Darren before I filed my dental-damage compensation claim,' I said. 'Maybe I'm selling myself short here.'

Farrell jerked the statement back and scowled. 'You want money, too?'

'The thought occurred to me,' I said. 'But things tend to get messy when money's involved. So I'll settle for a bit of personal satisfaction. Like you said, Darren Stuhl had it coming. Tell me what it was like when you killed the prick.'

Farrell raked me with a look of disgust. 'It didn't feel like anything,' he said. 'He wouldn't put his gun away, so I hit him. He went down. End of story.'

Beautiful, I thought. Come in spinner. Gimme more. 'You think there was any chance he was still alive when you shoved him under Maitland's truck?'

'He was stone dead, you sick fuck.' He nodded down at my feet. 'Are we going to do this or not?'

I had what I wanted. All that remained was to finish the charade, bring down the curtain and see him off. 'Okay,' I said. 'Slide the statement under the door.'

He crouched, reaching out with his free hand as he fed the paper through the gap. As it disappeared, I kicked the mobile forward. Farrell grabbed it and came back upright.

Now that the evidence was in his grasp, he wasn't taking any more chances. He whipped a can of lighter fluid from his hip pocket, doused the phone and set it alight with his slim gold cigarette lighter.

Grab, squirt, flick, whoomph.

He dropped it to the ground and squirted it again as it burned between his feet, a smokeless ball of blue flame. Frank was a man who liked a fire.

'What about Maitland?' I said. 'No remorse about feeding him to Bob Stuhl's wolves?'

The phone was shrinking to a molten blob. Farrell

prodded it with the scuffed toe of his elastic-sided boot, hurrying it along. 'You just don't get it, do you?' he said.

'Get what?'

He put a hand to his groin, made a hissing noise through his teeth and pretended to piss on the fire. Then he directed the stream from his invisible dick in my direction.

The scales fell from my eyes, washed away by a blast of imaginary urine. 'You were the guy who pissed on me?' I said. 'But why?'

Not just the pissing. I meant the entire exercise.

Farrell shrugged. No skin off his nose if I knew the truth. He had what he wanted. I prayed the tape was picking this up.

'Things weren't moving along quite as briskly as I hoped,' he said. 'The cops were taking their time buying the Maitland frame-up. So I thought I'd give the process a nudge. Rounded up an old army mate, told him we were doing a favour for Bob Stuhl. Coached him on his lines, of course. Didn't want you recognising my voice. That was a very busy night, believe me. We'd just finished winding you up when I got the call about the cars being vandalised. Had to rush off and attend to union matters, put Maitland out of the election business.'

'So Bob Stuhl was just a smokescreen?'

'And you bought it,' said Farrell. 'Lock, stock and shotgun barrel.'

Holy Christ, I thought. I am a fucking moron. If Stuhl hadn't sent the pantyhose twins, did that mean he hadn't had Donny killed either? A band of steel closed around my chest. Farrell smirked and twisted the knife.

'If you'd done as you were told,' he said, 'Maitland would

currently be awaiting trial on a murder charge. Manslaughter, even. Improper disposal of a body. Six or seven years, tops. But you had to get all hairy-arsed and start waving that gun around, didn't you? Forced my hand. After that, the only way I could be sure the fix would stick was to kill him. The pig-headed bastard. It took some considerable effort to get him to write that suicide note.'

I felt sick to my soul. Farrell had wound me up, all right. He'd played me like a Stradivarius. But that was nothing compared with what he'd done to Donny. I wished I had a gun so I could shoot him on the spot like the mad dog that he was. My eye darted to the cassette recorder.

Farrell didn't notice. He was stomping the remains of the phone beneath his boot. When he'd pulverised it, he kicked it aside. Then he turned and slammed his heel into the door of Room 23. As it flew back on its hinges, he reached down and snatched up his statement. 'You didn't really think I was going to let you keep it, did you?' he sneered. It flared briefly, then disintegrated into ashes.

A startled yelp came from inside the room. Our heads turned.

A woman was kneeling on the bed. She wore nothing but a studded dog collar and a leather harness. She held a riding crop in one hand and was straddling an albino sea-lion.

For a bizarre moment I thought it was a Helmut Newton photo-shoot. Except Helmut's people hadn't been in touch to ask if he could use my motel room. And the woman wasn't a model but the press secretary of the deputy leader of the opposition, the driver of the black BMW. She stared back at us in alarm, her arm shooting up to cover her naked breasts. They were okay but her legs were better.

'Very juicy,' said Farrell. 'Nothing like a bit of bondage.'

Golden showers were more his preference, I thought. Along with bashing, torture and cold-blooded murder.

'No way,' cried the woman, leaping off the sea-lion and scooping an armful of clothes off the floor. 'I'll go along with dress-ups and a little light spanking, but I draw the line at groups. This is too weird for me.'

Farrell's palm slammed into my chest and I reeled backwards. 'So long, sucker,' he crowed, and took off across the quadrangle.

'Baby doll,' gasped the sea-lion. 'Where are you going?'

Grabbing the tape recorder off the ice machine, I dashed into the stairwell. As I hit the rewind button, Madame Lash erupted from Room 23, a loose bundle of clothing pressed to her bosom. Her other attractions were now swathed in the voluminous folds of a man's shirt. It flapped around her knees as she wrenched open the door of her BMW.

I hit the play button and heard Farrell's voice: '...sexual misbehaviour on the part of...'

Angelo Agnelli burst out onto the walkway tucking a towel around his expansive waist. The black beamer roared into life and backed away, tyres screeching. 'Wait,' begged Ange. 'You've got my pants.'

'You sick fuck,' said the tape recorder.

The desk clerk emerged from the reception area and started along the walkway, preceded by his out-thrust jaw. I ejected the tape, slipped it into my pants pocket and backed deeper into the obscurity of the stairwell.

Angelo hurled himself at the BMW, signalling wildly and pleading for his daks. But the dominatrix was a woman without pity. She spun the wheel, laid rubber and sped away.

Propelled by his own desperate momentum, Angelo lurched after her for a dozen futile steps. Then he pulled up short and abandoned the chase.

He stood there in the middle of the floodlit quadrangle, clad in nothing but a bath towel and a gorilla mat of chest hair. Suddenly a screech of brakes resounded through the archway from the direction of the street. This was followed by the loud crump of an automotive collision. Then another, then another, then another. Then came the blare of a horn. The insistent, unremitting wail of a jammed horn.

Doors flew open all around the quadrangle. Inquisitive faces appeared on the balconies and peered downwards. Angelo was centre stage. Firming his towel around his midriff, he adopted the insouciant air of a man who had lost his way while looking for the swimming pool. There was no swimming pool.

'Hey, you,' shouted the desk clerk. He bounded towards Angelo, blocking his way back to the room. 'What have you done to my door?'

The horn continued to shred the air. More people emerged. The manager advanced. Panic swept the face of the Minister for Transport. Clearly baffled by the sudden turn of events, he knew only one thing for sure. Explicability-wise, he was in a very vulnerable situation. Casting about for an escape route, he spied the only one available. Taking a firm hold of his loincloth, he beat a hasty retreat through the archway to the street.

It was a popular destination. Others were also headed that way, drawn by the incessant bleat of the horn. I joined them.

The pile-up was impressive. A six-vehicle fender-bender.

Drivers, passengers and busybody onlookers were milling around, surveying the damage, yelling and gesticulating. The driver of the lead car, a dark grey Mercedes, was remonstrating with a cluster of people. Occupants of vehicles further down the line, judging by the way they were rounding on him.

'A black BMW,' he said, gesturing helplessly up the street. 'It shot out in front of me, so I hit the brakes. What else could I do?'

'You should've been paying attention,' accused a bystander. 'Instead of yapping on your mobile phone.'

The blaring horn was coming from the last vehicle, an orange transit van with the words 'Stuhl Couriers' along the side. It hadn't connected with the other cars. Swerving to avoid the pile-up, it had mounted the kerb and slammed into a wall. A young man in a long ponytail and a Stuhl Holdings shirt was standing at the point of impact. He was wringing his hands and staring with stricken disbelief at a body which was pinned between the wall and the front bumper of his van.

'Somebody call an ambulance, man,' he kept repeating. 'For Chrissake, man, somebody call an ambulance.'

It was too late for an ambulance. You didn't need to be a Fellow of the Royal Australasian College of Surgeons to see that much. The eyes of the hapless pedestrian were wide open, staring lifelessly ahead. Blood trickled from the corners of his mouth. One minute he was walking along the footpath, the next he was winging his way to eternity.

It was Frank Farrell. He didn't look quite so pleased with himself any more.

Traffic was building up. Cars in the southbound lane

were slowing to a crawl as the occupants craned for a look. Spectators were converging from all directions. Across the road in the gardens, a pale ghost was flitting from tree to tree, thighs flapping, disappearing into the night.

The ride was coming to an end. Three men were dead. One good, one bad and one capable of very nasty behaviour while drunk in a nightclub. It was time to hang up the Superman costume, crawl back down the limb and renew my trust in the due process of the law.

I went back into the motel, retrieved my jacket from behind the ice machine and ducked into Room 23. The bed was ravaged, smalls lay scattered across the floor and the atmosphere was pungent with the tang of body fluids and leather-care products.

Clearly, Farrell wasn't the only one who thought I belonged in a sheltered workshop. Ange had been playing me for a sucker, too. Our hush-hush pow-wows were simply a cover for his surreptitious rumpy-pumpy. To add insult to injury, he'd contrived to have me pay for the room. And his behaviour was even more scandalous than alleged in the shit-letter. Fooling around might be forgivable. Kinky is a matter of taste. But doing it with a member of the Liberal Party was beyond the pale.

I slumped on the edge of the bed, rang the Curnows' place and fixed it so Red could spend the night. 'I had a meeting and things got out of hand,' I told Faye. 'You know what it's like.'

Back out in the street, barriers were going up, ambulance and police lights flashing. I stood in the red-blue stroboscopic flare and watched as Farrell's body was strapped onto a gurney and whoop-whooped away. Then I sidled up to one of the cops and told him I had information pertaining to the deceased pedestrian. And to related matters of probable interest to the Criminal Investigation Branch.

By the time the uniforms passed me up the line and the dicks at headquarters had done listening to the tape it was past midnight. Detective Senior Sergeant Noel Webb joined the team at that point, not pleased to have been summoned from some Friday-night piss-up. 'If being a fuckwit was an indictable offence, Whelan,' he told me, 'you would've spent most of your life behind bars.'

The coppers would like to have arrested me, they made it plain, but couldn't think of a charge. Professional jealousy, I decided. Like me, they could hardly be expected to greet with delight the revelation that they'd been given the right royal runaround. With the tape in the hands of the authorities, however, the burden of responsibility at last moved back to where it belonged.

When I was shown the door of the cop shop, it was two in the morning and I was as spent as yesterday's lunch-money. I hailed a cab, gave the driver my address and sat numbly in the back. As the convent of Mary Immaculate flashed past, I offered up a silent prayer for Donny's repose. Not that there was anyone to hear it. Or that Donny would've looked kindly on such a lapse. At least his killer had not escaped retribution. The dead mightn't care, but the living take consolation from such things. I did, at least.

I stared into the gardens, too, as we drove by, and wondered what had become of Angelo. That question was answered the next morning, after I was dragged from my slumbers by a brief and enigmatic phone call from Lyndal Luscombe.

'Seen the *Sun*?' she asked eagerly.

'Huh?' I snuffled. 'Is there an eclipse or something?'

'Quick,' she ordered. 'Take a look.'

I tugged at the curtains, squinted at the cirrus-streaked sky and realised she meant the newspaper not the celestial orb. So I pulled on some track pants, padded down to the corner shop and bought a copy.

Ange was plastered across the front page. The photograph showed him with one hand raised in an unsuccessful attempt to shield his face while the other gripped his trusty Gardenview Mews towel. Flanked by two Parliament House stewards, he looked like a Roman senator being arrested at the baths by a detachment of the Praetorian Guard.

SEX CLAIM MINISTER IN NUDE ROMP declared the headline.

According to the report, the Minister for Transport had been disturbed the previous evening by parliamentary staff while trying to slip into his office in a state of undress. Not immediately recognising him, they had given chase. In an attempt to elude his pursuers, the government leader in the Upper House had taken a wrong turn and crossed the floor of the chamber during a debate on the deficit. The incident was witnessed by a *Sun* reporter, who was waiting for an opportunity to seek the minister's comments on allegations of inappropriate sexual behaviour circulating in his electorate.

Claiming he had been robbed of his clothes while taking a stroll in the nearby gardens, the minister lunged at a press photographer and attempted to destroy his camera.

The menials of Murdoch had struck paydirt and they mined it for all it was worth. Further pictures appeared on the inside pages, along with reports that a near-naked man had earlier been observed in the vicinity.

Poor Angelo. Timing is all in politics, and this was far from the ideal moment to go streaking through the corridors of power. By late morning, Ange's allies on the public office selection committee had hung him out to dry. Finding himself a faction of one, he was compelled to review his priorities. Citing stress, he submitted his resignation as minister and announced his intention to retire from parliament at the next election.

That left just me and Save Our Trains at the starting gate. On the following Monday, when the result of the preselection poll was declared, I became the endorsed Labor candidate for Melbourne Upper.

The state election was held almost exactly twelve months later. The result was a landslide that buried Labor so deep it might be the next century before we tunnel our way out. As always, Melbourne Upper remained solid and I was duly elected as its representative in the Legislative Council. I sit there now, one of a tiny rump of Labor members.

Unfortunately for my constituents, vengeance is the watchword of the new regime and my days in parliament are spent ineffectually voting against legislation that appears specifically designed to punish safe Labor seats for their traditional loyalties. Banished to the wilderness, the party has directed its energies into squabbling over the spoils of defeat.

Bob Stuhl is bigger than ever. According to Faye, he is diversifying into the telecommunications sector. Australia has one of the highest take-up rates of mobile phones in the world and Bob is positioning himself to capture a significant share of the traffic they are expected to generate. The size and cost of cell phones is shrinking before our very eyes and it will soon be difficult to believe that a fit young man could once have been beaten to death with one. I myself have finally succumbed. Twice. One for me for work-related purposes, the other for Red. He needs it, I feel, since he travels so far to and from school every day.

One of the first acts of the incoming Liberal government was to close two hundred government schools, Fitzroy High among them. Somewhere else had to be found for Red. Reluctantly, after considerable soul-searching, I decided to enrol him in a private school. To be frank, his academic performance at Fitzroy was disappointing and Wendy's ceaseless telephone tirades were beginning to wear me down. On top of which, sending your children to government schools is contrary to established practice for Labor members of parliament.

Red still thinks the purple blazer makes him look like a twat, but he's finally settled down to the two-hour daily commute. At least he doesn't have to wear a boater. He still sees Tarquin socially, of course.

What with the annual school fees, the mobile phone and the mandatory laptop computer, I'd probably be feeling the strain if it wasn't for my parliamentary salary. My interim year as a consultant was not as financially rewarding as I'd hoped and there wasn't much left of my lump-sum pay-out by the time the election rolled around. Angelo's spectacular fall from grace tended to tarnish me by association, despite the fact that our connection had been formally terminated three weeks prior to his self-immolation.

Angelo has returned to the law, where a tendency to lewd behaviour is a professional asset and a reputation for misogyny is a recommendation for appointment to the bench. His wife, Stephanie, stuck with him steadfastly in the aftermath of his ordeal. They were divorced, however, soon after his parliamentary term expired. She got the lion's share of his superannuation.

Howard Sharpe continues to rule the Haulers' roost, having been re-elected without opposition for his seventh successive four-year term. Soon he'll be looking for a new sidekick. There's a federal election coming up and Mike McGrath made the cut for the Senate ticket, so he's Canberra-bound. He'll doubtless find many kindred spirits in the national capital, particularly among those visiting from Sydney.

Miss Leatherette of the Liberals, by the way, is currently in charge of the new state government's prison privatisation program. Word has it that she's very close to the marketing director of the global corrections corporation, Wackanut Inc.

As arranged, Lyndal and I had dinner together on the Tuesday evening after the preselection poll. What with one thing and another, I didn't feel like Italian, so it wasn't candlelight and champagne at Florentino's. Instead, we settled on sake and tonkatsu in a shoji-screened alcove at Kenzan, the Japanese restaurant at the Regent Hotel.

'I'm keen to come to grips with that issue you raised prior to the closure of nominations,' she told me.

'And I remain curious about your preferences,' I said.

'Perhaps we can go upstairs afterwards and assess each other's credentials,' she suggested, taking a hotel key out of her purse.

'Waiter,' I called.

Soon after, she landed a job with the Department of Human Services, reviewing its needs-based service-delivery performance. I gave her an excellent reference, based on a personal assessment of her capabilities. She continues to harbour long-term ambitions for a federal seat. After almost eighteen months she and I are still bedding down the central plank in her platform.

Red approves of our relationship. 'She reminds me a bit of Mum,' he told me. I have no idea what he means.

The lad will be fifteen soon and Wendy has finally conceded defeat on the custody front. My status as a member of parliament makes it a tad difficult for her to cast me as a complete incompetent, although it hasn't stopped her trying. I'm reluctantly forced to agree with her on one point, however. Being an opposition member in the Upper House of an Australian provincial parliament is hardly the most high-powered job in the world.

Still, it meets my modest requirements. It keeps the bank at bay and the refrigerator stocked. I have time to devote to the tasks of fatherhood. I do what I can for my constituents. And I have absolutely no reason to visit the Melbourne

Wholesale Fruit and Vegetable Market at four o'clock in the morning in the middle of winter.

Anyway, that's the story of how I became a member of parliament. Whether you believe it or not is entirely up to you.

It's a big ask, I know.

SOMETHING FISHY

> Politicians also have no leisure, because they are always aiming at something beyond political life itself, power and glory, or happiness.
>
> Aristotle, *Ethics*

A fraction of a second, that's all it takes.

By my reckoning, Rodney Syce and Adrian Parish began their break-out from the Melbourne Remand Centre at precisely the moment I emerged from the trees in the Fitzroy Gardens and found Lyndal Luscombe sitting on the bench beside the birdbath fountain.

Her message said she'd wait there until six, hoping the Hon. Murray Whelan could make it. A personal matter. The Legislative Council usher must have liked that bit because he was even more inscrutable than usual when he passed me the note during the third reading of the Administrative Resources Amendment Bill (1994).

I got the note just after five-thirty, a welcome distraction from the drone of the Minister for Administrative Services. Rising from my place in the back row of the opposition benches, I bowed to the Speaker and sidled out of the chamber, hoping the party whip wouldn't notice I was gone.

Not that my presence in the upper house of the state legislature made a skerrick of difference, of course. Since our disastrous defeat at the last election, there were so few of us left in parliament that to describe the Victorian branch of the Australian Labor Party as an impotent rump would have seriously overstated both our size and influence.

I left Parliament House by the rear door, dodged a snaggle of peak-hour trams and made my way through Treasury Place, the pavement thick with homeward-bound public servants. Whatever it was, it must have been pretty important for Lyndal to summon me like this. Why not wait until parliament adjourned for dinner at seven, talk to me then? And why the gardens?

Oh Christ, I thought, picking up my pace as I entered the long avenue of overarching elms. She's in the gardens because of what borders them. The Freemasons Hospital. The Mercy. Medical suites and day-procedure centres and rows of Victorian terraces filled with specialists. She's been to a medico of some sort. Something's wrong and she wants to talk about it. Somewhere quiet, somewhere she'll have my full attention.

I came out of the trees and saw her before she saw me, bathed in a pool of late-afternoon sunshine, the light catching the chestnut hues in her hair. Her eyes were downcast and she was fiddling with the hem of her knit skirt where it ended just above her knees. Her lips were moving as if she were rehearsing lines. She definitely had something on her mind.

It was about then that the alarm must have gone off at the Remand Centre. Not that I could hear it, three kilometres away on the other side of the downtown grid. I was attending to my own, inner alarm bells. Don't panic, I told myself, wait until you hear what she has to say.

'Hi,' I said cheerfully, bending to plant a kiss on her cheek. Act natural, let her take her own sweet time.

Lyndal met my descending smile with a brisk, open-palmed slap. 'Don't you dare,' she warned. 'You filthy beast.'

I rocked back on my heels, jaw slack. What had I done to deserve this? It wasn't as though I hadn't tried to kiss her before. Or worse. And succeeded.

'What's got into you?' I said, hand pressed to my face.

Quickly glancing around, I checked that nobody was watching. Not exactly good for the parliamentary image, copping a biff from a woman, especially one as attractive as Lyndal. But the gardens were deserted. A mid-autumn chill was already rising from the lawns. A spill of white-clad nurses emerged from the Mercy Hospital across the road, but none of them looked our way. Cars rolled past, their drivers intent on making good time to the freeway.

'What's got into me?' said Lyndal. 'I'll tell you what's got into me. You have, Mr Sexpot. I'm pregnant.'

My jaw resumed the slack position. 'Pregnant?'

'Potted. Up the duff. Preggers. Bun in the oven. Expecting.'

Pressing both cheeks, I sank onto the seat beside her. 'Goodness,' I said.

Lyndal inched away. 'Goodness had nothing to do with it, pal.' Her counterfeit ire dissolved into a self-congratulatory grin.

'You're sure?'

'Sure as spermatozoa,' she nodded. 'And I've got the picture to prove it.' She fished in her handbag and thrust a

Polaroid at me. It looked like an underexposed satellite reconnaissance photograph of atmospheric turbulence over the South China Sea. 'She's the spitting image of you, don't you think?'

'She?' A grainy blob occupied the north-west quadrant of the photograph, a furball in a blizzard. 'How?' I said. 'I mean when?'

Lyndal's expression had become beatific, placid, wise. Christ, freshly duffed and she was already turning into the Earth Mother. 'By the usual method,' she said. 'Last January, during the summer holidays. One of those lazy afternoons with nothing better to do than.'

'Not that when,' I said. 'I mean, when's it due? I mean she.'

'Nine months from the time of conception, Murray,' she said patiently. 'Even you should be able to figure it out.'

My fingers did the sums. 'October.' But it was already April. 'How long have you known? And why didn't you say anything?'

'I wanted to be one hundred per cent sure that everything was okay before I told you.' She nodded towards the building beside the hospital. 'I've just seen the obstetrician. It's too early for amniocentesis but the ultrasound indicates a normal baby.'

'Normal?' I said, incredulous. 'With you for a mother? A sneaky minx who doesn't even bother to tell her poor dumb paramour that she's gone and got herself knocked up.'

Waves of relief broke over me, a treacly ocean of love and pleasure and pride. My feet executed a little jig. Slipping my forearm beneath Lyndal's thighs, I swung her legs up onto the bench and tilted her sideways so she sprawled on her back the length of the slatted seat. I dropped to my knees and gently pinned her shoulders.

'Under the circumstances,' I said, 'I don't see how you've got any choice but to marry me forthwith.'

She smirked back. 'Determined to make an honest woman of me, are you, Murray Whelan, MLC?'

Oh yes, indeed. I lowered my face to hers. She yielded, squirming beneath my caress, ripe and lush, letting her arms dangle. I laid a hand on her breast. 'Now that you mention it, I do detect a certain womanly fulsomeness.'

She smacked my hand away and swung her feet to the ground. 'Get up,' she commanded. 'You look ridiculous. Forty-two-year-old politician in a double-breasted suit, down on his knees, slobbering like a teenage Romeo.'

I stayed exactly where I was. 'Groping the tits of the fiercely independent thirty-five-year-old public policy analyst whose swelling belly is heavy with his love child.'

Lyndal tugged down her hem and smoothed her dress. 'Who are you calling heavy?' Her hands lingered on her abdomen for a moment longer than necessary as she adjusted the fall of her skirt. 'Let's go and have a celebratory drink. We've got things to talk about.'

I gave her my hands and let her haul me to my feet. 'Should you be drinking?' I tutted.

'Believe me, Murray,' she said. 'If it wasn't for drink, I wouldn't be in this condition.'

Hand in hand, we ambled towards the Hilton, the nearest licensed premises. 'This'll mean a lot of changes,' said Lyndal.

'About twenty a day for the first few months,' I agreed. 'There'll be crap everywhere. We'll need nappy service.

Lucky for you I already have some experience in these matters.'

'That's one of the things we need to talk about,' said Lyndal. 'How do you think Red will react to the news?'

Red was my thirteen-year-old son, the only good thing to come out of my marriage. After several years of Olympic-standard wrestling for custody with his mother, Wendy, I won the prime-parent medal when Red reached high-school age. Very convenient for Wendy, who had meanwhile plighted her imperious troth to a silvertail Sydney lawyer and spawned a brood of twins.

'Red adores you,' I said. 'He'll be just as pleased as I am.' An exaggeration, but only a slight one. Fact was, the two of them got along like a house on fire.

'He won't mind that his father has knocked up the babysitter?'

'That was a low blow. Red doesn't think of you like that.'

But it was a role she played well, tending to the home fires and riding herd on the lad's homework when duty compelled my attendance at an all-night sitting of parliament, a party meeting or a commitment in the constituency.

At a break in the traffic, we skipped across the road, hands still linked. The day was drawing to a close, the last beams of the sun slipping between the office towers of the central city, catching the filigree of cast-iron lacework on the rows of terrace houses that faced across the gardens. Had I looked over my shoulder, I might have noticed the police helicopter, a distant speck, still inaudible, coming fast out of the setting sun.

We entered East Melbourne, a district of well-heeled gentility, its appearance largely unchanged since the 1890s.

A block away, down a slight incline, lay the Hilton.

Conrad's pleasure-dome was a recent interloper, a tower of shit-brown bricks erected in the 1960s on the ruins of the Cliveden Mansions, an elegantly loopy late-Victorian lodging house for gentlemen bachelors. In place of four-poster beds and brass-potted aspidistras, the Hilton offered weekend-getaway packages and express checkout. Hardly our usual watering hole. But these were exceptional circumstances. Lyndal's news required immediate access to a flute of Moët.

'Anyway,' I said. 'You never complained about keeping an eye on Red from time to time.'

And she hadn't, of course. After all, we'd been shacked up together for the best part of a year. Informally at first, a matter of convenience. Then, after I sold the cramped little workman's terrace I shared with Red in Fitzroy and moved to a larger place in the electorate, officially.

We sauntered, our arms around each other's waists, our hips moulded together. 'If you're going to be a cry-baby,' she said, 'you'd better make the most of it before the real thing arrives.'

'Show me the picture again,' I said. 'I couldn't read the name-tag.'

Lyndal pulled the Polaroid from her bag and dangled it in front of my eyes. 'Lysistrata,' she said. 'See. Says it right there. Lysistrata Luscombe.'

I snatched it away and tilted it to the light. 'Lysistrata Luscombe-Whelan, don't you mean?' I said. 'A bit of a tongue-twister but it's got a certain ring. Wasn't Lysistrata that Greek chick who went on a sex strike? I hope you're not getting any ideas along those lines.'

To assure myself otherwise, I backed her against the

cast-iron fence rails of the nearest terrace, pressed my lips to her neck and began to work my way upwards. Lyndal squirmed against me in a gratifying manner. 'Get it while you can,' I whispered. 'Before your body is devastated by stretch marks and the ravages of childbirth.'

A car horn bleated in the distance, followed by screeching tyres and the faint metallic *clump* of a low-speed fender-bender. My head turned at the sound and Lyndal blew a raspberry in my ear. Snatching the Polaroid from my hand, she wriggled free.

I lurched after her, the two of us playing tiggy-tiggy-touchwood in the golden light. The only thing missing was a veil of gauze over the lens and a soundtrack of violins.

But it wasn't Mantovani and His Orchestra that surged in the background. It was the thunder of an approaching motor, a swelling chorus of sirens, the bass thump of a helicopter.

As we turned, wondering at the sudden ruckus, a powerful motorbike erupted from the gardens, its rider hunched low over the handlebars. A passenger straddled the pillion, the two helmeted figures clad in identical orange coveralls. Rocketing across the kerb, the bike cut the path of the oncoming traffic, then banked sharply to the right, coming our way.

A police car flashed past us, speeding to intercept, siren wailing, lights flashing. Cut off, the bike swerved and went into a skid, spilling its riders as it toppled over and skittered across the roadway. It came to rest against a parked van. The prowl car braked and two uniformed cops jumped out. Drawing sidearms, they crouched behind their open doors, bellowing for the riders to halt.

But the boiler-suited men were already back on their feet. One sprinted for the bike, the other hobbled to catch up. The cops were yelling, more sirens were converging, horns blared, tyres screeched. The first rider reached the bike, wrestled it upright and climbed aboard. His limping confederate struggled to cover the distance. A shot rang out. He was shooting at the cops. They returned fire. *Pam, pam, pam.*

We were thirty metres away. It didn't seem nearly enough. I caught Lyndal by the wrist and pushed at the front gate of the nearest terrace. The iron latch was down. I fumbled with it, letting go of her. *Pam, pam, pam.* Above the sound of the shots, the bike roared into action. My mind was clear but my fingers were putty. My legs turned liquid. The bike reared, front wheel spinning, then it burned rubber and shot forward, past the police car, up over the gutter and along the footpath, heading straight for us.

Lyndal pressed herself back against me as I finally managed to lift the latch. The gate sprang open and I stumbled through, reaching back to drag Lyndal with me. As I grabbed her elbow, the speeding motorcycle slammed into her, tearing her from my grasp and flinging her into the air like a doll.

Above the roar of the departing bike, I heard a crack as her head hit the stonework of the gatepost.

I dropped to my knees at her side, just in time to see the light go out of her eyes.

On the day the coroner's report was due to be released, I woke in darkness.

But not, it gradually came to me, total darkness. A faint, blood-tinged glow hovered at the edge of my consciousness. After a while, I rolled onto my side and turned my eyes towards it, the digital display on the clock-radio by my bed. For exactly eighteen minutes I stared at the numbers, counting them off. One minute for every month since the events in East Melbourne.

At 5 a.m., I threw back the bedclothes, planted my feet on the floor and cancelled the alarm just as the sting sounded for the news. The news could wait. As far as I was concerned, the whole world could fucking wait.

The house was cold and I cursed myself for having forgotten, yet again, to pre-set the timer on the central heating. Truth be told, the house was too big for just the two of us, much bigger than our old place in Fitzroy. But a member of parliament should live in his constituency and Fitzroy did not fall within the boundaries of Melbourne Upper, so a move was inevitable from the moment I was endorsed for the seat. Anyway, there were three of us when I bought the place. With more to come, I'd hoped.

I padded down the hall in slippers and bathrobe, straight into the kitchen without knocking on Red's door. Another ten minutes wasn't going to make any difference. And a growing lad needs all the sleep he can get. Thirty-six hours a day, minimum, if Red was any indication. I lit the gas, opened the blinds and stood at the window while I waited for the kettle to boil. Not that I could see anything. The October dawn was still an hour away.

In daylight, I would have seen a rectangle of dewy lawn, slightly overgrown and bordered with clumps of daffodils. Garden furniture, still sheathed in winter plastic. Drifts of japonica blossoms, turning to mush. My personal low-maintenance Gethsemane. And beyond the back fence, the rooftops of Melbourne's northern suburbs.

For more than thirty years, off and on, I'd lived and worked in this part of town, breathed its vapours, taken its temperature, counted its heads. I was a kid when my father took the licence on the Carter's Arms in Northcote. After university and a stint as a union official, I returned to run the office of the area's representative in the state legislature. A job which I now held in my own right, thanks to 69.52 per cent of its voters on a two-party preferred basis. It was my Province, to use the terminology, from the Ford factory in Broadmeadows to the Greek senior citizens home at Thornbury, in all its brick-veneer, blue-collar splendour.

Unfortunately, my election had coincided with the utter defeat of the Labor Party after a decade in office. The worm had turned and, for the past three years, my constituents had been punished for their traditional adherence to the party of social democracy. Their schools and hospitals had been closed, municipal councils abolished, a poll tax imposed.

About which, at that particular moment, I could not have given a tinker's. What did the voters of Melbourne Upper, asleep in their beds, know of loss?

Most days, I managed to keep a lid on my self-pity and heartache. But that particular morning, I felt entitled to the consolations of blame.

The kettle began to whistle. I poured boiling water over a tea-bag and carried the brew towards the bathroom. As I passed, I thumped on Red's door with a balled fist, threw it open and flicked the switch.

'Yes or no?' After a silent count of ten, I repeated the question. 'Yes or no?'

The lump on the bed shifted. Sock-clad feet emerged from the quilt accompanied by a compliant moan. 'Okay, okay.'

Exactly twenty-seven minutes later, we crossed the Yarra at the Punt Road bridge. The streets were almost deserted. As usual, Red hibernated the whole way, his school uniform stuffed into the backpack between his feet. He was fifteen now. His voice had deepened, fluff was sprouting on his upper lip and he would soon be taller than his father. But although no longer a cub, he was not yet the full grizzly. He was still my baby boy.

Over the river, I followed Alexandra Avenue along the bank, the ribbon of water veiled in a thinning mist. The sky was high and clear and the last of the stars were fading fast. A fair spring day was predicted. As we approached the boathouse, I shoved the *William Tell Overture* into the tape deck and cranked up the volume.

Red lunged for the eject button, swearing like a stevedore at a joke that was even more tired than he was. He fumbled for his bag as I nosed into the kerb. 'I've got play rehearsal after school, don't forget, and we're working on the maths challenge at Simon's place. Won't be home until eight-thirty.'

'Got everything you need?' I dug out a twenty. 'Rake the path and mow the lawn, I'll double it.'

'Weekend,' he yawned, feeding a tangle of limbs though the car door.

He was long and lanky, taller and thinner than I had been at fifteen. His teeth were straighter than mine, too, thanks to an orthodontic bill that would have financed a moon shot. But the similarities outweighed the differences. In the ways that mattered we were very alike.

As he closed the door, Red paused. 'That inquest thing,' he said. 'It's today, right?'

I nodded.

'Fucking coppers,' he said. 'Covering their arses.'

Other lads were already lowering sculls into the water and sorting equipment. Hoisting his backpack, Red shut the door and loped down the incline. When he reached the bottom, he looked back and raised his arm in farewell. He made his open palm into a clenched-fist salute. *Venceremos*, Comrade Dad.

I drove towards the city centre, following the course of the river.

I turned on the radio for the six o'clock bulletin. The

announcer's voice droned. Jury still out on O. J. Simpson. Federal election tipped for early in new year.

A butterscotch smudge was creeping upwards from the eastern horizon. Over the mist-shrouded river, beyond the tubular metal canopy of the tennis centre, lights were appearing in the office towers. A pod of joggers powered along the path beneath the newly mantled elms. This was the postcard view of Melbourne, the garden city on a river of bridges. It was a pretty sight at dawn, one that I enjoyed three times a week, thanks to Red. But the pleasure was qualified. My home town was changing fast. Not just the shape of the skyline but the spirit of the place.

Further downstream, a vast new casino was taking shape beside the Yarra. The plutocrats were at the helm and a veil of secrecy had descended over the processes of government. A cult of personality surrounded the Premier. The smirking bully was king and Fuck You was the official ideology. The public interest was a bankrupt notion in the heads of fools.

I switched off the radio, made an illegal U-turn and parked. Sculls began to appear from upstream. A quad, then a coxless four, their hulls half-concealed in mist, oars dipping rhythmically. Girls, I realised, their coach on a bicycle. Ducks rose as they skimmed past, flapped and settled. Then, a few minutes later, came an eight. Red's crew. Year Ten boys, C division, all knees and elbows, still settling into their stroke.

I stood beside the car and watched the boat glide past. Focused on his task, pumping away between Max Kline and Danny Chang, Red was oblivious to my presence. That was fine by me. Rowing was his thing, unprecedented in our branch of the Whelan family. But that's what you get when you send your son to a private school. Not that I had much choice. Not after they closed the local high school. Not with the senior bureaucrat in the education department being paid a cash bounty for every government school teacher fired or strong-armed into redundancy. Four thousand of them in two years.

So it was either have Red commute to an overcrowded classroom with a leaking roof and a demoralised teacher or bow to *force majeure* and go private. And it wasn't as if I was the only Labor politician to take his kid out of the public system. After all, it's only natural to want your child to enjoy the same privileges that you had. All the more if you never had them. And, Christ knows, it kept the boy's mother off my back, hectoring me long-distance about my paternal shortcomings.

Red had adjusted well to the change of schools. Some of his mates from Fitzroy High had also made the shift, which eased the transition. And he'd discovered rowing, an activity more benign than others available to his age group.

'Builds up the shoulders,' he argued, beefy delts being a self-evident good to the contemporary teenage male.

As I watched him pass, tending his oar, I suspected that the allure of the sport lay in the opportunity it provided for him to be both alone and part of a team. That, and a sort of aristocratic élan behind which a boy can conceal his adolescent uncertainties.

Flash motors were beginning to whoosh down the hill from the thicketed heights of Toorak. When Red's eight slid under the Swan Street bridge, I got back into my Magna Executive and joined the flow.

By six-thirty, I was pacing the treadmill in the gym at the City Baths, a towel around my neck, a newspaper draped across the console. I did my usual ten kilometres, going nowhere, reading as I went. The *Age*, the *Australian*, the *Herald Sun*, a summary of pending amendments to the Gaming and Betting Act, agenda papers for the Public Accounts and Estimates Committee. Anything to keep from thinking.

Lyndal had weaned me off cigarettes and making the effort to stay healthy had become a way of honouring her memory. But trudging along a rubber belt was never more than a chore and I still kept a packet of smokes in the glovebox of the car for moments of maximum stress. I finished my session with a couple of laps of the pool and a bowl of fibre in the chlorine-scented snack-bar, then crawled through the swell of rush-hour to Parliament House.

For all its neo-classical splendour, its colonnaded portico and gilded chambers, the House was feeling its age. A haughty Victorian dowager, it was inadequate to the demands of the late twentieth century. Behind the brass and marble, beyond the pedimented portals and wood-panelled halls, it was a rabbit warren of file-filled crannies and windowless cubicles. Only the biggest of the big chiefs warranted a private office and for opposition backbenchers like me, the lowest of the low, it offered a desk in a shared office in a permanently temporary outbuilding abutting the carpark.

The Henhouse, we called it. But despite its clapboard construction and nylon carpet, it met its obligations to protocol. The name-plate beside the plywood door listed me as 'The Honourable M. E. Whelan'.

The first to arrive, I turned on the lights as I walked along the corridor to my office. Twenty years of schooling and they put you on the day shift. I transferred the contents of my briefcase to the desk and hung up my overcoat. Aquascutum, a fortieth birthday present to myself, a bit the worse for wear. Like its owner.

Get a grip, I warned myself. Today would be hard, but there had been harder days. Much harder. Keep it in perspective, don't let them get to you. Lyndal's death was part of a big news story, a major episode in an unfinished saga. And with the cops keen to generate optimum coverage, it was inevitable the media would come after me when the report became public.

And what would I say? That I felt some sort of closure? Pig's arse I did.

Problem was, I couldn't say what I wanted to say. It wasn't just that it was impossible to express my feelings about Lyndal's death in a neat, five-second sound bite. If that was all they wanted, the platitudes could be found. I was a politician, after all. But what if I was quizzed about the subsequent events? If that happened, and if I didn't keep a tight rein on myself, the shit would really start to fly.

I sat down at my standard-issue, formica-veneer desk. Keep it moving, that was my watchword. Head down, tail up. In-tray to out-tray. The first item was a reminder letter from the state secretariat regarding the deadline for submissions to the party reorganisation review process. I stared down at it and yawned. The phone rang.

'Saw the light,' said a woman's voice. 'Thought it was you. Wondering how you're set today. Any chance of a favour?'

It was Della McLeish, administrative assistant to Jim Constantinides, leader of the opposition in the upper house, calling from Jim's office in the main building. Jim was the closest thing I had to a boss, so a request from Della carried a certain amount of weight. 'It's a last-minute stand-in job,' she explained. 'Out-of-town sitting of the Coastal Management Advisory Panel. Comes under Natural Resources, Moira Henley's brief. Moira's gone down with the flu and Jim feels we should show the flag.'

'It'll mean missing a day in parliament,' I said. 'And you know how much I enjoy sitting on the backbench with my thumb up my quoit. So what's the pay-off?'

'A chance to observe the democratic process,' said Della. 'And a free seafood lunch in beautiful San Remo.'

'I don't know anything about coastal management.'

'What's to know? The tide comes in, the tide goes out. Session starts at eleven, finishes at four. I'll send over the agenda papers, okay?'

'Might as well,' I said. 'And thanks, Del.'

'For what?'

'As if you don't know.'

San Remo was a hundred kilometres away. Good old Della had cooked up a reason to send me somewhere beyond the reach of journalists. Somewhere I wouldn't get my nose rubbed in it.

I was touched by the gesture. It reminded me that the Labor Party was a kind of family. Dysfunctional, certainly, but one to which I had belonged, man and boy, for almost thirty years.

I spent the next forty-five minutes drafting a speech opposing a forthcoming amendment to the Government Audit Act, a measure requiring that the Auditor-General carry out his duties with a bucket over his head. You do what you can. By the time I'd roughed up an outline, other MPs and staffers had begun to arrive for the day.

I found a half-dozen of them in the lunchroom, clustered around the coffee plunger, chewing the fat. The Honourable Kaye Clegg, Member for Melbourne West, had just returned from Sydney. She was talking about an event that happened there a year earlier, the murder of a Labor MP as he arrived home after a party branch meeting. The case was still unsolved.

'Word is, it was a professional hit by Vietnamese heavies,' she said, dunking a shortbread.

'At least somebody thought he was important enough to kill,' said Dennis 'Ivor' Biggun, the Member for Ballarat. 'Here in Victoria a Labor MP can't even get run over. People cross the street when they see us coming. What do you reckon, Murray?'

'I'm thinking of having a whip-around, see if I can raise enough for a contract on you-know-who.' I cocked my head in the direction of the Premier's office.

Ivor tossed a coin onto the table. 'Count me in.'

'Pay to have him whacked? I wouldn't give him the satisfaction,' said our deputy spokesperson on health.

Most of the others dredged change from purses and pockets, adding it to Ivor's ten cents. The total came to ninety-five cents.

'That's this party's problem in a nutshell,' sighed Kaye Clegg.

We drifted in a group to Parliament House for the weekly caucus meeting. A new leader had recently been installed, a thin-lipped automaton with television hair and the voter appeal of diphtheria. He gave us a half-hour lecture on the need to shake off our image as big spenders. I sat at the back and rested my eyes.

When I got back to the Henhouse, the agenda papers for the coastal management whatsit had arrived. I tossed them into my briefcase and rang my constituency office in Melbourne Upper. It had just gone nine-thirty, opening time. Ayisha, my eyeball on the ground, answered the phone.

'That cop, Detective Sergeant Meakes,' she reported. 'He rang a few minutes ago. Said to tell you that the coroner's findings'll be handed down mid-afternoon and the police media unit will issue a statement immediately afterwards. Said if you've got any questions, don't hesitate to call him.'

'Very thoughtful,' I said. 'Considering what the cops think about my questions. Anything else?'

'Three media calls, so far. "Today Tonight", the *Herald Sun* and ABC radio. You going to talk to them?'

'Think I should?'

'It might help,' she said.

'Do you really think I should allow myself to be made an object of pity because the cops can't do their job? Act like a politician who can't resist the chance to get his face on the news?'

'Maybe there's a chance it'll help, that's all I'm saying.'

'If only that was true, mate. But it's all bullshit. Call them back and tell them I'm not available.'

'That won't stop them looking for you.'

'They'll search in vain,' I said. 'I'll be in San Remo for the rest of the day.'

'San Remo? What's happening in San Remo?'

'Very little,' I said. 'I hope.'

An hour down the South-Eastern got me to the Bass Highway turn-off at Lang Lang, where the suburban sprawl finally gives way to the lush green of dairy farms, market gardens and wetlands. The forecast was holding and the only clouds in the powder-blue sky were thin shreds on the southern horizon. The highway forked again and Westernport Bay came into view, a verdigris slab fringed with mud-flats and tidal shoals.

Just before the bridge across the narrows to Phillip Island, I took the turn into San Remo. The venue for the day's meeting was a function room in a motel at the jetty end of Marine Parade. I found the place, parked out front and stood for a few minutes, breathing the ozone and contemplating the view.

At the public fish-cleaning benches on the foreshore reserve, a flock of seagulls squabbled over the innards of somebody's catch. Down at the jetty, commercial fishing boats were unloading tubs of whiting and school shark, fodder for the fish'n'chip shops of Melbourne. Near the war memorial, an elderly couple was sharing a thermos at a picnic table, squinting out at the water.

According to the paperwork from Della, the Coastal Management Advisory Panel had been established to provide input into government management of the state's coastline. A seaside location was chosen for its inaugural public meeting to facilitate the participation of what were called 'coastal resource user groups'.

It was just past eleven. I went into the motel lobby and followed the signs to the Cormorant Room. It had salmon-pink acrylic carpet, stackable furniture and wide windows that overlooked the Phillip Island bridge. The five-member panel was presiding from behind a long table on a platform facing a couple of dozen chairs, less than half of which were occupied.

I recognised one of the panel members as Alan Bunting, the National Party member for the Mallee, semi-desert country a long way from the wave-lapped littoral. A genial, slightly tubby thirty-year-old, he owed his seat in parliament to the depth of his father's pockets. The Nats were the junior partner in the ruling coalition, and Alan was very much a junior Nat.

The other familiar face belonged to the chairman, Dudley Wilson, a big bluff fellow in his sixties with bulldog jowls and tragic blow-dried hair. Wilson was the leading light of GoVic, a cabal of business identities and civic worthies that served as a kind of kitchen cabinet to the Premier. Slash-and-burn free-market ideologues to a man.

I wondered why a high-flyer like Wilson was chairing such a low-key advisory committee. Dudley Wilson didn't waste his attention on anything that didn't have a dollar in it.

The only other face I recognised belonged to the civil servant taking minutes. Her name was Gillian Zarek. During Labor's time in office, I'd worked with her briefly at Planning and Regional Development. Behind her butterball exterior, Gillian was sharp as a tack. She saw me at the door, gave me a wry smile and used her chins to indicate where I should sit.

I nodded hello to Alan Bunting, then sat and thumbed through the agenda papers. A bloke in a bargain-basement suit was making a submission on behalf of the Sporting Anglers Association, directing his words straight at Dudley Wilson.

'Last time I saw a face like that,' he was saying, 'it had a hook in it.'

Wishful thinking, I realised. He was, in fact, affirming the ongoing commitment of the recreational fishing sector to managed bio-diversity. It was already evident that the Coastal Management Advisory Panel was going to be an arid source of diversion.

Over the next ninety minutes, the bio-sustainable line-dangler was succeeded by speakers from the Surf Lifesaving Association, the Shipwreck Heritage Trust, Disability Access and a group opposed to the dumping of raw sewage into the Gippsland lake system. Proceedings drifted like the continents, the room was overheated and my attention soon wandered out the window.

The seagulls had quit the gutting-sink. They were perched on the railing of the bridge, grooming their plumage. An incoming tide inched across the mud-flats. A wet-suited sailboard rider tacked back and forth. A gaff-rigged couta boat sailed out of the marina at the tip of Phillip Island, then sailed back in. The customary Greeks bobbed for squid off the jetty.

At 12:45, Dudley Wilson announced the lunch adjournment.

Alan Bunting immediately pounced. 'Hello, Murray. You're doing duty for Moira Henley, so I've been given to understand. You'll be joining us for lunch, of course.'

He led me into a room where the official party was lining up, plates in hand, at a buffet table laid with platters of prawn salad, breadcrumbed calamari rings and a baked schnapper with a slice of pimento-stuffed olive over its oven-roasted eyeball.

'You know our chairman, of course,' Bunting said, manoeuvring me towards Dudley Wilson.

Wilson regarded me over his jowls. We'd once exchanged a brief handshake at some public event. Wilson nodded, remembering, and I nodded back. Then, casting a disdainful glance at the buffet, he pulled a mobile phone from his jacket pocket and walked away, dialling as he went.

Bunting introduced me to the other suits, a cross-section of the ruling demographic. An old boy, a wide boy and a bean counter. I made some tiny-talk over a plate of prawn salad, then slipped outside for a breath of air. I found Gillian Zarek sitting at a log picnic table on the foreshore, eating a sandwich from a paper bag. We exchanged hellos and agreed that the weather was indeed splendid for the time of year.

'So what's the story with Dudley Wilson?' I said. 'This is a bit downmarket for a big wheel like Dud, isn't it?'

Gillian wiped her fingers on a paper napkin, mock-dainty.

'Dudley Wilson is a well-known philanthropist, always attentive to the voice of the community.'

A trio of pelicans wheeled overhead, wings spread, then splashed down near the jetty.

'And that's a fine flight of pigs,' I said.

Gillian chortled. 'I could speculate, I suppose. But strictly in a personal capacity.'

I ran fingertips across my lips, zipping them shut. Gillian dropped her voice, although there was nobody within hearing range.

'This public input stuff, it's just window-dressing,' she said. 'A couple more meetings like this, then the real agenda will emerge. The privatisation of public assets along the coast. Camping grounds, piers, lighthouses, they'll all be flogged to commercial operators, turned into theme parks, resort hotels and pay-per-view whale-watching towers. This panel will recommend who gets what and how much they pay. As its chairman, Dudley Wilson will be uniquely situated to identify the easy-money opportunities.'

'Nice work if you can get it,' I said. The function of the government, after all, was to transfer wealth from public to private hands.

'Big cuts in the department's field staff are also on the cards,' Gillian continued. 'Park rangers, fisheries officers and so forth. They'll say it's more cost-effective to use contract labour.'

'Flexible types who can be persuaded that jet-skis and dolphins are a natural mix.'

Gillian balled her empty sandwich bag and flicked it into a nearby litter bin. 'Exactly.'

We contemplated the prospect in morose silence. For the

moment, it was just speculation. In time, it would be a *fait accompli*. Either way, there was nothing we could do about it.

I left Gillian with the pelicans, took a turn down the jetty, then returned for the afternoon session. The panel was settling back into place, preparing to hear from the Friends of the Ninety Mile Beach. Alan Bunting beckoned me over. 'Forgot to mention,' he said. 'There's a bit of a boat trip afterwards. A tour of Seal Rocks in the Natural Resources launch. You're invited, of course. Privilege of rank and all that. Three-fifteen at the jetty, unless you have to hurry back for some union conclave at the Trades Hall.'

I indulged his little joke with a self-deprecating shrug. 'I'll check,' I said. 'Thanks for the invite.'

Frankly there was scant appeal in the prospect of being stuck on a boat with a bunch of government placemen, a young fogey and a corrupt henchman of the Premier. Seals, I thought as I took my seat, waving their flippers and bellowing. It'll be just like parliament.

Proceedings resumed, first with the beach lovers then the Charter Boat Operators Association. As the voices droned, my thoughts returned to the coroner's report. Not that I had any doubt about the verdict.

The facts of the case were simple. Two career criminals, Adrian Parish and Rodney Syce, used smuggled explosives to blast their way out of the Remand Centre, where they were being held for sentencing. Both were looking at major time—Parish for robbing a bank, Syce for an aggravated burglary in which he bashed an elderly man.

Their escape was well planned and aided from the outside. The bike was waiting nearby, a stolen Kawasaki racer, key in the ignition. Syce was the rider. Taking advantage of the rush-hour traffic, the pair made a daring and dangerous dash through the congested streets of the central city and under the tree canopy of the Fitzroy Gardens.

They might well have got away if not for a couple of rookie cops en route to the bingle outside the Hilton. Responding to the radio alert, the young cops intercepted the escapees as they emerged from the gardens. Parish died in hospital that evening, a police bullet in his lung.

The Kawasaki was found in a laneway in nearby Richmond. But the police dragnet closed on empty air. Syce had evaporated.

Lines of enquiry were pursued, screws applied, trees shaken. The bike was supplied by one of Parish's crim associates, a small-timer. On Parish's instructions, he put two pistols in the pannier. Only one gun was recovered, so the other was presumably taken by Syce. But as to Syce himself, Parish's mate didn't know him, had no idea where he'd gone or might be.

Initially, the police were confident. Syce wouldn't get far, they swore. He was no mastermind. He would leave a trail. It was just a matter of time before he was back in custody, facing the consequences. Cold comfort, they admitted, but the only kind they could promise.

But that wasn't what happened. Fuck all was what happened. Weeks, months, a year passed. Old leads petered out. New leads failed to emerge. Finally, someone senior decided to bring on the coronial hearing into Lyndal's death. The attendant publicity might refresh the memory of the public. Or prick a guilty conscience.

So Lyndal's inquest, which should have been the formal

administrative response to a death in a public place, became a desperate media stunt.

I played my part. I stood in the box and gave my eye-witness account. I was the grieving widower at press conferences and Coroner's Court door-stops, appealing for anybody with pertinent information to come forward.

The net outcome was a fat zero.

And now, months later, the slow-turning wheels of justice were grinding out the formal verdict. Again the media would turn its fleeting attention to Lyndal. Again the coals of memory would be fanned. Again the police would call for anyone with information to ring the Crime Stoppers hotline. Again they would present themselves as resolute and tireless. In fact, they were clueless, incapable even of tracking down a petty crim with no known associates in the state.

Useless bastards.

The last speaker of the day, a representative of the Abalone Industry Association, was finishing his presentation. Sober of suit and careful with his words, he came across more like a lawyer than a man who made his living by scraping marine snails off submerged rocks, 'reminding the panel that the legal abalone catch is worth $50 million a year to this state. The ongoing sustainability of the industry depends on government willingness to tackle the issues confronting it.'

Dudley Wilson cleared his throat and peered down from the table. 'On behalf of the panel, I thank you for your input. Your views will be given every consideration when we are framing our recommendations.' He then declared the meeting adjourned until a date to be advised.

It was just on the dot of three o'clock. Unable to contain

the urge, I scurried out to the Magna and twiddled the radio dial across the hourly bulletins. French nuke Pacific atoll. Again. Princess Diana denies bonking rugger bugger. Government approves further casino expansion. No mention of the inquest.

I decided to take the boat ride after all. The temperature was holding nicely, the sky appeared benign and almost four hours of daylight remained. I shed my tie, traded my suit jacket for the sweatshirt in my gym bag, and headed for the jetty.

The Department of Natural Resources launch was moored at a landing near the berths of the commercial fishing fleet, motor idling, exhausts burbling at the waterline. It was a seven-metre fibreglass-hulled cabin cruiser with a covered cockpit and a small rear deck. A youngish bloke in a khaki windbreaker with DNR shoulder flashes was standing on the jetty, issuing life-jackets to Dudley Wilson and Alan Bunting.

Wilson had changed into boat shoes and a thigh-length navy-blue waterproof jacket with big flap pockets and cord piping. A regular outdoorsman, Dud. Must have cut quite a swell at the yacht club regatta. Bunting, still in his suit and tie, bulged from his bright yellow buoyancy vest like an animated grapefruit. I took a jacket and fastened it over my windcheater.

The three other panellists were coming along the jetty. Before they reached us, they were overtaken by a solidly built bloke of middle years in a DNR windbreaker. He spoke to them briefly, erasing the air with his hands and shrugging his shoulders. Then, leaving them milling uncertainly, he continued to where we stood beside the launch. He had

Popeye forearms, a pepper-and-salt buzz-cut and a face like a pontiac potato.

'Bill Sutherland,' he announced. 'DNR fisheries compliance. Sorry, gents. Trip's off.'

Wilson scowled. This smacked of disrespect, poor organisation. 'I'm Dudley Wilson,' he said. 'Chairman of the Coastal Management Advisory Panel. What's the problem?'

'Bottom line, Mr Wilson, operational priorities. Follow-up on tip-off re possible illegal activity.'

Commodore Wilson was dressed for seafaring and he wasn't about to be brushed off. 'What do you mean, illegal activity?'

'*Possible* illegal activity,' Sutherland repeated. 'Half an hour away. *Suspected* unlawful taking of abalone. Boat access only. And this is the only boat we've got in this part of the state. Long story short, got to gazump your sight-seeing trip. No choice. Sorry.'

He didn't look sorry at all. He looked like he could think of a hundred better uses for the departmental launch than ferrying freeloading pollies around Seal Rocks.

'Listen here,' said Wilson. 'This could be a very good opportunity to get a first-hand perspective on some of the issues being examined by our panel. What say we come along?'

Sutherland shook his head. 'No can do. Due respect, Mr Wilson, fisheries enforcement isn't a spectator sport.'

'Not spectators,' insisted Wilson. 'Official observers.'

Sutherland rubbed the back of his neck, not quite sure how to deal with Wilson's persistence.

'I'll make sure your superiors are made aware of your co-operation,' Wilson continued. Or the opposite, the implication was clear. 'We won't get in your way, I assure you.' He looked to Bunting and me to back him up. 'Isn't that right?'

Alan Bunting started to unfasten his life-jacket. 'I'm not sure about this, Dudley. There's probably regulations or something.'

'Suit yourself,' said Wilson. 'What about you, Whelan?'

As much as I disliked being co-opted by Wilson, I had to agree that reconnoitring abalone poachers sounded a lot more interesting than gawking at seals.

'Your decision,' Sutherland jumped aboard. 'But we haven't got all day.'

Wilson boarded. Bunting hesitated, then joined him. Me too. Sutherland took the console while the deck hand cast off the lines. Three minutes later, we were motoring down the main channel. When we cleared the sandbanks, Sutherland opened the throttle, veered east and let rip. The bow slapped the waves, raising plumes of spray.

We ran parallel to the shore, a kilometre or so out from a line of ragged cliffs and blunt headlands. The shelter of Westernport Bay lay behind us now. This was Bass Strait, a notorious stretch of water. Come a change of weather, it would rear up and throw huge waves against the coast, smashing a craft like ours to matchwood.

My innards were churning, rising and falling with the motion of the boat. Bunting, too, had gone a little green around the gills. Wilson was loving it. He stood at the stern, eyes narrowed, scanning the horizon. Captain Pugwash rides again. When spray swept his face, he wore it like a complimentary spritz of Old Spice.

Once we were well under way, the deckie took the helm and Sutherland joined us for a proper round of introductions.

He might not have been happy about running a passenger service, but he had enough professional sense not to waste an opportunity.

'One of the last viable abalone habitats in the world,' he declared, sweeping his arm along the line of coves and cliffs, his voice raised above the thrum of the engine. 'Shallow-water reefs, plenty of wave action. The abalone feed on specks of pulverised kelp.'

Wilson didn't want a natural history lesson. 'Tell us about these poachers,' he said.

'If that's what they are,' said Sutherland. 'Shore-based, most poaching. Less conspicuous that way. All you need's a snorkel and a lever to prise the buggers off the rocks. But our tip-off says these guys are diving off a boat, using breathing apparatus. Could be recreational, looking for an old wreck or something, forgot to hoist their blue-and-white. Could be not so innocent. Weather like this, chance to work a reef you can't get to from the land. Harvest as many abs as possible, take off before they're noticed.'

The wind bit through my pants and the sleeves of my sweatshirt. My stomach churned. An endless swell rippled towards us from the horizon and sludgy clouds were advancing from the west. The sky was the colour of a dirty sheep. I took deep, regular breaths and considered moving down into the cabin. Pride got the better of me. I didn't want to look like a wimp in front of Dudley Wilson.

'Lot of abalone poaching, is there?' I asked Sutherland.

'Enough,' he said. 'Used to be a cottage industry. Collect the public bag limit, ten a day, sell them to restaurants for cash. Huge demand in Asia these days. Big profits, professional crims.'

'I've never understood the appeal,' said Wilson. 'Underwater escargot, they call it. Tastes like shoe-leather to me. Give me a crayfish any day. Or a good feed of oysters.'

At the mention of food, my prawn salad lunch stood up and saluted. I clamped my jaws shut and breathed through my nose. Alan Bunting went a greener shade of pale.

'Can't be farmed,' said Sutherland. 'Unlike oysters. When it's gone, it's gone. California, Canada, Japan, nix. A high-value fish-stock…'

Fish-stock. The word conjured bouillabaisse. First the name, then the smell. My stomach lurched. 'So what's the drill if this lot are poaching,' I said quickly, chasing the subject elsewhere. 'You arrest them, or what?'

'Try,' said Sutherland. 'But if they resist, our options are limited. Like our means of self-defence. The minister's just taken away our sidearms.'

'Quite right, too,' said Wilson. 'Since when do fishing inspectors need to go armed? Let civil servants carry guns, who knows where it'll stop? Look at America.'

'With respect,' said Sutherland. 'For forty years officers of this department carried guns. Never once fired a shot.'

'So you're not going to miss them,' said Wilson.

'Good theory,' said Sutherland. 'Try standing on a rock platform, facing off some desperado with several grand of illegal ab in one hand and a diving knife in the other, nobody around for miles. Mere fact he knows you're armed can be a big help.'

Bunting took a deep breath and lurched into the conversation, obliged to support the decision of the minister, a fellow Nat. 'But you can call in the police, right?'

'True,' said Sutherland. 'Subject to operational availability.'

San Remo was far behind us, long vanished over the horizon. The next settlement on the coast, Inverloch, was fifty kilometres to the east. Five hundred metres away, the southern edge of the Australian continent was a line of abraded bluffs, sandstone cliffs rising to a wind-swept hinterland.

'And where exactly are the nearest police?' I asked.

'Wonthaggi,' said Sutherland.

Wonthaggi was somewhere inland. A three-cop town. Definitely no helicopter.

'Main strategy, deterrence. Patrolling. Maintaining a presence. Surveillance. Avoid confrontation until we've got full control of the situation.'

Sutherland resumed control of the helm and steered the launch closer inshore. The tide washed across a platform of pitted rock that extended outwards from the base of the cliffs, rising and falling like the breathing of some vast living creature.

We rounded a stubby headland and Sutherland dropped the motor into neutral, letting us drift across the mouth of a sheltered cove with a half-moon beach of crushed shells.

A boat was moored in the cove, a chunky beige-coloured craft, a box sitting on two fibreglass hulls. A wiry type in shorts, tennis shoes and a woollen sweater was emptying a bucket over the side. Fiftyish, grizzled, a short ponytail sticking out the back of his peaked cap. As soon as he saw us, he grabbed a hose that was running into the water and gave it a solid jerk.

'Shark-cat, twin 200-horsepower Yamaha outboards.' Sutherland raised binoculars. 'Registration number concealed with duct tape.'

It was about a hundred metres away. Bunting craned for a view. Wilson firmed his jaw, a representative of law and order. I wondered what the hell I was doing there.

A figure in a hooded wetsuit surfaced beside the shark-cat. He hurried aboard, hauling the hose up behind him. Ponytail was firing up the Yamahas.

As the shark-cat began to move, Sutherland opened the throttle.

As it gathered momentum, the shark-cat rose on hydroplanes, skimming the water. It raced for the far side of the cove, a Formula One shoebox.

The hooded diver ducked under the canopy, his shoulders hunched, no more than a black shape. Ponytail glanced back over his shoulder, his lugubrious weather-seamed face clearly visible. When the young DNR crewman emerged from the cabin with a video camera, he pulled down the bill of his hat and flipped us the bird.

We gave chase, heading to intercept. The shark-cat hugged the shore, taking advantage of its shallow draft. Sutherland swung the launch into deeper water, steering a curved course. As we chopped at the swell, the launch tilted and rocked. So did my stomach.

Whoah, I thought. Pass. Not today, thanks. Enough already. A surge of nausea lapped at my Plimsoll line, tasting of curdled mayonnaise and masticated crustacean. I wished I was anywhere else, as long as it wasn't moving.

Lunch wanted out. And it got what it wanted. A fountain of hot lava, it hurtled upwards. I lunged for the side and barfed into the briny. I retched again. Sour milk and corn flakes, this time.

Then, without warning, a stream of berley erupted from Dudley Wilson's mouth and hit Alan Bunting in the face. This was not how the Nats usually spoke to each other, except at woolshed dances. Aghast, Bunting staggered backwards, gagging. At that moment, the deck tilted as the launch banked, turning to intercept the shark-cat. Bunting, struggling to find his footing, skidded on Wilson's mess and toppled overboard.

He hit the water with a splash, then vanished in the churn of our wake. Wilson leaned over the side and finished parking the tiger. Bunting bobbed to the surface and raised an arm, as if attempting to hail a cab.

Sutherland was already on the case. The launch slewed around, circling back. My head throbbed and a bilious taste filled my mouth. Wilson wiped his mouth with the back of his hand, squared his jaw and resumed his Captain Queeg stance, as though nothing had happened. The deckie reached with a gaff and hooked Bunting as we came around. In short order, he was being manhandled up the stern ladder like a disconsolate dugong.

Wilson tried to help, but Bunting wasn't having it. 'B-back off,' he hyperventilated, snatching back his arm. His teeth were chattering and torrents streamed from his ruined suit and pooled around his sodden brogues. Unbuckling his life-vest with trembling fingers, he let the crewman lead him down into the cabin. 'Th-thanks, m-mate,' he said. 'Wh-what's your name?'

'Ian. Mind the step.'

The shark-cat was rounding the point, running for open water. 'That's torn it,' said Sutherland, his binoculars trained on the mocking V of its wake. 'Never get near them now.'

'But can't you radio...' started Wilson.

Sutherland lowered the field glasses. 'No point, pace they're travelling,' he said through clenched teeth. 'Didn't even get a chance to hail them. So if your stomach is now settled, Mr Wilson, I suggest you wait below while we try to find out what our thieving friends were up to.' He turned to me. 'You too.'

I followed Wilson down into the tiny cabin. Alan Bunting was already occupying most of the space. Stripped to his jocks, he towelled his pudgy, goose-pimpled flesh with ill-concealed irritation. The deckie, Ian, handed him a fluorescent orange wetsuit. 'This'll keep you warm until we get back.'

Bunting squeezed into it, looking daggers at Wilson. 'You might as well have pushed me,' he said.

'You've had a nasty shock,' said Wilson. 'But I hope you're not suggesting it was my fault.'

'You spewed in my face.'

'Not deliberately,' said Wilson. 'You're just not used to boats, that's all. No reason to be embarrassed.'

'*Embarrassed?*' He looked like a giant orange gum-drop.

I wedged myself into a seat and buried my face in my hands. I needed to wash out my mouth, but didn't dare move for fear of another up-chuck. The vibrations of the engine came up through the seat, compounding the movement of the boat. Bunting and Wilson bickered. Misery enveloped me.

We returned to the place where the shark-cat was parked when we first spotted it. Sutherland cut the engine and dropped anchor. Ian changed into a wetsuit and went over the side, snorkelled and flippered. He made a slow circuit, occasionally disappearing below the surface. When he climbed back aboard, he held up an abalone shell. The light caught its opalescent interior.

He and Sutherland conferred in an undertone at the stern, then Sutherland stuck his head into the cabin. 'How you feeling?' he asked Alan Bunting.

Bunting made a brave face. 'Sorry about this,' he said.

Sutherland nodded, then handed the crusted shell to Wilson. 'Hundreds of these down there. They were shucking them on board, probably stashing the meat in hidden compartments. Couple of grand's worth, just here. At it since dawn, different spots. Day's take, before we interrupted them, maybe ten thousand dollars.'

Wilson examined the palm-sized shell gravely, as if appraising an antique.

'Pity we had to abort before we IDed them,' said Sutherland. 'Top it off, I'll be carpeted for letting you lot come along.'

Wilson tried to hand back the shell.

'Keep it,' said Sutherland. 'Souvenir. Best get you back to San Remo ASAP.'

After we'd been under way for ten minutes, sipping sugary instant coffee from the launch thermos, Wilson broke our self-imposed silence. 'When this gets around, we'll be a laughing stock,' he said. 'Throwing up. Falling overboard.'

I slowly raised my head. 'Stuffing up a fisheries enforcement operation,' I croaked. 'The press are going to love it. Given any thought to your resignation letter, Mr Coastal Policy Chairman?'

Wilson narrowed his eyes and looked me over closely. 'This Sutherland.' He jerked his thumb upwards. 'You want him to lose his job?'

'The cuts you've got in mind,' I said. 'He'll probably lose it anyway.'

Wilson leaned forward and stuck his face in mine. For an awful moment, I could see the stream of spew flying from his rubbery gob. Worse, I could smell it. I flinched and turned away. Wilson gave a satisfied grunt and, dipping out of the cabin door, stood at the console talking to Sutherland.

'I don't think it's right,' whined Alan Bunting. 'Trying to make political capital out of a situation like this. I'll have to resign from the panel, too. And it wasn't my fault. If anyone's the injured party, I am.'

I didn't know where to begin to answer that one, so I didn't try. They mustn't have offered Politics 101 at agricultural college.

Wilson returned. 'He wants to talk to you,' he said.

I found Sutherland seated at the wheel, driving towards the low-slung sun, surveying the way ahead through oversized Sunaroids. 'Beautiful, isn't it?' he said.

I took a deep, stomach-settling breath of air and absorbed the view. It swept across a burnished sea from weathered sandstone cliffs at our starboard to pink-edged billows of cloud on the southern horizon. 'Magnificent,' I agreed.

'Like your job, Mr Whelan?' said Sutherland. 'Think it's worth doing?'

'Sometimes,' I said.

Sutherland tilted his head back, master of all he surveyed. 'Love mine,' he said. 'Pretty good at it too I reckon, all things considered. Less than fifty of us fish dogs, you know. More than seventeen hundred kilometres of coastline.'

'You've done a deal with Wilson,' I said. 'And I'm the fly in the ointment.'

Sutherland shrugged. 'What if that Bunting bloke had drowned?'

'No chance of that,' I said. 'Too buoyant. Completely empty head.'

'Tell that to the committee of enquiry, just before they transfer me to shore patrol ticketing dog owners for crapping on the beach. Thought you might understand. Being Labor.'

I heaved a defeated sigh. 'Yeah, all right,' I said. 'None of this happened. And if it did, I didn't see it. Just get me back on dry land pronto, okay?'

The light was fading when we cruised into the San Remo boat harbour. Up on the Phillip Island bridge, the coaches were bumper-to-bumper, packed with tourists bound for the twilight parade of penguins waddling ashore at the rookeries.

I hit the dock as soon as we tied up, glad to have something solid beneath my feet. Next time I got on a boat, I promised myself, it would be nothing smaller than the *Queen Mary*.

It was nearly six o'clock. I walked down the jetty, past the fishermen's co-operative and into the front bar of the Westernport Hotel. Three blokes in working clobber were nursing beers at the bar, swapping monotones. A bunch of bozos were playing pool, their banter lost in the plink-plink of the poker machines from the gaming lounge. 'Wheel of

Fortune' was showing on the box above the bar. I parked on a stool and ordered a Jameson's. 'Straight up,' I told the barman, a girl in a Jim Beam tee-shirt. 'Water on the side.'

I diluted the whiskey and sipped, letting it settle my stomach. When the television news began, I tipped the last of it down my throat and signalled for another.

The inquest story came after the first ad break. The state coroner, the newsreader reported, had found that Lyndal Luscombe, thirty-five, was murdered by convicted felon Rodney Syce during a break-out from the Melbourne Remand Centre.

Of course it was fucking murder. It was murder the instant that the motorbike slammed into Lyndal. You kill somebody while you're escaping from jail, it's murder. Not manslaughter. Not involuntary homicide. Not reckless driving. Not oops. Murder, plain and simple.

Lyndal's picture filled the screen, a full-length shot cropped from a portrait taken at her cousin's wedding in late '93. She was laughing, crinkling her nose at the camera like a naughty schoolkid.

'Despite an extensive search here and interstate, Syce remains at large,' continued the newsreader's voice.

The screen filled with a mug-shot. It showed a thick-lipped, round-faced man with a receding brow and dark, surly eyes. He looked like one of those guys who stand at road works, directing traffic with a lollipop sign. The sort of face you see, but don't register.

'Police are hopeful that the coroner's finding will result in new information that may lead them to Syce.'

Vision cut to a sleek, fortyish man in a fashionable suit and rimless glasses standing on the steps of the Coroner's

Court. A caption identified him as Detective Sergeant Damian Meakes. 'This man Syce is dangerous and absolutely desperate,' he said, leaning forward into the camera, one hand holding down his tie. 'Anyone who believes they might have seen him on the day of the escape or any time since, or has any other information, should contact the Syce Task Force or Crime Stoppers. Under no circumstances should members of the public approach him directly.'

And that was it. Sixty seconds, tops. My second whiskey was on the bar. I slammed it down neat and stomped out the door, fire raging in my belly.

The sea was purple with the last shreds of the day and the air was acrid with rotting seaweed and diesel fumes. I put the key in the ignition of the Magna and drove across the bridge to Phillip Island. I went past a tourist information booth and a flower farm, down streets with nautical names, following the road through the sand dunes to the rectangle of asphalt beside the Woolamai lifesaving club.

A half-dozen vehicles were parked overlooking the beach. Sedans, tradesmen's utilities and a panel van with roof-racks. Solitary men sat in two of the cars, gazing out at the monotonous pounding of the surf. Sad, lonely fucks like me, pining their lives away.

Should I ball my fist and bang on their windows, I wondered? Tear open my shirt and display the scar where my heart had been torn out? Defy them to outdo my wounds? Squat with them in the tufted dunes and howl like a stricken animal at the rising moon?

I lit a cigarette from my emergency pack in the glovebox and sat on the topmost plank of the wooden steps leading down to the sand, shoulders hunched against the deepening chill.

Aeons ago, I'd surfed here at Woolamai. Driven down with friends from university, spent a weekend catching the break that unfurled beyond the sandbank. But tonight the waves of Woolamai were not surfable, not by me anyway. They reared up, menacing black walls, their crests shredded by the wind, their glassy surface bursting open as they smashed against the shore.

The cigarette made my head spin. I gave it the flick and plodded down the steps to the empty beach, hands buried in my pockets. When I reached the edge of the water, I took off my shoes, stuffed my socks inside, hung them around my neck by the laces and rolled my pants to the knee.

Talk about a fucking wasteland. It wasn't supposed to be like this. We were going to have a daughter. There would be the father, the mother and the children. An affectionate, intelligent, playful, semi-blended family. We would adore each other. The big brother would cherish his little sister. She would worship him. The father would be a competent provider, the beloved butt of his children's teasing. The mother would outshine him and he would glory in her accomplishments. They would all live happily ever after.

Then had come a man on a Kawasaki racer.

The man of my dreams.

Rodney Syce was a light-fingered chancer with a tendency to lose his grip when things got slippery.

The third child of a Darwin construction worker, he was sent to live with elderly relatives in a one-silo town in Western Australia's wheat belt in 1974, after his mother was killed by flying debris during Cyclone Tracy. At fourteen, he was already in trouble with the law. Illegal use of a motor vehicle was the first entry in a ledger that grew to include breaking and entering, possession of stolen goods and trespass. The juvenile court gave him good behaviour bonds and suspended sentences.

I knew this because I'd made it my business to find out.

The cops had told me a certain amount, of course. In the beginning they were falling over themselves to keep me in the picture. Later, when the search became a long-haul operation, they were much less forthcoming. But by then, I'd started making my own enquiries.

Call it a kind of therapy. Or fuel for speculation in the absence of news. Information is currency, they say. I wasn't sure what the facts I was gathering could buy me. Not peace of mind, that's for sure.

I collected newspaper clippings and studied video footage. Read court transcripts. Talked to lawyers, journalists and jailbirds. Pulled what few strings I could still lay my hands on. Assembled a file. Sifted it. Pored over it deep into the night.

Height: 168 cm. Weight: 75 kg. Eyes: dark brown. Distinguishing marks: nil. Criminal history: extensive.

At seventeen, Rodney Syce quit school and headed for Queensland, and a string of short-lived rouseabout and labouring jobs on cattle stations. His first taste of jail came at nineteen, two months for assault and robbery after he rolled a drunk at the Cloncurry races. The magistrate was less exercised by the ninety-seven dollars lifted from the victim's wallet than the metal fence picket used on the back of his head.

Back on the outside, Syce fluctuated between low-wage jobs and petty crime. He worked in canneries, on a prawn trawler, down the Mt Isa mines where he was dismissed for pilfering from the employees' changeroom. Then came a two-year stretch in Boggo Road after he pushed a night watchman down a flight of stairs during a bungled factory break-in. On release, he took up with a gang of Brisbane car thieves. That ended when he bashed the employee of a dodgy panel-beater with a steering-wheel lock. She turned out to be the girlfriend of a local heavy. On the wrong side of both the cops and the crims, he hightailed it to Melbourne.

Within a month, he was back in custody. Disturbed during a daylight burg in South Yarra, he belted the householder, an eighty-two-year-old retired judge, with an antique inkstand. The old beak went down squeezing his heart-attack alarm. The ambulance arrived just as Syce was coming out the front door, making like he lived there. The paramedics, burly boys, sat on him until the cops arrived.

In his ten-year life of crime, Rodney Syce had generated enough paperwork for a psychological profile to emerge. In layman's terms, he was a gutless mongrel, a coward given to unprovoked outbursts of violence, a loner who had trouble maintaining relationships with other people.

Except in prison. There, Syce seemed to find the sort of society he craved. Quick to suss the pecking order, he found ways of attaching himself to a high-status inmate, some means of making himself useful to a top dog.

Someone like Adrian Parish. At fifty-three, Parish was king of the heap in remand. An armed robber and old-school all-rounder, he was a tiler by trade. He had a reputation for covering his tracks well and keeping his head down between jobs. He used violence only when he believed it was necessary. Shooting at coppers to avoid arrest, for example. And, although he'd been charged with dozens of offences, he had a knack for beating the rap. In a thirty-five-year career as a professional criminal, he'd served a mere eight years and seven months of jail time.

But Parish had run out of luck. An armoured-truck heist had turned to shit. Shots were fired. A guard had a coronary embolism and nearly died. Dye-bombs spoiled the cash. When fingerprint fragments were found in the burned-out getaway car, the driver rolled over. Parish was rousted from his marital bed at 5 a.m., charged with everything but indecent exposure, committed to the County Court for jury trial, found guilty and remanded for sentencing. The judge was poised to throw the book. The way things were going, Adrian Parish would be a very old man by the time he got out of prison.

But while he was waiting for sentence, Rodney Syce entered his orbit. And Rodney had qualities that Adrian appreciated. He could ride a motorbike and do what he was told.

The sands of Woolamai beach had turned to grey. The sky and the sea were seamless. The breaking waves advanced, line after line, roaring like distant artillery.

If I had a gun, I told myself, I'd kill Rodney Syce. Do it with my bare hands if necessary. If I ever found him, came face-to-face with him, saw him walking down the street.

But I knew that it was just as well I didn't have a gun. If I had a gun, I might already have taken revenge.

Three times I'd spotted Syce. The first was during the AFL grand final. The Eagles were thrashing the Cats. Late in the last quarter, Peter Matera darted from the pack and took a stab for goal. The ball went wide and sailed into the crowd. Fans rose, reaching to grab it. A camera tracked the action, magnifying the image on the electronic scoreboard. One of those who reached for the incoming pigskin was Rodney Syce.

I knew him as soon as I saw him. He had a beanie pulled down around his ears, a West Coast scarf swathing his neck. Probably figured he could pass unnoticed, one of thousands decked out in blue and yellow.

I came up out of my seat, fumbling for my mobile,

dashing down the stairs to the section of terrace where the ball had landed, jabbering at the task-force detective who picked up the phone. Then the full-time siren blew and the crowd was streaming for the exits, ninety-seven thousand people in motion.

Even before the last of the fans had dispersed, two dicks were sitting with me in the stadium's media centre, running the tape over and over, slow-motion and freeze-frame. Yes, they agreed, the guy did look a bit like Syce. It was possibly him. But within a week, it wasn't. The seat was bought with a credit card by a retired librarian from Warrandyte. The lead was scratched.

The second time I saw Syce, he was coming out of a service station on the Hume Highway near Wangaratta. It was Boxing Day and I was driving back after spending Christmas with Lyndal's parents at their orchard near Beechworth. It was their first Christmas without her, Red was in Sydney with Wendy, and I hadn't seen Lyndal's family since the funeral. We ate roast turkey on the screened veranda and sat not saying much in the listless afternoon heat and I slept on a trundle bed on the floor between two near strangers who would have been my brothers-in-law if not for Rodney Syce.

An hour into the trip home, I was filling the tank at a roadhouse pump when a man came out the gas-station door and got into a dust-covered Falcon. Wraparound sunglasses, stringy goatee, but Syce all right, no doubt in my mind. I bolted inside to the cashier. 'That guy just left, you know him?'

The cashier shook her head, I grabbed the phone and the Falcon was intercepted at roadblock just south of

Glenrowan. The driver came out with his hands in the air, babbling that he'd paid already, the cheque must have been held up in the Christmas mail. An unlicensed driver with $900 in outstanding speeding fines. A win of sorts, but not Rodney Syce. Not by a country mile.

After my third sighting, I had a house-call from Detective Sergeant Damian Meakes of the Syce Task Force.

I'd never warmed to Meakes. He seemed bloodless and far too style-conscious for a copper. Four-button suit and designer spectacles. Talked to me down his nose.

'A courtesy call, Mr Whelan,' he informed me. Courtesy my arse. He'd brought a social worker with him, a sincere young thing with spaniel eyes and a Masters in Hand-holding.

'Sightings of this kind aren't uncommon, Murray,' the Victim Liaison Officer reassured me earnestly. 'They're a recognised coping mechanism. A victim's way of dealing with feelings of helplessness and frustration. Even guilt.'

'Guilt?' I said. Syce was the guilty one. And so, I was beginning to think, were the rozzers. Guilty of gross fucking incompetence. 'First you let this prick escape, then you fail to catch him.'

'Your anger is perfectly understandable,' cooed the VLO.

'If I want my bumps read,' I told her, 'I'll find somebody better qualified than a cop shrink.'

There was no more counselling after that. I did, however, receive a phone call from the Chief Commissioner. One of the privileges of my parliamentary rank was to have the balm dispensed from the highest level. But it was the same old balm. The recapture of Rodney Syce, the CC assured me, remained an ongoing priority. But it was probable that he'd left the state, possibly even the country, so an arrest might be some time in coming. In the meantime, the chances of my lucking upon him were low. And I was helping nobody by cracking the shits with his officers.

I ate crow, right and proper. Thanked him for taking the time. Promised I wouldn't trouble the constabulary again, not unless I had substantial cause. Offered my assistance, should an appropriate occasion arise. That's when he pitched the idea of fast-tracking the inquest.

And now the inquest had come and gone, another milestone on the road to nowhere. Syce was the free man and I was a prisoner of self-pity and hunger for revenge, so bent out of shape that it sometimes took all my strength to keep hold of the things that made life worth living.

The surf raged and pounded. I let the icy tide wash over my feet, felt the tug into oblivion.

But this too solid flesh refused to melt. It stood there, barefoot in the freezing water, shivering. Get a fucking grip, I told myself.

Nothing could bring Lyndal back. It was time to stop wallowing in misery and dreams of revenge. Time to concentrate on the here and now. Count my whatnots.

For a year and a half, the folds of my wallet had held the ultrasound photograph of the embryo in Lyndal's belly. The girl-child with the joke name. Lysistrata Luscombe-Whelan. Had she been born, she'd be almost a year old, crawling around the kitchen, playing merry hell with the pots and pans.

I opened my wallet, took out the picture and touched it to my lips. I placed it gently on the swirling foam and watched the tide carry it away. As I waited for the moment when it disappeared into the embrace of the sea, the sharp clap of a breaker rang out. Above the far horizon, Venus was rising.

Then I was splashing forward, calf-deep, grabbing at the photograph, wiping it dry on my chest.

This wasn't over yet.

A soft rain was falling by the time I got home from San Remo. It continued to fall, in varying degrees of softness, for most of the next six weeks. In Melbourne we call it spring.

If the coronial circus provided any new leads, the police didn't share the fact with me. To the best of my knowledge, Rodney Syce remained no closer to capture than he was on the day he killed Lyndal.

From time to time, I bumped into Alan Bunting in the corridors of Parliament House. We did not speak of the sea. Red's eight came third in its heat at the rowing carnival. By early November it was still raining but the air grew a fraction warmer each day. I began to consider destinations for the summer break.

The Legislative Council of Victoria was designed by its colonial fathers as a brake on progress. It did the job well. As the spring session began to peter out, it sat for only two or three days a week. To fill the available time, the parliamentary party turned its energies to a new round of factional warfare.

The Australian Labor Party is composed of two main factions. Them and Us. Ideologically distinct only at their extremities, their function is the distribution of spoils. But fighting over the spoils of defeat was a ritual for which I could muster little enthusiasm. For the moment, I was content to lick my private wounds and leave the backstabbing to others.

Certain party obligations, however, remained inescapable. One of these was the annual Melbourne Upper fund-raising dinner and trivia quiz night. That year, it was held on the second Friday in November. As usual, the venue was La Luna, a restaurant near the Moonee Valley racetrack. Steaks and seafood a speciality.

La Luna's proprietor, Tony Melina, once fancied himself as something of a player and helped round up some stray Italian votes in the preselection contest for the local federal member. But that was years ago. Business had long since taken precedence over politics, and Tony's involvement in the party was ancient history. But he always gave us a discount price for the fund-raiser, so we stuck with La Luna. Whatever its faults, the Australian Labor Party has a great respect for tradition.

Starting as a check tablecloth and Chianti-bottle candlestick sort of place, La Luna had worked its way steadily upmarket, evolving into Tony's idea of contemporary Mediterranean. The wrought-iron torch sconces and bagged brickwork were superseded by murals in the manner of ancient Roman mosaics. Nymphs and satyrs now peeked from behind *trompe l'oeil* plasterwork. The floor space was expanded and a central bar installed, black marble with onyx inlays and overhead glassware racks. Messalina meets Maserati.

Tony's wife Rita pounced as I came though the door. 'Murray, you big hunk,' she said, offering her cheeks for a peck-peck. 'It's been ages. Getting too high and mighty for your old friends?'

Rita was petite, not yet forty, tight-packed and high-maintenance. She had a haystack of raven hair, sculpted nails and enough gold jewellery to drown a duck. She abducted my arm and dragged me to the bar. 'Your lot are upstairs, getting stuck into the nibbles,' she said. 'Have a quick drink with your auntie Rita before you go up.'

We perched knee-to-knee on tubular chrome barstools and the barman poured two glasses of white wine. Rita locked her big brown eyes onto mine and ran a hand down my arm. 'Still hurting, aren't you, baby?' Her hand settled on my knee.

I shrugged and hid behind my drink. 'Life goes on. And my boy keeps me busy.'

Rita nodded knowingly. 'He must be what, twelve, thirteen now?'

'Fifteen,' I said, glad to be off the hook. 'Doing okay at school. Couldn't ask for better. Yours?' I racked my memory. 'Carla and…'

'Lauren. Both fine. Carla's married now, threatening to make me a grandmother. Lauren's on the overseas trip, waitressing her way around Europe. Must be in the blood.'

'You were never a waitress, Rita,' I smiled. 'Your old man would never have stood for it.'

Rita's father Frank had a furniture emporium just down the street from the electorate office. Rococo, traditional and moderne. An immigrant success story, he had higher hopes for his only daughter than marriage to the boy from the fish'n'chip shop. But when his ambitions were thwarted by teenage passion and its unintended consequences, he copped it sweet. He bankrolled young Tony into the pizza business, but only on condition that his princess never knead the dough or sling the capricciosa.

'Maybe I should take it up,' sighed Rita. 'I need a career now that the chicks have flown from the nest and Tony's busy building an empire.'

She waved her drink with weary forbearance at the starched napery, floral centrepieces and mood lighting, as if fate had condemned her to sit by the fireplace like some shrivelled, black-clad nonna.

'Speaking of Tony,' I said. 'Is he about? I should say hello.'

A party of six were being led to their table by a waitress, a bit of a strudel, a fleshy blonde in her late twenties. One of the men made a joke and she laughed, a little too loud, too saucy. Rita's rings tightened around her wineglass and her lips thinned.

'Tony?' She raised her shoulders a millimetre, a gesture of utter indifference. 'He's around somewhere, handling something.' She lit a Marlboro Lite, exhaled a long stream of smoke and showed me her profile, also utterly indifferent. 'Handles everything around here, Tony does.'

Just then, rescue arrived in the form of Ayisha Celik, my electorate officer. Ayisha and I went back a good ten years, back to the time when she worked at the Turkish Welfare League and I took care of the electorate office in Melbourne Upper. Once upon a time I entertained certain delusions about my chances with the kohl-eyed Levantine looker, but Ayisha was long-since married to a Macedonian mother's boy and was now a mother of three herself.

Since her days at the TWL, Ayisha had worked for the Multicultural Resource Centre and, until the incoming government cut its funding, an advocacy organisation for self-help groups. Foster parents, women's shelters, recovering glue-sniffers, fur-allergic cat-fanciers, you name it. She also worked as Lyndal's campaign manager in the three-way preselection contest that sent me to parliament. She knew Melbourne Upper like the back of her hand. Me, I suspected, she knew even better.

'Started drinking already?' she said. 'Hello, Rita.'

Rita squeezed out a faint smile. 'Hello, Ayisha. Got everything you need?'

Ayisha laid a proprietary hand on my shoulder. 'Except an emcee,' she said. 'Our guest comedian hasn't shown up. Looks like you'll have to do the honours.'

'Duty calls.' I gave Rita a shrug, downed my drink and followed Ayisha's ever-broadening backside towards the stairs.

'What a classic,' said Ayisha over her shoulder. 'You know she's only here tonight because she knew you'd be coming. She had to satisfy her curiosity, get the gossip. Poor Murray, she'll be able to tell the other ladies-who-lunch, what that man needs is a…'

'You make me sound like a train wreck,' I said. 'What's the turn-up?'

'Thirty-two,' she said. 'Even fewer than last year. Frankly, I don't know why they bother. We'll be lucky to cover costs.'

'It's not the money, it's the participation,' I reminded her, as we started up the stairs. 'The only role left for rank-and-file Labor Party members is attending crappy fund-raisers that don't raise any funds.'

We found the party faithful seated at two long tables in the upstairs dining room, tucking into antipasto and forming themselves into teams for the trivia challenge.

The lighting was harsher than downstairs, there were no flowers and the tablecloths were paper. But Tony's special price included complimentary garlic bread and adequate quantities of wine and beer, so nobody was complaining.

I knew almost everybody in the room. They were the bedrock of the local membership. Handers-out of how-to-vote cards and veterans of a thousand pointless meetings. Sentimentalists and failed opportunists. A retired tool-maker and his librarian wife. Three schoolteachers and a nurse. A kid so young he thought the White Australia Policy was an ironic marketing push for a new laundry detergent. I shook a few hands, patted some cardiganed backs, kissed some cheeks. Then Ayisha handed me a list of questions.

'Good evening, friends and comrades.'

Jeers of amiable derision erupted.

'Let's begin with an easy one. For ten points, in what year was the shearers' strike that led to the foundation of the Australian Labor Party?'

'Point of procedure,' shouted somebody up the back.

By ten o'clock we were done. The questions were asked, the jokes shared, the raffle drawn, $235 raised for the collective coffers. For the thousandth time, the outrages of the current administration were reprised. I recited the party line that we'd fight our way back to power at the next election, but I didn't believe it and neither did the troops. Our last years in government were a shambles. We just had to take our lumps and wait for the tide to turn. In the meantime, all we could do was gnash our teeth, rend our garments and commiserate with each other over spaghetti con vongole and Caterers Blend coffee.

As soon as decency permitted, I split.

Back downstairs, the clamour of a hundred diners was bouncing off the walls. Staff flitted between tables, trays laden. There was no sign of Rita. I asked the barman if Tony was in. He pointed his bow tie towards the kitchen door. 'Office,' he said. 'Better knock.'

Beyond the kitchen was a greasy-floored alley stacked with drums of cooking oil and cartons of tinned tomatoes. 'Private,' said the peel-and-stick sign on the door past the staff washroom. I gave a brisk rap.

'Come,' came the command. If Tony was doing any handling, he was doing it very lightly.

I opened the door a fraction and peered though the gap. The office was a windowless cubicle, its every vertical surface layered with pieces of paper. Price lists, invoices, booking sheets, postcards, staff rosters, suppliers' phone numbers, fish identification charts, health department notices, a calendar with a scene of Mt Vesuvius. The horizontal surfaces were cluttered with ring-binders, ledgers, clipboards and phone books.

Tony was sitting at a desk that was pushed against the wall just inside the door, signing some documents. He finished with a flourish, looked up and gave me a broad smile. 'Hey,' he said, spreading his palms in greeting. 'Murray, my man, I was just gunna come up.'

'Sorry to disturb,' I said. 'Couldn't leave without saying

thanks. A friend in need and all that.'

Tony was a stocky, slightly paunchy Neapolitan with a van dyke beard and sleek black hair brushed back from a high receding brow. He wore a charcoal-grey polo shirt under a pale-lemon, crumpled-linen sports jacket, the cuffs pushed back to his hairy forearms, Miami Vice style. Give him a tunic and laurel crown, stick a bunch of grapes in one hand and a Pan pipe in the other, and he wouldn't have looked out of place amid his trattoria satyrs.

'Hey guys,' he said cheerfully. 'Meet Murray Whelan, our local MP. Labor, unfortunately, so knowing him ain't worth shit.'

I put my head around the door and found two other men in the room, one leaning against the filing cabinet, the other sunk in a worn-out armchair. They were observing Tony with amusement, like he was a novelty act, the genial wise guy. This, I imagined, was exactly the effect he was trying for.

The bloke at the filing cabinet was small and neat, well into his fifties. Thick-rimmed spectacles. Brown suit, bland tie. The total package suggested a clerical occupation. Accountancy or somesuch. 'This is Phil...' said Tony.

I nodded hello around the door and Phil nodded back. His eyes sideways behind his glasses, goldfish in a bowl.

'...and Jake Martyn.'

Tony delivered the name with the hint of a flourish. It was one I'd heard before. A name name.

Martyn was a culinary trend-setter, the proprietor of Gusto, a fashionable restaurant in seaside Lorne. A frequent mention in the epicure pages, he was the pioneer of the *dernier cri* in fine dining, a style eponymously called '*con gusto*'. Out with those finicky morsels of yesteryear, the smidgin of scallop on a wasabi wafer, the flutter of quail over an inference of artichokes. In with the hearty mouthful, the port-glazed porterhouse on a shitload of mashed spuds, the pan-seared swordfish with a bottle of beer and a burp.

An embodiment of the pleasures of the table, he was a barrel-chested, generous-gutted man in his early forties with a round, cheerful face, robust shoulder-length hair the colour of old oyster shells and an air of easy affability. He was wearing a just-folks sweater and scuffed hiking boots, as though making it plain he had no time for fussbudget fiddlers with sea-urchin roe.

He came up out of his seat a fraction of an inch, gave me a brief spray of charm and dropped back. 'G'day.'

His charm was the kind you can see coming but don't resent. Through it I sensed that he recognised my name. I was that guy whose girlfriend got killed and sometimes, when people met me for the first time, they didn't quite know how to respond to that fact. Whether to say something or not. Martyn went for not, which was the way I preferred it.

'Ah,' said Tony. 'Here it is, at last.'

The waitress with the flirty laugh appeared beside me in the doorway, a liqueur bottle in one hand, three snifters in the other.

'I'll leave you to it,' I said. 'Thanks again, Tony.'

'We're finished here,' he said, slipping the signed form and some other papers into a manilla envelope and handing it to the accountant type. 'Stick around. Have a drink with us. VSOP.'

The waitress squeezed past me and Tony rose to relieve her of the bottle and glasses. In doing so, he found it impossible to avoid pressing against her. She squirmed free with practised ease, but not before he managed to grind his groin against her rump.

'A tasty drop,' he smirked, sniffing the cork. 'Bring another glass, will you, honey?'

I stepped back to give the waitress plenty of exit room. She raised her eyebrows as she sidled past, and rolled her eyes.

'Not for me,' I said. 'Had a couple of beers upstairs and I'm driving. Don't want to end up blowing into a bag.' Or providing the pretext for a repeat demonstration of Tony's amatory technique. 'Nice meeting you, fellers.'

I went back through the kitchen, amused and wondering. Jake Martyn was a long way out of Tony Melina's league. Finding him at La Luna was like bumping into Coco Chanel in Woolworths. Whatever had lured him there, Tony was keen to impress. There was definitely business in the air. Was Tony trying to flog him something, I wondered?

Vice versa, as it turned out. And Tony paid far too much for it.

I drove down Mount Alexander Road in a thinning trickle of traffic, harness-racing enthusiasts home-bound from the track, then cut through North Melbourne to Dudley Street and parked behind Festival Hall.

The old boxing stadium was looking its age, a relic from the days of 'TV Ringside' and 'Rollerderby', a grimy shed redolent of hotdog water, cork-tipped cigarettes and extinct chewing gum. But, more than just a shrine to the gladiators of the glove, the House of Stoush was also a centre of excellence in the musical arts. Little Richard had played there. The Easybeats. George Thorogood and the Destroyers. The Clash. Dolly Parton.

Tonight, the bands were called Chocolate Starfish, Bum Crack and Toothbrush Messiah. The gig was a cut-price show for under-age punters, sponsored by a zit cream manufacturer. It had just finished and teenagers were pouring from the building, gathering in droopy-jeaned hordes at the kerbside and malingering around the kebab vendors and doughnut caravans. I double-parked across the road from the main entrance and scanned the crowd.

Red was standing with a cluster of kids beside the box-office window. His hair was gelled into a cockatoo crest, his shoulders were slouched and his clothes hung off his frame like a scarecrow. He merged, in short, with the crowd.

I recognised some of the gang, friends and classmates, male and female. They were full of beans, teasing and joking. Their weekend had already begun. I sat watching from the Magna. Red was looming over a smaller kid, listening intently. There seemed something self-conscious about his stance, as though he was making an effort to appear relaxed. His hands were thrust into the back pockets of his jeans and his hip was cocked in an attempt at nonchalance. Then the other kid turned a little and I saw that it was a girl. A wisp of a thing, a pixie-faced waif with chopped hair and cast-off clothes. Her arms were folded across her barely-there chest and she tilted her head sideways when she looked up at Red.

I couldn't place her among the usual suspects, the crowd from school. But, even from thirty metres away, it was plain that she was reaching parts of my boy that hadn't been reached before. Not, at least, to my knowledge.

Girls were nothing special in Red's circle of friends. They were peers, pals, members of the tribe. The boys and girls treated each other with the casual camaraderie of brothers and sisters. But this, if I was not mistaken, was something different. The lad was mooching like a man smitten. Was the young sap rising, I wondered? Was he feeling his oats? Or the unexpected sting of Cupid's dart?

The poor little bugger didn't know where to look. His gaze darted from the girl's shoes to his knees, alighted on her face for a moment, then moved back to his knees. The girl, too, seemed deliciously ill at ease. She tugged a thread from the shredded elbow of her tatterdemalion sweater and absently toyed with it.

A Landcruiser pulled into the kerb, blocking my view. A recent model, roof-racks, rear window plastered with surfwear stickers. Ripcurl. Balin. Hot Tuna. The driver stepped out and checked the crowd, standing in the angle of the open door. She was lean, crop-haired, a wading-bird with a cashmere shawl draped over her shoulders. It was just beginning to drizzle and, as she raised the shawl over her head, the flecked light caught a dark seam that ran down her cheek, hard against her ear, and crossed the angle of her jaw.

Urchin-girl saw the woman and waved, then detached herself from the gang, flapped her sleeve-ends in a collective goodbye and tripped to the Landcruiser. A boy I had seen before, maybe one of Red's classmates, straw-coloured dreadlocks, got into the front passenger seat. Red watched them drive away. He kept watching until the car turned the corner.

I tooted and he came, bringing a boy named Tarquin Curnow with him.

Tarquin and Red had been mates since kindergarten and their friendship had survived Red's years of exile interstate after my divorce from his mother. His parents, Faye and Leo, were my closest friends, family almost, pillars of strength and providers of casseroles in the dark days when I was fit for nothing. Back in Fitzroy, our houses were separated only by a cobbled lane and the boys spent so much time together whenever Red came to town that they might as well have been joined at the hip. After Red's permanent return to Melbourne, the boys went to Fitzroy High together. Now at different schools, they were still as thick as ever.

Adolescence had done wonders for Tark. Formerly a drip, he had transformed himself into a Goth. Spiky black hair, funeral weeds, fingerless gloves, high-laced Doc Martens. A pet rat, too, until the cat ate it. Purple candles and Nick Cave records. But Faye and Leo had drawn the line at the eyebrow piercing. And no tattoo, not yet.

Not that his parents were panicking that Tarquin was on the slippery slope to glue sniffing and satanic rituals. He was too smart for that. His maths were good enough to get him into an advanced studies program, his general aptitude test placed him in the top eight per cent for the state and he was vice-captain of the school debating team.

He and Red loped across the road and piled into the back seat of the car, like I was the chauffeur.

'Any good?' I said. 'The bands?'

'Wimpy pop,' declared Tarquin. 'Think they're alternative, but they're not.'

'He can't wait to get home,' said Red. 'Take the Marilyn Manson antidote.'

We drove past the market, windscreen wipers scraping the drizzle, and turned down Victoria Parade towards Fitzroy. The boys talked bands, names I'd never heard, until we were almost at the Curnows' place.

'Before I forget,' said Tark. 'Mum wants to know if you've decided about the holiday house.'

Faye Curnow had invited the two of us to spend part of the summer break at Lorne, a couple of hours west of town, in a rented beach house. I'd mentioned the idea to

Red, but we hadn't yet discussed it in detail.

'What do you reckon?' I asked Red. 'Any chance of an opening in your hectic social calendar for some time at the beach with your poor old dad?'

Red had been giving the matter some thought. 'I've got Christmas with Mum, so I'll be in Sydney until the twenty-seventh,' he said. 'We could go down to Lorne when I get back, take Tark with us. Then Faye and Leo can come down with Chloe after New Year when Faye's holidays start.' Chloe was Tarquin's nine-year-old sister. 'There's that non-residential rowing camp in mid-January, but I haven't made my mind up yet. Maybe we can stay at the beach longer, see how it goes.'

'With Jodie Prentice,' said Tarquin.

'Get stuffed,' said Red.

'Who's Jodie Prentice?' I said.

'A girl,' Tark informed me, authoritatively.

I glanced at the rear-view mirror. Tarquin clasped his hand to his breast, turned his gaze upwards and heaved a lovelorn sigh.

'Jeeze, you're an idiot,' said Red.

'This Jodie, she wouldn't have been the one you were putting the moves on, back there?' I said. 'Little Orphan Annie.'

'She's Matt Prentice's sister,' said Red, like I was supposed to recognise the name. And not notice that he was sidestepping the subject.

'The rasta?' I guessed.

'Surfer,' said Tarquin. 'He's in Year Eleven. She's in Year Nine. Their mother's an architect. Designs these ecological houses. They've got a place at Aireys Inlet, spend a lot of time there.'

I got the picture. Aireys Inlet was just along the coast from Lorne. A couple of weeks surfside would give Red ample chance to pitch his novice woo in the general direction of the elfin Jodie.

'That was her in the Landcruiser,' I said. 'The mother?'

'She's divorced,' said Red. 'Quite attractive, don't you think?'

'Fancy her, too, do you?' I said.

Red shook his head, despairing. 'It's known as sublimation, dad.'

'Actually,' I corrected him. 'It's called projection.'

By the standard measure, I was a man in the prime of life. My forties still lay before me, half of them anyway. I was moderately fit. I still had my own teeth, most of them. Secure employment, good pay, flexible hours, excellent pension plan. With the right lighting, not entirely repulsive. Hydraulic equipment in full working order.

So there were, of course, women after Lyndal. Three, to be precise. Brief encounters, regretted even before they began.

There was nothing wrong with the women. Except for the nut case, but she'd been so forceful as to represent a collapse of resistance rather than a lapse in judgment. Nor, with the passage of time, was fidelity to Lyndal's memory an issue. I missed her and thought about her every day, but nothing would bring her back. I nurtured no illusions about dedicating the rest of my life to the chaste remembrance of my lost lover.

Always pragmatic, Lyndal herself would have been the first to urge me to find a new squeeze. Although she might have had something to say about the randy desperation which led me to crack onto a half-sloshed twenty-four-year-old legal stenographer at the Lemon Tree by pretending to be a recently divorced commodities broker.

Problem was, I needed more than a hump. I needed what Lyndal had embodied. Passion plus compatibility. A shared bed, a shared world, a shared future. A combination it had taken me the best part of my life to find.

I'd met Lyndal during the '88 election campaign when she was doing some sort of voter-profiling work for the state secretariat, number-crunching the demographics in a raft of wobbly seats on the urban fringe. Taking the customers' measurements, she called it, so our wonks could tailor policy to a snug fit.

I loved it when she talked like that, her scepticism pitched midway between the earnest cant of the old guard and the blatant cynicism of the up-and-comers. I quite fancied other things about her, too. Eyes, lips, hips, those kinds of things. I planned to make my move at the election-night party, the victory knees-up. I left my lunge too late. It was three years later before I got a second shot, both of us on the rebound.

What I missed most about Lyndal, apart from the touch of her body, was her sharp eye for the nuances, her bedrock sense of justice and her bullshit detector.

And there's never a shortage of bullshit, not in my line of work. You don't even need to go looking for it. It seeks you out.

In early December parliament went into recess until the following March. I spent the next three weeks avoiding factional brawls, handling constituent matters, playing the minor dignitary at civic events and assisting with the disposal of free beer at end-of-year piss-ups. By then, the sky had begun to behave itself, the mercury was pulling its weight and summer appeared to have arrived. Like everybody else in Melbourne, I suspected a trick.

Christmas Eve was the last business day of the year. The only business of the day was to shut the electorate office for the four-week break.

At ten, I drove Red to the airport for his flight to Sydney. The baggage-handlers had turned on their customary peak-period go-slow and there was no danger that the flight would leave on time. I contrived to steer Red into the Mambo outlet.

'You'll be needing a surfboard,' I said. 'It can be your Christmas present.'

He beamed and picked out a three-fin thruster.

'Act surprised when your mother gives you a wetsuit,' I told him.

When I told Wendy that I planned to give Red a board for Christmas, she immediately suggested that she complete the package with a wetsuit. At first, I took the suggestion as her reminder of the deficiencies of my universe, like I was personally responsible for the water temperature in the southerly latitudes. As if to say that when he lived with her in Sydney, her son hadn't needed thermal insulation. Thinking the worse of my former wife was a reflex, but considering her previous form Wendy had been remarkably sympathetic about Lyndal, the whole mess, and since I was the victor in the custody war, I no longer had any true cause for resentment.

'And I got some of that fizzy bath stuff for her,' Red said. 'And this is for you. You can open it now, if you like.' He handed me an inexpertly wrapped object.

'A 48-piece socket set,' I said. 'This'll be really handy.'

'Get stuffed,' he said. 'At Christmas dinner, I mean.'

There was no point in Red schlepping the surfboard with him to Sydney, so I waved him off at the gate-lounge and carried it back through the terminal, a man in a business suit with a Balin thruster under his arm.

On the way to the electorate office, I stopped at AutoBarn in Tullamarine and bought a set of roof-racks for the Magna, then found a chain bookstore and picked up a present for Ayisha.

The electorate office was a shopfront in Bell Street, Coburg, near the municipal library. When there were no delivery trucks blocking the view from the back window, you could see all the way across the K-Mart carpark to St Eleptherios basilica and the dumpsters behind Vinnie Amato's fruit shop.

I arrived just after one o'clock and found Ayisha surrounded by bags of groceries, talking to her husband on the phone. 'Since when do Macedonians have roast turkey on December twenty-fifth?' she was saying. 'It's not even orthodox Christmas. And I'm a fucking Moslem, culturally speaking. You want it, you cook it.'

Reminded of lunch, I went into the kitchenette and scraped together a tub of low-fat cream cheese, a jar of kalamata olives, a packet of crispbread and the remnants of a bottle of chenin blanc. I waved the bottle in Ayisha's general direction. 'Fancy a quick one before you go? This won't be worth drinking by the time we get back.'

She gave me the thumbs-up and finished her call. I filled our glasses and handed her the present.

'*Lenin's Tomb: The Last Days of the Soviet Empire*,' she read, peeling back the wrapping. 'For the girl who has everything.'

In return, she presented me with a recent biography of the Prime Minister, 487 pages, hardbound. 'Take it to the beach,' she suggested. 'Bury your head in the sand.'

We toasted ourselves for having survived another year, then she gathered up her groceries and departed in the general direction of a month's holiday, leaving the locking-up to me.

The sign on the front door said the office would be open until two o'clock. Since it was unlikely that anyone would have urgent need of our services in the next half-hour, I figured I'd eat lunch then close up early.

Five minutes later, as I was brushing crispbread crumbs off my shirtfront and putting the olives back in the fridge, I heard the front door open and the buzzer on the reception desk ring.

It was Rita Melina. She was wearing pedal pushers, a loose blouse that hung to mid-thigh and big-framed Jackie O sunglasses. A glossy shopping bag with the logo of the Daimaru department store was slung over her shoulder.

'Happy Christmas, Rita,' I said.

'Maybe for some,' she said bluntly. 'Can you spare a few minutes, Murray? I need to talk to somebody official, but not too official, if you know what I mean.'

'I guess that just about fits my description, Rita,' I said. 'I'll be happy to help, if I can.'

I led her into my office. She drew up a chair, put her elbows on the desk and pushed her sunglasses up onto her hairdo. 'This is confidential, right?' she said.

I was about to make some kind of a joke, until I saw the look of flinty determination in her eyes. 'Up to a point,' I said. 'I'm a member of parliament, not a priest or a doctor. I couldn't conceal a crime, for example.'

'Say we were talking hypothetically?' she said. 'Or I was here on behalf of a friend?'

'Ms X, for example?' I said.

'Mrs X, actually,' said Rita.

'Ah, so,' I said. 'And what is the nature of Mrs X's hypothetical problem?'

'She's worried about something Mr X has done, or might have done, and she's wondering how she might raise her concerns with the appropriate authority.'

'And you're hoping I can provide some informal advice, steer you right,' I said. 'On behalf of Mrs X, that is?'

Rita flicked her wrist dismissively, dispensing with our tippy-toe pas-de-deux.

'I think we've established the ground rules, Murray,' she said. 'Tony's left me. Shot through. Not a word of goodbye, except for some half-baked message on the answering machine about having being called out of town urgently on business. I didn't believe a word of it, of course. He must think I'm an idiot.'

'Oh,' I said. 'I'm sorry to hear…'

She cut me off with another peremptory flap. 'I'm not here for marriage guidance counselling, Murray. Some sort of a bust-up between me and Tony has been on the cards for a while, ever since the girls left home. What's he expect me to do, sit around the house counting my wrinkles while some little gold-digger sinks her claws into him? Anyway, a few days ago I finally put my foot down. Told him I wasn't prepared to tolerate his womanising any longer. Told him that if he didn't get rid of that waitress, the one he's been slipping it to, I'd divorce him, take him to the cleaners.'

I sank deeper into my seat and wished that I'd locked the door while I still had the chance. 'Catholics don't get divorced, Rita,' I said. 'They stay together and fight to the death.'

Mrs X wasn't interested in my observations about matrimony. She took a pack of Marlboro Lites from her bag, fired one up with a disposable lighter and looked around for an ashtray.

'It's forbidden to smoke in government offices,' I said.

'Sunday night, I gave the prick twenty-four hours to make up his mind,' Rita exhaled. 'Next day, he goes to work, never comes home. Vanishes. So does mega-tits, his bit on the side. She quits without notice, moves out of her flat, tells the neighbours she's going on a long trip. So it's obvious what's happened. Tony's made his choice, taken off with this cow. And good riddance to him. Except for one thing. His passport's gone, too, along with a whole bunch of business papers he keeps locked in his den at home. Banking details and whatnot. The bastard's left me high and dry.'

I tipped the paperclips from a saucer and put it between us on the table. 'I can understand you being upset, Rita,' I said. 'But what you need is a lawyer, not a member of parliament.'

She held up her palm, not finished yet. 'I called Immigration, tried to find out if he's left the country in the last couple of days. They say they can't tell me. Some bullshit about the Privacy Act, even though I'm his wife. So naturally

I thought of you, thought that you'd be able to pull some strings, make some unofficial enquiries on my behalf, that sort of thing.'

As a former adviser to a Minister for Ethnic Affairs, I was not entirely unfamiliar with the labyrinthine back corridors of the federal Department of Immigration. So it was quite within the realm of possibility that I could find somebody who knew somebody who could get an informal peek at the information that Rita wanted. On the other hand, it is axiomatic that getting sucked into your constituents' marital disputes is a zero-sum game.

'I wish I could help, Rita. I really do. But Immigration's federal, I'm state. Different worlds. And frankly, I just don't have that sort of pull.'

'I thought you were my friend,' she said.

'I'm not a magician, Rita,' I said. 'Anyway, even if you confirm that Tony's left the country, what good does it do you?'

'Apart from wanting to know, one way or the other?' she said. 'Remember my friend, Mrs X?'

Here it comes, I thought. Whatever it is. Hell hath no fury like a woman stiffed by her spouse of twenty years.

'Mrs X is just a simple housewife,' said Rita. 'She knows nothing about her husband's business dealings. Never has. She's always been the home-maker, he's been the provider. A traditional marriage, strict demarcation. She's never had any reason to want it otherwise. After all, he's quite successful, business-wise. Starts out with a little pizza joint, builds it into a booming restaurant, branches out into the wholesale seafood line. Always some iron in the fire. Long as the bills get paid, Mrs X sees no reason to think twice about the situation.'

I nodded, letting her know that I could see where she was going. 'But now that Mr X has run out on her,' I said, 'maybe left the country, she's begun to worry that some of his business affairs, about which she knows nothing, might create problems for her. Perhaps he's run out on his debts, too, and she'll be left holding the baby.'

'Or holding nothing at all,' she said. 'For all the wife knows, Mr X is even now in the process of transferring his assets to wherever it is that he's gone. Or hiding them where Mrs X will never be able to find them, so that by the time she tracks him down the cupboard will be bare and she'll never see her share of the common property. She might even lose her home. Would that be fair, I ask you?'

'You really think Tony would do that to you?' I said.

'Not until he walked out on me,' she said. 'Now, frankly, I really don't know. Who knows what ideas that piece of trash has been putting into his head? It'd be different if I could talk to him about it. But nobody'll admit to knowing where he is. The staff at the restaurant say they haven't seen him. All I can be sure about is that I can't afford to take the risk he's doing the dirty on me.'

'So it's occurred to you that if some government agency had reason to suspect that Mr X was engaged in illegal activity,' I said, 'they might take steps to prevent him moving his assets out of the country?'

'Exactly,' she said. 'Freeze his bank accounts, something like that.'

Her brilliant idea lay there on the table between us, like a dead cat. I let it lie there for a while before speaking.

'I sympathise with your situation, Rita, I really do,' I said eventually. 'But you can't just go accusing Tony of criminal activity because you think he might be screwing you out of your potential divorce entitlements. You'll probably just make the situation worse with Tony when he eventually re-surfaces. Plus, you'll get yourself into trouble with the law. Making false allegations is a serious offence.'

'Even if they're true?' she said.

'So what's he done, Rita?' I said. 'Paid his casual staff cash-in-hand, watered the drinks, bribed the health inspector?'

'How about tax avoidance,' she said. 'Money laundering, stuff like that.'

'I thought you said you don't know anything about Tony's business activities.'

She ground her cigarette into the saucer, lit another and leaned forward conspiratorially. 'He's been going to Asia on business every few months for the last couple of years,' she said. 'Quick trips, just a day or so at a time. Hong Kong, Bangkok, Singapore. Meetings with his seafood export clients, he said. Last June, he took me along, made a bit of a holiday of it. Singapore. We went sightseeing, shopping, ate some fabulous food. But as far as I could see, the only business Tony did was visit the Oriental Bank to deposit some cash. A great big wad of it, $30,000 at least. Told me he was building up a nest egg for us.'

'It's a little unusual, I'll grant you that,' I said. 'But what makes you think there was something dodgy about the money?' I said.

She gave me a withering look. 'Get real, Murray,' she said. 'Even I know that there's a limit to the amount of currency you're allowed to export. And that banks in Australia have to report transactions that big. All I'm asking here is that you point me in the direction of the right government agency. Go into a cop shop with this sort of story, they'll put it down to a domestic, give me the bum's rush. A word to the wise, that's all I'm asking, Murray.'

'You're sure about this, Rita?' I said. 'You start the ball rolling, you won't be able to stop it.'

'It's Tony's ball,' she said. 'And right now, as far as I'm concerned, Tony's balls belong in a vice. As for me, I've done nothing wrong. I've signed nothing so I can't see how I can be implicated. I'm just an honest citizen doing her duty.'

She glowered across the table at me, as if any suggestion to the contrary would constitute a wilful obstruction of justice. 'You men,' she added gratuitously. 'I should have known whose side you'd be on.'

'That's unfair,' I said. 'And it's not a matter of taking sides. I'm just suggesting you give yourself a few days to think about this, not go off half-cocked.'

'And let Tony clean me out in the meantime?' she said. 'No way.'

I thought about Pontius Pilate. A much maligned figure, I reflected. I picked up the phone, dialled the state headquarters of the taxation department, identified myself and asked to speak with a senior officer.

I was put through to the state manager, a more senior seat-polisher that I'd expected, and explained that I was calling on behalf of a constituent with information relating to possible tax evasion and infringement of currency laws. Despite his understandable lack of enthusiasm for an unscheduled meeting on the afternoon of Christmas Eve, he agreed to spare said constituent fifteen minutes of his time, subject to her prompt arrival at the Moonee Ponds office.

'Can you be there in half an hour?' I asked, hand over the mouthpiece.

'Just try to stop me,' she said.

There was not the slightest chance of that happening.

As I escorted her to the door, Rita presented me with her Daimaru shopping bag.

'A little something for Christmas,' she said.

The bag held two brick-sized parcels wrapped in newspaper.

'A crayfish,' Rita explained, 'and a dozen abalone.'

'Thank you,' I said. 'That's very generous of you.' About a hundred dollars worth of generous by the heft of it.

'You've been a pillar, Murray,' she said. 'And Tony's got a freezer-load of this stuff in the garage.'

The instant she was out the door, I lowered the blind, shot the bolt and heaved a sigh of relief. Tony, I thought, you're a dead man. I was thinking metaphorically.

And then I wasn't thinking about it at all. As of that moment, my holidays had officially begun.

The house in Lorne was one of those sixties jobs, a cement-sheet box on stilts. Perched on a sloping block of land at the crest of the ridge overlooking the town, it had bare floors, throw-rugs, an antique television set with rabbit-ear antenna, ramshackle furniture and a timber deck from which the sea could be glimpsed through the raggedy tops of the surrounding bluegums. Sand had seeped into the nooks and crannies, pieces were missing from the board games and the bookshelf held only dog-eared fishing manuals, bird-spotting books and unfinished Peter Carey novels.

We arrived three days after Christmas, drove straight from the airport with a carload of holiday supplies and Tarquin Curnow. A three-man advance party, our mission was to establish base camp before the others arrived late on New Year's Day.

I had Christmas lunch with the Curnows, contributing

Rita's abalone to the spread, then trawled the Boxing Day sales for cut-price wardrobe essentials. My purchases included a selection of tropical shirts and a panama hat which, I felt, would serve me well in the resort-wear stakes.

I wore the panama hat to the airport. The day was hot, proper beach weather, with the promise of more to come. In deference to the season, Tark had shorn his Joey Ramone pageboy into a Travis Bickle mohawk and ripped the sleeves off his Nick Cave tee-shirt. The black jeans and mid-shin Doc Martens remained, however, welded to his lower body. For his part, Red was dressed for summer as God intended. Baggy shorts, a baggy shirt, blow-fly wraparounds, baseball cap and rubber thongs.

We drove across the Westgate Bridge, heat-haze rising from the oil depots, and fought our way down the Geelong Road with the rest of beach-bound Melbourne. Tarquin sprawled on the back seat, playing Tetris on his Gameboy, while Red gave me a run-down on his visit with mummy dearest, his twin half-sisters and Wendy's husband.

'Nicola and Alexandra are getting really fat,' he said, puffing out his cheeks. 'Biggest five-year-olds you've ever seen. I gave them swimming lessons in the pool and taught them to say fuck-bum. They're all going to Phuket for two weeks when Richard gets back from the Sydney to Hobart yacht race.'

'Phuket?' I snorted, flooring the pedal to pass a fish-tailing caravan. 'Fuck it! What's Phuket compared to this?'

I fed *Pet Sounds* into the cassette-deck and cranked up the volume. Tarquin groaned from the back seat but Red went with it, grooving on the antique vibrations. An hour later, it was Nirvana as we turned down the Anglesea hill and sighted the ocean. By then, we were following the Great Ocean Road, two lanes of blacktop threaded between the sea and the Otway Ranges.

We followed it past the Anglesea funfair and paddle-boat rentals, past the lighthouse at Aireys Inlet and along the straight stretch of surf beach at Moggs Creek. As we travelled further west, the hills became steeper, wilder, more thickly wooded.

The road began to climb, clinging to the forested slopes in a series of switchback curves, dropping away to wave-washed rocks, double lines all the way.

According to the annual report of the Australian Tourism Commission, the Great Ocean Road attracts more than four million visitors a year. Most of them, it was evident, should never have been allowed behind the wheel of a motor vehicle. For twenty minutes we were stuck behind a tortoise-shaming senior citizen in a spanking new all-terrain Nissan Patrol. When I pulled out to pass him, we were almost totalled by a dipstick in an Audi convertible.

At the Cinema Point lookout, I hit the left indicator and eased onto the gravel margin.

'Five minute break,' I said. 'Stretch legs, contemplate nature, allow blood to return to driver's knuckles.'

The sea extended to the horizon, vast and twinkling. Towering eucalypts and ragged scrub marched up the incline from the rocky shore, continuing past us, up into the grey-green vastness of the state forest. Looking back, we could see the surf at Eastern View, the breakers uncoiling in rows as regular as corduroy. Up ahead, beyond a series of blunt capes, we could just make out a broad arc of calico sand etched into the bush-covered ranges. And, packed tight around the sand, the township of Lorne.

'What's that pink blob?' asked Red.

'The Cumberland,' I said. 'A cutting-edge condominium-style time-share apartment complex.'

'Shipwrecks,' declared Tarquin, his hand sweeping the watery horizon. 'There's hundreds of them out there. Dozens, anyway. They sailed all the way from Europe, five months or more, then got smashed on these rocks.'

Red peered over the edge. 'Cool.'

'The dead bodies were washed ashore all along here. I did a project on it in Grade Six.'

An ancient kombi trembled to a halt beside us. Red nudged Tark and nodded towards a concert poster taped to its side door. Regurgitator. Hunters and Collectors. Spiderbait. Rock the Falls.

Two ferals got out of the van, little more than kids. He was covered in Celtic tattoos and she had feathers in her braids. A baby was slung across her chest in a raffia hammock. She sat on the lookout parapet, whipped out a tit and began to feed it. Magic Happens, read a sticker on the van window.

'So does shit,' muttered Tarquin, without apparent malice.

'Can I use the mobile?' said Red. He'd had his own, briefly, for emergency use and ease of essential son–father communications. Three hundred dollars worth of calls in a month, and I pulled the plug.

'Keep it short,' I said.

He strolled away as he dialled, reading the number off the back of his hand. 'Hey it's me. Wassup? We're almost there.'

Fifteen minutes later, the road dropped to sea level and

crossed the Erskine River where it tumbled out of the hills and turned into the lagoon beside the Lorne caravan park. We continued past the fruit shop called Lorne Greens, the joke lost on post-Ponderosa generations, and cruised along the main drag, an esplanade of shops that faced across the road to the foreshore carpark and the teeming beach. The old bait-and-tackle shops and milk bars were long gone, replaced by seaside-theme knick-knackeries and surfwear boutiques with swimsuit racks out the front. Holiday-makers ambled along the footpath, clinging to the shade, window-shopping. Some sat at tables outside coffee shops and juiceries, their hair still wet from swimming.

After a couple of passes, I found a parking spot between a Porsche and a Jeep Cherokee, then set off to pick up the house key while the boys found some lunch. As I headed along the footpath, I passed several nodding acquaintances. We smiled, delighted to see each other, even if we couldn't quite remember who we were.

I went into the real estate office and collected the key and directions to the house. As I came out, tucking the receipt into my wallet, a short man was rocking on his toes as he peered through the front window at the For Sale listings. He had less hair and more waist than the last time I'd seen him.

'G'day, Ken,' I said. 'Win the lottery, did you?'

Back when I was a ministerial adviser, Ken Sproule was factotum to a party heavyweight, the Minister for Police. Both Ken and his boss saw the chill weather ahead and jumped ship before the hull impacted the iceberg. Ken found himself a snug new berth as a consultant to the poker-machine business, a booming sector of the state's new growth industry.

'Hello, Murray,' he drawled. He did me the honour of tearing himself away from the array of ideal getaways with water views and in-ground pools. 'Checking the prices, mate. We've just built a place at Aireys Inlet, thought we might have over-capitalised. Look who's here, Sandra.'

Sandra was Ken's new cookie. Mid-thirties. Petite, well-toned, worked in PR. She was waiting her turn at the ice-cream counter next door. A small child was slung on her hip. Sandra was the chirpy type, foil to the blunt Ken.

'Hello, Murray,' she said, handing a cone to the kid. 'You in the market?'

'For an ice-cream?'

'A house, stupid.'

I showed her the key. 'We're renting for a few weeks,' I said. 'Sight unseen.'

'We?' She dropped her chin and looked over the top of her sunglasses. Wondering, I understood, if I had paired off since Lyndal.

'Me,' I said. 'My son. Some old friends.'

'Ah,' she said.

'Careful.' Ken lunged for the child's hand, narrowly averting a spilt vanilla crisis.

Sandra pulled a scrap of paper and a pen from the beach-bag slung over her shoulder. 'If you're free tomorrow evening,' she said, firming the paper against the estate agent's window as she scribbled. 'We're having a few friends around for drinks and a barbecue. A sort of housewarming for our new place.' She thrust the address at me. 'You will come, won't you?'

I made tentatively affirmative noises, then headed back to the car. The boys had connected. They were lounging in the shade of a big cypress, pizza slices in hand, communing with a mixed gaggle of teens. I recognised Max Kline from Red's rowing eight and some other kids from school. I waved the house key and Red and Tark came to the car, trailing a slim girl in a crocheted bikini-top and hipster board shorts with tousled, beach-wet hair.

'This is Jodie Prentice,' Red said. 'This is my father.'

The girl smiled shyly, displaying her retainer, and held out her hand, all very well-brought-up. Narrow hips, bare midriff, very little in the shirt-potato department. 'Pleased to meet you, Red's father.'

We shook, as though confirming a deal. She wore a butterfly ring, a puzzle ring and a black plastic spider ring. 'Charmed, I'm sure,' I said. 'Jodie Prentice.'

She was cute in a whippish, salt-flecked, young girl way. A bit cheeky. But no ditz, that much was evident. Heartbreak on the hoof.

Red shuffled in the gravel. 'I've got to go and, um…'

'He'll be back,' I told Jodie. 'After he's milked the cows, chopped the firewood and nailed Tark into his coffin.'

The gang began to gravitate beachward, trailing goodbyes. 'We'll be in front of Beach Bites,' Jodie told Red, hesitating for a second before dashing away.

'Ready to rock?' said Tark, drumming impatiently on the car roof.

I turned the Magna uphill and we climbed through the sunbaked town. Hemmed by inviolable forest, Lorne did not have room for lateral expansion. So, year by year, the old houses with their wide verandas, vegetable patches and couch-grass yards were giving way to low-rise cluster housing and sandstone mansions with garage access and touch-pad security.

But not our place, thank Christ. We found it at the end of the last street in town, nothing but bush beyond the back fence. We gave it a good going over, threw open the windows, checked the water pressure, tested the sofa, sniffed the empty fridge.

'Bit basic, isn't it?' concluded Red.

At six-fifty a week, it was no bargain. On the other hand, it was something of a classic, the last of its kind. Abalone-shell ashtrays, seventies stereo, flyscreen doors and a perforated surf-ski on the back porch.

'Nothing to maintain, nothing to keep clean,' I said. 'Perfect.'

Except for the noise. Every time Tarquin clumped across the bare floorboards in his Docs, it sounded like we were being raided by the Gestapo.

'No boots in the house,' I ordered. 'I'm here to relax, not have an Anne Frank experience.'

He clicked his heels. '*Jawohl, mein Fuhrer.*'

Opting for private quarters, the boys claimed a grove of tea-trees in the backyard and pitched an igloo tent. Until Faye and Leo arrived, the indoor accommodation was exclusively mine. I was stocking the refrigerator with Coopers Pale Ale and Pepsi Max when the boys ambled into the kitchen.

'New Year's Eve,' said Red, backside on the benchtop, bare feet dangling, Mr Casual. 'There's this music festival up in the hills.'

'Rock the Falls,' I said. 'I've seen the poster.' Not just on the ferals' kombi. They were taped to every light pole on the main drag. 'I'm getting a bit old for that sort of thing, but I'll keep it in mind.'

'Not you,' said Red. 'Us.'

'We were thinking we could maybe take the tent,' said Tark. 'Camp overnight.'

'Everybody's going,' said Red. 'We'll be social outcasts if we don't.'

'Pariahs,' said Tark.

I busied myself in the fridge, taking my time with the product placement. The boys were trustworthy, mature, capable. But they were only fifteen. And the music would not be the only experience they were seeking.

'Everybody?' I asked. 'That includes this Jodie Prentice?'

'Probably,' said Red. 'Her brother Matt is definitely going.' He rattled off some other names.

I shut the fridge and gave him the stop sign. 'I'll need to talk to Faye or Leo, see what Tark's parents think. And I'm not making any promises.'

The boys nodded, suppressing smirks of self-congratulation.

'In the meantime,' I said, hooking my thumb in the direction of the sea. 'Ready to rock?'

An hour later, I was sitting under a market umbrella at a table in front of Beach Bites, the snack bar on the foreshore. I was fresh from the water, togs still damp, legs bare. My Hawaiian shirt hung open, my panama hat was tilted low over my eyes and I was stirring the ice in my fresh-squeezed orange juice with a straw. A summery mix of ozone, hot chips, vinegar and sun-block hung in the shimmering air. Tarquin, dressed for a punk funeral, lounged beside me, sipping decaf macchiato and munching a vegan muffin. Spread before us was a tableau of the nation at play.

Innumerable near-naked bodies reclined on the baking sand, soaking up the full glare of the afternoon sun or sheltering beneath nylon hooches. Out from the shore, a row of surfers lay prostrate on the glistening water, staring seaward for the next break. Closer, where frilled curls dumped against the shore, swimmers bobbed in the water and little kids skittered though the shallows, dragging boogie boards behind them. Young men were playing cricket on the wet, hard-packed sand, defending plastic stumps against dog-gnawed tennis balls. A rainbow-tailed kite fluttered overhead. In front of the surf club, lifeguards with logo-emblazoned backsides stood sentinel in reflector sunglasses. Above the swish of the waves came the screeching of children and gulls.

'Uh-oh,' said Tark. 'Big brother.'

He nodded at a pile of bodies a few metres down the beach, the boys in peeled-down wetsuits, the girls in very little indeed. Young, free and girt by sea, they were chatting and joking and flicking each other with wet towels. Red lay sprawled in their midst, head turned towards Jodie Prentice. She was sitting, knees tucked up under her chin, squinting up at her brother Matt. He loomed above her, legs akimbo, proprietary.

'Protective type?' I said.

Tark shrugged and fluttered his hand. 'A bit,' he said. 'Not always friendly. Nothing weird or anything. They're pretty close, that's all. Real thick. Red's gunna hafta tread careful.'

Matt Prentice picked up his surfboard and padded towards the reef break at the far end of the beach. Jodie tapped Red on the shoulder, unscrewing the cap from a tube of zinc cream. He moved closer, offering his face and she began to paint his nose an iridescent pink.

Tark groaned in disgust. I, too, averted my gaze. It roamed along the shoreline, a frieze of nubile flesh. There were near-naked, magazine-strength babes everywhere. Face-down on towels, bikini straps undone. Jogging from the water, flanks glistening. Strolling in pairs, boobs straining at tiny scraps of lycra.

'Anybody looking,' said Tark. 'I'll be in the video arcade.'

My attention drifted to a woman dawdling barefoot along the edge of the water, sandals dangling from her hand, her straw hat pushed back on her short fair hair. She was long-legged, slender, a sarong knotted at her bosom, a billowy white shirt draped over her shoulders. Something about her bearing caught my eye, the poised way she held herself, her absorption in the play of the light on the water.

She drew nearer and I recognised her as the Prentice kids' mother, the woman who'd picked them up after the concert at Festival Hall. Jodie spotted her and waved. Their resemblance was obvious. The woman came up the beach, heading for the group of kids.

I should meet her, I decided. Make myself known, what with our children being friends. Say hello, in a purely social way. I stood, sucked in my stomach, ran my fingers through my hair, set my hat at a rakish angle and steered a converging course across the beach.

Rubber thongs sinking into the soft sand, I wove my way through the maze of prostrate bodies. Flip, flop, flip. Red spotted me coming, rose from his towel and shouted.

'Hey, Dad!'

He twisted, pirouetting on the ball of one foot, and whipped a Frisbee at me. It came low and fast. I took a couple of paces forward and firmed my stance to catch it. But the hurtling disc suddenly veered upwards. My arm shot into the air and I stepped backwards to intercept.

This was not a smart move. I immediately toppled over a pile of towels, ricocheted off a beach shelter and tripped over a child's bucket-and-spade set. My hat went west and my feet went east.

My fall was broken by a supine sunbather. A young woman. She was blonde, remarkably attractive, possibly Swedish, almost completely naked and glistening with oil. Her bikini top was unlaced. I registered these facts in the half second before my out-thrust hands closed around her busty substances. They were more than adequate to cushion my fall.

Blurting apologies, I leaped backwards, scrabbling in the scalding sand.

Bountiful Ingrid jack-knifed upright and lunged at me, emitting an outraged yelp. At that point, I realised I was clutching something. A wisp of floral fabric with a length of string attached. The string was taut. It was caught on something. A ring. A ring inserted through a nipple.

'Ikea,' yapped the Valkyrie, her face contorted with pain. Her right boob was coming at me like the nose-cone of an ICBM. 'Bang & Olufsen!'

She sounded like Marlene Dietrich gargling ball-bearings. Her companion, Sven Smorgasbord, loomed up and smacked the bikini top from my grasp.

'Häagen-Dazs,' he accused menacingly. 'Gustavus Adolphus? Björn Borg.'

No translation was required. His expression was sufficient. That, and the aggressive thrust of his posing pouch.

'Absolut!' I assured him, backing away. 'Hans Christian Andersen.' I realised my mistake immediately. Sven glowered.

'Ingmar Bergman,' I grovelled, displaying the Frisbee as

token of my innocence. 'Liv Ullmann.'

'Orrefors,' snorted the woman dismissively, and they sank back onto their towels.

Red was watching, writhing with embarrassment at his father's antics. I looked past him and saw that Jodie and her mother were occupied in conversation, apparently oblivious, beginning to walk away. Red glanced over his shoulder, following my gaze, then turned back, a relieved smirk on his face.

I unleashed the Frisbee, warp factor nine, and zapped the smarmy little smartarse.

The sign for Gusto stood at the corner of a narrow, bush-bordered road leading sharply uphill from the Great Ocean Road. The name was spelled in glazed turquoise tiles.

The moment I saw it, set in a curved adobe wall, I thought of Gusto's owner, Jake Martyn. And then of Tony Melina, in whose company I had met him.

I noticed the sign as I was driving out of town, taking Red to baptise his new surfboard. The surf scene at Lorne was tight and the local nazis took a dim view of blow-in grommets. I offered to drive Red to Fairhaven, just the two of us, so he could get some practice before strutting his stuff in full view of the gang. It was late morning, overcast and humid. The sky was the colour of dead grass, the swell even and glassy. According to the radio surf report the water temperature was eighteen degrees, the swell running at just over a metre.

It was two days after our arrival in Lorne and a week since Rita Melina had ambushed me at the electorate office, wanting my help to nail her husband's cheating arse to the wall. Since then, I hadn't given her or Tony a moment's thought.

In certain respects, a member of parliament is like a doctor, only less useful. An endless parade of people knocks on your door, each with their own problems. If you can, you help. If you can't, you refer them elsewhere. Either way, there's no mileage in busting your chops. And if the marital barricades are up, try not to get caught in the crossfire. Christ knows, you're never thanked, whatever the outcome. So when I shut the office door on Rita, I put the matter behind me.

But the Gusto sign set me thinking of Tony and, as I followed the twists and turns of the Great Ocean Road, I wondered if Rita had run him to ground yet. It revived my curiosity, too, about Tony's connection with Jake Martyn. According to Rita, Tony Melina was bent, at least a little. And the last time I'd seen him, he and Martyn appeared to be involved in some kind of deal. This offered scope for idle conjecture.

Idle being the key word. The restaurant game is a cash business. To those inclined, it provides ample opportunity to skim the till or dud the tax collector. If Tony was running some sort of scam, that didn't make Jake Martyn a crook just because I saw them together. After all, if it came to that, I myself had done business with Tony Melina over the years. Did that make the Melbourne Upper trivia nights a money-laundering operation?

'Forty dollars,' said Red. 'For that you get ten bands plus

a camp site. Pretty good deal, I reckon.'

'Hmm,' I said, hugging the cliff-face as we edged around a hairpin bend, a squadron of bikes roaring past, a sheer drop to the sea.

Value for money was Red's latest argument in support of the boys' plea to be allowed to stay overnight at The Falls festival on New Year's Eve. Tarquin had already phoned his parents and got the provisional nod, subject to my final endorsement, but the lads knew I wasn't going to announce my decision until I'd extracted maximum tease value from the situation. And that meant making them pitch their case.

'And this forty dollars?' I said. 'Where's it coming from?'

'Consolidated revenue,' said Red. 'I've got $63 in my bank account. And Tark's got even more, if he doesn't spend it all at the video arcade. He's met this girl there, Ronnie, one of the undead.'

'So you're both set for the night, then?' I said. 'Chicks-wise.'

'Guess so,' he said, not displeased with the idea.

'You'll be up there in the woods, no adult supervision, free to have your wicked ways.'

He gave a scornful snort, but he knew he'd fallen into a trap. 'Check it out,' he said suddenly, pointing to the view as we turned down the hill towards the long stretch of beach at Fairhaven. The waves were as advertised, a perfect beginner's break. Perfect, too, for an old guy who was long out of practice.

'Jodie's mother,' I said. 'What's she think about this overnight stay business?'

'Her name's Barbara,' he said. 'And I was wrong about her. She's not divorced.'

Fairhaven was a popular spot, a sandy bottom with even, regular sets. Vans and station wagons lined the tussocky dunes beside the road and it was hard to find a place to park.

'Let me know if you spot an opening,' I said.

'Actually, her husband's dead,' continued Red, eyeing me sideways. Checking my reaction, not getting one. 'Car crash. It happened when Matt and Jodie were little. They were trapped in the wreckage, all four of them. Jodie's still got this scar.'

He began to raise his right arm, his left hand reaching across his chest to show me where. The hand got half-way, then he changed his mind, wary, before I asked how he'd come to be so familiar with young Jodie's anatomy.

'Is that where her mother got that…?' I ran my finger from my earlobe to my collarbone.

'You've been checking her out, haven't you, Dad?'

'You should talk,' I said. 'You're the one planning to get her daughter into your tent.'

He shook his head, exasperated. 'Matt'll be there the whole time. They're hardly out of each other's sight.'

'That's reassuring.' I pulled into a spot at the Moggs Creek end of the beach, body-board territory.

'Yeah,' said Red, figuring maybe he'd found an angle he could use to his advantage. 'Anyway, in case you're wondering, Jodie says she's not involved with anyone at the moment. Her mother, that is. She lived with a guy called Dennis for a few years, but they broke up. He's married to someone else now, got his own kids. Matt was pretty cut up about it, apparently. So, like I said, she's up for grabs. I reckon you should go for it.'

'You're a sick puppy, you know,' I said. 'Trying to line me

up with your girlfriend's mother.'

'This thing with Jodie,' he said. 'I'm not a hundred per cent sure about it. She's nice, but she can get a bit clingy. Reckon I should play the field a bit before I commit. What do you think?'

'I think I should have you spayed while it's still legal.'

'No, really.' He went serious on me, man-to-man. 'If you're interested in her mother, don't let me stand in your way.'

'That's very considerate of you, son.' I mirrored his tone, meaning it.

'That's okay,' he said. 'You need it more than I do. Last chance before the retirement home.'

'Get fucked,' I said. 'Any other words of wisdom from the master of romance?'

'Just one,' he said. 'If you're fast enough, there's an empty parking spot next to that yellow station wagon up ahead.'

We hit the water and Red soon found his feet, the sharp-nosed thruster an easier plank to walk than my first board, a malibu. Or so it seemed, watching from the shore. When I finally managed to wangle a turn, it wasn't quite as manoeuvrable as it looked. We surfed up a hefty appetite, bought pies for lunch and drove back to Lorne through a squall that put coin spots on the Magna's dusty windscreen.

I spent the rest of the day lounging around the house. Intermittent showers, cricket on the radio, a book within reach, a nap. The lads were elsewhere, watching videos with better-resourced cronies, they claimed. Pressing their suits with the objects of their desire, I didn't wonder.

By seven-thirty, the cool front had passed, the streets were dry and the sky was clearing. Red and Tark were back, heads in the refrigerator, talking about having some friends over, kicking on. I dug out the address for Ken Sproule's place, changed into clean chinos and a polo shirt, forked over enough cash for a delivery of pizza, made a show of counting the beer, stuck a bottle of wine under my arm, then left the younger generation to its own devices and started for Aireys Inlet.

Sunset was still more than an hour away, but the ranges had already cast their long shadow across the Great Ocean Road. The beach at Fairhaven was murky and spray-shrouded, deserted by all but the most dedicated wax-heads. At the lifesaving club, I turned off the highway, climbed into the sunlight and followed the spine of the ridge that ran parallel to the coast.

Ten years back, a bushfire had descended from the hills and incinerated many of the houses along this section of road. New growth soon sprouted and new houses were built, but the inferno had left its mark. Charred trunks jutted from the greenery and many of the new dwellings had been constructed with an eye to the harsher realities.

Ken and Sandra's place was such a house. Low-slung and well clear of surrounding trees, it was recessed into a fold in the earth, the front cantilevered, the rear facing the road with a packed-gravel parking apron. Solar panels. External sprinklers. Slatted timber pergolas shading the north and west aspects. Slightly Spanish feel. Costa Monza.

The door was open. I gave it a passing rap and followed a short hallway into an open-plan space that was filled with convivial chatter and the smell of fresh paint. The furniture was sparse and modular. Ikea, I guessed. The feel was stylish but comfortable, tending to homey. Stray pieces of Lego littered the floor and cartoon noises leaked from behind a closed door. Pushing fifty, Ken was a come-again father.

About a dozen adults, none of whom I knew, were drinking wine and batting the breeze at a beechwood dining table. Past them, on a jutting deck, Ken was tending a Weber, aided by two blokes in fashionably lairish shirts, cans of beer in hand. He spotted me hovering uncertainly and beckoned with his barbecue tongs.

He introduced me to his friends, a Steve and a Boyd, ageing yuppies, then carved a wide circle in the air with his meat-grippers. 'Not bad, eh?'

It certainly wasn't. Undulating, scrub-covered hills extended from the deck, capped in the distance by the jade of the ocean. A froth of tangerine clouds rose from the horizon. Here and there, houses dotted the landscape and solitary trees emerged from the undergrowth, twisted into picturesque shapes by the sea winds. The building and the view were all of a piece, made for each other.

I whistled appreciatively, meaning it.

'We'll get built out eventually, of course,' said Ken. 'Lose the view. But not the capital gain.'

Sandra appeared, thrust a flute of bubbly into my hand, steered me inside and introduced me to her other guests. Couples, mainly. A few years younger, mostly. Media types and film people.

In keeping with the unspoken code of the beachside holiday, jobs were not mentioned nor shop talked. The topic was plans for New Year's Eve. Having none, I sipped and listened.

Ken, Sandra and some of the others had managed to get a table at Gusto, no mean achievement, apparently. 'We've got an in,' confided Sandra. 'The architect who designed this place also did Gusto. She had a word with Jake Martyn, fixed it up for us to join her party. We've become quite matey with her. Matter of fact, she said she might drop around tonight, see how the place works with people in it.'

What are the chances? I wondered.

My answer arrived twenty minutes later, a raw cotton skirt swishing at her ankles as she came down the hall. She hesitated for a moment before entering the room, examining the set-up. Unnoticed, possibly, except by me. She was buffed and moisturised, post-beach. Her ash-blonde hair was cut in an Annie Lennox crop and she wore a green coral necklace that might have matched her eyes. Hard to tell at the distance.

Sandra saw her and darted forward, smoocheroonie. The two women conferred, then waltzed around the room for a series of effusive introductions. In due course, it was my turn.

'Murray,' Sandra started. 'You really must meet…'

'Barbara Prentice,' I said. 'Jodie's mother.'

The architect raised a quizzical eyebrow.

'My son is a friend of your daughter,' I explained. 'Red Whelan. I'm Murray.'

'Ah,' she exhaled, putting it together. 'You're the polly, right?' Something in her tone conveyed the impression that my occupation wasn't the only thing she knew about me.

We held each other's gaze for slightly longer than was dictated by the requirements of common courtesy. Her eyes were grey.

'Quick,' called Ken from the deck, a rare enthusiasm in his voice. 'Showtime.'

A flock of sulphur-crested cockatoos had come flapping out of the hills, white plumage vivid against the darkening sky. There must have been a hundred of them, screeching and wheeling, then settling in the branches of a fire-blackened stringybark, the nearest tree to the house. We crowded the deck, all oohs and aahs, captivated by the wild splendour of the sight, children pressing to the front, television forgotten.

'Are they on the payroll?' somebody quipped. 'Ambience consultants?'

'All part of the design,' Barbara laughed.

The cockatoos worked on the tree for a while, their beaks shredding the foliage. Then they rose again, a restless whirlwind, and flapped away to feed elsewhere, screeching and carping. I thought of my ex-wife, Wendy.

Candles were lit and Ken's burnt sacrifice transferred to the dining table. As the other guests found their seats, I lingered on the deck, watching night settle over the lavender hills, and sea merge with sky. After a while, Barbara Prentice was standing there too.

'Nice house,' I said. 'It has such an open, welcoming feel. Wonderfully site-specific, too.'

'Sounds like you're out of practice,' she said.

'Badly,' I admitted.

'Your son, on the other hand, does not appear to be backward in coming forward.'

'I heard it was the other way around.'

She gave a derisive snort. 'Wishful thinking.'

'Well, that's no crime,' I said. 'Is it?'

Even in the waning light, the faint scar under her ear was clearly visible. A different haircut would have made it less evident, possibly hidden it completely. But she seemed to wear it almost as a badge of honour, the mark of a survivor.

There was something a bit dangerous about the woman. Smart dangerous, not whacko dangerous. Something challenging and, well, sexy.

'You comfortable about Jodie going to this Falls festival thing?' I said.

'Something I should be worried about?'

'Not Red,' I said. 'If that's what you mean. Born gentlemen, the Whelan boys.'

She gave me a sideways look that suggested both doubt and a degree of disappointment.

We're flirting, I thought. We're definitely flirting.

She waggled a hand, signifying ambivalence. 'The way I see it, Jodie will probably be a lot safer at the festival than hanging around in Lorne. It can get pretty ugly in town, all the boozing and brawling on the foreshore, yobbos coming from miles around. And her brother Matt will be there to keep an eye on her. He can be a bit of a tearaway at times, but he looks after his little sister.'

'So I understand,' I said. 'Not that…' I let the sentence fade away. Like she said, I was out of practice.

We leaned on the railing, saying nothing, watching the purple light seep away across the scrub.

'Murray,' she said.

'Yes,' I breathed.

'Did you bring your Frisbee?'

I didn't want to jump this woman, not straight off. I wanted to stand close behind her, put my arm around her waist, feel the fit. Just stand like that, looking out over the world.

'Get it while you can,' called Ken, summoning us to dinner.

Inside, Sandra was bustling with the seating arrangements, intent on placing us next to each other. But I wasn't about to have my match made. And neither, I could tell, was Barbara. We dithered, evading Sandra's attempts at shoehorning, and finished up at opposite ends of the table. Soon after dinner, Barbara made her goodbyes and left.

Later, as I was helping Ken and his mate Boyd with the washing-up, Sandra floated into the kitchen, pleasantly pickled, and sidled up to the sink. 'Spoke to Barbara about New Year's Eve,' she slurred into my ear as I scrubbed a sauce-smeared plate. 'Asked her if maybe we couldn't squeeze you onto our table at Gusto. You know what she said? Said you could always turn up and'—she glanced around conspiratorially—'try your luck.'

'Luck?' I said.

There'd been bugger all of that lately.

'Mummy,' squeaked a voice near the floor. 'Damon stuck a piece of bread in the video player.'

As soon as Sandra turned her back, I handed the dishmop to Ken, thanked him for a splendid housewarming, and slipped away.

With five or six drinks under my belt, I was close to the limit. So I pushed Barbara Prentice and all she represented to the back of my mind and concentrated on the twists and turns of the road, my headlights sweeping empty air like the wandering beam of a lighthouse. Perhaps it was more than six.

Back in Lorne, I found a boat trailer blocking the driveway, a neighbour loading fishing equipment. He signalled his willingness to shift, but I wasn't fussed and parked a little further along the street.

Although the lights were lit, there was no sign of movement in the house. As I sauntered up the driveway, I was met by sounds from the backyard. The low strumming of a guitar and a girl's voice, singing off-key. Mopey, strangulated vocals of the Tracey Chapman variety, subset of the Joni Mitchell whine. Along with the music came the background burble of youthful conversation. And, as I drew closer, the unmistakable smell of something burning.

Ah shit, I thought.

Shit, pot, hemp, grass, weed, ganja, mull.

Marijuana.

In certain situations, discretion is the better part of parenting. I went back to the car, waited until the driveway was clear, then returned anew, advertising my arrival with engine noises, headlights and a banged door.

As I climbed the front steps, a camel-train of teenagers came loping down the side of the house, half-obscured in the shadows. Three boys and a girl.

The point man was Matt Prentice, sister Jodie in his wake. The other two boys were unfamiliar, generic tagalongs.

A year older than Red, Matt was taller and more confident. Nothing of his mother or sister in his features, not that I could immediately discern. He communicated an attitude, though. A cockiness that didn't necessarily have much to do with self-assurance. Something chippish in the shoulder region.

'I'm Jodie's brother,' he said with minimal courtesy. 'Picking her up.'

The two other boys nodded, confirming his claim. Jodie gave me a little hello-goodbye wave. And then they were gone, flowing down the hill.

I clattered through the front door and made a general presence of myself in the house. There was no smell of smoking but there were empty beer cans in the kitchen bin. Not a lot, not mine, not an issue. A half-dozen mid-teens were hunkered down in the backyard near the tent, propped on the rental's assortment of chairs, their outlines familiar to some degree or another. A boy I knew as Max, one of the many Maxes of his age, was noodling on the guitar, displaying an unsuspected talent.

Red wandered upstairs. 'Home already?' he said. 'No good?'

'It was okay,' I said. 'Jodie's mother was there.'

He tilted his head. 'And?'

'And various other people,' I said. 'So what's been happening here?'

'Nothing much,' he shrugged. If he was stoned he was hiding it well. 'Starting to drift away.'

'I passed Jodie on my way in. Big brother strikes again?'

'Matt's cool,' he allowed. 'Hung for a while, him and a couple of mates, Year Elevens. Came around to pick up Jodie, get her home before curfew.'

'Good idea,' I said, yawning and having a late-night scratch. 'Same goes for you and Tarquin. I'm going to hit the sack. Keep it down, will you, and don't leave the premises, okay?'

He shrugged, not fussed. 'Sure,' he said. 'Cool.'

I tossed and turned, just catching the low murmur of boytalk from the backyard and the faint sighing of the waves, somewhere out there at the furthest reaches of my hearing.

And as I awaited oblivion, I thought of Lyndal. And of a night like this, two summers back, when we lay entwined, the sea in our ears, moonlight seeping through a chink in the curtains, and conceived a child.

Then I tried to remember how many days had passed since Lyndal had last come unbidden into my mind. And what, if anything, the answer to that question might mean. It meant, I decided, that time is an active verb. And pondering in turn the meaning of that observation, I drifted into sleep, sure of only one thing. That I was sleeping alone and I wished I wasn't.

The morning dawned hot. By ten, it had muscled thirty aside. I nailed the boys at breakfast, got them with their snouts in the Nutrigrain. 'Order in the House,' I declared, gavelling the kitchen benchtop with the back of a spoon and firming the knot in my sarong. 'The Honourable Murray Whelan has the floor.'

The lads regarded me languidly, cereal-laden implements poised in mid-shovel.

'Regarding the smoking of dope,' I began. 'I'd like to take this opportunity to point out that the possession and use of cannabis is illegal in this state. A bust could get you kicked out of school. Furthermore, some authorities believe that marijuana can trigger adolescent-onset schizophrenia.'

Tark and Red gave each other the sideways eyeball, brows furrowing.

'Not if you don't inhale,' said Tarquin.

'According to the President of the United States,' added Red, helpfully.

'I'm not going to be hypocritical and pretend that I've never smoked the stuff myself,' I said. 'I know it's out there and you'll probably have a lash at some stage. Just let's not pretend it isn't happening.'

They twigged, realising why I had chosen that particular morning to raise the issue.

'Wasn't us,' said Red.

I raised my palms. 'No names, no pack drill. Just play safe, that's all I'm asking. And you might consider waiting until you're a bit older. That way, you can combine it with alcohol and cars, get more bang for your buck.'

'Chill, Dad,' said Red. 'We're cool.'

'I'm glad we had this little talk,' I said. 'Pass the sugar.'

'Now there's something can really kill you,' said Tarquin.

'Depends how hard you get hit with the bowl,' I said.

After breakfast, we went squinting into the heat and drove down the hill, looking to get wet. Mountjoy Parade was thick with traffic as party animals poured into town for the evening's revels on the foreshore, horns honking, car stereos cranked to maximum doof. On the sward of couch grass between the esplanade and the beach a concert stage was taking shape, roadies swarming over the rigging like a pirate crew.

We headed for Wye River, fifteen kilometres further west, a sandy beach at the mouth of a trickling creek. The water was wet but the tide was out, the surf was nowhere and the heat was so wilting that our swims wore off almost before we left the water. Within an hour, we'd had enough.

Back in Lorne, we found council workers erecting crowd-control barriers along the main drag, heat haze rising from the asphalt. Police buses were disgorging coppers from Melbourne, all aviator sunglasses and peaked caps, and a mobile command centre was parked at the kerb outside the Chinese take-away. An FM radio station was broadcasting from the foreshore, its studio in the shape of a giant boom box.

I spent the rest of the day in a wilting torpor, the boys drifting in and out of frame. In due course, late afternoon, we set out for the Falls festival. The lads were tarted up for the festivities. Tark had gone for the romantic-consumptive look in a pleat-fronted dress shirt with a wing collar and no sleeves. Red's hair was sculpted into the vertical with enough gel to grease a Clydeside slipway. Taking the Erskine Falls turn, we followed the shuttle-bus up a meandering road that climbed past the town tip and fern-shaded picnic grounds towards the divide at the top of the ranges. Somewhere to our right, invisible in the dense bush, was the Erskine River and its eponymous falls.

For the last couple of kilometres, the traffic crawled, bumper to bumper. There was shade between the trees, but not a hint of breeze. The leaves hung motionless, limp, the light filtering through their drab greenery from a baked enamel sky. Then, at the top of a crest, they parted to reveal the festival site, a neat patch of grazing land that sat in the midst of the forest like a crop circle in a wheat field. A squarish circle, cyclone-fenced and sloping to an array of big-tops, canopied stages and food stalls, a bass thump washing up the hill to the main gate. A mini-Woodstock.

Eight thousand were expected. Most were there already, the rest arriving by the minute, the tribes gathering. I parked in the designated drop-off zone and told the boys that I'd pick them up in exactly the same spot at exactly noon the next day. After extracting sworn assurances that they would enjoy themselves without doing anything health-threatening or egregiously illegal, I issued a small cash bounty and left them to find their friends in the milling mass at the main gate.

On the way back down to Lorne, I passed a dark grey Landcruiser coming up the hill, Barbara Prentice at the wheel, a full load of teens. I gave her a beep and a wave but I couldn't tell if she recognised me.

By seven-thirty, I was back in town, replenishing my stock of grog at the pub drive-through. The show on the foreshore was firing up. Elements of the crowd were already well lubricated, and mounted police were patrolling the fringes on horses with clear plastic visors. I'd been giving some thought to my options for the evening and hanging with the headache crowd wasn't one of them. I took my beer back to the house, stripped to my jocks, put Ry Cooder on the CD player, ripped the scab from a Coopers Pale Ale, sat in the shade on the deck and watched the sinking sun reach over the ranges and caress the molten sea. Fuck it was hot.

One beer down, I was talking to myself out loud. 'Nothing ventured,' I said, far from convincingly.

Two beers down, I was staring into the rickety wardrobe beside my rented bed, looking for the right kind of statement. The pre-faded Hawaiian, I decided, with the dark hibiscus motif. Khaki shorts and loafers. Laid-back but snazzy.

I finished the third bottle under the shower, out-and-out Dutch courage, then dressed and drove to Gusto. It was nine, the sun was gone and a syrupy twilight was taking its place, the sea flat, the air motionless. Inbound traffic on the Great Ocean Road was backed up to the town limits, cops at a row of witches hats running random breath tests. I was safe, headed the other way, but I popped a mint anyway and summoned my sobriety. Chill, I ordered. Be cool.

If I was serious about this, I'd have done some spadework. I'd have called Sandra, made exploratory noises, got the low-down. Instead, I was playing an outside break sucking a peppermint, for Christ's sake. All dicked up in my new-bought leisure-wear, hot to trot with a mother of two who probably wasn't even in the market.

By the time I took the turn at the adobe signpost, I was moving beyond second thoughts, entering cut-and-run territory. But there was nowhere to run. The sharply ascending strip of asphalt was squeezed by tea-trees and there was a car behind me, pushing me forward. At the first opening, three hundred metres up the slope, I was extruded into the restaurant carpark.

I fed the Magna into the first available slot and sat there, engine idling, aircon blasting, fingers drumming on the steering wheel, sucking my mint.

The carpark was a quadrangle of crushed gravel toppings, fifty or so spaces, filling fast. The car that had followed me up the road, a big old banger of a Merc, decanted a party of four. Thirtysomething couples, the men in high spirits, the women in high heels. Passing a dark grey Landcruiser with roof-racks and Ripcurl stickers, they bantered and crunched their way down steps flanked with enormous terracotta pots sprouting an exuberant arch of raspberry bougainvillea.

Another carload arrived, then another, then another. This was getting ridiculous. Time to screw my courage to the designated place. But which one?

It wasn't rocket science. I had two choices. I could return to the house and get comfortably numb on self-pity, Coopers Pale Ale and *B. B. King's Greatest Hits*.

Or I could slip into the restaurant, ease my way into the evening's *joie de vivre*, suss my prospects with Barbara Prentice and play it as it came.

Go wild, I told myself, live dangerously. You're on holidays after all.

I turned off the motor, checked my charm in the rearview mirror and stepped out into the sticky night air. The twilight was thickening, thrumming with laughter and music, the sound of salsa. Gusto's facade was an eclectic amalgam of peeling weatherboards, fibro sheeting and rust-hued corrugated iron. The effect was of a beachcomber's shack slapped together by a castaway with an artist's eye. Gilligan meets Georgia O'Keeffe. Or Barbara Prentice.

A strip-door curtain of rope and crimped bottle caps marked the entrance. I parted the strips and found myself in a narrow, badly lit corridor. The sound and light and laughter lay ahead, drawing me forward. All part of the design, I realised. The customer as privileged insider, a mate of the owner. The cook's cousin, granted back-door access.

A gaggle of diners milled at the edge of the light, pressing their credentials on the head waiter. One wall of the corridor became a plate-glass window, a view into the kitchen. Another design flourish. No miserly dribbles of truffle oil here, no pernickety plating of filleted fava beans. This was

Gusto's fiery forge, a seething engine-room of white-clad minions, flaming sauté pans and flashing knives. I watched a cook emerge from a back door, a heavy bucket in each hand, and pour a stream of glistening black mussels into a huge pot on the cooktop.

Past the waiting customers, the lucky guests were roaring at each other across long tables covered with butcher's paper, carafes of wine and Duralex tumblers. Some of the tables were outside, running around the edge of a broad patio. Party lights hung in droopy loops, illuminating the scene.

At one end of the terrace a four-piece combo was doing a playful *mucho maracas* Carmen Miranda routine. Snack jockeys were circulating, aproned tweenies with nibbles on trays. Couples sat on the low adobe wall that surrounded the terrace, soaking up the view. All two-seventy degrees of it. A wedge of moon glowing through a thin gauze of clouds crept across the sky. The sea extended forever, eerily phosphorescent. And immediately below, the snaking lights of the cars on the Great Ocean Road.

Hooley-dooley, I thought. Whacko the did. All the senses, all at once. Count me in.

I scanned the moving bodies, peering into the muted, multicoloured light, searching for a slender woman with a talent for the casual chic, a mannish haircut and an elusively attractive way of carrying herself. The knot of supplicant customers dissolved, approved *en masse* by the head waiter. As I shuffled forward to plead for admission, Barbara emerged from a clump of conversation on the far side of the room.

She was wearing a sheathy jade-green thing with shoestring straps. One of them slipped off her shoulder and as she turned her head to fix it, our eyes met. Hers were still grey.

'Ay-ay-ay-ay-ay I like you verrry much!' warbled Carmen on the veranda.

Barbara gave a little self-satisfied smile. I knew you'd come, it said. Let the games begin.

I gave her a smile back, the hapless here-I-am one. I poked at my chest, then at the head waiter, shrugging. She nodded and began to make her way across the crowded room. Some enchanted evening, I murmured.

The kitchen door flapped on its hinges and a big man came sailing out into the restaurant. He wore a loose cotton shirt, cuffs rolled to the forearm, and an air of proprietary bonhomie. It was Signor Gusto himself, Jake Martyn. He paused for a moment, cast an appraising eye over the proceedings, then advanced into the throng, arm raised in hearty salutation.

A burst of flame drew my eye to the window into the kitchen. A flambé of prawns in Pernod, perhaps. Beyond the cooktops and the steaming molluscs, a man in a khaki work shirt and matching stubbies had also turned towards the sudden flash. He was glancing back over his shoulder from the semi-darkness of a doorway to the delivery bay. Stocky. Bushy beard. Ravaged baseball cap, the bill pulled down. A working man. Delivery driver, rubbish removal, hump and grunt.

Head tilted sideways, eyes peering out, his expression exactly mirrored an image which I had seen many times before. A still photograph printed from a few seconds of video footage, then enlarged. A three-quarter profile of a handcuffed prisoner being bustled into a remand hearing, tossing a sideways glance in the direction of the television camera. A picture at which I had stared long and hard, simmering with impotent rage.

A picture of Rodney Syce.

And then he was gone.

My stomach dropped away beneath me like an elevator in freefall.

I stood rooted to the spot, mind spinning, staring into the empty space where the man had been. Was it really possible that I had just looked through a plate-glass window at Lyndal's killer?

Only one thing was certain. I could not ignore what I had seen. Try, and the doubt would drive me nuts, poison the promise of the evening. And beyond.

I had to get another look at the man. Satisfy myself, one way or the other.

Dashing back along the corridor, I squeezed past a phalanx of incoming guests and burst through the rope-and-bottle-cap curtain. An irregular hedge of tea-tree separated Gusto's public entrance from its service area. I shouldered my way through the thicket and glimpsed a curved driveway leading from a loading bay at the back of the restaurant to the road above the guest carpark.

A runabout tray-truck was parked half-way up the driveway, a well-used Hilux utility. Its driver's-side door was open and the figure in khaki was hoisting himself aboard. He glanced back, not noticing me as I parted the shrubbery.

I was thinking very fast. His general description fitted Syce. Height, shape, approximate age. The beard didn't appear in the picture, but that proved nothing. Stood to reason that he'd attempt to disguise himself. More to the point, there was a nagging similarity between my snapshot and what I could see of the man's face. The oval shape, the full lips, the sloping cheekbones.

But still I couldn't be sure. The light was murky and he was a good ten metres away.

The door of the Hilux slammed shut and it started up. I began to run towards it, but its wheels were spinning, tyres spitting gravel, tail-lights glowing.

I pulled up short. But only for a heartbeat. And then I was running again, sprinting back to the Magna, slamming the key into the ignition, backing out of the parking slot. Acting, not thinking, except to think that I couldn't let him vanish into the night. That there was no way in the world the cops were going to believe me a fourth time.

The Hilux had turned right, heading uphill. Fifty metres past the restaurant driveway, the road became graded gravel. It climbed through low scrub for a couple of minutes, crossed the hump of the hill and emerged into a residential area, cars at the kerbsides, lights in the houses, party time.

But the utility was nowhere in sight. I arrived at a T-junction. Two lanes of asphalt, double yellow lines, cats-eye reflectors on white roadside markers. Deans Marsh Road, the back-door route across the ranges. Cars whizzed past, barrelling downhill, revellers heading into town. Which way had he gone? Downhill or up? Towards the activity or away from it?

Go back to the restaurant, I told myself. Make enquiries. Find out if anybody knew him. By the look of it, he'd been making a delivery of some kind. So even if nobody knew him, they'd at least be able to tell me who sent him. What could be gained by chasing him?

A better look at him, for a start. The chance to cross him off the list, mark him down as a false alarm. And without going through the rigmarole of interrogating the Gusto staff, parading my obsession. Without the risk of making a fool of myself in front of Barbara Prentice.

Uphill, I decided, away from town. I swung the wheel and floored the pedal, spraying gravel as my front tyres gripped the bitumen. The road climbed steadily, joined at irregular intervals by smaller side roads and tracks. Had he taken one of those? I stuck with the main road, a theory taking shape in my mind, consistent with what I knew about Rodney Syce. As scenarios went, it made as much sense as anything the coppers had told me.

On the lam, solo, Syce had gone to ground, grown some fungus. Stayed in Victoria, where he had no criminal connections, less chance of being fingered. Picked up jobs on the margins, cash-in-hand stuff, melded into the here-today-gone-tomorrow casual workforce. Maybe even built a new identity.

The road twisted and turned, climbing continuously, its course hemmed by thickening bush. The traffic was all downhill, oncoming headlights at the frequent corners. It was almost nine-thirty, night coming down. If I didn't spot the Hilux in the next few minutes, I told myself, I'd pack it in, turn around, contact the cops. Persuade them to make enquiries at Gusto. Let the appropriate authorities deal with it, like I'd been told.

I checked my watch, stepped on the gas. Two minutes, that's how much longer I'd give it. *Dangerous Turn*, read a yellow advisory sign.

Then it was there, right in front of me as I rounded a bend, nothing between us. I dropped back, not showing my hand, waiting for an opportunity to overtake, study the driver as I passed. I tried to read the number plate, but it wasn't lit.

It was double lines all the way, not a chance to swing around him. We continued uphill, north-west into the ranges. At some point, twenty or thirty kilometres further along, the road would pop out of the hills and run through farmland to the Princes Highway. If he went that far, he could be headed anywhere in Australia. Literally. The Princes Highway circled the entire fucking continent.

The road straightened and I moved closer, preparing to pass. But the Hilux slowed, indicated left and turned down a side road. I continued past for a hundred metres, then doubled back. The road was a single lane of asphalt, gravel-edged, tree-lined, a trench cut into the forest, well signposted. Mount Sabine Road. Never heard of it, or its mount. The ute's tail-lights bobbed in the distance, beckoning.

This is crazy, said the voice of reason. But since when has reason been reason for anything? I dipped my lights to low beam and kept going, deeper into the night.

Rodney Syce was an experienced bushman. And what were

the Otways if not the bush? Dense, virtually impenetrable bush, all just a few hours from Melbourne. A tall timber bolt-hole, exactly the sort of place where a wanted man could lie doggo, grow a beard, pass unremarked among the locals. Scruffy transients, back-to-nature hermits, hippy farmers, breast-feeding ferals, bush mechanics, timber cutters, sleep-rough surfers, mind-your-own-business truckies, law-leery bikers. The full panoply of tree-dwelling, kit-home, cud-chewing yokeldom. The only thing missing was a banjo-plunking soundtrack.

I twiddled the dial of the radio, caught wavering snatches of pop music and the hiss of static, the signals baffled by the timbered folds of the hills. The road rose and fell with the signal, snaking around tight-coiled corners. The trees got bigger, closer together, the understorey more dense. My headlights swept the fronds of giant ferns, bare rock walls, mossy clefts.

Occasional chinks opened in the curtain of bush. The brutal gash of a firebreak. Obscure clearings stacked with saw-logs. Unmarked forestry tracks. Machinery sheds, hunched in the middle of nowhere. All the while, up ahead, the pickup's tail-lights winked and blinked, luring me on.

The road meandered, lost its paved surface, became a rutted blanket of beige dirt, forever changing direction. As it followed the twists and turns, the pickup vanished for minutes on end. Then, just when I thought I'd lost it, I caught the flicker of headlights amid the trees ahead, slatted radiance. Or the abrupt flare of brake lights at some sharp bend.

Where was he going? A farm? That would explain the delivery to the restaurant. Strawberries? There were signs along the Great Ocean Road for pick-your-own berry farms. Kiwi fruit, maybe. Some sort of bush tucker, myrtle berries, gummy bears. Not very Jake Martyn, that sort of stuff.

And why the late-night delivery? An unexpected shortage of canapé garnishes? If this guy was indeed Rodney Syce, he should be hunkered down in the native shrubbery, not gadding about the place, running taste treats into a town crawling with coppers.

The road forked, then forked again, the Hilux nowhere in sight. I guessed, guessed again. Kept left, tightened my grip on the steering wheel, imagined it was Rodney Syce's neck.

The track kept getting narrower. Its surface was potholed and corrugated. It hammered my suspension, peppered my undercarriage with gravel, sent my tail slewing at the turns. A tight bend loomed and suddenly the track disappeared, replaced by a sheer drop into a scrub-choked gully. I stomped on the anchors, the steering juddered and the Magna went into a skid, wheels locked.

I wrestled for control, steering wildly for the inside edge of the road. The Magna slid to a halt, then stalled, side-on to the direction of the road. My fingers were rigid around the wheel, my ears roaring with adrenalin.

I killed the lights, got out and took stock. The car's rear wheels were sunk to the rims in a pothole, its tail dangling over the edge. Another half a metre and I'd have joined the choir eternal. Or worse, been trapped in the wreckage, ruptured and bleeding, lingering in agony for days, waiting for help that never came. Situation like that, a body could remain undiscovered for decades, like some shot-down Mustang pilot in a New Guinea jungle, a bleached skeleton buckled into a rusting machine.

I reached into the glovebox for another cigarette. My second in an hour. I was practically chain-smoking. Then, squatting at the side of the road, I tried to gather my wits. The bush was motionless, monochromatic, an ancient daguerreotype. Pools of black gathered at the feet of massive trees, grey slabs of bark peeling from their trunks. The milky wash of an overcast sky seeped through their dappled foliage. The humidity was oppressive and beads of sweat trickled from my armpits.

What the hell did I think I was doing? Right at the very moment that my life was regaining balance, when romance seemed not likely—okay—but possible, I'd headed for the hills in hot pursuit of a half-seen face. What was more important, settling the scores of the past or making something of the future?

It was nearly ten. Down on the Lorne foreshore, beer and sunburn were brewing a heady mix, testing the tolerance of the coppers. At the Falls, Red was moshing it up with Jodie Prentice. Back at Gusto, the Domaine Chandon was flowing and an intriguing, accomplished woman in a jade-green dress was wondering, I hoped, where that Murray Whelan fellow had disappeared to.

The bush, stilled by my noisy arrival, was coming back to life. Mopoke calls, cicada thrums, possumy ruttings in the canopy. I ground my cigarette under foot, making sure it was completely extinguished. It was time to stop chasing geese around the ranges.

As I rose from my haunches, I heard the clunk of gears being engaged, then the muted wheeze of an engine. I dropped back into a crouch and leaned forward, every fibre straining into the variegated night. Across the gully and slightly below me, a vehicle was labouring through the bush. I squinted in the direction of the noise, attempting to pinpoint its source. I caught the whine of a gearbox, the slow crunch of tyres. But no lights. The driver, it seemed reasonable to assume, didn't want to be noticed.

The sound receded. I got into the Magna, manoeuvred it back onto the track and crawled forward, aircon off, window down, ears cocked, headlights off. Whoever he was, the fact that he didn't want to be followed was reason enough to follow him.

The track hugged the rim of the gully, switched back, then turned again, heading away from the source of the noise. The ground became flatter, the vegetation less dense, stringybarks with an understorey of scrubby vines. I cut the motor, got out, and listened. Nothing.

I walked back along the track, eyes fixed on the ground.

Enough light from the overcast sky made it through the canopy to throw a faint shadow in the wheel ruts. Fifty metres from the car, tyre treads had squashed the edge of the track. The treads ran into the bush. I followed them. The ground was hard-packed and thick with tufts of native grass. The tyre marks petered out.

Maybe they'd been made by the Hilux. Maybe not. What did I know? I was no black tracker. But I'd come this far, so I figured I might as well exhaust the possibilities before turning around and going back to Gusto.

I slipped the Magna into neutral and rolled it off the track. I left the key in the ignition ready for a fast getaway and put my wallet under the seat. I took a torch from the glovebox, pocketed my mobile phone and set off.

Swinging the torch back and forth across the leaf litter, I

advanced into the undergrowth. After a few minutes, the beam found a patch of exposed earth, the clay ploughed by wheel ruts. Somebody had come this way in a wetter season, broken the surface. But the ground had turned back to iron and the trail faded away, lost in a thicket of bracken between towering gums.

The torch beam flickered, then faded completely. I pressed on, picking my way through a stand of flattened bracken. The terrain dropped away to a fern-filled gully, the ground spongy with rotted logs and leaf mulch. I climbed back up the slope and started again, casting about for spoor like an illustration in *Scouting for Boys*. Absurd figure in Bombay bloomers demonstrates correct technique for detection of rogue wildebeest. I might as well have been wearing a blindfold. It was so dark in places that a man would have been hard put to find his local member.

My shirt was sticky with sweat, my knees caked with dirt, the bare skin of my legs and arms livid with nicks and scrapes. Fuck this shit, I thought. Time to pack it in, come at the matter from a different angle.

For some reason, the track wasn't where I left it. I retraced my steps, scanning the forest for previously noted landmarks. A dappled gum with a skirt of shredded bark, a cleft boulder with a sapling sprouting from it, a quartz-strewn slope. But they, too, seemed to have wandered away. I began to suspect that I might not be headed in the right direction.

No immediate cause for alarm, I told myself. The track must be somewhere nearby, it's just a matter of taking a methodical approach, applying your mind to the problem. You are not lost. You have merely paused to orient yourself.

Five minutes later, I conceded that I was utterly bushed.

According to received wisdom, the correct procedure when lost in the bush is to remain where you are. Do not risk exacerbating the situation by wandering around. If you have a pack of cards, deal yourself a hand of patience. Before long someone will lean over your shoulder and point out that the red queen goes on the black king. Failing that, simply wait for your absence to be noted and a search initiated.

On the other hand, I could ring for help. I pulled out my mobile phone, switched it on and looked down at the keypad.

Ring who, I wondered? Roadside assistance. The Hansel and Gretel helpline. The House Ways and Means Committee? I dialled 000 and pushed the send button. 'Out of Range' glowed the LCD. I tried again, my number in Melbourne, testing. Same result. Zip.

I scrabbled uphill, hoping for a better outcome on higher ground. Still no luck. The ground kept dropping away, always some gully yawning before me. The understorey was so thick that I almost needed a machete to get through it. And still no signal. If I kept punching at the phone, it would go the way of the torch, battery flat. Panic began to take hold. I was trapped in a labyrinth, hoist on my own petard, an idiot.

I changed strategy. Rather than heading uphill in search of a signal, I hunted the lower ground, plunging down gullies, hoping to reach a creek bed. If I was not entirely mistaken, always a possibility, I was somewhere on the seaward side of the divide. If I followed a creek downstream, it would lead me in the right direction.

Down, down, I went, momentum building. Then my left foot hooked a root and I fell, crying out as a bolt of pain shot through my ankle. Flat on my arse, I skidded and skittered down a sharp incline, snatching at branches to slow my descent.

I landed hard, ankle throbbing, chest heaving. Keep thrashing through the mulga like this, I decided, and I'd do myself a serious damage. No point in continuing to buggerise around in the dark, risking a fatal accident. Follow the manual, stay put, wait until morning. I pressed my back against a tree fern and tried to get comfortable.

As the thump of my heartbeat slowed and the rasp of my breathing settled, I became acutely aware that night was filled with sound, alive with movement. Faint rustlings in the leaf litter, reptilian slitherings, bandicoot scuttlings, the snick and hum of insects, the omnipresent chorus of cicadas. Soon, my every sinew was tuned to the concert of the forest. I was in the dress circle.

Gradually, I became aware of an intermittent murmur at the far periphery of my hearing. Two distinct components, two alternating tones, snatches. It was coming from further along the debris-choked gully in which I was sitting.

I stood up and began limping towards it, picking my way over rotting logs and lichen-covered boulders. The sound grew clearer. Somebody was talking.

I heard the words quite clearly.

'A pizza.'

There was a contemptuous hoot, then silence.

I kept going, all my senses alert, creeping through the undergrowth. Maybe the owner of the voice was benevolent, a potential rescuer. Or maybe it was Syce.

A hundred metres along, the gully became a dry creek bed, a floor of sand and pebbles between sharply rising banks. High above, the canopy parted a little and a milky wash leaked down from the night sky, creating a chiaroscuro world of deep shadows and luminous space. I felt my way forward, ankle throbbing but not unbearable.

'Bag of ice. Any warmer, you could poach an egg in this beer.'

'I'm not your fucken errand boy, you know?'

The voices had started again, just above me now, at the top of a steep rock wall. Snatches. Two men, it sounded like. Bickering about who was responsible for the poor quality of the catering.

'Anything'd be better than this canned crap you've been feeding me.'

'Yap, yap, yap…nothing but bitch the whole time.'

The exchange was intermittent, lethargic, rehearsed, like the conversation of a long-married couple. But it offered no clue as to the identity of the speakers, apart from the fact that there were two of them and they were men. Neither was a member of the Royal Shakespeare Company. Both spoke a flat, workaday Australian, one with a tinge of second-generation wog.

Hunched, darting, all very commando, I worked my way along the narrow watercourse to where the bank became less steep and overhanging. Looking back, I caught a flicker of movement, elongated shadows reaching up into the branches, thrown by the white glow of a camping lantern.

I caught the glint of water, a necklace of shallow pools, hovering mosquitoes, the ribbit of a frog. A low wall of sand-filled plastic bags had been laid across the creek bed. Water was banked up behind it, its surface flecked with dead leaves, busy with bugs. A heavy-duty hose emerged from the pond and disappeared into the darkness. I raised a cupped palm of the tepid, musty-tasting water to my lips, then skirted the pool and continued, my ear tuned to the murmur of voices at the top of the bank.

A few metres past the dam, the creek bed widened into a flat wash of gritty sand and loose pebbles, maybe ten metres wide. Tyre tracks led downstream and a vehicle had been driven up onto a flat area on the bank. It was the Hilux. I put my hand on the hood to be sure, felt the lingering heat of the engine.

The bank was low, easy to scale, but the ground was

uneven and densely thicketed. I tiptoed up the bank, my left ankle still not pulling its weight, trying to get some sense of the set-up without betraying my presence. The dam and the creek bed roadway pointed to an established campsite. Illegal, in that the state forest was off-limits to campers, but playing fast and loose with forestry by-laws was hardly a federal case, not in itself. Point was, whose camp was it?

Wired, every nerve at battle stations, I circled around, looking for the best approach to the light. At least now I had a potential exit route, the creek bed. If the driver of the Hilux turned out to be Rodney Syce, or if things just got too hairy for me, I could follow the tyre ruts to the nearest police station.

In the meantime, I was edging through a clump of saw-toothed shrubs, the ground between them cut with shallow trenches. I plucked a leaf, crushed it between my fingers and sniffed. Cannabis. A small crop of it, irregularly spaced, twenty or thirty plants, head-high.

Okay. So we had a dope-growing operation of some sort. That accounted for the dam, the hose, the concealed location. And weren't petty crims sometimes employed to baby-sit dope plantations? The Syce scenario was firming.

And my nostrils were twitching, picking up a pungent smell. Not the dope but something fishy, its source closer to the light. I edged forward, the hiss of the gas lantern now audible. A square-edged structure loomed in faint silhouette.

I waited, letting my eyes adjust to the complexities of the near-total darkness, until the outline became an aluminium shed, garage-sized, its metal surface camouflaged with rough dabs of paint. The pong was coming from inside. A dark-on-dark rectangle suggested an open door. From the other side of the shed's thin walls came the voice I had come to think of as The Grumbler. It was grumbling.

'Jesus, what a way to spend New Year's Eve, hanging around this god-forsaken dump with a half-wit possum fucker. What's keeping him, for Chrissake? You said he'd be here in half an hour, it's been twice that.'

'Sooner he turns up the better,' said the other voice. 'Ten days of listening to your fucken belly-aching, I'm fed up.'

Easing the torch from my pocket, I stepped to the opening in the shed. The flashlight summoned its reserves, glowed wanly for a few seconds, then expired once again. Before it did, I glimpsed an earthen floor, a pump, a generator, gas bottles, a bench with a four-ring burner and grimy sink, a cooking pot. By the look of it, and the smell, the cultivation of marijuana was not the only illicit activity taking place here. If I wasn't mistaken, this was some sort of abalone-processing set-up. It seemed reasonable to assume that it was not a government-licensed, industry-standard, health-inspected facility. The fishy smell was vile, overwhelming.

A weathered aluminium dinghy on a boat-trailer was parked beside the shed, brick wheel chocks. Above it, a tarpaulin was slung between the shed and the branches of a tree. Even from a helicopter, the place would be almost impossible to spot. Peering between the shed and the boat, I saw a clearing lit by the spill from a Primus lantern, a gas bottle with a glowing white mantle above it. The lantern sat on a folding table in a tent walled with insect-screen, the side flaps rolled up. Tiny moths swarmed over the screen.

A man was sitting at the table, his back to me. Shorts, work shirt, the outline of a beard. My suspect. I could see that he was playing solitaire, hear the faint slap of the cards.

A man well equipped for the bush. But I couldn't see his face.

'Christ,' he said. 'How many fucken times I gotta tell ya? You want a slash, go into the bush. Stop fucken stinking up the place.'

The other bloke was standing a few metres away, at the far edge of the circle of light. He, too, had his back to me. He was stocky, roughly the same shape as the card player. He was naked except for a pair of mustard-coloured jockettes and rubber flip-flops. His hairy shoulders drooped above the sagging flesh of his torso. He was pissing loudly against the trunk of the tree.

'Yeah, like it doesn't stink already, those abs you been cooking up.' He shook himself and turned. Sweat glistened on his high, domed forehead and stubble crawled down his face, thickening into a goatee.

I saw but I didn't believe. It was Tony Melina, proprietor of La Luna restaurant, steaks and seafood a speciality. Tony Melina, runaway spouse.

Dumbfounded, I squeezed my eyes shut, shook my head and looked again. Yup, it was Tony all right. But what was he doing here? It didn't make sense. According to his wife, Tony Melina was disporting himself with some floozie in the flesh-pots of Asia. That, at least, was plausible. This was utterly baffling, as incomprehensible as Section 27(a) of the Health Insurance Act. More mystifying even than a Liberal's ethical framework. Tony Melina? Here? With Rodney Syce? I sniffed my fingertips. That dope, maybe it was some hybrid superstrain. Perhaps I was hallucinating.

Tony stepped forward into the light. He looked like a washed-up gorilla, the missing link between man and doormat. He raised his foot and shook it.

'You want a hygienic camp?' he said. 'Try showing a little trust.'

A chain rattled. It was connected to his ankle, running across the ground to the screened tent. The card player gave a derisory snort and shuffled the cards.

'And have you take off again? Not on your nellie.'

'Why would I take off now?' Tony whined. 'Soon as he arrives, we do the business, I'm out of here.'

'Just doing my job, pal. You'll get unlocked when he gets here, not before. You know the drill.'

Tony grunted, then shuffled into the tent, dragging the chain after him. 'Far as I'm concerned, it won't be a minute too soon,' he said, plonking himself down and curling his fist around a can.

Things were getting weirder by the second.

Tony was obviously a prisoner, yet his demeanour suggested that to some degree he accepted the situation. Did Rita have a hand in this? Was some sort of rough justice being dispensed here? It was one thing to dob her philandering husband in to the authorities, quite another to chain him up in the Otway Forest wearing only last week's underpants. Who was the card player? Was he Rodney Syce or not? And what was that fucking terrible smell?

Every fibre of my being was telling me to get the hell out of there, follow the creek bed downhill, find a road, summon the cavalry. Let the coppers sort it out.

But I couldn't leave yet, not without getting a clearer view of the card player's face, enough to satisfy me on the Syce front. Heart pounding, I inched into the gap between the boat-trailer and the shed. The inky shadow of the tarpaulin canopy ran right to the edge of the clearing, as close as I could creep without giving myself away. But to get a well-lit view of the man's face, I needed a bit of altitude and a better angle. Slowly, heartbeat by heartbeat, I put my right foot, the good one, on the mudguard of the boat-trailer. Easing down on the springs, I hoisted myself upright. Left leg jutting sideways for balance, I leaned over the boat, craning for a clearer view.

That's when I saw the mutt. It was lying on an old sack beside the screened tent, licking its balls. A short-haired mongrel of a thing, a stump with legs, some sort of kelpie-pitbull cross.

The trailer's springs squeaked beneath me. The sound couldn't have been softer. The dog pricked up its ears and raised its muzzle, did a radar sweep. I froze. The bloke at the table turned over a card, oblivious. The dog stood up. I stared at it, not daring to breathe, my mouth dry, my ears filled with the *boomf, boomf, boomf*ing of my heart.

The dog's ears quivered. It took a step forward, sniffed the air, tensed. Somewhere in its canine recesses, input was being assessed, conclusions drawn, sinews mobilised. It swung its snout in my direction and emitted a low, carnivorous growl.

'Wassat, boy? That feral again?'

The card player swivelled in his seat, following the direction of the dog's stare. But I didn't notice his face. I wasn't looking that way. My eyes were glued to the dog. It was hurtling towards me, a fanged missile, barking savagely.

My fight-or-flight instinct took the floor. Flight had the numbers. Run, Murray, run. Now. Fast.

But I wouldn't get far, not with a dodgy ankle and set of canine canines embedded in my fleshy extremities. Nor, prudence dictated, would simply revealing my presence be a good idea. 'Evening gents, Murray Whelan here, Member for Melbourne Upper.' For a start, I still wasn't absolutely sure if the solitaire-shuffler was Rodney Syce. I was pretty sure, however, that he was engaged in some sort of criminal activity and he was unlikely to be well disposed to a stranger blundering into his operation. A lost and vulnerable stranger.

And as for Tony Melina, although he wasn't hostile, not as far as I knew, he was in the unreliable category until proven otherwise. Besides which, he was chained to a frigging tree.

Instinctively, even as these thoughts were racing through my mind, I stepped into the dinghy and dropped to a crouch.

My hands swept the floor, searching for something with which to defend myself, should the situation so require. Furious barking rent the air. Creatures scarpered in the canopy. But the dog came no closer. It snapped to a halt at the end of a rope tether, capering and baying, filling the night with its clamour.

'Shuddup, you,' snapped the card player. 'Quiet.'

The dog reluctantly obeyed, firing off a final volley of yaps. But it continued to bristle, snout pointed my way, trembling eagerly. I sank lower on my haunches, eyes level with the edge of the boat, hand closing around a light metal object. The shaft of an oar, I guessed. A serviceable implement, if paddle came to whack.

The card player emerged from the screen shelter and stood beside the dog, staring out of his pool of light directly into the darkness in which I was immersed. The lantern behind him formed a nimbus around his head and threw his features into shadow. He was holding a shotgun.

That did it for me. I no longer needed a full-face close-up. Forget the Cecil Beaton portrait, the whole murky ball of wax spoke for itself. If the man with the gun wasn't Rodney Syce, I'd go down on the Premier in front of the entire parliamentary press gallery.

He stared long and hard, head tilted to one side, listening. My heart was pounding louder than the Burundi National Drum Ensemble. My mouth was so dry that the skin was making crackling noises. I had ceased entirely to breathe.

From somewhere behind me came the faint drone of an approaching motor.

Syce relaxed, reached down and ruffled the nape of the dog's neck. 'Good boy,' he said. Then, over his shoulder to

Tony, who was hobbling from the annexe, dragging his chain behind him. 'Here he comes now.'

The dog yapped, its muzzle still pointed directly at me. 'Settle,' Syce ordered. The mutt gave a disappointed growl, padded back to its bed and lay down.

Syce moved out of my frame of vision for a couple of seconds, then reappeared minus the shotgun. He busied himself with undoing the shackle at Tony Melina's ankle. 'Behave yourself and you'll be out of here tonight,' he said.

'Yeah, yeah,' said Tony impatiently. 'I know the score.'

I allowed myself to inhale. I needed to get out of there, fast and quiet. I let go of the oar, took hold of the rim of the dinghy and tensed, ready to vault to the ground beside the ab-processing shed. But the advancing vehicle was already labouring up the slope from the creek bed, headlights angled high into the treetops. Up the bank it came, *vroom, vroom*, a blaze of light preceding it. Light that began to sweep across the tarpaulin above my head.

I dropped flat, cheek pressed to the dinghy's aluminium hull. Fetid bilgewater rose in my nostrils. The vehicle came around the boat, very close, and pulled up. The engine cut out, but the lights stayed on, spilling their glow to the very edge of my hiding place. A door creaked open, then snicked shut. Footsteps crunched.

'Tony,' hailed a man's voice. 'Mate.'

'Nice to see you, Jake,' replied Tony, his tone heavy with sarcasm. 'Good of you to pay us a visit. Busy night at Gusto, I imagine.'

Jake Martyn. It couldn't be anyone else.

This did not compute. Nothing computed. My mental mainframe could not do the arithmetic.

'Busy enough,' came the reply. Relaxed. Hail-fellow. 'So what's the problem? Something in the paperwork you didn't understand?'

I managed to roll onto my back. Shadows flickered across the tarpaulin suspended above the boat. An unobserved exit was now out of the question. The voices were no more than ten paces away.

A million questions swarmed through my mind, not many of them finding answers. Jake Martyn and Tony Melina belonged in the same frame, that much I could grasp. Two men in the restaurant business. Men in the process of conducting a business deal of some sort. A dirty money deal, poached abalone in the picture. Some degree of duress involved, hence Tony's captivity. This had nothing to do with Rita. And the whole tall-timbers hideout set-up made sense in terms of Rodney Syce, wanted fugitive and experienced bushman. But what was the connection between Jake Martyn and Rodney Syce?

'What's the problem?' echoed Tony Melina, his tone incredulous, angry. 'I've been chained to a fucken tree, you ask me what's the problem?'

'Chained to a tree?' Martyn mirrored Tony's incredulity, but with a larding of mock outrage. 'I had no idea. Is this true, Mick?'

Mick clearly meant Syce. An alias was only to be expected. Tony, evidently, didn't know the true identity of his jailer. Or he was in on the act.

'Not to mention the bloody awful stink,' Tony went on. 'It seeps into your pores.'

Martyn laughed. 'That's the sweet smell of money, mate. Mick's little abalone kitchen might not be Health

Department approved, but we'd both be poorer without it.'

'You said I'd only be stuck here for a couple of days,' whined Tony. 'It's been ten, for Chrissake. What the fuck am I going to tell the missus, the staff.'

'It's been far too long, mate, I agree,' soothed Martyn. 'And you've been very patient. I appreciate it, I really do. And so would Phil, I'm sure, if he knew how uncomfortable you've been. But delays are inevitable at this time of the year, any kind of international transaction. Banks closed for the holidays, different time-zones, it's been frustrating for all of us. But I sent up the papers the minute they arrived, just like I promised. All you had to do was sign them, have Mick bring them back. If you'd done that, you'd be on your way right now. Instead, you send him to fetch me, busiest night of the year, insist on seeing me in person before you sign. And here I am. So, can we get on with it?'

I tensed my stomach muscles and raised my torso until I could just see over the bows of the boat. Jake Martyn—it was definitely him—had a briefcase in one hand. His other hand was on Tony Melina's hairy shoulder, leading him towards the screened tent with its table and hissing Primus lantern.

That wasn't the only thing I saw. Rodney Syce was walking directly towards me. I dropped back and felt the bows of the boat dip as he lowered his backside onto the trailer hitch. He grunted as he dropped into place and the springs of the trailer squeaked beneath his weight. My bowels turned to liquid. I clenched my buttocks, scarcely daring to breathe.

'I don't fucken believe this,' Tony Melina was saying. 'You act like it's perfectly normal to do business like this. Grab me, get me pissed. Keep me that way for days on end, pouring grog down my throat every time I wake up. Drag me up here, wherever the fuck this is, tie me to a tree like a dog, then expect me to sign on the dotted line, go home like nothing unusual's happened. This is the deal from hell, Jakey boy. I might as well kiss my money goodbye, right?'

Syce made a low, irritated noise, then stood up, restless. His footsteps moved away, into the bush.

'Not at all, Tony,' Martyn soothed. 'It's going to be exactly like we agreed in the beginning. We'll be partners in the restaurant, you and me. Fifty-fifty. Straight down the middle. I'll run things, you'll be the silent partner. Very silent. As long as you keep your mouth shut, things will be sweet. You'll get your fair whack of the profits. Believe me.'

'Sure,' said Tony bitterly. 'If there's any profits to share. Which there won't be, of course. Why don't you admit this whole thing's been a scam from the word go.'

'Listen, mate. Things got off to a bit of a rocky start, I'll admit. But there'll be plenty for everybody. You keep your side of the deal, I'll keep mine. It's a matter of trust. And, frankly, you've been the weak link in that department, you've got to admit. You were eager enough to come into the business when I first proposed it, you'll recall. Keen to play with the big boys. It was even you who first suggested we go the offshore loan route, remember?'

I could hear twigs snapping and the clump of Syce's footfalls as he stalked the perimeter of the camp. The hull was hard against my back, my mobile phone jammed against my kidneys. I hoped to Christ it was still out of range. The last thing I needed right then was an unexpected call, some cold-canvasser ringing to discuss my insurance needs at ten past eleven on New Year's Eve. Shifting position, I propped on my elbow, casting about with my free hand, taking blind inventory. Two lightweight metal oars, a tangle of fishing line, a life-jacket. Nothing remotely useful.

'And if you hadn't tried to back out at the last minute, upset the applecart, it wouldn't have been necessary to remind you of your obligations,' Martyn was saying. 'So stop being such a cry-baby, Tony. Sign the fucking papers, join the firm. Then Mick can see you out of here and I can get back to my guests.'

I hazarded a peep. Tony and Jake Martyn were facing each other across the table in the screened tent, the briefcase open between them. Martyn was reaching in, removing a sheaf of documents. The dog was reclining on its sacking bed, back to doing what dogs do because they can.

As far as I was concerned, Tony Melina and Jake Martyn could do the same. And the sooner the better. My interest was Rodney Syce. And if I'd understood what I'd just heard, as soon as Martyn and Melina finished transacting their business, Syce was going to escort Tony elsewhere. If I was patient and kept my head down, all three of them would soon be gone. This offered a much more satisfactory prospect than attempting to sneak past Syce, who was still lurking out there somewhere in the mulga.

I sank back down, immersing myself in the pool of darkness on the floor of the dinghy. My shirt and shorts were soaked with bilgewater and sweat, and a plague of mosquitoes was gorging on my skin. I didn't dare swat them but I managed to get the life-jacket under my head, ease the crick in my neck. Ears cocked for Syce, I could hear nothing but the drone of the predatory mozzies and the back-and-forth of Jake Martyn and Tony Melina as they talked about their deal.

As far as I could make out, a company owned by Tony, incorporated in the Cook Islands, was buying a half share in Gusto. This was somehow concealed as a loan to a company registered in Panama, a Chesworth Investments. The entire exercise was doubtless a means of concealing the transaction from the scrutiny of corporate regulators and the tax man. Was the Senate estimates committee aware of this, I wondered?

'Sign here, here and here,' said Martyn. 'X marks the spot. This authorises the transfer of funds from your account with the Farmers Bank of Thailand to Phil Ferrier's account with the National Bank of Cartagena.'

I cupped a hand around one ear, fingers splayed, fending off an insistent anopheles, straining to hear what they were saying. Who was this Phil Ferrier that Martyn kept mentioning? A faint bell rang in the west wing of my mind. It rang, but nobody came.

'Take no notice of the repayment schedule,' Martyn was explaining. 'As per our understanding, the debt is purely nominal. On receipt of your $750,000, Phil's company transfers its ownership of a fifty per cent share of the restaurant to you. As you see, he's already signed the relevant documents. Trust, Tony. Like I said, this is all about trust.'

'Yeah, yeah,' said Tony. 'No need to labour the point. Just show me where to make my mark.'

'Here and here.'

'And that's it?'

'Signed, sealed and delivered. Here are your copies. And here's your passport, your credit cards and the other ID that Phil needed to set up the relevant accounts. Congratulations, mate. You now own a half share in Gusto and the land on which it stands. And you're getting a bargain, if you don't mind me saying so. And all that dough you made selling my abalone is now nicely laundered.'

'Yeah,' said Tony drily. 'It's a real steal.'

'Don't be like that,' said Martyn. 'You'll be well looked after, I promise you. Now, if you don't mind, perhaps I can get back to our restaurant, schmooze our guests. I'd invite you to join me, toast our partnership, but you're not really dressed for the occasion, are you?'

I heard the snap of a briefcase closing, then the zip of the door flap on the screen tent.

'You there, Mick?' called Martyn. 'A quick word before I go.'

'Here.'

The response startled me with its proximity. It came from right beside the dinghy. Without my noticing, Syce had stepped into the gap between the boat and the shed. The slightest move and he would have heard me.

Martyn's footsteps approached and two men conferred in hurried whispers.

'You still up for this?' said Martyn.

'Leave it to me.'

'The places for him to sign are marked in pencil. Make sure he signs them all.'

'I'm not fucken stupid, you know,' hissed Syce. 'You sure his wife still hasn't reported him missing?'

'She's telling anyone who'll listen that he's fucked off overseas. It's perfect.'

'What about the plane ticket and the fifty grand?'

'I'll be back with them mid-afternoon. I can pick up the signed documents, shave back your hairline, trim your beard into a dapper little goatee, dab on a bit of grey.'

'You sure this'll work?'

'I guarantee it. You'll be a dead spit for his passport photo. Seven tomorrow night you'll be on a plane to Bali, just another tourist, fifty grand in your pocket. They won't look twice at you, I promise. And Tony Melina will have left the country.'

'Okay, leave it to me. See you back here tomorrow arvo.'

'Just one more thing. Make sure you don't get any blood on the documents, okay?'

Blood? What the hell did that mean?

The rest was clear enough. Aided by Jake Martyn, Rodney Syce was planning to leave the country the next day, using Tony Melina's passport.

It was a risky proposition, but not without a fair chance of success. Tony was ten years older but the two men shared certain general characteristics. Both had egg-shaped heads, for a start. Thick necks. Facial hair. Beyond that, the differences could be fudged with judicious tinkering. Australian passports do not specify the height or eye colour of the bearer. And a Bali-bound tourist was unlikely to get the fine-tooth-comb treatment from the overworked guy behind the outbound desk at the airport, not at the height of the holiday-season crush.

Spotting Syce was a lucky break. Spotting him in the process of leaving the country was even luckier. But my luck wouldn't be worth a pinch of shit unless I could raise the alarm. I shrank down into the hull of the dinghy, silently urging them to hurry up and go.

'Mick'll see you out of here,' Martyn was saying, his voice receding towards his vehicle. 'Pleasure doing business, Tony.'

The vehicle started up, backed away, beeping as it reversed. I risked a quick look and glimpsed a dark 4x4, a Range Rover or Landcruiser, tail-lights flaring as it angled down the slope to the creek bed. One down, two to go.

Syce was standing at the screen tent, watching Tony Melina pulling clothes from a plastic garbage bag, replacing them with documents scooped from the table. 'Let's get out of here,' said Tony. 'Sooner the better.'

Amen to that, I thought. Tony tugged a tee-shirt over his head and emerged from the tent, garbage bag in hand, clambering into a pair of pants.

'One more thing.' Syce brandished a document. A4, longwise fold. 'Jake needs a couple more signatures.'

'On what?' said Tony, irritably. 'Jesus, what a fucken shambles.' He snatched the papers from Syce's hand and turned them to the light. 'Why didn't he say so while he was here?'

The dog got up, yawned and trotted to Syce's side. Syce bent and scratched its ears, his eyes never leaving Tony Melina.

Tony moved closer to the light, lips moving as he read, brow furrowing as he flipped the pages. 'This authorises the transfer of my half of the business to some offshore company I've never heard of.'

'So?' said Syce.

'So it was never part of the deal,' he said. 'I've just forked over three quarters of a mill for a half share in Martyn's restaurant with fuck-all prospect of a return on my investment. Sign this, I'm out of the picture entirely.' He ran a cupped hand over his glistening scalp, then tugged at this goatee. His eyes darted nervously towards Syce. 'Must be some sort of mistake,' he said. 'Tell you what. Get me to a phone, I'll give him a call, clear it up.'

Syce took a step forward. 'He was pretty clear just then,' he said. 'Told me to make sure you signed before we left. Very specific, he was.' He took another step.

The tip of Tony's tongue flitted across his lips. Then he bolted for the trees. He hadn't gone three steps before Syce slammed into him, knocked him to the ground and snatched the papers from his hand.

The dog started yapping again, but Syce was too busy to notice. He had Tony in a head-lock, hauling him across the clearing. Tony flailed, bare heels scuffling as he tried to writhe free. With a sickening thud, Syce rammed his bare head into the trunk of a tree, the one Tony had been pissing against.

Tony slumped, stunned, the wind knocked out of him. You could almost see the little birdies twittering around his cranium. Syce propped him against the tree, legs splayed, and stuffed a rag into his mouth. Scooping up the chain, he passed it under Tony's arms and ran it around the tree. In a matter of seconds, Tony was trussed like a turkey.

'Go,' screamed every sentient atom in my body. 'Run, now, while Syce is looking the other way. Fuck caution, just run.'

Hands pressed against the sloping sides of the boat, I bore down, knees bending as I came into a coiled crouch.

Knees not bending. Legs not responding.

I'd been lying there for so long, body contorted, hugging the bottom of the dinghy, that my ambulatory extremities had gone to sleep. Dozed off, like the Minister for the Arts at the opening night of *Götterdämmerung*. I pounded my thighs with a balled fist, felt pins and needles. I sent jiggle messages to my toes and instructed my knees to bend, frantic to get going, desperate not to reveal my presence prematurely.

At the far edge of the pool of light, muffled protests were leaking through the gag in Tony's mouth. He writhed and thrashed, eyes rolling in his head. Syce kicked him in the ribs. He made a noise like a chihuahua being dropped down a lift-shaft, then went quiet.

Sensation was returning to my legs. I eased myself into a low crouch, levered myself up and down on the balls of my feet. Up, down. Up, down. Toe aerobics.

Syce planted a booted foot on Tony's knees and dropped the lid from a cooler into his thighs. He twisted his captive's right arm free of the encircling chain and shoved a pen into his hand. 'Do what you're told, stupid cunt.'

Tony tossed the pen away, flung it right across the clearing. It bounced off the side of the aluminium dinghy. Ping. As Syce turned to find it, I dropped back onto the stinking floor of the miserable, shitty little boat.

Light bobbed as Syce picked up the Primus and came towards the dinghy. Tony spluttered and coughed, spitting out his gag. 'I'll double it,' he gasped. 'Whatever he's paying you, I'll double it.'

He should have screamed at the top of his lungs, not wasted his breath trying to negotiate. Syce didn't bother to reply.

Tony started babbling, pleading, saying he wasn't going to sign anything. The light went back towards him and he made a gurgling noise as the gag was shoved back into his mouth.

'You'll sign, nice and proper,' said Syce. 'Even if it takes all night.'

I peeked over the gunwale, preparing again to make my escape. What I saw was a tableau from Hieronymus Bosch. A hallucination straight from hell.

The lantern sat on the ground beside the tree, hissing, pounded by kamikaze moths. Syce had one foot planted on Tony's chained legs, the other braced against the ground. There was a blade in his hand. Short and blunt. An oyster knife. He was sawing at the side of Tony's head with it.

A keening was rising from Tony's throat, a guttural groan of despair and pain. A combination of muffled scream, prayer, wail and whimper.

The dog growled, straining at the end of its leash. Moths battered the light. Shadows jumped in the leaf canopy.

Syce's arm sawed back and forth. Tony moaned.

Then Syce stepped back. The side of Tony's head was red raw, a blood-gushing wound. Syce held the knife in one hand, Tony's severed ear in the other. He held it up, dripping, then tossed it to the dog. Fido rose and its jaws clamped around the tasty titbit before it could hit the ground. A chomp, a snuffle and the gory morsel was gone.

The mutt licked its chops and stared expectantly at Syce.

But Syce was bending again to Tony. 'What next, you reckon? Other ear? Nose? Fingers? What about your dick? How about I cut off your wedding tackle?'

I shuddered and felt myself sink backwards onto the floor of the dinghy. My legs had again turned to jelly. But it wasn't poor circulation that was stopping me from moving. It was fear. Sheer, nameless, gut-wrenching dread. A kind of shame, too, as if my failure to intervene in what I was witnessing somehow made me complicit in it.

For more than a year and a half, I had fantasised about coming to grips with the man who killed my Lyndal. This scum-sucking piece of shit, Rodney Syce. This despicable, gutless loser. And now he was within reach, not more than ten metres away.

And me? What was I doing? I was cowering in the dark, watching him torture a man, feed the poor bastard's ear to his dog, for fuck's sake. If only I could get my hands on the shotgun. But I had no idea what he'd done with it. If only I could be sure that my legs would do what I told them, when I told them. If, if, if.

The dick threat had done the trick. Tony's hand was fluttering, signalling surrender. Syce pulled the plug from his mouth long enough for him to gulp down a lungful of air, then jammed it back. Tony was limp, a rag doll, the fight gone out of him, blood squirting from the side of his head. Syce ripped a strip from the towel, pressed the balled wad against the gash where Tony's ear had been, tied it in place. He tore Tony's tee-shirt from his torso, drenched it with water from plastic jerrycan and wiped Tony clean of blood. I caught the glint of a small gold crucifix in the dark mat of Tony's chest-hair.

Syce acted quickly, a man who knew what he was doing. He tilted the jerrycan, cleaning himself, then dried his hands and arms. Then he replaced the lid of the cooler on Tony's thighs, fitted the pen into his fingers and guided it towards the paper. 'Do it properly,' he commanded, holding Tony's head back. No blood on the documents, as per Martyn's instructions.

Tony's hand moved. Syce turned the page. Tony's hand moved again. Then Syce was stepping away, bending to the light, checking that all was correct. Satisfied, he folded the pages and slid them into his back pocket. Tony was slumped, forehead on the lid of the cooler, motionless, sobbing.

He knew what was coming next. So did I. Transfixed, incapable of action, I watched it happen.

Syce stepped out of the light and vanished behind the tree. Seconds later, he reappeared with a long-handled shovel. A latrine digger. A grave digger. Gripping the handle like a bat, he swung downwards, putting his full power behind the blow. The flat of the blade hit the back of Tony's head with a dull thud. For a brief moment, a metallic reverberation quavered in the air. When it stopped, Tony Melina was no longer sobbing.

Lizards and scorpions crawled up my spine. A python writhed in my stomach. 'Holy fuck shit Jesus Christ,' I thought.

Syce propped the shovel against the tree and began to unchain Tony's limp body. The logic of the situation unfolded before me. Syce did not intend to merely borrow Tony Melina's identity. He was going to steal it. A plan which wouldn't work if Tony's body was found. At the very minimum, a shallow grave would be required. Hope flared. While Syce was burying Tony, I could make myself scarce.

But instead of dragging Tony out of the circle of light, he was dragging something into it. Something heavy. A roll of chain-mesh fencing. He unrolled it and stomped it flat. Hauling Tony by the armpits, he manoeuvred his limp form onto the wire mesh and straightened his limbs. Grunting and pushing with his boots, he rolled up the mesh with Tony bundled inside.

He disappeared again, moving out of my line of sight. I heard an engine start, the Hilux. He was driving away, leaving the body behind. I scrambled to my feet, legs buckling beneath me. This was it. The moment had come.

But he wasn't driving away. He was driving up the slope from the creek bed, coming the way that Jake Martyn had come, headlights catching me as I stood in the dinghy, poised to spring over the side.

I froze as the beam passed over me, a prison spotlight. The light kept going, sweeping into the campsite. I dropped back to the floor of the dinghy. If this kept up, I might as well send for my furniture, have my mail re-directed. The Hon. Murray Whelan, The Old Runabout, Club Torture, Hidden Location, Otway State Forest.

The Hilux continued. Syce hadn't seen me. Fresh hope welled. He wasn't going to bury Tony near the camp. He was going to haul him somewhere in the back of the utility. Again, it was just a matter of keeping my head down and waiting until he'd gone.

I kept it right down, pressed myself to the floor of the boat. No peeking. Too risky.

The Hilux was reversing, beep-beep-beep. Then the door was opening, engine still running. Feet shuffled. Shuffle, shuffle. Syce grunted and wheezed, exerting himself.

There was more foot shuffling, then a flicker of movement at the periphery of my vision, a writhing in mid-air. It was coil of rope, first ascending, then slithering downwards. Then again. Syce was attempting to toss a line over the branch of a tree.

He succeeded on the fifth attempt. Then the Hilux was creeping forward. The rope went taut and the roll of chain mesh rose into sight. When it got to about three metres off the ground, the Hilux stopped. The mesh cylinder swung on the end of the rope, rotating like the needle of a compass.

Syce's intentions eluded me. Did he plan to conceal Tony Melina's body in the branches of a tree, I wondered, cocooned in fencing mesh? Was this a practice he'd encountered in remote backblocks of the country? Had he got the idea from some sort of aboriginal burial rite? It was certainly not a custom usually associated with the interment of second-generation migrants from Melbourne's inner-northern suburbs.

I heard the ratchet of the Hilux's handbrake above the idling of its engine, then footfalls headed for my hiding place. The bow of the dinghy dipped. It began to move. Syce had the boat trailer by the hitch. He was pulling it forward, steering it towards the dangling bundle. I began to get the idea. The mesh was weight. Tony's body wasn't going up into a tree. It was going down into the sea.

I pressed myself as flat as possible against the floor of the shallow dinghy. One glance and Syce would see me. But he was already back in the pickup, reversing. Beep, beep, beep. Down came the awful package. Thump. It landed right on top of me, pinning me to the floor of the boat.

Syce's footsteps crunched. The dinghy went horizontal and rolled forward a little. With a judder and a clunk, Syce hitched it to the tow-bar of the pickup. An arm reached out and jerked the rope holding the mesh. Its coils slithered into the boat. The mesh bore down on me. I writhed beneath it, discovery imminent.

Then, utter darkness. A covering had been flung over the load.

The door of the Hilux slammed shut and the trailer began to move forward, rocking and bumping. I put my palms against the mesh and pushed upwards, gasping for air. The dog started barking, wondering where the rest of its supper was going. Syce yelled for it to shut up. It did. A tepid, viscous liquid was seeping through the mesh. It dribbled onto my face, pooled in my palms and trickled down my wrist.

The boat tilted as if plunging over a waterfall. The load shifted, slipping towards the bow. As I tried to squirm free, something brushed against my cheek, swaying back and forth. It was, I realised, Tony's crucifix, dangling from the gold chain around his neck.

Fat lot of good it had done Tony. But the way things were going, I'd need all the help I could get.

I closed a sticky fist around it and squeezed tight.

Hell is other people, said Jean-Paul Sartre. Take it from me, he didn't have a clue.

Hell is being pinned on your back to the bottom of a cheap aluminium dinghy by a crushingly heavy roll of fencing mesh containing the mutilated corpse of a murdered trattoria proprietor from Ascot Vale, while being hauled cross-country through a trackless forest in the middle of the night by a criminal maniac with a propensity for gratuitous violence who's already slaughtered your pregnant lover, trapped in absolute darkness beneath a black plastic tarpaulin, drenched in sweat and struggling blindly to get out from under a shifting cargo of metal links and oozing body fluids.

As distinct from having to share your breakfast croissant with Simone de Beauvoir, for example.

Twigs and branches scraped the hull of the dinghy as it

bounced along the dry creek bed, plunging down invisible gradients and lurching over hidden obstacles. Desperately, I wriggled free of the pitching, bucking, bitching bale of wire and got my head clear of the suffocating plastic tarpaulin.

For all the bump and grind, our progress was slow. I rapidly assessed the situation. Syce's attention was focused on the way ahead. He was unlikely to notice if I rolled over the side and slipped into the surrounding scrub. With luck, I might even be able to find a phone signal, get a description of the Hilux and boat trailer to the cops, have them nail Syce with the corpse in tow.

I gave my pocket a reassuring pat. The phone was gone. Ducking back under the plastic tarpaulin, I put my shoulder to the mesh cylinder and groped the hull beneath it. As my fingertips found the phone, the load shifted, grinding my digits between steel mesh and aluminium hull. The mobile slithered beyond my grasp. By the time I succeeded in getting a firm grip on the elusive little fucker, the Hilux had found level ground. Shifting up a gear, it accelerated forward.

Hidden by the tarpaulin, I prodded at the touchpad of the phone. No light, no dial tone, no nothing. A shake and a rattle did nothing to improve the situation. The useless piece of plastic was kaput. And my chance of an easy exit had gone west. Or possibly south or even east. The pickup was moving along a proper track now. It was narrow and bumpy but our speed was increasing. A brisk leap overboard was off the agenda.

I was wedged into the gap between the side of the dinghy and the roll of wire mesh, swathed like a papoose in black plastic, the blade of an oar jammed up my kazoo. Branches flashed overhead. My chest rose and fell. The roar of adrenalin filled my ears, overlayed with the hum of the wheels, the squeak of the suspension and an intermittent, almost inaudible groaning.

At first I thought it was me. Gradually, I realised that the groan was emerging from the folds of wire. Sweet Jesus, was it possible that Tony Melina was still alive? I pressed my head against the mesh, all ears. Which was more than could be said for Tony.

Tony was a tosser and a letch, and his garlic bread was mediocre, but those aren't capital offences. So what if he'd fiddled his taxes and done business with crooks? Start killing people for that sort of thing and you'd have to execute the entire Australian corporate community. Apart from the Murdoch family, of course. And the Packers.

The moan became a gurgle. Melina must have been tougher than an overdone veal scaloppine. 'Hang on, mate,' I urged. 'Just hang on. We'll get you out of here.'

We? Me and my regiment of crack commandos.

The headlights of the Hilux lit up, sweeping the bush ahead of us. Syce's silhouette was visible in the rear window of the cabin. We moved onto a road, an even surface. No longer pitching wildly, the dinghy was hurtling through the night, speed increasing. The surface firmed, turned to bitumen. We were racing downhill, the cat's-eye reflectors on the roadside posts winking as we flew past. Down, down.

The roadside verge widened. Gaps opened between the trees, then closed again. For a fleeting moment, the sea glinted in the cleft between two humped-back crests, a distant mirror. The pickup's tail-lights flared. On-off-on. On-off-on. SOS.

A radiance lit the horizon, a spreading sheet of lightning.

A rocket rose, trailing incandescent showers, then burst into a glittering ball of emerald sparks. Even as it faded, a scintillating yellow cascade took its place, followed by an explosion of vermilion.

The midnight fireworks show in Lorne, I realised, squinting into the dial of my watch.

Happy New Year, Murray. My first resolution was to get out of that fucking dinghy toot sweet. My second was never again to act on impulse.

I thought about Red, imagined him in a sea of youthful faces. Goofing it up to a wah-wah Auld Lang Syne, flanked by a supercilious goth and a clinging pixie. Thought, too, about the festivities at Gusto. Jake Martyn presiding. Barbara Prentice in attendance. Me not.

We were flying now, the boat-trailer bucking and fishtailing. Fingers sunk to knuckle in the steel mesh, I clung for dear life. The tarpaulin flapped and rustled around my ears. If Tony was still breathing, I could no longer hear it.

The Hilux slowed, then jerked to a halt. The load slid forward, carrying me with it. Then we were moving again, turning right, the trailer swinging wide, the load sliding back. I heard the crashing of surf, saw the flash of oncoming headlights, felt the buffeting rush of passing vehicles.

I figured the geography, conjured the map. Sea to our left, hills to our right. We were west of Lorne, heading along the Great Ocean Road. Ahead lay a long stretch of sparsely inhabited coastline.

A car was approaching from the rear. I crawled to the very back of the boat and extended an arm, waving in a way that I hoped would be understood to be a sign of distress. The headlights moved closer and closer, blinding me. I continued to wave, hunched across the stern of the boat. The car veered to the other side of the road and accelerated, beginning to pass. A figure leaned from the passenger window.

'Whackaaaaa,' he yelled, raising a can of beer in salutation. The shitfaced peabrain in charge of the wheel hit the horn, a doppler wail of appreciation at my daredevilry.

The car picked up speed, overtook the Hilux and disappeared. On we drove, our speed unchanged. Hoping that Syce had not twigged to my presence, I ducked back beneath the tarpaulin.

We were moving fast, 90 k at least. Soon there would be fewer and fewer cars on the road. I needed a more compelling attention-grabber than a wave and a grimace.

The dinghy's outboard motor was held in place by a pair of salt-encrusted wing-nuts. Sprawled flat on my stomach, head down, I went to work on one of them. It was corroded tight. If I got it undone, I could drop the motor into the path of an approaching vehicle. That should do the trick. Or send some poor innocent hurtling off the road into the ocean hundreds of metres below us.

The nut refused to budge. I tried the other one. Ditto. I persisted, wincing with the pain of it. Same result. I pounded the inert metal with my mobile phone. Even as a blunt instrument it was useless.

From far behind us, headlights began to approach. But just then we began to slow down. The Hilux swung off the highway, cut its lights and bounced towards the sea. Dry sand spattered against the trailer mudguards.

I slid back into the gap between the hull and the freight and got my hands around the shaft of an oar. I lay there, staring up at the blackness of the covering tarpaulin. Oar clutched to my chest like a quarterstaff, I awaited developments.

We rocked across broken ground, then stopped. The cabin door opened. It snicked shut. The hitch fastenings of the trailer squeaked and clattered. The trailer moved backwards, bumpity-bump.

Now, I told myself. Go for broke. Toss the tarp aside, jump out of the boat, run, head for the highway. If tackled, clobber Syce with the oar, keep running, find somewhere to hide.

As I began to rise, the front of the boat jerked upwards. The top of my head slammed against the stern of the dinghy. The boat slid off the trailer, scraped across a hard, uneven surface and splashed into the water. It bobbed, righting itself, then rocked again as Syce jumped aboard.

I lurched upright, oar at the ready. But the tarpaulin didn't rise with me. Syce was standing on it, yanking the rope toggle to start the outboard. I pushed upwards against the unyielding sheeting, and flung myself recklessly in the direction of the stern. Flailing with the oar, I tried to bat the slippery plastic aside.

The motor fired. The boat rocked in the swell as it chugged forward. I bore upwards, jerking like a frog in a sock and tried to hoppo-bumpo the helmsman into the water.

Syce must have thought I was Tony, rising from the dead. Or some avenging spectre in black plastic.

'The fuck?' he said.

Spooked or not, he had a firm grip on the tiller handle. I bounced off him and sprawled backwards onto the roll of mesh, scrabbling free of the tarpaulin.

Syce was an ominous presence in a wrestler's stance, arms

spread, legs akimbo. I teetered on the mesh roll, the tarp wrapped round my shins, firming my grip on the oar. Lit by the phosphorescence of the sea, we confronted each other down the short length of the bobbing boat.

'The fuck are you?' demanded the dark shape.

That was for me to know and him to find out. Kicking free of the tarp, I lunged forward and took a swing. Syce dipped and the oar whistled over his head. He snatched it and tried to wrench it from my grip.

We see-sawed back and forth, fighting for ownership of the oar, the boat pitching beneath us. We were about fifty metres from the shore, moving parallel to it. Then Syce pushed instead of pulling and I felt myself toppling backwards. It was the Frisbee incident revisited.

'Mamma mia,' I thought. 'Here I go again.' I let go of the oar and dived overboard.

The sea was bracing cold, pitch black. I kicked hard and made as much distance as possible before broaching the surface. When I bobbed up, whooping for air, the boat was already turning. The vibrations of the propeller hummed in my ears as Syce gunned the throttle. The swell rose beneath me and the low outline of the shore reared at the periphery of my vision. I struck for the land, clawing at the water with a frenetic overarm.

The tempo of the outboard increased, closing fast. The sea was dark, the land darker. The boat sliced through the water, bearing straight at me. I filled my lungs and dived. The hull brushed my shoe and I kicked harder, deeper, lungs at full stretch, ears popping.

I broke the surface in the wake of the boat and immediately resumed my wild stroke for the shore. The boat came around, Syce trying for another pass. But before he could reach me, I was taken in the grip of a wave, hoisted aloft and pitched towards the shore.

The swell dropped, then rose again, clutching me to its heaving bosom. Directly ahead, just metres away, white water slopped over a shelf of jagged rocks. The rocks were mottled with seed mussels, thousands of tiny shells, sharp as razors.

For the moment, I was flotsam. Soon I would be jetsam. The difference being a fractured skull, a broken spine, a ruptured spleen and multiple lacerations.

The fatal shore rushed towards me. I hit it chest-first and rocketed forward, careering across slimy straps of wet leather. A bed of uprooted kelp. Limbs flailing, I skittered like a buttered duck. The wave subsided and my fingers closed around a projecting knob of rock. I dragged myself upright. White water streamed around my shins, trying to drag me back. I tottered forward, escaping its pull.

Somehow, miraculously, I was alive and ashore. I bent, hands on knees, shivering and retching. Then, I looked back to sea. Thirty metres away, the dinghy sat low in the water, a grey smudge. A dark shape crouched at the stern, arm on the outboard rudder, watching me.

I turned and headed inland, wading and hobbling across the pitted table of exposed rock. My shoes squelched and my ankle throbbed but I was well on my way to the highway, to a passing car, to the police.

I would have been, at least, if a cliff wasn't blocking my way. A sharp incline of crumbling sandstone, it rose almost vertically from the rock shelf. I groped along its base, sloshing through ankle-deep water, looking for a way up. It crumbled at my touch, showering me with sand and pebbles.

The boat was still there, outboard idling, Syce watching. My landing place was a shallow bite mark in the encompassing cliff, a dead-end street.

I started to scramble up the cliff, clefts and crannies crumbling under my weight. The putt-putt of the outboard came across the water and I glanced over my shoulder. The dinghy was moving, heading back the way it had come. I kept climbing.

The cliff face had all the substance of a coffee-dunked donut. I slipped back, advanced, slipped back again. Gradually, I gained height. Nearer the top, stunted vegetation sprouted from the loose rock. Seizing roots and stems, I worked my way upwards, clinging like Spiderman to the friable rock.

Eventually I reached the top. Greyish waist-high bushes extended for as far as I could see, melding into wind-bent trees at the top of a far incline. A figure was wading through the scrub. He was holding a long thin object.

Syce. He must have put the boat ashore.

Bent almost double, I fled along the clifftop and picked my way through the maze of bushes. But the soft ground gave way beneath my feet. Slithering downwards, riding my backside, grabbing anything within reach to slow my descent, I found myself back at the bottom of the cliff. A cascade of pebbles and sand rained down on my head. Syce was close, moving fast. A wave broke across the rock platform and lapped at my feet. The sea was my only way out.

Desperate for deeper water, I hobbled and limped, winced and pirouetted through the rock-strewn shallows. I stubbed toes, lost my balance, tripped and stumbled. The grunts and curses from above told me Syce was coming fast down the incline. A few more seconds and he would be at the bottom, raising the shotgun, getting a bead on me.

Water flooded my nose and mouth. I sank into deep water, a hidden rockpool. A wave washed over me and I grabbed the jutting rim of the pool, looking back in terror.

Syce had stopped, pulled up short by my sudden disappearance. He cast around, trying to spot me in the churning water. I held tight and ducked as the next wave passed over me. Syce advanced, scanning the roiling shallows. A bigger wave broke, sending water surging to his thighs. He swayed and teetered but held his ground. I gulped down a lungful of air and another wave washed over me.

The rock pool was maybe a metre and a half deep, jacuzzi-sized. I clung to the overhang, willing myself invisible, daring to raise my head only in the brief intervals between waves. Gasp, duck, cower. Gasp, duck, cower.

An eternity came and went. My teeth began to chatter. The tide was going out. If I stayed where I was, I would soon be exposed. Syce, if he was still there, would walk across the rocks and shoot me dead. I risked raising my head a little. Syce was not visible. But that didn't mean he'd gone.

Taking a punt, I edged my way to the seaward extremity of the rock pool. Then, flat on my belly in the surging foam, I slithered out towards the ocean.

A wave broke over the rocks and the ebbing tide sucked me off.

Nostrils at the waterline, I breaststroked along the edge of the deep water, rising and falling with the chop. The water was deep and dark, cool and creepy, but it was infinitely better than being shot.

The land lay to my left, about fifty metres away, so the current was running east in the general direction of Lorne. This was good. Once I'd put a bit of distance between myself and Syce, I could swim ashore. After that, all I had to do was make my way uphill to the Great Ocean Road, follow it to human habitation, sound the alarm and collapse in a convulsing heap.

The land loomed, a sheer wall, the sea foaming at its base. With no immediate opportunity for landfall, I rolled onto my back and sculled, letting the current carry me, conserving my strength for the push to shore. My shorts clung to my thighs, chafing the skin, and my ankle throbbed faintly. The leather of my watchband had shrunk, tightening around my wrist. My mobile phone and flashlight were long gone, dropped in the dinghy during my tussle with Syce. But I still had Tony Melina's cross tucked in my change pocket.

I heard a faint putt-putt, the signature of Syce's outboard. Treading water, I strained to get a fix on its position. Cool currents swirled around my legs. Gradually, the sound grew fainter, then faded away entirely.

The land, too, was fading. With a sudden sense of urgency, I struck for the shore, freestyle now. The continent appeared to be receding. I slogged on, pounding at the water.

Face down, arm over, turn and breathe. Face down, arm over, turn and breathe.

Urgency became panic. Despite my efforts, I was making no progress. I was panting, unable to suck down enough oxygen. My pulse was racing and so was my imagination. I was electric with fear. Freaking out, big time. Gripped by the gut-wrenching terror of a man adrift at night in the bottomless abyss, a puny speck in the immensity of the inky ocean. Shark bait.

Even now, a great white or a blue pointer was rising from the deep, circling for the kill. It would strike without warning, hit me like a freight train, clamp its monstrous jaws around me, shred my flesh with merciless, serrated teeth. Then others would join the attack, a pack of them, whipped to a frenzy by the blood in the water. My blood. Even now, myriad minor abrasions were spreading my scent, sounding the dinner gong.

A shark, or something worse. Some nameless horror from the primordial depths. A creature of suckered tentacles or poisonous spines. Anyone familiar with the leading personalities in the NSW branch of the Labor Party would know exactly how I felt.

Onwards I thrashed, adrenalin, sea water and my own asthmatic gasps roaring in my ears. Whatever they are, I told myself, you can't outswim them. Don't exhaust yourself trying. I slowed down, shifted to sidestroke, focused on the blurred smudge of the land. Specks of light showed along the coast, some of them moving. Houses and cars, all just beyond my reach. I let panic settle into mere hysteria, then struck again for the shore, aiming for a ragged line of white, the slosh of waves on rocks.

Churning through the black water, I collided with a pedestal of nubbled stone. It was slightly below water level, table-sized and flattish. I scrambled onto it. For several minutes, I knelt there, clinging to its uneven surface. My chest was heaving and relief surged through me.

When the gasping subsided, I climbed to my feet and took my bearings. Ankle-deep in the encompassing briny, I must have looked like a try-hard Jesus pausing for a leisurely look-see on my way across the Sea of Galilee.

The shoreline proper was about two hundred metres away. Here and there in the intervening water, dark patches could be faintly discerned, fragments of submerged reef. If the tide continued to fall, it might eventually be possible to get ashore by jumping from rock to rock. I decided to wait and see.

No man is an island, according to the constitution of the Australian Labor Party, but I certainly felt like one. At the very minimum, I was a shag on a rock. A shivering shag in sodden shoes squatting on an almost invisible rock, water swirling around me, waiting for the tide to ebb away.

'Aarrkk,' I cried, just to hear my own voice, reassure myself that I was still alive. 'Aarrkk.'

I raised my watch to my face. Waterproof to 30 m, it said. 1:33 a.m. Four hours since I'd got myself lost in the bush. For most of that time I'd been in imminent danger of being discovered, mutilated, shot, drowned or eaten by killer whales. By comparison, being perched on a semi-submerged rock waiting for the tide to ebb was a moment of quality solitude, an opportunity to reflect on what I'd seen. My chance for an end-of-year stocktake.

I reviewed the contents of my mental in-tray.

Rodney Syce was hiding in the Otway Ranges. He was calling himself Mick, growing marijuana and processing poached abalone for Jake Martyn, celebrity eatery proprietor. The two of them had abducted Tony Melina, a less celebrated but evidently cashed-up restaurateur. Someone called Phillip Ferrier was involved too.

On the promise of a cash pay-off and Martyn's help getting out of the country, Syce had tortured Melina, forced him to sign certain documents, then murdered him. He was currently in the process of dumping Melina's body in the sea.

Had Syce been hiding in the Otways ever since the Remand Centre break-out? Was the restaurant owner involved in the escape? If so, how? And why?

It was a bizarre scenario. Too bizarre.

A new fear suddenly took hold of me.

This was a story that strained credulity to the limit, even mine. How could I expect anyone else to believe it?

My credibility with the Victoria Police was not exactly money in the bank. Surely they would conclude that I was having one of my periodic visions. Maybe even that I'd mislaid my last marble.

How could I convince them that I was telling the truth? What evidence could I produce?

Syce had doubtless rolled Tony Melina overboard by now, so there was no body. I had no idea how to find the camp again. And judging by what I had seen of him, Jake Martyn wasn't likely to fess up the moment the coppers put the question to him.

No evidence, no admission, a lunatic witness.

I rummaged in my pockets as if they might possibly contain some means of proving my story. Or some means of getting off that damned rock. An inflatable life-raft, a signed confession, a map of the Otways with X marking the spot.

I found $125 in notes. Waterproof polymer banknotes, thanks to the cutting-edge washing-machine-proof technology of the Australian Mint. A half-full pack of Tic-Tacs. And Tony Melina's little gold crucifix.

It was circumstantial at best, but it was the only hook on which I could hang my credibility. Rita would be able to identify it. She could also attest that he was missing, whereabouts unknown. And the fact that I possessed an item of Tony's personal jewellery might persuade the police at least to investigate.

Poor Tony. He slept with the fishes tonight. At least he was getting some rest, which was more than could be said for me. I slipped his little Jesus back into my change pocket and gave it a reassuring pat. Then I ate the Tic-Tacs.

An hour passed, making no effort to hurry. My shirt began to dry out, the accumulated heat of the day radiating from the nearby landmass. The air was balmy, the ambient temperature still in the high teens. Little by little, the water level receded. My plinth became a pyramid. Add a deckchair and a daiquiri, I could have sold tickets.

Time crawled. I flexed my knees and windmilled my arms, shag-aerobics to keep myself from cramping up.

An archipelago slowly emerged from the sea, a path of stepping stones leading to the tide-exposed shore. Problem was, it fell far short of my perch. Walking ashore dry-shod was off the agenda. Apart from the fact that my shoes were soaked, the nearest visible outcrop was a good hundred metres away.

At 3:40 a.m., I climbed down from my shag-roost and lowered myself into the water. A hundred metres was nothing, after all. Four lengths of the pool at the City Baths. A mere bagatelle.

Small beer but big trouble. A powerful current was surging through the channel. For every metre I advanced towards the shore, I was swept five sideways, a cork in a stormwater drain. I tried to fight my way back to Whelan Island but soon lost the battle. Again, I was being swept out to sea.

I pounded for the land, relentless, determined. Kick, stroke, breathe. Kick, stroke, breathe. Thirty strokes, fifty, a hundred. My arms turned to lead and still I kept clawing at the water. My thighs were red-raw but still I waggled them. I shucked off my shoes, hoping it would help.

It didn't. I was going nowhere fast. Nowhere I wanted to go, at least. The current was running parallel to the shore, dragging me with it. The land remained in view, contours rising and falling as it rushed past, but I couldn't reach it, try as I might.

You're finished, Murray Whelan, I told myself. This is it.

You are going to die. And for nothing. By the time your body washes ashore, if there's anything left to be washed up, Syce will be long gone.

The sea wanted me bad and I no longer had the strength to resist. Water filled my mouth and visions flooded my mind. Deeds regretted, hopes unfulfilled, a terrible sense of waste. All the usual shit. And worst of all, the gut-wrenching, aching realisation that I would never see my little boy again.

I shuddered, gasped and groaned. Then, marshalling my strength, I made one last effort to reach the land. If I was going down, I'd go down fighting.

I went down.

Jesus, it was dark down there. My lungs were burning. My arms were flailing. My hand struck something slimy and ropy. A slimy rope. I grabbed it and hauled with the last of my strength.

Blood raged in my ears and a glowing ball of white rushed towards me out of the darkness. It grew larger and larger until it filled my entire field of vision. The mystery of life and death was revealing itself to me.

It struck my head with a hollow *bonk*. I broke the surface gulping for air and discovered that the secret of the universe was a basketball-sized polystyrene sphere. I grabbed it and clutched it to my chest.

Christ alone knew how long I hung there, and He wasn't telling. A bamboo cane extended from the centre of the bobbing white ball. A limp scrap of orange plastic hung at its far extremity. I was clinging to the marker buoy for a crayfish trap.

I grabbed the cane mast, wrapped my legs around the buoy and mounted it. It sank beneath my buttocks. Instead of being chin-deep in the water, I was now midriff-deep.

From my marginally improved position, however, I could see the shore. A faint light flickered on the beach, a fire perhaps. A sound came across the water. It was almost human.

'Tonight's the night,' wailed the voice. 'Gonna be all right.'

I didn't believe a word of it. Party noises joined the music, well-oiled revelry.

'Help,' I bleated. Help me if you can. I'm feeling drowned. But help was beyond earshot. My strangulated plea was a reedy vibration.

After Rod Stewart came Dire Straits. As if things weren't bad enough already.

My body heat was being leached away. My skin had turned to gooseflesh and my teeth were castanets striking up the overture to hypothermia. I had, at most, another two hours. By the time the music faded, half an hour later, my respiration rate was so high that I couldn't get enough air in my lungs to raise a decent shout.

I hugged the thin sliver of bamboo, jiggled up and down, braced for imminent shark attack and tried to distract myself with hot thoughts. The blazing sands of the Sahara. A steaming mug of cocoa. Nicole Kidman and Tom Cruise in bed. When that didn't work I pissed my pants, luxuriating in the brief suffusion of warmth.

But the cold was unendurable. I slid off the polystyrene ball and examined the orange nylon rope that moored it to the pot on the floor of the sea. Somewhere far below me, a trapped lobster was facing an identical problem, racking its crustacean brain for a means of escape.

The rope was spliced, tighter than a preference swap in a leadership spill. Impossible to untie. I bit a chunk from the polystyrene, then another. Gnawing with my teeth and tearing with my nails, I worked at the ball.

Water flooded my mouth. My fingers were numb. My jaw jack-hammered. After an eternity, I managed to break the buoy in half. The bamboo mast toppled into the water. The rope sank without trace. I'd done what I could for my incarcerated crustacean companion. He was on his own now.

All that remained of the buoy was two irregular hemispheres of polystyrene and a scattering of little white pellets. I stuffed the two lumps of foam up the front of my shirt and began to breaststroke, high in the water.

This time, I didn't fight the current. I let it carry me along, steering across it at an oblique angle, working my way gradually shoreward, alternating between backstroke and breaststroke. Gradually, the land moved closer. But Christ on a bike, I was fucking freezing.

It was nearly five o'clock. I was hyperventilating, numb and shivering. Rolling onto my back, I twitched and gave up the ghost.

High above me, the firmament faded to a blur. One by one, the stars went out. Through the water came the grind of icebergs. The sands of time turned to crystals of ice. A pale radiance was all that I could see. Faces looked down at me. Curious, not unkind.

It came to me that I was passing between rows of columns like those of a temple. And that the faces staring down at me were those of ancient Greeks.

My shoulder struck something hard. Thought flickered in my sluggish brain. The current had carried me all the way to

Lorne. I was passing beneath the pier. The faces belonged to old Greek men, jigging for squid. Was there some law, I wondered, some clause in the Fisheries Act which required that at least one male of Hellenic origin with a squid rig be permanently present on every pier or jetty in Australian territorial waters?

I rolled over and the swell surged beneath me. It hefted me forward as the current pivoted like a hinge around the point at the end of the bay. Beyond it, rimming the curve of Loutitt Bay, the town glowed. The shore was just a few metres away. I clawed at the water and felt the grainy drag of the bottom against my toes. Another surge of the swell and I was flopping through the shallows, Robinson Crusoe crawling up the beach.

You're alive, I told myself. Hallelujah. Praise be to Whatsisname. That little guy in your pocket. The one on the thingamabob.

My brain was frozen. My thoughts moved at the speed of glaciers. Fingers trembling, I fished the cross from my pocket. It was important, that much I remembered. But why?

A gaggle of youths materialised, staring down at a barefoot man with bloodshot eyes, his clothes sodden, two foam hemispheres bulging in his shirt like skewiff falsies. Unable to speak, I held up the cross.

'You're too late, mate,' slurred one of the juveniles, a pimply half-wit with his hat on backwards, his shirt tied around his waist and a can of rum and lolly water in his hand. 'We've already sold our souls to Satan.'

He snatched the cross from my hand and flung it into the sea.

Misery on a stick, I discarded my primitive flotation device and lumbered along the beach. Blue with cold, teeth hammering out the Rach 9. Heat, I needed heat.

A downy light suffused the scene with the pearl grey of pre-dawn. Empty cans and crumpled food wrappers littered the trampled sand, the detritus of a massive communal booze-up. A faint whiff of cordite hung in the air, a reminder of the fireworks five hours earlier. Figures shifted obscurely at the periphery of my vision, hunkered down in the boulders and vegetation at the edge of the beach.

'Not here,' whispered a female voice. 'I'll get sand in it.'

Lights were still blazing at the surf lifesaving club. I lurched towards it, shorts clinging, bow-legged as a crotch-kicked cowpoke. Two and a half hours deep-sea marination had done wonders for my twisted ankle. My hobble was now merely a limp. My jaw, however, was snapping so violently that I feared for my tongue. Goosebumps covered my flesh like a relief map of the Hindu Kush. Get to the lifesaving club, I urged myself, to people who know the art of defrosting. That's why it's called the lifesaving club.

I reached a door, yanked it open, found a concrete-floored corridor. I wobbled inside, tottered, careened off a wall, felt a door handle, smelled disinfectant. A light switch found my hand. The changing rooms. Metal lockers, slatted benches, a row of showers.

The water ran tepid. Tepid was encouraging. I cranked up the volume and stood beneath the stream, clothes and all. Miracle of miracles, it grew warmer and warmer, until it was so hot that I was reaching for the cold tap.

I don't know how long I stood there, turning from pale blue to pale pink, stripping off my clothes to find a penis so puckered and brine-bleached that it looked like an albino axolotl. I slumped to the floor and let hot water cascade over me, sobbing and retching and pissing down the plughole. Me, not the hot water.

Just as my inner permafrost was beginning to melt, a man appeared in the doorway. He was about seventy years old. Leather face, leather arms, leather legs, immaculate white tee-shirt, shorts, socks and trainers. He blazed with irritation and rapped at the sign on the door with his knuckles.

'Can't you read, bloody idiot?' barked the surfside ancient. 'This is the Ladies. Gawn, out you get.'

His steely gaze brooked no contradiction. I climbed back into my sodden clothes and beat a retreat, finger-combing my hair as I went.

The foreshore was deserted, its swathe of couch-grass mashed and litter-strewn. At its centre sat the skeleton of a cuboid whale, the scaffolding of the deserted concert stage. I thought again about Red, wondered what kind of a night he'd had up at the Falls.

Lorne was a hangover waiting to happen. Streetlights shone down on empty asphalt, their sodium glow bleeding into the grey wash of the imminent day. A girl in a bikini-top and denim mini tottered down the middle of Mountjoy Parade in absurdly-high platform sandals, her mascara smeared, a bottle of Malibu in one hand. Drunken shouts reverberated in the far distance, punctuated by the honking of plastic party horns. The mating call of the shitfaced dickhead. In the foreshore carpark, the flashing light of a stationary ambulance showed the limbs of crashed-out party animals protruding from car windows and the tail-gates of station wagons.

The police temporary command centre was gone, along with the reinforcements bussed from Melbourne for the revels. The only sign of the law enforcement community was a scattering of horse-shit and a few piles of orange plastic crowd barrier in the gutter.

It was almost six o'clock. Magpies were carolling and kookaburras cackling. Where the sky met the sea, the nicotine-stained fingers of dawn were already at work, levering open the first day of the new year. Even in my half-thawed state, I could tell that it was going to be a hot one, a real stinker.

The police station was up the hill behind the pub, a weatherboard building in a residential street, a small cellblock out the back. I took a deep breath, wiped my nose on my shoulder and pushed open the front door.

The counter was unattended. A ragged chorus of 'Born in

the USA' was coming from the direction of the lock-up. I pushed the buzzer. After a couple of minutes, the racket out the back subsided and a beefy young rozzer appeared. He had damp patches at the armpits and the demeanour of a man at the fag-end of a long shift. The tag on his shirt pocket identified him as Constable Leeuwyn. He gave me the once-over, unimpressed, and suppressed a yawn.

'Can I help you?' His tone implied that he hoped not.

'I'd like to speak to the senior officer on duty,' I said.

'I'm the watchhouse keeper, if that's senior enough for you. Or you can wait for the sergeant. He'll be here at seven.'

'Is there a CIB attached to this station?'

'Nearest CIB's Torquay,' he said. Torquay was nearly an hour's drive away. 'What's it concerning?'

'A murder,' I said. 'And the whereabouts of Rodney Syce. The Remand Centre escapee. He's got a bush camp somewhere up there.' I jerked my thumb over my shoulder at the hills behind the town. 'There's a fair chance of collaring him if you're quick enough.'

The cop narrowed his eyes, letting me know that he'd spent a long night listening to bullshit and his tolerance was pretty well exhausted. 'Is that right, sir?'

'I can assure you this is not a joke. I'm not crazy. I'm a member of parliament.'

Constable Leeuwyn's expression suggested he did not consider these categories to be mutually exclusive.

'And I'm not drunk, either,' I went on. 'If I look like crap, it's because I've spent half the night in the sea in fear for my life. I am not playing funny buggers here, officer. I'm here because I've just witnessed a number of very serious crimes involving a wanted fugitive.'

My high-horse tone did the trick. The copper, alert now, laid a clip-board on the counter between us. 'Do you have any identification, sir?'

'Not on me,' I said. 'But I'm sure you can check. My name is Murray Whelan. I'm the member for Melbourne Upper in the Legislative Council.'

The constable took down my name, address and DOB, then disappeared through a door into a muster room with computers on the desks. I paced the worn linoleum of the vestibule in bare feet, keeping the blood flowing to my still-chilled extremities. The walls were hung with framed certificates of appreciation and commemorative photographs of civic events. In one picture, a representative of the Rotary Club was shown presenting the results of a fund-raising fun-run to an officer of the Country Fire Authority. Jake Martyn was holding one end of the cheque.

After ten minutes, the constable reappeared. Word had evidently come down the line that I was to be treated with kid gloves. 'Sorry to keep you waiting, Mr Whelan,' he said. 'The sergeant will be here shortly to take charge of matters. In the meantime, you'd better tell me all about it.' He raised the flap on the counter, inviting me to step through. 'Can I get you a cup of something?'

'Tea with milk and sugar,' I said, my gratitude unfeigned. 'Please.'

We went through to the muster-room where I dictated my statement between sips of hot tea. Three cups, it took, and twenty minutes. Leeuwyn two-finger typed my account of the night's doings straight into a computer, interrupted only by periodic visits to the cells to quell outbreaks of communal singing. I stuck to the bare bones and he tapped at the keys without comment or question, even when I mentioned Jake Martyn, whose name was almost certainly known to him.

When I got to the part where Syce fed Tony Melina's ear to the dog, the young copper looked up from the keyboard and opened his mouth as if about to warn me that telling outrageous fibs to the wallopers is a chargeable offence. I held his gaze until he turned back to the computer.

He printed out the finished statement and, as I was signing it, the sergeant arrived.

He was a solid man in his iron-grey fifties, with a military moustache and the bearing to match. His cheeks and chin were still raw from the razor and, judging by the bags under his eyes, the shave had come on the heels of a minimum of sleep. The buttons of his powder-blue shirt were taut over a midriff like a sack of concrete.

He introduced himself as Sergeant Terry Pendergast, took the statement from my hand and led me into his office, his demeanour correct and businesslike.

The sergeant's office was a cubby hole off the muster room. There was a large map of the district on the wall and a stand of fishing rods in the corner. He wedged himself behind an almost-bare desk and invited me to sit on the other side of it. He put on a pair of reading glasses and studied my statement. He took his time. Occasionally his gaze shifted from the page to my face, then back again. He stroked his moustache once or twice. There was coming and going in the outer office. I may have tapped my feet and chewed on a knuckle or two.

'Hmmm,' said the sergeant at last. 'Quite a story.' He laid

down the statement, folded his reading glasses and slipped them into his shirt pocket. He pushed his seat back and crossed his hands on his stomach. The ball, I understood, was in my court.

'If you've spoken to Melbourne,' I said, 'you'll be aware that I have a history in regard to Syce. You might even have been told that I've got a tendency to imagine I've seen him.'

Pendergast gave a slight nod, confiming that he'd been backgrounded. 'And do you?'

'Syce killed the woman I loved,' I said, 'and our unborn child. So, yes, I'll admit to a degree of obsession. But this isn't like those other times. I realise it all sounds pretty far fetched, Jake Martyn's involvement and so on. And I don't have anything to substantiate my claims. But I'd have to be certifiably mad to make up something as unlikely as this.'

Pendergast gave me the copper's eyeball, as though considering the possibility. The salt encrusted on my printed hibiscus didn't help. Then, abruptly, he swivelled in his seat and directed his freshly shaven chin at the map on the wall. 'So where do you reckon this bush camp is, Mr Whelan?'

The map was large-scale, the contours of the hills so dense they showed as crumples in the paper. Filaments of blue ran between the wrinkles, dozens of creeks and rivers. I got up, put my finger on Lorne, ran it up to Mount Sabine Road and traced the route along the ridge of the ranges to an unnamed road that led back down to the coast.

'Somewhere here,' I said, placing my palm on an area of perhaps a hundred square kilometres. 'It's hard to be more precise. You'll need to get in a helicopter.'

'Let's start by trying to find your car,' said Pendergast.

A Constable Heinze was summoned. He didn't look more

than twenty, a sinewy lad with a flat-top and a lazy drawl.

'Any sign of this Syce,' the sergeant instructed, 'let me know immediately. Do not approach.'

'Understood,' said Heinze. 'No worries. This way, sir.'

He rustled me up a pair of thongs, fed me into a police 4x4, dropped a pair of mirror shades over his eyes and hauled me back up into the hills. It was a tad more civilised than the trip down.

The sun was climbing, turning the sea to tinfoil and flooding the town with a harsh light. Work crews were clearing the foreshore of rubbish and stay-over party beasts were emerging from parked cars, blinking and wincing.

I tried to make myself comfortable, damp knickers wedged up my bum crack, eyes puffy with salt and glare. I wished I had a pair of sunglasses and some lounging pyjamas. I wished I were waking up in Barbara Prentice's bed, but the last time I thought about her was a lifetime ago.

'Busy night for you blokes,' I said, making conversation.

'Not as bad as usual,' said the young constable. 'So they tell me. Only twelve arrests.'

'How about the Falls?' I said. 'How'd that go?'

'No problems, if that's what you mean,' he said. 'Hunters and Collectors stole the show, I heard.'

'Were they charged?' I said.

'Very amusing, sir,' said Heinze. 'Where to from here?'

At first, I had no great difficulty in retracing the route I'd taken the previous evening. Landmarks and side-roads appeared in the right places. The twists and turns of the track resonated in my memory. But as we advanced deeper into the bush, my self-assurance began to wane. The whole aspect of the terrain was transformed by the daylight, even if that daylight was strained through a rainforest canopy. The tracks and trails, no longer revealed by headlights, twisted and forked in ways I didn't anticipate. The sheer vastness of the bush threatened to overwhelm me.

I hunched forward in my seat, staring through the windscreen, scanning the sides of the track, directing Heinze down dead-end tracks that were little more than faint ruts in the hillsides. We backed up and tried again. And again.

'It's around here somewhere,' I kept repeating. 'It has to be.'

But the damned thing had vanished, swallowed up by the landscape like some dingo-snaffled Adventist infant.

After an hour of buggerising around, Heinze got a call on the radio, a string of letters and numbers, unintelligible code.

'A4, copy that, 7–11,' he replied, or words to that effect.

We'd been summoned back to Lorne. Developments had occurred.

'What developments?'

'Sarge'll fill you in,' said young Heinze.

Hitting the nearest scaled road, we dropped down to the sea. I scanned the outline of the hills, concluding that this was probably the road I'd ridden in the boat with Tony Melina. Syce had turned south-west at the Great Ocean Road. We turned north-east. The tide was coming back in. Tony's body was out there somewhere, catering to the bottom feeders.

Sergeant Pendergast was waiting outside the cop shop, lips compressed, thumbs hooked in his belt. There'd been developments all right. 'Your car's been located,' he announced. 'It's parked near the Cumberland River caravan park, twenty kilometres back along the Great Ocean Road. It's been there for several hours, apparently.'

My shrivelled dick shrivelled further. I stared at the copper, struggling to understand. I was back to square one.

'Somebody must have moved it…' I said.

The sergeant raised his hands, cutting me short. 'This obviously raises a number of questions, Mr Whelan. But I'm sure we'll soon get some answers. A member of the Syce Task Force is on his way from Melbourne to take charge.'

Was he bringing a straitjacket, I wondered? A ticket to the funny farm? Or just the Victim Liaison shrink, ready with some on-the-spot counselling for the bitter and twisted Murray Whelan, headbanging fantasist.

I nodded bleakly. 'The car?'

'For the moment, we'd prefer to leave it where it is,' said the sergeant. 'If you don't mind.'

As if I had any choice. I felt hollow inside. I must have looked it. Pendergast took pity on me.

'This time of year,' he said, 'Christmas and whatnot, it can be very emotionally difficult for some people.' The sergeant twitched his moustache in the direction of the cop shop. 'You can wait inside. We'll get you something to eat if you like.'

At the mention of food, I felt a sudden ravenous hunger.

'Okay,' I said. 'I'll have an orange juice, two fried eggs, bacon, mushrooms, grilled tomato, wholegrain toast, a selection of jams and a black coffee with sugar. And a cigarette, thanks.'

'Best we can do is a cup of instant and a slice of cold pizza I'm afraid, Mr Whelan. This isn't the parliamentary dining room.'

Delving into my cling-shrunk shorts, I confirmed that my

cash was still there. 'Maybe I'll just pop down the street,' I said.

The sergeant dispensed an indifferent shrug. 'Better make it quick,' he said. 'The officer from Melbourne will be here soon.'

'I'll try not to keep him waiting.' I hoisted my shorts, turned and hobbled away in my borrowed flip-flops.

It was getting towards nine and the early risers were up and about. The pock of ball on catgut came from the tennis courts on the foreshore. A man with a bowling-ball beergut was hosing the footpath outside the pub. Couples pushed toddlers in strollers. Kerbside parking places were filling fast. The air of normal life seemed discordant, bizarre.

As I trudged back down the hill towards Mountjoy Parade, I contemplated my situation, seething with frustration. The business with the car had trashed my fragile credibility with the coppers. This dick from Melbourne had been dispatched to hose me down. At best, I might be able to persuade him to contact Immigration and have Tony Melina's name put on a passport watch list. An immediate full-scale manhunt for Syce was clearly out of the question.

There were other law-enforcement buttons I could push, of course. Corporate Affairs. The tax department. But that was a long-term approach. In the meantime, Syce would slip through the net again.

I found breakfast being served at tables on the terracotta-tiled terrace outside the Cumberland Resort. Some of the other customers looked a little the worse for wear, although none of them came near my level of unkempt. The waitress asked for cash upfront when she took my order.

As I peeled off the notes, I recalled that I'd left my wallet under the seat of the Magna. Where it had probably been found by whoever moved the car. An image came to me of Rodney Syce in Bali, spending up big on my Visa card. But there was more than plastic in my billfold. As well as a creased ultrasound Polaroid, it also held my driver's licence and the rent receipt for the holiday house.

So, chances were, the person who moved my car also knew my name, my face and where I could be found. Was I being watched, even now? By Jake Martyn, perhaps? The mystery ingredient.

My eggs arrived. I wolfed them, warily scanning the dog-walkers and newspaper-buyers as they strolled past. Cars cruised the strip, the sunlight from the ocean searing their windows.

Lucky the boys weren't at the house, I thought. I'd have to get out of Lorne, of course. A draft agenda began to take shape. Deal with the cops, try to persuade them at least to organise a helicopter sweep of the camp area and have the airport watched. Get my car back. Pick up the boys as arranged at midday. Should I phone Faye and Leo, I wondered, who were due to arrive later in the day?

A man appeared on the other side of my toast. Wiry and fiftyish, he wore shorts and a threadbare tee-shirt. A towel hung over his shoulder as if he'd just come from an early-morning swim. Without asking, he pulled out a chair and sat down.

'Murray Whelan?' He squinted at me with a kind of cock-eyed leer.

Straggly greyish hair hung to the nape of his neck. His face was tanned and weather-lined. It was a face I had seen before, I realised, nearly gagging on my multigrain. Just once and very briefly. But I remembered. It had been a memorable occasion. The owner of the face had been tossing the finger over his shoulder from the helm of an escaping shark-cat.

There were maybe thirty or forty people in the immediate vicinity, sipping coffee, browsing newspapers, nursing hangovers.

'There's witnesses,' I said, loud enough to turn heads. 'Try anything, these people are witnesses.'

The abalone poacher looked at me like he'd been warned that I was somewhat eccentric. He chuckled, letting the onlookers know that he was in on the joke. At the same time, he made a small placatory gesture with his hands, stroking the air between us.

'My associates are hoping for a word.' He spoke softly, reasoning with me.

'I'll bet they are,' I said. 'But if you think I'm going anywhere without a fight, pal, you'd better think again.'

He furrowed his brow, disappointed and perplexed at the vehemence of my response.

'Before you make a scene,' he said, 'I suggest you take a look at this.'

He took something from his pocket and placed it on the table between us.

It was a business card.

The logo of the Department of Natural Resources was embossed at the top. Printed beneath it: Bob Sutherland—Director, Fisheries Compliance.

'Bob said to remind you, if need be, that you met him a couple of months ago in San Remo. He'd like a few minutes of your time, if possible. He's a couple of minutes' walk away.'

I picked up the card and studied it. It looked real enough.

'So you've got Sutherland's card,' I said. 'Doesn't prove he sent you.'

The man shrugged, stood up and handed me a mobile phone. 'Ask him yourself.'

He strolled away and stood on the footpath, a hand shading his eyes as he stared across the road towards the sea.

Two phone numbers were printed on the card, office and mobile. I punched in the office number. Sutherland's voice said he wasn't at his desk, that I could leave a voice-mail message or call him on his mobile. The number was the one on the card. I dialled it.

It was answered immediately. 'Sutherland.'

'Murray Whelan,' I said.

'Thanks for calling, Mr Whelan. Excuse the cloak and dagger. Appreciate a few minutes, face-to-face.'

'What's this about?' I said.

'Nutshell, hope you can clarify some matters.'

Typical skewiff priorities, I thought. Sceptical about my tale of a wanted fugitive, murder and mayhem, the cops report the shellfish-rustling aspect to the fish dogs.

'The police have been in touch, have they?'

'Not as such,' said Sutherland after a brief pause. 'Far as we know, they're not aware of our presence in the area.'

'I'm not sure I understand.'

'Coastal communities, all kinds of connections, family and whatnot. Word gets around pretty quick, fish dogs in the neighbourhood.'

That wasn't what I didn't understand. 'So how did you know where to find me?' I said.

The lank-haired man was watching me keenly, not pretending otherwise.

'Strayed onto our radar,' said Sutherland. 'And like I said, we think you might have information of interest.'

Damn fucking right I did. This was manna from heaven. If the cops didn't believe me, perhaps the fish dogs would. I'd thrown up on his boat and been seen with Dudley Wilson, but at least Sutherland didn't think I was a fruitcake.

'I'm just up the road,' continued Sutherland. 'My man will show you where.'

'With the department, is he?' I said.

'Not as such,' said Sutherland. 'Technically.'

'Seems familiar,' I said.

Again, a pause. Then, 'Employed by the Abalone Industry Association, the licensed divers. Liaises with us, enforcement-wise. See you soon.'

He hung up. The man in the falling-apart tee-shirt tilted his head sideways, a question. I nodded. He began to walk away.

I downed the last of my coffee and followed, weaving through the foot traffic. Twenty paces up the street, outside Tourist Information, I fell into step and gave him back his phone. 'You work for the licensed ab divers?'

He nodded, not stopping.

'Liaison with the fish dogs?'

He nodded again.

'Doing a little liaising down Cape Patterson way a few months ago, were you?'

He looked at me sideways.

'You must be mistaking me for someone else.'

I heaved a heartfelt sigh of exhaustion. 'I've been a member of the Labor Party for more than twenty-five years,' I said, 'so I've been bullshitted by grand masters. And I've had a long night. I'm not in the mood to be treated like a moron.'

We were passing a surfwear shop with racks of swimsuits on the footpath. New Year Special, announced a sign on a bin of footwear just inside the front door.

'Give my regards to Bob Sutherland,' I said. 'Tell him maybe some other time.' I turned into the shop, rummaged in the bin and selected a pair of rubber-soled strap-overs. I paid a not very special price and tossed my perished police-issue thongs into the wastepaper basket under the counter.

My escort was waiting on the footpath. 'Was it that obvious?'

'Fooled me,' I said. 'At the time.'

'What about Dudley Wilson?'

'He was the target, was he?' I said.

'He's the influential one. Ear of the Premier and all that. We thought it'd be a good way to dramatise the poaching problem.'

'It was dramatic, all right.'

'The guy overboard? Yeah, that was a real bonus. We only planned on a chase sequence and a bit of show and tell. But Wilson ended up believing he'd compromised a real operation.'

'How did you know he'd insist on gate-crashing the expedition?'

'Calculated gamble. And if he hadn't risen to the bait, it would've been no problem to cancel. We were only fifteen minutes ahead of you. Bob would've got on the blower, pulled the plug. Nothing ventured, nothing gained.'

'I can see Sutherland's motives,' I said. 'Fending off staff cuts. How about your lot? What was in it for the Abalone Industry Association?'

'The same thing,' he said. 'Our members pay up to a million dollars for a licence, then find themselves competing with poachers. Complain that the resource is under pressure, we run the risk the government will respond by lowering the quota rather than beefing up the enforcement.'

I was impressed. Behind his sturdy bosun exterior, Bob Sutherland was a crafty bugger.

'So what's all this about a hush-hush operation?' I said. 'Not another pantomime, I hope.'

The pretend poacher shook his head. He'd said too much already. 'Talk to Bob.'

He moved ahead and I followed in silence, dodging pedestrians. At the corner of Erskine Falls Road, the shuttle bus arrived from the concert. A horde of tired-but-happy campers tumbled out, chattering in a range of foreign languages, several of which might have been English.

We turned up the hill, tramping along the nature strip past a shop window where a woman in a sailor's hat was arranging a display of distressed sheet-metal pelicans. After that, it was mostly houses. There were few other pedestrians and most of the road traffic was flowing the other way, down from the festival. It was a little after nine-fifteen, still almost three hours before I was due to pick up Red and Tarquin. A police divisional van came down the street. The driver was Constable Heinze from the wild goose chase for the Magna. I raised my forearm in a gesture of recognition as he cruised past.

Just before the water supply reservoir, we entered a side road and went through a gate into a compound of utilitarian, shed-type buildings surrounded by tall trees. My guide indicated a door marked 'Forestry Survey', then turned and walked away.

My skin was sticky with sweat and I was puffing from the hike up the hill. I was just a tiny bit short of sleep, standing alone on an apron of sun-baked concrete, not sure why I was there.

I'd jumped at the chance to talk to Sutherland, who represented another way of getting at Syce. But now I was beginning to think I had been a bit rash. What if this was a set-up?

'Appreciate your assistance, sir.'

Bob Sutherland stepped from the doorway, hand extended. He was dressed for a round of golf. Pastel yellow polo shirt, beige slacks and a wide-brimmed white hat, shark logo on the band.

He gave me the once-over, but said nothing.

'I hope this isn't another of your theatrical productions,' I said. 'No use lobbying me, you know.'

Sutherland grinned. 'Told you, did he?'

'Sang like Pavarotti,' I said. 'Couldn't shut him up.'

Sutherland guided me to the open door. 'Low on resources, high on resourcefulness, that's us,' he said. 'And I'm not wasting your time today, sir.'

The door opened into a room with frosted windows and a row of tables running down the middle. Grey steel map cases lined two of the walls. An all-in-one television–video sat on a desk, together with some kind of radio communications equipment. Looked like the fish dogs had borrowed the place from their tree-counting colleagues. A boyish bloke was sitting on the desk, legs dangling, murmuring into a mobile phone. About thirty, he wore hiking boots with khaki socks, shorts and shirt.

Sutherland took off his Greg Norman hat and wiped his brow with the back of his wrist. 'This is Geoff Crowden,' he said. 'Runs things for us in this part of the world.'

Crowden snapped the phone shut and clipped it to his belt. He pumped my hand, a real eager beaver. Cheerful as Chuckie the Woodchuck. 'You look like you could do with a cold drink.'

Not to mention a shave, a comb, a change of clothes and twelve hours' shut-eye.

He reached into a bar fridge and tossed me a tetra pack of apple juice. I half-expected him to break out the trail mix and rub two sticks together.

'So what's this all about?' I said, lowering myself into a chair at the table.

Sutherland was propped on the edge of one of the map cases, hat in hand.

Crowden climbed back onto the desk and picked up a clipboard. He leaned forward, bare elbows on his bony knees. When he spoke, his tone was formal, interrogatory. 'You drive a dark green Mitsubishi Magna sedan?' He checked the clipboard and recited the registration number.

'That's correct.'

'Your vehicle was observed in a remote location in the state forest last night.'

I felt a surge of elation. 'By who?'

'Officers of this department.' He turned the clipboard towards me, displaying a list of rego numbers, makes, models and times. 'We have the area under surveillance.'

'Excellent,' I said. 'That's great news.'

Crowden and Sutherland exchanged perplexed glances.

'We'd like to know why you were there,' said Crowden. 'And if you encountered any other vehicles or individuals.'

I wanted to leap to my feet and cheer.

'Before I answer,' I said, 'can you tell me the target of your surveillance?'

Crowden looked at Sutherland.

Sutherland looked at his hat.

'These enquiries relate to an ongoing investigation into a

poaching and distribution ring,' said Crowden. 'You'll appreciate we can't say more than that.'

'This ring,' I said. 'Does it include Tony Melina and Jake Martyn?'

Sutherland's hat was suddenly less interesting. His head came up sharply. 'You know these individuals? You saw them last night?'

I made the stop sign. 'Another question before we go any further. The man with the beard, drives the Hilux utility. Is he still at his camp?'

Crowden looked to Sutherland, got the nod. 'That's our understanding,' he said.

'You know who he is?'

'First name Mick,' said Sutherland. 'Surname currently unknown. Plates on the utility were stolen. Wrecker's yard in Colac. This matter—you know something we don't?'

'I know that I'm very grateful for your diligence,' I said. 'And I'll tell you why.'

I laid it out for them, pre-dinner drinks at Gusto to breakfast on Mountjoy Parade. The whole blood-drenched kit and caboodle.

This time, there was no question of diminished credibility. The fish dogs listened without interruption, galvanised. When I'd finished, Crowden gave a low whistle.

'Incredible,' he said.

'That's what the police think, unfortunately.'

Sutherland picked up the clipboard. 'This should sort them out. Log of all traffic in that part of the state forest between 6 p.m. and 3 a.m.,' he said. 'The Hilux was also observed at the Gusto restaurant.'

'And you had no idea that you were watching Syce?'

Sutherland shook his head. 'Came to our attention a year or so back, courtesy of our friend from the divers' organisation. Seen to be a regular buyer of abalone and crayfish from small-time poachers along the west coast. Not a priority target at the time. Had our hands full with a major Asian gang. Then, lo and behold, up he pops on a video surveillance tape. Routine monitoring, carpark at the Cape Otway lighthouse. Same frame, Jake Martyn.'

'We already had our eye on Martyn,' explained patrol leader Crowden.

'Tip from the federal money monitors,' said Sutherland. 'Questionable transfers. Period of time, we pegged him as a mover of illegal abalone and crayfish. Selling it to other restaurants and certain seafood exporters.'

'Such as Tony Melina,' I said.

Sutherland nodded. 'Been looking for a chance to bust him. Big time possession. But he's cagey. Doesn't shop around for product. Supplier unknown. Then he's spotted with this Mick character.'

Crowden dropped off the edge of the desk and turned to a map pinned to the wall. 'We finally managed to tail him to a sector of the state forest designated as a reference area.' He pointed to the spot, like a student teacher launching into a geography lesson. 'Pristine bushland. Kept that way for long-term study purposes. No forestry. No tourism.'

Bottom line, as Sutherland put it, several months of intermittent surveillance and a quick look-see of the man's camp confirmed that he was operating a makeshift abalone processing plant.

'He was cooking them up, vacuum-sealing them,' said Sutherland. 'Large quantities, buyer unknown. Martyn suspected. But no firm evidence. We were getting ready to bust him, see if we couldn't get him to roll over on his buyer. Then, week before Christmas, bingo.'

Crowden explained. 'Our phone scanner started to pick up calls to Jake Martyn's mobile. Our man Mick, calling from a payphone up the coast. Coded references, something about a guest. We cranked the surveillance back up. Martyn made two visits to the camp.'

'Late at night,' said Sutherland. 'Thing is, no warning. No chance for us to act. Then, last night, a flurry of activity.'

Crowden put his clipboard on the table in front of me and ran his finger down the log entries.

Hilux to Gusto. Hilux to camp. Magna enters area. Jake Martyn's Range Rover enters area. Range Rover returns to Gusto. Hilux emerges, towing a boat. Hilux returns, no boat. Hilux leaves area, towing Magna. Hilux returns. Surveillance ends, 3 a.m.

Surveillance recommences, 6 a.m. Police vehicle from the local station enters area. Appears to be searching for something. Police officer and civilian.

'We'd checked the registration of the Magna, identified you as the owner,' said Crowden. 'Thought that you must've strayed into the area, got bogged or had a breakdown, walked out and left your car behind. Figured our man had found it, decided to move it further from the camp. That was our thinking when we approached you after you left the police station.'

Which brought us back to square one.

'Better escort you back there pronto,' said Sutherland. 'Get the ball rolling.'

As we got to our feet, the door swung open. A figure

stepped into the frame, side on, backlit by the glare of the sun. Coiled tight, he scrutinised us through rimless sunglasses. The jacket of his lightweight suit was drawn back at the hip and his right hand rested on the butt of a holstered pistol.

'Who the hell are you?' demanded Sutherland.

'Allow me,' I said, 'to introduce Detective Sergeant Meakes of the Victoria Police.'

Within an hour, I was surplus to requirements.

I'd been conveyed back to the station house, pumped dry, offered tea and trauma counselling, then left to cool my heels in an interview room while assorted components of the law-enforcement community got their ducks in a row.

Everybody was lining up for a suck of the Syce sausage. Two other members of the task force had arrived with Meakes. Homicide turned up soon after. The Special Operations Group was on its way with kevlar vests, shin-high combat boots and surface-to-surface missiles. The fish dogs were having a field day, the drug squad was sniffing around, the local cops had been conscripted and, for all I knew, the Man from Snowy River was galloping Lorneward with a detachment of alpine cavalry.

'You should've informed the sergeant of your intentions,' Meakes reprimanded me as we drove back to the police station. 'Naturally we were concerned about your safety when we arrived to find that you were missing. Particularly when one of the local officers reported seeing you with a unidentified person.'

'I appreciate the way you came to my rescue,' I said. 'But until that point I was under the impression you lot didn't believe me.'

'Why would you think that?' he asked.

Back at the police station, Meakes loosened up. I had, after all, delivered Syce to him. Done his job for him. Once Syce was back in custody, DS Meakes would be the man of the moment, his mug on the box, his pic in the paper, his tailoring the envy of the aspirational classes. So he rapidly recast himself as my confidant and collaborator.

As we worked our way through the details, he brought me up to speed on the background investigation.

For starters, I was wrong to assume that the moving of the Magna had scuppered my story. It was irrelevant. Meakes and his crew were half-way to Lorne by the time the car was found. Their scramble button had been pushed by two names that appeared in my statement to the Lorne coppers. Persons already of considerable interest to them.

One was Jake Martyn. The other was Phillip Ferrier, who was a Melbourne solicitor, Meakes informed me. And one of Ferrier's clients was Adrian Parish, the hold-up man who masterminded the motorbike escape. It was Ferrier who briefed Parish's barristers. He also assisted Parish with financial matters. Investments and the like.

After Parish's untimely death, his estate went to probate. It came to light that his goods and chattels included a shelf company whose sole asset was a half share in Gusto. It further emerged that Parish had assigned his share in Gusto to his lawyer as security against any outstanding fees, should he find himself unable to pay.

'Because he was doing fifteen years in prison, for example,' explained Meakes.

Adrian Parish died owing his lawyer money and so, in due course, Phillip Ferrier became half-owner of Gusto.

In the meantime, Meakes and his merry men were putting Jake Martyn under the microscope.

When interviewed, the restaurateur denied all knowledge of Parish. As far as he knew, the equity in his restaurant was owned by a trust fund operated by a reputable solicitor named Phillip Ferrier, a man he had met several years earlier when seeking investors for Gusto. Solicitors' trust funds are not an unusual source of capital for enterprises such as restaurants, he pointed out, and his dealings had been exclusively with Ferrier, an arm's-length investor who took his share of the profits but played no role in the business. Martyn was shocked to discover that the actual investor had been a notorious criminal. So he claimed.

Ferrier backed Martyn's account. Parish had wished to remain anonymous, he explained. Client confidentiality, blah, blah.

As to Rodney Syce, Martyn claimed to know only what he'd read in the newspapers.

Lacking hard evidence to link either Martyn or Ferrier directly to Syce, the police had no option but to bide their time. And when I was washed ashore with their names on my lips, lights flashed and buzzers buzzed.

'You hit the trifecta,' said Meakes.

My eye-witness account of the previous night's events,

combined with the investigative work done by the cops and the fish dogs' surveillance, produced a working hypothesis to explain the connection between Jake Martyn and Rodney Syce.

It ran like this. When Parish escaped from the Remand Centre, he planned to rendezvous with Jake Martyn, his bent business associate. After Parish was shot, Syce connected with Martyn, who hid him, then put him to work. First in the illegal seafood racket, then as an extortionist and killer.

Had I not spotted Syce, the two of them would probably have got away with it. As Meakes generously conceded, I'd been a very real help to the investigation.

Once the big picture came into focus, police attention moved to operational issues, the tactical implementation of Operation Snaffle Syce.

Surveillance was upped on the bush camp and Jake Martyn was kept under observation at Gusto, where he was choreographing preparations for New Year's Day brunch. And, presumably, preparing for his assignation with Syce at the bush camp.

No contact had been detected between the two men since Martyn's trip into the hills the previous night. This indicated that Syce was now playing a lone hand, the cops concluded. That he was keeping quiet about the complications that had arisen during the disposal of Tony Melina's body. That he was waiting for Martyn to arrive with the blood money, Tony's passport and the airline ticket out of the country.

Martyn had told Syce he'd bring the dough and the getaway kit to the camp during the afternoon. The moment he got there, the police trap would spring shut.

By eleven-thirty, I was out of the loop and growing bored

with sitting around waiting for my underpants to dry. Besides, if I didn't do something I would fall into a coma. My request for a lift to the holiday house for a change of clothes was denied—it would be better to wait until the dust settled. Just in case. Likewise, pending forensics, the Magna was to remain at the Cumberland River caravan park.

Meakes had taken over the sergeant's office as a field headquarters. Busy, busy. I waited until he finished a phone call, something about a helicopter landing area.

'I have to pick up my son and his friend from the Falls music festival,' I reminded the detective.

He beckoned over my shoulder to the muster room, a minor hive. 'One of the boys will drive you.'

But I didn't want a free trip in a police car. What I wanted was an hour's respite from the thump and grind of the previous twelve. A chance to feel normal again. Not a victim, not a witness, not a man possessed. Just a father doing his fatherly thing. Meeting his boy, asking him about his big night out. Not a man with a police escort and awful things to explain. In time I'd have to explain them, of course. But not yet.

'Thanks,' I said, 'but I'll take the shuttle-bus.'

'It's no problem,' insisted Meakes.

'It is for me,' I said. 'I need a bit of breathing space.'

'Not a good idea. We don't want a repetition of that earlier business, do we?'

'You think I'm in danger? Think you might have to rescue me again?'

'No, it's just better this way.'

Better for him, he meant. Better to keep me filed away until after his moment of triumph. We batted it back and forth for a couple of minutes, but short of arresting me, he couldn't detain me against my will.

'I'll keep my head low,' I said. 'And I'll be back in an hour with two teenage boys.'

'Suit yourself,' he said. 'But you're acting contrary to my advice.'

Outside the copshop, I found the weather turning, the heat dissipating before it reached its threatened peak. Concrete-coloured clouds scuttled across the sky. A gusty onshore breeze was raising whitecaps and rattling the treetops. Frankly, I was more than a little rattled myself. Rats-arsed, anyway. It had been a big night, what with one thing and another, and I was fuzzy-headed and heavy-limbed.

I was also not in a fit state to been seen on the main drag of a fashionable resort in the middle of a public holiday. The Labor Party's reputation was already at an all-time low. Sticking to residential side-streets, I steered an inconspicuous course to Erskine Falls Road and hailed the mini-bus as it returned up the hill.

I was the only passenger. Picking my way towards the back, I found a yellow terry-towelling hat on the floor. I sprawled across the back seat and laid it over my face, resting my weary bones and red-rimmed eyes.

Fifteen minutes later, the bus jerked to a halt at the festival gate. Yesterday's pasture was now a mosh-trampled cow-paddock littered with abandoned tents, wayward groundsheets and half-dismantled vegan-burger stalls. A bunk-chukka-bunk beat was washing up the slope from the direction of the circus bigtop that housed the main stage. Youthful punters were straggling from the scene of the all-night beano, their duds crumpled and flecked with grass.

Here, at least, I was dressed for the occasion.

I found Tarquin on the grassy verge beside the pick-up area. He was dozing, mouth open, his back against a big grey-gum. His dress shirt was scrunched and sweat-stained, the wing collar gone entirely. He was buttressed on one side by two backpacks, his and Red's, and on the other by a girl in a black knee-length slip. She had black, magenta-streaked hair, purple lipstick, flour-white make-up and Cleopatra eyeliner. Around her neck was a black velvet ribbon. She was about fourteen years old. She, too, was slumbering, slack-jawed.

I looked around, but saw no sign of Red.

'Wakey, wakey,' I croaked, nudging Tark's prostrate form with a rubber sandal.

He came upright. He looked at me, looked around, looked at his watch and looked around again. His little friend from the Addams family came awake and stretched fetchingly.

'This is Ronnie,' explained Tark.

Veronica gave me a watery smile. Then she stood, flapped her wrist in Tark's general direction, mumbled something about seeing him later, and wandered away.

'No need to ask if you had a good time, then,' I said.

'Likewise,' said Tark. 'Love the hat. It's very you.'

'Get fucked,' I said. 'Where's Red?'

Tark clambered to his feet, smacking the dust off his backside. Shading his eyes, he took a long look around. No result. He scratched his scalp-tuft and shrugged. His put-upon air suggested that he'd been left to guard the baggage while Red amused himself elsewhere. 'Not back yet,' he said.

'Back from where?'

'Nature ramble.' He said it with disdain. 'Red, Jodie, Matt

Prentice, bunch of them. Been gone a while. Supposed to be back by now.'

I sighed and slumped down onto the backpacks. They were very comfortable, stuffed with tent and sleeping bags. So Red was a bit late. No big deal. Busy enjoying himself, he'd probably lost track of time. He'd turn up. I settled back to wait, shoulders against the grey-gum, my new head-wear pulled down against the glare.

'Good, was it?' I yawned in Tark's general direction. 'I hear Hunters and Collectors stole the show.'

'If you like that sort of thing,' he allowed. 'Think I'll get a drink. Want one?'

'Uh-huh.'

I dozed, lulled by the swish of the leaves above my head. Images from the previous night flashed past. Barbara Prentice at Gusto. The pursuit into the ranges, tail-lights dancing ahead. Bafflement at the discovery of Tony Melina. Dark and horrible things. White knuckles, severed ears. The immensity of the ocean.

'Mineral water.'

'Huh.'

'Mineral water,' repeated Tarquin. 'It's all they had left.'

He lifted the towelling hat and dangled the bottle in front of my face. Deep Spring.

Deep mouthfuls, then a glance at my watch. A half hour had slipped past. I eased myself upright and scanned the scene. Vehicles were coming and going in the pick-up area, parents collecting offspring. Red was still nowhere to be seen. Nor Jodie or her big brother.

'Still not back?' I said.

Tarquin prodded the ground with a steel-capped toe, a

man on the horns of a dilemma.

'Better tell me what's going on,' I said.

Tark heaved a sigh. He'd talk, but only because I'd beaten it out of him. 'They went to get some plants.'

'Plants?' I said, 'What do you mean plants?'

Tark shrugged. Not tomato plants. Not hardy perennials. Not specimens of endangered native vegetation.

'Little bastard,' I said. 'I'll wring his fucking neck.'

Tarquin shook his head furiously. 'It wasn't Red's idea. He doesn't even smoke, honest. Okay, maybe a puff now and then. But he doesn't inhale. Only reason he went was because Jodie went. And she only went because Matt was going and she wanted to make sure he didn't get into any trouble. The whole thing's down to this dickhead eco-warrior called Mongoose. He's the one found the plants, talked Matt and the others into going with him. Reckoned they were just sitting there for the taking.'

Great timing, I thought. Today of all days, rope-a-dope Red decides to join a band of bhang-burglars.

Then came an even more disturbing thought. I stared past the fences to the featureless bush. There's bound to be more than one clump of hemp out there, I reassured myself. And the one I happened to know about was at least two hours solid hiking to the west.

'And where exactly are these plants?' I said.

Tark shrugged. 'Mongoose was pretty vague. They left about eight. Mongoose said they'd be back by midday.'

'Which way did they go?'

He looked around, settled on a direction and tossed his mohawk west-ish.

'On foot?' I said.

Tark nodded. 'You think they might have got lost or something?'

I wasn't sure what I thought. I was fully occupied trying to calculate the chances that the target of the half-baked dope raid was Rodney Syce's camp.

'Who is this Mongoose guy anyway?' I said. 'Friend of Matt Prentice, is he?'

Tarquin shrugged again. 'Friend of a friend of a friend sort of thing,' he said. 'He's a feral. Walked here cross-country from a logging protest camp with a bunch of tree-huggers.'

'I want to know exactly where they went,' I said.

Tark caught my antsy tone. 'I dunno,' he pleaded. 'Honest. But that lot over there might.'

A pod of ferals was moving towards the exit, a half-dozen soap-shy, low-tech, bush-dwelling hippies. Crusty chicks in shaman chic, fabric-swathed and spider-legged. Bedraggled boys in scrofulous face-hair and army-surplus pants, matted dreadlocks stuffed into tea-cosy tam-o'-shanters.

'They're the ones Mongoose came with,' explained Tark. 'Want me to ask if they know anything?'

'Go,' I commanded. 'Ask.'

Tark jogged after the ferals and hailed them. They encirled him, bobbing in time with the faint pulse of the music, beaming at him like he was a strange and fascinating artifact. A conference commenced. Everybody had something to contribute. I hung back, impatiently awaiting the outcome.

The talk continued, back and forth, heap big pow-wow. The People's Consultative Congress. Then, abruptly, the ferals resumed their march for the exit. Tark returned.

'Off their faces,' he reported. 'But they know where Mongoose took Red and the others. They camped near the place on their way here, night before last. They heard this dog barking somewhere in the bush, nobody around, houses or anything. Mongoose went for a look, came back with fresh leaf. Said he'd found a dope patch. He wanted to go back in the morning, check it out, maybe rip it off. They said no, so he convinced Matt and his mates to help them instead.'

I didn't like the sound of that dog.

'They're headed that way now,' said Tark. 'They reckon they'll probably meet Red and the others on their way back.'

The ferals were trucking out the gate, disappearing down the road. Should I wait here? Should I follow the furry freaks, hope to connect with Red and the Prentice kids?

Should I contact the cops and share my concerns?

I decided on all three.

'You wait here,' I ordered Tark. 'If I'm not back in half an hour, or if Red hasn't shown up, contact the Lorne police. Mention my name. Tell them what you told me and what the ferals told you. Tell them I think these dope plants might be the ones at Rodney Syce's camp. Tell them I've gone to find Red and the others. Okay?'

Tark was a fast study. 'Rodney Syce?' he said, 'Wasn't that the guy…'

'Later,' I said, stuffing the bottle of mineral water into my back pocket and starting after the vanishing ferals.

They were setting a cracking pace, moving faster than a runaway budget deficit. I hurried to keep them in sight as they powered along the roadside.

A dark-grey surfwear-stickered Range Rover came up the hill and whizzed past, Barbara Prentice behind the wheel.

Come to collect Jodie and Matt, no doubt. Chances were, Tark would spot her, fill her in. Good.

Or was it? Barbara had connections with Jake Martyn. Could word leak back to him somehow?

The ferals had walked into a picnic area. Tree ferns, log tables, families. They entered a slot between the trees, the beginning of a hiking track. I pursued them along the narrow defile. The bush rustled around us. The path rose and fell.

I put on a spurt of speed and caught up with the rearguard feral. She was a thin girl, her collarbones jutting above a flat chest bandoleered with ragged scarves. A wide headband and a ring though her septum, she looked like the door knocker from a Mayan temple. She was sucking a Chupa-Chup and making a vibrating noise in her throat as she marched.

'Excuse me,' I panted, falling into step beside her.

She shook her head briskly and continued to hum, lips tight around her lollipop stick. Headphone plugs stoppered her ears, leading from a Discman in an embroidered sack on a cord around her neck.

'I'm trying to find out...'

She shook her head again, making it clear she wasn't going to speak.

Suppressing the urge to rip the wires from her lugholes, I hurried up the line to the next crusty. He was bare-footed with vulcanised soles, Celtic tattoos, a braided beard, a moonstone pendant and a walking staff incised with a rainbow serpent. All of twenty years old.

'Excuse me,' I gasped. 'I'm looking for my son. He's with a guy called Mongoose. I'm worried...'

Gandalf did not break stride. He beamed benignly and stroked his beard. 'You've got to learn to let go, man. You can't, like, stifle the people you love.'

'I'm not trying to stifle him,' I said. 'I'm trying to find him.' And then, it was true, I'd throttle him.

'Find yourself first, man,' opined the wizard. 'The answer lies within.'

More likely it lay ahead. Stacking on the pace, I reached a brace of feralesses. One was tall and ethereal, all bracelets and bells. The other was stocky and wore a shearer's blue singlet. ''Scuse me,' I wheezed. 'I'm looking for my son.'

Tinkerbell slowed a little and smiled beatifically. 'What's his name?'

'Red,' I said.

'Cool,' she said. 'It's, like, very vibrant.'

The little shearer sheila clocked me for a suit in mufti. She eyed me suspiciously. 'We don't know anyone called Red.'

'But you know a guy called Mongoose, right?'

Grasping my line of enquiry, she shook her head. 'It's nothing to do with us.'

The wind was getting stronger, snatching at our words. I had a stitch in my side and a raging thirst. My ankle was throbbing and my new sandals were rubbing at my heels. I downed the last of my water.

'I just want to know where they've gone,' I pleaded.

Tinkerbell extended a long delicate finger threaded with silver rings. The trees on the side of the trail were thinning. Through them I could see a vast open space. A firebreak. The lead ferals, a cluster of young bucks, had left the path and started across it.

I checked the time. It was past one-thirty. The half hour

had come and gone. Either Red and the others were safely back at the concert pick-up area or Tark had contacted the coppers. Should I go forward or back? I decided to press on, give it another few minutes.

The firebreak was a desolate gash in the grey-green fabric of the forest. Two hundred metres of torn earth, flattened vegetation and chain-sawed tree stumps. By the time I was half-way across, the pathfinder ferals had vanished into the bush on the far side.

Pixie and Poxie and Whacko the Wizard were nowhere in sight. The sky roiled with clouds. My brain was turning to mush. What was I doing?

A rutted track intersected the firebreak, two shallow undulations in the hard-packed dirt. I followed it into the trees for a couple of minutes, then sank onto a fallen branch.

Time to pack it in, go back the way I'd come.

The wind roared in the canopy and stirred up willy-willies of leaves and dust. Shards of bark and dry twigs flew through the air. The temperature dropped. Rain coming.

I pulled the empty water bottle from my pocket and cursed my stupidity. So much for my New Year resolution about going off half-cocked. I unpeeled the velcro tabs on my sandals and massaged my raw heels.

The Australian bush. I hated it. The sooner it was turned into woodchips, toilet paper and florists' accessories, the better.

As I climbed to my feet, a spanking new Nissan Patrol came lumbering along the track from the direction of the firebreak. Bullbar on the front grille. It juddered to a halt beside me and a flush-faced, silver-haired man in a crisply ironed check shirt leaned out the window.

'G'day,' he said, in an unconvincing attempt to sound as if he hadn't spent his entire adult life in a corporate boardroom.

'G'day,' I responded, spotting an opportunity. 'Got myself a bit bushed here, mate. Any chance of a lift back to civilisation?'

A brittle-coiffed matron scrutinised me from the passenger seat, not entirely thrilled by the idea. Her R. M. Williams collar was rakishly turned up. Protection against the harsh outback sun for both a well-preserved neck and a string of rather good pearls.

'Hop in,' said the silverback.

I climbed into the back seat, inhaling the ambience of the leafy suburbs. The vehicle had a dashboard like a B-52. Traction control, six-speaker CD, floating compass, artificial horizon, dual airbags. 'Murray's the name,' I said.

'Douglas,' said the man. 'And my wife Pamela.'

The massive machine crawled forward. Douglas craned over the steering wheel, concentrating on the narrow, rutted track.

'Bit new to this,' he explained. 'We're planning a big trip to the Top End later in the year. I thought I'd get some off-road experience first.'

We bumped and rocked to the top of an incline, then ploughed downwards. Douglas hadn't counted on an audience. He kept wiping his hands on his thighs. Wet patches darkened the armpits of his shirt.

'Sure this is the way?' I said. 'You got a map?'

The wife had one on her knee. 'This track leads to the Mount Sabine Road,' she said primly.

You're the one who got lost, her tone implied.

I lapsed into grateful silence.

Pamela stared fixedly ahead. I couldn't tell if her tension was caused by her husband's driving or a suspicion that the rough-looking stranger in the back seat was about to cut their throats and steal their expensive new car.

The track was little more than a fissure between close-packed trees. Branches scraped the doors and the vehicle yawed from side to side.

'Honestly, Douglas,' said his wife, clinging to the handrail. The minutes ticked past. I grew prickly with impatience.

'I really appreciate this,' I said.

Suddenly, Douglas hit the brakes hard and the Patrol lurched to a halt.

A wild-eyed figure was blocking our path.

He was compact and sinewy, his scalp razored back to a braided topknot. Sweat and grime covered his nut-brown skin and his bare chest heaved beneath a shark-tooth necklace. His army surplus pants had been sheared off mid-calf and cinched at the waist with a tattered saffron scarf.

He was semaphoring desperately for us to stop.

I hit the ground running and reached him in ten seconds flat. He had a sharp, tapered face, small ears and darting eyes. A mongoose if ever I saw one.

He teetered on the spot, sucked down air and steadied himself. He was much older than I'd assumed. Twenty-five at least.

You prick, I thought, bracing for the worst.

'Need help, man,' he panted. 'I was, like, taking these young dudes to check out this place where I'd, like, seen this amazing platypus and next thing there's this loony pointing like a shotgun at us and sort of herding us into this kind of shed but I'm like basically behind a tree and he doesn't see me so I, like, see my chance to go get help so I make a break and…'

The torrent dried up and he paused to catch his breath. I clamped a hand around one of his Polynesian wrist tattoos.

'Cut the outdoor-education crap, Mongoose. I know all about you ripping off the dope.'

The twerp stared at me, eyes wide with astonishment. His mouth did a passable impression of a dying carp.

'Are those kids okay?' I demanded. 'Tell me exactly what happened.'

Mongoose licked his lips, cowering slightly. Probably because I was twisting his arm behind his back.

'There's five of them,' he said. 'Four guys and a chick. We were doing a run-through of this guy's crop. He springs us, and suddenly he's waving this gun around, yelling out stuff like, "Hands in the air, shuddup, get in the shed." The others, they're like totally freaked but, "Sure, man, whatever you say" and I'm out of there, so I don't see what happens next. But there's no shots, nothing like that. He's, like, taken them prisoner or something. I think.'

Douglas was hovering apprehensively. All this, and he wasn't even in the Northern Territory yet. He glanced back at the Patrol. Pamela stood a few paces behind him, fingering her pearls. In her other hand she held a bottle of water.

'Where's this happening?' I said.

Mongoose flapped his free arm. 'Back that way. Along a creek, bottom of a ridge.'

'Take me there.'

He wrenched free. 'What for, man? Take me to the cops, I'll show them the way.'

'The cops already know where it is.'

'Bullshit. How could they?'

'You don't know the half of it, you dopey deadshit,' I said, with more assurance than I felt. 'Take me there and I'll put in a good word for you at the trial.'

He accepted a swig of water from Pamela and gulped, his adam's apple pulsing. As he drank, he eyed me warily as though I might snatch the bottle from his grasp and deck him with it.

'You're out of your fucken tree, man. No *way* am I going back there. Not without an army of cops.'

I turned to Pamela and Douglas and adopted my doorknocking-in-a-marginal-seat tone. 'This sorry specimen has put a group of teenagers in serious danger. They're in the hands of an escaped convict, a murderer. One of them is a young girl. We need to get to the police, ASAP.'

'That's what I'm telling you, man,' bleated Mongoose. 'Except I didn't know he was a murderer, just some dude with a dope plantation. Dead set.'

I shoved him towards the Patrol. He shoved back. 'Fuck, man,' he said peevishly. 'No need to get so heavy.'

I balled my fist, seething with anger, frustration and anxiety. 'I'll get as heavy as I like, pal,' I said. 'One of those kids is my son. And if anything's happened to him, I'll have you up on so many charges you'll be meeting parole conditions for the rest of your sorry-arsed life.'

The sky was darkening, the trees groaning in the wind. I shivered, a coldness creeping through me. Finger by finger, I unballed my fist.

Douglas and Pamela had gone into whispered conference beside the Patrol. Now Pamela turned on her heel and strode towards the driver's door. 'For God's sake, Douglas,' she said. 'This is an emergency.'

I followed Mongoose into the back seat. Douglas took the front passenger slot. Pamela got behind the wheel and turned the key in the ignition.

'Seatbelts,' she commanded.

She slammed the Patrol into gear and gunned it along the rutted outline of the track. Lips tight, pearls swaying as the leviathan powered forward. She was, I knew at once, a formidable presence on the tennis club social committee.

Mongoose retreated into his corner. He smelled of sweat and fear and patchouli oil. But even in his deflated state, there was a hint of nervy charisma about him, an expectation that people would turn towards him. I could understand how his bush-warrior pose might appeal to a surly, insecure kid like Matt Prentice.

Redmond Whelan, on the other hand, should have known better.

I tried to picture the scene at Syce's camp, imagine his reaction to the sudden appearance of a stampeding herd of plant-plundering adolescents. At least, if the funked-out Mongoose was to be believed, he hadn't starting blasting away with his shotgun. On the other hand, he didn't need a gun to be lethal. A shovel would do, or even an oyster knife. I didn't want to think about it. Drop my bundle now and I'd be no use to anyone.

Pamela was boring ahead like a three-time veteran of the Paris–Dakar. I leaned into the gap between the seats and gave them a thumbnail of the situation. A police operation was in progress, I told them, but this was a new development. I said I was worried the police might get there too late. Didn't mention the doings of the previous night. Fudged the reasons for my involvement. Clear as mud, but it covered the ground.

'Dreadful,' said Pamela above the grunt and thrash of the engine.

'You're a member of parliament, you say?' Douglas sounded sceptical.

'Labor,' I explained.

'Ah.'

The track divided. The right-hand fork, better-defined, ran uphill. Douglas fussed with the map.

'Go right,' said Mongoose. He shot a furtive glance down the side track.

'Stop the car,' I said.

Pamela hit the anchors and hoisted the handbrake. We propped precariously, bullbar angled upwards.

I loomed over Mongoose like a cobra. 'It's down there, isn't it?'

'I'm not going back, man. Not without…'

'Yeah, yeah,' I cut him off. 'At least give me directions.'

'Surely you're not thinking of going alone?' said Douglas.

'How would you feel if it was Verity?' said Pamela.

Douglas said nothing, but if I wanted to get myself shot, it was fine with Mongoose. 'Track ends at a fallen tree,' he said. 'Somebody's had a go at it with a chainsaw. Slope drops away, totally steep. Creek's at the bottom. Follow it downstream, ten, fifteen minutes.'

I repeated the instructions to myself and opened the door.

'What's your shoe size?' said Pamela.

'Nine,' I said. 'Why?'

'Give him your shoes, Douglas,' she said. 'And socks. He can't go tramping through the bush in those sandals.'

Douglas unlaced his Timberlake hikers. A Christmas present, judging by their mint condition. He peeled off his cream cotton socks and handed them over. Socks and boots both were a perfect fit.

'Take care,' Pamela said, laying a motherly hand on my shoulder. 'Good luck.'

The Patrol grunted upwards. I jogged down the left fork in my brand new seven-league boots, plastic bottle in hand. I ached in some parts and chafed in others, but the exhaustion had evaporated. I was hyper. Dark possibilities coursed through my brain.

The faint ruts, the barest figment of a track, sank deeper and deeper into the swaying grey-green immensity of the ranges. After ten minutes of thudding footfalls and heaving lungs, they were just a gap in the vegetation, a narrow seam weaving through the trees.

The trunk of a long-dead stringybark blocked my way, a decaying giant notched with incisions. Once upon a time, an optimist had tried to clear the path, given up. I vaulted the log and traversed the shoulder of a ridge. The ground dropped away to one side. Like, totally steep, man.

This looked like the place. Unless Mongoose had been winding me up. He wouldn't dare, I told myself.

It was nearly three o'clock. Jake Martyn was expected mid-afternoon. Any time now. The cops, I assumed, had already established some sort of perimeter. With luck I'd connect with them or the fish dogs as I approached the camp. I half expected to see a hovering helicopter, squaddies abseiling down ropes into the tree canopy.

I plunged down the incline, skidding though clumps of parrot-pea and careening off grey-gums. The drop was almost vertical. Hurtling headlong, I snatched at anything in reach. Thorns and blades of native grass ripped my skin, wiry, like frayed cable ends. I fell on my arse and rode the seat of my pants to the bottom, steering with my feet.

The creek was a chain of tea-coloured puddles, midges swarming. I caught my breath, examined my abrasions, took an abstemious slug of my bottled water and started to work my way downstream.

The watercourse meandered through a tangle of rotting logs and moss-covered rocks, its fern-crowded banks never more than three or four metres apart. The air smelled peaty and primeval. Bellbirds pinged. The air was almost still, the wind a distant moan.

The slopes on either side gradually became less steep. Dry, undergrowth-choked gullies converged with the creek bed. At the mouth of one, I found footprints in a spill of quartz-speckled sand. Mine, I concluded. My lost-at-sea loafers. I spent half my political life going round in circles, but this was beyond a joke.

Nerve-ends tingling, I began to move more cautiously, half-recognising features of the terrain from the previous night. The wind picked up again, sighing and whistling in the treetops. The creek bank became a redoubt of weathered, lichen-colonised granite. Edging around it, I caught a glimpse of the sandbagged dam, hose running up to Syce's camp.

I turned and crept back the way I had come, assessing the lie of the land. A hundred metres upstream I scrambled up the bank. I began to circle the camp, dreading what I might discover.

Where were the police, I kept asking myself? Surely they were somewhere nearby, monitoring the comings and goings. Surely they were up to speed on the desperately changed situation by now. My old lack of confidence in the constabulary was back with a vengeance.

The cloud was breaking apart, the light flickering and shifting as it fell through the swaying leaf canopy. I approached the camp from high ground, duck and dart, bent in a half-crouch.

I spotted the Hilux, caught a fishy smell on a gust of wind. The abalone kitchen was a camouflage-dappled cube in the dusty green. The screen-wall tent was gone, struck.

Nothing moving. Nobody talking, weeping, groaning.

No barking. Not yet, anyway. I changed position, keeping well back. Now I could see the whacky-backy patch, a deeper green, half of it uprooted. And Syce. I could see Syce.

He was standing beside a tree, the one Tony Melina had been chained to. He was staring at its trunk, very close, his back to me, his hands moving at the sides of his head as though batting at his ears.

Jesus, I thought. He's wigged out, gone Lady Macbeth.

My blood ran cold. His nerves were fine when he was torturing and murdering Tony Melina. It must have taken a far worse atrocity to whip him into such a psychotic lather. Far, far worse.

I got down on my belly with the snakes and the lizards and slithered through the leaf-litter.

'I need to pee,' pleaded a girl's voice.

'Shuddup,' grunted Syce. 'You peed already.'

The voice came from inside the shed. It had to be Jodie Prentice. And she wasn't too terrified to speak. And Syce was not too deranged to respond. These were good signs, I told myself. A minuscule ripple of relief ran through me.

I manoeuvred until I could see the doorway of the shed. It was a black rectangle, the interior obscure. I now also had a profile view of Syce. He wasn't flipping out. He was snipping his hair with a small pair of scissors, checking his reflection in a shaving mirror hooked on a nail hammered into the tree.

A fine drizzle descended, a momentary sun-shower, bathing the scene in a brief, sugar-sprinkled incandescence. In the sudden flash of light, a cluster of figures took shape in the shed. They were sitting on the earth floor, hugging their knees, blindfolded. One, two, five. Jodie, Red, Matt, two boys I didn't know. The mongrel dog lay on its sack in the doorway, scratching.

Relief again. A small tsunami this time.

But where were the frigging cops? And did they know yet that Syce was not alone? That abalone shed was just a tin box. If push came to gunplay, the kids could get caught in the crossfire.

I backed up the slope, hunkered down in the shrubbery and did the trigonometry. It was the police plan, last I'd heard, to wait until Jake Martyn arrived at the camp before making their move. Until then, they were probably holding back, wary of spooking Syce. Martyn would come up the creek bed. So, in all likelihood, would the main force of plods.

I needed to connect with them before things started happening, give them the low-down on the set-up.

As I started toward the creek, the dog began to bark. Syce said something brisk, the word inaudible. The woof-woofing ceased immediately. I crouched, frozen, hearing nothing but the creak and rustle of the bush, the buzz of bugs. Syce spoke again, the words lost, the tone instructional.

Instant replay of the previous night. Martyn was arriving. Syce was telling the kids to behave themselves.

Skirting the shed, I navigated for the creek bed. But a vehicle was already emerging from the tunnel of vegetation. I pulled up short and took cover behind a thick stringybark.

The car was a dark green Range Rover. Syce was watching it, too. He was standing in the lee of a towering bluegum, double-barrel shotgun in the crook of his arm. He'd whittled his full beard down to a rough stubble, thicker at the chin. Likewise the front of his scalp. Got a head start on the big make-over. Charles Manson meets Fu Manchu, the rough-cut.

The Range Rover laboured onto the slew of sand below the camp and stopped. Jake Martyn got out. Big shirt, comfortable pants. Syce came down the slope to meet him, shotgun angled to the ground. Martyn toted a sports bag. That'd be the money. Tony's passport, the airline ticket, the salon accessories. Avon calling.

They walked back up towards the shed, Syce doing the talking. Explaining. Persuasive hand gestures. The shed doorway was out of sight, around the corner. The dog padded out to meet them, metronome tail, sociable as a parish priest in a public bar.

The guard has deserted its post, I thought. Syce must have realised the same thing. He increased his pace, still pitching his line. Jake Martyn was asking curt questions, not liking the answers.

The cops, the cops. Where, sweet Jesus, were the cops?

Then the dog was woofing again. This time, Syce didn't silence it. He turned towards the shed, the shotgun swinging around with him, rising as it came. Martyn reached out and grabbed the barrel. The gun went off. Boom. Astonishingly loud.

Birds erupted from the trees, an explosion of screeching feathers. Jake Martyn went down, keening like an air-raid siren, blood gushing from his thigh. As if responding to a starter's pistol, figures bolted from the shed and scattered into the bush. The kids were breaking out. The dog took off in hot pursuit, barking and snapping.

Syce recoiled from the accidental discharge. Even from thirty metres away, I could tell that he was losing it. The best laid plans were turning to shit, coming apart at the seams. He swept the shotgun in a jerky, erratic arc. Then, snatching up Jake Martyn's tote bag, he bolted for the Range Rover.

Just as he reached the creek bed, a stick figure in hipsters and a halter-top burst out of the undergrowth and skidded down the bank. Jodie Prentice. The dog had its fangs in the hem of her jeans, slathering and thrashing. She kicked out, trying to shake it loose.

Syce swung around, dropped the sports bag and brought up the shotgun.

Then Red appeared, sprinting, an upraised stick in hand.

Jodie was yelling and swearing, dragging the dog behind her. 'Fuck off, shit-bastard animal.'

Jake Martyn was back upright, one hand clutching his wound, mouth opening and closing.

Screaming girl, rabid dog, rushing boy, desperate maniac, ruined plan, pointed shotgun. I didn't like the way the dominoes were falling. Not with one barrel to go and Syce's history in tight corners.

And where were the pinhead pigs?

I stuck my head out from behind cover. 'Hey, you,' I shouted. 'Up here.'

My words were lost in the cacophony. Windwhip,

dogsnarl, birdscreech. Jake Martyn's gunshot yabbering and Jodie Prentice's industrial-strength cursing.

I stepped into plain sight and thundered down the slope, weaving through the saplings, a bellowing buffalo. 'Syce,' I screamed. 'Over here, arsehole.'

He spun around and I dived behind a tree. The shotgun came up to his shoulder and the barrel swept the hillside.

Red started belting the dog. It turned on him, sabre-toothed. Syce swung the shotgun around at the sound.

He'd run out of rope. I could see it in the way he was tensing, his grip whitening on the stock of the shotgun, finger crooked at the trigger.

Again, I stepped from cover and yelled. The shotgun came around again. The business end was pointed directly at my chest. I was maybe ten metres away.

Red and Jodie were in retreat, Red beating at the dog with all his rower's strength. Snarl, snap.

A thunderclap rang in my ears and a blow struck my chest, powerful as a runaway bus. I felt myself lifted off my feet, thrown backwards through the air.

Everything went black.

A heavenly chorus filled my ears.

'Drop it.'

'Police.'

'Don't move, police.'

'POLICE!'

My shoulder slammed into the ground with a lung-flattening *womph*. The runaway bus landed on top of me, pressing my face into the earth. The hubbub of voices swelled. Two shots rang out in rapid succession. In their echo came the unremitting battle-cry of the dog. A voice started yelling, 'Don't shoot, I'm not armed. Don't shoot.'

Over and over, a mantra.

I spat gumleaf crud and unscrewed my eyelids. A body was straddling mine, a black-clad blur, pinning me flat. It shifted aside to let me breathe but maintained the pressure between my shoulder blades. I twisted my head and registered the black as a coverall uniform. Special Operations Group. The Sons of God.

Heavy footfalls drummed past my head. Jake Martyn stopped his shouting. A shrill whistle pierced the bush and the hubbub abated a little. The weight on my spine eased. I was being helped to my feet.

The soggie hauling me upright had a boxer's nose and Tartar cheekbones. He squinted into my face and spoke, his voice beamed from a distant planet.

'Yoke, eh?'

My hearing was MIA, still ringing with the din of the gunshots and my impact with the forest floor.

'R. U. O. K.?' he repeated.

I nodded stupidly. Okay enough, I guessed. Nothing a month in traction and a bionic ear wouldn't fix. A blood-curdling snarl pierced the fug. I spun around, searching for the source of the sound.

The dog was still on the job, fangs bared as it snapped at Red's groin. My boy was engaged in a desperate holding action. His stick was no more than a shredded stump. Tight-lipped, he was fighting a losing battle.

As I launched myself towards him a soggie appeared, cocking his leg. He sank a high-laced boot into the slathering beast's belly. With a startled yip, the dog rose high off the ground and flew ten metres though the air. Straight through the middle of two tall saplings. It hit the embankment, gave a terminal yap and was finally silent.

Red's head turned to follow the trajectory of the punted pooch. The goal-kicking copper grabbed him by the arm, steadying him, and said something. The kid's shell-shocked grimace dissolved into a tension-draining laugh. Then the anxiety flooded back and he looked around urgently.

I raised an arm. He spotted me and took the salute, his relief evident. Then he buckled at the knees. The cop supported his weight.

Between us, on the broken slope of creek bank, Jake Martyn was lying face-down in the forest debris. Two soggies with pump-action shotguns loomed over him while a third cuffed his hands behind his back.

Nearby, Rodney Syce was flat on his back, motionless. His neck was twisted at an unnatural angle, about 328 degrees at a guess. His arms were flung out from his torso. A swarm of soggies surrounded him, pump-actions converging at point-blank range. One of the troopers nudged the double-barrel shotgun from Syce's limp grasp. Another dropped to a crouch and pressed his fingers to the prostrate felon's neck.

Up the hillside, a line of dark shapes was advancing through the trees. Two police four-wheel-drives roared from the canopy of vegetation over the creek bed and pulled up behind Jake Martyn's Range Rover. The doors flew open and cops piled out, DS Meakes among them. Jodie Prentice was limping across the gravel towards Red, escorted by a uniformed officer in short sleeves and a bullet-proof vest.

'This way, sir,' said the squaddie at my side. He put a hand on my shoulder and steered me down the slope.

'You saved my life,' I said.

He shrugged. 'We get time and a half on public holidays.'

'Taxpayers' money well spent,' I said. For once.

Jake Martyn was whimpering, not so full of zest now. The soggies rolled him onto his back and one of them clamped a wad of bandage to his wounded thigh.

The cop with his fingertips on Syce's carotid shook his head and stood up.

For a clearing in a forest wilderness, the place was busier than the federal tally room on election night. Cops were pouring in from all points of the compass. Matt Prentice and his mates straggled out of the mulga, each with an attendant officer. Jodie and Red stood in the creek bed, watching me approach. She was hanging onto his arm, stroking it like it was a pedigree Siamese. When I got to the bottom of the bank, Red detached himself and ran to meet me.

We clung to each other for dear life, hearts pounding together.

'I was so scared,' he said.

Me too. I pressed his head to my chest and buried my face in the glutinous spikes of his hair.

'I'm sorry, Dad,' he said. 'I'm so sorry.'

'You are so fucking grounded,' I said. 'You'll spend the rest of the holidays locked in your bedroom.'

Over the top of his head, I could see Jodie Prentice laying into her big brother with balled fists, kicking him in the shins. He was copping it, making no attempt to defend himself.

Our manly embrace ran its course. Red started to speak. One question now, I knew, would quickly become a torrent of explanation and justification.

'Later,' I said, raising my hand. It was trembling. 'The main thing is, you're okay and I'm okay. Only the bad guys got hurt. Go stop Jodie killing her brother while I have a word with the police.'

'I'll kill him myself,' muttered Red. 'Bloody idiot.'

'Let's wait until there aren't so many cops around.'

I looked back up the slope towards Syce's body. Two cops

stood beside it. Damian Meakes in his light brown summer-weight suit, and a nuggety man with a bony forehead and close-cut iron-grey hair. A homicide cop called Kevin Hayes. One of the many jacks I'd met that morning at the Lorne cop shop.

A uniform blocked my path. I called Meakes' name. He turned and stared at me from behind the rimless ovals of his green-tinted sunglasses. After a long moment, he nodded.

The uniform stepped aside and I trudged up the incline. The wind had dropped away and the clouds were breaking up, but the air still had a damp feel to it. I rubbed the bare skin of my arms and shivered.

I'd wanted to see Syce lying dead on the ground, no denying it. I'd lived with the want aching in the marrow of my bones for almost two years. From the instant the gutless prick did what he did to Lyndal. I'd felt it burst into a raging fury when he pointed his shotgun at my son. But now the moment had arrived, I felt only an unexpected emptiness.

The two cops moved apart, wordless. I stared down at the corpse.

He was dead, all right. No doubt about it. His shirt was unbuttoned, the bullet wounds clearly visible. Two in the side, one where his neck joined his shoulder. Very little blood, a quick death. Flies were already buzzing at the dark-rimmed punctures. My gaze moved up to his face. There were flies there, too. They crawled across the rough remnants of his beard and swarmed at his lips. His skin was the colour of putty, the lividity already draining away.

For the first time I looked at the man properly. Close up. Broad daylight. When my gaze reached his lifeless green eyes, a shudder started deep in my body. My stomach clenched and my mouth filled with a bitter taste.

The fruit of knowledge.

I stared until the silence grew unbearable, then turned to Meakes. His face, too, was motionless. He looked back at me, hands clasped in the small of his back, eyes invisible behind the lenses of his sunglasses. He was waiting for me to speak. But speech, at that moment, was not within my power.

It was Hayes who broke the silence, his tone conversational. 'Your second message didn't get through until events were already in progress, Mr Whelan. Your presence here came as something of a surprise to the officers on the ground.'

'It's been a big day for surprises,' I said stiffly, looking at Meakes. 'Sorry for the inconvenience.'

I turned and walked back down the incline. Gutted. Meakes fell into step beside me.

I'd been overly harsh on DS Meakes. Maybe it was the fashion-plate suits. Or the Heinrich Himmler eyewear, or the cold-fish personality. But that was all water under the pier now. When it came to the crunch, the detective sergeant acquitted himself well. Did his legwork. Came out of his box like a greyhound. Crack of dawn, New Year's Day. I couldn't fault that.

Meakes waited until we reached the creek before speaking.

'I'm heading back to Melbourne,' he said. 'Homicide will be handling things here from now on.'

'Better luck next time, eh?'

I extended my hand. Meakes accepted it. We shook, a moment of silent communion.

'We'll get him,' he said. 'No matter how long it takes.'

'I know,' I nodded sombrely. 'I know.'

The action sequence was over. The wash-up was beginning. Uniformed cops were running crime-scene tape around the area, tying yellow ribbons round the old gum trees. Jake Martyn's bulk was being manoeuvred onto a stretcher. Intermittent squeaks and gasps indicated that his condition was painful but not critical.

Kevin Hayes took charge of me. He said the parents of the other teenagers had been informed that their children were safe. Everything else would be sorted out back in town.

A police four-wheel-drive ferried us along the creek bed to a dirt track and a row of cars. The kids were subdued but physically none the worse. If there was other damage, it was not yet evident.

Red and I had the back seat of a prowl car to ourselves for the trip down to Lorne. His tee-shirt was streaked with sweat and dirt.

He looked so young and vulnerable and brave that it almost broke my heart.

'What a maniac,' he said, stroking his jaw like a war veteran at a reunion. 'And how about you, charging through the trees, going ballistic?'

'I thought he was going to kill you,' I said.

While a uniformed constable steered us along dirt tracks to the asphalt hardtop, Red told me all about it.

Mongoose had sucked them in, he said. He kept leading them deeper and deeper into the bush, their destination always just a little further ahead. He told them the crop probably belonged to some hippie surfer who only visited it occasionally to water the plants. It'd just be walk in, walk back out with the smoke.

'We wanted to turn back, Dad,' he said. 'Me and Jodie. But Matt and the others…' he shrugged. 'And after a while, we knew we'd get lost if we didn't stick together.'

They reached the camp about eleven. Mongoose scouted ahead and reported. The dog was out and about, the surfer asleep in a tent. Mongoose's plan was to distract the dog while the others crept into the dope patch, grabbed a couple of plants each and scattered into the bush.

It went fine until, mid-harvest, the plantation owner appeared. Not a spaced-out seaweed sucker but a bearded redneck brandishing a shotgun and screaming questions.

He calmed down when they said they were just hikers, lost in the bush. Told them he'd let them go in a while if they did what he said. Then he herded them into the shed and blindfolded them.

'We were scared,' Red said. 'But he didn't hurt us, so we sort of believed him.'

In the rear-view mirror, I saw the cop at the wheel of the prowl car tilt his head, the better to hear.

'And we thought Mongoose was maybe out there somewhere, getting help or figuring out a way to spring us. That's why we didn't say anything about him first up.'

'You did the right thing,' I reassured him. 'Exactly the right thing.'

It was past four o'clock when we reached Deans Marsh Road and began our descent to the sea. Thirty hours since I'd risen from my bed. Red, too, looked buggered. We yawned simultaneously. When he started up the questions again, I fended him off with the minimum. There were things it was better he didn't know, too much that I didn't yet understand.

'Tell me something,' I said. 'When that cop booted the dog, what did he say to you?'

He grinned. 'He said not to dob him in to the RSPCA.'

My boy, I sensed, would get though his experience intact.

A small crowd was milling on the street outside the Lorne cop shop. The other kids had arrived a few minutes ahead of us and family reunions were taking place. Barbara Prentice was huddled with Jodie and Matt, her sunglasses pushed back on her head. Her expression was a mixture of relief and admonishment, both kids talking at once. Across the street, Faye and Leo Curnow leaned against their Volvo wagon. Tarquin sat in the front passenger seat, door open, elbows on his knees, thumbs working his Gameboy. His sister Chloe combed through a *Who Weekly*. Our driver continued past and deposited us at the back door.

Proceedings inside were brisk, almost perfunctory. With my permission, Red was taken away to give a brief preliminary statement. I was parked in Sergeant Pendergast's office with a cup of tea and a Tim Tam. An officer would be with me in due course.

I sat there and counted the number of ways a man can be a fool. A slat of sunlight inched its way across the wall map. My tea went cold. And then Hayes of Homicide was dropping a wallet on the desk in front of me.

'Yours,' he said. 'We found it among Surovic's stuff up there at his camp.'

'Surovic?' I said. 'That his name?'

Hayes looked down at me, hands sunk deep in his pockets. 'Michael Surovic,' he said. 'According to items found at the camp.'

I thumbed through my wallet. Credit cards and whatnot were still there. The Polaroid. I took it out and looked at it.

'For what it's worth,' Hayes said, 'in my opinion he does look a bit like Rodney Syce.'

Perhaps that was supposed to make me feel better. I waited for the shard of ice to melt, then put the photo away.

'And Jake Martyn?' I said. 'Enlighten me.'

Hayes rubbed his nose thoughtfully. 'A superficial wound, but painful. And there was an awful long wait for the ambulance.'

'Terrible delays, apparently,' I said. 'Since the privatisation.'

'We did our best to make him comfortable. He was very grateful. Opened his heart to us. Told us about his run of bad luck at the blackjack table.'

'High roller?' I said.

'Deep shit,' nodded Hayes. 'Spiralling debts and a business partner impatient to be paid out. Desperate frame of mind.'

'And an easy mark in Tony Melina,' I said. 'Did he

really think he'd get away with it?'

Hayes shrugged, a man who'd seen it all. 'He still might. What he told us back up there in the hills isn't admissible evidence. The actual killer is dead. And Tony Melina's body is somewhere on the bottom of Bass Strait. A lot will hang on your testimony, Mr Whelan.'

I lowered my head and groaned.

'All in good time,' said Hayes. 'Right now, I suggest you get some shut-eye. We'll talk again when you're rested up. Your son's waiting outside.'

So was Barbara Prentice.

As I stepped into the glare of the late afternoon, she came forward to meet me.

I must have looked like an insurance assessor's nightmare. But there was understanding in her eyes, and gratitude, and the promise of consolation. Before I knew it, her arms were reaching to enfold me.

She drew me close and held me tight, my head cradled in the hollow of her hand. The short blond hairs behind her ear gleamed in the afternoon sun.

A long time had passed since I'd felt the warmth of a woman's arms, the press of a woman's body. A small sigh escaped me. A dam burst.

I began to cry.

Not just a sob and a sniffle. Not just a quiet weep. Great shudders racked my body. Tears gushed from my eyes. I blubbered, whimpered and gasped.

Barbara rocked me, soothing me with strokes and sympathetic murmurs.

Women say they appreciate vulnerability in a man. Admire it, even. So they say. But nothing can convince me they find it sexy. Not the full waterworks. Not the pathetic bawling that dribbles gooey strings of snot onto the downy hairs at the back of their necks.

You've blown it, sport, I told myself. And I didn't mean my nose.

'You're a good man, Murray Whelan,' said Barbara.

That sealed it. I drew a shaky breath, extricated myself and firmed my upper lip.

'Better be going,' I snuffled.

It never would have worked anyway. A potential minefield. That son of hers, for a start. What a ratbag. And Velcro Girl, the daughter. And when it came to the clinch, as it just had, she was a bit too skinny for my taste.

'You okay, Dad?' said Red, stepping deftly into the gap.

They say that time is a great healer.

So is pursuing your personal demon to the heart of the labyrinth. Confronting him one on one, and seeing his fly-blown carcass in the dirt.

Okay, so it was Mick Surovic, not Rodney Syce. But as far as I was concerned, the rage was spent. The evil spirit was exorcised.

We went back to the holiday house and I slept like a felled tree, twelve hours straight, Red on a blow-up mattress on the floor beside me.

'Just in case you need anything in the night,' he said. Also because he had no choice in the matter. He and Tark had ripped a hole in the tent at the Falls, so they had to find sleeping space in the house. The ban on the Docs remained.

Early next morning, I went down to the beach.

There was a secluded spot not far from where I'd staggered ashore. I walked barefoot into the lapping foam and stood for a moment, watching the fall of the waves. Then I laid the photograph of my never-born little girl on the gently ebbing tide and watched it float away.

Lyndal, I felt sure, would have approved.

A few days later, back in Melbourne for a meeting with the coppers, I tossed the Syce file into the garbage. Didn't even open it. Lyndal was beyond caring about Rodney Syce and so was I. He lived a crappy life and he'd die a crappy death. I had better things to think about than the form it might take.

That was six months ago. There's been plenty to keep me busy since then.

The federal election has come and gone, with all its attendant demands on the party faithful. We lost, of course. Routed. The Labor Party is now in the wilderness at national, state and municipal level. And you know how I feel about wilderness.

Jake Martyn is languishing in the Remand Centre, awaiting trial for murder. Not conspiracy, not delegation of a messy unpleasant chore, not possession of illegal abalone. Certainly not oops.

As predicted, he reneged on his forest-floor fess-up. Went the clam. The Director of Public Prosecutions is concentrating on the paper trail, working to buttress my eyewitness testimony. Visibility from that aluminium dinghy wasn't too hot, after all, and the absence of a body in a homicide case is always problematic.

Gusto has gone into receivership. One of the creditors is Prentice & Associates, Architects. Another reason I haven't returned Barbara's calls.

Red still sees Jodie, but only in passing at school. For the moment at least, he has forsworn romantic entanglements. Girls are more trouble than they're worth, he tells me, although I suspect he's got his eye on one of the munchkins in the Year Eleven production of *The Wizard of Oz*.

The big loser among the living is poor Rita Melina. The Black Widow of Melbourne Upper, as Ayisha calls her.

What with the tax office and the fish dogs and the overseas bank accounts, Tony's estate still hasn't passed probate. The way things are looking, Rita will be lucky if she ends up with enough dough for a decent root perm. Worse still, she has to live with the fact that she ratted out a husband whose infidelity was limited to feeling up the hired help. And did it while he was chained naked to a tree, pleading to be allowed to call her.

The bodacious waitress, Tony's supposed elopee, had in fact upped tits without notice to accept a lucrative job offer as a hostess in a Tokyo nightclub.

Out of concern for Rita's finer feelings, the business with Tony's ear has not been divulged.

Likewise, I've never disclosed the promise I made to blow the Premier's bugle in public if the man in the shadows wasn't Rodney Syce. There was nobody there to witness my pledge, after all. And anyway, that particular service is more expertly and frequently provided by the organs of the mass media.

Nor have I yet found an appropriate use for the videotape that was waiting in a plain envelope on my desk at Parliament House when I returned from the summer break. It was unlabelled and the first few seconds of vision were so jumpy and jerky that I thought it must have been a misdirected submission to the film funding commission.

Then the focus sharpened, the camera steadied and I found myself watching crystal clear footage of Dudley Wilson chucking his chunks over Alan Bunting on the deck of a Natural Resources launch near Cape Patterson.

I think I'll wait until Dudley's Coastal Whatsit Panel submits its draft recommendations to the government. If he proposes further reductions in DNR staffing levels, I'll slip a copy to every parliamentary member of the National Party. It might not affect the final outcome but it should sow some acrimony in the ranks of the enemy.

Parliament is currently in recess for the winter and I'm spending my working hours at the electorate office. Detective Sergeant Meakes called me here a few days ago. It was the first time we'd spoken since New Year's Day.

'I thought you should know,' he said. 'A man's body was found yesterday morning.'

It was discovered in an old storm-water drain during excavation work on the new freeway tunnel under the Yarra at Richmond. It had been lodged there for a fair while and there wasn't much of it left. There was enough, however, to get some partial fingerprints.

It was Rodney Syce.

The way Meakes figured it, Syce ditched the Kawasaki in Richmond after the shoot-out, then went to ground down a manhole cover. Perhaps he was injured from his spill off the bike, perhaps he got lost in the maze, perhaps he had an accident in the subterranean darkness. Whatever the case, however he died, his body was swept into an ancient section of piping.

As to the other aspect of closure, I won't say too much. Suffice to mention that I've met someone who shows signs of playing a significant role in that regard.

We live in hope.

What else can we do?

SUCKED IN

The author gratefully acknowledges the support of the Ghirardelli Foundation, the Cape Liptrap Lodge for Demented Writers, the Patramani family of Episkopi, Crete and Señora Luisa Guzman of Cochabamba, Bolivia.

*To my sister, who saved my life in Puno,
and my wife, who helped.*

The author of this book, its setting and characters, are entirely fictitious. There is no such place as Melbourne. The Australian Labor Party exists only in the imagination of its members. The process by which it selects its candidates for public office is a source of ongoing bafflement.

Prelude

On a cool and overcast April afternoon, a retrenched Repco salesman from Benalla named Geoff Lyons and his fishing mate, Craig Kitson, drove the forty-three kilometres to Lake Nillahcootie in Geoff's Toyota 4 Runner. When they got to the boat ramp, they sat for a minute, staring out the windscreen.

'Jeeze,' said Craig. 'That was quick.'

Geoff said, 'Told ya.'

The lake, an eight by three kilometre reservoir on the Broken River where it flows out of the High Country, was almost completely empty.

At the end of January, VicWater had commenced stabilisation work on the weir wall, a concrete dam constructed in the 1950s. They were sinking new reinforcement plugs, a project which involved opening the sluices and draining the lake. Since Craig and Geoff last saw it, the water level had dropped ninety percent. For the first time in forty years, the course of the original river bed was visible, its meandering progress marked by an intermittent line of truncated, long-dead trees.

The two men walked out onto the lakebed, testing the surface. The gradient was slight and the hot summer and long dry autumn had dried the clay pan to a firm crust. Craig said, 'Think it'll take the Toyota?'

'We get bogged,' Geoff warned, 'you're the one walks to town.'

Closer to the trees, the clay was covered with cracks like the stained fissures in an old teacup and the sharp edges of blackened stumps broke the surface of the ground. When the Toyota's traction started to slip, they got out and walked the last hundred metres, carrying their waders. Craig took a plastic bucket, just in case they found anything worth keeping.

They had fished Lake Nillahcootie many times over the years, although they preferred Eildon or, better still, Lake Mulwala. But Nillahcootie was handy, only half an hour out of town and too small to interest the watersport crowd. There was a camping ground near the weir and holiday houses scattered along the shoreline but some weekends they'd virtually have the place to themselves.

Mostly it was redfin and brown trout on live bait from Geoff's tinnie, but they'd also taken some nice rainbows on spinners from the shore, particularly in the shaded shallows where the trees ran right down to the water. The Murray cod that preferred the deep holes of the old river bed had eluded them, however, and cost them some top-shelf trolling lures on hidden snags.

So they'd come up with the idea of doing a bit of reconnaissance while the water level was down. A better idea of the lay of the lakebed might improve their chances when it was again hidden beneath opaque, red-brown water.

The old riverbed was now a chain of shallow pools linked by a feeble trickle of muddy water, its surface swarming with midges. All the useable timber had been cleared before the dam was flooded, leaving only dead or diseased trees. Their denuded trunks now jutted out of the sludge, bleached and sepulchral, surrounded by fallen, half-buried logs. The men followed the river's meandering course upstream, checking their location against the undulating paddocks and clumps of trees that marked the shoreline.

Oddments of litter were scattered across the lake floor, mainly old bottles and cans. They fossicked as they went and within half an hour they'd picked up some metal lures in pretty good nick, an assortment of wire traces and a slime covered Tarax lemonade bottle. By then, they'd given up the idea of discovering the hiding places of the fabled cod. No way were they going to start sloshing around in the murky black water that now filled the riverbed.

'Careful.' Geoff pointed to a sinuous grey shape draped over a fallen tree-trunk. 'Snake.'

'You reckon?'

Whatever it was, it wasn't moving. Craig waded through the ankle-deep water and took a closer look. 'A deadly nylon python,' he called. One end was buried in the mud, the other disappeared into dark water between two logs. 'Could be an anchor rope.'

He straddled the logs and hauled. The rope offered little resistance. It came up in a loose tangle, slimy and thick with a black mass of rotted vegetation. Trapped within its coils was a ball of fibrous mud, an oversized coconut.

'Hey, check this out,' he called back to Geoff.

'What is it?'

'Looks like a skull.'

Geoff came closer, primed for one of Craig's lame jokes.

Craig reached down gingerly, hooked his fingers through the eye holes and held it aloft for Geoff to see. 'Human, I reckon.'

The bone was stained tan, the bottom jaw was missing and the nasal socket was eaten away at the edges, but the shape of the cranium was unmistakable.

Geoff shaded his eyes with his hand and took a long hard look.

'Well I'll be fucked.'

I stood at the edge of the grave and sprinkled a handful of soil onto the lid of the coffin, adding it to the mound of clay and carnations. It was a classy box, rosewood with silver handles, befitting its distinguished occupant.

Charles Joseph Talbot, MHR. A cabinet minister in three successive Labor administrations, twice as Minister for Industrial Relations and, until the previous week, member for Coolaroo and manager of opposition business in the House of Representatives of the Commonwealth of Australia. A pillar of the community. An elder of the tribe.

At sixty-four, Charlie Talbot was as dead as a man can get. It was hard to believe he was gone, even though it had happened right in front of me.

'You're in good hands, mate,' I murmured. 'The Lord's a Labor man.'

Charlie and the Lord went way back. Back to when he

was a lay preacher, whatever that means, in the Methodist church. It was down that obscure tributary that Charlie had floated into the union movement, and thence into the Australian Labor Party. A world in which the Lord's name is not often invoked, except in vain.

I couldn't say if Charlie's faith survived the journey. It was not a subject we had ever discussed, although we'd talked of many things, often at great length, in the decades of our friendship. But whether he was now enrolled in the choir eternal or merely, as I suspected, compost, I knew I'd never forget him.

Ceding my place to the next mourner in line, I wandered a little further into the cemetery. It was an autumn afternoon, late in the twentieth century, and there was still enough lustre in the stainless-steel sky to have me squinting against the glare. I pulled a pair of sunglasses from my breast pocket, lit a pensive cigarette and took in the scene.

After the interminable eulogising of the funeral service, the graveside formalities had been brief. The crowd was drifting away, gravitating down the gravel pathway to the cars at the graveyard gate. The widow was escorted by the federal party leader, a stout man, if only in the physical sense. She was still a good looking woman, Margot, no diminution of assets there.

Charlie's three daughters kept their distance, husbands and children clustered around them as they accepted condolences. Although she'd been married to Charlie for almost ten years, Margot was still the Other Woman as far as his children were concerned. The Jezebel who'd snared their grieving father while the flowers were still fresh on their mother's grave.

She slept elsewhere, the sainted Shirley. She was taking

her eternal rest beside her mother and father at Fawkner cemetery, fifteen minutes up the road.

But even in death Charlie had civic obligations. And so it was here in Coburg cemetery, ceremonial burial site of the electorate he had represented for almost twenty years, that his mortal remains were interred. Here, cheek-by-jowl with the district's other deceased dignitaries, a hundred and fifty years of extinct aldermen and mouldering worthies. I suspected Charlie would find them dull company. Not that he was any too lively himself anymore.

Still, he had a pretty good view.

Melbourne is a city of many inclinations but very few hills. Its northern suburbs are almost unremittingly flat but the cemetery occupied the slope of a low ridge, screened from six lanes of traffic by a row of feathery old cypresses, so even the slight rise of the bone yard offered a rare vantage point. To the west stood the grim shell of Pentridge prison, a crane jutting from its innards. The old bluestone college was currently being made over into luxury apartments and B Division, home of the hardened, would soon be equipped for designer living. A gated community of the newer kind, vendor finance available.

The last two mourners were lingering at the graveside. Men of Charlie's vintage, dark-suited, they were conducting a hushed but animated conversation across the pit. I contemplated the bleached inscriptions and grievous angels for as long as it took to finish my cigarette, then crushed the butt with the toe of my shoe. At the sound, the pair turned and looked my way.

One of them cocked his head sideways, a summons. He was a compact, beetle-browed man with wavy black hair above an alert, self-assured face. His companion, a stoop-shouldered scarecrow of a man with thinning gingery-grey hair and a matching beard, opened his mouth as if to object, then closed it again. He pushed his thick-framed spectacles back up the bridge of his nose and watched me approach.

'Senator,' I said, dipping my head to the darker one.

Senator Barry Quinlan. The grey eminence of the Left faction of the Victorian branch of the Australian Labor Party. Punter, bon vivant, all-round philanthropist and currently the Shadow Minister for Telecommunications.

'Murray,' he nodded back. 'Sad occasion.'

As befitted a champion of the underdog, Quinlan took great care with his appearance. His tailored three-button suit and immaculate white shirt were set off with a Windsor-knotted black tie and expensive cufflinks. The morose beanpole beside him, by contrast, was so nondescript that he might almost have been invisible. But that, I reflected, was Colin Bishop's greatest talent.

'G'day, Col,' I said. 'Or is it Professor Col these days?'

When I'd last seen Colin Bishop, he was running the Trade Union Training Authority. Now he was Pro Vice-Chancellor of Maribyrnong University, a federally funded provider of post-secondary education in the fields of tourism, food technology and hospitality studies.

'Show some decorum, you cheeky bugger,' said Quinlan. 'A bit of respect for your elders and betters.'

Unholstering a silver hipflask, he toasted the coffin, took a shot and offered it around. I obliged, for form's sake, and passed the flask to Bishop. Col hesitated, then took a long slug.

'Lard-arse Charlie,' he intoned, peering downwards. 'Wonder how they got him in that box?'

'Levered him in with fence pickets,' Quinlan suggested.

There was no malice in the banter. Life goes on. Big boys don't get soppy. We were just four blokes, chewing the rag. Charlie was the quiet one in the rosewood overcoat.

'And you were there when it happened?' said the senator, suddenly serious again.

I nodded. 'Sitting at the same table in the dining room of the Mildura Grand Hotel.'

It was a story I was already sick of telling. But these two were entitled. They'd known Charlie even longer than I had.

'We'd just finished our back-to-the-bush roadshow. *Labor Listens.*'

Half a dozen of us trooping around the back-blocks in shiny new Akubras, listening to the yokels bitch about the axing of government services that everybody knew we had neither the present ability nor the future intention to restore. It had been a proper pain in the bum. A thousand kilometres in four days, preaching to the converted in community recreation facilities and civic halls.

'Charlie was in Mildura for some regional and rural gabfest in his capacity as Shadow Minister for Infrastructure. We all ended up at Stefano's for dinner.'

'As you would,' said Quinlan. Stefano's was the town's landmark eatery, five toques in the *Age Good Food Guide*. 'Did you try the saltbush lamb?'

Colin Bishop looked up from the coffin and sucked his cheeks impatiently.

'Let's just say we made a night of it,' I said. 'First thing next morning, the rest of the team took the early plane back to Melbourne. Charlie and I were booked on the noon flight, so we had time for a leisurely breakfast.'

Poor Charlie, under doctor's instructions to watch his weight, had settled for the fresh fruit compote. If only he'd known it was his last meal, he'd probably have ordered the lamb's fry and bacon.

'We were taking our time over coffee and newspapers when he started to make groaning noises. Not particularly loud so I didn't pay much attention. Just assumed he was muttering to himself as he read. Then, suddenly, the paper cascaded to the floor and he was clawing at his collar. He'd gone all pale and clammy and his eyes were bulging out of his head. Heart attack. Cardiogenic shock.'

Despite the repeated tellings, I still didn't quite believe it.

'What paper?' said Bishop, pushing his glasses up his nose, avid for detail.

'The *Herald Sun*.'

'Can have that effect,' nodded Quinlan. 'Although it's rarely fatal.'

Bishop eyed me keenly. 'Went quick, did he?'

'Here one minute, bang, gone the next. One of the hotel staff gave him CPR and the paramedics got there pretty fast but he was cactus by the time we reached the hospital.'

On the far side of the cemetery, a back-hoe started up. We were the only ones left now, three men in dark suits, perched on the lip of a grave. A trio of crows. Not a trio. What the hell was the collective noun for crows? A parliament? No, that was owls.

'Heart attack,' said Quinlan as we started towards the gate, hands in pockets. 'It's a caution. None of us are getting any younger.'

Bishop and Quinlan were well into their sixties, older than me by a generation. Quinlan seemed fit enough, buoyed by inexhaustible reserves of self-regard, but Bishop looked well past his use-by date, his skin loose and mottled.

'Let's hope he didn't suffer too much,' said Quinlan. 'I

hear you were with him in the ambulance.'

I nodded. It was a short trip, just long enough to make me feel completely fucking useless.

'Unconscious, was he?' said Bishop.

'In and out.'

'No famous last words?'

'More a case of unintelligible last mumbles,' I said.

'Like what?'

'Jesus, Col, you want me to do a fucking impression?'

'Just asking. No need to get shitty.'

We clomped down the slope a bit further. There was a hint of humidity in the air and my skin prickled under my shirt.

'You mean to keep in touch, but somehow you never find the time.' Col was trying to make amends. 'Then you wake up one day and it's too late. Must be donkey's years since I last saw Charlie.'

Quinlan nudged the subject sideways. 'Our young protégé Murray has done well for himself, hasn't he, Col?'

'Mail room to the state legislature,' agreed Bishop, falling back into step. 'Who'd've thunk it?'

'Always a bright one, our Murray,' said Quinlan. 'I saw his potential right from the start, flagged him to Charlie.'

That was news to me. Very late news indeed, two decades old. Colin and I had been working for Charlie well before Barry Quinlan came on the radar. But claiming credit was one of Quinlan's trademarks. He'd even been heard to maintain that he cut the deal that first got Charlie into federal parliament, all those years ago. If so, he hadn't got much out of it. Charlie was ever his own man.

'The transition will be smooth, I trust,' said Quinlan. 'No hugger-mugger from the locals?'

'How about we let Charlie get cold first?'

'Ah, Murray,' sighed the senator. 'Always the sentimentalist, God love you.'

Simultaneously we checked our watches, busy men, and stepped up the pace. The quick deserting the dead.

We made our brief goodbyes at the gate. As I headed for my car, I glanced back. Quinlan and Bishop had resumed their private conversation, leaning close and speaking intensely. Quinlan's finger was stabbing the air and Bishop kept screwing his neck back towards Charlie's grave. Maybe it was yawning a little too loud for comfort.

My electorate office was less than ten minutes away, a refurbished shopfront between Ali Baba's Hot Nuts and Vacuum Cleaner City in an arcade off Sydney Road. The mid-afternoon traffic was light, so I took the direct route along Bell Street through the heart of my electorate. Melbourne Upper, my seat in state parliament for the previous five years.

Those years had not been kind to the Australian Labor Party. The voters hadn't just shown us the door, they'd bolted it shut behind us. We barely held enough seats to play a hand of Scrabble, let alone influence the running of the state.

Fortunately for me, Melbourne Upper was one of the safest Labor seats in the state. Rusted-on blue-collar meets multicultural melting-pot, a stronghold in our besieged heartland. With 54 percent of the primary vote and an eight-year term in the Legislative Council, I was, at least, secure in my employment. Many a colleague had gone down, better men than me among them. Better women, too.

Now Charlie had also vanished from the political landscape. Not turfed by the electors of Coolaroo but felled by a fit of fatal dyspepsia while leafing through a Murdoch rag. Suddenly his seat was up for grabs.

Not that I had a dog in the fight. Charlie was federal, I was state. But the borders of our electorates overlapped and there were party branches and personalities in common. As a responsible member of the parliamentary team, I'd be expected to see they toed the line during the anointment of Charlie's successor. I knew this. I didn't need to be reminded of the fact by Barry Quinlan, the presumptuous prick.

As long as most people could remember, Quinlan had swung a very big dick in the Left faction of Labor's Victorian machine. Over a twenty-year period, he'd risen from union official to federal senator to a member of the federal cabinet. And even though our electoral battering had eroded his influence, he was still a major player. It was axiomatic that Barry Quinlan would have a finger in the Coolaroo succession pie. Which finger and exactly how deep remained to be seen. Nor would his be the only digit in this particular opening.

By long-established custom, the ALP is loath to pass up any opportunity to erupt into a full-fledged public brawl, particularly with a safe seat at stake. As the long years of opposition grew ever longer, however, the faction bosses had called a truce in the internal bloodletting. Rather than carrying on like a sackful of rabid badgers, we now tried to pretend we were one big happy family.

But old habits die hard. Top-level jostling continued behind closed doors and some of the rank-and-file persisted with their delusions of democracy. Hence Quinlan's graveside remarks.

A block after Bell Street crossed Sydney Road, I turned left and drove into the carpark behind the shopping strip. At three-thirty on a Wednesday afternoon, the place was chockers. Italian senior citizens loading groceries into modest sedans. Somali women, swathed in turquoise and aquamarine, waddling down the ramp from Safeway. Schoolkids on skateboards slaloming through the parked cars. I nabbed a spot vacated by a fat new Landcruiser and parked my taxpayer-funded Mitsubishi Magna next to the overflowing skips behind Vinnie Amato's Fruit and Veg Emporium.

I locked the car and entered the arcade. Exchanging familiar nods with the track-suited layabouts at their table outside the nut shop, I bought two takeaway coffees at Vida's Lunch'n'Munch, then pushed open a plate-glass door with my name on it.

Murray Whelan—Member of the Legislative Council—Province of Melbourne Upper.

My reception area contained six metal-frame chairs upholstered in fish-belly vinyl, a side-table strewn with information brochures, three framed prints from the Victorian Tourism Commission, an artificial fern, *Philodendron bogus*, and one modular reception desk, off-white.

A teenage girl in track pants, a Mooks sweatshirt and a hijab was leaning on the desk, a slumbering child in a cheap fold-up stroller parked beside her.

'Anyway,' she was saying. 'I reckon it sucks.'

Sitting behind the desk was my electorate officer, Ayisha Celik. 'Sucks big-time,' she said. 'But Supporting Mothers Benefits are a commonwealth matter. We're state. You've come to the wrong place, I'm afraid.' She clicked her tongue and gave an empathetic shrug.

Empathy was one of Ayisha's strong suits, along with a good memory for names, extensive networks, an inside knowledge of the bureaucracy and a well-tuned political antenna. The package made her indispensable to the smooth functioning of my retail operations. Parliamentary matters, the upstream side of the business, she left to me.

The girl in the hijab heaved a resigned sigh and angled the stroller towards the exit, another dissatisfied customer. I held the door open and gave her my most benign smile. She looked at me with a mixture of contempt and pity. The baby started to wail. A normal reaction all round. It came with the territory.

Ayisha reached across the desk and relieved me of one of the coffees. Done up in her funeral weeds, a navy pants suit and cream blouse, her jet black hair piled up in a mushroom, she could've passed for an SBS newsreader. Back when I first met her, the resident radical spunk at the Turkish Welfare League, she favoured skintight jeans and a *keffiyeh*. But that was before a career in public administration had dampened her activist zeal and two children had gone to her hips.

'So Charlie Talbot is laid to rest.' Ayisha raised her polystyrene cup.

I returned the salute. 'And now the games begin. I've just had Barry Quinlan pissing on my lamp-post.'

She cocked her head at the glass wall that separated the reception area from the inner office. Through the angled slats of half-closed slimline venetians, I could see a dark-suited figure sitting at the conference table.

'Speaking of which, Mike would like a word.'

I locked the front door, hung up the CLOSED sign and

followed Ayisha into the windowless heart of my political fiefdom. A laminex-topped conference table occupied most of the room. The rest was taken up by an Uluru-sized photocopier-printer, a row of filing cabinets, a steel stationery cupboard and three colour-coded recycling bins. Office Beautiful.

Our visitor was a slim, good-looking man in his late thirties with close-shaved olive skin and the liquid eyes of an Orthodox icon. He, too, had come straight from the cemetery. Come, I assumed, to ventilate the pressing topic of the moment, Charlie Talbot's succession.

'*Yasou*,' I said.

Michelis Kyriakis had trodden the well-beaten path from immigrant childhood to university to local politics. He'd worked for Charlie Talbot for a while, keeping the home fires burning while Charlie was busy running the country. Now he was mayor of Broadmeadows, the *primus inter pares* of the coterie of Laborites who controlled the sprawling municipality at the centre of the seat of Coolaroo. Capable, energetic and well-motivated, he was going to waste in the small world of roads, rates and rubbish. This fact had not escaped his attention.

'Sorry if it looks pushy, mate, turning up like this straight after the funeral,' he said. 'But things are moving pretty fast.'

I sat down, facing him across the table. 'I've been a bit tied up, Mike, dealing with the undertakers and so forth, but I've heard murmurings about the FEA being convened ASAP.'

A conclave of local branch members and delegates appointed by the central machine, the Federal Electorate Assembly would select Charlie's successor.

'Saturday week,' said Mike. 'Ten days away. That must be a record.'

Ayisha perched herself on the desktop, legs dangling. 'The FEA's just a formality, you know that,' she said. 'There's a cross-factional agreement that the next federal vacancy in Victoria goes to the Left.'

'Yeah, but who in the Left?' said Mike. 'Charlie promised me that I'd get the seat when he retired. But now that he's gone, I've been sidelined. I'm out of the loop and it's obvious somebody else has been given the nod.'

I shrugged and showed him my empty palms. 'Your guess is as good as mine, Mike. Better, in fact. You are a member of the Left, after all.' I turned to Ayisha and raised an eyebrow. 'You heard anything?'

'Not a whisper,' she said. 'None of the usual suspects at state level have been mentioned, not that I've heard.'

'Maybe they're airlifting somebody in from Canberra,' I shrugged.

Mike made an acid face. 'Fucking typical,' he said. 'You put in the time, pay your dues, bust your gut, then some prick nobody knows gets handed a seat on a platter. Waltzes in, brushes you aside and you're expected to grin and bear it.'

'Welcome to the Labor Party,' I said. Or any party, for that matter. Mike knew the rules. You pays your money and you takes your chances.

'What would you say if I told you I'm thinking about throwing my hat into the ring?' he said.

I glanced sideways at Ayisha. She widened her eyes in mock horror. Mike had a lot of friends, us included, but he lacked clout in the places that counted.

'I'd say you'll be pushing shit uphill,' I said. 'It's obviously a done deal.'

'Even so,' he said. 'It's a matter of principle.'

Principle. The weeping scab of the Australian Labor Party.

'Climb aboard your saw-horse if you like, Mike. Point it at the windmill. Wave your lance around. But tell me, end of the day, what'll you get for your trouble?'

Mike straightened up and fixed me with the earnest expression he used for citizenship ceremonies. 'I feel very strongly about this, Murray. And I'd like your support. You've got a lot of sway in this part of the electorate.'

I ought to, I thought. I was paying the annual dues of half the branch members.

'You'd be an ornament to federal parliament, Mike,' I said. 'And I'm not the only one who thinks so. But you know the current party line. Heads down, bums up, noses to the grindstone. Strictly no muttering in the ranks. I'd need some pretty compelling reasons to buck company policy. Apart from my profound admiration for your personal qualities, of course.'

'Fuck you, too, comrade,' said Mike, letting out a little air. 'It's not like a bit of grass-roots democracy is going to damage our electoral prospects, since we currently have none. And by the time the next federal election rolls around, the punters will have forgotten all about it anyway.'

'Probably,' I agreed. 'But you've got to appreciate my situation.'

Mike nodded. 'I know I've got nothing to offer in return,' he said. 'I'm just trying to be straight with you, that's all. Your help would mean a lot to me.'

I leaned back in my chair, crossed my arms, pursed my lips and impersonated a man wrestling with his conscience.

'Tell you what,' I said at last. 'Why don't we sleep on it? Nominations don't close until next week. By then, we'll know the identity of the mystery candidate and meanwhile you can do your arithmetic, see how the numbers stack up. We'll talk again after the weekend.'

Mike knew it was the best he could expect for the moment. He stood and extended his hand. 'Fair enough.' We shook on our mutual good sense. 'See you at the wake, then. Broady town hall, right? Sundy arvo.'

Mike had taken upon himself to organise an informal send-off for Charlie, one for the constituents rather than the apparatchiks. Broadmeadows Town Hall was Mike's home turf. A good choice of venue for a man with his eye on the empty saddle.

Ayisha showed him to the door and came back grinning. 'Did that sound to you like a wheel squeaking?'

Mike Kyriakis hadn't come down in the last shower. He was well aware that he didn't stand a snowball's chance of elbowing his way into serious contention. But he also knew that by threatening to upset the apple cart with a grass-roots lunge, he might be offered an inducement to drop out. The promise of a seat, possibly, or even a paying job. At the very minimum, he'd be noticed—the essential requirement of political survival. Either way, it would cost him nothing to take a shot.

'He can squeak all he likes,' I said. 'But I don't think it'll get him any grease.'

Ayisha fished a blank sheet of paper from the photocopier feeder tray and put it on the table between us.

'Coolaroo,' she said, drawing an elongated circle with a black marker pen. 'An aboriginal word meaning "the Balkans".' She drew a second circle, overlapping the bottom edge of the first. 'Melbourne Upper.'

She hatched the circles with a series of crosses. 'Coolaroo's got about a thousand party members spread across ten branches. Four of the branches are down here, inside

Melbourne Upper. Those four only account for about a quarter of the total membership.' She jabbed her pen into the top circle. 'Anybody considering a run will need major support here.'

'In other words, somebody acceptable to the Turks, the Lebanese and the Greeks,' I said.

'An Anglo,' confirmed Ayisha. 'Somebody neutral who can balance out the competing sensitivities of those wonderfully inclusive communities.'

'I guess we'll know soon enough,' I said, glancing at my watch. 'Won't your kids be wondering if their mother's still alive?'

'Shit!' Ayisha grimaced and dashed for the door. 'Mail's on your desk. Usual bumph, nothing urgent. Bye.'

I ambled into my private office, a glass-walled cubicle distinguished only by a view across the K-Mart carpark towards the Green Fingers garden centre. I yawned, sprinkled some slow-release fertiliser granules on my African violet, plonked myself in my ergonomic executive chair and waded into my overflowing in-tray.

Even in opposition, the flag must be flown, the good fight fought, the flesh pressed, the creed recited, the candle kept burning. Over the next couple of weeks, according to the priorities flagged by Ayisha's multi-coloured post-its, my presence was required at the Housing Justice Roundtable, the Save the Medical Service Action Committee, a performance by the Glenroy Women's Choir, the Greening Melbourne Forum, Eritrean Peace Day, the Sydney Road Chamber of Commerce, the Free East Timor Association and a citizenship ceremony at Coburg Town Hall.

I checked the dates against my parliamentary schedule, then moved on to constituent matters, correspondence for signature and an urgent memo on Y2K compliance.

Apparently some inbuilt computer glitch was going to cause planes to plummet from the sky and hospital operating theatres to black out at the stroke of midnight on 31 December 1999. This global catastrophe was still more than two years away but meanwhile an incessant stream of paperwork had to be completed, with the usual object of ensuring that nobody could be blamed.

I stared down at the pages of techno-babble, thoughts wandering. I was going to miss Charlie Talbot. He'd been one of the good guys. Spent his life getting us into power, keeping us there when we won it and reminding us why we made the effort.

'If we don't do it,' he'd say, 'some other bastards will, and they'll be even worse bastards than us.'

Bastardry, in Charlie's language, was a political attribute, not a personal one. He bore no personal animosity towards his opponents. Not even back in the snake pit of the Trades Hall, back when he was state secretary of the Federated Union of Municipal Employees.

Then, as now, Labor was out of power, state and federal. Whitlam had crashed in a blaze of futile glory and we were back in the wilderness. Blind Freddie could see that we'd be there forever if we didn't get our house in order. Pronto. It was the Reformers versus the Shellbacks. The arena was the union movement and the battle was long and bitter.

Charlie's tolerance must have been sorely tested on quite a few occasions during those decisive tussles. But it was all ancient history now, water over the dam, a mere footnote. The millennium was approaching, bringing new and urgent challenges. I focused on the computer compliance paperwork.

Come the apocalypse, nobody could say it was my fault.

One by one, the afternoon-shift shelf-stackers trickled through the employees' door of the Bi-Lo food barn. When Red appeared, I gave him a bip and a wave. He sauntered over to the car, school backpack slung across his shoulder, shirt-tail hanging out his pants.

'Good funeral?' Red knew Charlie. Sporadically over the years, Charlie had taken a vaguely avuncular interest to which Red had responded in a vaguely nepotal manner. Gifts had never been exchanged.

'His best yet.' I started to open my door. 'Want to drive?'

Red looked around and scanned the scene. 'Now?'

On quiet Sunday afternoons, Northcote Plaza carpark was a perfect spot for introductory lessons in three-point turns and parallel parking. But this was a midweek evening at the intersection of homebound rush-hour and pre-dinner shopping flurry, dusk blurring the visibility, road courtesy somewhere between endangered and extinct. Out on High

Street, the trams were crawling, every stop a stop, the backed-up traffic seething with latent rage.

Red got into the passenger seat. 'Not worth it,' he said.

'I thought you wanted some practice.'

He rolled his eyes and snorted. 'Proper practice. Not ten minutes shitting myself in peak-hour traffic.'

We were built to the same genetic design but Red was half a head taller and two shoe sizes up. And when he was exasperated he was every inch his mother, Wendy.

'You sure?' I said. 'It all adds up.'

'Shut up and drive,' he said. 'I'm starving.'

He'd had his learner's permit for three months and he knew the basics, but it'd take more than an occasional inner-city shuffle to clock up the hundred hours recommended by the Transport Accident Commission. He'd need a few decent runs up the freeway, some night driving, a bit of wet-weather work, the odd long haul. It wasn't going to happen tonight.

'Suit yourself,' I said. 'Can't say I didn't offer.'

I moved into the traffic flow and turned at the corner where the Carters' Arms Hotel had once stood. The spot was now occupied by Papa Giovanni's Pizza and a branch of the Bank of Cyprus. In the olden days, back when I was younger than Red, my father was the licensee at the Carters'. We lived upstairs, hotel-keeping then being a family business. A peripatetic one, in our case, my father being my father.

A crawl-line of tail-lights stretched ahead. I dodged down the first side street, opting for the longer but less congested route. The dusk had taken a Turnerish turn, the clouds tinged with pink, the fresh-lit lamps of the outspread suburbs glinting in the gloaming, flecks of mica in a slurry of wet sand. In the far distance, the Dandenongs were a low bulge blurring into the horizon. There was a damp chill in the air, harbinger of the encroaching winter.

'Payday, eh?' I said, slowing for a speed bump.

'Uh-huh,' he nodded. '$81.60, after tax.'

I extracted four twenties from my shirt pocket. The supermarket job was Red's idea, a token of his commitment to self-reliance and financial independence. But his wages, notionally earmarked to buy a car, tended to get frittered on six-packs, taxi fares and mobile phone top-ups. Still, the gesture was laudable, parentally speaking, so I matched his earnings dollar for dollar.

'Don't drink it all at once,' I said.

We hit Heidelberg Road, crossed the Merri Creek bridge and turned down a short cul-de-sac abutting the parkland leading down to the Yarra.

The neighbourhood dated from the beginning of the century, built to cater for the Edwardian petit bourgeoisie. From its neat brick maisonettes and double-storey terraces, shopkeepers and artisans who had risen above the proletarian morass of nearby Collingwood could turn their aspirations towards the big houses across the river, the boom-era mansions of Kew.

Our place was a single-storey duplex, half of a matched pair. Its interior had been considerably remodelled over the years but the original façade remained intact, complete with a fretwork arch above the front door and leadlight magpies in the windows.

It was smaller than the house in Thornbury I'd bought with Lyndal not long after my election to parliament. But with Lyndal gone, the Thornbury place felt like an empty shell, an echoing reminder of her and the child she was carrying when she was killed.

Over time, my rage had burned itself out. I'd learned to live with my grief, to mourn and to move on.

Or at least to move house. So what if Clifton Hill was outside the boundaries of Melbourne Upper where, convention dictated, I ought to reside among my constituents? Such scrupulousness was more honoured in the breach these days, and Clifton Hill was only a spit and a piddle from the electorate anyway. More to the point, it was very convenient for Red, what with the network of bike paths just beyond the back gate, the railway station and the bus to school a few minutes' walk away.

Not that he'd need bike paths and public transport for much longer. Or me, for that matter. Come the end of this final year of school, the bird would fly the coop, hurtling towards the new millennium in the car I'd helped him buy, leaving me in an empty nest.

But that was months away. I parked at the kerb and Red hauled his books and laptop inside and retreated to his room on the pretext of homework. Doubtless this would entail much tele-conferencing and net-surfing.

I exchanged my suit for jeans and a sloppy joe, poured myself a short snort, stepped through the sliding glass doors onto the back deck and fired up the gas barbecue. In the dying light, the sky was the colour of ancient rust and I stood for a moment, drinking it in.

'At the going down of the sun,' I said to myself, 'we will remember them.'

I went back into the all-purpose eating-living area and pointed the remote-control at the television for the ABC news headlines. The Prime Minister was refusing to say sorry for something. Bill Clinton's penis was facing impeachment. Peace talks, astonishingly, had collapsed in the Middle East.

I gave some rocket a spin, ran the sniff test on a block of feta, sliced a cucumber and nuked a couple of kipflers. By then, the hotplate was ready. I seared two slabs of rump and hit the mute.

'Grub's up.'

Red materialised at the refrigerator door and scouted the interior, his broad shoulders filling the open gap. Physically, he was nearly a man, the stuff of gladiator sports and conscript armies, bulletproof and bound for glory. But as he crouched there, contemplating the cling-wrapped leftovers, tousle-haired in an oversize sweatshirt and bare feet, he was once again a little boy.

'Beer or wine?' he said.

It was five years since he'd opted to join me in Melbourne rather than remain with his mother and stepfather in Sydney, and it felt like five minutes.

Five years, three houses, two schools, one major freak-out and a fair smattering of the ups-and-downs that come with having a politician for a father. A loser politician, at that.

'Don't forget to call your mother,' I said, watching him set the table. 'It's her birthday tomorrow, you know.'

'It was yesterday,' he said. 'I already rang.'

I dished up and we ate in companionable silence. Two honest toilers, home from their workbenches, tucking into a manly repast of meat and potatoes accompanied by a tossed mesclun salad lightly drizzled with extra-virgin olive oil and served with crusty ciabatta and fresh-broached Stella Artois.

The television was burbling in the background, volume low. Half-way through the news, the reporter caught my attention. A big-eyed, round-faced blonde named Kelly Cusack. It wasn't often that she made the prime-time bulletin. Her usual gig was anchoring 'On the Floor', a weekly round-the-nation digest of state political affairs that went to air after the religion show on Sunday nights. Question Time kerfuffles in Hobart, redistribution brouhaha for the Nationals in Queensland, men in suits go yakkity-yak.

It was a program strictly for the hard-core politics junkies. But for Kelly Cusack it was a foot in the door of current affairs, a step up from her previous gig as host of a gee-whiz techno-buff show.

'Hello?' Red was leaning sideways to block my view of the set.

'Say again?'

He tapped the side of his head. Wake up. 'Driving lesson? Saturday?'

'Haven't you got a rehearsal? Bunking off won't get you into NIDA, you know.'

'It's just a run-through,' he said. 'We'll be finished by one o'clock.'

Red's ambition was pointed in the direction of drama school. Theatre Studies was his top subject and a lot of his off-hours went into a youth theatre based in an old knitwear sweatshop in South Melbourne. It was a semi-professional operation with a resident grant-funded dramaturg; more than one alumnus had gone on to feature in a distinctively quirky Australian film.

His mother, of course, took a dim view. Her idea of a proper career was law, medicine or one of the other money-harvesting professions. But the kid was hot to tread the boards. He'd already scored a walk-on in 'Heartbreak High' and two lines in 'Blue Heelers', and in my wild erratic fancy visions came to me of him holding aloft a gold statuette and thanking the father who'd backed him all the way. If only to give his mother the shits. Currently, he was codpiece-deep in an upcoming production of *Rosencrantz and Guildenstern Are Dead.*

'Dunno why you're pissing around with this poncey thespian stuff,' I said. 'What's wrong with plumbing? Steady work and the money's good. You could start by learning how to operate the dishwasher, not just fill it up with concrete-encrusted cereal bowls.'

'Don't change the subject. If you haven't got a fete to open or a ship to launch, we could put in a couple of hours.'

If memory served, my schedule was clear.

'Let's call it a strong maybe,' I said. 'Die young, stay pretty. Worked for James Dean.'

Well pleased, Red microwaved a brace of individual self-saucing butterscotch puddings which we ate on the sofa watching 'The Simpsons'. When he drifted back to his homework, I pulled a cork and retired to my hermitage.

Ah, gentrification. What started life as a laundry at the rear of the building was now a snug little hideaway, just big enough to accommodate my Spooner cartoons, archive boxes, books and music, and an authentic op-shop Jason Recliner. Its side door opened onto a small patio—a bed of white pebbles beside the ivy-clad wall of the next-door neighbour's garage.

I kicked off my shoes, cued an audio cassette and declined on the davenport. There was a hiss, then a male voice spoke.

'Μαθημα Δεκα,' it said.

'Μαθημα Δεκα,' I responded.

Melbourne swarms with Grecians. And having spent half my life up to my taramasalata in the progeny of Hellas, I'd decided it was high time I learned how to order my souvlaki in the demotic. So, earlier in the year, I'd enrolled in a beginners' course in Greek.

'Στο σταθμο του τραινου.'

So far, by diligent application, I'd managed to acquire the conversational skills of a speech-impaired three-year-old. On the up side, most of my classmates were female. And a man in my situation takes his opportunities wherever he can find them.

One classmate in particular had caught my eye. Her name was Andrea Lane, but she was Lanie to her friends and that was the tag by which she'd introduced herself to the class. Our teacher mistook it for Eleni. It was an apt elision. Helen, she who eloped with the Trojan Paris.

Lanie's may not have been the face that launched a thousand ships, but it definitely floated my little rubber duckie. She was cheerful, sardonic and fetchingly full-figured. Naturally, she was already taken.

Hubby had picked her up after one of the first classes, their pubescent daughter in tow. He was a dopey-looking dork, reeking of academia. With any luck, he'd be struck by some fatal skin disease, turn into a mass of weeping pustules and retire to a leper colony. I would comfort his lonely wife and one thing would lead to another. Until that happened, I could only put my hopes for conjugation on hold, try not to ogle her too obviously during class and buff my conversational skills.

'Εχεις πολυ ωραια ποδια,' I recited. '*Ti ora fevgi to treno?*'

After thirty minutes and four glasses of Penfolds Bin 28, my concentration was flagging. I stopped the tape, took my wine out to the wrought-iron table in the pebbly courtyard and fired up an ultra light. SMOKING KILLS, it said on the pack.

So does an out-of-the-blue coronary occlusion in the

dining room of the Mildura Grand Hotel. Funny thing, I thought, Charlie dying in front of me in a restaurant. We first met in a restaurant. Toto's, a pizza joint near the Trades Hall.

In 1978 I was a political science graduate, still in my twenties. I'd been working on a health and safety campaign for the Combined Metalworkers, a futile attempt to convince welders at the naval dockyards to stop getting shitfaced at lunchtime and falling off their gantries. My tenure had just fizzled out and I was pondering my employment prospects.

Charlie was sitting at a table up the back, having lunch with Colin Bishop. Purged from the public service in the aftermath of the Whitlam dismissal, Col was carving a niche for himself as education guru to the unions. From time to time, he'd employed me as a casual teacher at the Trade Union Training Authority. He waved me over and introduced me to Charlie.

I knew him by reputation, of course. He was state secretary of the Federated Union of Municipal Employees, elected on a reform ticket. A former bible basher, he had a reputation among the more hard-nosed blue-collar types as a bit of a boy scout. Somewhere in his forties, he was a stocky, sandy bloke. Teddy-bearish, you might say. Soft spoken, no side, real smart. I liked him straight up.

We made some chit-chat, ate some spaghetti, drank some coffee and I walked away with a job. Assistant Publications and Training Officer. Six days a fortnight, beginning immediately.

My job was producing the monthly newspaper that went out to the Municipals' fifty thousand-odd members. Boilerplate stuff—a paste-up of reports from the state branches, advertisements for the credit union, updates on award negotiations. Between issues, I slaved over a hot photocopier, organising the schedules and study materials for Colin Bishop's weekend seminars for shop stewards. Spiral-bound folders with diagrams of the Conciliation and Arbitration Commission, that sort of thing.

I worked out of the state office, a modern, low-rise building in Queensberry Street, not far from the crumbling mausoleum of the Trades Hall. Our queen bee was Mavis Peel, a woman of indeterminate age and towering coiffure who directed the daily ebb-and-flow from behind a golf-ball Selectric, a PBX and a Rothmans.

Mavis had been with the union since the days of the dunny men and she brooked no cheek from anyone. In her twin-set and diamante frames, she looked like a character from an Ealing comedy, fielding calls from shire clerks with brisk efficiency and guarding our two typists, Margot and Prue, with the ferocity of a mother lioness. Never mind that they were grown women, both already into their thirties, and well able to look after themselves. To Mavis, they were her 'girls', targets of opportunity in the blokey world of the unions.

Years later I wondered if Mavis had registered what was going on between Charlie and Margot. If so, she certainly kept it very close to her twin-torpedo chest. I definitely didn't twig, nor did anyone else at the time, far as I was aware.

Not that I was paying much attention. My relationship with Wendy was moving inexorably towards cohabitation, home-ownership and parenthood and it simply didn't occur to me that hidden fires might be burning behind Charlie Talbot's well-ironed shirtfront. He was just too straight for that sort of thing. Too married. And Margot, lovely Margot, she had more than enough to keep her hands full elsewhere.

And then there was the quite unlovely Mervyn Cutlett. Merv had ruled the union since the mid-fifties. He was a wily old throwback, half class warrior, half lurk merchant. A product of the Depression and the War, he regarded the Municipals as his personal property, maintaining his tenure by sheer bloody-mindedness intractability and a sharp eye for potential challengers.

When he wasn't interstate, shoring up the loyalty of the various state secretaries, he was ensconced in his nicotine-drenched, pine-panelled, shagpiled lair in the basement of the Trades Hall, holding court with his well-stocked bar fridge, his kitsch collection of wartime memorabilia and his attendant gopher, an ageing rocker named Sid Gilpin.

Merv and Charlie were the union's yin and yang, its past and future. As one of Charlie's appointments, yet another university-educated smartarse, I was bound to be viewed by Merv as an object of suspicion.

'Just make sure his picture appears on every page of the union news,' Charlie counselled. 'And try to keep out of his line of sight.'

I took his advice. And later, after he made the switch to parliament and I'd become a minister's minder, I kept taking it. No matter how busy, Charlie was always good for a word of wisdom when I needed one. That was something else I was going to miss about him.

I finished my cigarette, took the bottle back inside and restarted the tape.

'Ας ξαναρχίσουμε πάλι.'

Lesson Eleven. Future Conditional.

The Premier stood on the topmost step of the broad terrace leading to Parliament House. His chest was thrust forward, his chin tilted upwards, his hands on his hips. The tuft of his trademark cowlick stood erect, the comb of a strutting cockerel. A great strutter, the Right Honourable Kenneth Geoffries. He could strut standing still. All this is mine, his stance announced. The legislature behind me, the city at my feet.

'This cutting-edge development will guarantee Melbourne a place in the front row of the world's leading cities for generations to come,' he declared.

A semi-circle of reporters and photographers clustered around him, scribbling and snapping. Flunkies patrolled the perimeter of the scrum. Tourists paused to observe the goings-on from between the Corinthian columns of the portico.

'…enhanced competitive advantage…international landmark…'

It was nine-thirty the following morning and I was on my way to a caucus meeting. The sky was clear and the morning fair. Mild sunlight suffused the rich, contented lawns of the parliamentary gardens. The forsythia were still in bloom but the shrubbery borders had begun turning to russet.

The end of the autumn session was imminent and the legislature was dawdling towards its winter hibernation. Not that Joe and Joanna Public would take much notice. Parliament was a dull spectacle at the best of times and its current configuration made for monotonous viewing. The Liberals had an iron-clad majority, a steamroller legislative agenda and a bullet-proof leader. They outnumbered us two to one in the lower house, five to one in the upper house. We weren't just a minority. We were an endangered species, a puny splinter with little option but to keep our heads down, our seatbelts buckled and our powder dry. Not that we had any powder. We'd lost the formula two elections ago.

I trudged up the steps towards the main door. Skirting the mini-scrum, I paused for a second to catch the topic of the Premier's spiel.

'The massive contribution of the gaming industry to the people of this state…'

He was barking for the new casino, one of his pet projects. Hyped as a magnet for tourists, a generator of jobs and an all-round good thing, the casino had been slowly taking shape on the south bank of the Yarra. Its grand opening was now only days away and media interest was intense. Mick and Keef were rumoured to be flying in, Wham had got back together and Freddy Mercury was rising from the dead for the occasion.

And the Premier, you could bet on it, was claiming his share of the limelight.

'This is the kind of vision that drives my government...' he was saying.

Trotting up the last of the steps, I went into the grand old pile. The entrance was crowded with management types. They were queueing for admission to the Queen's Hall, the main parliamentary lobby. I nodded hello with the doorman, stuck my head through the door and took a quick squizz.

Fifty or so suited figures were milling around the swathe of red carpet between the two legislative chambers, helping themselves to coffee at a temporary muffin buffet. Many wore V-shaped gold lapel pins, the official insignia of the Premier's insider-trading, head-kicking, nest-feathering regime. Public service mandarins and Liberal backbenchers were mixing and mingling, not a spine among them. A rostrum had been set up, framed by banners. 'Victoria—On the Move', they declared.

On the take, more likely, I thought. You could smell the greed in the air.

The Premier's presidential style, an innovation in Australian politics, was built on events like this. Announcements of landmark accomplishments. Policy launches. New initiatives. *Son-et-lumière*. Colour and movement. A torrent of proclamations and pronouncements that kept his highness on the front page and his critics scrabbling to keep up.

Towards the rear of the room, beside the statue of Queen Victoria, camera crews were uncoiling cables and erecting tripods. Senior members of the parliamentary press corps stood nearby, idly rocking on their heels, waiting for the curtain to go up. Among them was Kelly Cusack, the presenter of *On the Floor*.

She was standing with the other hacks, half-listening to

the half-wit who did the rounds for Channel 10, her gaze skimming the room. Without the television make-up and studio lighting, she had a sexy-librarian quality, the look emphasised by her pairing of a dark suit with a form-fitting, pastel-yellow cowl-neck cashmere sweater.

She noticed me looking her way. She held my gaze, tilting her head to one side as if trying to place me.

At that exact moment, a hand clamped itself around my elbow. It jerked me abruptly sideways as the Premier swept into the room, flanked by a phalanx of ministers and minions.

'Out of the way, sonny. Who do you think you are, standing in the way of progress?'

I turned and found myself looking down at a tubby, leprechaun-faced man with wiry grey hair and twinkly eyes. He wore a crumpled tweed jacket and a cord around his neck with his spectacles attached.

'Let's rush him, Inky,' I said. 'I'll grab him, you bite his knees.'

Dennis Donnelly, universally known as Inky, was a Labor Party institution. A spin doctor *avant la lettre*, he'd been press secretary to prime ministers and premiers, and eye witness to the rise and fall of more Labor governments than I'd had taxpayer-funded taxi rides. Officially retired but impossible to keep away, he was our roving media watchdog, a sniffer-out of potentially damaging press stories.

'I been looking for you.' His voice was a whispery undertone that sounded like two press releases being rubbed together. 'Got a tick?'

I checked my watch. The caucus meeting was still fifteen minutes away.

'For you, Inky,' I said. 'Any time.'

His hand still gripping my elbow, he shunted me into the

corridor outside the Legislative Assembly. 'I understand you worked at the Municipals at one point.'

'Long ago,' I nodded. 'In a galaxy far, far away.'

He pulled a folded copy of the *Herald Sun* out of his jacket pocket and handed it to me. 'Seen this?'

The tabloid was folded open at an inside page. It had a furry, handled feel. Most of the page was occupied by a photo of a lanky young footballer with blond tips in his hair and a cast on his arm. A horde of grinning kids were jostling to sign the plaster.

'It's a cruel world,' I said. 'I've been praying to the Blessed Virgin for a speedy recovery.'

Inky and I were Lions supporters. And if the forced merger of our club with an interstate team was not indignity enough, the loss of our most promising new recruit to a shattered ulna in the first quarter of the first game of the season had rubbed salt into the wounds.

'Bugger the Blessed Virgin,' said Inky. 'Check the sidebar.'

The column contained a half-dozen brief news items. One of them was circled with an orange felt-tip pen. It was headed *Remains Found in Lake*.

> Human remains were discovered in Lake Nillahcootie in central Victoria yesterday afternoon. They were found in the bed of the lake which has been recently drained as part of maintenance work on the dam wall.
>
> Consisting of bones and a skull, the remains were removed by police for examination at Melbourne's Institute of Forensic Medicine. Police said it could take some time to identify them.
>
> 'They appear to have been at the bottom of the reservoir for a considerable period of time,' said Detective Acting

Senior Sergeant Brendan Rice. 'Items recovered from the scene suggests that they belong to the victim of a drowning which occurred at the lake a number of years ago.'

Inky watched me read, head slanted sideways, an expectant expression on his classic Hibernian dial.

'Well, well,' I said. 'It took long enough, but it looks like they've finally found Merv Cutlett.'

'You reckon it's him?'

'The odds would have to be pretty good. There can't be too many other bodies on the bottom of Lake Nillahcootie, can there?'

'You wouldn't think so,' he rasped. 'Is this first you've heard about this?'

'News to me.'

Inky reached over and laid a stubby finger on the date line at the top of the page.

A memory flashed before me, so fresh I could smell the bacon and eggs. A breakfast table at the Mildura Grand, Charlie tearing at the buttons of his shirt, vomit at the corners of his mouth, his open newspaper cascading to the floor.

'Last Thursday,' I said. 'The day Charlie Talbot died.'

What with one thing and another, I realised, I'd never got round to finishing the papers.

'Ironic, isn't it?' said Inky. 'Charlie being there when Merv drowned, then carking it on the very day the body turns up, twenty years later.'

I nodded, sharing the old flak-catcher's appreciation of life's little quirks. 'You wouldn't read about it, would you?'

Inky gave a world-weary sigh. 'If only that was true, Murray,' he said. 'Thing is, I've had a call from a journalist.

He's picked up on the unidentified remains discovery, put two and two together, come up with Merv Cutlett. He's got the idea there might be a story in it.'

'*Union Boss Slept with Yabbies*?'

'Something like that,' he said. 'He's keen to rustle up some background on the union. Problem is, I spent the late seventies in Canberra, scraping Whitlam-flavoured egg off the face of the national leadership, so I'm a bit behind the eight-ball on the twilight of the Municipals. Right now, you're the horse's mouth.'

Mouth? It was usually the other end. I glanced through the double doors at a buffet laden with coffee dregs and muffin carnage.

'Tell you what, Inky. Buy me lunch and I'll spill my guts.'

Inky patted his paunch and made a mournful face. 'My lunching days are over, mate. Gastric ulcer. Talk about guts, mine are completely cactus.'

The name Inky Donnelly was synonymous with the long Labor lunch. I puffed my cheeks in astonishment and gave a doleful shake of my head. 'No wonder the party's rooted.'

As if on cue, a handful of listless suits shuffled through the entrance archway to Queen's Hall. The remnants of my decimated tribe massing thinly for the scheduled caucus meeting.

'Tell this journo, whoever he is, he's wasting his time.' I handed Inky back his *Herald Sun*. 'Merv Cutlett's death is old news, bones or no bones.'

Inky took the paper. 'It's Vic Valentine,' he said.

I pricked up my ears. 'Accidental drowning's a bit prosaic for Vic, isn't it?' I said. 'All this gangland action going on, you'd think Melbourne's ace crime reporter would have more newsworthy leads to pursue.' We strolled out onto the clattering mosaic of the Parliament House vestibule.

'You can see where he's coming from, though,' shrugged Inky. 'A union official. An influential senator. A recently-deceased former minister. Three men in a boat, one of whom goes to a watery grave. It's got to be worth a sniff.'

'He sniffeth in vain,' I said. 'It was just a stupid accident. And Merv Cutlett wasn't exactly Jimmy Hoffa.'

Inky gave a pessimistic shrug. Crime or politics, a story was a story. And stories had a tendency to grow legs and start running in all sorts of undesirable directions.

'You know him? Personally, I mean.'

'We've talked on the phone a couple of times,' I said. 'Struck me as an okay sort of bloke.'

In the aftermath of Lyndal's death, the cops were beating the bushes, hoping to flush out the maniac who ran her down. Valentine rang me for a quote. Later, when a group of teenagers were taken hostage, Red among them, he asked my permission to interview my son. It was a messy business and I didn't want the kid turned into grist for the media mill. Valentine had respected my wishes.

'They tell me he's a straight shooter,' nodded Inky. 'But once the police ID the body, it'll be open slather. Rumour and insinuation, the Liberals can say anything they like under parliamentary privilege. They'll have a field day. Mindful of which, I think it'd be advisable to stay ahead of the pack, not risk getting blind-sided.'

In the doorway, a man in a somewhat better suit than mine was batting back a routine pleasantry from one of the Parliament House staff. Alan Metcalfe, star attraction of the imminent party meeting. He took a deep, bracing breath, inflated his chest to leaderly proportions and advanced on the staircase.

Inky retrieved some folded sheets of paper from the inside pocket of his tweed. 'I happened to be down the State Library, doing a bit of work on the memoirs, so I took a quick gander at the original newspaper reports.' He tapped his wrist with the sheaf of photocopied clippings. 'They cover the drowning, but they're a bit thin on context.'

I nodded at Metcalfe as he strode by and checked my watch. It wouldn't do to be too much later than the boss.

'Context?' I said. 'In other words, you want to know if the union was corrupt?'

'Was it?'

'There might've been the odd little fiddle here and there, but nothing systemic. The employers were government agencies, so there wasn't much scope.'

'And there was never any question that the drowning was an accident?'

'Nope,' I said. 'Not that I heard.'

'Three blokes go fishing, one of them falls overboard, that's it?'

'Pissed as a parakeet, probably,' I said. 'Cutlett.'

'Consistent with form,' Inky said. 'And Charlie Talbot was state secretary, right?'

I nodded. 'The way I heard it, Charlie jumped in, tried to save him.'

'They were pretty thick, were they?'

'Chalk and cheese,' I said. 'Mortal enemies, so to speak. Charlie was trying to drag the union into the twentieth century. Merv preferred the early nineteenth.'

'But pally enough to go fishing together?'

I tried to imagine Charlie Talbot in an aluminium dinghy with a bucket of worms and a six-pack. The image didn't come readily to mind.

'That's another irony,' I said. 'Charlie wasn't the outdoor type. Merv must have twisted his arm. Probably dragged him along just to give him the shits.'

'The union had a place on the lake, right?'

'The Shack,' I nodded. 'Notionally a training and recreation facility for the members. In reality, it was Merv's private retreat.'

Inky put on his specs and quickly flipped through his collection of newspaper cuttings. 'So what was Barry Quinlan doing there? I can't see him and Merv Cutlett as mates.'

'They weren't,' I said. 'Quinlan was working for the Public Employees Federation. He had some nebulous title like development officer or liaison co-ordinator or some such. Essentially, he was their mergers and acquisitions man. The PEF was very pro-active on the amalgamation front, always on the lookout for a takeover target. Charlie knew that amalgamation with a bigger union was the only way forward for the Municipals. He and Quinlan were working a tag team, trying to swing Merv on the issue.'

Inky nodded along, connecting the union dots to the bigger political picture. 'The PEF backed Quinlan onto the Senate ticket for the 1979 election. That would've been his pay-off for bringing the Municipals into the fold. The amalgamation must have increased its membership by a hefty swag.'

'A well-trod route,' I said. The more members, the more votes a union has at party conference.

Inky patted his pockets, found a half-gone roll of Quik-Eze and peeled away the foil.

'Tell you what,' he popped a couple in his mouth and started to crunch. 'How about we have a drink with your mate Valentine? Nip this thing in the bud. How're you set tonight after work?'

It was a rare Friday night that Red didn't have a social engagement. Tonight was no exception. Come knock-off time, I'd have no reason to go rushing home to an empty house.

'Sure,' I shrugged. 'I'll shout you a glass of milk.'

'I'll give Valentine a call, get back to you with the when and where.'

I was already turning away, pushing it to make the meeting on time. Inky grabbed my sleeve and thrust his collection of cuttings into my hand.

'Extra! Extra!' he rasped. 'Read all about it.'

The party room was a grand salon on the first floor, all neo-classical architraves and french-polished sideboards. I arrived just as the pre-meeting burble was dying down and found a seat in the back row.

The entire parliamentary party was there. All twenty-nine of us.

As usual, the Right sat on the left and the Left sat on the right. An apt demarcation since the two factions were indistinguishable in both principle and practice. The Right had long been dominant, having successfully pinned responsibility for our demise on the Left, a situation akin to the cocktail waiters blaming the dance band for the sinking of the *Titanic*. They called themselves the Concord faction, thereby staking out the moral high ground. The Left, demonstrating its usual measure of political imagination, just called itself the Left.

Those without factional affiliation, myself included, sat

at the back. In due course, if I wanted to retain my endorsement, I'd probably be forced to choose a side. For the moment, however, I was content to keep my entanglements to a minimum. Even if it meant sitting at the back.

Up front, facing us, sat Alan Metcalfe, along with his deputy, Peter Thorsen, and a select group of senior frontbenchers. Metcalfe stood up, cleared his throat and called the meeting to order.

'*Harmf*,' he said. 'Let's get on with it, then.'

Metcalfe was a former federal MP who'd been shoehorned into state politics after losing his safe seat in a redistribution. He was capable, earnest, deeply ambitious and utterly boring. He had the head of a shop dummy, the mannerisms of a robot and the charisma of a fish finger.

Notwithstanding these excellent credentials, the electorate had failed to warm to our glorious leader. Under his tutelage, our state-wide primary vote had plummeted to new depths. Nobody, probably not even Alan himself, believed that he could reverse this trend in time for the next election. In the most recent preferred-premier poll, he'd rated somewhere lower than viral meningitis. But what he lacked in voter appeal he more than made up in tenacity. He clung to his job with fingernails of steel, a testament to inertia disguised as stability.

'Fair to say, and I think you'll all agree with me,' he started, 'we've put up a pretty good show in recent weeks. The public is tiring of this government's high-handed attitude. It's looking to us to keep up the pressure.'

Metcalfe was whistling dixie. The fact was, we'd been comprehensively trounced in every fight we picked. And successfully painted as a rat-pack of financial incompetents who couldn't be trusted to run a primary school tuck-shop.

As Metcalfe continued, chopping the air for emphasis, an air of lethargy filled the room. In the seat beside me, Kelvin Yabbsley, the member for Corio East, lowered his chin to his chest and closed his eyes.

He was dreaming, I fancied, about his superannuation payout. After twenty-two years on the back bench, Yabbers was due to retire at the next election. With his parliamentary pension and a pozzie on the board of the Geelong Harbour Trust, he would want for nothing for the rest of his natural life.

Play your cards right kid, I told myself, and one day that could be you.

Eventually, Alan Metcalfe's air-karate pep-talk petered out. 'Fair to say, all things considered, we've got our work cut out for us,' he concluded. 'And on that note, I'll hand the floor to the shadow ministers who'll brief us on their respective portfolio areas.'

Shoulders sagged lower and backsides sank deeper into seats. Con Caramalides, our point man for planning and infrastructure, began to outline his plans to stick it up the government over a raft of issues connected with increased domestic electricity charges. If anybody needed a raft, it was Con. He sounded like he was drowning in molasses.

'...the flow-on of cross-ownership to low-voltage...'

I did my best to stay awake, just in case there was any mention of my current parliamentary duties. Shadow Secretary for Ethnic Affairs, Local Government and Fair Trading. Acting assistant manager of opposition business in the upper house, *pro tem*. Various other bits and bobs. With our numbers so short, it was all hands on deck.

And what a motley crew of deck-hands we were.

Most of our frontbench were yesterday's heroes, so busy undermining one another that they'd lost sight of any other reason for existence. Circling each other like burned-out suns, they were kept in place only by the centrifugal force of their mutual loathing. Of the fresher faces, few stood out as foreman material. For my money, our best hope was Peter Thorsen, the deputy leader.

Thorsen was a cleanskin, untarnished by our period in government. Not yet forty, wheaten-haired with the hint of a tennis tan, he was the very picture of a golden boy on the cusp of middle age. One of the Concord faction, he carried himself with a breezy self-confidence that played well on television. He'd scored some hits on the floor of parliament and he was popular with the troops. But so far, he'd given no indication of having his sights set on the top job. Whether motivated by caution or timing or loyalty, he seemed content to play second fiddle to Metcalfe.

'Natural gas, on the other hand,' said Con, 'is a two-edged sword...'

Thorsen had one arm draped across the back of his chair, browsing a document. He glanced up, saw me looking his way, and gave me a sly grin. Ho-hum, it said, here we are again. I replied with a resigned shrug and put a balled fist to my mouth, stifling a yawn.

By eleven-thirty, the shadow ministers' round-ups had ambled to a conclusion. The room came out of its collective coma. Members began gathering up their papers. Kelvin Yabbsley opened his eyes, blew his nose and pulled up his socks.

'Fair to say that covers the overall thrust,' said Metcalfe, raising his voice above the resurgent murmur. 'But before I close the meeting, I've got a brief announcement to make.'

There was a communal deflation and bums again descended onto seats.

'We're all deeply grieved,' said Metcalfe, 'fair to say, at the untimely death of Charlie Talbot.'

'Hear, hear,' murmured a smattering of voices.

Metcalfe signalled for silence, then raked us with his sternest stare. 'And I believe the best way to honour his memory is to avoid a distracting and divisive preselection brawl over the seat he left vacant. Accordingly, I've assured our federal colleagues that the Victorian branch can be relied on one hundred percent to adhere to the current agreement regarding the prompt filling of the vacancy in Coolaroo.'

There was a low burble of assent from the Concord ranks.

'So who's the lucky boy?' chipped in Nanette Vandenberg, one of the independents. 'It *is* a boy, I presume.'

Heads swivelled, then turned back to Metcalfe. 'I've been given to understand that the choice is Phil Sebastian,' he said. 'He'll bring a strong background in policy development to the federal team.'

In other words, he was a policy wonk with fuck-all experience of ground-level politics. He also happened to be Barry Quinlan's chief-of-staff. At least now I knew which particular finger the good senator was giving the voters of Coolaroo.

A lukewarm murmur of approval wafted from the thin ranks of the Left. The choice had evidently not been met with unanimous enthusiasm among the comrades. Nothing remarkable there. Nelson Mandela would've got the same reception.

'I'm confident I can rely on you all,' said Metcalfe pointedly. 'A hundred percent.' He brought the edge of one hand down hard on the open palm of the other. 'Understood?'

All heads nodded in unison, a row of toy dogs in the rear

window of a slow-moving vehicle.

'In that case, I declare this meeting closed.'

As the room began to empty, Peter Thorsen caught my eye. Angling his head slightly, he twitched his chin upwards in the direction of his second-floor office.

Whatever it is, I thought, it can wait until I've had a cup of tea. I headed for the urn on the sideboard to dunk myself a bag. Jenny Hovacks, a Concord spear-carrier, was ahead of me in the queue. She'd been buttonholed by Eric Littler, one of the Left.

'We're not unhappy with the result,' he was saying fiercely. 'It's the process we don't like.'

'Murray,' Jenny turned to greet me. 'What do you think of your chances tomorrow?'

Jenny was an Essendon supporter. The Lions would be up against them at the MCG, their first Melbourne match since the merger.

'I think we'll make a good showing,' I said. 'Then you'll shit on us from a great height.'

'Just as well you're used to it, eh?' said misery-guts Eric, snaffling the last of the teabags.

I didn't like the turn this conversation was taking. I settled for a butternut snap and trudged upstairs to Thorsen's office.

His admin assistant, Del, was busy at her keyboard, fingers flying. 'Go on in, Murray,' she said, flipping a wrist towards the open door of the inner sanctum.

Thorsen's office overlooked the Gordon Reserve, a triangle of lawn studded with memorials to dead poets and imperial warriors. He was standing at his desk, a massive block of native hardwood incised with an *art nouveau* gum leaf motif. His jacket was draped over the back of his chair and he'd loosened his tie. A cluster of silver-framed photographs was arrayed in a semi-circle on a credenza behind him, family snaps of his barrister wife and their brood of tow-headed children, four at last count. A phone was pressed to his ear.

'Yup, yup,' he said into the mouthpiece, waving me inside and signalling that I should shut the door. 'Yup.'

Peter's political base lay on the other side of town, in socially liberal seaside suburbs that had long since traded their working-class credentials for off-the-rack bohemianism, grouchy gentility and rampant property speculation. Our relationship was cordial, but it had yet to be tested where the poop meets the propeller.

He hung up, nodded for me to sit down, ambled across to the window, propped his backside against the sill and stuck his hands in his pockets.

'Everybody appreciates the job you did with Charlie Talbot, Murray, the funeral arrangements and so forth. It must have been pretty rough.'

'The least I could do for an old mate.'

'Big shoes to fill,' he said. 'You know Phil Sebastian, do you?'

'We've met in passing,' I said. 'But I imagine I'll be seeing a lot more of him from now on. Squiring him around the shire, familiarising him with the southerly boroughs of his new fiefdom,' I fluttered a regal hand. 'Introducing him to the peasantry.'

'Will the folks in the local branches be welcoming?'

'There's bound to be some bitching about being taken for granted,' I said. 'Always is.'

'Think any of them will feel aggrieved enough to take a tilt?'

I shrugged. 'Somebody might have a rush of blood to the head, but I doubt they'll go the distance. The result's a foregone conclusion after all, isn't it?'

'Alan certainly hopes so. The push for a change of leadership is building up steam. Keeping this cross-factional deal on track will be the litmus test of his authority. But if the wheels come off, he'll have laid himself open to a challenge.'

'Only if there's a challenger,' I said.

A wolfish glint flashed in Thorsen's eyes. Hello, I thought. Could he be making a move at long last?

I looked around, mock furtive, and dropped my voice to a conspiratorial whisper. 'Strictly between you and me, Peter,' I said. 'Nobody could be worse than Metcalfe. Not even a ponce like you. And if you can cook up a spill, you've got my vote.' I put my hand on my heart. 'True dinks.'

He gave a sardonic smile. 'The Murray Whelan seal of endorsement.'

'But,' I said. 'Throwing the Coolaroo deal off the tracks, that'll take some doing. You'd need a spoiler candidate, the fly in Metcalfe's ointment.'

'Do you think there's any chance such a person might emerge?'

'Anything's possible. Plenty of wannabes out there. What you're after is a kamikaze pilot.'

'Quinlan has the numbers on the panel, so they'll get creamed in the final count,' he agreed. 'The important thing is to make a decent showing in the first round, the district plebiscite. The ideal stalking horse would be some local identity with a branch or two up their sleeve.'

The description fitted Mike Kyriakis to a tee.

'Somebody encouraged to run by a friend in the

parliamentary ranks?' I said. 'A hidden hand to steer him in the right direction.'

'Precisely. An MP without a vested interest in the current arrangements. Somebody committed to the renewal of the party. Somebody with an eye to the future.'

'Put away the trowel, Peter,' I said. 'What's in it for me?'

'Assuming this all pans out,' he said. 'How does a shadow ministry sound?'

'Like a hollow carrot,' I said. 'More work for very little gain.'

'But an assured seat at the grown-ups' table when we get back into office.'

'*If* we get back into office.'

Thorsen smiled placidly, conceding the point. 'Sooner or later the pendulum will swing back our way. And when it does, we'd better be ready. Not sitting around with cobwebs up our quoit.'

He went back behind his desk, the loyal deputy leader once more. 'We're speaking hypothetically, of course.'

'Naturally.'

If Peter had finally decided to take a shot at the boss cockie's job, he was approaching his target at a very acute angle. In all likelihood, he was simply testing the waters, sniffing the wind, flying a kite, laying some pipe. Whatever the case, I felt no pressing temptation to sign up for the ride.

Wait and see, that was the motto emblazoned on my escutcheon. Head down, tail up. There was fuck-all mileage in getting sucked into the machinations of the upper echelons.

Thorsen scrutinised my face with a look of bland innocence. I chuckled, shook my head slowly and stood up.

'Before you go,' he said. 'Brian McKechnie is heading off on a study tour of Europe at the end of the month. Looking into export opportunities for the alfalfa industry. We'll need somebody to cover his portfolio.'

'Agriculture?' I said. 'What do I know about agriculture?'

'Messy business, apparently. Sometimes you have to get your hands dirty.'

I went downstairs to the back door, heading for my office in the prefab annexe behind the House. The Henhouse, we called it. A cool front had arrived from the west, turning the sky into a roiling mass of rain clouds. The temperature had dropped ten degrees and gusts of damp wind whistled across the carpark. As I hunched my shoulders, bracing for the dash, my mobile phone rang.

'Mr Whelan? It's Kelly Cusack from the ABC. I wonder if you could spare me a moment of your time?'

She was perched on one of the banquettes in the vestibule, a laptop open on her knees, too deeply immersed in her work to cast more than a cursory glance at the comings and goings around her. From time to time, she compressed her telegenic lips and looked up absently, as though hunting an elusive phrase. I ambled past in the slipstream of a tour group, then detoured into the now-empty Queen's Hall, confident that she'd registered my presence.

Thirty seconds later, she found me waiting beside the statue of Victoria Regina, concealed from casual view by the royal plinth. A press pass was clipped to the lapel of her jacket and her laptop case was slung over one shoulder. She was all business.

'I don't have long,' she said. 'I'm on a flight back to Canberra at three. Is there somewhere we can go?'

Heavy drapes hung on brass rails across the archways at the back of the hall, separating it from the gallery outside the parliamentary library, an area off-limits to the public. I checked the way was clear, we slipped through the curtains and I led her down a carpeted corridor past the office of the Usher of the Black Rod, closed for lunch. Ten steps along, I pressed my shoulder against a section of the wood panelling. It swung open, revealing the dimly lit chamber of the Legislative Council.

The shop was shut, the portals locked, the lights switched off. A pale wash of daylight spilled through the high transom windows, illuminating the elaborate plasterwork of the barrel-vaulted ceiling and the gilt finials of the Corinthian columns. Reflected off the crimson plush of the benches, it bathed the whole space in a rosy glow. I shepherded the journalist inside and slipped the latch on the door, a discreet hatch used by the clerks when sittings were in progress. Up close, I could smell her perfume, musky and elementally feminine.

My hands found her hips and guided her back against the scalloped canopy of the President's podium. Her peripherals slid to the floor as I took one of her lobes between my lips and sucked her pearl stud.

She pushed me away, hoisted her skirt and peeled off her pantyhose. In the five seconds this took, I shucked off my jacket and tossed it across the back of the President's chair.

With a quick glance to double-check that we were still alone, we went back into our clinch. Her response was eager, a real buttock-gripper. As my lips slid over her cheek, she ran her palms up my chest and ground her hips against me. 'Is that a ceremonial mace in your pocket or are you just glad to see me?'

Too glad for words, I lunged for her earlobe again, running my hands up the inside of her jacket, one cupping the contents of her cashmere, the other savouring the sexy slither of her back, my fingers splaying as they neared the nape of her neck. 'The hair,' she squirmed. 'Don't muss the hair. You know the rules.'

No kissing was the other rule. It played havoc with her lipstick, she said.

Obediently, I slowed my pace, allowing things to take their time, what little time we had. Lust-flushed in the half-light, we gazed glassily into each other's eyes, confirming our mutual understanding of the situation.

This wasn't romance. It was an itch. And by Christ we were scratching it.

'Saw you at the Premier's casino thing.' My breathing was heavy with anticipation. 'Not exactly hard news.'

'Not as hard as something I could name.'

'Name it,' I begged. 'Name it.'

She did more than that. She put her mouth to my ear and tendered some encouraging recommendations regarding its employment. My fingers delved beneath her skirt. She was likewise engaged, negotiating a break in my strides. As I found the passage I sought, she seized upon the pressing issue.

'I hear there's a spill in the offing.'

With a handshake like that, she should have been in politics. She definitely had my vote of confidence. Maintaining her grip on proceedings, she edged towards the despatch table, towing me along behind.

'You want spill,' I muttered through clenched teeth. 'Keep glad-handing me like that, I'll give you spill.'

She shoved aside the chief clerk's chair and bent forward across the despatch table, cheek pressed to the baize. 'Thorsen's almost got the numbers, I hear.' She widened her stance, toes gripping the carpet, fingers curled around the bevelled edge of the hardwood. 'He's making all sorts of offers, they say. Thinking of putting your hand up?'

Not just my hand. I hefted her skirt, exposing her ivory orbs. My head spun with the sheer recklessness of it, the wanton folly. We could be sprung at any moment. The main doors would burst open and the chief steward would usher in a tour party of school children. It was utter madness. Again I scanned the room, confirming that we were unobserved.

'Who's this "they"?' My trousered thighs slid forwards into a valley of bare skin.

'My lips are sealed.'

'Liar,' I gasped, pressing home my point.

The slap of flesh on flesh, the carnal squish of congress, urgent and rhythmic, ascended to the chandeliers. Regal beasts, the lion and the unicorn, stared speechless from atop the President's podium. Mythic champions brandished their frescoed spears. The locomotive of progress hurtled onward, pistons pumping.

We'd been at this, intermittently, for almost a year. It had begun with a spur-of-the-moment, alcohol-fuelled shag on the fire stairs at the Meridian during some interminable awards dinner, something to do with medicine and the media. She was there to accept a Golden Goitre for a doco on pharmaceutical kickbacks. I was there as the shadow of the Shadow Minister for Health, who was recovering from a colonoscopy.

Introduced at the pre-dinner booze-and-schmooze, we'd let our eyes do the talking across the floral centrepiece during the leek tartlets, given our dates the slip half-way through the pan-seared spatchcock, and found ourselves going the slam against a concrete wall in the emergency exit somewhere between the Most Outstanding Contribution to Obesity Awareness and the Best Jingle in a Cough Suppressant Commercial. Fifteen minutes later, she was stepping onto the stage to accept her trophy, not a hair out of place.

No visible hair, at least. Several of her short and curlies were stuck to the roof of my mouth, a piquant textural counterpoint to the passionfruit panacotta.

Ours was a no-strings, no-promises, no-assumptions arrangement. It suited us both. She was married, I was amenable. If Kelly Cusack needed attention, I was happy to provide it, even at short notice and close quarters. We hardly ever talked politics. Or much else, for that matter. Too busy with the wham-bam.

Although she was fastidious about her appearance and circumspect in regard to our assignations, Kelly had a taste for quickies. What stoked her fire were knee-tremblers in risky locales, situations with a high prospect of having our coitus interrupted in flagrante. Since the episode in the hotel stairwell, we'd abandoned caution in the kitchenette of a corporate box at the tennis centre during the mixed doubles final of the Australian Open, in a fitting cubicle in the Myer menswear department, in the back of an ABC outside-broadcast van and between the buttress roots of a Moreton Bay fig in the Fitzroy Gardens. On the solitary occasion we'd taken a hotel room, she'd unpacked my lunch in the lift on the way upstairs.

But going the goat on the despatch table in the Legislative Council really did redefine the parameters of parliamentary privilege. My heart was thumping. My loins were pumping. My pulse was ringing in my ears. Ring-ring, ring-ring, ring-ring.

Not my pulse. A mobile phone. Close. Very close. Kelly abruptly jack-knifed upright, bucking me off at the exact moment my honourable member reached the climax of his oration.

She dived for her carry-all and tore it open. 'Helloo,' she warbled, chest heaving. 'Oh hi, darling.' She rose from the carpet, Eriksson pressed to her baize-burnished cheek. 'What? No, fine, just run up some stairs, that's all.' She mouthed her husband's name, as if I needed telling. 'What, right now?'

I teetered unsteadily, my legs jelly, my lap a swamp, my standard at half-mast, and plonked myself down in the President's chair. Kelly continued her conversation, domestic and therefore private, simultaneously wiggling back into her hosiery, counting her earrings, fluffing her cashmere and otherwise repairing her dishabille.

By the time I'd reclaimed my wetlands, zipped my fly and run my tie back up the flagpole, she'd finished her call and traded the phone for a vanity purse. She reapplied her lippy, checked herself in the mirror, then turned to me for confirmation that she didn't look like she'd just been schtupped in the consistory.

'You're a true professional,' I said. 'Best interview technique in the business. Pumping while you're humping.'

'I didn't get much out of you.' She patted her hair and smoothed her skirt.

'More than you realise,' I said. 'Miss Lewinsky.'

She reached for her rump, then jerked her hand back. 'Ick!'

I crouched behind her and sponged away my memorandum with a spit-wetted handkerchief, copping a feel while I was at it. 'Now what's this about Thorsen?' I said.

'I'll call you later.' She scooped up her kit. 'Must rush.'

I surveyed the corridor and gave her the all-clear. She sidled past, giving my bum a squeeze and my cheek a parting peck, then glided away, not a backward look, poised and purposeful. I plopped down in the place customarily occupied by the government whip, heaved a sigh and waited for my blood to settle. Seven minutes twenty-nine seconds had elapsed since we entered the chamber, a zipless PB.

As the coital fog ebbed, I contemplated Kelly's crack. The one about putting my hand up. What did she mean about Thorsen and the numbers? Was she working up a story? Was the cat already out of the bag, or was she just fishing?

I'd have no answer until she called me back. Even then, I'd be lucky to get anything out of her.

I consulted my watch. One o'clock. No wonder I was feeling peckish. Time for a smidge of the fast and easy.

Outside on the front steps, a photographer was posing a wedding party at one of the antique light stanchions, the bride's gown billowing. Nearby, a pair of teenage constables were keeping a bored eye on a cluster of subversive geriatrics, a thermos-fuelled vigil against the Formula One circuit in Albert Park.

I joined the lunchtime throng on the Bourke Street footpath, and spotted an empty stool at the window-bench of Tojo Bento.

Equipped with a plastic tray of yakitori nori and a squishy-fishy soy-sauce sachet, I parked myself at the bench and pried open a pair of disposable rainforest-timber chopsticks. As I sank my fangs into the seaweed, I unfolded Inky Donnelly's slim collection of photocopied newspaper clippings and began to read.

Alert and purposeful, Merv Cutlett stared into the middle distance, his jaw clenched in unwavering resolve, steely determination glinting in his gimlet eyes. His hair, thin but tenacious, was slicked back over his scalp and deep lines were etched into his sentinel face. He looked like a cross between a fox terrier and a sack of hacksaw blades.

The photograph was Merv's personal favourite. His Great Leader shot. He also liked Merv at Work, which showed him at his desk, staring out importantly from behind a redoubt of papers, important files weighed down by a hefty ring of keys, his emblem of office. For lighter stories, he favoured Merv Shares a Laugh, in which he appeared surrounded by a mob of admiring garbologists at the annual union picnic.

All three were regular features of the *FUME News* during my stint as editor. I'd not been at the Municipals long when the incident at Lake Nillahcootie occurred. Six months or so. Thinking back, I had no firm recollection of hearing the news about Merv's disappearance. No JFK moment. Many concerns occupy a man in his twenties, and the office is sometimes the least of them. Cutlett's drowning was a notable event, of course, but all I could recall with any certainty was the almost palpable sense of relief it brought to the Queensberry Street office.

As I studied Merv's photograph, tears flooded my eyes. Bloody wasabi. Honking into a paper napkin, I turned to the next photocopy.

It was a page from the *Herald*, Melbourne's long-defunct evening broadsheet. The date was written in the margin in Inky's shorthand scrawl. Saturday 27 July 1978. Refugee Influx Raises Fears, I read. Terrorist Bombing Shakes London. Record Profit for Qantas. Unionist Feared Drowned.

> *A search has failed to find any trace of prominent union official Mervyn Cutlett, 58, who disappeared this morning while fishing on Lake Nillahcootie north of Alexandra. According to police, Mr Cutlett was reported to have fallen overboard in rough weather conditions. Despite repeated attempts, his companions were unable to pull him from the water. Police said that heavy rain at the scene has hampered the efforts of emergency services to locate Mr Cutlett, who is head of the Federated Union of Municipal Employees. The alarm was raised by fellow union officials Barry Quinlan and Charles Talbot. Mr Talbot was treated at the scene for hypothermia.*

The story concluded with a statement from the officer in charge about the police being short-handed due to a call-out to assist victims of flooding in other parts of the district.

I'd forgotten about the weather, I realised. Even by Merv's standards, it was particularly perverse to drag a pair of reluctant fishing companions out onto a lake in what must have been miserable winter conditions. No wonder Charlie had copped a dose of hypothermia. The water must have been freezing.

The next report was lifted from the *Herald*'s stable-mate, the *Sun*. It was dated two days later, the Monday morning edition. It described a more extensive search, including the use of divers and a line search of the shore, but the headline summed it up. *Hunt fails to find unionist's body.*

A similar story appeared in the next day's *Age*. It was slightly better written but contained no fresh information.

Out on the street, the lunch crowd was thinning, scurrying back to the grind, shoulders hunched against the breeze. A young woman of the Oriental persuasion materialised at my elbow, washcloth in hand. A Chinese student, probably; about as Japanese as a California roll.

'Jew finish?' she said, whisking away my plastic tray and giving the benchtop a perfunctory swipe. 'July a trink?'

I ordered green tea. When it comes to coffee, the Nips are the pits. While I waited, I pondered the newspaper reports. Although they told me nothing I didn't know already, they'd begun to prime the pump of my memory.

Now that I thought about it, I seemed to remember that there were others up at the Shack that day. Colin Bishop? Someone else, too, but it eluded me for the moment.

In any case, the incident had faded into the background pretty quickly. With Merv out of the picture, the amalgamation proceeded apace. By the end of the year, FUME had been absorbed into the PEF. The Municipals' staff being surplus to requirements, jobs were slated for slashing and mine was high on the hit list. Charlie saw me right, though. Found me a full-time spot at the Labor Resource Centre, a policy think-tank tasked with cooking up a strategic vision to be enacted in the event that Labor ever got itself elected into government.

Which, in due course, it did. By then, both Charlie and Barry Quinlan had seats in federal parliament, Charlie in the Reps, Quinlan in the Senate. Our glory days were upon us. I was married to Wendy and Red was on the way. And Mervyn Cutlett, like the stegosaurus, had receded into prehistoric oblivion.

My green tea arrived, pallid but piping. While it was cooling down, I sucked air over my scalded tongue and ran my eye over the last of Inky's pages. An obituary from the *Labor Star*, official organ of the ALP, it summarised the salient features of Merv's biography.

> Born 1920, youngest son and third child of a slaughterman. Apprenticed as a motor mechanic, then worked at Footscray Council maintenance dept before volunteering for the AIF in 1940. Service in North Africa, repatriated, rejoined the council. Shop steward, then elected to union executive in 1948. Sailed close to the communist wind but never carried a card. Emerged from the splits and ructions of the fifties as national secretary, a position he continued to hold for the next two decades. One of the longest-serving union officials in Australia, survived by wife and daughter, to whom the labour movement extends its sincere condolences.

As intimate and revealing as your average obit, it revealed nothing about his personality, such as it was. On that subject, the Great Leader photo offered more clues.

In line with Charlie Talbot's advice, I'd kept my contact with Cutlett to the bare minimum. But once a month, I was compelled to enter his office in the Trades Hall to get his approval for the layout sheets of the *FUME News*.

'Look out,' he'd say. 'It's Scoop Whelan, our very own Jimmy Olsen.'

That'd get a big guffaw from Sid Gilpin, his spivvy sidekick. 'Charlie Talbot's bum boy,' he'd chorus.

Low-grade monstering, it might have got a rise out of a first-year apprentice. But it was like water off Merv's Brylcreemed comb-over to me. I wasn't there to bat the breeze. I was there to get the national secretary's sign-off so I could send the union newsletter to press.

Merv would put on his thick, big-framed reading glasses and carefully study the layout boards, all the while eyeballing me as if I was trying to pull a swiftie on him. Once he'd confirmed that his photograph did indeed appear on every second page, he'd grunt grudgingly and reach for his signing pen.

The pen was part of a brass desk-set fashioned from an expended shell casing. Merv's desk was a repository of such items. An ashtray on bullet legs. A cartridge cigarette lighter. A letter-opener with an anti-tank round for a handle.

At first I'd assumed Merv's cherished collection of museum-quality trenchware was a souvenir of his war service, a reminder of his front-line participation in the global conflict against fascism. But not according to Col Bishop.

'Merv never heard a shot fired in anger,' Col once told me. 'He was in the sanitation corps. The Royal Australian Shitshovellers. Got clapped up in Cairo then invalided home after the provos beat him to a pulp in a street brawl. But that's not something Merv cares to advertise. He just happens to like that sort of crap. And if people want to jump to the wrong conclusion, that's hardly Merv's fault, is it?'

Nor, contrary to the suggestion in his obituary, was Cutlett much of a family man. The wife might have survived him, but she was long gone. Gave him the flick some time back in the fifties, according to office rumour. The daughter—her name escaped me, perhaps I'd never known it—was sighted in his office occasionally, a listless lump of ageless frump whose resigned demeanour reinforced the assumption that old Merv was not worth breeding off.

He was definitely a dinosaur in his general attitude to women, for all his leftist posturing. The office 'girls', Margot and Prue, clearly did not relish their frequent trips to the Trades Hall to fetch or deliver documents. It was not for nothing, apparently, that they called him Merv the Perv.

I had no idea how his daughter felt about his disappearance, let alone the prospect that his remains had been resurrected from the mud at the bottom of Lake Nillahcootie. If identification of the remains involved DNA tests, she'd probably already had a visit from the police.

I pocketed the clippings and downed the dregs of my tea. Like I'd told Inky, Merv Cutlett's disappearance was a non-story. Even the most imaginative journalist would be hard put to suggest otherwise. If and when the ownership of the remains was confirmed, the whole business wouldn't be worth more than a couple of paragraphs, a historical postscript.

Vic Valentine, crime beat specialist, was probably just giving the trees a passing shake, see if anything interesting fell out. I'd be telling him not to waste his time.

As I was standing at the register, paying for lunch, my mobile rang. It was Inky.

'Re that drink with Valentine,' he rasped. 'He suggested somewhere in Fitzroy, a place called the Toilers Retreat. You know it?'

Valentine obviously had a sense of humour. The Toilers Retreat was a watering hole in Brunswick Street, a former milk bar that had been refurbished in the faux proletarian style. The name was part of the design. At least it wasn't the Hammer and Tongs or the Rack and Pinion.

'I used to live around the corner,' I said. 'What time?'

'Six-thirty,' he said. 'If your car's at the House, I'll cadge a lift with you. See you at six in Strangers Corridor, okay? Oh, and by the way, the odds have shortened on the deceased being Merv. Nothing official yet but I've just picked up an interesting bit of static from a mate at the Peaheads.'

The Peaheads were the PEA, the Public Employees Association, the government sector super-union. Originally the Public Service Association, it had become the PEA after absorbing the Public Employees Federation subsequent to the PEF's amalgamation with the FUME.

'Couple of days ago, they had a call from the constabulary wanting to know if they've still got the Municipals' old records.'

'Something in particular?'

'Membership rolls, payroll, financial accounts, that sort of thing,' he said. 'Circa 1978.'

'You reckon it's got anything to do with Merv Cutlett's bones turning up?'

'No names mentioned. A routine enquiry, whatever that means. Nobody at the Peaheads seems to have joined the dots. The Municipals were three amalgamations ago and corporate memory doesn't exactly run deep at the PEA. Lucky if they can remember as far back as breakfast.'

'They give the cops the records?' I said.

'In my experience, unions are reluctant to hand over their internal documents,' said Inky. 'But being a helpful lot, the

Peaheads said they'd have a poke around, see what they can find. Which will be exactly zip. The old FUME records were definitely BC. Before Computers. Nobody's got the faintest idea where they ended up. Long gone, probably.'

'How can twenty-year-old financial records help identify an old skeleton?' I said.

'You tell me, Murray,' said Inky. 'You tell me.'

Not much was happening in the Parliament House library.

A pair of dust motes were dancing a slow waltz in the air beneath the crystal chandelier. A century of Hansard was snoozing on the shelves, silent in its calf-leather covers. A scatter of documents and a writing pad lay unattended on the big octagonal reading table beneath the cupola.

The duty librarian, a studious-looking, carrot-haired young man in a boxy suit and tiny diamond ear-stud, was languidly staring into a monitor, occasionally tapping a key.

'G'day, Pat,' I said. 'Busy?'

'Frantic,' he said, deadpan, then tore his attention away from the screen. 'How may I assist you today, Mr Whelan?'

The parliamentary library prided itself on its ability to hunt down and capture almost any publication in the global vastness of the public domain. And do so with absolute confidentiality. I could have asked for the Olympia first edition of *Swedish Stewardesses on Heat* and Pat wouldn't have batted a pale-pink eyelid.

'I'm after the findings of a coronial inquest,' I said.

'That shouldn't be a problem.' He was clearly disappointed that it was not something more professionally challenging. 'Recent?'

'1978,' I said. 'Sorry.'

On my way back from lunch, it'd occurred to me that I might be able to rustle up a tad more information on the circumstances of Merv Cutlett's drowning than the sketchy outline provided by the newspaper reports.

At its last meeting, the Scrutiny of Acts and Regulations Committee had considered a slate of recommendations from the State Coroner regarding the mandatory wearing of lifejackets. Too many teenagers were dying in canoeing accidents and the rules on mucking around in boats needed tightening. Supporting documentation had included inquest summaries pertaining to accidental deaths on inland waterways, some going back twenty years. The proposed legislative amendments were uncontentious, so I hadn't bothered wading through the files.

'It might even still be here,' I said. 'Pending return to the Coroner's office.' I gave Pat the details and he jotted them down.

'I'll get right onto it.' His attention was drifting back to the monitor.

'ASAP will be fine,' I said.

By then it was two-fifteen, time for the monthly meeting of the Public Accounts and Estimates Committee. I went upstairs to the conference room and took my seat at the table. It was a bi-partisan conclave, with Labor outnumbered six to two. The other Labor member was Daryl Keels, our

Shadow Finance Minister and chief number cruncher.

The meeting was chaired by the Treasurer, an abrasive, pug-faced Liberal dry with eyebrows like cuphooks and a Gorgon's stare guaranteed to freeze the wee in a Liberal backbencher's underpants. The main agenda item was gambling revenues.

In other states, poker machine licences were issued to sporting clubs, the earnings earmarked for community facilities. In our case, the Liberals had dished them out to friendly plutocrats in return for a slice of the action. And the action was going ballistic. Hundreds of millions of dollars were slipping through Lady Luck's fingers and into the state's coffers.

Social consequences be damned, it was money for jam. A bottomless goodie-bag that no future Labor government would be able to keep its hands off. As a policy issue, gambling was a lost cause. We were all sons of bitches now. All that remained was to dicker over the distribution of the whack, and Daryl did the dickering. Labor wanted more of the revenue allocated to health and education. As usual, we were defeated on party lines.

The meeting finished at four and while we were all packing up our papers, I chatted with Keels.

'Get your invite to the big event?' he said, shovelling a small mountain of facts and figures into his briefcase. He meant the casino opening. The proprietors had invited all state MPs and every federal MP from Victoria, irrespective of party.

'You bet,' I said.

As I spoke, I realised that I still didn't have an escort for the evening. What with Charlie's death, the whole thing had slipped my mind. It wasn't like I could ask Kelly. I knew who

I'd like to invite, but she was unavailable. Unattainable, I told myself sternly. My classmate from Greek lessons was not a potential date, she was a married woman. I should stop fantasising about her and get serious about finding somebody else.

It couldn't be too difficult. Even Keels had managed it, for all his bony arse and non-existent hairline. Recently divorced, he was putting himself about a bit, or so the gossip went. Doing okay, too, apparently. As the last of the Liberals left the room, he lowered his voice.

'This Coolaroo business,' he said. 'Alan's very keen that it goes without a hitch. This is no time for disunity. You're pretty close to the ground out there. No one's got it into their heads to play funny buggers, I trust.'

'You know me, Daryl,' I shrugged. 'Nobody ever tells me anything.'

When I got to my cubicle in the Henhouse, a couple of phone message slips were waiting for me. I returned Ayisha's call first.

'Barry Quinlan's office called,' she reported. 'The senator would like a word at your earliest convenience. I imagine he wants us to organise a meet-and-greet for the soon-to-be member for Coolaroo.'

'You've heard?'

'Phil Sebastian?' she said. 'It's going through the grapevine like a dose of the salts.'

Phylloxera, I thought, or sap. That's what runs through grapevines. Not doses of salts. 'Mike Kyriakis? Any word there? Is he still planning on making a run?'

'Far as I know.'

'Do me a favour,' I said. 'Press your shell-like a bit closer to the terra firma. Find out if any other hopefuls are lurking in the woodwork.'

'Sounds like you've been promoted to boundary rider,' she said.

'Let's just say I like to keep abreast.'

Just as I hung up, the phone rang. It was the library.

'I've got your report,' said Pat. 'Do you want the summary or the full transcript?'

As I'd hoped, the files had not yet been returned to the Coroner's office. Even better, some included the evidence tendered at the inquest in addition to the finding itself. I told Pat I'd come straight over.

'We close in half an hour.'

'I'll read fast.'

But first I called Barry Quinlan's office. I flipped open my diary as I dialled, expecting one of his buffers to organise the meeting with Phil Sebastian. The buffer, it transpired, was Phil himself.

'Murray,' he cooed. 'Listen mate, I'm sorry I missed you at Charlie Talbot's funeral. It must have been a shocking experience, you being there when he, er, went and everything. I wanted to personally tell you how much everybody here appreciates the job you did with the arrangements.'

'Yeah, well,' I mumbled. 'It wasn't the best of days.'

'Anyway,' he moved right along. 'As you've probably heard by now, I'll be his replacement.' He managed to make it sound like an onerous but inescapable burden, one he'd agreed to shoulder out of duty. 'So Barry suggested we get together, the three of us, and have you brief me on some of the specifics of the demographic. He's in Sydney at the moment, Telecommunications matters, but he'll be back in Melbourne on Monday. How does ten-thirty sound, here at Barry's office?'

One time's as good as another when you're being taken

for granted. 'It's in the book,' I said, scribbling it into my diary. 'See you then.'

'Before you go,' he said quickly. 'This thing on Sunday at Broadford town hall. I was thinking it might be a good opportunity to meet some of the locals. And to pay my final respects, of course. Two birds with the one stone, so to speak.'

'*Broadmeadows*,' I said. The idea of him working the room at Charlie's wake was too appalling to contemplate. 'I can see where you're going, Gil. But Sunday'll be very much a family affair, know what I mean. Bit of a closed shop.'

'Point taken,' he said. 'Monday, then.'

We kissed goodbye, I hung up and headed over to the library. The weather had changed yet again. The wind had dropped and the cloud ceiling had lifted to a high grey sheen. To the west, beyond the office towers of the central city, it was breaking open to reveal clear skies. By the look of it, Red would get his hoped-for wheel-time. As I walked, I fished out my mobile and dialled the other call-back number on my list. It belonged to Charlie's electorate officer, Helen Wright.

Helen had been hit pretty hard by her boss's death. Not only because they'd been friends and workmates for many years, but also because she was now facing an uncertain future. Phil Sebastian owed her nothing and once he was securely installed, he'd probably dump her and use the job to buy some local personal loyalty. Such was the nature of political patronage, and Helen knew it.

She'd called, she explained, to ask my advice.

'You've heard about Phil Sebastian getting the guernsey, I take it? Thing is, he's been trying to get in touch with me. The electorate office is closed for the duration, so he's been leaving messages on my voicemail. He wants us to meet as soon as possible, and for me to line up some introductions with branch secretaries. And, get this Murray, he wants to come to the wake.'

Helen was not just a brick, but a mate. I'd do my best to steer her right.

'It's up to you, Helen,' I said. 'You can always lie low for the weekend, plead family matters or whatnot while you make up your mind what you want to do. As for the wake, I've already spoken with him about that.'

'What did you say?'

'I told him to fuck off.'

She laughed. 'Nah, you didn't. You're better brung up than that, Murray.'

Since she was on the line, I asked if she knew of any other possible contenders. She didn't, but she'd heard talk that Dursun Durmaz, a state lower house member whose seat also overlapped Coolaroo, had been sniffing around, asking the same question.

Durmaz was a Concord faction footsoldier, Turkish by birth and thicker than chick-pea dip. If the Metcalfe forces were using him as their watchdog, they obviously weren't expecting problems.

'See you Sunday,' I said, ringing off as I stepped through the back door of Parliament House.

Climbing the stairs to the library, I wondered if Durmaz, too, had been made an offer by Peter Thorsen. He wasn't the brightest bauble in the bazaar, but he was a political opportunist of the first water. If the tide was beginning to turn against Metcalfe, Durmaz would be among the first to jump ship.

Up in the library, Pat handed me the coroner's file and

pointed to the clock, a reminder that my time was limited. I pulled up an antique chair, flipped open the file and began to read.

Thirty minutes later, as arranged, I found Inky Donnelly waiting in Strangers Corridor, an elongated antechamber that served as a public restaurant area for Parliament House visitors. He was nursing a coffee, absently gnawing a shortbread as he studied that morning's *Australian*.

'Hold the presses,' I said. 'Breaking news in the Cutlett carcase case.'

Inky peered up at me, biscuit poised in mid-air, waiting.

'He's not dead,' I said.

Inky stubbed out his coffee and brushed the crumbs from his lapels, and we plunged into the entrails of Parliament House, weaving our way along corridors lined with portraits of forgotten politicians and bronze busts of colonial mugwumps.

As we steered for the rear exit, we were met at every turn by the hail-and-farewell of scarpering MPs, pub-bound young staffers and home-heading bureaucrats. Five-thirty on a Friday night and the joint was emptying faster than a pensioner's pocket at the pokies.

'Officially, Mervyn Cutlett is not dead,' I repeated. 'He is merely missing.'

Inky grunted impatiently. 'I've got that much,' he said. 'I'm not fucking senile, you know. What I'm asking is why the inquest?'

The sooner I got that glass of milk into the grumpy old codger the better.

'Normally, the proceeds of an estate can only be distributed on production of a death certificate. No corpse, no certificate.'

'No certificate, no probate.'

'Exactly,' I said. 'Only way to expedite execution of his will was have an inquest.'

'Who were the beneficiaries?'

We went out the back door into the carpark and I pointed my keys at the Magna. 'No idea,' I said. 'The family, presumably.'

Inky made a pained face, lowered himself into the passenger seat, popped an antacid and eased the seatbelt over his dyspeptic midriff. The boom gate rose and I turned towards Fitzroy, joining the line of cars backed up at the lights beside St Patrick's cathedral.

'The Coroner's verdict was death by misadventure,' I said. Inky gave a belch of relief. 'An interim finding,' I added, '*Pro tempore.*'

'*Coitus interruptus*, eh?'

'In theory, I suppose. But for all intents and purposes *consummatus est.*' The lights turned green and we inched forward. '*Per omnia secula seculorum.*'

'Let's hope so, Murray.' Inky eyed me sideways. 'Let's just fucking hope so.'

At any other time, Brunswick Street was a five-minute trip. Peak hour, the traffic was moving with all the urgency of a sedated sloth. To aggravate the situation, a fire engine emerged from the Eastern Hill fire station, sirens blaring. As I negotiated a stop-start crawl through the fray, I gave Inky the gist of the testimony in the coronial record.

The Benalla magistrate heard the case eight months after the event. Under oath, the witnesses confirmed their original statements to the police and answered detailed questions.

According to Charlie's testimony, the purpose of the weekend trip to the lake was to discuss work-related issues at the union's purpose-built country retreat. They travelled there in separate parties, making the three-hour trip from Melbourne in two cars, one driven by Charlie, the other by Quinlan.

Charlie and Merv got to the Shack about eleven-thirty in Charlie's union-issue Falcon. Barry Quinlan and Col Bishop arrived half an hour later in Quinlan's car. Sid Gilpin had been left behind, due to a mix-up about the departure time.

Immediately prior to leaving Melbourne, Merv had been drinking at the John Curtin Hotel. He was 'somewhat intoxicated' when Charlie picked him up at the Trades Hall. Charlie, who had not been drinking, did the driving. Merv slept for most of the trip. On arrival, they each had a can of beer, then several more when Quinlan and Bishop turned up at midnight. Before retiring for the night at one a.m., Merv took a nightcap of rum and cloves.

'Yum, yum.' Inky smacked his lips. 'The working man's all-purpose tonic.'

Cutlett woke the others about seven and proposed that they go out in the Shack's boat and catch some redfin for breakfast. Despite the cold and fog he insisted, claiming the conditions were perfect for fishing. Colin Bishop refused but 'for harmony's sake', as Charlie's testimony stated, the other two reluctantly agreed. Under Merv's direction, the boat was wheeled from the shed, launched and tied up at the Shack's short jetty. Merv consumed a 'phlegm cutter' of Bundaberg rum but appeared to be in full control of his faculties.

All three were dressed heavily against the cold and they took along a thermos of coffee laced with rum. Nobody wore life-jackets. Merv drove the boat, a 6.3 metre Catalina with a half-cabin canopy. Visibility on the water was poor, but Merv was familiar with the lake and navigated the boat confidently into an area some two hundred metres from the jetty, then stopped the motor and tied-off to a dead tree projecting from the water. They fished for around fifteen minutes without success before moving to another spot, again tying off to a tree. The fog began to rise and a heavily timbered section of the shoreline was visible, but neither Quinlan nor Charlie had a definite sense of their exact location.

After about twenty minutes, the fish still weren't biting and they had finished the coffee. Prompted by questions from the court officer assisting the Coroner, both Charlie and Quinlan stated that it contained 'a high proportion' of alcohol. The weather was rapidly becoming threatening and they decided to immediately return to the Shack. As Merv was casting off from the dead tree, a squall front hit. Torrential rain began to fall. As Merv hurried to untie the rope, the boat turned in the wind and he toppled overboard.

He thrashed wildly in the widening gap, the wind pushing the boat beyond his reach. Quinlan and Charlie tried to grab him, but he went under almost immediately. While Quinlan tried to get the boat started and bring it back around, Charlie jumped in and attempted to reach him but he'd disappeared beneath the surface. Charlie duck-dived, trying to find him, but his efforts were futile. The water was pitch black, lashed by the rain and freezing cold.

By the time Quinlan got Charlie back into the boat, he was shivering uncontrollably. They returned immediately to the Shack to get help. When they got there, they found that

Colin Bishop had been joined by Sid Gilpin, who had arrived while they were out on the lake.

Gilpin tried to ring for help, but the phone at the Shack was locked—standard procedure when the place wasn't in use—so he drove to the nearest roadhouse and raised the alarm. While this was happening, the other two helped Charlie out of his wet clothes and thawed him out in front of the fire.

A police constable on traffic patrol near Mansfield was directed to attend. On the way, he stopped off at the home of the regional State Emergency Services captain and within forty minutes there were six boats on the lake. They included the Catalina, which Gilpin had taken back out on his return from summoning help. Charlie and Quinlan gave fairly precise directions to the scene of the accident, but the wet and blustery conditions doomed search efforts to failure.

By the time the diving team arrived the next day, the worst was assumed. Efforts to locate the corpse were fruitless. Underwater visibility was zero and the compression ratios at that depth limited dive times to a matter of minutes. According to the officer in charge, there'd have been a better chance of winning Tattslotto than finding a body. Weighed down by clothing, lungs filled with water, it would soon discharge its gases and settle on the bottom, between five and fifteen metres down, depending on the precise location.

Citing alcohol and the absence of life-jackets as contributing factors, the magistrate handed down his interim verdict and consigned the case to the files.

'Straightforward enough,' summarised Inky. 'But it doesn't tell us why the cops want to get their hands on the Municipals' old records.'

We cleared the tangle of traffic and I cruised down Brunswick Street, scouting for a parking spot.

'Maybe this sensation-mongering jackal of the gutter press can shed some light on the subject,' I said, slowing as we neared our destination.

'Yeah but let's keep it under our hats for the moment,' said Inky. 'See what Valentine has to say about it first.'

Spotting an opening, I threw a U-turn in the face of an oncoming tram and snaffled a spot directly across the road from the Toilers Retreat.

In the five years since I'd moved from Fitzroy, its landmark strip of pubs, funky cafes, knick-knackeries, record stores, bookshops and kebab boutiques had continued to creep up the hill towards the city. With their usual eye to the revenue potential, Yarra Council had jacked up the parking meter fees and erected time-limit signs of such baffling complexity that a team of Philadelphia lawyers armed with atomic clocks would've been hard put to escape a ticket. I double-checked the sign and fed every coin I possessed into the meter.

The Toilers Retreat was buzzing with a boisterous Friday evening crowd. Young persons on heat, the weekend ahead, anticipation in the air. Over-loud music ratcheted up the drinking rate and pool balls clicked. Vic Valentine wasn't hard to identify. Apart from us, he was the only one in the joint over thirty.

He was tending a beer at a corner table, eye to the door. By way of identifying himself, he raised his chin.

The journalist was a spare, spindly type with a sharp-featured rodent face. His head, almost perfectly spherical, was shaved as clean as a burnished hazelnut. He wore a hairline moustache, a faint, self-deprecating smirk and a black leather motorcycle jacket. He was maybe forty.

'Fuck me,' muttered Inky. 'It's Zorro.'

I nodded towards Valentine's glass. He held it up. Beer, almost empty. Same again, thanks. While Inky elbowed his way to the bar, I went over, sat down and introduced myself. Valentine asked after my son and explained how he'd picked up on the Merv Cutlett connection. At the time of the drowning, he was a cadet, working general rounds at the *Herald*. One of the more senior journalists had covered the original search, but the discovery of the remains rang a bell when Valentine picked it up in the daily feed from police media relations.

Inky arrived with two beers and a Guinness, its foamy head as close as he was prepared to come to a glass of milk. '*Sláinte*,' he said.

We all took a convivial sip. Then Inky put his glass down, wiped the foam from his lip and leaned across the table towards Valentine. 'Ground rules,' he rasped. 'This conversation is strictly off the record. Background only.'

Valentine stared around, innocence itself. 'Noisy, isn't it? Can hardly hear myself think.'

That settled, we got down to it.

'What do you want to know?' I said. 'There's slim pickings in the Municipals for a crime reporter.'

'Maybe,' said Valentine. 'But if those bones turn out to be Mervyn Cutlett's, there might be a three-course banquet.'

He paused while Inky and I exchanged wary glances.

'Go on,' said the Ink.

Valentine took a sip. 'Two-way street,' he said. 'I'll show you mine if you show me yours.'

'Okay,' said Inky. 'Show.'

83

'You first,' said the journalist. 'What can you tell me about a bloke named Sid Gilpin?'

'He was one of the union's organisers,' I said.

'And what exactly did he organise?'

I shrugged. 'The usual stuff, I assume. Resolved minor workplace disputes. Liaised with the shop stewards. Kept an eye on membership subscriptions. Out and about, on the road, maintaining a presence.'

As I said it, I realised something that didn't quite gel. All the other organisers worked out of their respective state offices. Gilpin reported directly to Merv Cutlett. Whatever his job description, it wasn't on the organisational chart.

'Mate of yours?'

I made a noise like I'd swallowed a fly. 'Not my speed. I was mid-twenties. He was a fair bit older. One of the safari-suit squad. University of Life and don't you forget it, pal. He thought I was an over-educated, up-myself nancy boy.'

'How about him and Cutlett?'

'Thick as thieves, so to speak,' I said. 'Matter of fact, he was on the scene the day Merv drowned. The first to go out looking for him.'

Inky shot me a warning glance, reminding me not to get ahead of the game. 'What's your interest in this Gilpin, Vic?' he said.

'He rang me. Unsolicited. He said he'd heard of me, asked if I was aware of the recent discovery at Lake Nillahcootie. Flagged the name Cutlett. When I expressed interest, he claimed he had evidence that Cutlett was the victim of foul play.'

He took a long, slow sip, studying our reaction over the rim of his glass.

Inky snorted dismissively. 'What evidence?'

'Proof of corruption, he said. But he wouldn't go into specifics, not without being paid. Started talking telephone numbers. I told him it didn't work that way. If he had reason to believe a crime had been committed, he should go to the cops.'

I glanced at Inky. Could this explain the police visit to the Peaheads?

'And did he?' Inky pondered his Guinness. 'Go to the cops?'

'You'd have to ask them,' Valentine shrugged. 'I was hoping you might be able to shed some light on the subject.' He meant me. 'Any intimations at the time?'

The bar was getting noisier and more crowded by the minute, all elbows and belt buckles and tribal tattoos. I wondered why Valentine had chosen it.

'If there were, I never heard them,' I said. 'Which isn't to say there might not have been some pub talk. It was the seventies. Conspiracy theories were thick on the ground.'

Valentine took a tin of baby cigars out of his motorbike jacket, unwrapped one and tapped the end idly on the lid. 'And the Municipals were clean, you reckon?'

'As the driven?' I said. 'Maybe not, but the opportunities for graft were minor league. As for foul play, the idea's got whiskers all over it. The cops were there within minutes. There was a full-on search of the scene. Anything suss went down, somebody would've noticed something. And Gilpin testified at the inquest. He uttered not a peep about anything untoward.'

'Perhaps he found out later.'

'Perhaps he's pulling your chain.'

'Why would he bother?'

'Buggered if I know. He got the bum's rush from the

union soon after Cutlett's demise. Maybe he's been pining for revenge. Maybe he's just trying to hustle up a dollar.'

'Fishing in troubled waters?' said Valentine. 'Stirring up the mud?'

Inky grunted. 'Mud's got a tendency to stick. What's this Gilpin do now? Who does he work for?'

'He's a dealer.'

'Drugs?' I was genuinely surprised. Sid had chancer written all over him, but drugs were something else entirely.

'Junk.' Valentine smirked. 'Rubbish.'

He waved a demonstrative cigarillo at the Toilers Retreat's tone-setting collection of blue-collar nostalgia. Bushells Tea and Castrol Oil signs adorned the walls. An old Bundy clock stood on the bar. Toolbox assortments embellished the bottle shelves.

'He did quite well for himself in the eighties, I hear. He had a big old barn of a place up Upwey way. A former foundry or superseded smithy or some such. Stuffed it full of brass doorknobs, cast-iron lacework, Golden Fleece petrol bowser lights, all the usual crap. Called it a flea market and made a killing in Australiana.'

Sid would've been ideally placed to go into the junk business, I thought. The Municipals' members included garbage collectors and rubbish tip attendants. The Outcasts of Foolgarah. Gleaners and fossickers with their treasure troves of the cast-off and chucked-away. A man with Sid's connections could really clean up. Buying the stuff at fifty dollars a trailer-load, recycling it into instant authenticity and selling it for whatever the market would bear. Turning old tin into pure gold.

'About ten years ago, the joint burnt down,' Valentine continued. 'Suspected arson. Nothing proved but the insurance company wriggled out. Gilpin lost the lot. Lock, stock and Early Kooka. After that, everything turned to shit. Wife left him, children turned their backs, dog died. He hit the skids and hit the bottle. The whole country music ball of twine. These days, he's down to his uppers, flogging dross out of an old nissen hut across from the cargo sheds at Victoria Dock.'

I vaguely remembered a rusting wartime relic half lost in the eyesore industrial jungle between the wharves and the railyard.

'Has he tried to sell this so-called story to anyone else?' said Inky, back to the point.

'He spoke to some of my esteemed colleagues. We all told him the same thing. If you've got evidence, take it to the police.' Valentine shook his head, benignly amused at the human capacity for self-delusion. 'People read something in the paper, they start seeing dollar signs.'

'But you're not dismissing him out of hand,' said Inky. 'So either you've got a lot of free time or there's something you haven't got around to sharing with us.'

Valentine eyed me sideways. 'Is he always like this?'

'Dyspepsia,' I said. 'It makes him crabby as all hell.'

Valentine twiddled his Wee Willem. 'What happened to our quid pro quo?'

Inky picked up his stout, poured a long draught down his throat, wiped his mouth with the back of his hand and nodded.

'I've been given to understand the rozzers are making enquiries about the Municipals' old membership accounts,' he said.

Valentine was nonchalant, wheels turning in his hairless head. 'Interesting.'

'Is it?' said Inky. 'Why?'

The journalist made a show of mulling his response. Then he leaned forward and dropped his voice, drawing us into his huddle.

'Because it might tie into something else the boys in blue are keeping very close to their silver-buttoned chests. Something a little birdie told me about those remains.'

Inky and I leaned closer, elbows on the table, all ears.

'It's a dry argument.' Valentine sat back and surveyed the bottom of his glass. 'A man could perish.'

As I fought my way back through the press of bodies, crab-gripping three glasses, the corner of a bag of peanuts clenched between my teeth, my phone began to ring.

I let it ring off to voicemail and deposited my load.

Inky had gone for a slash, leaving Vic to hold the table. The journalist picked up his beer and nodded towards a guy coming through the door, a beefy young lump in a buzz cut and Cockney-crim pinstripe suit, tie loosened, eyes darting around the room like startled goldfish.

'My next appointment,' he said. 'Jason's in the wholesale pseudoephedrine business, or so it's been alleged in a slate of charges currently before the County Court. He's taking me to see a man about a dog. Or maybe it's vice versa.'

Jason spotted the journalist's chrome dome and began homing in. Vic flashed him ten fingers, buying us some time, and the speed-vending slugger veered off to join a group of hyperactive boyos who were hogging the pool table.

Inky returned, drying his hands on a handkerchief. 'So, Vic,' he said sceptically. 'You were saying?'

Valentine tore open the bag of Nobby's finest, laid them out on the table. 'You know the Institute of Forensic Medicine? AKA the morgue?'

I'd done the tour, part of some committee or other. The place was new, state-of-the-art, disaster-ready. It was housed in the same complex as the Melbourne Coroner's Court.

'Did they tell you about their in-house wireless communications network?'

I nodded, then explained to Inky. 'There's an internal radio link between the autopsy suites and the typing pool. By the time the pathologist has rinsed his scalpel and binned his gloves, a print-out of his notes is ready for checking and signature.'

Valentine moved his head forward, again drawing us into a conspiratorial hunch. 'That little birdie I mentioned, he's a technology buff. He's also a forensics fan. He likes to combine his two hobbies. He sits outside the Institute with a scanner and a set of earphones.'

He paused while we conjured the image.

'Sick, isn't it? I really should report him to somebody. But he's harmless enough and whenever he picks up a transmission he thinks might interest me, he gets straight on the blower. Which is what happened last week after they brought in the hessian sack from Lake Nillahcootie.'

Inky's eyes were growing less twinkly by the second.

'For what it's worth, I've got the tape,' continued Valentine. 'The examination is categorised as preliminary but what it boils down to is this. Only the larger bones remain—pelvis, thighs, upper arms, cranium. Reasonably well preserved considering the passage of time and the ravages of the creepy-crawlies. The owner was a mature male aged somewhere over fifty, approximately 170 centimetres tall with mild osteoporosis. Teeth in the upper jaw were long gone, indicating the corpse wore dentures.' He paused and flicked a peanut into his mouth. 'How are we doing so far?'

'Fits Mervyn Cutlett's general description,' I said. 'Shortish, right age group, probable chopper wearer.' Dentures were virtually standard issue for members of Merv's class and generation. You got a full extraction and a pair of clackers on your twenty-first birthday, save yourself further trouble and expense.

'Now here's the interesting bit,' said Valentine. 'Wear on some of the bones consistent with rope friction. Plus trauma to the parietal plate in the form of a circular perforation of approximately six millimetres diameter.'

He leaned low over the table, displaying the bare back of his depilated noggin. Using the tip of his miniature cigar, he gave it a sharp, demonstrative tap.

'Conclusion,' he said. 'He'd been tied up and shot in the back of the head.'

My eyes widened in disbelief. 'You've got to be kidding.'

I tore the parking ticket off my windscreen and read the penalty by the light of the lava lamp bubbling in the nearest shop window. Fifty bucks, straight down the toilet. Inky shovelled a handful of Quik-Eze into his face and grunted.

Across the street, outside the Toilers Retreat, I could see Vic Valentine getting into an illegally parked BMW, his dope-dealing informant Jason behind the wheel. 'It's extortion, pure and simple.' I squinted up at the four paragraphs of fine print on the parking sign.

The implications of Valentine's startling revelations about the pathology examination were still sinking in. They were alarming, unfathomable and as welcome as a prawn cocktail in a kosher deli.

'The whole idea's ludicrous,' I said. 'If the remains are really Merv Cutlett's, then Charlie Talbot and Barry Quinlan must've shot him and dumped the body in the lake.

Assisted by Colin Bishop. We've got two MPs and the pro vice-chancellor of a university guilty of murder and criminal conspiracy. It beggars belief. Did they kill him somewhere else? Did they lure him up to the Shack and do it? Did something happen while they were there that escalated? Where did they get a gun? Who pulled the trigger? It's patently absurd.'

Inky nodded. 'You don't kill somebody over a union amalgamation,' he pointed out. 'No matter how tempting.'

Which was what we'd told Vic Valentine when he dropped his bombshell. And he admitted that it did seem an unlikely scenario. Fortunately, for the moment at least, he wasn't actively pursuing the story. For a start, the pathology report wasn't publishable, given its provenance. And the remains were yet to be definitely identified as Cutlett's. Matters were now in the hands of the Homicide Squad and he was content to let the story play itself out before writing it up.

Meantime, he had the imminent outbreak of a gang war to occupy his attention. The Beamer peeled away and we watched it disappear down the street.

'What do you think Gilpin's playing at?' I said, pocketing the poxy parking infringement notice.

Inky's mind was elsewhere. 'I think it might be a good idea if you had a word with Barry Quinlan,' he said.

'Me?' I asked. 'Why me?'

He crunched his antacid and gave a choleric scowl. 'Me and Bazza aren't exactly Bogie and Bacall. It's a long and tedious story dating from the Hawke–Keating showdown. Suffice to say, I wouldn't get through the door.'

'Yeah, well,' I said grudgingly. 'So happens I'll be seeing Quinlan on Monday. You think it can wait until then?'

'It's been waiting for nearly twenty years, it can wait

another couple of days. No point getting our underwear in an uproar. Like the man said, it's still provisional.'

'If this is what it looks like…'

'If this is what it looks like, it's going to be the shitstorm from hell. We don't want to find ourselves anywhere near it.' He held out his arm and a taxi pulled up. 'You hear anything else, let me know.'

And on that less-than-illuminating note, the leprechaun climbed into the cab and fucked off, leaving me holding the crock. And it most definitely wasn't full of gold.

The street was coming alive with dreadlocks, pierced appendages and ravenous vegans. I fished out my mobile and called Red. The lad was at home, divesting the refrigerator of its remnant leftovers before heading to a farewell party. His mate Tarquin was flying out on Sunday for six months' study in Japan.

'Say sayonara from me,' I instructed. 'Don't get wasted. Don't take any of my beer. And be home by one-thirty.'

'Are we still on for the driving thing tomorrow?' he said. 'The weather report says fine and mild.'

'We'll see,' I said. 'But all bets are off if you're not home before curfew.'

I checked my voicemail. I got the last caller first.

'This is Detective Constable Stromboli, Mr Whelan,' said a male voice. 'Homicide Squad. If you get this message before eight, please call me back this evening.'

By ten to eight, I was at the northern limits of the Coolaroo federal electorate, out where the tract housing finally gave way to market gardens, stud farms, small wineries, golf courses and bare paddocks. Tullamarine Airport was ten minutes behind me, a phosphorescent glow in my rear-vision mirror.

The house stood at the end of a gravel driveway, both sides planted with rows of vines, a curtain of natives shielding it from the road. As I turned off the asphalt at the letterbox marked TALBOT–FOLLBIG, my headlights swept the outbuildings.

First the old dairy shed in which Charlie turned his minuscule *vendage* into Chateau Coolaroo, a quaffing red guaranteed to put fur on the tongues of his Christmas list of friends, colleagues and constituents. Then a triple carport, swathed in Virginia creeper, where his maroon Lexus was parked beside Margot's Audi and a little red Mazda 323 that

I assumed belonged to the young woman who looked after Margot's daughter Katie. And finally the chateau itself, low, sprawling and unostentatious, the brick of the original homestead rendered in whitewash.

Katie heard my car arrive. She was waiting behind the screen door, her chubby face beaming.

'Mum, Mum,' she called. 'It's Muh-ree.'

I waited for her to open the screen, knowing she liked to do it herself. She was almost thirty, stocky in a dusty-pink tracksuit, with the slanting, ageless eyes that announce Down Syndrome.

'Hello, Katie.'

As I stepped inside, I touched the back of her plump hand. She went shy, blushed and gave me a disconcertingly coquettish look. I followed her rolling gait into the living room, a welcoming space with muted lighting, soft cushion-strewn couches and a large refectory table from which Margot rose to meet me.

Her eyes were tired, her face was scrubbed and her ash blonde hair was drawn tight behind her ears but she was still easily recognisable as one of Mavis Peel's girls from the FUME office. The original Charlie's Angels, the big-hair brigade.

'Murray,' she said. 'Good to see you.'

We hugged gently, motionless in each other's embrace. Television sounds came low from somewhere deeper inside the house and Katie's carer appeared.

'Hello, Sarah,' I said, remembering the girl's name. She was a serious young insect with bobbed hair and glasses, a part-time student who lived in a self-contained flat attached to the house.

'Hi,' she said. 'C'mon, Katie. Let's say goodnight to Mr Dobbs.'

They disappeared, off to the stall where Katie's elderly pony was stabled.

Between them, Charlie and Margot had done well. Their pooled resources had funded a comfortable set-up and Margot would never need to worry about money. But it had been a struggle for her, especially in the early years. A single mother, a disabled child, no formal education past secretarial school. And now what? Picking up the pieces, facing the future alone, the material comforts scant compensation.

'Help yourself to a drink,' she said, sliding open one of the glass doors onto the flagged patio that overlooked the side lawn. 'Let's have a fag.'

There was an open bottle of white on the table beside a heap of unopened envelopes. I got a glass from the usual cupboard.

We stood, wine in hand, smoking and staring into the darkening space where they'd pitched the marquee that summer day, eight years earlier, when she and Charlie finally tied the knot.

'How's Katie taking it?' I said.

'She's still waiting for him to come home, I think. It's all a bit much for her to grasp.' Margot exhaled hard and sucked her cheeks, holding herself back. 'I think I'm still waiting, too. But that's normal, isn't it?'

A dead partner, that was something else we had in common.

'You never really get used to it,' I said. 'But you get on with it.'

'I'm sorry,' she said. 'It's just...' The sentence trailed off and silence hung between us, more expressive than words.

She abruptly extinguished her cigarette, screwing it into a terracotta pot-plant saucer on the heavy redwood garden table. 'You'll stay for dinner, I hope.' She started back inside. 'I've got a lot of casseroles need eating.'

The refrigerator was stacked with funerary meats. Gestures of sympathy in plastic tubs and floral pattern Corningware, the offerings of neighbours, friends and constituents. A fortnight's supply at least.

'Got any tuna mornay?' I scanned the collection. 'Apricot chicken?'

'Don't be mean,' tutted Margot. 'You'll eat what you're given and you'll like it. Open another bottle while I heat something up.'

She blitzed some condolence stew in the microwave and we sat at the big refectory table and poked at it. I asked about her plans.

'Back to work,' she said. 'Everyone's been wonderful, of course. Staff, clients, everybody. But the place won't run itself. Or maybe it will, which would be even worse.'

She owned a travel business, Fliteplan. A niche outfit with three staff in the Melbourne office and two in Sydney. Together with Prue, the other typist at the Municipals, she'd set it up when the amalgamation made them redundant. Charlie helped arrange finance, making good on his promise that he'd see everyone right. With their experience of organising travel for FUME officials and their contacts among the women who did likewise at other unions, the pair soon had a thriving operation. They broadened out into the corporate sector and by the late eighties they were doing well enough for Prue to sell her half to Margot and take early retirement.

'So, you're not tempted to pack it in?' I said.

'And do what?' She swept the air with the back of her hand. 'Revive my career as an international supermodel?'

I shrugged. 'Something different.'

'Maybe,' she conceded. 'Eventually. But it's not something I want to think about right now.'

'No, no,' I said. 'Of course not.'

She gave me a reassuring smile. 'How's your goulash?'

'Rubbery,' I said. 'Dericious.'

'Gina Schiavoni's tiramisu might be a safer bet.'

I ate two helpings and made some coffee to finish off. While it was perking I asked if she was going to the wake. She shook her head firmly. That side of Charlie's life was now a closed book. 'But tell them thanks for all the support,' she said.

The bottle I'd opened with the alleged goulash was almost empty. Margot was out-drinking me, two to one.

'Snort of port with your coffee?' she said.

'Better not. Run into a booze bus on the way home, it's more than my job's worth.'

Katie came through the archway leading to the bedrooms. She had Sarah by the hand, as if for moral back-up.

'We've come to say goodnight,' announced Sarah. 'Say goodnight, Katie.'

Katie blushed furiously. 'Goodnight, Muh-ree,' she declared, then scuttled away with the ambivalent finality of a woman terminating an over-long engagement.

While Margot went off for the bedtime ritual, I took a cup of coffee outside for a smoke. After a few minutes, she joined me once more on the terrace. I nodded towards the lawn, a rectangle of deep darkness where the lights of the house bled out into the night.

'You were like a couple of teenagers that day,' I said. 'Prancing around the dancefloor, that god-awful cover band playing old Buddy Holly tunes.'

'Teenagers?' she snorted. 'Hardly.'

'Okay, thirtysomethings.'

'That's better. Barefaced flattery, but closer to the mark.'

She lit a cigarette and tapped the ash on the edge of the terracotta saucer. I screwed my courage to the sticking point.

'I don't know if you heard about it,' I started, 'but they found part of a skeleton up at Nillahcootie. The lake's been drained apparently, some sort of maintenance work. They're still working on the ID, but it looks like it might be Merv Cutlett.'

'So I understand,' she nodded. 'As a matter of fact, the police came to see me this afternoon about it. A man and a woman. Plainclothes. They were very nice, sorry to intrude at a time like this and all that. They asked if Charlie had told me much about the accident. They're trying to get a more precise picture of exactly what happened. To help with the identification, they said.'

She inhaled deeply, as if catching her breath, and looked upward towards the faint engine roar of a northbound plane. Its wingtip lights were pulsing pinpricks of red in the encompassing void of the sky.

'I don't think I was much help. Charlie never really spoke about it, not back then and not after we got together properly. I think he felt guilty.'

'Why would he feel guilty?'

'You know what Charlie was like,' she said. 'Probably blamed himself, thought he should have done more.'

The moon was rising, a pale crescent above the raked vines. Margot shivered slightly and wrapped her arms around herself.

'Did they know you were working at the Municipals when the accident happened?'

'They didn't say. I was Margot Barraclough back then, of course.'

I knew the story. Barraclough was Katie's father's name. When she fell pregnant, Margot had told her parents they were married. She and Barraclough had gone their separate ways by the time the child was born, but Margot continued with the pretence. It was only when she was starting the travel business that she went back to Follbig, her maiden name.

'It's just that I've had a message to call them,' I said. 'I think they might be doing the rounds of anyone who was at the union at the time.'

Margot furrowed her brow. 'Why?'

'You remember Sid Gilpin?'

'Oh yes,' she said. Her tone made it clear she remembered him only too well.

'Thing is, he's bobbed up in the wake of these remains, trying to flog some yarn about corruption at the union.'

She turned to me, fierce. 'That little weasel. He's not saying Charlie was corrupt is he?'

I patted the air, a mollifying gesture. 'So far nobody's taking him seriously. But Charlie not being here to defend himself, you never know what kind of bullshit might find its way into circulation.'

'The union was a long time ago.' Her voice had taken a flinty edge. 'But I'll tell you one thing for sure. If I ever hear anyone cast the slightest doubt on Charlie Talbot's honesty, I'll wring his neck, so help me. Charlie was the finest, most ethical man I ever met. He could've had me anytime he wanted. An affair, anything, and he knew it. But he was married to Shirley. He'd made his vows and he kept them. Never so much as touched me until he was a free man, more's the pity. You think somebody like that is going to put his hand in the till for a few dollars? Sid Gilpin wasn't fit to tie his bootlaces.'

I sat there, abashed, until the heat went out of her.

'I'm sure it'll all blow over, Margot,' I said. 'I just thought you should know, that's all.'

She sighed wearily, then reached over and squeezed my forearm. 'I know, Murray,' she nodded. 'I'm sorry.'

She took her hand away and used it to brush her eyes. Then she stood and gathered up my cup, her glass and the ashtray.

'Anyway,' she said. 'It wasn't Buddy Holly. It was Chuck Berry.'

'It wasn't Jimi Hendrix,' I said. 'That's for sure.'

She walked me to the front door, pausing on the way to press a Pyrex dish of non-specific pasta bake into my hands.

'If there's anything,' I said. 'Anything at all.'

'I know.' She smiled tightly. 'I know.'

We embraced again. This time, she seemed as fragile as a sparrow. And when I stood at the car door and waved back at her, framed there in the doorway, she looked brittle enough to snap in half.

At six the next morning, I tossed back an orange juice and laced up my trainers.

Twice a week for three years, I'd risen in the dark to drive Red to rowing, then run for thirty minutes on a treadmill in the gym at the City Baths, reading the newspapers while I jogged. It wasn't much but at least I was making an effort. After Red switched from dipping his oar to treading the boards, I slipped out of the habit of regular exercise. Another winter of puddings and gravy and my decline would be irreversible.

It was do or die. I went out the back gate and began thumping down the path to the river.

A heavy dew had fallen and the lawns were dark and sodden, still untouched by the pearly tinge spreading from the eastern horizon. By the time I reached the bottom of the slope, my lungs were raw and I was dizzy from exertion. Where the grassy slope ended and the path entered the trees,

I stopped for a second to catch my breath.

On the high ground across the river, the old lunatic asylum was taking shape against the dawn sky. It, too, would soon be luxury apartments. A waste, I thought, what with madness on the rise.

I jogged for half an hour, easing my body back into the groove. As I ran, I thought about the scraps that had blown across my path the previous day. Politics abhors a vacuum, and Charlie Talbot's death had created one. Ambition was being sucked in from all directions. And despite myself, I could feel the inexorable tug.

It was a dead-set certainty that we'd lose the next state election. If we were lucky enough to win the one after that, I'd have spent ten years in opposition. Even if I entered government as a junior minister, I'd be shin-deep into my fifties, my future behind me. It wasn't an encouraging prospect. On the other hand, I wasn't exactly spoiled for choice, career-wise. After a lifetime in politics, I was ruined for useful work.

And then there was the business of the Nillahcootie bones and Sid Gilpin's mischief-making. Having slept on it, I was even more convinced that I'd been slipped a tinfoil sixpence. The remains might not even be Merv's. Even if they were, there could be any number of explanations for the hole in his head. And anyway, Sid Gilpin had no credibility. The coppers would soon have it sorted.

The day was shaping up as forecast, the opening act of what might be the last weekend of fine weather before the onset of winter.

As I staggered through the back door, aching in unaccustomed places, a girl was coming out of the bathroom. She was bleary-eyed and tousled and creeping softly so as not to wake anybody. Glancing back down the passage, she noticed me, gave a little wave and let herself out the front door.

Her name was Polly, or perhaps Molly, or Milly. She was one of Red's school friends, part of the gang. Her parents, if I remembered right, were both medicos of some kind.

Red had arrived home just after midnight, a small entourage in tow. He'd stuck his head around the bedroom door, found me reading and we'd made our goodnights. Around one-fifteen, my sleeping ears registered muffled shushes and heavy-footed tip-toes at the front door. Evidently, not all of Red's visitors had departed at that point.

By the time he emerged from the Stygian gloom of his bedroom, I'd showered, donned my Country Road casuals, breakfasted and almost finished working my way through the weekend broadsheets. It was pushing nine and he was running late for the train that would get him across town to the Knitting Mill Youth Theatre.

'All systems are go for your driving lesson,' I said, watching him simultaneously inhale a muesli bar, fall into his clothes, brush his hair, find his travel card and grab his script. 'I'll pick you up at one, okay?'

He nodded enthusiastically, gave me the thumbs up and rushed out the door. I checked the number on my voicemail and rang DC Stromboli.

'Thanks for getting back so promptly, Mr Whelan,' he said. 'We're attempting to identify some human remains recently found at Lake Nillahcootie which may possibly be those of Mervyn Cutlett, the former secretary of the municipal employees' union. In the course of our enquiries, we're seeking the assistance of a number of people who used to work for the union. Is there a convenient time in the next few days for me to ask you a few questions?'

'Fire away, Constable.'

'I'd prefer to speak with you in person, if possible.'

He didn't need to explain how he knew that I'd worked at the Municipals. I'd had enough dealings with the law over the years, not least during the business with Lyndal and matters arising, to warrant an entry in the police database. A keyword search of the union would've thrown up my name. Not everybody who worked there would be quite so easy to track down, I suddenly realised. Which possibly explained the police interest in the old union records.

'Your place or mine?' I said. 'Whichever you prefer. I'll be catching up with some paperwork at my electorate office between ten and twelve this morning if that's convenient for you.'

It was. I gave him the address and rang off.

Larder, refrigerator and cellar were all looking wan, so I ducked into Safeway on the way to the office. As instructed, Red had refrained from nicking off with my last half-dozen cans of beer. He'd simply invited his friends home to consume them *in situ*. I made a mental note to dock his allowance and give him a sound thrashing. Just as soon as I'd interrogated him about his overnight guest.

I'd made some work-related calls and shuffled some paper around my desk by the time Detective Constable Stromboli knocked on my door around eleven-thirty.

He was younger than he sounded on the phone. A tall, solid man with close-cropped hair that was starting to whiten, he wore his suit like he still trying to get the hang of it.

'Robert Stromboli,' I said. 'I did wonder about the name. You're the bastard cost us the 1985 semi-final, aren't you?'

A Robbie Stromboli had played three seasons with Collingwood in the early to mid eighties, one of those patchy footballers who has his occasional dazzling moment, then fades away. Stromboli's flash of glory happened when he snatched the ball from the pack at the first bounce of the 1985 semi, went through the Fitzroy backline like cod-liver oil and booted it straight between the big ones. Twenty seconds, go to whoa. We stayed behind for the rest of the game.

'I did my bit,' he said. 'But I can't claim credit for the entire thirty-seven-point margin.'

'You broke our spirit,' I said, extending my hand. 'Come in, Detective Constable, tell me how I can be of assistance.'

He gave me a brief pump and a resigned, collegial look. The sooner we get this nonsense out of the way, the sooner we can get back to our proper work. The manner was relaxed but the shake was all copper.

'I won't keep you long, Mr Whelan,' he said, settling into my visitors' chair and taking out a small notebook. 'If we could begin with a brief outline of your history and duties at the union and the extent of your contact with Mr Cutlett.'

I obliged, trying to keep it succinct. He nodded along and made a few scribbles.

'Do you happen to know if Mr Cutlett wore a wrist-watch?' he said.

I thought for a moment and answered truthfully. 'Can't say I ever noticed.'

The detective took an envelope from his jacket pocket and handed me two Polaroids.

'Anything here jog your memory?'

The photos showed a yellow-metal watch, front and back views.

'A number of items were found in the vicinity of the remains,' explained Stromboli. 'Buttons, some one and two cent coins, but this was the only personal object. We're hoping somebody might recognise it.'

It was a sports watch, a thing of winders and knobs and subdials. The clasp-lock band was undone and the hands were stopped at 11:17. Seiko Sports Chronometer, read the name on the face. Limited Edition.

'Still under warranty?' I said. 'It says "Guaranteed waterproof to 60 metres".'

Stromboli smiled. 'It's a knock-off.'

I studied the Polaroids carefully. The watch face had a distinctive rotating bezel, day and date, and an alarm function, but it didn't ring any bells. I shook my head and handed back the snaps. 'I thought it was all DNA and whatnot these days.'

'In the works.' Stromboli pocketed the Polaroids. 'But it takes time. We're still in the process of locating family members.'

The sentence ended on an interrogative note. I shook my head again. Sorry, couldn't help there either.

'Meanwhile, it's old-fashioned methods,' he said, the footslogger who'd copped the door-knocking job.

'But you're pretty sure it's Merv Cutlett?'

He crossed his legs, keeping it conversational. 'On the balance of probabilities, it seems likely. The only other reported disappearance in that area was a child who drowned back in the sixties. The nature of the remains rules that one out.'

He consulted his notebook, flipped some pages then asked if there was anybody else connected with the union who I thought might be able to assist. 'Interstate officials and so forth?'

I thought for a moment and gave him some names. Three of them were still involved in union and public affairs. One worked for an employer organisation. Stromboli noted the names and details.

'I assume you've talked to Barry Quinlan and Colin Bishop,' I said.

He nodded. 'It's a pity we can't speak with Mr Talbot, who was also there at the time,' he said. 'I understand that you had a close relationship with him over a number of years. Did you ever talk about the incident?'

I put my elbow on the desk, rested my chin on my balled fist and had a think.

'Not that I can bring to mind,' I said, eventually. 'I was well down the union totem pole. Our friendship developed later. By then, we'd both moved on a fair distance and the subject never came up.'

'How did Cutlett get along with his associates, the ones at the lake the day he disappeared?' He consulted his notebook. 'Colin Bishop?'

'They had a reasonable working relationship, far as I know.'

'Charles Talbot? Barry Quinlan?'

'Likewise.'

'I understand that there was a degree of friction in the union.'

Understood from where, I wondered? 'Friction?'

'Cutlett was a bit of prick, wasn't he?'

I had to laugh. 'Obstreperous, let's say. And, yes, there were differences of opinion concerning the direction of the union. Management issues. Nothing of a personal nature, if that's what you're getting at.'

'And the assistant secretary, Sid Gilpin?'

'Gilpin wasn't assistant secretary,' I corrected him. 'That's an elected position. Gilpin was a sort of personal assistant. I wasn't privy to their relationship.'

He scribbled something in his pad. 'One last question, Mr Whelan. Were you ever at the union place up at Lake Nillahcootie?'

'The Shack?' I said. 'Afraid not, Constable. The decadent pleasures of Lake Nillahcootie were the preserve of the elect, not minions like *moi*.'

The detective pocketed his notebook, uncrossed his legs and stood up. 'Thank you for your time, Mr Whelan.' He indicated the clutter on my desk. 'I'll leave you to it.'

I showed him to the door and waved him off, hoping I'd played it right.

Stromboli wasn't giving anything away, which was only to be expected. But our little chat had raised more questions than it answered, at least for me.

There'd been no mention of the forensics, for a start. Was that because they'd arrived at a different explanation from the one Vic Valentine was trying out? Something a bit less melodramatic?

The questions about relationships within the union, on the other hand, didn't seem relevant to ID-ing the remains. So were the cops going with the shooting scenario, but still not showing their hand? Were they looking for a possible motive?

And the watch. What the hell was that about?

It was true I'd never noticed if Merv wore a timepiece. But I was damned sure of one thing. If he had, it wouldn't have been a flashy chunk of tomfoolery like that boy-bangle in the Polaroids.

Merv was the sort of bloke who wore a cardigan with his suit. For special occasions, he might've had a Timex Oyster self-winder with an expandable strap. Day-to-day wear was more likely to have been a Casio digital one-piece with a black plastic band. Merv, to strain a threadbare metaphor, wouldn't have been seen dead in a Seiko Sports Chronometer with stopwatch, day/month calendar and phases of the moon.

So who did the watch belong to?

I slid back my cuff and examined my own timepiece. It was ordinary but accurate. The time had arrived, it told me, to extract my digit.

Red's grip loosened a notch and the blood flowed back into his knuckles. We both heaved a sigh of relief as the massive semi-trailer moved further ahead of us, taking its buffeting slipstream with it.

'Speed,' I said.

Red flicked a glance at the dash, checked the rear-view mirror, eased back on the accelerator and turned his head just far enough to give me a wide smile. Pilot to co-pilot. So far so good.

The first half-hour had been stressful, both of us anxious during his neophyte negotiation of the cross-town traffic. Still, I thought, anxious was good. Better than overconfident. When I proposed a spin up the Hume, some open-road motoring, he'd jumped at the chance. Now that we were on the dual carriageway, he was cruising, pace steady, alert but not alarmed, enjoying himself. There was even scope for conversation.

'So what's this play about?' I said. 'Rosybum and Goldenpants Are Deadshits?'

'*Rosencrantz and Guildenstern Are Dead*, by Tom Stoppard,' he said. 'You know *Hamlet*?'

'Not personally. But I'm familiar with the type. Chronic existential indecision interspersed with fits of violent rage. You see a lot of it in my line of work. You're drifting into the emergency lane.'

He corrected his steering. 'Well, this is a play about the play within the play.'

This Stoppard geezer should be writing for the Labor Party, I thought. Red took a hand off the wheel for a second and jerked his thumb back over his shoulder, indicating the dog-eared script on the back seat.

'Hear me my lines,' he said. 'I was fluffing big time at the walk-through.'

'Hands at ten-to-two,' I said sternly. 'Stay in the left lane, no faster than eighty, and watch out for dickheads. We're in the country now.' Bypassing Kilmore to be precise, seventy kilometres north of town. Not exactly the mulga, but you can't be too careful once the houses run out. 'And no fluffing in the car.'

I flipped through the script, a mass of scribbled annotations and post-it notes.

'Tell me again, which one are you?'

'The Player.'

'Ah, yes,' I said. 'Which reminds me. That little friend of yours I noticed leaving the familial premises at the crack of dawn. Ellie? Polly? Molly?'

'Madeleine,' he said. 'Maddie.'

'I knew it was something like that. The point being, is this something serious?'

'Or what?' he said. 'Am I just using her for sex?'

'Well, are you?'

'Maybe she's just using me.' He eyed me sideways. 'Are you giving me the third degree?'

'That comes later,' I said. 'For the moment I'm simply exercising some natural parental interest in your activities.' Jesus, I thought. Listen to yourself. You'll be talking about your roof next, insisting on your right to know what goes on under it. 'You're being careful, I hope.'

'I won't knock her up, if that's what you mean.'

I winced at his bluntness. But Red's age-group had been raised on condoms, so to speak. If nothing else, AIDS had reconnected sex and consequences, two concepts my generation thought it had sundered forever. But it wasn't the idea of an unwanted pregnancy that worried me as much as the prospect that he'd mistake the ride for the destination. That what began as a fumble on the futon would end with a stomped-on heart. His.

'Abstinence has a lot to recommend it,' I said.

'The voice of experience?' He put his hand on the indicator lever and checked me sideways for the go-ahead to pass a puttering tractor.

I cleared him to overtake. 'The old dog's got life in him yet.'

'Yeah?' Red did the Groucho eyebrow dance. 'Anyone I know?'

We were going places I'd rather avoid. As we swept around the Massey Ferguson, I gave the driver a cheery wave. The constipated old cockie ignored me. Probably a One Nation supporter. Didn't he know tractors aren't allowed on the freeway?

'I'm glad we had this little chat, son. I'll reassure

Madeleine's parents next time I see them.'

Red moved back into his lane. 'They don't mind.'

Oh well, great then. Clearly, I was the last to know. As usual. I flipped through the pages. 'So where do we start?'

'Page 17, half-way down. You're Rosencrantz.'

The place was marked. '*What's your line?*' That was the line.

'*Tragedy, sir,*' declaimed the young Olivier. '*Death and disclosures, universal and particular, denouements both unexpected and inexorable…*'

The speedo was creeping towards ninety. 'Ease back a little,' I instructed.

'No, it's supposed to be hammy,' he said. 'I'm in character.'

By the time we were shot of Elsinore, he'd been behind the wheel for two hours straight and we were almost in Benalla.

'Need a break?'

He gave his head a vigorous shake. Nothing short of a crowbar would've got him out of the driver's seat. 'Then hark us hence homeward via the scenic route, what sayeth thou?'

'Aye, my lord.'

We turned south along the Midland Highway, two lanes of blacktop that curved through open, rolling farmland and scrubby bush, double lines for long stretches. The traffic was light, but the driving took all of Red's concentration.

We were coming back over the hump of the Divide. The Strathbogies lay to our right and the peaks of the High Country reared distantly to our left, bare bouldery shapes emerging from thick timber. The radio commentary had the Lions down 51–77 and the weather was looking iffy. The sky had turned from high and hazy to low and broody. I was splitting for a piss.

'Pull in here,' I said. 'We'll stretch our legs and I'll spell you for a while.'

Red eased it back nicely and turned into the landscaped picnic area at the Lake Nillahcootie weir. I directed him along an unpaved track between some big shade trees until we reached the high-water mark.

'Wow,' he said. 'Somebody pulled the plug.'

The bare bottom of the lake sloped away to dark, wind-rippled water at the sheer concrete cliff of the dam wall. The waterline reached no more than a quarter of the way up the 25-metre embankment, leaving the spillways at each end gaping uselessly, high and dry.

The water extended for half a kilometre or so, then narrowed to an elongated tadpole-tail that snaked away across the exposed lake-bed. An intermittent picket of long-dead trees marked its path. Those closer were footed in water, the more distant fully exposed.

We got out and drained our personal reservoirs against the trunk of a big redgum. No call for modesty. We had the place to ourselves.

'Let's check out the weir,' I said.

Access to the dam wall was barred by the chained gate of a cyclone fence. The construction camp was locked down, its cluster of Porta-sheds and heavy equipment deserted for the weekend. YOUR TAXES AT WORK, read the sign. KEEP OUT.

'So, Dad,' said Red. 'What are they doing?'

Once upon a time, I'd been a policy advisor to the Minister for Water Supply, so I was able to give him the benefit of my expertise.

'Buggered if I know,' I said. 'But I guarantee it's both

necessary and expensive.' Necessary, most likely, to the ongoing job security of the local National Party member. Expensive in that it cost a packet.

The weir had been thrown across a choke-point where the Broken River narrowed to a gorge. From the footpath above, we looked down into the rocky cleft, thick with trees and undergrowth. The clouds were glowering and the wind, heavy with the smell of rain, was rattling the treetops. I didn't know why I was there.

We went back to the car. I slid the driver's seat forward a notch and drove further along the highway, its course running parallel to the elongated bed of the lake. Trees marked the far shoreline, a kilometre away, thinning to pasture. The situation at the MCG had not improved, 64–91 at three-quarter time.

'A bloke I knew was killed out there,' I said. 'A couple of years before you were born.'

'How?'

Good question.

'Fell out of a boat while they were fishing. He'd been drinking and he wasn't wearing a life-jacket.'

'Let that be a lesson, young man.'

''ken oath,' I said.

The Shack, in whatever form it now took, lay somewhere on the far side, invisible up a short inlet formed by the undulations of the terrain. The inquest papers I'd scanned in the Parliament House library included a sketch map of the lake showing the location of the Shack and the spot where Cutlett was last seen. A photocopy would've been handy but I hadn't thought to make one. Why would I?

'They never recovered the body,' I said. 'But about ten days ago a couple of blokes found bits of a skeleton while they were poking around out there, looking for old stuff.'

'Yeah?' Red was interested. 'Where?'

'Let's have a squizz,' I said, 'see if we can work it out.'

The road and the lake diverged, separated by a low rise capped with a cluster of buildings surrounded by trees. A school camp, some sort of private religious college. Just past it, a weathered sign announced BARJARG ROADHOUSE 300M, the paint peeling. An unpaved side road led back towards the lake. I turned down it and found the claypan again.

Despite the general dryness of the season, Melbourne had seen two rainy days and a smattering of intermittent showers since the middle of the previous week. Up here, it had possibly been even wetter. In any case, it was impossible to miss the churned-up margin and the deep ruts running about two hundred metres out towards a cluster of bleached tree-trunks and a string of shallow pools.

'Over there,' Red pointed. 'See the bits of plastic tape?'

The ground was gouged open and the tracks included deep caterpillar treads. I wondered what sort of equipment the police had brought in to sift the sludge.

'Looks like they did a pretty thorough job of trying to find all his bits and pieces,' I said.

I tried to conjure up a mental picture of the Coroner's sketch map. If I had it right, the Shack was somewhere in the trees beyond the fence line where the edge of the cleared paddocks ran ruler-straight to the shoreline. But Charlie and Barry had certainly got their geography skewiff. The place they reported losing Merv was a good five hundred metres closer to the dam wall. The search had been concentrated in the wrong area.

I cruised along the road another couple of hundred metres, hunting for the turn-off to the Shack. A well-maintained road led in the right direction but it was barred by a locked gate. Private Property. Trespassers Prosecuted. Cows lifted their heads and loped towards the fence. I turned the car around and we went back to the highway.

The Barjarg Roadhouse was somewhere between picturesque and primordial, a weatherboard throwback that looked like it had been erected to cater to the passing bullock-dray trade. In front of a bull-nosed veranda enclosed by expanding garden trellis, the petrol bowsers stood naked on a raw dirt apron. The only concession to amenity was an arbour at the side, an outdoor eating area roofed in shade cloth with a tan-bark floor, two pine-log tables and a green wheelie bin.

'If we can't get a sausage roll here,' I said, 'I'll eat my socks.'

'If I don't get something into me soon,' Red replied, '*I'll eat your socks.*'

The interior was a dim, lino-floored general store whose main lines were apparently fishing tackle, dust and jumbo tins of Pal. A man in a faded flannel shirt with a beer gut and a head like a pontiac potato sat on a stool behind the counter, talking to a man in a faded flannel shirt with a beer gut and a head like a glaucomic wombat. Strangers to the service economy, they ignored us.

I peered across the counter at the pie warmer. Its solitary sosso roll looked like it had been smuggled through customs in a body cavity. 'See if they've got any chocolate-coated socks,' I told Red.

We hunted up a late lunch of BBQ crisps and lolly water and piled our selections on the counter. Flannel-back number one broke off his riveting monologue about what he'd told Kev about Brian's attitude to Goose for long enough to ring up the damage. $7.85. I took a five out of my wallet, emptied my pants pocket onto the counter and sifted through my small change for correct weight. Red gathered up the comestibles and went out to the car.

I caught up with him as he was opening the driver's-side door. The little bugger had snaffled my keys. 'Hold up,' I said. 'You've done okay so far, but it's getting dark and looks like rain. Let's not push it.'

'Just a bit longer,' he pleaded.

'Give,' I said, holding out my palm.

He stood his ground. 'Just a few more kilometres.'

As we faced off, a fully loaded logging truck barrelled past, spitting volleys of gravel in our direction. A few seconds later, we heard the crunch as it shifted down a gear.

'You want to sit behind that monster for half an hour?' I said. 'Or are you planning on overtaking it?'

Red considered the options, shrugged and slapped the keys into my open hand. 'Worth a try.'

I floored the pedal, hit the radio button and we laid into the carbohydrates. The final siren was two minutes away but it might as well have been two hours for all the difference it made. At the close of play the score was 71–102. Our nineteenth consecutive loss at the MCG, said the word from the commentary box. Not bad. After all, this was our first season, *per se*.

We overtook the logging truck in good order and headed back through Mansfield.

'Any plans for the evening?' I asked.

'Videos at Max's.' He was making an early night of it, due to a shift-swap deal that would have him shelving cornflakes for most of the following afternoon.

'Seeing Madeleine tonight?'

He waggled his hand, *que sera sera*. 'You?'

'Probably not,' I said. 'She's playing hard to get.' This was greeted with the silence it deserved.

'Since you're asking, I'm presenting the trophies at the Somali Youth Association regional basketball finals.'

'Hope your arms are long enough,' he said. 'Some of those kids are so tall they have to reach down to shoot for goal.'

My gig was at seven-thirty. I sat on the speed limit and took no prisoners as dusk descended around us. I kept thinking about the lake, wondering how Charlie and Quinlan had managed to be so far off the mark. Even allowing for the lack of distinctive landmarks, it was a wide margin of error. Yet both swore that's where Merv went down.

On a long straight strip just before Tallarook, crows were picking at a carcase by the side of the highway. A fox maybe, or a possum. They flapped upwards at our approach, and when I glanced back in the mirror, they'd settled again, beaks in the mess. It was an image that stayed with me until the sky broke open and torrents of rain threw themselves against the windscreen.

After that, there was no room for thought of anything but the way ahead.

Obsessive punctuality is a vice rarely practised by those who have fled to these shores from the war-torn Horn of Africa, so nobody at the Somali Youth Association was fussed by my slightly tardy arrival at its northern region basketball final. The official start time was merely indicative, after all.

Abdi Abdi, the association president, showed me to my place with the other dignitaries in the Fawkner Park Sports Complex gymnasium just as the whistle sounded. On the bleachers opposite sat an undemonstrative crowd of snaggle-fanged Mogadishu matriarchs, egg-shaped and taffeta-swathed, each attended by a retinue of long, lissom girls with oval faces and gazelle eyes. The menfolk of the community were not much in evidence. Presumably they were busy driving taxis and drinking glasses of tea.

The collective clout of Melbourne's Somali population was yet to be tapped but its potential had not gone unnoticed. The evening's fixture had attracted a number of representatives of the body politic whose interest in both Somalia and basketball was tangential at best.

I, of course, was one of them. As was the mayor of Darebin, whose bailiwick included the housing commission estate in West Heidelberg, and the Legislative Assembly member for Yorta Yorta, Ken Crouch.

Ken sat two seats away, on the other side of the imam from the Brunswick mosque. The holy sheikh was blind and wore dark glasses. He spent the match smiling wildly and rocking in his seat, Stevie Wonder in a green turban. Ken spent most of it on the phone, a frown on his dial and a finger jammed in one ear.

At the half-time break, he unbuttoned beside me in the urinal and revealed the reason for his distraction.

'This fucking preselection deal,' he groused. 'It's turning pear-shaped.'

Ken was the Shadow Minister for Community Services and a steadying hand on the tiller of the Left. His state lower house seat overlaid the Coolaroo federal electorate to an even larger extent than mine, so he had a territorial as well as a factional interest.

'ALP preselections don't turn pear-shaped, Ken,' I said. 'They're born that way.'

In this case the paternity of the pear rested with Barry Quinlan.

As soon as word of Charlie Talbot's death got around, Ken explained, the party's national executive was besieged by aspirant replacements. Every come-again kid, voter-ousted ex-minister, wannabe-politico union official and me-next machine oiler was knocking on the door, flourishing their credentials. All claimed to be perfect for the job, due to either proven experience, self-evident talent, string-pulling skills or the principles of affirmative action.

Sensing a major affray, and constrained by the deal already cut guaranteeing the next federal vacancy in Victoria to the Left, the executive handballed the fingering job to Barry Quinlan. Barry had dibs on the spot, but nobody specific lined up to fill it. Finding common cause with Alan Metcalfe, who didn't want a drawn-out brawl in his backyard, Barry nailed down a fast-track timetable and shoe-horned Phil Sebastian into the slot. Phil's major qualification being that he wasn't owed or owned by anyone else.

All this had happened while I was escorting Charlie Talbot's corpse from Mildura, seeing it into the tender hands of Tobin Brothers Family Undertakers and conferring with the various stakeholders as to the manner, location and scheduling of its interment.

'Made sense at the time,' said Ken, directing himself to the stainless steel. 'And it still makes sense.'

But no sooner had the bell sounded on round one than the would-be contenders were up off the mat and shaping up for round two. Quinlan had exceeded his brief, they were muttering.

Unsurprisingly, the loudest mutterers were those he'd given to understand could count on Barry's support whenever the next vacancy arose. And Barry being a master of the dangled expectation, there were plenty of those. All of them members of his own faction.

'I've been on the blower 24/7 since Phil Sebastian's name came out of the hat,' complained Ken as he shook the drops off the end of his dick. 'Hosing down half the Left.'

'You're in an unenviable position, Ken,' I said, hitting the flush button.

'I think there's a very real chance of a split.'

'In the Left?' I zippered up. 'You're kidding. You've already split more times than a hyperactive amoeba. Do it again and you'll be holding your meetings in a Petri dish. For Chrissake, Ken, there's only eight of you still standing.'

'Not the *state* Left, Murray.' He spoke as though to a particularly obtuse child. 'The *federal* Left. If the right candidate steps forward, he or she could drive a wedge through Barry's numbers on the selection panel. Split the Left wide open.'

'The right Left candidate?' I said.

'That's right. And that'll leave the Left in a right mess.'

'I see,' I said, washing my hands. 'Better get back to the game. I think the Kensington Giraffes stand a very real chance of a comeback in the second half.'

But Ken was already back on the blower, damping down the embers of smouldering discontent.

By ten o'clock my duty was done. I'd stood with assorted Abdis, the shadow minister, the mayor and the mufti and handed cups and trophies to a line of slope-shouldered, toothy youths. I'd shaken the tips of their feather-light fingers, partaken sparingly of the potato-crisp and Fanta supper and called it a medium-long day.

While performing my bedtime ablutions, I studied my face in the mirror. More shop-worn cases walked the earth, to be sure, but my lifelong battle with gravity was entering its decisive phase.

At fifty, they say, a man has the face he deserves. Fifty wasn't far away, almost as close as the millennium. What had I done to deserve this particular countenance?

'At least you've still got your own teeth,' I reassured myself. I took a closer look. 'Most of them.'

As I fell into that slumbering state that passes for the sleep of a parent—a sober one, anyway—a sharp sound cut the faint swish of the distant traffic. The jarring, metallic screech of brakes.

It sounded like an axe being ground.

The rain that sluiced the roof that night had cleared to a persistent drizzle by seven-thirty, so I togged up and hit the exercise track again, drawstring tight on the hood of my lightweight nylon slicker.

Where it wasn't drizzling, it was either dripping from the trees or leaking through my elastic. A pair of kayakers hurtled downstream, chasing thrills down the Yarra's swollen bacterial brew. Head down, I focused on the way ahead, mouth working as I pounded the pavement.

'Γρηγορα,' I croaked, pushing the guttural γ from the back of my throat onto my palate, then rolling the ρ across the tip of my tongue. 'Ο γατος γρηγορα ηπιε το γαλα.

'The cat drank the milk,' I translated for my own benefit. Bloody wet cat, this morning.

On Sunday mornings, an informal gathering of my classmates from the Greek course met for coffee, cakes and conversation practice at the Archeon Cafe in Lonsdale

Street. My participation was intermittent at best, but I'd missed the last three lessons, so it would be a way of getting back into the linguistic swing. That's what I told myself anyway, as I sloshed along the riverbank, sweating into my slicker and performing unnatural acts with the fleshy folds of my maxillary tuberosity.

By the time I'd showered, downed my cereal, read the papers and made my leisurely way into town, Lonsdale Street was parked out by the first-sitting yum cha crowd streaming into Chinatown. I wasted twenty minutes cruising for a vacant space, then put the Magna in the carpark under the Daimaru cookware department and walked the two blocks to the Archeon. At the hoardings surrounding the Queen Victoria Hospital site, I couldn't resist looking through one of the viewing windows into the massive hole which had once been the maternity wing. Eventually, an international hotel would arise in the spot where Red had first drawn breath. Or a shopping complex, or an office tower, or some indispensable combination of all three. For the moment, it was just an empty, puddle-dotted crater and the prospect of a year's work for a thousand construction workers.

Finally, fully half an hour late, I reached the intermittent string of tavernas, pastry shops, worry-bead emporia and travel agencies that constitute Melbourne's official Greek precinct. In fine weather, we had our practice chit-chats at one of the tables on the footpath outside the Archeon. But the rain-specked tables were deserted. Even by hardy Melburnian standards, this was no day to go alfresco.

I peered through the window and scanned the interior, a tasteful combination of chrome-frame chairs, ripple-glass tabletops and mirror-tiled walls. Wogarama Deluxe. The

Archeon was a popular Sunday brunch spot and business was brisk. The place was chockers. Women with brass hair, men in expensive tracksuits, their fat kids and people who couldn't get into yum cha.

I spotted our little *kafeneon*-klatsch at its usual table in the back corner, away from the worst of the bustle and shielded from the turbo-pop blare of the ceiling-mounted television. There were six of them, a good turn-out.

I could make out Terri, a children's book illustrator who claimed to have picked up a smattering of Greek on Mykonos during her hippy days. Her smatter was long scattered but she was doing her best to round it up again. As she spoke, she rotated her wrist in the air, as if uncoiling the tentative thread of her thoughts. The others were leaning forward, the better to catch her drift. I recognised one as Simon, a palliative-care nurse in his early thirties with plans to explore the Peloponnese. And some of the Peloponnesians, too, I assumed. The others, three females and one male, had their backs to me.

Lanie, I registered immediately, was not among them. My shoulders sagged and I mouthed a silent curse. *Malaka*.

I shouldn't have come. I'd been bullshitting myself. Truth be told, it wasn't the prospect of refreshing my feeble, faltering Greek that had lured me to the Archeon. It was the dumb, wistful hope that Lanie would be there.

My gaze dropped to the display of pastries. The syrup-drenched *kataifi* cocoons, deep-fried *loukoumades* and sugar-dusted *kouranbiethes*. The moist walnut cake and flaking *bougatsa*. The oozing babas and sticky halva. The suppurating *galaktoboureko*.

Butterflies danced a lead-footed Zorba in my stomach. I started to turn away, back the way I'd come.

Jesus, Murray. Behave yourself. Get a grip. So what if she's not here? You hardly know the woman, for Christ's sake.

But I did know some things. She had a wide, confident mouth and heavy-lidded sensual eyes. She was pleasingly full-figured and her thick mane of chestnut hair went down to her shoulders. She didn't get impatient when other students slowed down the class because they hadn't done their homework, even though she always did hers.

I knew she was a piano teacher. In the first lesson, she'd told us so, fluttering her fingers across an imaginary keyboard. From our practice dialogues, I knew she lived in Abbotsford in an apartment near the river. So I didn't know nothing.

Which didn't excuse the fact that I was pining after her like some smitten teen. I slapped some sense into myself and turned back towards the door.

But my appetite had gone. For cakes, for company, for coffee. This whole conversation thing was a waste of time. I'd be better off alone, working on my vocabulary or taking dictation from a tape.

So, was I staying or leaving? A wispy drizzle began, not quite heavy enough to qualify as rain. Even the weather couldn't make up its mind.

A Daihatsu hatch-back pulled up, double-parking in the inside lane. The passenger door flew open and a woman jumped out, a flurry of seasonal browns and burgundies. A chunky adolescent girl clambered from the back and took the empty seat. Hasty goodbyes were exchanged, and the car drove away.

Lanie Lane, looking a little cross, flung her scarf back over her shoulder and marched towards the coffee shop.

'*Ti kanis?*' I said brightly. '*Kala?*'

'*Kala.*' She twitched her mouth, erasing the frown.

'Better late than never, eh?' I said.

She grimaced and tossed her chin in the direction the car had taken. 'My bloody ex. You'd think an IT expert could tell the time, not turn up an hour late.'

'I've just arrived myself,' I said.

Her ex! Things were looking up. Potentially.

I held the door open, then followed her into the filo-and-cinnamon scented fug of the coffee shop. 'Θελετε καφε κυρια?'

'Latte, *parakalo*,' she smiled, 'as they say on Santorini.'

We joined the others. Space was made, greetings exchanged. '*Kalimera, kalimera. Kala?*'

Everybody was *poly kala*. Simon, the palliative-care nurse, was explaining that he had been to the *kinimatografos*. Was it *enhromo* asked Julie, the florist, or an *aspromavro*? It was a *komodhia*. Yesterday, I informed them, I had visited *exohi*. I had not gone by train. I went there by *aftokinito*. Lanie had been to a *sinavlia*. Her friend played the *klarino*. Friend, masculine. Just who was this tootler, I wondered?

After half an hour of mangling our generatives and spraying our fricatives, slipping in and out of English to encourage and correct each other, our number began to dwindle. Other customers were impatient for tables and the waitress confiscated our chairs as fast as they were vacated. Eventually, it was down to me and the object of my desire. We dawdled, guarding our cups, neither of us in a hurry.

A waitress started clearing the table. I scooped up the book illustrator's leftover baklava as the plate was whisked away. Nothing wrong with my appetite now.

'Abbotsford, eh?' I said.

She nodded. 'Bought if off the plan. Saved a fortune in stamp duty.'

There are places in the world where conversation revolves around subjects other than real estate. Melbourne is not one of them. Lanie told me about her place. I told her about mine. In the process, we sketched the bones of our personal histories.

She'd bought her apartment, she told me, with her pay-out from the Education Department. A high school music teacher, she was one of the thousands made redundant in the wave of school closures initiated by the incoming Liberals. As well as her job, she'd lost her husband. Given him the flick for fooling around. He was now shacked up with a marketing consultant. No great loss, she said, and the divorce had left her with half their house in Balwyn.

'Fifteen years of capital gain, tax free,' she said, scraping the bottom of her coffee cup and licking the spoon.

She'd bought the Abbotsford place because she liked the location and it had enough room for her grand piano.

'It's leased. But nothing impresses the customers like a grand. Means I can charge twenty dollars an hour above market rates to teach little Griselda her scales.'

Talk came easy to us. We got and gave in equal measure, and Lanie learned at least as much about me. From real estate and work, we moved to children and education. Her daughter, Nicole, was in year seven at McRob Girls' High. She had the second bedroom in Abbotsford, plus a room at her father's place in Prahran. I reciprocated with the potted history of Red and Wendy.

The only subject I deliberately elided was Lyndal, but I read in Lanie's eyes that she had an inkling. Many people did. The murder had generated a fair amount of press.

The waitress came back, a bottle-blonde dragon with a cat's-bum mouth. She stared at our empty cups and flicked her towel. We were getting the heave-ho. But there was still one subject yet to be broached.

'Stop me if I'm speaking out of turn or making a fool of myself,' I said. 'But I wonder if you'd be in a position to accompany me to a sort of semi-official, semi-social event thingo on Thursday evening?'

Lanie smiled at the construction. 'A semi-official semi-social event thingo?'

I made a sheepish face. 'The casino opening, actually.'

'I thought the Labor Party didn't approve of the casino?' Her tone was teasing.

'It's a reconnaissance mission,' I said.

We stood up and made for the cashier, my eyes on the sway of her hips. She looked back over her shoulder. 'So a hand of blackjack and a spin of the roulette wheel would be out of the question?'

'Fan tan, craps, two-up, you name it,' I said. 'We can even pull some slots with the hoi polloi if you like.'

I tried to pay for her coffees. She wouldn't let me.

'Is this a dress-up event?'

'Whatever you like. Long as you're not wearing a balaclava and carrying a sawn-off shotgun.'

She chewed her lip, hesitant. 'Thursday evening, right?'

'I could ask them to change it,' I said. 'But Mick and Keef might get shitty.'

'Could take a bit of juggling,' she said. 'Can I let you know in a day or two?'

I nodded, a little too eagerly, and borrowed the cashier's pen to write my home number on the back of a business card. Lanie glanced at the number, then read the other side.

'Parliament of Victoria.' She shook her head dolefully. '*Malaka.*'

Broadmeadows Town Hall was a vision of drear in the afternoon rain, a brick monolith distinguished only by its lack of distinction. As the venue for a wake, it was hard to imagine anywhere more depressingly institutional.

I directed the cab to the agglomeration of buildings between the K-Mart and the municipal library, hoping that Mike Kyriakis had at least laid on an adequate supply of grog. A wake is not a wake without booze. It was basic multicultural courtesy. The rites were over. The tomb was sealed. It was time to get ragged and maudlin.

When I was a teenager, Broady was the very end of the earth. Beyond lay only factories and thistle-infested paddocks. Its residents were blue-collar workers, their feet tentatively planted on the first rung of the ladder to affluence. Many were recent migrants whose oily-rag thrift had allowed them to scrape together the deposit on a stake in the Australian Dream.

Community facilities were basic. The opera rarely performed there. Ballet classes were few and far between. Childbirth often preceded wedlock. The mullet ruled supreme. Sheepskin moccasins were high fashion. Broady boys were generally not a calming presence.

In the following decades, however, the frontier of suburbia galloped further north. Target and K-Mart colonised the council carpark, school retention rates had risen and a tertiary campus sprang up. It had got to the point now where real estate agents were describing the place as a 'desirable location' without the faintest hint of irony or even deception.

Pity there wasn't a decent pub in the area. Still, there's a limit to what social engineering can achieve.

I paid my chauffeur and followed the hand-lettered signs up the Prussian-blue polypropylene pile to the council chamber, the locus of the gathering.

The chamber had recently been decommissioned following a forced rationalisation of local government by the state Liberals. While the surrounding offices continued to operate as an administrative centre, decision-making had moved elsewhere. It was now a general function room and storage area for municipal artifacts. Honour rolls of mayors previous. Mementoes from sister cities. Winning bushscapes from the annual acquisitive art award.

About fifty people had turned up. They were milling around the room, drinks in hand, chatting and raising a gratifyingly loud hubbub.

Somebody had taped old campaign posters and press photos to the walls. Serious-faced Charlie in front of the party colours. Dark-suited Charlie opening the Community Health Centre. Hard-hatted Charlie inspecting progress on the Meadow Heights adventure playground. Just-folks Charlie living large at the Upfield Senior Cits dinner dance.

Mike Kyriakis spotted me the moment I arrived. He beckoned me over to a bunch of old ducks who were stripping the buffet of four-point sandwiches and meatballs on toothpicks. At their centre was Mavis Peel, former doyenne of the Municipals' typing pool. Her bosom had vanished and her hair had thinned to a blue-rinsed wisp. She was deaf as a post and didn't know me from Adam. But she remembered Charlie Talbot, all right.

'Such a nice young man,' she reminisced. 'So considerate.'

Her companions from the Craigieburn Home for the Terminally Bewildered nodded agreement and sank their talons into the pink salmon sangers.

'Have you got a drink, love?' asked one of them.

I couldn't tell if she was cadging or inviting. Mike grabbed me like a life preserver and steered me to a trestle table where a council hall keeper in a clip-on bow-tie and a neat blue mohawk was pleased to offer me something from his comprehensive selection of wines, beers and spirits.

'This is a fine thing you're doing, Mike,' I said, hoisting a stubby of VB. 'Here's to Charlie.'

A lead weight descended on my shoulder. It was the open hand of Sivan Demiral, one of Charlie's office auxiliaries. He was an old mate, a Kurd who'd helped run the Turkish Welfare League alongside Ayisha when I was the electorate officer for Charlene Wills, many moons prior.

'Murray, my friend,' he boomed. 'We have lost a good man.' He raised his stubby and I seconded the motion.

An ebullient optimist with the build of a Hittite shithouse, Sivan was forever launching ill-fated business ventures, all the while keeping his hand in local Labor politics. His current project was a Turkish video store, its precarious earnings underwritten by a part-time job in Charlie's electorate office. Customers with a valid ALP membership card got a ten percent discount.

We swapped some Charlie Talbot anecdotes and I gravitated towards Helen Wright. She was part of a trio that included Ayisha and a woman from the Broadmeadows Neighbourhood House toy library. They were taking a punt on the white.

'Courtesy of Domaine Diggers Rest, the winery just up the road from Charlie and Margot's place.' Helen puffed her cheeks, swished and swallowed. 'An argumentative little drop with an aftertaste of aviation exhaust.'

I accepted a glass and took a tentative sip. Helen wasn't just a fine electorate officer. She had a cast-iron stomach. Perhaps these facts were not unrelated. Ayisha was downing the stuff like a trooper.

'Margot sends her apologies and her thanks,' I said. 'If you ladies will excuse me, I think I'll stick to the suds.'

I collected a cleansing ale and made the rounds. I knew perhaps half the people in the room. Ron Tragear, secretary of the Anstey branch and C-grade juniors football coach. Signor Panebianco, the Cicero of the Calabrian Club. Lauris Foxe, deputy principal of Strathmore Primary. Doug and Vera Ahern of the Anstey Progress Association. Ada Ahmet from the Disability Resource Centre. Working-bee regulars and old-school true believers, bedrocks of their communities. As big a pack of dags and busybodies as you could ever hope to assemble. The more I drank, the more I loved them.

'Your attention for a moment, folks.'

I was saved from total immersion in the well of sentimentality by Mike Kyriakis. He rapped on the table with a spoon and Helen Wright hauled her low centre of gravity up onto a chair.

She made a short speech, reminding us why we were there. It centred on a funny story about the time computers were first installed in members' offices in the old Parliament House in Canberra. To Charlie's bafflement, the technician sent to explain their operation kept using an acronym current in the computer jargon of the day. WYSIWYG, pronounced Wizzywig. What You See Is What You Get.

'Charlie Talbot was a Wizzywig man,' she said, drawing her tale to its point. 'What you saw was what you got. A man who knew what he stood for, did what he could to the best of his abilities, recognised his limitations and honoured his obligations. The sort of person who restores your faith in politics. I'm not sure if they make 'em like that anymore.'

And we all drank to that, and shared a silent sniffle. I realised my stubby was empty and, as I turned towards the bar, banged into a vaguely familiar middle-aged woman. She clicked her tongue and gave a reproving shake of her head.

'Jesus, Murray Whelan,' she said. 'Still as hopeless as ever, I see. You don't recognise me, do you?'

'Course I do.' I smiled widely and racked my fibbing brain. A committee? A delegation? A primary school pageant?

'Nadine,' she said. 'Nadine Medlock.'

'Of course, Nadine,' I said, my ears turning pink. 'It's been a long time, that's all.'

'Twenty-three years, four months and five days.' She eyed my livid lobes, amused, then appraised the rest of me. 'Don't worry, Murray. I almost didn't recognise you, either.'

The last I'd seen of Nadine Medlock was her bare arse.

I had a force ten hangover and I was crawling out her bedroom window, shoes under my arms, trying to remember where I'd parked the car. She was flaked out on her doona, her bum in the air and her head buried under a pillow. It took me three days to find the car.

'So,' I said, bouncily. 'What've you been up to? What brings you here? Didn't realise you knew Charlie.'

She cupped an elbow in one hand, sipped her wine and slipped into chatty mode. 'Been living in Darwin,' she said. 'Husband, kids, the full catastrophe. No, it's been great, actually. Len's in the PS, Department of Environment and Natural Resources. Transferred back here last year so the girls could finish school. I've been working with young offenders and Charlie was a big help with a program at the Sunbury juvenile centre. Thought I'd drop by and pay my respects. What about you?'

Nadine was, I remembered, a pretty good sort.

'I'm in state parliament,' I said.

'No!' she said. 'You poor bastard. What did you do to deserve that?'

'I'm in it for the glamour,' I said. 'My electorate's just down the road.'

We stood at the plate-glass window, looking down at the K-Mart carpark, and traded ancient gossip about half-remembered acquaintances from our long-gone twenties.

For a while, I recalled, Nadine was a barmaid at the John Curtin Hotel, the watering-hole directly across the street from the Trades Hall.

The Curtin was an institution in those days. ACTU headquarters was just down the road in Swanston Street and it drew thirsty union officials like flies to the proverbial. In its beery swill, sanctified by the name of Labor's most revered and contentious prime minister, loyalties were affirmed and animosities stoked, rumours circulated and deals done, old alliances eroded and new ones forged. Every inch was staked out. The Right sat by the window, the Left near the cigarette machine. The pragmatists held the bar, leaving just enough room for the Maoists. People went there as much to fight as to drink.

'You don't happen to remember Merv Cutlett, do you?' I wondered.

'How could I forget? The old letch cost me my job.'

'Yeah?' I topped up her glass. 'How so?'

Nadine shrugged. 'Usual story.'

'Got a bit frisky, did he?'

'Downright grabby,' she said.

'Tell all,' I said. 'Paint me a picture.'

She heaved a reluctant sigh. But reminiscence, after all, was our pretext for an afternoon on the grog.

'It was a Friday night, right. Bedlam hour. Cutlett was perched at the bar, usual pozzie, with his bandicoot-faced little hanger-on.'

'Sid Gilpin?'

'I forget the name. A cut-price Bob Hawke, always cracking his knuckles and twiddling his pinkie ring and tugging at his earlobe.'

She smoothed back the hair at her temples, mimicking one of Gilpin's grooming gestures. She had him down pat. I laughed appreciatively, egging her on.

'As per usual, the little grease-ball had his head so far up Merv's bum you couldn't see his neck. Anyway, this night, for some reason, the two of them were particularly full of themselves. Carrying on like they'd just pulled a major swiftie. Sold Sydney Harbour Bridge or something. Patting themselves on the back. And hitting the amber pretty hard in the process. Eventually, whatsisname, Sid, got totally legless and lurched off. So Cutlett turned his attention to yours truly. Stupid old fart tried to crack onto me. Really laid on the charm, told me how much he admired my tits.'

Nadine's tits weren't bad, if memory served, but they weren't anything to write home about. My eyes started slipping downwards but I got them back to Nadine's face before they disgraced me.

'Of course sexual harassment was an occupational hazard at the Curtin,' she said. 'Bar work, it's no job for a shrinking violet, but even you proto-SNAGs assumed it was open slather.'

Before she got any further down that particular detour, I steered her back to Merv.

'He was pissed and arrogant and I wasn't in the mood to be nice. So I tried for a swap with Terry, the barman upstairs. He reckoned he was flat out, too, and I should just cop it and carry on. Anyway, Cutlett keeps it up, so I banged his next beer on the bar so hard it slopped into his lap.'

'Bet he loved that,' I said, the scene vivid in my mind.

'Went off like a pork chop. Said he knew exactly what I needed and he was just the man to give it to me. There's a scrum of drinkers three deep at the bar, waving their money in the air, grabbing glasses off me. Every time I lean across the bar, he puts his hands on me. I go to the boss again, said I couldn't work under those sort of conditions, tried to get shifted. He said "Later", so I cracked the shits. "Take this job and shove it," I told him, "I ain't workin' here no more."'

'Johnny Paycheck,' I said.

'Dead Kennedys, the way I did it,' Nadine laughed. 'Felt

good at the time, but I was jacked off about it later. Turned out to be the weekend the old goat got himself drowned. He never went back to the Curtin, so I needn't have quit on his account.'

I shook my head at the injustice. 'And here we are,' I said. 'Twenty-odd years later, at the wake of the man who jumped into a freezing cold lake trying to save the bastard.'

'Yeah, well,' she said. 'That's the difference between the Merv Cutletts of this world and the Charlie Talbots.' She held out her glass and I topped it up with Domaine Diesel. We gave a desultory toast and I sucked meditatively on my stubby. Down in the K-Mart carpark, Sunday afternoon shoppers were dashing though a downpour, their purchases clutched tight.

'Cutlett and Gilpin,' I said. 'You don't happen to recollect what they were so pleased about?'

Nadine gave a derisive snort and eyed me like I was nuts. 'Christ, Murray, it was twenty years ago.'

I tried a little charm of my own. 'Still,' I said. 'You do have amazing powers of recall.'

'Careful, Murray.' Nadine fixed me with a wry look. 'I might start remembering things best forgotten.'

My ears flared again. I racked my brain. What exactly had happened between me and Nadine? 'Yes, well…I, er…'

'Anyway,' she said, letting me off the hook. 'It ended well. I walked straight into a job at the Dan.' The Dan O'Connell was a folkie pub. Wack-fol-the-diddle, electric bush bands and outlaw crossover. 'That's where I met Len. And I'm still with him. Just goes to show that things work out for the best sometimes, eh?'

'Sometimes.'

By seven o'clock it was down to the hard core.

Somnolent, we sprawled among the ravaged platters, devastated dips and knackered plastic glassware. Helen Wright had taken off her shoes and propped her stockinged feet on a stackable vinyl chair. Sivan toyed with a bottle of raki, unscrewing the cap, thinking about it, then sealing it back up. Ayisha began clearing up. Mike Kyriakis told her not to bother, the cleaners would take care of it in the morning. Sam Aboud, the administrator of the Meadow Heights Community Health Centre, managed to scavenge enough sachets of Nescafe to make a round of coffees.

Darkness had fallen outside. One of the fluorescent ceiling lights spluttered sporadically. Mike took the Australian flag from its stand and poked the tube with the pole. It hummed, plinked and expired.

There were a couple of other lingerers, faces I knew less well, their names slightly out of range. A young psephologist with an attempted beard, one of Charlie's part-timers, sat on the floor with his knees cradled in his arms. One of Mike Kyriakis' council confreres, an official with the printing industry union. He'd souvenired one of Charlie's campaign posters, rolled it up like a telescope and was trying to focus down the tube.

We were all somewhat oiled, but I was probably the worst offender, flopped in an armchair and sinking gently into the west.

'I've done my sums,' said Mike, dragging a chair into the circle and dropping into it with an air of finality. 'And I gotta say, I'm more tempted than ever to put my hand up for Charlie's old seat. I reckon he'd want me to, too. What do you say, Helen, how about seconding me? And Sam, you too? Between the lot of you, I reckon there's just about enough signatures for the nomination form.' He gave the flagpole a slow wave. 'It'll be a glorious defeat. Gallipoli all over again.'

Sivan languidly returned the wave with his bottle of raki. 'Didn't we win that one?'

Mike was warming to his theme. 'I've got no illusions about my chances, but I reckon I can make those know-it-alls in Canberra sit up and take notice.'

He'd been though the membership rolls with a fine tooth comb, and he'd come up with a strategy.

'Everybody's been stacking branches for years, right? And both sides have about equal numbers, right? But it's like the nuclear balance. It only works if it isn't tested in practice. As long as they've got the numbers on paper, they never need to actually mobilise them. All they need in any vote is enough to make a symbolic showing. So next Saturday, come the plebiscite of local members, there'll probably be a turn-out of less than fifty percent of the eligible voters, right?'

The question was rhetorical. We settled further into our seats and let him answer it.

'If I can round up three hundred surprise punters, which I think might just be do-able, I really put the cat among the pigeons.'

He paused pregnantly, awaiting a reaction. Eventually Ayisha obliged with the obvious questions.

'Where are you going to get three hundred stray votes, Mike, and how are you going to keep them up your sleeve until Saturday?'

In Coolaroo, as in most ethnically diverse electorates, membership management was a highly developed science. Between the six of us, we knew every trick in the branch-stacking book.

The game had begun in the sixties when party rules were amended to allow branches to conduct their meetings in languages other than English. This, it was believed, would encourage migrants to join.

The Left started the meatball rolling with mass enrolments of Italians and Greeks. For a while, it was all Mikis Theodorakis and Bernardo Bertolucci. Then the Right followed suit by signing up a grab-bag of deracinated Indochinese, irredentist Chetniks and assorted Middle Eastern minaret polishers.

Before long, the so-called ethnic warlords emerged. Bottom feeders with murky affiliations and interchangeable surnames who enrolled hundreds of their most compliant compatriots, paid their membership dues and sold their votes to the highest bidder. All with as little regard for ideological distinction as any other influence peddler.

As they debated the merit of Mike's figures, I rested my

eyes and let the talk ebb and flow around me.

'You can discount the Italians completely,' Mike said. 'For political purposes, they're no longer ethnics. Three generations here, they might as well be skips.'

'Not like the Greeks,' said Helen. 'They don't migrate, they colonise. They could be here forever and never dream of giving up their political muscle.'

She's right about that, I thought. The heirs of Aristotle and Pythagoras know in their bones that politics is all, numbers are everything.

'Yeah,' said Sam Aboud. 'But did you ever try to get fifty Greeks to do what they're told? It's like herding cats.'

'You leave the Greeks to me,' said Mike. 'And what's the story with those Montignards or whatever you call them that you've stacked into the Attwood branch?'

'Hmong,' said Sam. 'A proud warrior people from the headwaters of the Mekong, currently residing in Meadow Heights. They worship me as a god, or at least the guy who can get them on the waiting list for a hip replacement.'

'How many have you got?'

'Sixty.'

'Bullshit.'

'Okay, forty-seven.'

'AK-47 you mean,' cracked Sivan, slapping his knee.

Ayisha said, 'You'd need five times that number to counterbalance the Croatians. With Metcalfe backing the deal, you've got to take the Right into account, too, don't forget.'

'The Croatians'll be a no-show,' said Mike. 'The Right's lost its key Croat head-kickers. They took their fat fascistic arses back to Zagreb when Yugoslavia fell apart. Welcomed with open arms and government jobs by their fellow Ustashi exile, Tudjman. And thanks to Milosevic, nobody wants to know the Serbs, so we can count them out, too.'

'I might only have forty-seven Hmong,' said Sam Aboud. 'But I've also got a minibus to ferry them to the polling point.'

'And somebody in Canberra doesn't know Muslim calendar,' said Sivan. 'Saturday is Miled an-Anabi, birthday of Mohammed. Nobody from Izik mosque gunna vote, too busy having big party.'

'Bullshit, Sivan,' said Ayisha. 'Since when was Miled a feast day?'

'Since new mufti arrive. Very go-ahead feller.'

And so it went, back and forth, as they amused themselves with the speculative scenarios of a theoretical campaign.

'No good without the element of surprise,' said Helen.

'That's where you come in,' said Mike. 'Let's face it, Helen, working for Charlie was a labour of love. You don't really want to end up the housekeeper for this time-server, Sebastian. Be my secret agent. Feed him misinformation, lull him into a false sense of security.'

'Tempting,' she yawned, a smile in her voice. 'Poison the wells. Go out with a bang not a whimper.'

I was drifting off, settling into a boozy miasma, Sam Aboud's instant coffee going cold in my lap. I was thinking about Nadine Medlock seeing Merv Cutlett and Sid Gilpin at the Curtin, their high spirits on the eve of Merv's death. Neither of them was the most demonstrative of blokes. What were they celebrating? More to the point, was it connected to the union?

'What about it, Murray?' The sound of my name dragged me back to the present.

Mike Kyriakis was asking me a question.

'You've got enough pull with those schoolteacher intellectuals and old retired boilermakers in those branches of yours. How about signing up to the crusade?'

I kept my eyes closed. This was Ayisha's department.

'Why would Murray want to stick his head above the parapet?' she said. 'Just so you can get your name in the papers and get a reputation as a man to watch.'

The talk was all still theoretical, the question academic.

'She right, Mike. Better he don't support you. Better he run himself.' Sivan picked up the baton. He'd been doing some thinking. 'Imagine if panel splits. They don't like Sebastian. They don't like you neither, Mike. So Murray, he decides to run. He don't support you. He runs against you. You both draw votes from Sebastian. He gets eliminated. Second round, you give Murray your preferences. He falls over the line. He gets Coolaroo. Thank you, Mike. You can have Melbourne Upper, he don't need it no more. He's in Canberra. He takes Ayisha, big new office up there. Helen, she gets Ayisha's old job, runs Melbourne Upper for you. I get Helen's old job, run Murray's office down here. Everybody happy.'

It was so elegant, so improbable, that they all burst out laughing and gave him a clap.

'What about me?' said Sam Aboud. 'What do I get?'

'You get to be Mayor of Broadmeadows,' said Ayisha. 'But first you get to call Murray a taxi. He's fallen asleep.'

I opened my eyes. 'Huh?' I said.

They poured me into a cab and I got home just in time to crash on the couch in front of the television. The usual ABC Sunday night fare. Women in hooped dresses and long-faced, sinister toffs in top hats. Red woke me when he'd packed up his books at eleven-thirty. 'On the Floor' was just finishing. Whatever Kelly Cusack had reported, I'd missed it.

I was thinking about Kelly as I climbed into bed. But then I was thinking about Lanie. Eleni of Troy.

With whom I had a date. Maybe.

We were on a boat, a sailing boat, skimming across a sparkling sea, the Aegean, destination unknown. The sun was warm. The sky was blue. I was wearing a tunic and sandals. Lanie was wearing a chiton and there was a diadem in her hair. She was standing at the prow playing 'Advance Australia Fair' on a piano accordion. There were others on the boat, somewhere behind us. I could hear them scuffling. Somebody fell into the water. Splash. I turned to look and the sea was gone. Lanie was gone. Everyone was gone. I was alone and the boat was sitting on dry land. I was stark naked and burning up. A parching dryness filled my mouth. I tried to swallow but I was suffocating, dying of thirst.

I groped blindly for the glass on the bedside table. My hand knocked it over, spilling water on the clock-radio. I swung my feet to the floor, stumbled to the bathroom, gulped from the tap, peed, gulped again. The sudden flare of the bathroom light set stars spinning behind my eyes. There was something I was trying to remember. I couldn't remember what.

Then I was standing at the door of my study, looking into the dark, thinking about my archive boxes. All that old paper. The silverfish would be eating it, nibbling it into powder. I'd put mothballs in the boxes, but that was long ago. They'd be gone by now, all used up. Buy mothballs, that was what I was trying to remember.

Mothballs, I told myself. Hold that thought.

And then the alarm clock went off.

Senator Barry Quinlan was advancing to greet me even as the polished glass security door into his reception area was clicking locked behind me.

With a state-wide electorate and therefore no particular constituency to pander to, senators pleased themselves as to where they located their offices. For the Nationals, it was always somewhere in the boonies, where they'd be visible to the cud-chewers. Those from the other two parties hung out their shingles wherever it suited them. Some liked the leafy 'burbs. Others bunged on the common touch, setting up shop at street level and opening their doors to all comers. Some found a comfortable pied-a-terre in the Commonwealth offices in Treasury Place with its ankle-deep carpet and uniformed doorman. In Barry's case, it was a corner suite in a mid-rise office building at the legal and banking end of Bourke Street, a short stroll from nowhere in particular.

He extended his hand, not for me to shake, but to

shepherd me through to his office. As well as the woman at the computer behind the reception desk, I counted four other staffers in small, glass-panelled side offices as we made our way towards the bridge of *HMAS Quinlan*. They looked up as we passed. One of them was Phil Sebastian. He was on the phone and signalled that he'd join us as soon as he finished the call.

Quinlan was well turned out, as usual, minus a jacket. Crisp and businesslike, but cordial. A man who'd spent a long time at the top of his profession. Warm, but not toasty.

'Thanks for coming, Murray,' he said, directing me to one of the comfortable chairs at the small conference table that shared the space with a file-stacked desk.

There was a fairly good painting of a racehorse on one wall, gilt-famed. A whiteboard on the other, erased but bearing evidence of much use. We could have been in a well-heeled bookie's office on settling-up day.

'I appreciate it,' he said. 'I really do. And so does Phil. I was probably a bit out of line the other day at the cemetery. Insensitive, bringing up this preselection business in a situation like that, you and Charlie being close and all.'

'That's all right, Barry,' I said. 'No offence taken.'

'Good,' he said, sitting down across the table, pinching up his trouser leg at the knee so as not to ruin the crease as he crossed one leg over the other. 'I felt sure you'd appreciate the need for a smooth transition. We've got a load on our plates right now, dealing with this Telecom privatisation push, pressing our advantage on the travel rorts scandal and so forth.' His hand swept the air expansively.

I gave an understanding nod. Many are the toils of those who would clean the Augean stables.

'This fast-track decision-making is not ideal I know,' he

said, forestalling any qualms I might have been poised to express. 'Under normal circumstances, we'd've been content for things to take their natural course. But a mid-term preselection tussle, if it gets out of hand, it costs us points at the by-election. That hands the government a chance to say we're running out of steam. It's like pissing in your own pants. Feels pretty hot to you, but the only thing anyone else notices is the smell.'

'I understand the party's concern, Barry,' I said. 'And I share it.'

'Good,' he said, that settled. 'I suppose you wouldn't be here if you didn't.'

Phil Sebastian came into the room. He was slightly younger than me, but he didn't have as much hair. The crown was the thin spot, leaving him with a monkish tonsure. His face radiated intelligence and goodwill. He had a brisk collegial handshake and a slightly harried manner, like the school dux interrupted midway between handing in an assignment and getting togged up for cricket practice. It was hard to dislike him and I saw no reason to try.

'I appreciate this, Murray,' he said. 'I really do.'

It's always nice to be appreciated. We'd met on a handful of occasions, he recalled, naming them. Party conferences and state–federal confabs back when we were in government. He'd worked for the ACTU, I recalled, and I'd read some of the papers he'd written for the Evatt Institute.

From a competence point of view he was no liability, that much was an evident fact. If the world was a meritocracy, Phil Sebastian had a ticket to ride. But that's not the way it works, of course. Sometimes it's down to kissing arse.

'I understand that your opinion carries a lot of weight in

parts of the electorate,' he kissed. 'I'd very much like the benefit of your insights, help steer me right in my approach to the local branches. No doubt they're feeling a bit sidelined at the moment and even though their votes only add up to half the total, I'd like to feel I'm coming into the job with their support.'

I nodded. 'I'm sure if they're handled in the right way, they'll do what's expected of them.'

'It doesn't have to be unanimous,' said Quinlan. 'Just overwhelming.'

We had a chuckle, fine fellows that we were.

'I've just been on the line to Helen Wright,' said Sebastian. He adjusted the knot in his tie, giving me time to send up a flare if one was required. His tie had an oblique dark green stripe on a maroon background. Corporate camouflage, fifty dollars at The Tie Shop.

'Keeping her on then, are you?'

'It's a good idea, I think,' he said, glancing at Quinlan. 'She does know the lie of the land.'

'She does indeed,' I said. 'Lined up some appointments, has she?'

He reeled off a list of names, most unknown to me. The few I recognised were minor players, all points of the Coolaroo compass.

'You'll be a busy boy for the next five days,' I said. 'It's a big electorate, lots of territory to cover. Tell you what, I'll have a chat with my electorate officer, nut out a list, have her call you back later this afternoon. You've caught me on the hop a bit. Parliament's rising this week and I've got my work cut out, but let's see what we can do for you.'

Sebastian handed me a card with his contact numbers. 'Anytime, anywhere. Just call me and I'll be there.' Phil had missed his vocation. He should have been a lyricist.

One of Quinlan's back-room beavers stuck his snout around the door. 'Your car's here, boss. And the select committee papers are ready. Christine'll brief you in the car on the way to the airport.'

Quinlan stood up and donned his jacket, tugging it into good order and shooting his cuffs. 'Sorry to rush,' he said. 'I've got to go and make the case against the full privatisation of a rapacious monopoly. Try to explain why it isn't a great idea to let a five-hundred-pound gorilla out of its cage to a pack of ideologues who'd sell their sisters to sailors and call it asset rationalisation.'

Phil Sebastian stayed seated, clearly anticipating my further assistance.

'Bit pressed myself,' I said. 'I'll come down with you, Barry.'

I followed Quinlan to the lift, just the two of us there waiting for the doors to open, Barry raising and lowering himself on the toes of his tiny, well-buffed shoes.

'Funny thing,' I said. 'I had a visit from the police the other day. Seems they've found Merv Cutlett at long last. What's left of him, at least.'

'Yeah,' said Quinlan, eyes on the floor numbers. 'I heard they were doing the rounds.' One lift went past, going all the way to the top, stopping to take on cargo. The other had taken up permanent residence in the basement. 'They talked to me last week. I was surprised there was anything left after all this time. Odd coincidence, eh, Charlie dying the day after they found him.' He tapped a toe, time-strapped. 'Showed you the watch, did they?'

'Yes. I didn't recognise it.'

'Me neither. I wish I'd had the presence of mind to say I

did, though. I should've told them I'd seen Merv wearing it. Save the taxpayer the expense of further buggerising around. Those forensic tests cost a poultice.'

Quinlan didn't sound like a man with anything to hide. He reached over and pressed the button again.

'I got asked some other questions as well,' I said. 'They wanted to know all about internal relations in the union. How everybody got along and so forth.'

'Yeah?' Quinlan raised an eyebrow. 'What did you tell them?'

'One big happy family. A veritable Woodstock.'

Quinlan snorted. The lift arrived and we stepped aboard, the only passengers.

'I got the impression they were giving the original reports a pretty thorough going over, like they were suspicious of something.'

'Well it was the Homicide Squad, right? That's the found bodies department. If they don't act suspicious, people think they're not on the job.'

The doors opened at the fourth floor and two women got in, talking some kind of finance language. Barry smiled and they smiled back, not drawing breath.

'So,' I said, just chatting. 'How did Merv manage to lure you up there that weekend, middle of winter? My idea of hell.'

'Well it wasn't for the fishing, that's for sure.' Quinlan adjusted his drape in the mirrored wall of the lift. 'That part was just Cutlett being bloody-minded. Actually, we'd gone up there to make him an offer, try to seal the deal on the amalgamation. The old coot had been playing hard to get, seeing how much he could squeeze out of the proposed new set-up before he'd agree to it.'

We followed the two women into the foyer. An officious looking young apparatchik in a navy pants-suit was standing by the door with a briefcase beside her and a fat folder in her hand. She looked towards us expectantly, but Barry signalled her to wait. We continued our conversation beside the tenants list. Orion Investment Planners. Cohen, Bullfinch and McGill. The Marasco Group of Companies. Leicester and Associates.

'It all came down to money and face. The golden parachute and its rate of descent. Cutlett wanted three years' salary, a term on the PEU executive and life access to the Shack. All of which wasn't going to happen. We were prepared to top up his super, which was already generous, and hang his picture in the hall of fame, but we weren't going to let him screw us. If he didn't accept, Charlie would go around him, swing the other state secretaries and he'd end up out in the cold.'

Quinlan was telling me this, his tone implied, for no other reason than to satisfy my curiosity. It was an act of courtesy.

'Cutlett being Cutlett, he would not go gently. Dug his heels in, made the whole exercise as difficult as possible. Always had to have the last word. He was the hairy-arsed champion of the underdog. We were a cabal of limp-wristed pen-pushers. Of course the big irony was that by getting himself drowned, he made the amalgamation both easier and cheaper. Charlie was assistant national secretary, *ex officio*. With Merv gone, he was in charge. The amalgamation sailed through under budget and ahead of schedule.'

'Earning you a seat in the Senate,' I said.

'Indeed,' he said, acknowledging the point with a courtly dip of his head. 'Indeed. And Charlie a place in the Reps. A most fortuitous outcome all round.'

One worth killing for? It would have been impolitic to ask.

Quinlan put his hand on my sleeve, signalling his departure. 'Just before I go,' he said. 'There's nobody out there in your neck of the woods looking to make an issue of Phil, is there? He'll be a real asset, you know.'

'These things are rarely uncontested,' I said. 'Nature of the beast.'

'Anybody in particular?'

'Nobody you need worry about, Barry.'

'But you'll keep your ears open?'

'I always do.' It was simple anatomy.

'Good man.' He patted me again and started for the door.

'Matter of fact, I did hear something might interest you,' I said. Quinlan paused mid-stride and turned. 'Apparently Sid Gilpin has resurfaced. He's trying to peddle some story about corruption at the Municipals, something involving you and Charlie.'

Quinlan creased his brow. 'Sid Gilpin?' He tried to place the name. 'Cutlett's off-sider? What story?'

'Dunno,' I said. 'He approached a journo I know, reckons he's got evidence of dirty deeds. Won't specify what until he sees a cheque-book.'

Quinlan made a world-weary face. 'Sounds like he hasn't changed. Your journo mate buying?'

'I don't think so.'

'Somebody should tell Gilpin we've got defamation laws in this country.'

'Specifically designed to protect politicians.'

'My oath,' said Quinlan. 'Who do you think made them?'

The aide approached, displaying her wrist to urge haste. Quinlan took the folder and gave me a parting nod. I watched them get into the back seat of his Comcar and drive away.

You can't defame the dead, I thought. Not within the meaning of the act. Once a man is gone, you can say anything you damned well like about him. And if you say it loud enough or long enough, it'll find its way into print. And if it's in print, it must be true.

A row of cabs was waiting outside the hotel across the street. I headed for the start of the line, hand raised, and gave a whistle.

The entire area between the waterfront and Spencer Street railway station looked chewed up and spat out. The shunting yards had been uprooted, the cargo sheds demolished, the oily earth churned by bulldozers.

From this blasted heath a glorious future would soon arise. The sod had been turned on an astroturf colosseum with a receding roof and fifty thousand pre-warmed seats, due for completion in 1999. The docks were destined for transformation into luxury apartments, high-rise mortgages with water views. Surprise, surprise.

The old nissen hut was virtually the only remaining evidence of the area's industrial past, a hump of curved tin marooned between dead-end roads and freeway feeder ramps. Grimy engine blocks, gutted washing machines and doorless refrigerators stood out the front with their hands in their pockets, looking bored and propping up weathered signs spray-painted on warped bits of plywood. CLOSING

Down Sale. All Stock Must Go. Last Days.

The big double doors were shut, so I gave the cabbie a twenty and asked him to wait.

A Docklands Authority notice-to-quit was tacked to the splintery timber of one of the doors. Its plastic sleeve was torn and the ink had bled on the tenant's name, rendering it illegible. From inside came the sound of machinery, a cutting or drilling device of some sort. A heavy chain hung loose, dangling an open padlock. I pushed at the door and it moved inwards.

The vaulted interior was lit only by filthy safety-glass windows. Worthless crap of every variety was laid out in aisles on the concrete floor. Obsolete computer monitors. The carapaces of busted stereo speakers. Rough stacks of chipped crockery. Milk crates and plastic baby-baths overflowing with disembodied chunks of kitchen appliances. Cracked wash-tubs. Scaly coils of perished garden hose. Rag-stoppered oil bottles and drip-encrusted paint tins with lids hardened on.

The aisles terminated at a chain-mesh partition running across the rear quarter of the shed. On my side of the wire, a figure was hunched over a bench, his back to me, working the screeching machinery. I waved off the cab and went inside.

I walked down the central aisle past a row of derelict Space Invader machines. Cracked screens, holes punched in their chipboard carcases. Inside the fenced section of the shed was a roofless room, its interior visible through an open door. Television sets were stacked haphazardly on a bench inside. One was running, its volume inaudible. Jerry Springer was working his audience. In front of the sets was a sagging sofa, a repository of yellowed bed linen. A boxy electric radiator glowed red, sending its heat upwards to a row of lights that hung from the ceiling. Their globes were screwed into basin-shaped enamel shades. Probably the only marketable objects in the place.

An open door led out the back. It had a Yale lock on the inside and a heavy-duty bolt on the outside. Standing just inside it was a slide-top ice-cream chiller. Magnum. Cornetto. Paddle Pop. Through the door I could see the tray of a ute and a 44-gallon drum, lidless and toppled. Flattened hessian sacks lined the drum and bleached dog turds surrounded it.

The din filled the shed, amplified by the curve of the walls. Its source was an ancient electric grinder bolted to an oily bench. The hunched figure was oblivious, engrossed in his task. He was picking tarnished brass pipe fittings out of a milk crate, polishing them on a spinning wire brush, then tossing them into another crate. He worked with the pointless mechanical monotony of a man shovelling mercury with a pitchfork. A can of beer sat by his elbow. From time to time he took a slug, maintaining a constant pace.

I stood at the end of the bench, trying to catch his eye. He wore leather work gloves, a frayed Collingwood beanie and a grot-marinated gabardine raincoat. When he'd finished the brass elbow-joints, he pushed back the armature, fitted a grinding wheel and started on a rusted pair of hedge clippers, sending out a spray of sparks. The bench was strewn with similar detritus. Corroded shears, rusted machetes, the heads of mattocks and axes. At this rate, I'd be waiting all day.

A lead ran from the grinder to a power board at my feet. I reached down and pulled out the plug. The motor shuddered to a halt, its bearings screaming. The bent figure straightened up and turned.

It was Gilpin all right, although it took me a moment to be certain. He must have been about sixty, but he looked at least ten years older. Time had not dealt well with Sid and little of the spivvy cockerel remained. Patchy stubble covered his cheeks and his eyes were half-buried in sagging pillows of flesh.

He tore off his ratty gloves and glowered at me.

'This is fucken harassment,' he exploded, spit flying from his lips. 'You lot, you think you can just barge in here any time you like. I've got until 5 p.m. Friday. Until then, I'm legally entitled to quiet possession. Now fuck off or I'll have the dog on you.'

I looked around reflexively. The dog was nowhere in sight.

'You've got the wrong end of the stick,' I said. 'I'm not here to evict you.'

Gilpin peered at me and wiped his mouth with the back of a bloated hand. His arm swept the merchandise. 'You want something?'

'I'm not a customer, Sid. I was at the Municipals when you worked there.'

He narrowed his gaze, trying to place me. Eventually, a tiny spark flickered.

'Talbot's bum boy? Whadda *you* want?'

'I've just come from Barry Quinlan's office,' I said. 'Senator Quinlan. He's heard you've been talking shit about him. Charlie Talbot, too.'

'Quinlan.' He spat out the name. 'Arsehole.'

'You'd be making a mistake to aggravate him.'

'He's the one made the mistake.' Gilpin raised his chin and widened his stance, the old Sid coming back. 'Sending some goon down here to intimidate me.'

Nobody had ever called me a goon before. Perhaps my new exercise regime was bearing fruit already.

'I'm not here to intimidate you, Sid. I'm here to deliver some free advice. You shouldn't go round telling porkies, trying to flog something you haven't got.'

Gilpin's breath was a laboured wheeze. For a long moment, we stared at each other. He hadn't just aged badly. He was not a well man. His eyes were filmy and jaundiced. He was mixing his medication with alcohol.

'Fucken Quinlan,' he said. 'And that weasel Charlie Talbot, you'd think he was Christ almighty, the stuff they've been printing about him in the papers. They'll be singing a different tune when they see what I've got.'

'And what's that, Sid?' I said. 'Water on the brain?'

He took a gulp from the can on the bench. In the sullen silence that followed, I could hear the slosh and stew of some half-formed idea slithering into life.

'You go back to Quinlan,' he said. 'Tell him I've got evidence he's a thief and a liar. Maybe worse, even. Talbot, too.'

'What sort of evidence?'

'Doc-u-mentary evidence,' he said. The can tilted high, almost empty. It wasn't much past noon.

'Doc-u-mentary evidence?' I said. 'Like what?'

'The sort I can stick in an envelope and send to the coppers. Really give them something to think about.' He licked his lips with relish. 'Maybe they'll begin to wonder if those two didn't have good reason to want Merv Cutlett dead. And who knows, maybe I'll get my memory back? Tell the coppers a few things that slipped my mind last time I talked to them.'

I felt sorry for him, the wretch. Flat broke. Sick as a dog.

High as the Goodyear blimp on a cocktail of ill health, pills, booze and malice.

'Let me get you to a doctor, have someone take a quick look. Maybe some income support.'

His face hardened into a snarl. 'Don't you fucken patronise me.'

Abruptly, he scooted backwards, coat-tails flapping, through the gate in the Cyclone partition. He swung it closed and shot the bolt, securing it with a twisted coat hanger.

'I'll show youse all,' he sneered through the wire. 'Just you wait and see.'

Prancing around and rubbing his hands like he was auditioning for the role of Fagin in a Julius Streicher production of *Oliver!*, he reached into the ice-cream chiller, pulled out a fresh can and disappeared into the roofless room, shutting the door behind him.

He didn't just need a doctor. He needed the burly chaps in white with the butterfly net.

The door flew open and he emerged with something in his hands. Small items bundled together with a rubber band. He stripped off the band and advanced towards the fence.

'Know what these are?'

I hooked my fingers on the links and peered through the chain mesh. He held two thin booklets, one in each hand.

'Passports?' I ventured.

'Bankbooks.' He stuffed one in his pocket and opened the other, extending it towards me at eye level.

I hadn't seen a savings passbook for years. They were obsolete, gone the way of the whalebone corset and the Betamax VCR. Gilpin shoved it at my face, close enough to read. Commonwealth Bank, 341 Victoria Street, Melbourne.

I remembered the branch. It occupied the building on the corner of Lygon Street, an august two-storey structure from the 1880s. It was something else now. Luxury apartments, probably. The side entrance of the Trades Hall was straight across the street.

The account holder's name was typed in a punch-card font. Barry Quinlan, it said. The columns showed a sequence of deposits over a six-month period, the first in February 1978. The amounts varied, averaging between one and two thousand dollars. The total balance was $18,022.07. It was withdrawn in a lump sum, all but the small change.

He held up the second passbook. The name at the top was Charles Talbot. The sum withdrawn was $14,225, leaving a balance of $2.04.

'More than thirty grand all up,' he said. 'Big bikkies in those days.'

I nodded. A year's wage, pre-tax, for a specialist tradesman or a mid-level manager. My own income that year would've been lucky to reach fifteen grand. He wrapped the rubber band around the passbooks and stowed them inside his coat, swapping them for his fresh can of beer. He popped the tab and foam oozed out. He licked it off his hand and waited for my reaction.

'They had bank accounts,' I said. 'So what?'

'And they cleaned them out on 27 July,' he said. 'Recognise the date, do you?'

I shrugged. 'Should I?'

'It's the Monday after Merv Cutlett went down,' he sneered. 'Interesting, eh?'

It was. Unfortunately.

'You've lost me, Sid,' I said. 'I've got no idea what you're talking about.'

'Quinlan will, though.' He took a long swig. 'So you get on your bike, sport. Go tell the senator that unless he sees me right, I'll make sure these little babies come to the attention of the coppers.'

I stayed where I was, fingers threaded through the wire. 'If these bankbooks are such hot property, how come Quinlan and Talbot let you get your mitts on them? It all sounds like crap to me, Sid.'

He flicked his wrist forward, shooing me away. I was merely the messenger, and a dumb one at that. 'Off you go, then. Scoot.'

'What do you want, Sid?'

He sneered. 'What do you reckon I want?'

'Money won't help if you're too crook to spend it. Let me get you to a doctor, eh?'

He sucked his breath inwards sharply and his eyes went hard. 'Fuck your doctor and fuck you and fuck Quinlan.' He pounded the front of his coat with the flat of his hand. 'These are going straight to the coppers.'

There was real menace in his voice. The guy was barking mad. Maybe the kennel and the chalk-stick turds were his.

'The senator's in Canberra for the next few days,' I said. 'Is this something I should talk about on the phone? Calls to federal parliament are recorded, you know.'

Gilpin's paranoid cunning was racing ahead of itself. Whatever his plan, he hadn't thought it all the way through. 'When's he coming back?'

'Later in the week.' I had to say something. 'Thursday.'

'Tell him he's got until Wednesday, close of business.'

'You have a figure in mind?'

'Tell him to make me an offer.' He fixed me in his yellow, puffer-fish gaze, an idea crossing his eyes like a fast-burning fuse. 'And while you're at it, take the same message to whatsername. That stuck-up bint from the office. The one Talbot had his tongue out for. Married her, didn't he? She must be worth quite a few bob now. Careful bloke like him would've been insured to the hilt. And the super. Politicians have always got a shitload of that.' He chugged on his can. 'Oh, yeah. She'd pay almost anything, I bet, to preserve Charlie-boy's good name.'

He stayed in his cage as I walked up the aisle of worthless trash. As I neared the door, he called out.

'Don't get any smart ideas. They're well stashed. And if I see you or anyone else around the place, the deal's off.'

When I looked back at the shed from the kerb, he was standing at the back corner, his coat drawn around him, watching me go.

Fliteplan Travel operated from a low-rise art deco apartment block in St Kilda Road, the vestige of a bygone era on an avenue of glass-clad office buildings. The elms were shedding their foliage and eddies of brittle brown chaff swirled around the angular metal sculptures in the granite forecourt of the advertising agency next door.

I climbed the stairs to the second floor, found the flat with the sign on the door, gave a light rap and went straight in.

Fliteplan did most of its business over the phone, so Margot hadn't wasted any money on décor. The living room doubled as her office, and I could hear muted female voices and computer tapping noises from the direction of main bedroom. A big window overlooked Fawkner Park, level with the treetops, and the wall of the kitchenette had been replaced with a laminex bench.

Margot was sitting at her table, working her way through the mail. She'd painted up and fluffed her hair, but her face was still drawn and a bit emptied-out. She looked up and gave me a convalescent smile.

'Murray, love,' she said. 'What a pleasant surprise.'

'A surprise,' I agreed sombrely, 'but not too pleasant, I'm afraid.' I shut the door leading towards the rooms where the staff were working. 'I've just been to see Sid Gilpin.'

Margot cocked her head sideways and stared at me, mystified.

I sat down at the table. The neat piles of envelopes were the same sort as I'd seen at the house. Condolence cards. Margot had been slicing them open with a letter opener and making a list.

'He's all hopped up,' I said. 'Mad as a cut snake. He showed me his so-called evidence of corruption at the Municipals. It's a couple of old bankbooks. One in Charlie's name, the other in Barry Quinlan's. Substantial sums were deposited in the months before Merv Cutlett's death, then withdrawn immediately afterwards.'

Margot gave me a blank look and shrugged.

'You don't know anything about this?'

She shook her head. 'You told me nobody was taking Gilpin seriously.'

'That might change.' There was no point in pussy-footing. 'A journalist, Vic Valentine, has taken an interest.'

The thin wash of colour drained out of Margot's face. 'The crime reporter?'

'He's not a bad bloke, as journalists go,' I said. 'Gilpin tried to flog him the corruption story but Valentine gave him the bum's rush. Since then, unfortunately, another angle has come up. Valentine's got inside information on the state of the remains. The forensics suggest that Cutlett was shot, then dumped in the lake.'

Margot furrowed her brow. 'Shot?'

'There's a hole in the skull, apparently.'

'A bullet hole?'

'It's absurd, I know.'

Margot reached into her handbag, its strap slung over the back of her seat, and fished out a pack of cigarettes. 'Open the window, will you, Murray?' she said. 'Can't smoke in here. Hell to pay.'

I slid open the glass. A concrete windowbox was built into the ledge. Red geraniums. Margot held a cigarette to bloodless lips. I found my lighter and summoned up a flame. Margot inhaled sharply, her hand trembling.

'The police think Charlie shot Merv Cutlett?'

I shrugged my shoulders. 'Far as I know, they still haven't got a positive ID on the remains. They're waving around photos of a wristwatch found at the recovery scene, trying to establish if it belonged to Merv. I'm pretty sure it didn't. But even without a confirmed identification, it seems a fair bet they're proceeding on the assumption it's him. The hole in the skull can't be ignored and there's some inconsistencies in Charlie and Barry Quinlan's original testimony. Exact location of the accident and so forth. So they've got a potential victim and possible perpetrators. Right now, I imagine they're casting about for a possible motive.'

'And you think these bankbooks might give them one?'

'Gilpin certainly does,' I said. 'He's threatening to send them to the cops anonymously. Set the cat among the pigeons. He's prepared to back off, he says, but it'll cost.'

She drew back hard and exhaled. 'The little shit.'

I went into the kitchenette, found a saucer and put it on the table between us. Margot tapped her gasper hard against the rim. It didn't need ashing.

'How much does he want?'

'Money won't fix it,' I said. 'Sid's off with the goblins.'

She tapped a couple more times, her thoughts turned inward. 'What about Barry Quinlan? Have you talked to him?'

'I came straight to you,' I said.

A draft came through the window, ruffling the pages of Margot's notepad. She used the saucer as a paperweight and stood, staring out over the windowbox, one hand on her throat. She suddenly looked about a million years old.

'"Don't worry",' she said. 'That's what Charlie told me. "It's over and done with". And I believed him because that's what I wanted to believe. But of course it's not over, is it?'

She left her cigarette burning in the saucer, sending up a thin curl of smoke. I picked it up and took a drag. It tasted of nothing. 'I'll do whatever I can to help,' I said. 'These bankbooks…'

'I don't know anything about them.' Her tone was sharp. She turned her back and stared out into the park. 'But I do know that Charlie didn't kill Merv Cutlett. And neither did Barry Quinlan.'

'Of course not,' I started. 'I'm not…'

'It was me,' she said. 'I'm the one who put a bullet in his brain.'

A woman, late twenties, with funky specs and a hedgehog haircut bounded out of the work area, a coffee mug in each hand.

'Oops,' she blurted. 'Didn't realise we had a visitor.'

I hastily grubbed the cigarette out in the saucer. Margot didn't miss a beat.

'Jodie, this is Murray,' she said. 'A friend.'

Jodie had registered the tension in the air. She gave me a cagey nod. Friend or not, I was obviously the bearer of bad news. A smoker in other people's workplace, come to heap even more sorry business on her boss's shoulders.

She clanked her mugs down on the metal sink top and began to run a stream of water into an electric jug. 'Can I get you a cup of something?'

Margot slid the window shut. 'That new lunch place next door,' she said. 'Today might be a good time for you and Michele to give it a try.'

Jodie took the hint. Shooting daggers at me through her Jenny Kee eyewear, she collected her workmate Michele and the two of them scuttled through the pregnant silence and disappeared out the front door.

'I want a full report,' Margot called after them, reassuringly.

Then she turned and stared through the window, her elbow cupped in one hand. An elegantly turned-out businesswoman in her fifties, shoulders square, her hair just a shade lighter than the overcast sky. Down in the park, the spindly fingers of the treetops clawed uselessly at the air.

The silence stretched out, taut as a piano string. The bell had been rung. There was no unringing it. I extended a fresh cigarette. She smiled bleakly and let me light it for her, steady now. When she sat down, I reached across the table and gave her hand a reassuring squeeze. It was ice.

She took a deep breath and began to talk.

'Charlie would never tell me what happened up there at Nillahcootie,' she said. 'He'd only ever say that it wasn't my fault, none of it, Cutlett's death included, and that nobody else knew. About me, I mean. But whatever happened at the lake, it gave Barry Quinlan some sort of a hold over him, at least for a while. If this comes out, Quinlan will blame Charlie for everything. I won't let that happen. I'll go to the police myself.'

The words were gushing out, tumbling over each other, dissolving her hard-maintained self-control. A fearful and frightening look had entered her eyes. I held up the palm of my hand.

'Stop,' I said. 'Wait.'

I went into the kitchenette, switched on the jug and opened the top door of the refrigerator. On the shelf beside the ice-cubes was a bottle of Stolichnaya. I poured a tot, put the glass on the table in front of her, sat down and lit myself a cigarette. Margot blew her nose on a tissue, downed the vodka and shuddered.

'There's no hurry,' I said. 'Take your time.'

She breathed deep, nodded and started again.

'It happened the Friday night,' she began. 'We'd been flat out all day at the office. Prue was home sick with the Hong Kong flu, the temp was out of her depth and the photocopier was on the blink. There were the phones, the fortnightly pay figures. Organisers in and out. Heaps of typing and copying. To cap it off, Charlie landed Mavis with a last-minute job, typing up some documents for a meeting up at the Shack that weekend.'

She scratched her ash on the rim of the saucer. 'Remember how we all felt sorry for him, the way Merv dragged him up there whenever they had something important to settle?'

She was circling, trying to find a way to tell it.

'Anyway,' she continued. 'Five o'clock came and Mavis still hadn't finished. It was her wedding anniversary, one of the big ones. Her family was throwing a turn and there was no question of her working late. Charlie was getting anxious, so I offered to stay back and finish the job. Kind of hoping, I suppose.'

I'd been too dense to notice it at the time, but for months there'd been an unvoiced attraction between Charlie and Margot. Lingering looks and hungry glances, never acted upon. Her offer, and Charlie's acceptance of it, must have been loaded with implicit possibilities.

'Mum was minding Katie, so I rang and told her I'd be a bit late. Charlie went home to Elsternwick to have tea with Shirley and the kids. He said he'd be back at seven-thirty to pick up the papers. After that, he'd collect Merv for the drive up to the Shack.'

Margot went back to the window and stood staring out into the park. I leaned into the fragile silence, letting her take her time.

It was past seven when Charlie phoned to say he was running late. 'He said he'd swing past in half an hour, to wait with the stuff at the side door of the Trades Hall, outside Cutlett's office. I could hear his kids in the background and I knew there was no hope of anything happening between us that night.'

Disappointed, dutiful, Margot did as she was asked. As she hurried along the footpath, Merv Cutlett and Sid Gilpin staggered out of the John Curtin.

'Pissed, of course,' she said. 'I walked faster, tried to shake them off, but we were all going in the same direction and they started trying to crack on to me. Nothing heavy, just a bit of drunken teasing. They were in a pretty good mood, and I didn't want to get them offside, so I slowed down and walked across the street with them.'

I could picture it clearly. Margot, hugging the buff envelope of papers to herself against the evening chill. Two blokes rolling out of the pub, full of beer, full of themselves. The three of them waiting at the traffic light, the suggestive joviality, Margot's resigned acquiescence.

'I was hoping that Charlie had already arrived, that he'd be waiting when we got to Merv's office. But he wasn't. Merv and Gilpin were both a lot drunker than I first thought. Merv wanted to get something from his office, something he had to take up to the Shack with him. The side door was locked and he kept dropping his keys. When Gilpin tried to help him, he told him to fuck off, there were still some things he was capable of doing himself. He told him to make himself useful, go get some fish'n'chips for the drive. Gilpin was rabbiting on about whether he should get flake or couta and did Merv want a bloody potato cake, and Merv was fumbling with the door. I was just wishing that Charlie would hurry up and arrive so I could go and pick up Katie.'

Margot absently fingered her wedding ring, a plain band with a row of small diamonds, twisting it round and round. I took the vodka glass into the kitchen and threw the switch on the electric jug.

'As soon as Gilpin was gone, Merv got the door open. He went down the steps and unlocked his office. A few seconds later, he called up to me. "Hey, girlie. Come and give me a hand."' She rolled her eyes. 'Like an idiot, I went down.'

A phone started to ring in the work area. Margot ignored it, butted out her half-smoked cigarette and lit another.

'He was standing behind the door. As soon as I stepped inside, he jumped me. Put his arms around me and tried to kiss me. He was always a bit of a letch, but this was the first time he'd ever got physical. I didn't really take it seriously, just pushed him way. But he stumbled backwards and dragged me down with him. And when I tried to stand up, he shoved his knee between my legs and pinned me underneath him. He was slobbering all over my face and telling me I was beautiful.'

She spoke in a flat, drained monotone, paying out the words one at a time. It was as if she was making an accounting to herself, as well as to me.

'I told him not to be stupid, that he was hurting me, but he wouldn't listen. He held his hand over my mouth and started tearing at my clothes. I was kicking and struggling, trying to get up, but he had my hair pinned to the carpet.

That awful brown shagpile. I couldn't breathe. He ripped my pantyhose and started to undo his pants. He was only a skinny bloke but he was strong, a lot stronger than me. I was really, really scared.'

The jug boiled and switched itself off with a sharp click. I gingerly rinsed Jodie's mugs and spooned coffee into a plunger, my attention wavering no more than an inch from Margot's face.

'I was struggling, trying to get out from under him. I grabbed the lead to the desk lamp and pulled it. The lamp crashed onto the floor and I grabbed it by the stem and hit him with it,' her hand bludgeoned the air. 'Hit him as hard as I bloody could.' Abruptly, she stopped, her fist poised as if still closed around the stem of the lamp. 'You ever see Merv's desk lamp?'

I put two mugs of coffee on the table. 'Solid brass shell casing, right?' I said. 'One of Merv's very tasteful items of militaria.'

She nodded. 'The base was a kind of starburst of bullets.' She fanned out her fingers. 'Anyway, it did the trick. Knocked him out cold. I rolled him off me and managed to find my feet. At that exact moment, Charlie came through the door.'

I pictured what he saw. Cutlett, insensible on the floor, his pants undone. Margot, dishevelled and terror-stricken, standing over him with the lamp in her hand.

'Charlie immediately took charge of the situation. He was so calm, so gentle. He took the lamp away from me, put his arms around me, just held me until I stopped trembling. Then he sat me down in a chair and examined Merv. He was still out cold. I thought I'd killed him, but Charlie said there was no blood, he was just stunned, that he'd be okay.'

She went into the kitchenette and came back with a jar of sugar and the bottle of vodka. She poured a nip of Stoli into each of our coffees and sat back down.

'He was wonderful,' she said. 'He wanted to know if I was hurt, did I need a doctor. He was going to call the police, but I wouldn't let him. We all knew stories about girls who'd gone to the cops and wished they hadn't. I wasn't thinking straight. The main thing I was worried about was being late to pick up Katie. Charlie said he'd sort things out. He made sure I was okay, escorted me to the toilet to clean up, called a taxi and sent me home. He told me not to worry, that he'd take care of Merv.'

She started to light another cigarette. I took it from her and slipped it back in the packet. There were five butts in the saucer and only one of them was mine.

'And so he did,' I said.

'Yeah.' She laughed harshly. 'Splish, splash.'

She took a sip of her coffee and grimaced at the taste. But at least the tension was draining from her face.

'I did exactly what he said. I picked up Katie and went home. All that night and all the next day, I kept thinking he'd ring me. He didn't. I realised why when I saw the Saturday evening news.'

Charlie had taken care of Merv all right, successfully disposed of his body, evidently aided by Barry Quinlan. He'd taken care of Margot, too, made sure that she wasn't called to account for Cutlett's death, spared her the ordeal of the judicial process.

'I can't even begin to guess what he told Barry Quinlan and Col Bishop. All he'd ever tell me was that neither of them knew that I was responsible,' she said. 'I knew he couldn't possibly have told Shirley. Whatever he did, he'd done for me. I didn't need to know the details. Does that make sense?'

I nodded. The vodka gave a bitter aftertaste to the coffee. I added sugar, but it didn't help much.

'I couldn't bear the idea that he should have to explain himself. To me, or anyone else. The important thing was that he understood how grateful I felt. If he ever tried to raise it, I'd just put my fingers to his lips and turn away. And when he died…well there was nothing left to say.'

Nor was there anything I could say. I reached across and gave her hand another squeeze. It wasn't so cold anymore. That was something. Certain things were clearer now, but we were still only half-way there. We faced each other across the rims of our mugs, sipping the vile coffee. Margot waited for me to speak.

'Got any biscuits?' I said.

She laughed, and the tension in the room slackened a little. While she searched the kitchen cupboards, I digested the implications of her confession.

If Vic Valentine was right about the forensics, Merv's lamp accounted for the hole in his skull. The rope had probably been used to weigh the body down. Getting him into the car wouldn't have been a problem, not if Charlie was parked right outside the door. He was burlier than Merv and it would only have been a few seconds' work to get him across the footpath. Anybody who happened to notice would've just seen a bloke helping his pissed-legless mate, not an unusual occurrence in that neighbourhood at the time. By the time Sid Gilpin arrived with the flake and chips, they'd already left.

'So,' said Margot, putting an open packet of Tim Tams on the table. 'There you have it. I didn't mean to kill Merv

Cutlett, and I didn't ask Charlie to do what he did. But those bankbooks haven't got anything to do with it. And if Sid Gilpin or Barry Quinlan or anybody else tries to make out they do, that Charlie was some kind of a crook, I'll...' She was angry again now. 'I'll...' She broke one of the biscuits in half. 'Jesus, Murray, I don't know what I'll do.'

'Then don't do anything,' I said. 'As soon as you're okay to drive, go home. If the police get back in touch, which I doubt, just tell them you're not feeling well. You've done your fair share of confessing for the moment. Just leave things to me for a while, okay?'

'What are you going to do?'

'I'm not completely sure,' I said. 'I'll ring you later.'

She looked down at the half-opened pile of condolence letters. I gathered them up, along with a Tim Tam, and got to my feet. 'I'll take care of these. You go home.'

We embraced. The brittleness was still there, but there was something else as well. Something steely I hadn't registered last time. 'It'll be all right,' I said. 'I promise.'

I hoped to Christ I was right.

'Parliament House,' I told the cab driver.

Whatever else I'd got myself into, I still had a living to make. In twenty minutes the Health and Social Services Policy Committee would be looking at my empty chair and making tut-tutting noises.

'Permanent House?' said the chirpy sub-continental behind the wheel. 'Near airport.'

'No such luck,' I said. '*Parliament* House. Big joint, top end of Bourke Street. More columns than the *Weekend Australian*.'

We cruised towards the CBD, stopping to have a cup of tea and a chat with every red light on the way. I pulled out my phone and called Inky.

'Another record-breaking performance on Saturday,' I said, mouth full of chocolate biscuit.

'Leppitsch played well.'

'If you don't count getting reported for striking.' As we

reached the Shrine of Remembrance, it started to drizzle. 'I've spoken with Barry Quinlan. I've also had a word with Sid Gilpin.'

'And?'

'Well, Quinlan didn't let any cats out of any bags, if that's what you're asking. He seems pretty relaxed. Didn't give me any openings. Gilpin, on the other hand, is wound up tighter than a clockwork monkey. He's talking all sorts of crazy shit. Little wonder the media's giving him a wide berth. But it might be an idea to give Vic Valentine a buzz, see if there's any further activity on the walloper front.'

'Something in particular you're concerned about?'

'Just curious about progress on dem bones. No point in spinning our wheels if it isn't even Cutlett.'

'I'll see what I can find out.'

The cab driver had found the slowest tram in Melbourne to follow, peering at it through the slapping wipers as though intrigued by the sight. He bore not the slightest resemblance to the official driver ID photo on the dashboard. Perhaps it was the first tram he'd ever seen.

I checked my message bank, hoping that Lanie had called to accept my invitation to the Croupiers' Gala. No such luck. Ayisha was the only caller. I dialled the electorate office. Mike Kyriakis had phoned, she reported, wanting to know if I'd made up my mind.

'He's talked himself into running,' she said. 'What do you want me to tell him?'

'Tell him if he holds off announcing his bid until tonight, I'll take readings of the branch secretaries, see if I can't rustle him up some support. First round votes only. Nobody's going to die in a ditch for him.'

'By you, I presume you mean me.'

'You don't keep a dog and bark yourself.'

'Careful Murray,' Ayisha said. 'I know where you live.'

'But first, can you please call Phil Sebastian at Barry Quinlan's office,' I said. 'Tell him we're poised to assist and you're setting up some appointments with local movers and shakers on Wednesday. Turn on the charm.'

'Appointments with who?'

'Nobody,' I said. 'We're blowing smoke.'

'Does that mean…?'

'Anybody else call?' I said, cutting her off short. 'An Andrea Lane?'

While I was talking, I flipped through Margot's pile of condolence cards. A parchment-quality envelope with a heraldic device in the corner caught my eye. A lion rampant surmounting the words *Mildura Grand Hotel*.

'No Lanes,' said Ayisha. 'Just the usual. Nothing that can't wait.'

When I left the Grand, I hadn't thought to enquire about Charlie's bill. It suddenly occurred to me that he'd flagged out, but maybe he hadn't checked out. Surely the hotel hadn't forwarded his bill to his widow? I thumbed open the envelope. It contained a letter of condolence, signed from the management and staff, and a courtesy slip with Charlie's uncollected messages attached. Calls he'd missed while he was busy eating breakfast and dying of a heart attack. There were only two. One was taken at 7:45, the other at 9:15. Please call urgently. Two different numbers, but the same name on each slip.

'Before you do anything else, do me a favour, will you?' I said to Ayisha. 'Call the House and give my apologies for the Health and Social Services Committee meeting.'

I rang off and dialled the number on the second slip, the

one left at 9:15. Business hours. The phone was answered after three rings.

'Pro Vice-Chancellor's office,' said a plummy female voice.

'I have a message to ring Colin Bishop urgently.'

'The professor isn't here at the moment. He's at a conferring ceremony at our city campus.'

'The one in Flinders Street?'

'That's correct. If it's urgent, perhaps I can assist.'

I doubted it. I thanked her, hung up and tapped the cabby's elbow. 'Just here, thanks, mate.' We were at the lights outside Flinders Street station.

'Parmalat House?' He looked uncertainly towards the railway station, the finest example of Indo-Colonial architecture in the southern hemisphere.

'That's right, mate,' I said, scribbling a voucher and thrusting it into his hand. 'Good job.'

The city campus of the Maribyrnong University was a twelve-storey office building above a shopping arcade near the corner of Queen Street. Student types were dawdling around the lifts, toting folders and chatting in Cantonese. I scanned the directory and decided the top-floor Assembly Hall was the likeliest prospect for the diploma-bestowing solemnities.

The Assembly Hall owed less to the traditions of Oxbridge than the aesthetics of a hotel-basement ballroom. The seats were crammed with polyglot parents and well-wishers while graduands wearing rented academic gowns and their best trainers stood in a shuffling line waiting for their names to be called. One by one, they stepped forward to receive the rolled parchment in a cardboard tube that certified them to be fully credentialled Bachelors of Food

Handling and Spinsters of Tourism Marketing. The faculty, doing its best to add lustre to the occasion, was sitting solemnly on the dais in floppy velvet scholars' caps and colour-coded gowns. They looked like a high school production of *A Man for All Seasons*. Colin Bishop was standing centre stage, dishing out the diplomas.

There seemed still to be another fifty or so customers waiting their turn, so I sidled along the back wall and slipped outside onto a long balcony that overlooked the river and Southbank. The drizzle had lifted and a couple of rough-nut fathers were sneaking a quick fag at one end. I botted a light, took my smoke and my phone out of earshot and dialled Peter Thorsen's office. After a short wait, the deputy leader came on the line.

'That matter we discussed,' I said. 'Still in the market for a kamikaze pilot, or has your Turkish mate Durmaz already found one for you?'

'Durmaz couldn't find Anatolia in an atlas,' said Thorsen. 'Got a taker, have you?'

'Two conditions,' I said. 'First, if I get this bloke to run, I want a definite commitment that I'll be a member of any shadow cabinet you form if and when you're elected leader, and that I'll remain there until the next election.'

Across the river, work crews were erecting stages in the forecourt of the new casino building, getting everything chip-shape for the grand opening on Thursday evening. This gambling caper, I thought, it can really suck you in.

'Second,' I continued. 'This stalking horse, he's a mate. I don't want to see him completely humiliated. I need your assurance that you'll do your best to get him some central panel votes, at least for the first round.'

Thorsen thought for a moment. 'Done and done.'

'In writing.'

A written commitment to include me in his putative frontbench team would be a token of Thorsen's good faith, nothing more. If niggle came to nudge, it wasn't worth the paper it was written on. An undertaking to steal votes from Phil Sebastian, however, was documentary evidence that he was conspiring to white-ant his liege lord, Alan Metcalfe.

Thorsen didn't hesitate. 'Yes to the first, no to the second.'

'Done,' I said. Some you win, some you just try for size.

'So who's your candidate?'

'Mike Kyriakis, Mayor of Broadmeadows, hero of the rank and file, pillar of the influential Greek community, valued member of the Left.'

'Beautiful,' said Thorsen. 'Fits like a glove. I'm penning my promise as we speak.'

A sustained, concluding burst of applause came from the conferring ceremony. The Exalted Ones were processing down the central aisle, followed by the newly minted graduates. The audience was on its feet, clapping proudly. I went back inside and contributed to the goodwill. May Providence smile upon them and all who consume their portion-controlled comestibles.

The procession arrived at an area lined with tables laid out with teacups and self-serve urns. There, it broke into its constituent parts and began milling around, joined immediately by members of the audience. Cameras began to flash and a congratulatory din arose.

I waded into the crowd and found Colin Bishop being dragooned into a photo-op with a beaming, tube-brandishing young lady and her camera-wielding mother. He recognised me and projected a telepathic plea. If this wasn't nipped in the bud, he'd be fair game for the rest of them.

'Pro vice-chancellor,' I cried, charging into shot. 'Come quickly. You're needed in the symposium. The dean's had an aphorism. He's defalcated on the bursar again.'

Grabbing him by the vestments, I dragged him into the lift lobby, shouldered open the fire door and steered him into the stairwell.

'Thank you, Murray.' He shook himself free, pushed his glasses back up the bridge of his nose and checked that his beard was still attached. 'It's the clobber. They always want a picture with the robes. You've got someone graduating today? One of your kids? I'll just go and hang this up.'

I blocked his way. 'Before you do,' I said. 'A word in your Thomas Cranmer-like orifice, if you don't mind.'

He registered my stance and the edge in my voice. 'What's wrong? Are you upset about something?'

'I'm upset that you lied to me, Col. I'm upset that you think I'm an idiot.'

'Lied?' He furrowed his brow and blinked, owl-like behind his spectacles. 'Idiot?'

'Is there an echo in here?' I said. 'You heard me. Out at the cemetery at Charlie Talbot's funeral, you said you'd lost touch with him, hadn't spoken with him in years, that you'd been meaning to catch up but never seemed to get around to it. Turns out that you rang him at seven-thirty on the morning he died. At a country hotel. Funny time and place to call somebody out of the blue. Slip your mind, did it, Col?'

His mouth did the goldfish thing. 'I…'

'What was so urgent that morning, Col?' I brandished the message slips. 'That's what your messages said. "Urgent".'

He took a step backwards and stumbled. I grabbed him

and didn't let go, even after he had a steadying grip on the tubular steel banister. His eyes were wide with fear. But that didn't stop me. I wasn't going to hurt him, just ask a few questions.

'Something you read in the paper that morning, was it? Human remains found in Lake Nillahcootie, presumed to be a long-lost drowning victim. You thought it might be a good idea if you all got your heads together—you, Charlie and Barry—make sure you still had your stories straight when the cops came around checking the details again?'

He stared at me, open mouthed, like I was Mario the Magnificent, mind-reader extraordinaire. He made a blustery noise and started shaking his head.

'You didn't tell them anything you might regret, I hope.'

Bishop shook his head, then nodded, then shook it again. His floppy velvet hat bounced around, adding to the pathos. To think this man had once taught self-assertion to officials of the Nurses' Federation.

'I wouldn't…'

'You wouldn't what, Col? You wouldn't have a fit of the wobblies and decide to make a clean breast of it? Of course you wouldn't. Because that would mean dobbing in Barry Quinlan. And Barry wouldn't like that, would he? Told you to get a grip, did he? Told you when you rang him that morning and told you again at the funeral?'

I was winging it. Firing wildly and hoping for a reaction. Bishop's mouth was opening and closing, but nothing was coming out.

If nothing else, I'd managed to freak him out. He started sweating, actual beads of moisture forming on his forehead. He took off his extra-large chocolate beret and wiped himself. I'd pummelled him into submission. He was on the ropes. I paused for breath and he summoned up his indignation.

'Now listen...'

The door bumped against my back. Somebody wanted to use the stairs. I held the door shut.

'No, you listen, Professor,' I said. 'You're in deep shit right now, and I'm here to throw you a lifeline. Take me somewhere we can talk in private.'

He gulped, turned and trotted down the fire stairs. I followed him down three floors and along a corridor to a door with a name plate that read VISITING FELLOWS. That was us, all right.

The room contained two empty desks with cheap office chairs and a window that looked onto a blank wall. I herded him ahead of me into one of the chairs and loomed over him.

'Now tell me what happened when you got to the Shack and found Merv Cutlett dead.'

'Dead?' The pro vice-chancellor blinked. 'Where on earth did you get that idea? He was alive as you and me.'

I sank into the vacant chair. Its hydraulics were kaput and it deflated slowly beneath me, folding my knees into my chest.

Colin Bishop took off his silly hat and scratched at his thinning hair, staring at me like I'd lost my marbles. I suddenly realised I was his Sid Gilpin. A raving lunatic spinning wild fantasies out of random scraps of information.

'Are you okay, Murray?' he said soothingly. 'What's all this about?'

Now that I'd stopped raving, he was going all pastoral care on me. Next thing, he'd be suggesting a doctor. I had to find a different approach before he smothered me in solicitude. I elevated my posterior and fiddled with my piston. The seat rose beneath me.

'Those questions you asked at the cemetery about Charlie's final last words and so forth, they've been playing on my mind, Col. Truth is, he did say something. It didn't make sense to me at the time. I thought it was just heavy breathing. But now I think he was saying, "Merv, Merv".'

The rabbit-in-the-headlights look came back into Bishop's face.

'I didn't see the report in the *Herald Sun* about Lake Nillahcootie until after the funeral. And then, when I found those message slips from the hotel in Charlie Talbot's effects, I thought…well, the heart attack and everything. I thought maybe there are things I'm entitled to know. Especially now that the police have been to see me, asking questions about Charlie and his relationship with Merv Cutlett.'

My apologetic, wounded tone had the right effect. The voltage dropped and Bishop gave an understanding nod. He opened his mouth. Before he could apply the soft soap, I changed tack again.

'It's pretty clear the cops think something untoward happened to Merv Cutlett,' I said. 'And now that the press is taking an interest, there's some concern among, well, certain people as to the potential fall-out. Since I happened to have a background at the Municipals, albeit minor, I've been tasked on a very confidential basis to appraise myself of the essential facts of the situation and to minimise the prospect of an adverse outcome.'

Col was going cross-eyed trying to unravel this combination of obfuscation, misrepresentation and management-speak.

'There are a number of issues of concern here,' I said, counting them off on my fingers. 'First, Charlie Talbot's reputation. Second, Barry Quinlan's exposure to risk. Third, the overall standing of the party.'

Bishop nodded along with the beat.

'So far your name hasn't come up,' I said. 'But it's there in the Coroner's report and…well, suffice to say, I'll do my best to see that your interests are protected. Assuming, of course, you're frank with me.'

Bishop took off his glasses and massaged the bridge of his nose. There was no getting around the fact that I knew considerably more than I should about this matter. Also, I was clearly capable of going off like a Catherine wheel if he didn't at least go through the motions.

'What do you want, Murray?'

'The truth, Col,' I said. 'My objective is to keep the lid on this thing. I can't do that if I've only got half the picture.'

He didn't exactly look enthusiastic. Rain washed across the window, darkening the room.

'I've told you the truth,' he said. 'Cutlett was alive and well when Barry and I got to the Shack.'

'Have it your own way then, Col.' I stood up. 'But if anybody takes the fall over this, you can bet it won't be Barry Quinlan.'

Bishop gestured for me to sit back down. 'He was alive,' he said glumly. 'But he wasn't too well. He usually got blotto on the drive up from Melbourne, so we expected he'd be a bit the worse for wear, but we'd never seen him in such a bad way. He was sprawled on a couch, semi-conscious, groaning and grunting. Charlie said he'd slipped and hit the back of his head on the corner of the car door when they stopped for a roadside leak. His hair was matted with dried blood, but he wouldn't let Charlie near him to clean it up.'

So Charlie had told Margot the truth, I thought. Her blow with the lamp wasn't fatal. Merv must have come round at some point, probably while he was being bundled into the car. Charlie probably assumed that he'd recover on the way to the Shack. And when he got his wits back, he'd be both chastened and grateful that his behaviour with

Margot had been covered up. That would also account for Charlie's fabrication about his condition.

'The three of us got hold of him and tried to take a look, but that just stirred him up. Bastard kicked me in the shins.' Bishop rubbed his lower leg, demonstrating the precise location. 'We waited until he flaked again, then dragged him into a bedroom and dumped him on the bed. We took off his shoes, tossed the bedspread over him, turned on his electric blanket and left him to sleep it off.'

'But he didn't wake up?' I said.

Bishop took a handkerchief from his pocket and wiped his glasses, fully committed now. 'We had a drink, went to bed. Next morning, it wasn't even light, I got up for a pee. On the way back from the bathroom, I stuck my head in Merv's door. He was flat on his back, just like we'd left him. Something didn't look right. All this gunk had leaked out of the back of his head onto the pillow. It was…' he smiled weakly, 'very unpleasant. And he didn't seem to be breathing.'

'So you woke up Charlie and Barry.'

He nodded. 'We tried to revive him. CPR, mouth-to-mouth. It was useless. His body was warm but that was probably because of the electric blanket. It was set on high and it had been running all night.'

'Why didn't you call an ambulance?' I said.

'I wanted to,' Bishop said. 'So did Charlie. He was at his wits' end. I think he blamed himself for not being more forceful. He thought if he'd got Merv medical attention earlier, he'd still be alive. But Barry didn't agree. It was too late for an ambulance, he said. Cutlett was obviously dead. It wasn't like they could bring him back to life.'

'And Barry was concerned about the way it might look?' I said.

'You know what he's like,' Bishop nodded. 'Always one step ahead. Cutlett dying under those circumstances, at that time, alone with three of his known political adversaries. Years of patient work were at risk. Something like this could have made us pariahs in the union movement. Or laughing stocks. Or worse still, a bit of both.'

'He told you that it would be better to stage an accident. Drop Merv's body in the lake, make it look like a tragic boating mishap.'

'He was very persuasive.' Col Bishop stared down between his knees, studying the carpet. 'Play it right and the body might not be found for hours, days even, he said. The head injury could easily have been down to a knock from the boat.'

'What did Charlie say?'

'Not much.' He thought about it. 'Actually, he was a lot less resistant to the idea than you might expect.'

And so it was done. In the pre-dawn darkness, the boat was launched and the body loaded. Charlie and Barry pushed off onto the fog-shrouded lake while Bishop remained behind, lit the fire, burned the fluid-stained pillow and waited for the others to return.

'Barry said they'd be back in fifteen or twenty minutes at the most,' he said. 'But they were gone for much longer than that. A storm blew up and rain was bucketing down. I thought they'd capsized or hit a submerged tree or something.'

He wanted me, I could see, to understand what an ordeal this had been for him. That he, too, had shouldered his share of the terrible burden. The blank-faced window behind him was a tremulous, rain-streaked shimmer. A wintry pall suffused the small room.

'It was getting light and there was still no sign of them. Then Sid Gilpin turned up. He'd driven part of the way the previous night, been breathalysed going through Seymour and the cops had confiscated his car keys. He'd had to spend the night in a motel before he could get them back.'

'He was party to the planned discussions, was he?' I said.

Bishop shrugged. 'I told him the story we'd concocted, that Merv had insisted on taking the other two out fishing and they were still somewhere on the lake. Then the boat turned up. They'd had trouble with the motor. Charlie was soaked to the skin and turning blue. His teeth were chattering so hard he could hardly speak. But Gilpin being there was a plus. You know, a witness from the other side. Barry said that Merv had fallen overboard and Charlie had jumped in and tried to save him. Merv had gone under and they'd lost sight of him.'

'And Gilpin bought it?'

'Hook, line and sinker. He tore back into the house to call the police and get a search happening, but the phone was locked. That's the way Merv kept it when he wasn't in residence. In case somebody broke in and used it to make free long-distance calls. The key must still have been on the ring in his pocket. Gilpin jumped in his car and tore off to the Barjarg roadhouse to raise the alarm. Barry gave them directions to where the accident had happened, misleading I assume, and they started to search.'

Bishop turned out his hands and stared me square in the face with his baleful owl eyes. 'So there you have it. We kept it under wraps for twenty years. Stuck with our stories when the police interviewed us again last week. As far as I know, Charlie took it to the grave with him. You're the only other person who knows what really happened.'

He tugged back the flap of his academic gown, glanced at his watch and looked around the visiting fellows' office with an air of impatient captivity.

'Sid Gilpin seems to have a talent for turning up,' I said. 'He's done it again. The prospect of Merv's resurrection has got him all excited. He claims to have evidence of a scam at the Municipals.'

Bishop tilted his scarecrow neck sideways. 'Such as?'

'A pair of bankbooks,' I said.

'Jesus,' Bishop snorted. 'Not *them* again?'

'Again?' I said.

Bishop squirmed in his seat. 'I really should go back up and let myself be seen. My absence will have been noted.'

I'd overplayed my hand badly in the stairwell and getting this far had been sheer good luck. 'Yes, of course,' I said, reaching for the door handle. 'You've been very generous with your time.'

'No need to get unctuous, Murray,' he said. 'I've got more at stake here than you, or the Labor Party. Just let me get this academic rigmarole out of the way.'

We hurried along the deserted corridor, Bishop's gown swishing as we passed the empty tutorial rooms and silent offices of the Department of Outdoor Recreation. Evidently the staff and students were outdoors somewhere, recreating in the rain.

'You remember how the union dues were collected?' he said.

'The usual way, I assume. Payroll deductions.'

'In most workplaces, public utilities, big municipalities and so forth, that was the case. But with some of the smaller employers, shire councils, say, it was handled by a union representative. The rep got a ten percent commission and a bonus for each new member signed up or every arrears brought back into the fold. Small beer, but a nice top-up for somebody on a base-grade wage.'

We reached the lifts and I pushed the button. 'What's this got to do with the bankbooks?'

'Those training programs you and I ran, they were very educational,' he said. 'While you were back at base, filling ring binders with diagrams and photocopying course materials, I was doing more than raising industrial education standards among the toiling masses. I was doing a bit of digging.'

The lift arrived, empty, and we stepped in. Bishop firmed his university-monogrammed tie and donned his velvet sombrero. I hit the button for the top floor. The doors slid shut and the lift began its ascent.

'I'd picked up some whispers that Sid Gilpin was extorting kickbacks out of some of the collection agents, threatening to give the job to someone else if they didn't pay up. He created the impression he was acting on Merv's behalf. But that didn't ring true to me. For all his faults, dipping into the till wasn't Merv's style. Charlie agreed.'

The lift doors opened. We'd been gone for a good half-hour and the crowd was thinning. A blue-edged gown, one of the big chiefs, spotted Bishop. 'Ah, there you are!' he declared. 'We've been wondering where you got to.'

Bishop cocked his scraggly beard in the direction of the balcony, indicating I should await him there. 'I've been hiding from the paparazzi,' he declared jovially, allowing himself to be led away.

It was well past three and a hasty Tim Tam was the closest I'd come to lunch. I was hungry enough to fang the furry dice off a Ford Falcon. I fronted the buffet table, but the best I could scrape up were a couple of quarters of picked-over tuna and mayonnaise sandwich. I took the fishy cardboard and a styrofoam cup of tea onto the balcony. The rain was back down to a fine drizzle and I savoured my repast with my back against the wall, sheltered by the overhanging eaves.

A string of flat-topped boats chugged up the river and parked in front of the casino. Entertainment stages, I wondered? Fireworks launch platforms? Premier Geoffries' royal barge on a practice run? I thought about Lanie, wiped the fish oil off my fingers and got out my phone to check my messages.

No joy. But while I had the phone out, I rang Fliteplan. As instructed, Margot had gone home. I'd call her there later, see if she was okay. It had been a busy and relentlessly informative morning. I wondered what I'd got myself into.

After a while, the drizzle stopped and people came out onto the balcony to look at the view or smoke cigarettes. I had one myself, just to be sociable. The crowd had drifted away and the caterers had started to pack up when Colin Bishop appeared, now minus the bonnet and frock.

'Where were we?' he said, leaning on the balustrade beside me.

'Cutlett and Gilpin,' I reminded him. 'Corruption and bankbooks.'

'Ah, yes,' he nodded. 'Poor old Merv. Behind that gruff exterior he was a deeply lonely man, you know. His war service had cost him his youth and his long-term health. Politics alienated him from his family—hard-line Catholics, the Cutletts, rabidly right wing. His wife divorced him and he bullied his daughter into a life of domestic begrudgery as his housekeeper. He couldn't relate to women at all.'

You don't know the half of it, I thought.

'The union was his entire life, but men like Charlie Talbot were trying to steal it from under him. Technocratic types spouting jargon about rationalisation, consensus and the social wage. Gilpin was just a bottom-tier organiser, an ex-garbo, but he read Merv like a book. He got alongside him, pandered to him, drank with him, made all the right noises. Played Tonto to Merv's Lone Ranger. Gave him loyalty and got trust in return. Not to mention a meal ticket.'

Col had obviously become quite reflective since his pro vice-chancellorship, but while this psychologising was all very interesting, it wasn't exactly germane. And the cold wind blowing up the river was threatening to freeze my nuts off.

'The bankbooks,' I prompted.

'Yes, of course.' Bishop swerved back to the point. 'Charlie didn't believe that Merv was corrupt, but he knew a trump card when he was dealt one. He got me to put together a full dossier on Gilpin's little fiddle. Names, amounts, statutory declarations, the irrefutable works. Then, at the height of Merv's intransigence on the amalgamation issue, Charlie showed it to him. Quietly, in confidence, and out of deep concern for his reputation.'

In the past five minutes, I'd learned more about the Federated Union of Municipal Employees than I'd picked up in all the months I'd worked there.

'Merv realised that Charlie had him by the short and curlies. Not only was he unaware of what was happening in his own office, he was at risk of having his reputation trashed in the eyes of his members. At that point, he stopped stonewalling and began to seriously negotiate the terms of his departure. What he wanted, above all, was to retain his dignity and his historic connection with the union.'

'A seat on the board and an appropriate honorarium,' I said. There was one cigarette left in my pack. That made a total of six smoked so far that day, well over my limit. We're all dead men on furlough, I told myself. Turning my back on the breeze, I cupped my hands and lit up.

'Gilpin knew there'd be no golden parachute for him,' said Bishop. 'So he'd bought himself some insurance, just in case Merv ever got backed into a corner. He opened accounts in Charlie and Barry's names at the bank across the road from the Trades Hall. You remember how easy it was in those days. No ten-point checks or photo ID. A gas bill was enough for most banks. Gilpin channelled his kickback earnings through the accounts, making it look like Charlie and Barry were trousering regular pay-offs of some sort.'

'Pretty smart,' I said.

Bishop stroked his beard and nodded. On the street below us, I could see a busker in a kilt playing the bagpipes at the underpass entrance to Flinders Street station. Fortunately, he was too far away to be heard.

'Merv wasn't going to look a gift like that in the mouth. He showed the bankbooks to Charlie and Barry. Quietly, in confidence, and out of deep concern for their reputations.'

'Mexican stand-off.'

Bishop nodded again. 'That's what the meeting at the Shack was supposed to be about. Cutting a deal that accommodated all parties. They'd get the dossier, we'd get the bankbooks. Merv would sign off on the amalgamation, Gilpin would get some fuck-off money. But once Merv had the bankbooks in his hand, he didn't need Gilpin anymore. When Charlie picked him up at his office on the Friday night, he'd sent Gilpin off on some fool's errand. The two of them left without him. But Sid must have realised that Merv was cutting him out of the loop and barrelled after them in a blue streak. If the cops hadn't picked him up for driving over the limit, the whole thing would've played out very differently.'

I knew that wasn't the real reason Gilpin had been left behind. Charlie obviously wasn't going to stick around and put himself in the position of having to explain why Merv was prostrate on the shagpile with his dick hanging out and a hole in the back of his head.

'If Merv had the bankbooks,' I said. 'How did Gilpin get them back?'

'He pinched them.'

Jesus, if this got any more complex, I'd need a degree in nuclear physics to follow it. And if it got any longer, I'd catch pneumonia. I shivered and shook myself, hinting that we should move inside. Bishop continued, oblivious. Fucking fresh-air nut.

'Barry took the books off Merv when he was non-compos and tossed them in his briefcase. They were just sitting there in plain view when Gilpin made his dash into the Shack to use the phone. He was only inside a few seconds, but it was long enough to take a quick shufti and grab them. We discovered what he'd done almost immediately, of course. But there was a lot going on by then, and bigger matters at stake.'

'You didn't try to get them back later?' I said.

'That would only have complicated matters. Gilpin cleaned out the accounts and made himself scarce. We wrote off the money and let sleeping dogs lie.'

It started to drizzle. I flicked my cigarette butt in the general direction of the casino and we hurried inside. Staff were stacking the seating and dismantling the dais. We headed into a quiet corner, our voices hushed.

'The sleeping dog kept the passbooks,' I said. 'He's picked up that the police suspect things are a bit iffy in the manner of Merv's death. He's threatening to send the books their way, just to stir things up. Unless, of course, somebody makes him a better offer.'

'He's crazy,' said Bishop. 'Their threat value is twenty years past its use-by date.'

'He's crazy all right,' I said. 'Certifiable. But you and Barry illegally disposed of a body and perjured yourselves at an inquest. Not a good look for men in your current positions. And your story's already springing leaks, otherwise I wouldn't be here.'

Bishop stroked his fungus and gave it some thought. 'Does Quinlan know about this?'

'He will as soon as I tell him,' I said.

'Don't use the phone,' said Bishop. 'Barry was very clear on that point.'

'He's a very wise man,' I said. 'By the way, did the police show you a picture of a watch?'

'Yes,' he nodded. 'What's that all about?'

'Buggered if I know,' I said.

For want of a better idea, I decided to put in an appearance at my place of work.

As I was walking into the vestibule, Alan Metcalfe emerged from the direction of the Legislative Assembly at the pointy end of a flying wedge of frontbenchers. Daryl Keels of the Right, Ken Crouch of the Left, deputy Peter Thorsen and a small phalanx of spear-carriers.

Metcalfe gave me a curt, magisterial nod as they swept past. Without breaking stride, Thorsen reached into his jacket and handed me an envelope.

'Good timing, Murray,' he said, tipping me a jovial there-you-go wink. 'That letter you wanted, re the constituent matter.'

'Good on you, Peter,' I said, pocketing his treasonous pledge as we each continued on our way.

It was one of those moments that makes politics a sport worth playing.

After an hour or so of dutiful paperwork at my desk in the Henhouse, I adjourned to the carpark and thence to the Safeway in Smith Street, Collingwood, which lay exactly twixt House and home.

Out of respect for the street's heritage status, the Victorian-era façade of the supermarket building had been retained. Its windows empty, it stood attached to the front of the strip-lit modern grocery emporium like the plywood set from a Western movie. I drove up the ramp to the rooftop carpark, then walked though the cluster of buskers and ferals sheltering in the entranceway.

One of them stepped into my path, cold-sores on her lips and track marks on the backs of her bony hands. ''Scuse me, mate,' she started up. 'You couldn't help me could you, 'cause I've lost me train ticket to Frankston and…'

'Forget Frankston,' I poured my loose change into her palm, all three dollars of it. 'Get yourself a hit.'

The supermarket was busy with home-bound shoppers and desperate singles cruising for a pick-up. Toilet paper, breakfast cereal, tea-bags. I browsed the condoms.

Lanie still hadn't called. Don't get your boxers in a knot, I told myself. It's only Monday. Give it time.

The classic plain ones, I decided. Ribbed might look a bit kinky.

In the meat section, I phoned Red to check on his whereabouts and discuss ongoing menu issues. He was home hitting the books. Did I have any thoughts on the consequences of the French Revolution?

'Too early to tell,' I said. 'How does spaghetti bolognese sound?'

He made a slurping noise. I took it for a yes, loaded up on mince and joined the line at the register. All the check-out chicks were Vietnamese students and all the bag-boys were Ethiopian. While I waited in line, I tried to imagine the results if they ever had children together. Long distance runners with doctorates in chemical engineering? Very tall restaurant owners?

'Proice check on gwuckermoley?' bellowed the Oriental pearl at the register, unequivocally true-blue.

I humped the groceries to the car, shuffled home through the drizzly rush-hour and conscripted Red into the unpacking. 'Mothballs?' he said, emptying the cleaners and chemicals bag.

'No thanks. They give me heartburn. Let's stick with the spag bog.'

Spaghetti bolognese was the bedrock of Red's culinary repertoire. He browned some mince, added a jumbo jar of tomato puree and phoned a friend while he stirred. I took the mothballs into my den of antiquity and hauled my archive boxes down off the top shelf.

I'd got there just in time. As I levered the lid off the first cardboard carton, a startled silverfish slithered back into the haphazard pile of documents that filled the box. I reached in and removed the contents. A fine powder of insect-droppings had accumulated in the crevices at the bottom. Not a whiff remained of the naphthalene flakes I'd scattered there only three or four years earlier.

Dropping a handful of mothballs into the box, I began replacing the pages, scanning them as I went. This was the archaeological record of my life and times, the hieroglyphs of a vanished civilisation, intelligible only to the expert eye. Why I'd saved this stuff in the first place, and why I continued to store it, was a mystery to baffle the Sphinx. Here were my initials, scratched with a stick in the sands of time. Or, in the instance to hand, scribbled in biro on the menu of the 1972 Young Labor Conference dinner.

In total, the evidence of my passage filled two and three-quarter pop-up Ikea storage boxes. A Politics 201 essay on Checks and Balances in the Australian Constitution. A diatribe addressed to the editor of *Rabelais*, the student newspaper at La Trobe University. The notification letter of my acceptance as a graduate trainee in the Commonwealth public service.

The papers were stored in no particular order. Cataloguing them could wait, something to occupy my sunset years at the Old Apparatchiks Home. Only occasionally did I pause between mothballs to peruse a memory. A staff photo from the Labour Resource Centre, Wendy beside me, her belly big with the imminent Red. A well-received position paper I'd written in 1980 on the untapped potential of co-operative credit agencies. All the vanished dreams of social democracy were mouldering in my boxes, snacks for the weevils. Sic transit Jack Mundey.

Half-way through the second box I found what I was looking for. The cheap newsprint had faded to a parchment yellow and the creases were permanent, but the silverfish hadn't yet done their worst. The eight issues of the *Federated Union of Municipal Employees News* that I had edited, probably the only copies still in existence. I knelt on the floor and carefully turned the pages.

Charlie's photograph appeared at the top of his monthly reports as Victorian State Secretary. The same photo every time, a simple passport-sized head-shot. He was somewhere in his early forties at the time, slightly younger than I was now. His face had aged over the years, but it hadn't really changed.

There was a magnifying glass among the oddments in my top drawer. I switched on the desk lamp and took a closer look. The eyes, crescents of old ink in a genial teddy-bear visage, contradicted nothing I thought I knew about the man.

Something about the story of that morning at Lake Nillahcootie was nagging at me. Something didn't quite gel. I could accept the fact that Charlie had hauled Merv Cutlett's limp form into his car and driven him, semi-comatose, to the Shack. His judgment was clouded by his concern for Margot and he had obviously misread the seriousness of Merv's injury. The disposal of the body, too, had its desperate logic.

But Charlie jumping into the water? It was an unnecessary embellishment. The man-overboard story didn't need it. Not only that, it smacked of self-aggrandisement. Not Charlie's style. Something else had happened out there in the boat, I was sure of it. A piece of the jigsaw was missing.

I leafed through the pages, scanning the other photographs. Most were of Merv Cutlett. Merv the Great Leader and Merv at Work, stern-faced defender of the working class behind his redoubt of logs-of-claim and keys-of-access. I found Charlie again, one of the figures in the background of Merv Shares a Laugh. *Annual Picnic December 1977*, read the caption.

The crowd basking in the great one's presence included Sid Gilpin. He was wearing a wide-collared short-sleeved sports shirt, the top buttons open to better display the medallion around his neck. His left arm was draped around one of the skylarking crew. On his left wrist was a chunky metal band.

My heart skipped a beat. Could it be a watch, I

wondered? A Seiko Sports Chronometer, as seen in the Polaroids that Detective Constable Robbie Stromboli had shown me at my electorate office? I put my nose to the lens and squinted at the blurry monochromatic image. Sid's jewellery was a name bracelet. I couldn't read the engraving, but I knew what it said. *Wanker.*

'Grub's up!'

Red banged a spoon on a saucepan lid. The dinner gong had sounded.

We tucked into our pasta with gusto, washing it down with orange cordial. Beer and wine were only for shelf-stacking nights. Not that Red's day hadn't been busy. Monday was his heaviest timetable and there'd been post-school toil over a hot assignment, due within the week. Unusually, Theatre Studies was giving him the pip.

'Motherfucking Courage,' he complained through a forkful of saucy tagliatelle. 'Brecht.'

His school had a reputation for liberality, giving it a roomy niche among the progressive element in Melbourne's middle class. To offset parental qualms about elitism, its curriculum offered Marxist agitprop along with interschool rowing and the international baccalaureate. But Red found Bertolt far too preachy, especially when he was expected to turn in a six-hundred-word essay on the cigar-chomping old Stalinist's dramaturgical critique of bourgeois ethics.

'Give me Lorca any day,' he said, mopping his plate with a crust.

'They didn't have any,' I said. 'You'll have to settle for Yoplait.'

'Not Jean-Louis Yoplait, founder of the Comédie Française?'

'Apricot Yoplait, his temptingly luscious mistress.'

After we'd eaten, Red returned to his homework. I took a half bottle of sav blanc into my den and hit the phone. First I called Margot and made reassuring noises. She sounded washed out, but she didn't put up a fight.

Next I rang Mike Kyriakis. Both his home and mobile numbers were engaged. I had a few sips and tried again. And again.

He was working the phones too. So far, so good.

I put everything but the *FUME News* back in the archive boxes, added the last of the moths' knackers and stowed them away again. Then I reclined on the couch, wine in hand, and contemplated the situation.

The proper, responsible course of action was obvious. Wait until the remains were officially identified. If the police continued to regard the death as a possible homicide, try to persuade Margot and the others to appraise them of the true circumstances.

It would be the best thing for all concerned. Given the passage of time, the police might well decide not to pursue the matter further. Even if they did, they'd probably have a hard time convincing the Director of Public Prosecutions they could make the charges stick. The physical evidence was questionable and sworn admissions were unlikely to be forthcoming. In the meantime, I should butt out and stop making promises I had no idea how to keep.

But I wasn't going to do that, was I? Not while mad, bad Sid still had those fucking bankbooks.

The phone rang. It was Helen Wright.

'We've just sent out a press release for Mike Kyriakis, alerting the media to his intention to run for Coolaroo,' she said. 'And you remember that kid there on Sunday, the young tyro sitting on the floor? Well, he spent the whole day tooling around the electorate with the membership lists. Seems there's a lot more party members on the books than on the ground. Unless some of them are living six to a room, the Right has been padding the books. Heavily. We're running up a hit list for the returning officer. If the central panel wasn't stitched up so tight, we'd actually have a real chance.'

'We?' I said. 'You sound like Mike's campaign manager.'

'It's just a hobby,' she said. 'During the day, I work for Phil Sebastian.'

'You're a very wicked woman, Helen Wright,' I said. 'To think that until last week, you worked for the straightest man in Australian politics.'

'Ah, Charlie was such a square,' she said, a smile in her voice. 'I haven't had this much fun in years.'

When Red stuck his head around the door at bed time to say goodnight, I told him there was a chance I'd be late for dinner tomorrow.

'I'm going out of town,' I said. 'When I get back there's something I'd like to talk to you about.'

That something was our respective putative careers.

For years I'd been telling myself that I was standing aloof from the petty squabbles. Truth was, I'd been sitting on the fence for so long I had a crease in my arse the size of the Mariana Trench.

Suddenly, and to my surprise, Thorsen's offer of a shadow ministry had fanned the few slumbering embers of my ambition into life. But state Labor was a dead end. I'd be in a twilight home before we got back into power. Federal politics at least offered the prospect of a shot at office.

It was shit or get off the pot, I'd decided. And Canberra was the only place worth shitting.

I caught the eleven-thirty shuttle from Tullamarine, the first flight available at short notice, after a brief but comprehensive meeting with Ayisha at the electorate office on my way to the airport. The cab dropped me at the Senate-side entrance to the federal parliament building just before one o'clock.

Say what you like about Australian politicians, we make no effort to conceal our delusions of grandeur. And there is no better evidence of our robust self-image than the seat of national government.

Part-boomerang, part-bunker, all modern conveniences, it tunnels into the heart of the nation like a glorified rabbit burrow. A pharaonic tumulus crowned with a metallic flagstaff of such monumental banality as to make a rotary clothesline look like the Eiffel Tower.

Before I left home, I contacted Barry Quinlan's office and was told he might be able to find a few minutes before Question Time. So after I'd been scanned for hidden weapons and issued with my visitor's pass, I shook off my escort and headed to Ozzie's for a snippet of lunch before our little chin-wag.

It was a typical, glorious early-May day in the Australian Capital Territory. The sky was Delft-ware blue, streaked with the white vapour trail of a high-flying jet and the maples in the parliamentary courtyards were a claret blaze amid the ornamental pools.

Ozzie's, the in-house coffee shop, occupied a wide, glass-walled intersection at the apex of the bicameral boomerang. Its tables were deployed to catch the traffic, offering its customers an excellent view of the passing political wildlife. Politicians and media hacks converged there to graze on light refreshments and freshly made gossip.

As I stood in line for a salad roll, I cast an eye over the faces and configurations. Given the hour, there was considerable coming and going. I spied the federal Treasurer, a moon-faced ponce, quipping with a table of journalists, pretending to have a sense of humour. A notoriously eccentric National Party backbencher from Queensland was treating a couple of his ruminant constituents to a cup of tea and a scone.

And there, amid a group of men so badly dressed that they could only have been ABC journalists, was Kelly Cusack. She was wearing a delectably snug navy-blue skirt-suit and a cream silk blouse. As she saw me see her, she smiled to herself as if struck by a slightly amusing idea.

'Uh-oh,' I thought.

She walked straight towards me, then reached through the queue to tug a paper napkin from the dispenser on the counter, contriving to brush against me in the process.

'Oh hello, Murray,' she said, like she'd just noticed me. I heard the faint rustle of her blouse and there was a lilt in her voice that needed no clarification.

Taking her napkin, she departed along the window-lined corridor, twitching her tail behind her. I put my salad roll on the back burner, waited twenty seconds and nonchalantly followed. The corridor turned and I found her standing alone at the open door of an empty elevator.

'You're kidding?' I said.

'You game?'

This wasn't on the schedule, but I was prepared to be flexible. I followed her into the lift and the doors whooshed shut.

'I've got a meeting in twenty minutes,' I said.

'So let's skip the foreplay.'

There were three buttons. She pushed the one marked M.

Five seconds later, the doors slid open and we stepped out. We were facing a blank wall with a sign that read 'This room is not intended for eating, drinking, smoking or any other purpose.'

'Mezzanine?' I said.

'Meditation.'

The meditation room was a long and narrow curve with light grey carpet and a series of alcoves set behind low blond-wood screens. Slit windows, one per alcove, offered views of the encircling Brindabellas. A selection of devotional texts sat on a lacquer table. *The Book of Mormon. The Tibetan Book of the Dead. Steps to Christ.* The space radiated a calming, vaguely Japanese feel. We had it to ourselves.

Kelly led me down a step into the furthermost of the alcoves. Unless there'd been some recent changes in church policy, it was not one of the steps to Christ. Behind the privacy screen was a cushioned bench. Kelly pushed me backwards onto it and unsnapped her suspenders.

Suspenders! My hesitation vanished. I heard the sound of one fly unzipping and my little bald monk emerged from his place of seclusion. Kelly turned her back and lowered herself onto my lap, assuming the position known to the sages as Reverse Cowgirl. I sought the four-fold path to nirvana.

'God,' I exhaled, my jewel within the lotus.

'*Om*,' came a nasal hum. '*Om mane padme hum.*'

'*Om*,' answered a second, different voice.

'Shit!' hissed Kelly, clenching her kundalini. 'It's the WA Greens!'

Through some unprecedented quirk in the electoral system, Western Australia, the most racist, development-worshipping state in the nation, had returned two Green Party senators at the previous national poll.

Derided by the major parties as fruit-bats in the political canopy, the Greens had risen to the occasion. In a country where politics is mostly the province of besuited men apparently cloned from the same suburban solicitor, the WA Greens were neither men nor besuited. Nor did they dwell within sight of any known constellation. They were a matching pair of bona-fide superannuated hippy Earth Mothers. In the straitlaced environs of the Senate, they were truly a breath of fresh incense.

'Ting,' said a brass finger bell.

'*Om mane padme hum*,' chanted the two voices.

We had failed to notice their presence when we arrived. And the image of two middle-aged tie-dyed tree-huggers communing with the tantric ineffable in the next alcove, so close I could smell their patchouli oil, instantly neutralised the effect of Kelly's nylon-clad thighs.

Her yoni bore down, enclosing my lingam. But the bald bonze was already backing out of the temple, retreating to his lonely sanctuary, renouncing all desire. Kelly squirmed irritably.

'Sorry,' I whispered. 'I just don't have it in me today.'

She gave a sharp, irritated click of her tongue, and dismounted. 'You're not the only one.'

We refastened our clips and zips, summoned the lift and stepped inside.

I was contrite. 'It was just too freaky, man.'

Kelly pouted. 'I've always wanted to do it in there.'

'And I'm sure you will one day, my dear.'

She laughed. 'I'm sure I will, too.'

We stepped out into the real world and walked back towards Ozzie's together. We both knew, I suspected, that it was our moment of parting. But it couldn't end without words.

'I can't do it anymore,' I said. 'I don't have the nerve.'

What I wanted was a woman I could make love to, lie

beside all night, wake up with, then do it all over again, then go out for breakfast for all the world to see. I missed kissing, too. Those were things Kelly could never give me. Not that it hadn't been fun.

'Our relationship…' I started.

'Relationship?' she raised an amused eyebrow. 'I thought I was fucking you against a tree in a public park, you thought we were having a relationship?'

'Our serial shagathon, then…'

'That's more like it.'

A Liberal minister hurried past, bound for the Reps, nodding to Kelly as he passed. We paused at a Fred Williams, one of the many primo-quality artworks that hung along the corridors, and pretended to discuss it.

'You're a sexual Maserati, Kelly,' I said. 'Zero to a hundred in twenty seconds flat. It's a brilliant ride but I just can't take the pace. I keep expecting us to flip over and burst into flames. It's a sad admission, I know, but I think I'd be more comfortable with a Subaru. Last Friday in the Legislative Council, I've been sweating about it ever since. And this bareback stuff, it makes me feel guilty.'

She patted my cheek and smiled kindly. 'You want out, eh?'

I gave a wan nod and gazed contemplatively at Fred's daubs.

'You're just an old softie, aren't you?' said Kelly. 'No offence intended.'

'None taken.'

'Then out you get, sport. No root, no ride. You were only ever a pit-stop anyway.'

'No hard feelings?'

'No hard anything, unfortunately.'

'Come on. That was just today.'

Already we were joking about it, veterans of many a hairy scrape. We continued along the corridor, our fork in the road just ahead. 'Moving right along,' I said. 'Can I ask what you meant last Friday about Peter Thorsen getting up the numbers for a spill?'

Kelly twitched her coiffure dismissively. 'Old news,' she said. 'That's why I rarely talk politics with you, Murray. You're always two steps behind the play. Haven't you heard?'

'Heard what?'

'About an hour ago, Alan Metcalfe announced that he's commissioned an independent review of internal party procedures in Victoria. He's found a top legal eagle from Labor Lawyers to chair it and given him an open brief. Says he wants to encourage participation, end branch stacking, make the party more accountable to its members, all the usual piffle. A thorough, broad-ranging review, conducted without fear or favour. He's given it until the end of the year to hand down its recommendations.'

I gave a low whistle of admiration. 'During which time nobody can challenge him without looking like they're trying to forestall a democratic overhaul of the party. Six months for the submissions and recommendations, add another six for discussion of implementation and he's bought himself another year.'

'If Peter Thorsen was planning on doing a Fletcher Christian, he's left it too late. Captain Metcalfe still holds the helm.'

We were almost back at Ozzie's. I was expected in Barry Quinlan's office in five minutes.

'By the way,' said Kelly. 'Since our relationship is now strictly professional, mind if I ask what brings you to Canberra?'

'A meeting with Barry Quinlan,' I said. No reason to conceal it. She'd know soon enough anyway. Somebody was sure to notice me and Quinlan together and this place leaked like a surplus Soviet submarine.

'Don't tell me,' said Kelly knowingly. 'The Coolaroo connection. It overlaps your electorate, doesn't it? Poor Senator Quinlan, he's really got himself in deep shit buying into that exercise.'

'I wouldn't call Mike Kyriakis deep shit,' I said. 'A piece of poo on the footpath, perhaps. Something Barry won't have any trouble wiping off his ballerina-size shoe.'

'Mike Kyriakis?' She furrowed her brow. 'That guy in the *Herald Sun* this morning, the local mayor throwing his hat in the ring? That's not what I mean, Murray. Wake up and smell the coffee.'

We'd got to Ozzie's and there was plenty of coffee to be smelled, most of it congealing in the bottom of cups left on the tables by the departing lunch-hour crowd.

'Please explain,' I said. It was the phrase of the moment.

'The local plebiscite is just a side-show, Murray, you know that. The central panel delegates will have the final say. Quinlan thought he had them sewn up, but the unions don't like his choice of candidate. They want one of their own. Word is, they're going to drop somebody into the ballot at the last minute. It'll be the unions versus the parliamentary party. If there was a way for Quinlan to dump Sebastian and find another candidate, someone with both a union and a parliamentary background, he'd jump at it. If he loses this one, his days as power-broker are over. Or so I've been led to believe.'

'It's all above my head,' I said. 'See you round, Kelly.'

'But not quite as much of me, eh, Murray?'

Away she went, heels clacking, and I went to meet the man I'd come to Canberra to see. I could only hope that my next conversation would end as amicably.

In accordance with the Westminster tradition, the House of Representatives and the Senate are demarcated by the tint of their floor coverings and soft furnishings. Green for lower, red for upper. Apart from anything else, this helps the less acute members of the federal parliament find their way back to their seats.

Although both the Reps and the Senate were sitting, and thus a fair fraction of the 226 federal legislators employed by the Australian taxpayer must have been taking advantage of the colour-coded décor, I encountered nobody as I hurried along the rhubarb-toned carpet leading to Barry Quinlan's suite.

Barry was coming out the door just as I hove into sight. Judging by his pace, he was keen to take his seat before Question Time kicked off.

Not so fast, Barry, I thought. I've got a few questions of my own.

'Thought you'd dipped out,' he said amiably. 'We'd better make it quick.' He tilted his head, inviting me back inside his office.

This time, I wanted him alone. Somewhere beyond the reach of watch-tappers and file-handers, the providers of pretexts if he started looking for an easy out. I turned back the way I'd come, back towards the central nub of the vast building, the direction of the Senate chamber.

'We can do this on foot,' I said.

He fell into step with me, brushing a fleck of invisible dandruff off the lapel of his beautifully cut jacket. 'So, what can I do for you in person that I can't do on the phone?'

'You can talk to me about that day at Lake Nillahcootie,' I said.

He gave a sidelong glance and registered that I was serious. 'You seem to be taking a great deal of interest in this matter, Murray.'

The corridor was hung with botanical illustrations by Joseph Banks, priceless originals every one. Quinlan was still looking at me, his shrewd eyes narrow.

'Frankly Barry, I'd rather not know about it. But that's not the way events have transpired.'

We reached an internal courtyard, an expanse of black marble surrounding a low, shallow fountain. The ceiling was open to the floor above and a party of schoolchildren were standing at the railing, looking down at the tops of our heads. Shoulder to shoulder, our voices muffled by burbling water, we slowly began to circumnavigate the ornamental pool. Looking, I imagined, as if we were discussing weighty matters of state.

'I know what really happened,' I said. 'Not that cock-and-bull story about Cutlett getting pissed and falling overboard.'

Quinlan's jaw tightened. 'Murray, mate,' he said. 'I've got no idea what the fuck you're talking about.'

'How about you cut the crap, Barry? I'm trying to do you a favour.'

'What makes you think I need any favours?'

Muted giggles descended from above. The schoolkids were dropping coins into the water.

'Suit yourself,' I said. 'It's not my problem if the genie gets out of the bottle. I'll tell Sid Gilpin to go ahead, do his worst, Barry Quinlan has nothing to hide.'

'Gilpin?' he snorted. 'What's Gilpin got to do with anything?'

'He asked me to give you a message. That's why I'm here. He showed me a couple of bankbooks.'

'Bankbooks? What bankbooks?'

'Cast your mind back, Barry,' I said. 'The bogus accounts Gilpin opened to make it look like you and Charlie Talbot were scamming the Municipals. The ones he nicked from your briefcase.'

Quinlan put his hand on his forehead and moved it back over his wavy black hair. 'You've been talking to Colin Bishop, haven't you? The silly fucking goose.'

'Don't worry,' I said. 'The cone of silence is still intact. Your problem's not Bishop. It's Gilpin. He's back for a second bite of the cherry. He kept the bankbooks. He's threatening to send them to the police anonymously. Stir things up. Then he'll start making allegations.'

Quinlan narrowed his eyes. 'What sort of allegations?'

'Think about it, Barry. Why do you think the Homicide Squad is asking questions about relations in the union? They obviously suspect there's more to Cutlett's death than originally reported. Right now I'll lay you odds they're looking for a motive. And Sid Gilpin is offering to supply them with one.'

Quinlan made a dismissive gesture, like flicking water off his wrist. 'Old bankbooks,' he said. 'Not exactly a smoking gun.'

'But intriguing enough to keep the cops on the boil, poking around, asking questions. You're a big target, Barry. You don't want something like this hanging over your head.'

Quinlan's well-polished toe was tapping a tattoo on the black marble floor. His eyebrows had moved so close they were almost touching.

'Gilpin wants money, I assume.'

I reached down, dipped my fingertips in the fountain and stirred the water slightly. 'Gilpin's stony broke and woofing bonkers, Barry, and he thinks you're the cut-and-come-again pudding. You'll have to find a more effective way of dealing with him.'

'Like?'

I let the drips fall from my fingers. 'It seems to me that you need someone willing to apply himself to the problem. Somebody who can see that your good name remains untarnished. The way things sit right now, Barry, you need a friend.'

'A friend?' He gave a derisive snort. 'Are you trying to horsetrade with me?

'Not at all,' I said.

'But you want something?'

'Of course.'

'Let's hear it then.'

'Just your assurance that if any of this comes out, for any reason whatsoever, you won't try to shift the blame to Charlie Talbot, hang his reputation out to dry.'

'Why would I do that?'

'Because you're a realist, Barry,' I said. 'Because you're alive and Charlie's dead, and the dead don't care.'

Quinlan stared me hard in the face, taking my measure. 'You think I'm a cunt, don't you?'

'I don't really have an opinion, Barry. I'm just the messenger boy. But I do know that even if Charlie no longer cares what happens to his good name, Margot does. And his three daughters and all the other people who looked up to him.'

Quinlan broke eye contact and turned his head away. I should have left it there. But I had to sink in the boot. I couldn't stop myself.

'You thought of everything that morning, didn't you? Even having Charlie jump overboard. Nice detail, that. Lent a real touch of verisimilitude to the lie. Easy to convince, was he? Take all your powers of persuasion? Or did he need a helping hand? Bit of a shove?'

Quinlan's face remained averted. I'd gone too far. He was going to walk away. My stomach was churning.

'Well?' I said. 'If the shit hits the fan, Charlie doesn't feature. You cop it all. Deal or no deal?'

He turned, slowly, and I was facing a naked man. The carapace of his tailoring had cracked open. All front had dissolved. He took a deep breath.

'I'm going to tell you something that nobody else knows, not even Col Bishop. Something I've lived with for nearly twenty years. Something Charlie Talbot lived with until the day he died.'

I waited. Water trickled over the edge of the fountain.

'Merv Cutlett,' he said at last. 'He wasn't dead when we threw him into the lake.'

And they reckon Rasputin was hard to kill. By comparison, Merv Cutlett was Lazarus on a trampoline.

My jaw almost hit the black marble floor. Barry Quinlan registered my shock.

'Oh, we thought he was,' he said. 'We were convinced of it. He wasn't breathing and he didn't have a pulse. Not that we could detect, at least. He was limp as a rag doll when we rolled him out of the boat. But the moment he hit the water, he came alive. The shock must have kick-started him.'

Quinlan shuffled uncomfortably, a man unaccustomed to candid admissions.

'He went under, then bobbed straight back up. He took this great gasp of air...' Quinlan inhaled demonstratively, the inrushing breath resonating against the back of his throat like a plaintive moan, '...then he sank back under the water.'

He paused, conjuring the image into the space between us.

'And, no,' he said. 'For your information, Charlie Talbot

didn't need a lot of persuading. Truth be told, I was surprised how easy it was to convince him that dumping Merv was something that had to be done. But disposing of a dead body was one thing, letting an injured man drown was another. It was a different matter entirely. For both of us.'

He looked me briefly in the eye, then dropped his gaze.

'Charlie drew the line, Murray. He drew it without a moment's thought or hesitation. He was in the water like a shot. Bang, straight over the side. He got hold of Merv and dragged him back up to the surface and tried to keep his head above the water. But the rain came plummeting down like some fucking judgment from above, and the wind started blowing the boat away. And I was bloody useless.'

Quinlan's hands were moving, moulding and shaping the empty air. 'I grabbed the wheel and slammed the lever into reverse but the motor stalled. The rain's absolutely sheeting down and churning up the surface. I'm looking back over my shoulder and trying to get the thing started and the rain's running down my face and getting in my eyes.'

He wasn't talking to me anymore. He was telling himself what happened, trying to put it into words.

'I push the starter and push it and finally it kicks over. The rain is almost horizontal, pelting down and I see this arm sticking up and I steer towards it.' His arm carved a wide, sweeping arc though the air, the trajectory of the boat. 'And I slam the lever into neutral and rush to the side and grab hold of the sleeve as I go past and I almost get dragged overboard and it's Charlie and I'm pulling him back into the boat and...'

Abruptly, the torrent of words stopped.

The schoolchildren had moved away, bored. The faces looking down at us were Asian now. Flat, incurious. Korean?

They started taking photos and dropping coins. Plop, plop, plop. What were they wishing for, I wondered? A job for life at Daewoo? A year's supply of kimchi?

'He was spluttering and shaking. He said he'd lost hold of him, that he'd gone back under. I circled around again, but there was no sign of him. Charlie was shivering so much I thought he was going into shock. We weren't going to find Cutlett without help, but I had no idea where we were by that stage. You could just make out the shoreline and some of the dead trees sticking up looked familiar. I tried to get my bearings but the only way back was to head for the shore and follow it. The whole way, I'm thinking "Maybe it's not too late, maybe we can get help soon enough to save him," and I'm wondering how we're going to explain things if that happens and Charlie, he's just a devastated shuddering wreck.'

He cleared his throat, raised his chin and inhaled deeply through his nose. There was a long moment of silence.

'So now you know.'

He squared his shoulders and began to fix his cuffs, making sure the amount showing was just right, marshalling his composure. I looked at my shoes. Compared with Quinlan's they looked cheap and shabby.

'I don't need your absolution,' he said. 'And I don't give a rat's arse about your opinion of me. But if you think Charlie Talbot's good name is something I'd treat lightly, you're a very poor fucking judge of character. Now tell me what you really want and I'll do my best to see that you get it.'

Ayisha was hunched over the conference table in the general work area when I let myself into the electorate office just after five o'clock. Her hair was pinned up, she had a phone glued to her ear and her much-chewed pencil was cross-hatching an asterisk against a name on a list. Other lists were laid out in a line on the table in front of her, all heavily marked and annotated. I recognised them as the ones we'd roughed out at our meeting before I left for Canberra.

Empty take-away coffee cups littered one of the bench-desks, along with copies of that morning's *Herald Sun* and *Age*. The newspapers were open at their coverage of Mike Kyriakis's announcement of his intention to contest the Coolaroo preselection. *ALP Bid Clash* headed the *Herald Sun* report, its most prominent page three story. The *Age* had gone with *Labor Mayor in By-election Contest*. Page eleven, below the fold, six pars.

Beneath the *Age* piece was a pointer to a 2000-word

Michelle Grattan eye-glazer on the op-ed page. *Labor Needs to Regain Trust of Core Supporters*. I'd read it on the flight to Canberra between the safety aerobics and the artisan-crafted macadamia-chip cookie. The cookie was easier to digest and the crash procedure lecture contained more useful information.

Ayisha's pencil inscribed a question mark against one of the names on her list, over-wrote it several times, drew a circle around it and underlined it. 'Just a tick,' she said, then covered the mouthpiece with her hand and turned towards me. 'Well?' she said. 'Yes or no?'

'Yes.'

She gave me a sceptical look. 'Are you sure you're not having a mid-life crisis?'

'Call it a mid-life epiphany,' I said. 'Mike?'

'He'll be here at six. Helen, too.'

'Peter Thorsen?'

'In his office until five-thirty. And the whip wants you to ring him.'

'Any other messages?' My mobile was still drawing a blank, Lanie-wise. Please God, I prayed, I've been a good boy. Let her have called.

Ayisha shook her head. 'Nothing pressing.'

'No Andrea Lane?'

Ayisha gave me a cunning look. I ignored it and went into my office. I hung up my jacket, loosened my tie and rolled up my sleeves. Whenever the temperature dropped below twenty, Ayisha turned the heating on full bore. My African violet must have thought it was back in Angola. I gave it a drink and hit the dog.

'Yes, what now?' barked Inky, answering his phone after one ring.

'It's Murray.'

'Sorry, mate. Thought it was my ex.'

'Which one?'

At last count, Dennis Donnelly had been married three times and begotten offspring on two other women. He was rumoured to have paid maintenance on seven children over a thirty-year period. Little wonder the poor bastard had an ulcer.

'Mind your own beeswax,' he said. 'I suppose you want to know the latest from Vic Valentine? I'm still waiting on his call. But in the meantime, I gave the police media liaison mob a bell. A very obliging young lady constable told me they're still working on identifying what she coyly described as the material remains. To that end, they've located the burial site of Cutlett *mater* and *pater*, to wit the Mooroopna cemetery, and they're awaiting an exhumation order for DNA purposes.'

There was a pause followed by the muffled crunch of an antacid meeting its match. 'I also had a call from an old mate in Adelaide, a former assistant secretary of the South Australian branch of the Municipals. He's had a visit from the local rozzers, acting on behalf. They showed him a photo of a watch, said it was found with the aforementioned material remains, and wanted to know if it was Merv's.'

'And was it?'

'Not unless he was moonlighting as a *Cleo* centrefold. Quite a flashy piece of tick-tockery apparently.'

'So it's not Merv,' I said.

'We live in hope.'

I left Inky to his domestic altercations and rang Peter Thorsen's office. Del was just finishing up for the day. She said Peter was on a call and put me on hold with instructions to ring back if he didn't answer within five minutes. Chopin's concerto for solo telephone kept me riveted for four and a half. Then Thorsen picked up.

'A wide-ranging, open-ended and time-consuming review,' I said. 'That should keep you out of mischief for the foreseeable future.'

'Some you win, mate, some you lose. Some you don't even get to fight.'

'Too true,' I agreed. 'But before you fold your tents and steal off into the night, I'm calling to remind you that we had a two-part agreement.'

'Meaning you still expect me to go into bat for kamikaze Kyriakis.'

'Is that a problem?'

'I told you I'd do my best and I will.' He sighed wearily. 'But the market in central panel votes has gone through the ceiling in the past twenty-four hours. I can't do more than try.'

'That's all I've ever asked,' I said. 'Care to put a number on your best possible projection? No names, no pack drill.'

'Phew,' he exhaled. 'Hard to say. How long's a piece of string? Four, tops.'

'Love that Motown sound,' I said.

'I'll be there.'

'Standing in the shadows of love?' I warbled as I hung up.

Darkness was falling fast and the strident beep of a reversing fork-lift was coming from the direction of Vinnie Amato's Fresh Fruit and Veg, crates of produce being shunted inside for the night. The rain had dried up while I was in Canberra and long pink-grey mares' tails streaked the skyline above the Green Fingers garden centre like a flock of attenuated galahs.

I dialled Margot's number.

'Murray,' she said. Her voice was an equal mix of fatigue and anxiety.

'How're you doing, sweetheart?'

'I'm okay,' she said.

'I can't chat,' I said. 'I'm at the office. But I'll drop round to the house tomorrow night and we can talk face-to-face. Things aren't as bad as you thought, Margot. It wasn't your fault. None of it. Not here, not there. You've got no cause to beat yourself up.'

'You mean...'

'Gotta go,' I said. 'You know what it's like, a politician's lot and all of that. See you soon, eh?'

I hung up, trusting she'd understand my briskness. Then I rang Red and told him to go ahead and eat without me, but leave me some of the spag sauce.

Ayisha rapped on the glass wall. Mike Kyriakis and Helen Wright had arrived. I joined them at the conference table, where they'd pulled up seats and started comparing their lists with ours.

'Evening all,' I said, assuming the chair position at the head of the table. 'As you know, Ayisha's been complaining for some time that her job doesn't give her enough opportunities for travel.'

My electorate officer gave a derisory, mocking hoot. 'My fault is it?'

'Politics is all about self-sacrifice,' I said.

Ayisha made a jerk-off gesture. The other two were looking mystified, Helen in a round, dimply way, Mike in a solemn, arms-crossed way.

'He means that he's decided to take a leaf out of your book, Mike,' said Ayisha.

Comprehension began to dawn. Mike looked at Helen, Helen looked at Mike, they both looked at me.

'That's right,' said Ayisha. 'This fool is putting his hand up for Coolaroo, too.'

Mike and Helen were looking at me like I'd mislaid my marbles.

'Bullshit,' said Helen. 'You can't be serious.'

'No, he's fair dinkum,' said Ayisha. 'And before you ask, it's not a mid-life crisis. It's a mid-life epiphany.'

The time had come to put my cards on the table. 'It's true,' I said.

Mike's disbelief was turning dark. He began gathering up his lists. 'You'll split the vote,' he said. 'By myself I had a pretty good chance of drawing blood. With two of us, it'll be a joke. Why are you doing this Murray? You're already sitting pretty. Why cruel my pitch?'

His sense of betrayal was palpable. Helen and Ayisha watched us in breathless silence.

'Hear me out, Mike,' I said. 'I think I've found a way to make this a win-win situation, or rather a win-lose-win-draw-lose-win-win situation. And I haven't come to the table empty-handed. I've got some cards up my sleeve.'

Mike looked dubious, but he put down his lists and leaned back in his chair. 'Well, since I'm here.'

'You remember on Sunday at Charlie's wake,' I started. 'That hypothetical scenario that Sivan cooked up, the one where a split opened up in the central panel?'

They leaned forward, all three of them, and I reached for a blank sheet of paper.

'Just hand me that abacus,' I said.

The President's gavel descended with a brisk, resounding clap and we lowered ourselves onto our red velvet cushions. It was ten-thirty on Wednesday morning and the Legislative Council of the Parliament of Victoria was now officially in session.

Beside and below me on the opposition benches sat my ten fellow Labor members. Facing us from the government benches were twice as many Liberal and National members. Between us was the Clerk's table where Kelly Cusack and I had conferred the previous Friday.

In six hours I was due to meet Sid Gilpin to relieve him of the bankbooks. In the meantime, however, there was work to be done.

Of a sort. In this particular instance, it consisted of listening to my colleague, Judy Mathering, the Manager of Opposition Business in the upper house and strong proponent of well-fitted foundation garments and sensible footwear, move and speak to a motion.

I settled my backside on the upholstery, and watched as Judy turned her stocky frame towards the President's podium, cleared her throat and begged leave to introduce a Condolence Motion on behalf of the people of Victoria to the family of the recently deceased Mr Charles Talbot, MHR.

My gaze moved up to the well-stocked public gallery where Charlie's three daughters were seated with various of his grandchildren, sons-in-law, nieces and nephews. They sat sombrely, as though in chapel. After almost two weeks of formal farewells, this was the last of the official elegies and I sensed that they would be relieved when it was all over.

Margot was there, too, at the other end of the pew, flanked by Charlie's older sister Jeanette and his younger brother Ray. This gesture of solidarity, I hoped, signalled an eventual thaw in overall familial relations.

The President granted leave and Judy began to read her speech. Her theme was Charlie's service as a parliamentarian and his contribution as a minister in the various portfolios he held during Labor's tenure in Canberra. Judy was no spellbinder and her reedy voice carried an unintentionally hectoring undertone, but this was not an occasion for politicking.

For once, members on the government benches made an effort to uphold the dignity of their office. Most refrained from their usual crotch scratching, nose picking and gum chewing. Several lowered their multiple chins reverently.

I, too, bowed my head and consulted my thoughts. They concerned my plan to deal with Gilpin. There was nothing sophisticated about it. Cunning would be wasted on the mercurial Sid. A blunt instrument was called for. Success depended on wielding it effectively.

Judy Mathering's voice was a steady, hypnotic cadence, rising and falling in the echoing space of the chamber.

> *...the loss of a man whose contribution to public life in the country, and to the welfare of so many people, sprang from a deep-seated commitment to the principles of social justice and...*

I lifted my eyes and studied Margot. It was hard to tell at that distance, but she seemed a lot more tranquil this morning. As tranquil as is proper, at least, for a grieving widow on public display.

She'd met me at the door when I arrived at the Diggers Rest house just after nine the previous night. Katie was tucked up in bed and Sarah the Carer was off duty for the evening, living it up at some student soiree. Margot had a glass in her hand and several under her belt, making me glad I'd come in person. She could sound misleadingly sober on the phone when she tried.

'I'm missing him hard,' she slurred, falling into my reassuring embrace. 'Charlie, oh Charlie, come back.'

For an hour I sat with her on the couch, recounting most of what I'd learned since our talk in the Fliteplan office.

> *...which demonstrated his capacity for creative solutions to the problems of the day...*

Not all of it, of course. But enough of the essentials to convince her that she'd been mistaken in assuming that she'd left Merv Cutlett dead on the floor of his Trades Hall office. Both Quinlan and Bishop had credibly attested to Merv's grouchiness when they arrived at the Shack, painting him more like a bear with a sore head than a man on his last legs.

Neither of them knew about her involvement, I assured her. By the time I left, she was prepared to accept that he had indeed accidentally drowned and Charlie had truly done his best to save the old prick's life.

> *...before going on to play an important role as one of the architects of Labor's return to power in 1983 and its subsequent long and eventful period in government...*

I lowered my eyes and nodded along with Judy's words. I'd helped her polish them that morning after I clocked on at the Henhouse, so I knew them almost by heart.

Apart from lending Judy a hand, I'd spent the morning sequestered in my cubicle, catching up on neglected paperwork and performing acts of administrative contrition for the Whip, whose calls I'd failed to answer in the five days since Inky Donnelly ambushed me with his copy of the *Herald Sun* and his questions about the Municipals.

In between pushing my pen, I'd spent a fair bit of time on the phone, conferring with Mike Kyriakis and Helen Wright.

Their reaction when I hit them with the news that I intended to enter the Coolaroo Derby was understandable. It had taken some heavy paddling, but eventually Mike had copped my proposition. Our interests, I'd argued, were congruent and with luck and good management we might both get what we wanted. He wanted to make a name for himself as a player. I wanted a reason to stay in politics.

> *...where his talents could be best used to safeguard and advance the interests of those who had elected him...*

Like working to defend universal health insurance, say. Reconciliation, and a regulated labour market and multiculturalism and a fair suck of the sausage. All the good stuff the Labor Party was supposed to stand for. And like Mike

Kyriakis, I really didn't have anything to lose by giving it a shot.

The plan I'd pitched in the electorate office was a leap-frogging preference-swap that called upon every iota of the knowledge I'd accumulated in my thirty-year membership of the ALP. It involved a hitherto-untested combination of the five basic moves in Labor decision making—the stack and whack, the roll and fold, the shift and shaft, the Brereton variation and the whoops-a-daisy.

A volatile brew indeed. But ultimately, it came down to Mike Kyriakis' spadework plus delivery on the pledges I'd exacted from Peter Thorsen and Senator Quinlan. And they were far from certainties. Particularly Quinlan's.

> ...*a minister in a wide range of senior portfolios, all of them demanding an ability to reconcile widely divergent pressures...*

By the time I got home from Margot's place, Red had hit the hay. I checked the answering machine in the vain hope that Lanie had called, shovelled down some spoonfuls of cold spaghetti sauce, threw myself on the sofa, and thought about my next move.

The police were obviously not slacking off on the identification of the remains. Nor, presumably, had any suspicions aroused by the bullet-shaped hole in the skull been allayed. I'd promised both Margot and Quinlan, each for different reasons, that I'd make sure that Gilpin did not succeed in fanning those suspicions. The mad bastard had given me until Wednesday afternoon to respond to his threats. Problem was, I didn't have the foggiest inkling of what to do.

I lay there for a long time, my feet on the armrest, staring between my socks, before I came up with an idea.

It was a feeble idea, but it was the only one I had.

I took down the archive box and found the issue of the *FUME News* with the picnic photo. Then I went into the loo and collected the pile of newspaper supplements off the floor. I worked my way through the fashion pages until I found what I wanted. I tore out the page, put it in a large manila envelope with the newspaper and drove to the service station in Heidelberg Road. I spent half an hour and five dollars using the photocopier in the convenience store section, then went home to bed.

> *...in the hope that this gesture will offer some consolation to his family and those many others who share the loss of his passing...*

Judy was nearing the end of her speech. I again tilted my head upwards, this time looking directly at Charlie's daughters.

Having a politician for a parent can be hard on a child. For most of their early lives, Charlie was an absentee father. Shirley raised the kids while Dad, like a shearer, followed the work. And now that he was gone, all that remained was his reputation. If I could, I'd see they weren't robbed of that too.

Abruptly, Judy stopped speaking. The President called for a seconder and I raised my hand. The motion was put, a unanimous chorus of ayes rose to the gilded ceiling and Charlie Talbot's name was officially consigned to the history books.

My job was to make sure it stayed on the right page.

What I needed now was a short length of chain and a padlock.

The city skyline was a palisade of glistening steel as the mirrored walls of the office towers caught the last rays of the afternoon sun. Down on the ground, darkness was expanding to fill the space available. The commuters converging on Spencer Street station were already hunched against the imminent chill.

I drove around to approach the Tin Shed from the west, skirting the worst of the traffic, dipping beneath the railway bridge at Festival Hall and turning into what used to be Footscray Road. It had a new name now, but nobody knew what. It was a government secret, commercial and confidential. In the torn-up space between the docks and the future, the only points of reference were the words on the cranes. Transurban. Balderstone-Hornibrook. Nudge-Nudge. Wink-Wink.

I cruised past the shed's corrugated hump and spotted Gilpin feeding a fire in a 44-gallon drum at the back door.

Doubling back, I parked among the doorless refrigerators and wheel-less wheelbarrows and went around the back.

The drum was the one I'd taken for a kennel. Oily flames were flickering from the top, fuelled by Sid from a heap of broken furniture, old garden stakes, ink cartridges and stuffed toys. I wondered if he was cremating the dog. Turds aside, there was still no sign of it.

He watched my approach through a veil of dancing fumes, his puffed-up face giving him the look of a pestilential toad risen from some witch's cauldron.

'Evening, Sid,' I said. 'Glowing with health, as usual.'

'Knew you'd be back,' he sneered malevolently. 'Quinlan's shitting himself, is he? Mr High and Mighty in Canberra. Or did he pass the parcel to that Marjory, whatever her name is? Called himself a bloody unionist, wouldn't know one end of a shovel from the other.'

I gave him the wind-up. 'You want to deal or flap your gums?'

He sniffed and tossed a tattered *Readers' Digest* into the flaming drum. 'Whad've you got?'

I took an envelope from my pocket, lifted the flap and fanned the contents. The top bill was a real fifty. The rest were colour photocopies, cut to size. It looked like a lot of money. 'Where are the bankbooks?' I said.

He licked his lips avariciously and jerked his chin at the open door. I took a step towards it.

'Not so fast,' he snapped. 'Go round.'

I shrugged and started back the way I'd come. Gilpin scuttled though the door, swung it shut behind him and shot the bolt. I scooted over and closed the outside bolt. The door was now locked from both sides. I pocketed the real fifty and tossed the envelope of fakes into the fire. Then I walked around the rusting hulk of the building and sidled through the gap between the front doors.

The interior was even gloomier than before, lit now by low-wattage globes in the dangling row of Chinaman's hats. Gilpin was in his wire-mesh enclosure, twisting a coat hanger through the gate latch. The bench with the electric grinder had been cleared of its rusty blades. They were inside the cage, freshly sharpened and stacked on the floor.

'Ready to do business?' I said, walking down the aisle between the rows of merchandise. Tip-top stuff.

Tip-ready, more like it.

Sid fished in his gabardine and pulled out the bankbooks, fastened together with a rubber band. 'Depends,' he sniffed, giving them a waggle. 'How much you offering?'

So far, so good. The books were out in the open.

I reached into my side pocket and pulled out a cable lock I'd bought at a bike shop in Bourke Street near Parliament House. Looping it through the gate latch in the cyclone fence, I snapped the locking mechanism shut and thumbed the combination tumbler closed.

Gilpin jumped backwards and stuffed the bankbooks back into his folds.

'Fair trade requires a level playing field,' I said. 'The back door's locked, too. I can't get in, you can't get out. What could be fairer than that?'

Gilpin grunted, dragged a can of beer from his raincoat pocket and picked off the scab. Foam spurted out and dribbled over his hand. He licked it off and took a chug.

'You want to know what those bankbooks are worth to Quinlan and Mrs Talbot?' I took an envelope, identical to the other, out of my inside pocket. 'Same as what this is worth to you.'

The envelope contained a photocopy of the picnic page of the union news. The original image had been slightly modified. Gilpin was now sporting a watch. A chunky sports chronometer clipped from the wrist of a rather fetching male model. Some doctoring with a fine-point pen and White-out had been required, but the overall result was passably convincing.

I unfolded it and held it to the wire mesh. 'Recognise this, Sid? It's from the Municipals' rag. See it clearly, can you?'

Sid moved close and squinted through the wire.

'You were a real picture that day, Sid. The vibrant patterned shirt, the wide collar, the medallion. A very snappy combination. And the watch set it off a treat. A Seiko Sports Chronometer, if I'm not mistaken. Just like the one found with Merv Cutlett at the bottom of Lake Nillahcootie.'

Gilpin's eyes were narrow slits in puddings of flesh. His nose was touching the wire. He was obviously having trouble seeing.

'Take a closer look.' I rolled the sheet into a tube and slid it through the mesh. Gilpin unfurled it, grunting and snuffling, and tilted it to the light.

'This is bullshit. I never owned a watch like that.'

'Really?' I said. 'That's not the way Senator Quinlan remembers it. Me neither. Now that we've had a chance to think about it, we distinctly remember you flashing it around. Powerful man like the senator, I'm sure he won't have any trouble finding lots of other people who remember it, too.'

Gilpin crumpled the paper, dropped it to the floor and sneered at me contemptuously.

'Plenty more where that came from,' I said. 'I've got one in an envelope addressed to the police, matter of fact.'

He kicked the paper ball with the toe of his dirty trainer. 'This doesn't prove anything.'

'Who said it did, Sidney?' I asked sweetly. 'You seem to be missing the point. That thing,' I pointed to the paper at his feet, 'is just an example. An illustration, if you like. You send your piece of cir-cum-stantial evidence to the coppers, we send ours. You point the finger, we point the finger. This stir-the-possum game, two can play at it.'

'Evidence of what?' He sucked at his can and wiped his mouth on his sleeve. 'Smartarse.'

I gave an exasperated sigh. 'Jeeze, Sid, do I have to spell it out for you? You reckon the bankbooks will make the cops think Charlie Talbot and Barry Quinlan were on the fiddle, giving them a reason to knock off honest Merv Cutlett. By the same token, this photo of you and your watch will make them wonder why you lied to them. Maybe even wonder if you mightn't have given Merv a helping hand on his way to the bottom of the lake. You had a chance. You were out on the lake looking for him. You had a motive. He was selling you out. Just your bad luck that he grabbed your watch while you were pushing him under.'

Gilpin laughed, spraying spit and beer at me. 'What a load of crap,' he said. 'Give me the money or fuck off.'

He crumpled the can and tossed it aside. Then he shuffled over to the ice-cream cooler and got himself a fresh one. There were cans all over the floor. Christ, the bloke was a bottomless vat.

The last of the daylight was fading from the dirty windows. I'd been too optimistic, I realised, thinking I could bluff Bozo Brainiac with a bit of cut-and-paste and a tangle of half-baked logic.

'You've had your money already, Sid.' I said. 'There's no second helpings. Do yourself a favour, just give me the bankbooks.' I extended my open palm and waited patiently.

Gilpin stared at me sullenly. 'Fuck off,' he said.

I gave a disappointed shrug, took out my mobile and pushed a couple of buttons. While I pretended to wait for an answer, I gave Sid a you-asked-for-it look.

'Senator,' I said, turning my expression serious. 'No go, unfortunately.'

Gilpin moved closer to the mesh, head tilted. He pulled off his beanie, the better to hear me. I listened again, nodding into the phone. 'Understood. You're the boss.' I thumbed the phone off and put it back in my pocket.

Casting a saddened glance at Gilpin, I grabbed a couple of old paint cans and tossed them at the base of the mesh fence. I added another pair, then another. I prowled through the array of old junk spread across the floor, selecting items and flinging them towards the partition. Speaker cases, rotary phones, a wooden stool, a milk crate of old textbooks. Anything flingable, all of it flammable.

'You're a greedy bastard,' I said, shaking my head dolefully. 'And this time you've bitten off more than you can chew.'

Gilpin stood rooted to the spot, comprehension dawning across his puffy, booze-ravaged dial as I poured a bottle of sump oil over the pile. I wiped my hands on a rag, tossed it aside, and looked around.

'This joint's a hazard, mate. One spark from that grinder and *whoompf*.'

Gilpin scratched his stubble and spat on the floor. 'You're bluffing,' he said. 'You'd never get away with it.'

I took out my cigarette lighter. 'If the senator can't have them, nobody can. And let's face it, Sid, you won't be missed.'

Once again, I extended my palm to the latch and waited.

My other hand held the lighter, thumb on the striker. If this didn't work, I was fucked.

It worked. He fumbled in his coat, pulled out the bankbooks and poked them through the gap. I snatched them from his grasp. Sweat was trickling down my back.

Gilpin hooked his fingers through the mesh and rattled the cage. 'Let me out, you prick.' He looked pathetic. Sad, sick, trapped, abandoned.

'You need help,' I said. 'You shouldn't be mixing your medications. I'm going to call a doctor, get somebody down here to see to you.'

'Fuck you,' he said.

Yeah, I thought, and fuck my doctor. We'd been through this before. I turned and walked up the aisle to the front door, the chain mesh rattling behind me.

'I'll fucking kill you,' Gilpin shouted. 'That prick Quinlan, too.'

I consigned the bankbook in Charlie Talbot's name to the toxic inferno of the petrol-drum incinerator, slid open the bolt on the back door and drove away without a backward glance.

The bogus Quinlan I tucked snugly into my back pocket.

When Inky Donnelly stuck his leprechaun phiz around my door in the Henhouse at nine-thirty the next morning, it had hot dispatch plastered all over it.

'I've just been chatting with your mate Vic Valentine,' he said, rubbing his hands together with satisfaction. 'Looks like we're off the hook with the Merv Cutlett rigmarole.'

I was unaware that Inky had ever been anywhere near the hook, but I let it pass. His usual dishevelled self, Inky plopped himself down in my visitors' chair, eager to explain the nature of our un-hooking.

As part of my penance to the Whip, I'd agreed to put in a couple of extra sessions of bum-time in the Council chamber. Inky had caught me trying to get on top of the morning's agenda before kick-off time at ten. I leaned back and gave him my undivided.

'Seems that our intrepid chrome-domed ace reporter was present during a long and well-lubricated session at the

Wallopers' Arms last night. In the course of which he picked up the latest mail on the bones-in-the-lake saga. Apparently forensic science has run into a dead-end, so to speak. DNA has met its match, you might say.'

Inky was clearly enjoying himself, so I simply sat and enjoyed the show.

'You'll recall in the last nail-biting episode, the coppers were gearing up to exhume Cutlett's parents' grave in the Mooroopna cemetery, where they have been enjoying their eternal rest for some several decades? Well, it seems that the passage of time has taken its toll on the headstones in that forgotten corner of a Mooroopna field that will be forever Cutlett. The exact location of their graves cannot be determined with sufficient precision to meet the requirement of modern science. So, no parental DNA.'

'What about the daughter?' I said.

'Killed in a car accident in New Zealand in 1990 and cremated,' he beamed. 'And what with the watch drawing a blank at all corners of the compass, the remains have now been relegated to the Unsolved Mysteries file.'

'The hole in the head?'

He shrugged. 'Borers?'

'So there was never anything to worry about all along?'

'Who was worried?' He massaged his stomach. 'Cautious, that's all.'

'Well that's certainly good news, Inky,' I said.

'I knew you'd be pleased.' He slapped his knees and heaved himself into the vertical. 'And good news about Leppitsch being cleared by the tribunal. He should be worth four or five goals against the Eagles on Sunday.'

'And we'll need every one of them,' I said, returning to my reading material. 'But do me a favour, Ink. Next time you're curious about something, just look it up in the fucking encyclopaedia, will you?'

He tossed me a parting cheerio as he went out the door. 'Looking sharp today, Muzza.'

I had to agree, for Inky's was not the only welcome news I'd received that morning. While he was waiting his turn at the toaster during the breakfast rush, Red had got around to mentioning there'd been a phone call on Tuesday evening.

'Didn't you see the note?' he said, hovering impatiently as my post-run slices of multigrain took their own good time to turn brown.

I most certainly hadn't. 'What note?'

'It's round here somewhere.' He said, elbowing me aside and prematurely ejaculating my toast. 'Her name was Anthea Lean or something like that. From your Greek class, she said. Wanted you to ring her. I wrote down the number.'

He simultaneously fed bread into the toaster, stuffed his homework into his backpack, did up his shoelaces and gestured vaguely towards the midden of scrawled notes surrounding the telephone.

He'd been out the door for ten minutes before I managed to find and decode his hieroglyphics. The deplorable penmanship of the younger generation was a matter that had long concerned me in a general sense. Now it had come home to roost. Was that a three or a five? A nine or a seven? Dammit, I'd try all of them if necessary.

But seven-fifteen in the morning was a tad too early to call on a matter like this, however impatient I was. So, hoping for the best, I dusted off my Hugo Boss dress-to-impress suit, drove to Parliament House and bided my time until nine-twenty.

A chirpy young voice answered. 'You've called the Lanes,

Nicole and Andrea. Please leave a message and we'll return your call when we can.' There followed an encouraging tinkle of classical piano music. Mozart, or one of those guys.

'Er, this is Murray Whelan, returning your call, Andrea,' I said. 'Sorry I missed you. Um, please call me back on my mobile. The number's on the card.' To be on the safe side, I recited the numbers. My fingers were still crossed when Inky arrived.

What with speed-reading the agenda papers and chatting with Inky, I barely made it to the chamber in time for the kick-off. Not that the legislative pace was exactly cracking that morning. The condolence motion had drawn a near-full house, but that was just good form. The second reading of the brucellosis clauses of the Livestock Disease Control (Amendment) Bill had pulled only eight members. Five of theirs, three of ours.

We were the short-straw corps. Kingers of Geelong, Butcher of Dandenong and Whelan of Melbourne Upper. Personing the post was our sole role. Kingers and Butcher took the far extremities of the front bench and I sat in the middle up the back. The expression 'thin on the ground' came to mind as I subsided into the plush.

Across the floor of the chamber, the enemy ranks joshed among themselves until the siren sounded and the President bounced the ball. The Minister for Agriculture, an old-style National with a military moustache and enviable silver hair assumed the position and began to read from a bulldog-clipped sheaf of papers.

'Pursuant to the matters covered in section five, subsection nine...'

The public gallery was deserted. Kingers was doing a crossword puzzle, his newspaper buried in a departmental file. Butcher was checking the government benches, scouting for a possible interjection. Ambitious fellow, Butcher.

The preselection vote was Saturday afternoon, less than forty-eight hours away.

Unless Barry Quinlan already knew that the police investigation into the Lake Nillahcootie remains had been shelved, he still had very good reasons for wanting the bankbook out of circulation. By early next week, however, he'd probably be better informed, and its threat value would be nil.

A personal savings account, decades old. That's all it was. A name. Some dates. Money in, money out. Like the man said, not exactly a smoking gun. Its sole significance lay in the construction that might be placed upon it at a certain time under certain circumstances. Sid Gilpin had opened and operated it with exactly that point in mind. Two decades later, he thought he'd found a different purpose for it. Now it was my turn.

Blackmail is an ugly word. Perhaps that's why it appears only twenty-seven times in the official ALP rule-book. If Senator Quinlan was doing what he promised me beside the wishing well in Canberra, it would never need to be uttered. In the meantime, it wouldn't hurt to mouth it silently in his direction.

Ayisha had already let me know he was back in Melbourne, shoring up his authority. When we adjourned for lunch, I scuttled down to the Henhouse and gave him a call.

As we talked, noises leaked through the thin partition wall from the staffroom next door. Staffers and MPs were tucking into cut lunches, opening take-away containers, microwaving Cup-a-Soup and nattering among themselves. Outside, the sky was overcast. The temperature had risen overnight and an almost-pleasant humidity had superseded the previous day's damp chill.

'That thing we discussed,' I said, when Quinlan came on the line. 'It took quite a bit of doing, but I've got it in my possession. I thought you might like it as a souvenir.'

'That's very thoughtful of you, Murray.'

'My pleasure,' I said. 'You haven't forgotten your promise, I hope?'

'I said I'd do my best and that's exactly what I'm doing. But the situation is very fluid at the moment.'

Fluid? From what I'd heard, it was forming an oil-slick under his hand-stitched size sevens.

'So I understand,' I said. 'You wouldn't care to hazard some numbers?'

'Later in the day perhaps.'

'I look forward to it,' I said. 'You don't happen to be going to this casino shindig, I suppose.'

As well as every state parliamentarian and city councillor, the casino bosses had invited all Victorian members of federal parliament to partake of their hospitality. Barry was a big man for the gee-gees and a keen plier of the knife and fork, so it was odds-on that he'd taken up their offer.

'Excellent suggestion,' he said. 'We'll get our heads together over a post-prandial snifter. They'll be laying it on in spades, I daresay.'

I called Ayisha. She was out of the office, escorting Phil Sebastian to lunch with a Frank Abruzzo, a salami manufacturer with an over-inflated sense of his influence with the Italo-Australian small business wing of the Melbourne Upper component of the Coolaroo rank and file.

My mobile had been switched off while I was sitting in the chamber. I'd turned it on the moment I got out, but it still hadn't rung. I checked the message bank. Lanie had called.

'It's about tonight,' said her recorded voice. 'I'm not really contactable at the moment. I'll call you back, okay?'

There was a questioning tone in her voice. I'd been too late getting back to her. She wasn't sure we were still on for it. Damn, shit, bugger.

I hung up and rang Mike Kyriakis. He'd been sussing out the likely disposition of the union votes on the central panel through his wife's brother-in-law, an assistant state secretary of the Construction Workers Federation.

'Len Whitmore's considering a last minute jump into the ring,' Mike reported.

Whitmore, National Secretary of the CWF, had long been touted as a parliamentary contender. He ponced around the country in a bomber jacket, getting his photo in the paper at every non-industrial opportunity. A blatantly obvious attempt to position himself as a common-sense, good-bloke candidate should the parliamentary seat allocators ever have the wit to utilise his talents.

'Here's hoping,' I said. The CWF was militant. If Whitmore nominated, the moderate unions would be backed into Quinlan's corner.

We talked for a while, then I rang Helen Wright to touch base. She was out and about, so I grabbed a slice of quiche in Strangers Corridor and hit the benches for the afternoon session.

With the sick cows out of the way, our numbers had been beefed up to five for Question Time. I slung the Health Minister a curly one about the negative impact of hospital waiting times on senior citizens in the northern suburbs, then proceedings moved to final passage of the Gas Industry

Privatisation (Further Amendments) Bill. Carriage was a fait accompli, but the least we could do was put our objections on the record. Con Caramalides had supplied me with a magazine of bullets, which I fired at the required moments, working from Con's crib-sheet.

Thereafter, when I wasn't contributing to the general spear-rattling and name-calling, I ducked outside to the portico, switched on my mobile and checked the messages.

And a fat lot of good it did. Still no Andrea Lane.

The session adjourned at six, giving me a comfortable thirty minutes to drop my bundle in the Henhouse, try Lanie's home number again, stick a collapsible umbrella under my arm and trudge the five despondent blocks to the Adult Education Centre.

As usual, the stairs and corridors were congested with self-improving mature-age students of Introduction to Computers and Resume Writing for Success. I got to Greek for Beginners with five minutes to spare. Lanie hadn't yet turned up. Exchanging *yasous* with my arriving classmates, I lingered in the hallway.

And lingered and lingered and lingered. By the time everybody else was seated and Agapi, our teacher, was making starting noises, Lanie still hadn't shown.

When Agapi gave me the coming-or-not, I took a seat at the back next to the children's book illustrator and we proceeded immediately to Στη μπισινα.

Lanie arrived just as we were ετοιμοι να βουτηξουμε στο νερο. She broadcast an apologetic look to the room in general and grabbed the only spare seat, two rows in front of me. She was wearing a pair of jeans and a sweatshirt and carrying a sports bag. She'd just come from the gym or she was bound there immediately afterwards; either way the casino clearly didn't feature in her plans for the evening.

'*Malaka fungula*,' I muttered silently.

The rest of the lesson passed in a self-pitying funk. I'd been stood up in favour of a Stairmaster. But then maybe the gym wasn't such a bad idea in Lanie's case. Those jeans did nothing for the woman's bum.

At seven-thirty, Agapi collected our worksheets, handed out fresh ones and closed the lesson. In the general mill of departure, Lanie made straight for me. 'I'm really, really sorry,' she gushed. 'You must think I'm hopeless.'

'No, no.' I shrugged and laughed. *Aha-ha-ha*.

'I've been on tenterhooks all week,' she said. 'We've had the state netball finals and we didn't know if Nicole's team would be playing tonight or not. That's why I couldn't be sure on Sunday. Depended if they got through the semis, and in the end they didn't. Got knocked out last night. Still, she played well and there's a good chance she'll be selected for the national under sixteens.' She beamed proudly. 'And I've been up to here with new students.' Her finger drew a line across her redoubtable poitrine. 'And on top of everything else, bloody Telstra cut the phone off on Wednesday because of some mix-up with the bill. You were probably getting the no-longer-connected message when you called. How embarrassing. So, when you finally got through…' She paused abruptly. 'You must have asked someone else by now.'

I'd been drinking her in with rapt attention. 'No, no.' I shook my head furiously. 'It's my fault. My son's a half-wit. Chip off the old block. He only gave me your message this morning. I'd've called earlier but I didn't have your number. I haven't, um…' I glanced at her casual outfit. 'We could, er, go somewhere else instead, if you like.'

256

Not really. Not tonight, anyway. I couldn't jeopardise my chance for a discreet tête-à-tête with Barry Quinlan during the post-banquet mix-n-mingle.

'And miss the fun and games?' said Lanie brightly. 'No way.' She hoisted her gym bag. 'Do you know the Duxton Hotel?'

'Used to be the Commercial Travellers'?'

The Duxton's place in Melbourne hostelry history wasn't the point. She reached over and firmed the knot of my tie, an eighty-dollar silk Armani I'd bought myself for Christmas.

'328 Flinders Street. Meet me in the lobby in half an hour.' She spun on her heels and took off at a rapid clip.

Her bum wasn't big at all, not really.

I re-inflated my male ego, edged through the Understanding Modern Art crowd milling at the classroom door and went down to street level. The Duxton was less than two blocks away. I sauntered towards it, rehearsing some studly moves in the shop windows and whistling under my breath.

People were coming from all directions, heading towards the river. Some carried rolled-up banners, protesters bound for the anti-casino rally. Others were evidently angling for good vantage points to watch the fireworks or do some star-spotting. Kylie and Kerry would be representing the A-list and a who's-that cast of B and C celebrities would soon be debouching from hired limos for exclusive private dinners, before the doors were flung open to the punting public.

The Duxton was one of Melbourne's first skyscrapers. A fine example of Belle Époque Moderne, its twelve storeys had spent most of the twentieth century descending into shabby gentility as a home away from home for suitcase-and-sample men. Recently, it had been refurbished for the Asian package-tour trade. I found the lobby full of heaped suitcases and gregarious gents in comfortable trousers with faces like Genghis Khan. Not the trousers, the Chinamen.

I bought a Jamesons and water at the bar, sat in a new-smelling club armchair and re-read my entrée card to the blackjack dealers' beanfeast. Ribbon cutting and banquet, Crown Towers, eight for eight-thirty. Hotel entrance.

The evening was still mild but there was a promise of drizzle in the air. With luck, it would hold off until we'd walked across the Queen Street bridge to the designated entry-point.

At ten past eight, Lanie descended the wide staircase from the first floor, displaying herself for my appraisal.

Her chestnut hair was twisted up, a few strands left artfully free to draw the eye to the sculptural curve of her neck. Her torso was tightly wrapped in a bolt-width of titian-red brocade that accentuated her full figure and left her shoulders bare except for a rain-fleck of freckles. The skirt was black and multi-layered and flared out slightly as it dropped over her hips, falling just past her knees. She was wearing Medea mascara and loose-fitting silver bangles, giving her the sultry look of a wilful slave-girl. Her shoes, thank you Jesus, were flat.

She was like a store of plundered treasure. Truly here was a woman who made you want to rush out and steal a horse, lead a raid, sack a city. It was all I could do not to jump up on my chair and let out a howl to rouse the Duxton's venerable Mongol horde.

For the moment, however, I'd be satisfied just to take her to the fun-fair. We'd share a sarsaparilla and I'd win her a kewpie-doll. On the way home, we'd sneak a quick pash in the back of the cab and I'd find out what sort of a kisser she was. Important, that. The *sine qua non* of all that might follow.

'Ready?' she said.

I presented the crook of my arm and strolled her towards the door, the man who broke the bank at Monte Carlo. As we passed reception, she took a key from her small black clutch and handed it to the girl behind the desk.

'Thanks, Amie.'

The girl beamed helpfully and returned the key to its slot. 'Anytime, Miss Lane.'

'Amie's one of my ex-students,' Lanie explained. 'She's just got her diploma in Hospitality Studies at Maribyrnong University.'

We crossed the road to Banana Alley, pulled along by the throng. When we reached the Queen Street bridge, we were confronted by a scene part Dante, part Cecil B. DeMille, part situationalist manifestation.

On the southern bank of the Yarra squatted the long, low lump of the casino. Here was the Temple of Mammon, intermittently lit by huge balls of flame belching from square, chimney-like pillars on the riverside promenade.

Facing it across the shimmering ribbon of water was the Multitude of the Righteous. This polyglot host of protesters had assembled in a featureless strip of urban park to display their opposition to the plutocratic–autocratic conspiracy behind the sucker-fleecing works on the opposite bank.

On the next bridge, King Street, the suckers were queued, bumper-to-bumper, scarcely able to contain their impatience to be fleeced. And on our bridge, Queen Street, milled those who had come for the show. Or, in our case, a free feed and party favours.

We stepped up our pace, mindful of the time and the density of the crowd. Every few metres, flyers were thrust at us by baby-faced Trotskyists, Gamblers' Helpline volunteers and touts for the Santa Fe titty bar.

'When do the fireworks start?' said Lanie, rubbing her bare arms against the faint chill rising from the river.

'They seem to have started already.'

I pointed from the bridge railing to the speaker's platform at the centre of the protest crowd. The clergyman at the microphone had just been upstaged by an actress who was baring her breasts in a statement of objection to media superficiality. That'll show 'em, I thought. The poor pastor didn't know whether to cheer, go blind or head for the Santa Fe.

As we reached the far side of the bridge, we hit a thick cluster of gawkers who were backed up behind a low wall of crash barriers. Across the street, cars were pulling up at a red carpet, disembarking their cargo of league footballers, former lead singers of former one-hit bands and various other VIPs. I spotted Vic Valentine's speed-pushing informant Jason as he stepped from a stretch limo with a soap opera starlet. Or was she a current affairs host? Hard to tell.

'That's where we need to get,' I told Lanie.

Putting my arm around her, I steered her through the fringes of the crowd. This gave me a pretext to press my face against her hair and inhale her slightly-musky, slightly-spicy fragrance. I was strongly tempted to nibble her neck, but decided that munching her jugular at this formative juncture in our relationship might send the wrong message.

We got to where the crowd petered out to a thin line with a lousy view. I let go of Lanie and squeezed through a narrow gap in the crash barriers. A constable detached himself from a strung-out line of bored cops. He advanced, arm extended, palm vertical, in a creditable impersonation of a real security guard.

Socialise the costs, I thought, privatise the profits.

'Sir,' he said. *Sir* as in get your arse back behind the barrier pronto, pal, Hugo Boss or no Hugo Boss.

I held up my entrée card. 'Sorry officer, I'm afraid I've come the wrong way.' Silly-billy me. 'My companion and I are invited guests.' I twisted my head back helplessly towards the well-dressed woman I'd left stranded behind me. 'I'm a member of parliament.'

The cop gave me a look of censure just short of outright contempt, inspected my ticket and beckoned Lanie through the gap. He pointed across the road. 'That way, *sir*.'

I took Lanie's hand and we walked towards the kerb where the red carpet started.

'Pity the Rolls is being washed tonight,' I said. 'Still, it's nice to see how the little people live.'

Lanie was lapping it up, already having fun. A cheeky minx, laughing at it all with her eyes. A white Fairlane with Commonwealth plates drew up at the roll-out Axminster and a compact, dapper, mid-sixtyish man in a dinner suit stepped from the back seat. The senator extended his hand and drew a woman of the same vintage from the interior, dark-haired in a tight perm and ankle-length evening gown.

'Do you know who that is?' I asked Lanie.

She shook her head. 'He looks vaguely familiar. Have I seen him on TV?'

'He's one of the world's greatest living actors,' I said.

'Two days ago he gave me a private performance that would've made Al Pacino weep tears of envy.'

I was half-turning to half-explain my little joke when a shout came from behind us. At the section of the crowd with the best view, a figure in a raincoat had climbed over the barrier. He was heading towards the red carpet.

A cop was moving to intercept him, and he increased his pace to a jog, then began to sprint. It was Sid Gilpin. He was heading straight for Barry Quinlan, pulling something from beneath the flaps of his coat. *Christ*, a machete. The blade was wide and dark and its edge was honed to a silver strip.

Security toughs in bomber jackets appeared out of nowhere. Cops were shouting and uniforms were converging on Gilpin. They were closing fast, but not fast enough.

Quinlan, oblivious to the ruckus, was advancing up the carpet, Mrs Quinlan beside him. Gilpin was ten paces away, fifteen, ten. For a sick man, he was moving astonishingly fast. I let go of Lanie's hand and raced forward.

I got to Quinlan a step ahead of Gilpin, slamming into his back with my lowered shoulder. Definitely a reportable offence. Quinlan bounced off me and flew forward. I hit the ground, maximum impact, just as the fireworks went off. They were really good. Worth every cent of the five million.

I could see them even with my eyes closed.

'Dad?'

Red's voice pulsated out of the void.

'How are you feeling?'

How did the damn fool boy think I felt? And why wasn't he doing something about the crazed monkey that was trying to break my head open with a sledgehammer?

'Dad?'

He was close, a moving shape on the other side of my eyelids. If I tried, maybe I could see him. I commanded my eyelids to open. No, they said. Yes, I insisted. Red's worried face filled my vision, then drew back. I was lying in a bed. A green curtain surrounded us. We were in a hospital.

'Okay,' I said. 'Feel okay.'

'That's good.' He still looked worried.

I leaned forward and he propped me up with a pillow. The throbbing rushed back, then subsided. My mind was clearing, remembering what had happened.

First came the jarring impact, then the sensation of flying as my limp body was grabbed and rushed inside the building by a thicket of security men. In a vertiginous rush, they propelled me though a series of doors, my head reeling. I must have gone nighty-nights for a moment. Next thing I knew, I was lying in a moving ambulance. And then on a gurney in a corridor with somebody shining a light in my eye and asking me if I could remember my name. I must have got the answer wrong because the next time I surfaced I was being fed into a giant white plastic doughnut.

'You sure you're okay?' said Red.

A motherly, vaguely familiar woman in scrubs came through the curtain. 'Feeling better, Mr Whelan?' she said. 'How's the head?'

'Not too bad.' Apart from the white-hot harpoons that shot through my brain whenever I spoke.

'Doctor will be round to see you soon.' She checked my vitals, gave Red a reassuring smile and floated away.

Soon, in hospital parlance, meant three hours. Not that I could do much but wait anyway. Whenever I tried to get vertical, it was spin-out city.

Red told me that a woman called Andrea Lake had rung the house to say that I'd been clobbered by a protestor at the casino and been taken to Prince Henry's. He'd come straight over in a taxi. She was outside in the waiting area, dressed up like a bon-bon. There were a couple of guys, too, but he didn't know who they were.

I had a pretty fair idea.

Not being in any position to entertain a lady, I sent the lad out to tell Lanie that I was all right, and please not to wait. I'd call her as soon as I could. I was feeling a bit groggy, so I closed my eyes and wondered where my clothes had gone. Next thing I knew, the registrar was waking me. I was suffering from concussion, he told me, but the scan indicated no serious damage. To be on the safe side, they were keeping me overnight. By then it was two o'clock and I didn't see any point in objecting.

Red spent the night in the chair beside my bed, bless his sweaty socks.

Just after six, I went to the loo. Borneo dayaks had done something to my head, but my legs were back on duty and the giddiness was gone. Red found my suit in a plastic box under the bed. While I was putting it on, he went to find whoever needed telling that I was ready to go home. The bankbook had vanished.

Red came back with two men, plain-clothes cops from headquarters in St Kilda Road. They were there to drive me home, they said. And if I felt up to it, perhaps I might answer some questions.

Fine by me, I had a few of my own.

We drove through the empty streets with Red in the front seat while I talked to the more senior officer in the back. By the time we got to Clifton Hill, Red's ears were as pointy as Spock's and I had a reasonably clear picture of the situation.

Twinkle-toes Quinlan had taken it on the fly. He was a bit scuffed around the edges, but he'd responded well to a touch of five-star valet service and a steadying drink in the Bugsy Siegel Suite. The casino appreciated my self-sacrifice and trusted that I was prepared to overlook the rougher-than-usual handling meted out by its security staff in the confusion of the moment. Their representative would speak with me personally in the very near future.

The attempted assailant was a man named Gilpin. He was currently in custody. He claimed that Senator Quinlan had been persecuting him. Could I shed any light on the subject?

My lights, I reminded the officers, had recently been punched out. When I'd had a chance to recover, I'd be happy to provide a full statement and answer any further questions. In the meantime, I'd had a bitch of a night and thanks for the lift.

The honcho cop, a likeable fellow, escorted us to the door. 'A man in your position,' he said. 'I don't need to remind you that since charges have been laid this matter is now *sub judice*.'

'Ah jeez,' said Red. 'That means I can't tell anyone.'

As the cops drove away, young Tyson from the newsagent's rode past and threw the papers over the fence. The *Age* described the casino event as 'a hoop-la the likes of which Melbourne had never seen'. The knock-'em-downs didn't get a mention. The *Herald Sun* was similarly mum, and so was radio news.

The lid was on and that's where I hoped it stayed. Reports of a machete-wielding maniac taking swipes at its patrons were not something the casino was likely to welcome, and I had some valid reasons of my own for concurring.

Red begged off school and retired to catch a kip. I changed out of my silly galoot into trackie daks and a sloppy joe. Under the circumstances, seven-fifteen didn't seem too early to ring Lanie. I tried to sound hale. 'Great first date, eh?'

'You've got some interesting moves, I'll say that for you.'

She wanted to come straight over, but I fended her off. Domestic squalor and a walking-wounded shuffle were not the ideal follow up to my display of heroics. What I wanted most of all was a cup of tea and a good cry.

I'd barely got those out of the way before the phone

started ringing and the rest of the day kicked in. It didn't take Nostradamus to predict it was going to be busy.

Mike Kyriakis called first.

'We're fucked, mate,' he said. Overnight, *inter alia*, the wheels had started to fall off our Coolaroo strategy. The last-minute surprise candidate wasn't to be Len Whitmore of the concrete gang. That was a furphy. The contender now being touted was Andrew McIntyre, Vice President of the ACTU. And with McIntyre's name on the ballot, it was *arrivederci* Canberra.

'You sure?' I said.

Mike was pretty sure. If the unions were looking for a way to take Quinlan down a peg, McIntyre was custom made. On the other hand, there were a lot of rumours flying around. We decided to keep a weather eye on developments and get together around lunchtime.

I went out onto the deck. The sky was overcast and the weather was still trying to make up its mind which way to jump. I downed a couple of Panadol and answered the phone.

'You sound ratshit, Murray.' It was Ayisha. 'Hit the turps at the big event, did you?'

'Hit something else,' I said. 'I'll tell you about it later. But I'm not feeling too sprightly, so I'll be working from home today.'

'Nominations close at four,' she said. 'I'll lodge the form at quarter to, okay?'

Hiding my hand until the death knell was integral to the plan. The way things were turning out, it might just save me falling flat on my face. I told her about the McIntyre rumour and lined her up for the confab with Mike. Then Peter Thorsen rang.

'Didn't spot you at the opening last night,' he said. 'I heard you were attacked by one of the anti-casino lot.'

'It was a non-violent protest,' I said. 'You can't believe everything you hear. Or can you?'

'McIntyre?' he said. 'Looks like it. But your mate Kyriakis will still get the first-round votes I promised. Just wanted you to know.'

'If McIntyre runs, Mike will probably withdraw,' I said. 'And that nice letter you wrote me, I've already shredded it.'

'You're a gent, Murray. If I can ever do anything for you…'

'Don't make promises you might regret,' I said. 'And I know whereof I speak.'

The next caller was offering free quotations on cladding. I told her we were happy with our current clad, but thanks for ringing. I finished the papers and emptied the dishwasher, then Helen Wright rang.

'I've heard the McIntyre rumour,' I said. 'Tell me something I don't know.'

'Phil Sebastian's on the run,' she said. 'He cancelled the meetings I set up this morning with various of the branch secretaries. He's locked down with Barry Quinlan. They're putting the blowtorch to Quinlan's people on the central panel, trying to extract written guarantees of support.'

My mobile started to ring. I asked Helen to hold.

'Cop this.' Ayisha again. 'Alan Metcalfe's office rang. Apparently there's a story doing the rounds that you joined the protest rally last night and rugby-tackled one of the silvertails as he was getting out of his limo. People have been ringing them to say it's a good thing at least some Labor members have got a bit of fight in them. Seems you're becoming the emblem of rank-and-file dissent.'

Oh deary dear. This was all getting out of hand.

'The leader wants a word, of course. I think he'd like to run you out of town on a rail. I said you were down with the lurgie.'

No doubt about it. I had no choice but to pull the plug.

'When you come around, bring my nomination form,' I said. 'And a box of matches.'

I went back to Helen, included her into the midday get-together and took the phone off the hook. The least I could do was tell them all to their faces. Until then, what I needed most in the world was a little lie down in a darkened room with a cold compress.

The damp face cloth was just beginning to work its magic when somebody banged on the door. Two somebodies. Senator Quinlan and Alan Metcalfe. Barry had brought a bunch of flowers and Alan had a box of chocolates.

Not really. But they might as well have.

'I hope you're feeling better, Murray' said Metcalfe. 'Fair to say I know all about last night's incident. Both your actions at the time and your subsequent…'

'Cut the cackle, Alan.' Quinlan elbowed him aside. 'Thing is, Murray, Phil Sebastian's had a fit of the colly-wobbles. He's only prepared to run if it's a lay-down misere. Which, as of Andrew McIntyre's nomination an hour ago, it isn't. If Phil pulls out, we'll both have the credibility chocks kicked out from under us. Unless, of course, we put our pooled resources behind another candidate.'

I stepped back, waved them inside and padded down the hall ahead of them in my extra-thick, extra-comfy socks.

'We're looking for somebody with parliamentary experience and good local credibility. Somebody capable of mobilising rank-and-file support at short notice. Somebody who's not averse to taking a risk.' Quinlan tapped me on the shoulder. 'Oh, and by the way, thanks for saving my life.'

'You're welcome,' I said, and took them into the den.

The Coolaroo by-election was held in September.

Diana, Princess of Wales, hit a post in a Paris underpass the same week, so it didn't rate much coverage. Labor's overall vote dropped three percent, but nobody blamed me. It fitted the national trend.

I made my maiden speech in the House of Representatives in November. My theme was the need to maintain a bi-partisan commitment to multiculturalism. Ayisha, acting in her capacity as my federal staff advisor, suggested the topic. My Coolaroo electorate officer, Helen Wright, came up for the day to watch from the gallery. Overall, they rated me nine out of ten for content, seven out of ten for presentation.

As promised, I backed Mike Kyriakis as my replacement in Melbourne Upper, but he was pipped at the post by one of Metcalfe's people. He was disappointed, naturally. Still, as I reminded him afterwards, a Labor victory in Victoria is about as imminent as the second coming, so it wasn't exactly the end of the world. He doesn't see it that way, of course, and I suspect I'll need to keep a sharp eye on him when it's time to re-nominate.

In the meantime, I've got more than enough to keep me busy. As well as the regular commute to Canberra, where I'm sharing a pied-a-terre in Campbell with dull old Phil Sebastian, there's plenty of running around in my capacity as assistant to the Shadow Parliamentary Secretary for Quarantine and Customs. It's just the first step on a very long ladder, but you've got to start somewhere.

And it gives me an excuse to drop in on Red from time to time. He's in Sydney now. At NIDA, if you please. All that extra-curricular youth theatre stuff paid off big-time. It was probably his performance in Rosencrantz *v* Guildenstern that did the trick. Lucky break, really, that Whatsisname Bell, the Shakespeare bloke, happened to catch a performance. The bit where Red stabbed Polonius in the arras was a real ball-tearer. Brought the house down, and not long after he received an invitation from NIDA to audition. An invitation!

Anyway, he's saving money by living with Wendy and Richard in their palatial spread. And Wendy's so chuffed about the status value of a son at NIDA that's she's turned into a regular stage-door mother. Poor bugger. Every now and then I swing through for a briefing on parrot-trafficking or Y2K readiness in passport-control and we have a meal together. If the Swans are playing a home game against the Lions, we catch the match.

They finished fifth at the end of the season, by the way, and their form is gradually improving. Margot's in good form, too. Quite a story to it, matter of fact.

She put the Diggers Rest place on the market and one of

the prospective buyers happened to be Terry Barraclough, the boyfriend who'd fathered Katie. He didn't know about Katie, or her condition. That was something else Margot had concealed.

He was mortified at the thought of the situation he'd left her in. Turned out he's been living overseas for the past two decades and has a very successful international career as a marketing consultant in the wine industry. He's divorced with grown-up children, and Margot and Katie have gone to stay with him at his place in the Napa Valley for three months. What Margot calls her trial re-marriage. If Katie settles in, she'll consider staying.

On the other side of the ledger, Sid Gilpin is currently enjoying confinement and treatment in a medium-security psychiatric institution, pending a review of his suitability to stand trial.

That eventuality appears to be something of receding horizon. By all-round implicit agreement, attempted assassinations of Australian politicians are considered a matter best swept under the carpet.

As for Kelly Cusack, our encounter at Parliament House was the last I saw of her. In the flesh, that is. Shortly after, she was promoted to doing the prime-time news for the national broadcaster's Queensland network. Doing very well, too. They like her up there because she looks so, well, *nice*.

And although it was fun while it lasted, I'm glad she and I went our separate ways before the thing with Lanie started. It made things so much simpler.

Coy as it sounds, Lanie and I came at it slowly after the excitement of our first, aborted get-together. We gave Greek conversation a miss that Sunday and she asked me around for a late lunch instead. Nicole was off at her father's, and we had the place to ourselves. Nice little split-level with a view over the peppercorn trees to Dights Falls. She fed me a chicken couscous and we drank a bottle of wine. There was talk of going for a walk by the river, but it started to rain.

So she opened another bottle and played me a lovely bit of Satie and we ended up flaked out on a pile of cushions on the floor with a tub of Norgen-Vaaz melting beside us.

We had the hots, all right, but both of us had been around the agora enough times to know that jumping into the sack can just as easily end things as start them.

We got there eventually and we're still there, almost a year later. Two sacks, actually, turn and turn about. Neither of us are quite ready for the full meld. And there's Nicole to consider.

As well as the freelance teaching racket, Lanie's picked up a regular gig tickling the ivories in the atrium bar at the Regent. Show tunes and jazz standards. And oh boy, does she look the goods, mood-lit behind a Steinway.

I drop by sometimes, just to bask. Then I take her home and roger her brainless.

We still haven't made it to the casino. The restaurants are pretty good, from all accounts, and the management is offering full comps, but it's just not our scene. When we do eat out, it's at Pireaus Blues, a great little Greek place in Brunswick Street that does a sensational rabbit *stifado*.

Haven't been there lately, unfortunately. As well as my parliamentary duties and whatnot, I've had my shoulder to the wheel of the republic referendum. The minimum-change model may not be very imaginative, but it's obviously the only way to go at this stage. I admit that the Resident for President slogan is a bit cheesy. Still, you can see the appeal in certain quarters. As I reminded Red over half-time pies at the SCG, an actor–president is not without precedent.

If things go according to plan, we'll have a republic by the new millennium. And a Labor government to inaugurate it.

I could be wrong, I suppose. What do I know?

Nobody ever tells me anything.